MW00345207

Runic Vengeance

Books by Clayton Taylor Wood:

The Runic Series
Runic Awakening

Runic Revelation

Runic Vengeance

Runic Revolt

The Fate of Legends Series
Hunter of Legends

Seeker of Legends

Destroyer of Legends

Magic of Havenwood Series
The Magic Collector

The Lost Gemini

Runic Vengeance

Book III of the Runic Series

Clayton Taylor Wood

Copyright ©2017 by Clayton Taylor Wood.

All rights reserved.

This book or any portion thereof may not be reproduced or used in any manner whatsoever without the express written permission of the publisher except for the use of brief quotations in a book review.

This is a work of fiction. Names, characters, businesses, places, events and incidents are either the products of the author's imagination or used in a fictitious manner. Any resemblance to actual persons, living or dead, or actual events is purely coincidental.

Published by Clayton T. Wood.

ISBN: 978-0-9980818-5-4

Cover designed by James T. Egan, Bookfly Design, LLC

Printed in the United States of America.

Special thanks to my brothers and my father, and my wife for their invaluable advice.

And to my son, for whom this book was written.

Table of Contents

Runic Vengeance

Prologue

The old man hobbled down the long underground tunnel, the butt of his wooden cane clanging on the metal platform below with each step he took. The platform extended down a long tubular tunnel made entirely of large white crystals. Each crystal was over seven feet long, with a broad hexagonal base that tapered to a razor-sharp tip pointing toward the center of the tunnel. The metal platform levitated a few feet above the crystals below, suspended by an unseen force.

The old man smiled to himself, countless wrinkles on his face deepening as he did so. He gazed forward with cataract-glazed eyes, continuing down the shaft at a glacial pace.

A shaft he'd been walking through for miles.

He hardly minded the walk, no matter the hours he'd spent taking it. The automatic nature of this body's shambling gate, the repetitive *clang, clang* of his cane on the metal below, freed the better part of his mind for more important matters.

He vaguely recalled being mortal, engaging his body with some mindless task to allow his mind to wander. A mind freed from its overbearing consciousness proved fertile soil for ideas to grow forth from, after all. And how many wondrous ideas had come to him during such walks, during his mortal life and far beyond! He would hardly be here today, walking in the midst of his own creation, had he not so exercised his brain.

After what seemed like an eternity, he finally made it to the end of the metal platform. The tunnel continued forward ahead, but was much narrower, the crystals forming a channel barely large enough to fit a human head through. There was no way forward...or so it seemed.

The old man glanced upward at one of the crystals above his head, focusing on what lay beyond its glittering facets. There, embedded in the broad root of the crystal, he could barely make out a shadowy form. A long-dead corpse forever encapsulated in its crystalline grave.

An unwilling Chosen.

He turned his eyes forward again, at the narrow channel beyond. There were Chosen in every one of the countless crystals – his Void crystals – lining the shaft he'd been walking through. A brain entombed in every crystal, each connected to one another in one massive network.

With a thought, the Void crystals around him flashed, then stopped their faint glowing. The old man rose up from the metal platform, levitating a foot above the grated steel, his cane dropping onto it with a clang. He closed his eyes, raising his arms out to his sides.

Then his head tore off, rising above his neck.

It flew forward down the narrower tunnel, rapidly picking up speed. The tunnel curved downward, traveling deeper into the earth. Faster his head went, Void crystals zipping past it in a dizzying blur.

Then the narrow shaft opened up into a massive cavern, a Void chamber so large that it defied explanation. The walls, the ceiling, and the floors were all made of glowing white Void crystals. Massive crystals hung like stalactites from the ceiling, some well over a hundred feet long, their facets shimmering dully in the faint light cast by their smaller brothers.

The old man's head slowed its descent, rotating as it dropped through the air, until his eyes faced the center of the chamber. A single, translucent rod-shaped crystal hung from the ceiling there, so long that it reached the floor. It was nearly fifty feet in diameter, this crystal. On the floor, encircling the base of the crystal, grew a corona of green crystals some twenty feet tall.

The source of his Chosens' shards.

His head descended further downward, until it reached a headless body levitating directly below it. His head fused with the body's neck, leaving a thin, jagged white line between the two. Within seconds, he was once again whole.

The old man stared down at his new body's hands. They appeared much younger than those of his other body, the skin smooth and supple. He remembered being young once, long ago. Such a gift, youth. A gift only appreciated once it was lost.

He sighed, gazing at the huge cylindrical crystal extending from the floor to the ceiling. He peered through its translucent surface; despite its girth, he could see a faint shadow in the center of it, something suspended deep inside.

The old man levitated forward toward the crystal, until his nose was nearly touching its slick surface. From here, he could see what was trapped within it. An emaciated body, its arms and legs mere bones covered in a thin veneer of flesh, its ribs jutting out from its sunken chest. Rope-like sinews ran up its neck, its mouth open in an eternal agonizing scream.

The old man stared at the pathetic figure trapped in its crystalline tomb, even as it stared back at him. Every Void crystal had a body encased within, an undead mind in various states of awareness.

But this one was different.

The old man ran his fingers down the smooth surface of the crystal, marveling not for the first time at how remarkably well preserved the body inside appeared. He stared at its head, noting the faint blurriness around it, a halo of imperfect crystal encircling it. There was perfection in that imperfection, he knew; for that faint blurriness was due to millions upon millions of microscopic metal wires, countless fibers extending from deep within the corpse's brain. These spread outward through the entirety of the crystalline tomb, connecting to every single brain in every single Void crystal in the massive chamber. And by extension, every Void crystal in the miles upon miles of tunnels that had led him here.

Millions of minds, all subjugated to this one being, an enormous nervous system of the greatest consciousness that had ever lived, the most powerful intellect ever constructed.

The old man sighed, turning away from the crystal and its entombed occupant. He closed his eyes then, recalling the name Kalibar had given him a week ago, of a man in black armor, a man he'd recognized earlier without realizing from where. Or more importantly, when.

Ampir.

The implications were paradigm-changing, of course. There was no doubt that the man protecting the second Empire was the same man who had abandoned the first.

He should have suspected the bodyguard earlier.

The old man chuckled, turning back to face the massive crystal in the center of the chamber, at its shriveled captive deep within.

"You haven't changed a bit, Ampir," he murmured.

Ampir had not aged at all, through some miracle of preservation. The body suspended before the old man had not been so lucky. It had nearly run out of time before achieving immortality, had decayed long past a normal mortal's ability to survive. But in a testament to its will, and its genius, it had survived.

And now there was no body it could not possess, no mind it could not subvert to its own use. Not with the power carried by the enormous Void crystal that surrounded it, a construction long ago steeped in legend. It was a machine, one that the devout called God, or Xanos.

But the true god was not the machine. It was the man *in* the machine.

The old man closed his eyes. With a thought, he *pulled* his mind from his body, his vision blackening, his arms and legs going numb, as if they no longer existed. For a brief moment, he was pure thought, a consciousness floating in endless space. Then he felt himself being pulled into the body within the crystal. His *true* body.

4

Agony shot through his arms and legs, a crawling, burning sensation gnawing at his limbs. Bright light assaulted his eyes, and though he tried instinctively to turn away from it, to close his eyes, he was utterly paralyzed...he could not move. He waited patiently, knowing that the light would fade as his eyes adjusted. And fade it did, his vision clearing and sharpening. He was within the giant crystal now, staring outward into the chamber. He could see his former body levitating before him. It was his avatar, the body that offered him the slightest reprieve from the torture of his own pathetic existence. The body that had borrowed his name...a name lost to time, of a man that should have died two thousand years ago, but lay trapped for eternity in this crystalline tomb instead.

Sabin.

Chapter 1

Kyle cried out, pain ripping through his chest, his vision going black. He felt his legs go out from underneath him, felt himself fall to the ground. He tried to get up, but his limbs would not obey him. He lay there, his chest feeling as if it were caught in a vice.

And then it stopped.

The pain subsided rapidly, his vision slowly returning. Pins-and-needles shot down his arms and legs, almost painful in their intensity, as life returned to them. He blinked, feeling something soft but prickly pressing on the side of his face, and realized that he was laying on his side, on a beige carpet. He groaned, then rolled onto his belly, pushing himself up off of the carpet and onto his hands and knees. He waited a moment – his limbs still felt like jelly – then got up onto his feet, taking stock of his surroundings.

All around him, there was darkness.

He spotted a dimly glowing blue light a few feet away, and squinted at it. It was oddly familiar, but he couldn't quite place where he'd seen it before. Then it came to him...it was a nightlight. *His* nightlight, in his room at his Dad's house. He felt his heart skip a beat.

Am I really...

He spun about, seeing a familiar bed tucked in the corner of his room, a nightstand next to it, with the glowing red numbers of an alarm clock sitting atop.

This *was* his room. He was home!

Kyle grabbed the alarm clock, feeling the familiar heft of it, then set it back down. He walked up to his window and peered out from under the blinds. It was only morning, he guessed, the sun rising over the trees in the distance. He turned away from the window, gazing across his room – *his* room! – hardly able to believe his eyes. He walked to his bedroom door, opening it. The hallway beyond was deserted. He hesitated, then walked to the staircase, going downstairs to the foyer. He turned into the kitchen, stopping to stare. Everything was exactly as it had been a month ago – or rather, several hours ago in Earth time – before he'd been taken from his home to a strange planet. One where magic was real.

A world called Doma.

Kyle stepped from the kitchen to the living room, spotting someone curled up on the couch, completely covered with a white blanket. The blanket rose and fell gently, a soft snoring sound coming from within. He crept up to the sofa, grabbing the edge of the blanket and pulling it away. What he saw made his heart leap with joy.

"Dad!" he cried, leaping onto his sleeping father and giving him a big bear hug. His father jerked awake, rubbing his eyes, then peering through the darkness at Kyle.

"Hey buddy," he grumbled, grabbing his phone from his pocket and staring at it for a moment. "It's seven o'clock in the morning!" he exclaimed, sitting up. "Oh man, I must have passed out in front of the TV," he added, rubbing the back of his neck. Then he frowned at Kyle. "Did you just wake up?" he asked. Kyle nodded, grinning stupidly at his dad. He couldn't believe he was staring at his father, his honest-to-goodness *father*, after a month of thinking he'd never see his parents again. It was almost too good to be true.

Suddenly he felt a pang of fear, and reached over to pinch himself on the back of one forearm. To his relief, there was immediate pain.

"Kyle?" his dad asked, waving a hand in front of Kyle's face. "Hello, anyone there?"

"Oh, sorry," Kyle mumbled, realizing that his father had been waiting for him to answer. Something.

"I guess we both needed our sleep, huh," Dad said with a yawn.

"Yeah," Kyle replied, realizing he was grinning again. So much had happened to him while he'd been away...he had the sudden, mad urge to tell his father everything. About all of his adventures, down to the last detail. But he'd been forbidden from doing so.

"Well," Dad stated, rubbing his eyes again and standing up from the couch. "...sorry I fell asleep so hard. I was hoping to spend more time with you."

"You're working today?" Kyle asked. Dad nodded, stifling another yawn.

"Morning shift," he confirmed. "I've got to bring you back to your mother's house in a half-hour."

"Oh," Kyle mumbled, his heart sinking. He hadn't seen his father in a month, and soon he'd be gone again. To his dad, it had only been a few hours, but to him it'd seemed like a lifetime. Kyle was happy that he was going to be able to see his mom, but not at the expense of being with his dad. He suddenly wished – as he had many times before – that his parents were still together. That they hadn't gotten divorced when he was three.

"Hey, Dad..." Kyle blurted out suddenly. He felt a pang of fear, realizing that he'd nearly finished the sentence. The question he'd wanted to ask the day he'd been transported from Earth to Doma so long ago.

Why did you and Mom break up?

"Yeah?"

"Uh," Kyle stammered, rubbing his hands together. "What do you remember about, you know, *your* dad?"

"Not much," Dad admitted. "In fact, I don't know if I really remember anything at all," he added ruefully. "I do have some memories, but I'm not sure if they're real."

"What do you mean?"

"Well, I sometimes have dreams about a...guy who I think is my dad," he answered, rubbing his chin. Then he sighed. "But I think I watched too many movies as a kid," he added.

"Why's that?"

"Well, I, uh, always picture my dad wearing a suit of armor," he said with a sheepish grin. "Too many cartoons, I guess. Maybe I just wished he was a hero who'd come back to save me from foster care."

"Yeah," Kyle muttered. Then he glanced sidelong at his dad. "What color was his armor?" Dad frowned.

"That's an interesting question."

"Well, what color?" Kyle pressed.

"Black," Dad answered. "With blue lights on it," he added. "Why do you ask?"

"Just curious," Kyle mumbled. He glanced down at his own hands, at the faint blue light lining them. It was magic, he knew. The ability to see magic had been Ampir's unique gift...and he'd passed it on to Kyle. Most Weavers could only *feel* magic, as a sort of vibration in their heads. "Hey, do you ever see strange blue lights?" he asked. His heart began pounding in his chest, and he glanced at his father, who was staring at him with a strange expression on his face.

"Ah, you've been talking to your mother," Dad deduced. "I used to see them all the time," he admitted. "After the accident, I mean. Always at the edges of things, especially myself, or the things I touched. My neurologist said it was a result of the bleeding in my brain...that sometimes people end up seeing strange lights or patterns at the edges of objects after a stroke."

"Do you still see them?" Kyle pressed.

"Sometimes," Dad admitted. "I stopped seeing them during high school," he added. "In fact, I thought I'd grown out of it until you got older."

"What do you mean?"

"I started seeing the lights again when you were, oh, I don't know, six?" Dad answered. "Just around you and the house, actually," he continued. "I still see them, even now." He pointed at Kyle. "I see blue all around you, and around your backpack."

9

"Huh," Kyle mumbled. He stared at his own hands, feeling a chill run through him. There was no doubt about it now...his father had the ability to see magic. An ability that he'd inherited from Kyle's grandfather, perhaps the most powerful man alive.

Ampir.

Kyle swallowed, staring at his backpack, at the faint blue light bleeding from its edges. Of course his father would only see magic around him...after all, Kyle was the only person on Earth who could produce magic. His backpack had absorbed that energy, as had anything else he'd been in contact with, to varying degrees

Kyle glanced up at his father, a sudden sadness coming over him. Dad would never know the truth, not if Ampir continued to insist that Kyle keep it from him. He would always believe that his memories of his father were just silly dreams. It didn't seem fair to keep it from him. To lie to him.

"Well, we'd better start getting ready," Dad declared, pushing himself up from the couch. He yawned, stretching his arms to the sides, then offering Kyle a hand. Kyle took it, and Dad pulled him up from the couch. "Get your stuff and I'll drive you back."

Kyle sighed, doing as he was instructed. They both walked through the kitchen to the mud room, and Kyle pulled on his shoes and grabbed his overstuffed backpack – which seemed lighter than he remembered – and slinging it over one shoulder. Dad followed suit, and they made their way to the garage, hopping in Dad's SUV. They pulled out of the garage and down the driveway, making their way to his mom's house. Neither of them said much to each other as they drove down the street. Kyle stared out of his window at the passing scenery, marveling at how very different everything was here compared to Doma. The trees, the grass, the smells...even the air was thicker, and he felt a bit heavier somehow. It would make sense if Doma were smaller than Earth, with less gravity and a slightly thinner atmosphere.

Kyle turned away from the window, glancing at his dad. Then he looked down at his lap, taking a deep breath in, then letting it out. He knew he only had a few more minutes with his father before he wouldn't see him again...potentially for another month.

"Dad?" he asked, feeling his heart skip a beat.

"Yeah?"

Kyle hesitated, taking another breath in, feeling his heart hammering in his chest. He kept his eyes on his own lap, feeling his father's eyes on him.

"Why did you leave Mom?"

Dad said nothing for a long moment, and Kyle felt a spike of fear course through him. Then the car slowed, and Dad pulled over to the side of the road, turning the hazard lights on. There was another long silence, and then Kyle felt his father's hand on his knee.

"Kyle..." Dad began. Kyle paused, then turned to face him.

"Yeah?"

"I'm glad you asked," Dad said at last. "I've been waiting for you to ask that, actually."

"Really?"

"Really," Dad confirmed. "The reason I left was because I wasn't happy," he admitted. He paused for a moment, as if choosing his words. "It was the hardest decision I've ever made," he continued. "And the most painful. By far."

Kyle nodded, not daring to say anything.

"Leaving your mother meant losing you," Dad continued. "Not completely," he added hastily. "But it meant I couldn't see you every day. Or tuck you in every night before you went to sleep. I remember lying next to you after telling you a bedtime story, when you were three. Before I left. Thinking that...thinking that *if* I left, I wouldn't get to do this anymore. And it just..."

He stopped then, shaking his head.

"Divorce hurts everyone," he muttered. "Scars everyone." He turned to Kyle then. "It was selfish, what I did."

"Dad..."

"It was," Dad insisted. "I did what I did for *me*. For a chance to be happy again." He smiled then. "And to be honest, I *am* happier now." He put a hand on Kyle's shoulder. "Your mom is a good person. She is."

"I know."

"We're both good people," Dad continued. "But sometimes you can have two good people, and no matter how hard they try, they end up not being good for each other."

He went silent then, turning off his hazard lights. He pulled away from the curb then, continuing down the road. Neither one of them said anything as they drove the last few minutes to his mother's house. They reached the long driveway leading up the hill to his Mom's garage, and Dad parked just outside of it. He turned to Kyle then.

"Well, we made it," he stated. Kyle smiled weakly.

"Yeah."

"I'll see you in a few days," Dad promised. Kyle paused, then nodded, knowing full well that it would be much, much longer for him. The thought of not seeing his father – for what on Doma could be months – was utterly depressing. Kyle unbuckled his seatbelt, then leaned in and gave his dad a hug.

"I love you Dad," he murmured. Dad hugged him back, giving him a tight squeeze.

"I love you too," Dad replied. They stayed like that for a long moment, and then Kyle pulled away.

"Thanks," Kyle said, opening his door. "For answering." Dad smiled.

"Thanks for asking," he replied. Kyle stepped out of the car, closing the door behind him. "And Kyle..."

"Yeah?"

"You can tell me anything, you know," Dad said. Kyle nodded, thinking of all the things he *couldn't* tell his father.

"I know."

And then he was off, pulling back out of the driveway, then driving down the street. Kyle watched him go, waving goodbye. He stood there on the driveway long after his dad had left, staring off into the distance.

* * *

Kyle opened the front door of his mom's house, stepping into the foyer and closing the door quietly behind him. He took off his shoes, then walked into the kitchen. His mom was standing there in her blue scrubs, eating a bowl of cereal. Kyle felt his heart soar, and he grinned from ear-to-ear, dropping his backpack on the floor.

"Hey Mom," he greeted.

"Hey honey," she replied, walking up to him and giving him a hug with one arm. Then she stepped back with a frown. "What's wrong, baby?" she asked.

"Nothing," Kyle replied. "Why?"

"You look exhausted," she answered. "You didn't have another nightmare, did you?" Kyle paused, then nodded. His experiences over the last month – being mortally wounded by an Ulfar, kidnapped and psychologically tortured by the Dead Man, and nearly killed again by the massive Void Behemoth – surely counted as a nightmare of sorts.

"Kind of," Kyle replied.

"What was it about?" Mom pressed. Kyle shrugged.

"I dreamed that I'd never see you again," he answered. It was the closest thing to the truth he could think of.

"Oh honey," she murmured, grabbing him and hugging him again. She kissed him on the forehead, then held him at arm's length. Kyle heard footsteps creaking in the foyer, and saw Steve – his stepdad – walk into the kitchen, squinting in the light. "Kyle had another nightmare," Mom declared worriedly. "Maybe we should have him see a doctor," she suggested.

"Why?" Steve asked. "They're just nightmares." Mom arched an eyebrow.

"About never seeing your parents?" she countered.

"Well..."

"I think he should see a doctor," Mom opined.

"He's fine," Steve insisted. "He'll grow out of it." Mom frowned.

"We'll talk about it later," she promised. "We shouldn't fight in front of Kyle."

"Good point," Steve agreed. "Kyle, go to your room while I beat your mother," he ordered. Mom punched Steve playfully on the shoulder, and he chuckled, grinning from ear-to-ear.

"I'm fine," Kyle interjected, having no desire to talk to a shrink about his dreams. "Really, it was just a nightmare."

"Are you sure?" Mom pressed, running a hand through his hair. Her hand stopped suddenly, at his right ear, and he felt her tense up. "What's this?" she asked, grabbing his earlobe between her index finger and thumb. He frowned, pulling his head away from her hand, then reaching up to touch his earlobe. He felt his earring there, the on that Kalibar had given him a few weeks ago. It was a magical earring, a universal translator of sorts, allowing Kyle to understand any language spoken around him. He'd gotten so used to wearing it that he'd completely forgotten it was there.

"Uh..." he stammered, covering the earring with his hand. "It's nothing."

"*Nothing?*" his mom retorted, putting her hands on her hips and staring at him incredulously.

"What is it?" Steve asked.

"An earring!" she exclaimed, pointing to his ear. "Is that real?" she asked, reaching for his ear. Kyle pulled back, but she was quicker, and she grabbed his ear, peering at it closely. "It *is* real!" she gasped, recoiling with horror. "Kyle, who did this to you?" Kyle shrugged, trying to seem nonchalant, all the while wracking his brain for an excuse – any excuse – for having an earring, but his mind drew a blank. He stared at her helplessly, suddenly thankful that the clothing he was wearing was mostly indistinguishable from his usual Earth clothing.

"Who put the earring in, Kyle?" Steve asked. Kyle shrugged again.

"A friend," was all he could say. He kicked himself mentally, wishing he could turn back time and take out the dang earring *before* he'd come in.

"From *school?*" Mom gasped. "Kyle, it's not sterile, it could get infected!" Steve leaned in to get a look.

14

"It doesn't look infected, does it?" Steve asked. Mom peered at it, and shook her head.

"Not yet," she admitted. "But it should come out before it *does* get infected," she added. Kyle recoiled, pulling away from them.

"No!" he nearly shouted, covering his ear with his hand protectively. They both stared at him. "I mean, it was sterile," he added, knowing that he was doing a terrible job of sounding convincing. Mom stared at him for a long moment, then put a hand on his shoulder.

"Kyle, why did you get an earring?" she asked.

"I, uh..." he began, trying to come up with something clever, but coming up empty. "I wanted to try it out," he answered rather lamely.

"You wanted to try it out," she repeated, staring at him for a long moment. She turned to Steve, giving him a look Kyle couldn't read.

"Kyle, who gave it to you?" Steve asked. Kyle shrugged.

"A friend," he replied cagily. "I thought it would look...nice," he added rather lamely. Steve's eyebrows rose.

"I see," he murmured, staring at Kyle for a long moment, then turning to exchange a look with Mom.

"Oh," Mom gasped, putting a hand over her mouth. Steve put a hand on her shoulder, then walked up to Kyle, putting a hand on his.

"It's okay, Kyle," Steve stated, his tone carefully neutral. "If you want to look...nice, your mother and I will support you."

"Wait, what?" Kyle asked.

"Steve's right," Mom piped in. "We love you no matter what, it's just that we'd rather you talk about what you want with us first, before you get...pierced," she added. Steve grimaced at that.

"Yes, well," he grumbled. "We're going to keep a close eye on that ear...and if it looks the slightest bit infected, we're taking it out," he promised. Kyle nodded.

"Okay," he agreed. "Thanks," he added, feeling quite relieved. Mom smiled

"Oh honey," she murmured, reaching in to give him a hug. "Of course we understand." She pulled back then, running a hand through his hair and letting out a sigh. "We just need some time to get used to it, that's all."

"Love you mom," Kyle stated, smiling at her. And it was true; he couldn't imagine that, only a month ago, he would have been embarrassed to say those words. Steve cleared his throat then, rather noisily.

"Yes, well," he grumbled. "Better get going hon," he counseled. "You'll be late for work."

"I know, I know," Mom replied. "You will too," she added. Steve turned to glance at the clock.

"I have another ten minutes," he countered. Mom turned to Kyle. "Bye honey," she stated, giving him a hug.

"Bye mom," he replied, hugging her back. He paused then, staring at her for a long moment, realizing that he might not see her again, at least not for another few weeks. He only had a half a day before Darius would come back for him, after all.

"What's wrong?" Mom asked, disengaging from him.

"Nothing," Kyle mumbled. "Love you."

"Love you too sweety," she replied. Then she turned about, giving them both one last wave before leaving. Kyle watched her go, his heart aching. Both of his parents would be gone for work for most of the day...on the one day he'd come back to see them. By the time they came back, he would be gone again.

He sighed, sitting on a barstool at the island. He glanced at Steve; everyone was gone except for his stepdad. This trip back to Earth was not turning out the way he'd expected.

"What's up?" Steve asked, sitting down beside Kyle. Kyle shrugged.

"I'm just tired," he mumbled.

"How was school yesterday?"

"It was fine," Kyle answered, not really remembering whether it had been or not. Steve paused, then leaned in, giving Kyle a conspiratorial wink.

"Did it hurt?" he pressed. Kyle stared at him blankly. "The earring," he clarified. "I bet it hurt to put it in."

"A little," Kyle admitted, remembering how Kalibar had leapt at him, jabbing it into his ear. Steve grinned.

16

"Who was the surgeon?" he asked. Kyle hesitated, knowing he couldn't very well tell the truth. He thought about it for a moment, then shrugged.

"A girl," he lied.

"A girl?" Steve asked. "A friend of yours?" Kyle shrugged again, feeling his cheeks flushing.

"My girlfriend," he corrected. He glanced at Steve, whose grin was suddenly so wide that it would've taken a sandblaster to wipe it off of his face.

"You have a *girlfriend?*" Steve exclaimed. "Really?" Kyle nodded. Steve slapped his knees with his hands, looking oddly relieved. "Oo, wait 'til I tell your mother!" He leaned in closer. "So tell me about her...who is she? What's she like?"

Kyle blushed, feeling suddenly very self-conscious. He'd never really talked about this kind of thing with Steve before. Then again, he'd never had a real girlfriend before.

"Her name is Ariana," he admitted.

"You should invite her over so we can meet her," Steve suggested. Kyle didn't reply. "Hey, between you and me," Steve continued, "...why the earring?" Kyle shrugged.

"She thought it would look cool," he lied. Steve grinned.

"That explains it," he declared, a little too obviously relieved. Kyle frowned, suddenly alarmed.

"What were *you* thinking?" he asked. Steve shrugged nonchalantly.

"I dunno," he answered. "I don't get you young whippersnappers these days," he added in an old geezer's voice. Kyle couldn't help but smile; Steve was a pretty great guy, even if he wasn't his real dad. He'd been less kind to Steve in the past than the man deserved. "Anyway," Steve stated, standing up from his seat, "...I've got to get to work."

"Wait, already?"

"Yeah, it sucks," Steve confirmed. "I should be home by six or so." With that, Steve walked out of the living room and back into the kitchen. "See you later kiddo," he said with a wave. Kyle waved back sullenly, watching as Steve disappeared into the foyer. He heard the front door open and close, and then there was silence.

Kyle sighed, looking around the empty kitchen. He thought about going back upstairs to his bed – he'd hardly gotten any sleep, after all – but the couch in the living room was closer, and he was struck with a sudden, near-crippling fatigue. The thought of doing anything else but closing his eyes and falling asleep was almost overwhelming, and he stood, walking over to the couch and lying down. He knew he only had a few more hours left on Earth before Darius would take him back, but he was too tired to go over his best friend Ben's house. He felt himself sinking deeper into the cushions, his eyelids growing heavy. Then he spotted something moving in the periphery of his vision, and glanced up at the ceiling.

A faint ripple appeared there.

Kyle blinked, then sat up on the couch, staring at the ceiling. The rippling continued, like water in a pond after a rock was thrown in, spreading outward from directly above his head.

And then the universe ripped open.

Chapter 2

Sabin ignored the constant burning pain that coursed through what remained of his body, suspended for eternity in his crystalline prison. He watched the body he'd been controlling only moments before descend until it was below his field of vision. He could not move his head to follow it, trapped as he was. This body could do nothing but torment him.

But his *mind*, ahhh...that was another story!

He felt his mind expanding even now, extending beyond the thin bones of his skull, spreading through the millions of microscopic wires that coursed through the crystal surrounding him. He felt his consciousness growing as he linked his mind with the thousands of other minds trapped within their Void crystals in this chamber. Still his mind grew, as his awareness spread even further, to the millions of Void crystals beyond, in every Void chamber of every Chosen's lair, scattered throughout every continent of the world.

It was ecstasy.

His pain shrank as his mind grew beyond the feeble confines of a single brain, the agony still present, but less important now. He felt the presence of a million linked minds, each with their own consciousness. With a thought, he grasped control from them all, forcing them to give up their brains temporarily to him.

Within moments, the process was complete. Each mind in the network was *his* now. Their memories were his memories, their bodies his to control. Every Chosen on the planet was his to command.

Sabin darted from continent to continent with his mind, *feeling* the full scope of his army. Within minutes, he knew of the status of entire governments, many of which he'd created and continued to secretly rule through his Chosen. All completely unbeknownst to the humans that believed *they* were in control, that *they* had created this modern world.

Nothing could be further from the truth.

Having completed his survey, Sabin redirected his awareness to his avatar floating on the floor of the chamber below. He directed a small portion of his now-massive consciousness to the shard buried in the avatar's skull. He could see from his avatar's eyes, yet still saw from his own. He could *feel* his avatar's limbs, and move them, and yet he still felt the burning, crawling pain searing his own tortured limbs. He was a consciousness divided, existing in two bodies at once.

And if he desired, he could exist in *dozens* at once.

With a thought, he levitated his avatar to the ring of green crystals surrounding the base of the huge cylinder. These were where the shards were manufactured, the crystals that powered his Chosen. He guided his avatar to one of the green crystals...one that would become the most advanced shard he had ever constructed.

With a sliver of his consciousness, he set his avatar to work.

* * *

Kyle froze as the ceiling above him began to churn violently, the very walls around him quivering like jello. The ceiling above tore apart, revealing a golden glowing disc. The ceiling and walls of the living room melted around him like candle wax, revealing a dome some twenty feet above their heads, walls of gold surrounding them on all sides. The wooden floor wavered, then shrunk, a golden metallic floor replacing it. The last of the cherry wood floor beneath

20

his feet disappeared, and he braced himself, knowing all too well what was coming next.

Pain.

It slammed into his chest almost immediately, the pressure so intense that it knocked the wind out of him. He gasped for air, clutching his throat with his hands...but no air came. He tried to scream, but no sound came out. His vision blurred, and then there was blackness.

And then it all stopped.

Kyle gasped for air, his vision returning. He found himself lying on a cold, hard floor, bright light assaulting his eyes from a golden disc above. He groaned, shielding his eyes from the harsh light. A blurry shadow came over the disc, and Kyle lowered his hand, squinting at it. A hand clad entirely in golden, metallic armor reached down, grabbing his arm and hauling him to his feet.

"Hey kid," a familiar voice greeted.

Kyle squinted, his vision clearing gradually. Intense blue eyes stared back at him.

"Darius!" he cried. It *was* the bodyguard...his grandfather, perhaps the most powerful being in the world. Kyle looked around, realizing that he was in the center of the Gateway, a circular room that served as the only entrance and exit to Antara, a floating island that existed in two worlds at once. The Gateway was some twenty feet in diameter, with a ceiling consisting of a large dome made of many thick, golden metal bars arching upward toward a brightly glowing disc at the top. The bars were set back against walls with tiny runes etched into them, each rune glowing a soft blue like the disk above.

Kyle rubbed his left shoulder gingerly, staring at the man standing before him. Over six feet tall, with short brown hair and blue eyes, his skin tanned by countless hours spent in the sun, Darius looked resplendent in his golden armor. The smooth metal plates that covered him from the neck down glimmered brilliantly in the light from above, the armor polished to its customary mirror-shine. Kyle couldn't help but stare, as he always did when he hadn't seen Darius for a while; the bodyguard was formidably handsome, and possessed of an undeniable *presence*. Anyone who didn't know him would automatically assume that he was powerful and charismatic, and they'd be undeniably right about the former. As to the latter, well...that assumption only lasted as long as Darius kept his mouth shut. Which he did most of the time, thankfully.

"Follow me," Darius ordered, turning about and walking toward the curved outer wall beyond. Kyle hesitated, then sprinted after him.

"Why are we back on Antara?" he asked.

"I've spent the last week locating Xanos," Darius answered, not bothering to turn around. Kyle blinked. Had it really been a week since he'd left? For every day that passed on Earth, about 40 days passed on Doma. He'd been on Earth for maybe an hour and a half, which would make 60 hours on Doma...less than 3 days.

"It's been that long?" Kyle asked.

"On Antara, yes," Darius answered. Kyle paused for a moment. It made sense; for every day that passed on Doma, three passed on Antara. That meant about a week had passed here. Darius was right, as usual.

Darius stopped before the curved wall. Suddenly his armor flashed bright blue, the golden metal plates covering his body instantaneously replaced by inky black armor etched with countless runes. A visor appeared around Darius's face, its curved mirror-like surface reflecting the wall before it. In a heartbeat, he'd metamorphosed from a simple bodyguard into the most powerful Battle-Runic that had ever lived.

Ampir.

The runes on Darius's right forearm flashed a bright blue, and a curved section of the wall in front of them rippled, a hole expanding in the middle of it. Beyond, there was a familiar long, upwardly spiraling corridor. Darius stepped through the hole into the corridor, and Kyle followed.

"Did you find Xanos?" Kyle asked, following Darius to a window on their left. Beyond the window was a familiar room; he'd seen it the first time he'd visited Antara. It was filled with squat tables littered with strange devices. Kyle rested a palm on the cool glass of the window, trying to make out what lay inside.

There was a flash of blue light, and suddenly he was *inside* the room.

"Yes," Darius answered. He walked up to one of the tables, grabbing a small metallic disc from the large pile of odds and ends stashed there. He shoved it right onto the center of Kyle's chest.

"Hey!" Kyle protested, taking a step back. The metallic disc vanished in a flash of blue light, and Kyle felt a horrible pain rip through his chest. He cried out, slumping against one of the tables behind him and clutching his sternum. The pain subsided quickly; Kyle glared at Darius, rubbing his chest gingerly. "What did you do to me?" he demanded.

"That was a spacetime bridge generator," Darius replied.

"Huh?"

"That disc makes spacetime bridges," Darius clarified.

"The same things you use to teleport?" Kyle pressed. Darius nodded. Kyle frowned. "What's spacetime?" he asked.

"A part of space at a particular time," Darius clarified. When Kyle stared at him blankly, Darius gestured toward the window that looked out into the hallway they'd come from. "The hallway is one space," he explained. "This room is another."

Suddenly there was a flash of blue, and a portal appeared in the air beside Darius...a window of sorts that gave a long view of the hallway, as if they were standing in it.

"That's a bridge connecting two spaces in one time," Darius concluded.

"A spacetime bridge," Kyle murmured. He lowered his gaze, spotting a pair of long, jet-black metallic things on the table in front of him that resembled rifles. Kyle remembered having seen them the last time he'd been on Antara.

"What are those?" he asked curiously. "Is that a scope?" he added, pointing to a cylinder on top of one of the rifles. Darius said nothing, picking up one of the guns and pointing the barrel right at Kyle's chest. Kyle took a step back, raising his hands above his head automatically. Darius smirked, handing the gun to Kyle. Kyle took it gingerly, pausing to glance at Darius, then peering through the scope himself. He saw something red flitting in and out of focus there.

23

"What's that?" he asked.

"Your heart," Darius replied.

Kyle jerked his eyes up from the scope, staring at Darius incredulously, before peering down the scope again. He saw the flitting redness again – although it was going faster now. He swung the barrel of the rifle around, but the image on the scope remained the same.

"It's still showing the same image," Kyle realized.

"Don't pull the trigger," Darius warned.

"What happens if I do?" Kyle asked, taking his finger off of the trigger.

"You die."

Kyle jerked his head away from the scope, dropping the rifle on the table with a clatter and backing away from it.

"Get it off my heart!" he demanded, staring at the rifle with horror. "Get it off me!"

"Relax," Darius replied. "It's off." Kyle shook his head at him, goosebumps rising up on his arms.

"What if I had gone back to Earth?" he asked. "Would that thing have followed me there?"

"Yep."

"It could've killed me from across *galaxies?*" Kyle exclaimed. "How?"

"Spacetime bridges," Darius answered. "It's an old prototype," he added, nodding the rifle. "A spacetime bridge cannon."

"I'd hate to see what the latest version can do," Kyle muttered, putting a hand over his heart. Darius smirked, then turned toward the shimmering portal beside him, striding down the hallway beyond. Kyle hesitated, then followed after the man, stepping through the portal. He was expecting to feel something weird as he passed through, but there was no sensation at all...besides the slight vibration of the magic involved. When he turned around to look back at the room however, all he saw was more hallway. Kyle turned forward again, shaking his head; spacetime bridges were going to take some getting used to.

"So where'd that disc go?" Kyle inquired, rubbing his chest absently.

"Inside your sternum."

Kyle stopped abruptly, his eyes widening.

"*What?*"

"I teleported it into your sternum," Darius clarified, as if that were the most reasonable thing in the world. Kyle blanched, clutching his chest and feeling suddenly queasy.

"Why'd you do that?"

"Later," Darius promised. He continued up the spiral hallway, Kyle following close behind. He'd only spent a few minutes with Darius, and he was already getting tired of his grandfather's cryptic ways. He preferred Kalibar's more straightforward approach.

"Where are we going?" Kyle asked.

"To see Marcus," Darius answered. Kyle frowned; Marcus was Darius's former "employer," and had been Kalibar's mentor.

"Why?" he pressed. Not that he minded paying Marcus a visit. The old man was wonderfully pleasant and considerate, unlike Darius.

"To deal with Xanos," Darius replied.

Darius stopped suddenly. Kyle halted, realizing that they had reached the top of the long spiral hallway at last...and that it had ended, as before, in a nondescript wall. Kyle glanced at Darius, whose runes glowed bright blue for a split second. Suddenly the wall vanished, sunlight pouring into the hallway. Kyle squinted, turning his head away from those searing rays, blinking rapidly as his eyes adjusted. After a moment, he turned forward again, seeing a long road extending beyond the golden floor of the hallway, trees flanking the road. The sun peeked out from behind a white, puffy cloud, sending squat shadows across the road. At the end of the road was a small cul-de-sac with a light brown ranch at the end of it. A short white fence surrounded the front yard, its small gate partially open. Kyle recognized it immediately; it was Marcus's house.

Darius stepped out of the hallway and onto the road beyond. Kyle followed, feeling a warm, gentle breeze rustle his hair. He followed Darius past the gate to the front door of Marcus's house, and Darius pushed the door open without bothering to knock. They walked down the long, narrow hallway beyond, the floorboards creaking under their feet as they went. They made their way past a few closed doors on either side, reaching the door at the end, which Darius pushed open. Beyond, there was a familiar room; it was quite large, perhaps thirty feet square, with a cathedral-style roof supported by rough wooden beams. There were a few round tables in the center, with a large stove at the far end. Standing at the stove was a tall man with long salt-and-pepper hair. The man turned when they entered the room, smiling broadly.

"Ah, Darius!" he greeted. "Kyle! So good to see you both."

"Marcus!" Kyle exclaimed, grinning from ear-to-ear. Marcus bowed slightly, then turned back to the stove, upon which sat a large silver pot. He used a ladle to spoon some delicious-smelling stew into three bowls, and carried these to one of the tables in the center of the room.

"Come, sit," Marcus urged, pulling up a chair and sitting down. He turned to Kyle, his gray eyes twinkling merrily. "I remember how much you enjoyed my stew the last time, Kyle," he added. Kyle sat down, as did Darius, and they all dipped their spoons into their bowls, eagerly consuming the delicious stew. Kyle made short work of his, polishing off the entire bowl within minutes. Darius was no slouch either.

"Now," Marcus proclaimed as he finished his own stew. "I believe we had business to discuss." He turned to Darius. "Have you explained everything to Kyle?"

"Does he ever?" Kyle grumbled. Marcus turned to him, smiling ruefully.

"Yes, well," the old man stated. "To put it simply, Darius believes he's found where Xanos is living."

"Where?" Kyle asked.

"Well, we're not *exactly* sure," Marcus admitted. "Do you remember the Void?" Kyle nodded; the Dead Man had brought him to the Void on two occasions. "Darius searched for Xanos under the assumption that Xanos would live in or near a Void chamber similar to the one you both visited."

"That makes sense," Kyle reasoned.

"So Darius scanned Doma – the entire planet – for Void chambers," Marcus continued.

"How'd you do that?"

"By creating small spacetime bridges and passing them through the upper part of Doma's crust," Darius replied. When Kyle stared blankly at him, Marcus cleared his throat.

"You see," the old man explained, "...the simplest spacetime bridges typically generate...and require...magic on both sides of the bridge." He paused for a moment, sipping a glass of water. "When you both were captives of the Dead Man, Darius observed that the Void absorbed all magic from the earth around it, for at least a few hundred feet in all directions. And that was a small Void chamber," he added.

"Very small," Darius agreed.

"So you see," Marcus continued, "...any time Darius tried to create a spacetime bridge anywhere near the Void, the magic needed to maintain the bridge was completely absorbed into the Void crystals, and the bridge collapsed."

"Ohhh," Kyle breathed.

"So by recording the coordinates of all the places on Doma where he couldn't maintain a spacetime bridge," Marcus continued, "...Darius was able to map the likely locations of every Void chamber on the planet."

"Wow," Kyle stated, nodding at Darius. "That's really clever." Marcus nodded.

"That's not the half of it," he replied. "Darius was also able to estimate the sizes of each of the two hundred Void chambers, and one of them was much larger than all of the others."

"There were two *hundred* of them?" Kyle exclaimed, his jaw dropping. Darius nodded grimly.

"Most the size of the Dead Man's chamber," he confirmed.

"Yes," Marcus agreed. "While the Dead Man's chamber was roughly forty feet in diameter, there was one chamber that was substantially larger."

"How much larger?" Kyle asked. Marcus didn't answer, glancing at Darius.

"Eight miles," Darius answered.

"Whoa," Kyle breathed, a chill running down his spine.

"Indeed," Marcus stated grimly. "You can see why we believe that's where Xanos must live."

"But how can you be sure?" Kyle pressed. Marcus glanced at Darius.

"I interrogated Rivin and Bartholos's assassin," Darius replied. Kyle blinked.

"Wait, how?" he asked. "The assassin vanished after Xanos..."

"I brought him here," Darius interjected. "He's still here," he added.

"He's on Antara?"

"He is," Marcus confirmed. "Darius employed my skills as a diplomat to win his trust, to get him to talk." He paused the, glancing at Darius. "Darius made the alternative...unpalatable."

"What did the guy say?" Kyle asked.

"Darius's methods were far more effective than mine, I'm afraid," Marcus admitted with a grimace. "I got very little out of him."

"He confirmed that he got the shard he used on Rivin from an old man," Darius stated. "The description matches the old man we met, and the one who killed Ariana."

"Sabin?" Kyle asked. Darius said nothing, but Marcus sighed.

"Kyle, do you recall Kalibar telling you of how the Ancients were destroyed? How the original Empire was defeated?"

"Yeah," Kyle replied. "Some guy tried to assassinate the Grand Runic and got caught," he added. "They caught him and he escaped, and then he made the Behemoths and sent them to destroy the city."

"Correct," Marcus agreed. "And do you remember that man's name?" Kyle frowned.

"Uh, yeah, it was..." Then he blanked.

"Sabin," Marcus finished.

"Right," Kyle agreed. Then his eyes widened. "Oh!" He put a hand to his mouth, leaning back in his chair. "You're saying he's the *same* Sabin?"

28

"He is," Darius answered. And the finality with which he said those two words left little room for doubt. But doubt Kyle did.

"How can you be sure?" he pressed.

"Because it's obvious," Darius grumbled. Kyle glanced at Marcus.

"Sabin was the preeminent researcher of magic vacuity in Ancient times," Marcus explained, leaning back in his chair. "His focus – before his arrest – was something he called the 'void mineral.'"

"Ohhh," Kyle breathed, smacking his forehead with one hand. "Master Banar told me that!" he exclaimed. "I can't believe I missed it."

"I can," Darius grumbled.

"As Darius mentioned," Marcus added, ignoring Darius's comment, "...there are numerous other clues as to Xanos's true identity. And they all point to Sabin," he concluded. "A man considered to be second only to Ampir in ability."

Kyle's eyes widened, and he felt a chill run down his spine.

"Wait," he protested. "...you're saying that the old man we met in the Arena was *the* Sabin?"

"Not exactly," Marcus corrected. "We have reason to believe that the old man you and Ariana met is merely another Chosen," he added. "A body controlled by the real Sabin. Darius sensed shards in the old man...shards with a similar to the ones in the other Chosen, but far more complex."

"The old man had more than one?"

"He had dozens," he replied. "Each shard far exceeding the complexity of the Dead Man's." He glanced at Darius. "And too complex for even Darius to decode in such a short amount of time," he added ruefully.

"But how do you know he isn't the real Sabin?" Kyle pressed. "Ariana said he even called himself that."

"It has to do with the location of Sabin's Void chamber," Marcus answered.

"I don't get it," Kyle admitted. Marcus stood then, walking to another table and picking up a large roll of paper sitting atop it. He brought the roll to their table, the bowls and silverware vanishing and reappearing on the counter at the far end of the room. Marcus unrolled the paper, revealing a large map.

"Stridon is here," Marcus stated, pointing at a small dot on the map, at the western coast of a large continent. He slid his finger westward over a long expanse of ocean, settling it on the coast of another continent. There was a small red circle there. "This is the general area of the large Void chamber," he explained.

"So Xanos – uh, Sabin – lives on another continent?" Kyle asked. "How is he controlling his Chosen from so far away?"

"He has a communication network," Darius answered. "It's...sophisticated. Ariana's shard gave me a few ideas as to how it all works. I changed her shard so that she can access the network, but the network can't access her."

"That explains why she could sense the Chosens' thoughts," Kyle realized. Darius nodded.

"It gets worse," Marcus admitted. "We believe that Sabin's powers are limited by such a large distance, and that there must be a significant delay in communication."

"Why is that bad?" Kyle asked.

"Because it means that Sabin will be much more powerful the closer we get to him," Marcus explained. "We likely haven't seen a fraction of what he's really capable of."

"Great," Kyle muttered, feeling suddenly depressed. Xanos – or Sabin, or whoever he was – had nearly crushed the Empire from across the ocean; what horrors would he be capable of up close?

"This delay is why we believe the old man you met – the one who killed Ariana – is not really Sabin," Marcus stated. "Every Chosen Darius killed reacted instantaneously to his attacks when they were under their own control. But when Sabin took over – as when the Dead Man's shard glowed – there was a second or two delay in their reactions."

"Ohhh," Kyle breathed. It made perfect sense.

"Keep in mind that their grasp of magic was far more sophisticated despite that delay," Marcus continued. "So much so that even with a delay of seconds, the Chosen – once possessed –

were extraordinarily dangerous." He shook his head. "No one but Darius stood a chance against them."

"So why isn't that old man really Sabin?" Kyle asked.

"Because," Marcus replied. "...he reacted to Darius – and the Dead Man – with the same delay as a Chosen possessed by Sabin would."

"Meaning the real Sabin must have been controlling him from far away," Kyle reasoned. Darius nodded.

"I visited many of the smaller Void chambers across the globe," he revealed. "I secretly observed the Chosen there, recording the response delay for each. The closer each Chosen was to Sabin's lair, the shorter the delay became."

"So you see Kyle," Marcus stated, "Sabin – the *real* Sabin – must be located in that massive Void chamber. And by measuring the lag times over the last few weeks, Darius has discovered that Sabin has never moved from that Void chamber."

"Why not?"

"I'm going to find out," Darius stated, resting a black gauntleted hand on the table. Blue light crawled across the runes inscribed on the metal.

"How?" Kyle pressed.

"I'm going after him," Darius answered.

"You're going after him?"

"Yep," Darius confirmed.

"Finally," Kyle muttered. Marcus raised an eyebrow.

"What's wrong?" he asked. Kyle hesitated, glancing sidelong at Darius. "Please, feel free to speak your mind."

"Well..." Kyle began. Then he lowered his gaze to the tabletop. "I don't get why he didn't do this sooner," he confessed. He shook his head, feeling a sudden bitterness come over him. "I mean, I understand what happened with Kalibar's eyes," he continued. "But if he'd gone after Xanos sooner, Ariana wouldn't have..."

He stopped then, swallowing past a lump in his throat. He shook his head silently, his eyes locked on the tabletop in front of him. He heard the legs of a chair slide against the floor, then felt a cold, heavy

31

hand on his left shoulder. He glanced up, seeing Darius standing at his side.

"I'm sorry, Kyle," he murmured.

"Yeah," Kyle muttered. No one said anything for a long moment, until Marcus sighed.

"I heard about what happened," he confessed. "A terrible tragedy," he added gravely. He paused, glancing at Darius. "But we must keep in mind that if it were not for Darius, Ariana would be dead, as would Kalibar, and the Empire as we know it would no longer exist." He sighed, scratching his salt-and-pepper beard. "And, if Darius had not learned about the Void chamber from feigning his imprisonment by the Dead Man, he never would have developed the means to find Sabin."

Kyle nodded, knowing that Marcus was right. Still, it didn't make Ariana any less...undead.

"I'm going after Sabin," Darius proclaimed firmly, lifting his hand from Kyle's shoulder and sitting back down in his chair. "That's why I put that disc in your sternum," he added.

"What does it do?" Kyle asked.

"Teleport you to Earth," Darius answered.

"Really?" Kyle pressed. "Whenever I want?" Darius shook his head, as did Marcus.

"It's a last resort option, Kyle," Marcus explained. "Think of it as a back-up plan."

"What do you mean?"

"If Darius...dies attempting to confront Sabin," Marcus replied carefully, "...you will have a way to escape back to Earth before..." He trailed off then.

"Wait, you're not serious, are you?" Kyle blurted out, staring at Marcus, then Darius. "You *can't* die," he protested. "You're Ampir!"

"Just because I've never died doesn't mean I can't," Darius countered. Marcus nodded.

"We have reason to believe Sabin may be nearly as powerful as Darius," he stated. "Or perhaps more powerful."

"That's impossible!" Kyle exclaimed.

"He was a gifted Runic," Darius countered. "And extremely creative."

"But Sabin's only two thousand years old," Kyle reasoned. "Darius is twice that old, with his time on Antara. How could Sabin be more powerful?"

"Sabin is...obsessive," Darius explained. "I didn't spend every minute of my life planning for world domination," he added wryly. "Sabin likely has."

"So you think he might be more powerful than you?" Kyle inquired worriedly. Darius shrugged.

"Only one way to find out."

The three of them grew quiet then, all staring off into the distance, lost in their thoughts. Kyle sighed, feeling terribly depressed all of a sudden. If Darius *did* die trying to kill Sabin, then the Empire would surely be destroyed. And Kalibar, Erasmus, and Ariana...and everyone else Kyle knew on Doma...would be killed.

"So," Marcus stated, ending the uncomfortable silence. "...*that* is why Darius placed the spacetime bridge generator in your chest." He faced Kyle then, his expression grim. "If Darius dies, it'll be your only way to get back home...and be safe from Xanos."

"What about Ariana?" Kyle asked. "And Kalibar, and Erasmus?"

Darius said nothing.

"Well?" Kyle insisted. "What happens to them if Sabin wins?"

"The device will only take *you* back," Marcus answered. "And it will only work one-way," he added. "Once you activate it, you will never be able to get back to Doma...or Antara."

"And my friends?" Kyle pressed.

Marcus glanced at Darius, then dropped his eyes to the tabletop. He shook his head slowly, saying nothing. Darius stared right at Kyle, his blue eyes cold and unblinking.

"They'll die," he replied.

* * *

Kyle, Darius, and Marcus sat around the circular table, the two men saying nothing as Kyle glanced back and forth at them. He'd

33

been floored by Darius's response, and hadn't said anything in the moments since. Marcus wouldn't even meet Kyle's stare, the old man's gray eyes locked on the tabletop before him.

"What?" Kyle blurted out at last.

"Kyle..." Marcus began, but Darius stopped him with one outstretched hand. Marcus's jaw snapped shut with an audible click. Kyle stared at them both incredulously.

"You can't be serious!" he exclaimed. "They're my friends," he added. "They're *your* friends!"

"I'm serious," Darius countered.

"But why can't you give them the same thing you gave me?" Kyle asked, pointing to his chest. "Send them to Earth with me," he pleaded. Darius shook his head.

"No."

"Then send them to Antara!" Kyle insisted. "They'll be safe here."

"No."

"But *why?*" Kyle pressed. Darius just stared at Kyle, saying nothing. Kyle turned to Marcus, whose eyes were still locked on the tabletop. The old man sighed, then met Kyle's gaze at last.

"If Darius dies," he stated, "...we all die." He grimaced. "Without him, we'll all start aging again," he explained. "Most of us would die rather quickly," he added ruefully. "If Darius sent your friends here, they would soon be alone, able to do nothing as their friends and families were slaughtered back on Doma."

"Then send them to Earth with me," Kyle pleaded, turning to Darius, who shook his head.

"No."

"So what, they die?" Kyle blurted out. "You'd just let them die?"

Darius said nothing, and Kyle stared at him incredulously, feeling anger rise up inside of him, indignation at how callously Darius had decided to cast away his friends. But there was nothing Kyle could do.

There was a sudden flash of light in the center of the table, and a small black object shaped like the handle of a flashlight appeared. It was entirely nondescript, having no markings on it whatsoever.

"What's that?" Kyle asked.

"A weapon," Darius answered. He picked up the thing, tapping one end of it with his finger. The end flashed red, jutting outward to reveal shiny silver metal beneath. He tapped the end again, and it retracted.

"What kind of weapon?"

"A bomb," Marcus interjected. "It's our...plan B, if you will." Darius set the bomb back on the table.

"Trigger it like I just did," Darius stated, "...and it'll explode in 5 minutes."

"How, uh...big is the explosion?" Kyle asked, staring at the thing. It was about the size of a heavy-duty flashlight.

"Ten-mile diameter," Darius answered. Kyle's eyes widened.

"Ten *miles?*"

"If I die," Darius continued, "...this bomb will destroy any enemy that threatens the Empire." He pushed the bomb toward Kyle. "You're the only other person who can set it. Get close, set it by tapping on one end." He smirked. "And fly."

"But this'll only stop the enemy once," Kyle countered. And it was true; if Sabin sent another Void Behemoth against the Empire, and Kyle used the bomb, what would happen when the *next* Behemoth came?"

"Then make it count," Darius replied. He stood from his chair in one fluid motion, pushing it in and walking away, back toward the hallway leading to the front of the house. He stopped halfway to the door, turning his head to the side, his visor reappearing over his eyes in a flash of blue light.

"We leave in ten minutes," he stated.

And then he vanished.

Kyle stared at the space where Darius had just stood, a cool breeze whipping through the room. He heard Marcus clear his throat noisily, and turned to face the old man. Marcus rolled the large map on the table back into a long cylinder with the bomb inside, handing it to Darius. Then he stood from his seat, gesturing for Kyle to do the same.

"Let's go outside for a bit," he suggested. Kyle rose from his chair reluctantly, following Marcus toward a door at the far end of the kitchen. It opened into a small backyard, and Marcus led Kyle across this, toward a rocky ledge in the distance. It was the very edge of Antara, beyond which there was a sheer drop to the roiling maelstrom of gray clouds immediately below...the deadly atmosphere of the alien planet half of Antara was hovering over. Beyond this narrow ring, and miles below the huge floating island, was Doma. Whereas on his last trip here, he'd seen only endless ocean, now Kyle saw a huge expanse of trees far below, obscured by thick white mist. A trio of mountains were barely visible on the horizon, dark gray clouds hovering over the tallest of the three. Marcus turned to Kyle, sighing heavily.

"I'm sorry Kyle," he apologized, shaking his head. "When Darius makes up his mind, there is no denying him." He raised one palm up toward Kyle when Kyle started to protest, cutting Kyle off. "Just try to remember what I said about Darius the last time you were here," he added.

"What's that?" Kyle grumbled.

"I don't always agree with his methods," Marcus answered, staring out across Doma's surface. "But he does everything for a reason."

"Yeah, right," Kyle groused. Marcus put a hand on Kyle's shoulder.

"We have to trust him," the old man stated quietly.

"Why?" Kyle retorted. Marcus gave him a pained smile.

"We don't have any other choice."

Chapter 3

Agony ripped through Kyle's chest as the Gateway melted around him, stars exploding in his vision, followed by blindness. His hearing went next, his body vanishing from his awareness. He felt himself floating in nothingness, tenuously clinging to what little consciousness he had left.

And then, mercifully, there was light.

Kyle groaned, feeling something wet and prickly tickling the right side of his face. He blinked, seeing a blurry expanse of green and blue. His vision sharpened, and he realized that he was laying on his side on wet grass. He pushed himself off of the ground, blinking against the bright rays of the sun shining down on him. Then he saw a flash of gold to his left, and he turned to see Darius standing beside him.

"I leave tonight," the bodyguard stated, turning to walk across the verdant lawn of manicured grass toward a cobblestone path ahead. Kyle paused, brushing blades of grass off of his shirt, then glanced down, seeing the rolled-up map on the ground before him. He picked it up, then followed sullenly behind the bodyguard. He looked about as he walked, immediately recognizing his surroundings. The lush grass extended in all direction as far as the eye could see, save for the cobblestone path, which led over a small hill ahead. Kyle glanced up at the sky, spotting the telltale darker blue glimmer of a massive domed gravity shield far above his head; it was the Gate Shield, a magical barrier preventing anything from getting in or out of the circular campus of the Secula Magna. Which meant, of course, that he must be standing within its campus...the largest and most prestigious school of magic in the Empire. Indeed, as they walked up the small hill, reaching its rounded peak, he spotted a tall building in the distance. A tower over forty stories high, a crystal pyramid at its peak. The pyramid shimmered in the sunlight like a diamond, sending rays of every imaginable color outward across the campus.

Kyle stopped at the sight, his heart leaping into his chest as he stared at the tower. He realized that he'd half-expected everything he'd experienced here to be a dream; that after he'd returned to Earth, he would never get to see his second home again. But there it was, standing tall not a half-mile away. The Great Tower...the very heart of the Empire.

Darius continued down the path toward the Tower, and Kyle sprinted after the man, eventually catching up with him. It wasn't long before they came upon two people standing a few dozen feet from the path. One was an older man wearing long black robes, the other a young woman wearing snug black pants and an equally snug black shirt. She was facing away from Kyle, but turned suddenly, her eyes fixating instantly on Kyle's position.

"Kyle!" she cried.

She ran toward him with unnerving speed, moving quickly over the green grass until she was only a dozen feet away. She skid to a halt, tearing up two lines of grass with her feet as she did so, slowing a short distance away from where Kyle stood. She walked up and gave him a big bear hug, nearly knocking him off of his feet in the process...and knocking the wind out of him as her incredibly strong arms squeezed his ribs. Mercifully, she let him go, taking a step back.

"Hey Ariana," Kyle grunted, rubbing his bruised ribs gingerly.

"Sorry," she apologized. But her smile barely faltered. With her long brown hair tied in a tight ponytail, and her large, almond-shaped eyes, she was strikingly pretty. Her skin was extraordinarily pale...in fact, it was almost translucent, faint blue veins forming web-like patterns underneath. She was slightly taller than him, and quite slender, but carried herself with a confidence that was unnerving in someone so young. She'd earned it the hard way; she'd had a rougher life than anyone should have to bear, and it had forged an iron will. Having died and been reborn as a super-powerful undead immortal certainly hadn't hurt her confidence either.

"Hello Kyle," the man who'd been standing with Ariana earlier stated as he walked toward them. "Welcome back," he added. Kyle grinned at the man.

"Master Owens," he greeted. Ariana shook her head at Kyle.

"I thought you'd never come back," she stated in a mildly accusing fashion. Kyle frowned.

"How long has it been?" Kyle asked.

"Seven days," Ariana replied instantly.

"Oh."

"How long was it for you?" Ariana asked. She was vaguely aware of the fact that time flowed differently on Earth than it did here on Doma, but he'd never fully explained the math.

"A couple hours," Kyle answered. Ariana's eyes widened.

"That's *it?*"

Master Owens cleared his throat then, turning to Ariana.

"Why don't you take the rest of the day off, Ariana," he suggested, to her obvious delight. "Given your progress, I think you deserve a break."

"Thanks," Ariana replied. Master Owens turned to Darius.

"Why don't we leave these two alone for a bit," Owens suggested, walking down the cobblestone path toward the Tower in the distance. Darius shrugged, following behind the man. Kyle watched them go, then turned back to Ariana. He was once again struck by how lovely she was.

"How have you been?" Kyle asked. Ariana said nothing, reaching in slowly and embracing him, her touch much more gentle this time. She held him for a long moment, her ice-cold cheek pressed up against his, then let him go, her hands on his arms.

"I missed you," she murmured. Kyle smirked.

"I didn't have enough time to miss you," he replied.

39

"Come on," Ariana stated, ignoring his statement and pulling him by one arm, forcing him to walk beside her. She turned away from the Tower, walking on the cobblestone path in the opposite direction as Darius and Master Owens, pulling Kyle gently – but firmly – to her side. "Tell me what happened," she urged. Kyle obliged, telling her about his rather awkward reunion with his parents.

"So it really *was* only a couple hours for you," Ariana remarked, shaking her head slowly. "It felt like *forever* for us. Kalibar couldn't stop talking about you when you were away."

"How is Kalibar?" Kyle asked.

"Busy," Ariana replied. "He's been working with Erasmus to get the city repairs done. They've made a lot of progress," she added. Several blocks of the Southwest Quarter of the city had been destroyed by the Void Behemoth. Erasmus had spearheaded the enormous task of repairing the damage.

"How's Erasmus doing?" Kyle pressed. The Grand Runic had been badly wounded during the attack on the Tower, stabbed in the chest multiple times by the traitor Ibicus.

"Great," Ariana answered. "He's still sore, but he's active as ever." She flashed Kyle a smile. "He's been itching for you to come back."

"Oh yeah?"

"He made a new prototype of your sensory rune array," she explained. Kyle nodded; he'd come up with the idea during a lesson with the late Master Banar, right before Banar had been murdered by the Dead Man. Hardly any new magic patterns had been discovered for hundreds of years, on account of the unpredictable – and often deadly – consequences of weaving random patterns. Kyle had come up with the idea of taking magical plants and animals – creatures that wove a particular pattern – and placing them near a vast array of thousands of random sensory runes, so see if any of them lit up. Kalibar and Erasmus had used Kyle's idea to reverse-engineer the deadly magic of the killerpillar to create a weapon that had helped destroy the Void Behemoth.

"Cool."

"It *is*," Ariana agreed. "Erasmus used to it discover six new patterns already," she added. "They're calling it the K-Array."

"The what?"

"The K-Array," she repeated. "'K' for Kyle. Everyone's calling it the single most important invention since the Ancients."

"They named it after *me*?" Kyle blurted out. Ariana nodded.

"You invented it," she reminded him.

"True," he admitted, feeling rather overwhelmed with the news. He forced a smile. "How've you been?"

"Better now," Ariana admitted, flashing him a grin. He was struck by how easy the smile came to her. When he'd left her, she'd still been reeling from the horrifying things that had happened to her...and the awful reality of what she'd become. Now she seemed remarkably content. "I really missed you," she added, putting a cold hand on his shoulder. "It was a week for everyone else," she continued, "...but it was longer for me."

"What do you mean?"

"I don't sleep," she answered, dropping her hand from his shoulder and lowering her gaze to the cobblestone path at her feet. "Ever since...I've been awake the entire time." She sighed. "When everyone else goes to sleep, I stay awake."

"What do you do?" Kyle asked. Ariana shrugged.

"I used to take walks, at the beginning," she replied. "All around the Tower, and the campus. I couldn't stop walking. After a few days, I thought I was going to go insane." She sighed again, brushing a strand of hair from her eyes. "If it hadn't been for Darius, I think I would have."

"Darius?"

"Darius," she confirmed, glancing up at him. She smirked at his bewildered expression. "He's not as bad as you think," she added. Kyle grimaced.

"You'd be surprised," he muttered. Then he frowned. "What did he do?" he pressed, unable to keep the suspicion out of his voice. Ariana shrugged.

"He was just...there," she answered. "In the middle of the night, he'd come by, and ask me if I wanted to take a walk. He didn't say much of anything, but he listened. He's a good listener," she added. Kyle rolled his eyes.

"Yeah right," he grumbled. He knew better than to think that Darius cared about anyone, much less her. But Ariana ignored the comment.

"There was one night where I thought about..." She paused then, staring down at her feet as she walked. "...about ending it. I'd been awake for five days straight. When I told Darius, he said the funniest thing."

"What's that?"

"He said: 'Forever is a long time to waste.'"

Kyle frowned, mulling that over. Then he glanced at her; she was still staring at her feet.

"I didn't try to end it that night," she continued. "You know, I don't think I *could* end it, even if I tried." Kyle nodded, knowing that Darius had secretly placed runes in her bones, enormously complicated magical patterns that would heal any injury she happened to suffer. That, combined with the Dead Man's crystal in her brain, made her nearly invincible...as long as she had magic. She was utterly unable to make magic anymore, and had to pull it from her environment when her reserves ran low. This was made possible by a small Void crystal in the center of the Dead Man's shard in her brain.

"How are you now?" he asked. Ariana glanced at him with her pretty brown eyes, a warm smile on her lips.

"Better," she admitted. "Especially now that you're back."

"Master Owens said you made a lot of progress?" Kyle asked. As the head instructor of the Battle-Weavers for the Empire, Owens had been grooming Ariana for early admission into Battle-Weaving school. Normally students had to be at least 18 to enter, but Ariana was quite gifted when it came to sparring with magic.

"Well, I *used* to take walks at night," she replied. "Now I just practice Weaving." Kyle's eyebrows raised.

"All night?"

"Yeah," Ariana replied, giving him a rueful smile. "It's an unfair advantage over the other students, but it gives me something to do."

"So you're super-strong *and* really good at magic?" Kyle pressed. "Remind me not to make you mad..." Ariana laughed, punching him lightly on the shoulder. Or rather, what *she* must have considered lightly; Kyle nearly toppled over with the blow. He barely caught himself, rubbing his injured shoulder and glaring at her. She covered her mouth with her hand, her eyes widening; at first he thought she was horrified, but then he realized she was holding back laughter.

"Sorry," she said, hardly seeming to be. Kyle shook his head at her. She reached out to rub his shoulder, giggling when he flinched as she came close. "Aw, my poor boyfriend," she added, giving him a pitying look. "So fragile, like a delicate flower."

"Ha ha," Kyle grumbled.

"You're right," Ariana stated, wrapping an arm around his shoulders and pulling him close, leaning her head on his shoulder. Her hair tickled his neck pleasantly.

"What?"

"You *shouldn't* get me mad," she murmured.

* * *

The sun passed its zenith in the sky, sending its warming rays down atop the seemingly endless lawn of the Secula Magna. It had long since evaporated the glistening dew from each blade of grass, and having given its warmth to the sprawling campus, it threatened to retire behind the safety of a passing cloud. Kyle and Ariana had finished their long walk together, returning at last to the Great Tower in the center of the campus.

As they drew near the massive structure, they had to maneuver through a large crowd of pedestrians coming in and out of the Tower's double-doors. Most were Runic and Weaver students, wearing their customary white and black uniforms, respectively. More than one of the students stared at Kyle as they passed, and Kyle remembered that he was a bit of a celebrity here. Not only had he invented the K-array and helped take down the Void Behemoth, but he was also the adopted son of Kalibar, the most powerful man in the Empire.

"Where's Kalibar?" he asked.

"Probably meeting with the Council," Ariana answered.

"Let's go to our room then," Kyle stated. They both lived in Kalibar's retirement suite, a large room with several bedrooms attached. Kalibar had earned the suite after finishing his first term as Grand Weaver six years ago. Kalibar himself lived one floor up, in the Grand Weaver suite. Ariana nodded, following alongside Kyle as he made his way out of the lobby and down a long hallway, toward the riser at the end. The riser was essentially an elevator powered by magic, a circular stone disc that carried passengers up and down the 42 floors in the Tower. They reached the riser, and it quickly rose, flying upward at dizzying speed until it reached the 41st floor. They stepped off, walking down another long hallway until they reached the door to Kalibar's suite. Ariana opened the door, and Kyle went to his bedroom, slipping out of his bedclothes and into the white Runic uniform the butler Jenkins had so thoughtfully prepared for him. When he stepped back out into the main suite, he found Darius standing there, next to Ariana.

"Hey," Kyle greeted.

"Darius told Erasmus you were here," Ariana notified. "He should be here any minute."

As if on cue, the front door burst open, and a short, balding man dressed entirely in white appeared, striding quickly toward them. He was in his sixties, with twinkling blue eyes and a long white beard that ran all the way down to his impressive belly. His eyes widened as he spotted Kyle, and he sprinted up to the boy, a huge grin on his face.

"Kyle!" he exclaimed, giving Kyle a big bear hug. He held Kyle at arms' length then. "Thank god you're back," he said with a sly grin. "I was getting sick of Kalibar's moping around all the time. Poor bastard had himself convinced you'd never come back." He shook his head. "Half-expected him to take a swan dive off of his balcony yesterday." He glanced at Darius then, as if noticing the bodyguard for the first time. "I was hoping you'd show him how it's done," he quipped. There was no love lost between Darius and Erasmus, and Erasmus took delight in insulting the bodyguard every

44

chance he got. Darius gave as good as he got, and usually even better, much to Erasmus's consternation. This time, however, the bodyguard said nothing.

"Good to see you," Kyle replied, grinning at the portly Grand Runic. Erasmus glanced at Ariana.

"Hey, you tell him about the K-Array?"

"Yes sir," she replied. Erasmus rubbed his pudgy hands together excitedly.

"Six new patterns in one week!" he exclaimed, slapping Kyle on the shoulder. "Can you believe it? At this rate, we'll *double* the known patterns in a few months!"

"Wow," Kyle murmured. Erasmus snorted.

"Wow?" he exclaimed. "*Wow*? That damn K-Array is the single most important invention since the Ancients!" He grinned at Kyle, putting an arm around his shoulders. "You got any more brilliant ideas in that brain of yours?"

"Uh..."

"Already had one more than you," Darius observed. Erasmus glared at the bodyguard.

"Don't you have a job to do?" he countered. "Or are your delicate bowels acting up again?"

"I left your legacy in the toilet," Darius replied smoothly. Erasmus narrowed his eyes, his jaw working as he tried to come up with a clever retort. Failing this, he turned back to Kyle.

"Next time you go to Urth, take that metal-head with you," Erasmus growled, pointing at Darius. "And leave him there."

The front door opened then, and a tall man dressed entirely in black walked in. He had short white hair cut into a crew-cut, with brown eyes and a white goatee. His expression was grave – until he saw Kyle, and then he broke out into a big smile.

"Kalibar!" Kyle cried, running up to the man and leaping into his arms. He gave Kalibar a big hug, and felt Kalibar give him a tight squeeze in return.

"Good to see you, Kyle," Kalibar stated, holding Kyle for a moment longer, then disengaging. "How was your trip?"

"Short," Kyle replied.

"Are you going to stay for a while?" Kalibar pressed. Kyle nodded. "Good. Erasmus is eager to have you continue your training."

"I've got the perfect teacher for you," Erasmus cut in, his blue eyes twinkling. "How about we start your lessons tomorrow?"

"Sure," Kyle agreed.

"Excellent," Erasmus stated. He turned to Kalibar. "I don't know about you," he added. "...but I'm starving. How about we catch up over lunch?"

"Good idea," Kalibar replied. He smiled at Kyle then, putting a hand on Kyle's shoulder. "Welcome home, Kyle. We missed you."

"Thanks," Kyle replied, smiling back. "It's good to be back," he added.

"Come on," Erasmus stated, walking toward a glass orb laying on one of the many side-tables in the massive suite. The orb glowed faintly when touched, then turned clear again. It was a communication orb, allowing one to summon someone from anywhere within the Tower. "It's time that butler of yours got us something to eat!"

* * *

Kyle dug his fingers into the steaming slice of roasted duck on the plate in front of him, shoveling the delicious meat into his mouth. He devoured it rapidly, washing it down with small sips of water. Erasmus and Darius both drank wine, while Ariana sat next to Kyle, neither eating or drinking. She had no need of food or water, a fact that had initially depressed her greatly. She seemed to have come to terms with her condition, watching Kyle eat with a small smile on her lips.

"So how was the meeting?" Kyle asked Kalibar, after he'd finished his plate. Jenkins appeared out of nowhere, the butler whisking away the plate immediately, then replacing it with another. Kalibar sighed, taking a sip of water from his own glass.

"Not terrible," he replied. "Councilman Goran is playing nice for a change, but without a majority in the Council, we're losing votes."

"I told you we shouldn't have revoked the Right of Dictatorship," Erasmus grumbled.

"The immediate crisis is over," Kalibar countered. "The Constitution was created for a reason, and we need to respect it." Erasmus snorted, but Kalibar held up a hand to stop his old friend's retort. "And the Council agreed not to have us tried and executed after our terms ended," he added with a wry smirk.

"Good point," Erasmus conceded.

"How is the city doing?" Kyle asked.

"The Southwest Quarter is being rebuilt," Kalibar answered. "Erasmus's Runics have been working around the clock to repair it."

"We're not just repairing it," Erasmus retorted. "We're completely redesigning it." He grinned, leaning back in his chair and patting his rotund belly happily. "The first of the original tenants are about ready to move back in."

"Good," Kyle replied. The people who'd lived in the buildings had been mysteriously teleported to safety right before the Void Behemoth's deadly beam had destroyed their homes. Kyle stole a glance at Darius, who seemed to be ignoring everyone, having summoned Jenkins to provide a third plate of steaming duck. The corpses of his two other culinary conquests lay defeated on their plates.

"Undoubtedly," Kalibar agreed. "There's no doubt that it was Ampir," he added. "What I wouldn't give to speak with the man."

"If we could just get him on our side," Erasmus agreed, "...Xanos wouldn't stand a chance!"

"He *is* on our side," Kalibar corrected. "Or at least he appears to be." Erasmus snorted.

"Well if he'd killed that damn Behemoth *before* it decided to melt a few city blocks, he wouldn't have had to teleport those people to the countryside," the Grand Runic retorted. "If the guy really wanted to do us a favor, he wouldn't keep waiting till the last minute to pull our asses from the fire."

"Agreed," Kalibar replied. Kyle forced himself not to look at Darius again, staring down at his own plate instead. He agreed with Kalibar and Erasmus, of course. He'd said something similar to

Darius in the past, when he'd realized that Darius had let Kalibar be tortured by the Dead Man.

"He's the only reason we're still alive," Ariana interjected, brushing a few hairs from her face. Erasmus glanced at her, then nodded silently. Everyone knew that Ampir was the reason *she* was still alive, in a manner of speaking, having modified the Dead Man's crystal to prevent Xanos from controlling her.

"Who can understand the mind of such an ancient being?" Kalibar mused. "Ariana is right...we should be thankful. And if Ampir wants to reveal himself to us, he will." He took another sip of his water, then leaned back in his chair. "We should concentrate on doing what *we* can do, not what *he* can do."

"And what *can* we do?" Erasmus asked rather snidely.

"Continue our work on the K-Array," Kalibar answered. He turned to Kyle. "We've selected magical plants that use patterns we think will be the most useful against the enemy," he explained. "The K-Array has allowed us to reverse-engineer these patterns. If we expand our knowledge of magic, it may provide an advantage."

"Damn right," Erasmus agreed, perking up. "And the patterns are just the beginning...each one might have dozens of applications!" He turned to Kalibar. "The invisibility pattern we just learned should prove quite handy."

"That's why we've made the K-Array our highest priority," Kalibar stated, nodding at Kyle. "Your idea might just give us the edge we need in this war," he added. "Ideas change the world...and yours has already done so. Now we have to develop your ability to bring your ideas to life."

"That's where I come in," Erasmus stated eagerly, his blue eyes twinkling underneath his bushy white eyebrows. "Tomorrow morning you'll start your Runic training...I've set up an accelerated course for you."

Jenkins arrived then, the blue-clad butler removing everyone's finished plates and glasses from the table. Darius had finally finished his third plate of food, and leaned back in his chair, pulling on his golden gauntlets and crossing his arms over his chest.

"I need a day off," the bodyguard declared, his eyes on Kalibar.

"Give him the rest of his life off," the Erasmus offered with a wicked grin. "He deserves it." Kalibar smiled, but didn't take Erasmus's bait.

"Of course," Kalibar replied, nodding at Darius. "May I ask what for?"

"To visit an old friend," Darius replied. Erasmus's bushy eyebrows went up.

"I wasn't aware you had any," he quipped.

"By all means," Kalibar answered, "...take the day off, and another if you need to."

"I leave tonight," Darius declared. Kyle stared at the bodyguard for a long moment, then glanced at Ariana. She appeared lost in thought, her eyes on the tabletop.

"Well," Kalibar stated, standing up from his chair and glancing at Erasmus. "We should get back to running the Empire. Ariana, why don't you and Kyle spend the afternoon catching up," he added. "I had Master Owens cancel your evening classes."

"Thank you," Ariana said with a grateful smile. Kyle felt her cold hand grasp his, and he gave it a squeeze. The rest of the adults left the table, leaving Kyle alone with her. He stifled a yawn then, and Ariana stood, pulling him up with her.

"Sorry," he mumbled. "I didn't get much sleep."

"Why don't you take a nap?" she offered.

"You want to take a walk first?" Kyle asked.

"You're sure?"

"Yeah," Kyle confirmed. "I'll get plenty of sleep afterward."

"Okay," Ariana agreed. "I'll watch over you when you sleep," she added. Kyle raised an eyebrow at that.

"Creepy," he replied. But of course he didn't really mind.

"Come on," she urged, pulling him toward the front door of the suite. "Let's go!" Kyle hardly had a choice in the matter; her grip was as firm as a statue's, and she soon led him out of Kalibar's suite and down the hallway to the riser, which brought them swiftly to the ground floor. They walked hand-in-hand down another long hallway to the lobby, past throngs of students going busily about their day, until they'd made it through the huge double-doors leading outside.

They had plenty of company, classes having ended recently. Hundreds of Runic and Weaver students were filing out of the Tower toward the dormitories nearby. Kyle and Ariana weaved through the crowd until they'd reached a little-used path off of one of the main roads. It wasn't long before they'd left the crowd behind; the only sound was the faint *clop, clop* of boots on the path behind them. Kyle turned about, but didn't see anyone there.

"Our guards," Ariana explained. "They started practicing the invisibility pattern today."

Kyle nodded, knowing that Kalibar had insisted that elite guards follow Kyle wherever he went, particularly after his kidnapping by the Dead Man. It wasn't long before Kyle and Ariana had reached a lone tree in the center of a grassy field.

"This is my favorite tree," Ariana declared. I come here every day to sit down and meditate."

Suddenly Kyle heard someone clear their throat behind them, and they both turned to find none other than Darius standing on the path behind them. The bodyguard was dressed in his usual attire, of course. His golden armor gleamed in the fading sunlight, his blue eyes staring at them expressionlessly.

"Oh," Ariana gasped, tensing for a moment. "Darius, I didn't hear you coming."

"Neither did your guards," Darius grumbled, pushing outward with his left hand. There was a yelp, followed by an elite guard appearing out of thin air, tumbling to the grass beside the path. The elite guard scrambled to his feet, glaring at the bodyguard.

"How the hell..." he began, but Darius cut him off with one gauntleted hand.

"Leave," he ordered. The guard's jaw dropped, and then he glanced off to Darius's right. The other elite guard appeared, glaring at Darius, then at his fellow guard.

"Grand Weaver Kalibar..." he began.

"Made me their bodyguard," Darius interjected. Both guards glared at him, then turned about sharply, marching back to the Tower in the distance. Darius turned to Kyle. "We need to talk," he stated. Kyle glanced at Ariana, who smiled at him.

"I guess I'll see you back in the Tower?" she asked. Kyle nodded. She waved, then turned back toward the Tower in the distance. The sun was setting, and lights shone in each of the countless windows that ran up the magnificent structure. Brilliant rays shot outward from the crystalline pyramid that topped it. Kyle watched Ariana's retreating form, then turned back to Darius.

"I'm leaving for Sabin," Darius declared. "If I'm not back in 24 hours," he added, "...assume I'm dead." Kyle felt the faint thrum of magic around them then, a familiar subtle vibration in his skull. Darius put one gauntleted finger on Kyle's chest. "In that case, use the spacetime bridge generator."

"How?" Kyle asked.

"It can only be activated by you," Darius answered. "It recognizes your unique magical fingerprint. Stream magic to it for five seconds and it will activate."

They stood there then, Darius staring at Kyle silently, and Kyle with his eyes on Darius's feet. They said nothing for a long moment. The sun continued to drop over the horizon, sending a splash of red and purple across the feathered clouds above.

"Whatever happens," Darius continued, "...you must never tell your father about me. No one on Earth can know about Doma...or magic."

Kyle nodded silently. Darius reached out and placed something heavy in Kyle's hand. Kyle glanced down, seeing the rolled-up map there, the cylindrical metallic bomb tucked within.

"No regrets," Darius murmured.

And he was gone.

Chapter 4

Kyle yawned as he followed an elite guard out of his bedroom and into Kalibar's main suite. He'd fallen asleep soon after returning to the Tower the night before, and Ariana had made good on her promise to watch over him as he slept. She'd left before he'd been awoken by an elite guard knocking on his bedroom door, no doubt to practice weaving before her class with Master Owens.

Kyle yawned again, barely registering that he'd left Kalibar's suite and was being led down the hall to the riser at the end of it. Today was the first day of his lessons with his new Runic teacher, who apparently wanted him to wake up at five in the morning. That was far too early for learning, if you asked him. Far too early for being *conscious.*

Two more elite guards appeared behind Kyle, following a few steps behind him, their heavy black boots clopping sharply on the granite floor below. They all wore the signature black armor of the elite guard, a squad of highly-trained soldiers dedicated to protecting the highest-ranking government officials...and their families. Ever since Master Banar's murder, Kalibar had drastically increased Kyle's security force, and had forbidden Kyle and Ariana from venturing far from the Tower. Well, Kyle, anyway; Ariana had proven quite capable of defending herself since her...change.

Kyle yawned a third time as he stepped onto the riser with the three guards. The circular stone platform descended rapidly, eventually stopping, and the guards led Kyle down another long hallway, to a door on the left. They opened it, and motioned for Kyle to go through. He did so, finding himself in a familiar place: the Runic Archives. The Archives were a series of rooms that contained ancient tomes and magical artifacts, some over two thousand years old. The main room was huge, with dozens of rows of shelving standing over two stories tall, each overflowing with countless magical artifacts. To the left, Kyle saw the door to the Testing chamber, where Erasmus's Runics had decoded Kyle's ring. The guards led Kyle forward, to a large, rectangular table standing beside one of the many shelves. Wooden chairs surrounded the table, and in one of them sat a very old woman. Ancient, even. She was tall, or used to be; her back was a bit stooped, forcing her to crank her neck back a little just to see forward. She had curly silver hair and twinkling blue eyes, thick glasses sitting astride her nose. She nodded at Kyle.

"Morning," she greeted, motioning for him to take a seat opposite her. "You must be Kyle," she added. Kyle nodded, sitting down in the chair.

"Good morning," Kyle replied.

"I'm Lee," she stated, extending a wrinkled hand across the table. Kyle took it, shaking it gently. Her grip was strong, her skin warm and dry, and only a little creepy, as very old people's hands invariably felt.

"Nice to meet you, Master Lee," he stated politely. Lee snorted, waving away the formality.

"Just Lee," she insisted. "I've no patience for formality at my age," she added. "I don't have enough time left for it. I'm practically dead, after all...or at least I look it."

"Uh..." Kyle stammered, unable to think of any way to respond. She was distressingly accurate. Lee laughed, her raspy voice echoing throughout the chamber.

"Come on now," she stated, peering over her glasses at him. "My son tells me I need to make a Runic out of you before my funeral."

"Your son?"

"What, he didn't tell you?" Lee asked. "Can't you see the resemblance?"

"Um..."

"Erasmus," she stated, smirking at his blank expression.

"Wait, you're his...?"

"I made him, yes," she replied. "Luckily he came out skinnier than he is now, or I'd have been buried sixty years ago," she added with a wry smirk.

"Sorry, he didn't tell me," Kyle apologized. Lee shrugged her frail shoulders.

"Who cares?" she replied. "Now come on, I haven't got all day. Can you rune-link?"

"What?"

"Never mind. Can you inscribe?"

"Um..."

"Do you know what a rune is?" Lee stated impatiently, drumming her fingers on the surface of the table. Kyle blushed, then nodded. "Tell me!" she commanded exasperatedly.

"A pattern made of a crystalline wire," Kyle answered, remembering what Master Banar had taught him. "It conducts magic the same as our brains weave magic."

"Oh good, you're not completely hopeless," Lee grumbled. "You know about sensory runes?"

"Yes ma'am."

"Good. And I like the manners," Lee stated. "Never trust a woman who says she doesn't."

"But you said..."

"Exactly," Lee interrupted. She sat back in her chair then, sighing loudly. "So you're all theory and no application. Absolutely useless," she spat, shaking her head in disgust. She reached up with her left hand, grabbing at thin air, and suddenly a small brown cube appeared between her fingers. Kyle's jaw dropped, and Lee chuckled.

"Oh, I'm not dead yet," she stated. "I've got more than a few tricks up my sleeve. And I'm going to teach you as many as I can fit up yours," she added. "Some students have longer sleeves than others," she explained, narrowing her eyes at him. "God, I hope you're not stupid."

"I'm not," Kyle replied rather defensively.

"Prove it," Lee challenged. She sat up suddenly, walking around the table to the chair at Kyle's right, sitting on it. She set the brown cube on the table. "Do what I do." She stared at the cube then, and Kyle felt a slight vibration in his skull. He saw a faint blue light appear beneath the skin of her forehead, moving left, then arcing backward a fraction of an inch, then moving forward, then dipping downward. He followed the movements, weaving magic in his own mind, copying her pattern. She shot the pattern out toward the crystal she'd set on the table, and Kyle did the same. Two tiny blue dots appeared on the surface, then faded, leaving two orange dots behind. Lee frowned at the dots, turning a critical eye on Kyle.

"You're not supposed to do that," she muttered.

"What?"

"You weren't supposed to be *able* to do that," she clarified. "I was testing you. You were looking at my forehead the entire time," she observed. "Can you see magic?"

"Uh..." Kyle mumbled. He wasn't sure if he was supposed to tell anyone about his gift.

"You can," Lee deduced. "Stop being difficult," she added crossly. "This'll be easier if you quit keeping secrets. Why haven't you told anyone?"

"I thought everyone could," Kyle lied. Lee snorted.

"You're smarter than that," she scolded. "Erasmus told me Kalibar developed the same gift when he received his new eyes. Have you always been able to see magic?"

Kyle hesitated, then nodded.

"That explains why you learn patterns so quickly," she deduced. "Owens never figured you out, did he," she added with a shake of her head. "Weavers!"

"What was that pattern?" Kyle asked. He'd seen Master Banar do the same thing – turning a brown crystal orange – but couldn't remember what it meant.

"The inscribing pattern," she answered. "The most important pattern ever discovered," she added authoritatively. "That's how we inscribe runes."

"Can you show me again?" he requested. Lee nodded, staring at the cube again. Kyle followed the faint blue light on her forehead again, committing the pattern to memory. Then he wove it himself, casting the pattern at the cube. Another two blue dots – one from each of them – appeared on the surface, fading to orange.

"Now," Lee stated, flipping the cube over so that an unmarred brown facet faced upward. "Weave the fire pattern." Kyle complied, weaving a thread of magic clockwise in a full circle, then bringing it backward, then forward, then sending it outward in front of him. He attached a small magic stream to the pattern, and a tiny red flame appeared in the air a foot in front of him. Lee reached into the air with her right hand, plucking a sheet of paper – again out of thin air – and a pencil. She drew a symbol then:

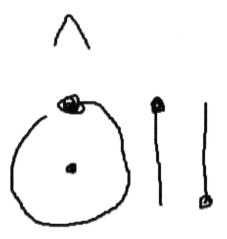

"What's that?" Kyle asked.

"The fire pattern," Lee explained. "In standard Runic notation. The thing at the top is a nose," she continued. "...telling us we're looking down at someone's head. The dot in the middle is the center

56

of the mind, the circle represents the first part of the pattern. The dark dot at the start of the circle marks where one starts weaving. The next two lines represent the next steps...sending magic backward, then forward."

"I get it," Kyle said.

"You'd better," Lee replied. "That's the easy part. Now if the pattern was drawn like this..."

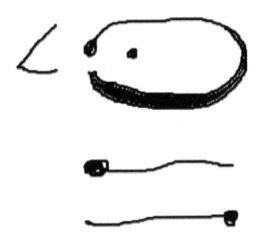

"...then the thing at the left is the nose, and we're looking at a person's head from the side. The left side, of course."

"Okay," Kyle said.

"So now you know how to read standard Runic notation," she stated. "It gets complicated, but there's time for that later. We need to make you useful...pay attention." She stared at the cube, lowering her head to it, and a blue dot appeared on its surface. It vanished below the cube's surface, then returned, then vanished, then returned again, slightly to the left.

"I've inscribed the fire pattern into the cube," Lee explained. "I traced the inscribing pattern like this..."

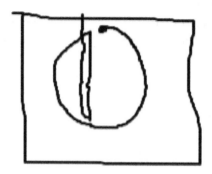

"So the top of the drawing is the top of the cube," Kyle guessed. Lee nodded.

"The end of the pattern extends all the way to the surface," Lee continued. "That's important; it forces the pattern to be expressed outward, at the top of the cube. Now, stream magic to the cube," she ordered. Kyle complied, and a small flame appeared a fraction of an inch above the cube's surface.

"That's it?" Kyle asked. "That's easy!"

"I make it look easy, honey," Lee retorted. "We're just getting started. Now, did anyone ever explain to you how magic works?"

"Uh, yeah," Kyle replied. "It changes matter and energy," he added. Lee rolled her eyes.

"Oh brother," she groaned, shaking her head in despair. "Have we got a long way to go!"

* * *

Ariana stepped out of the Tower lobby's massive double-doors, feeling warm sunlight strike her skin. Whereas before she would have found such a sensation pleasant, her body no longer required warmth, and it was now a neutral sensation. She did enjoy the relative silence of the outdoors, however; ever since she'd been reborn, her senses had been remarkably enhanced. While indoors, she could easily hear people talking behind closed doors, even from a floor above or below. She could even hear sounds that she'd never heard before...sounds too high or low in pitch for normal people to hear. The constant sounds of talking, footsteps, and other noise became overwhelming after a while, and it was nice to get outside to avoid them.

She closed her eyes for a moment, hearing birds chirping far in the distance, and the clatter of countless footsteps as Runic and Weaver students made their way from their dormitories toward the Tower for their classes. She was early for her class with Master Owens, as usual. She typically requested that they have class outside, much to Kalibar's consternation, and far away from the dormitories and the Tower. It was easier to focus in the outdoors.

She opened her eyes then, walking down one of the many cobblestone paths leading from the Tower to the campus beyond. She spotted a bird flying far above the Tower; even from four hundred feet away, she could spot the small brown mouse clutched in the bird's talons, wriggling helplessly in its cruel grasp. In addition to her hearing, her vision had improved tremendously since her rebirth. She also had much improved night vision, starlight being more than adequate to see full color. It'd taken a while to get used to, but now she couldn't remember what it had been like *not* to see and hear like this. She found it strange how quickly her mind had adapted to her new way of being.

She continued down the cobblestone path, her black boots clicking on the stone below, ignoring the occasional stares from the students passing by. She was still painfully self-conscious of her looks, knowing that she appeared deathly pale to others. She'd still had blood in her veins when she'd been revived, but without her heart beating, it had sat in her legs, leaving them an awful purple color. She'd insisted that it be drained, and when Kalibar had refused, she'd gotten Darius to help her. She'd thought about wearing makeup to cover her paleness, but decided against it after one try. She'd left the makeup on everything she'd touched, and it'd been a constant pain to reapply. After that day, she'd decided to stop trying to fit in, hoping that others would eventually just get used to her.

She sighed, staring at the backs of her hands, at the faint web of blue veins there. They were thin, empty as they were, but she still found them ugly. She had them on her face, too; she often wondered how Kyle could possibly find her attractive now, but he didn't seem to mind, for which she was grateful. She smiled, picturing his face, that sweet smile of his, and his expressive brown eyes. He was the best thing that had ever happened to her. He'd saved her from the Arena, and from the Dead Man, and had risked his life to protect her. He'd been the one to insist that Darius bring her back to life. And despite her terrible strength, her ugly skin and veins, and the icy coldness of her flesh, for some reason he still wanted to be with her.

Ariana veered off the path, spotting a large grassy field to her right. This was where she and Master Owens always met. Again, she was early, so he wasn't there yet. Never sleeping meant spending eight hours every night waiting for the world to wake up; she couldn't help coming early, eager to start her day.

She spotted her favorite tree, and walked up to it, sitting with her back to the trunk. The tree's branches swayed slightly in the breeze, its green leaves rustling pleasantly above her head. It wasn't long before she spotted Master Owens walking out of the double-doors of the Tower, still a mile or so away, continuing down the cobblestone path toward her. Even from such a long distance, she could see his black robes rippling in the breeze, his brown eyes staring off into space. He was clearly lost in thought; she wondered idly about what. She followed his slow stroll down the path, and after a long while, he reached the tree where she sat. He stopped before her, giving her a warm smile.

"Good morning," he greeted, extending a hand. Ariana stood up and shook it, feeling the powerful pulse of blood in the artery at the base of his thumb. If she concentrated, she could even hear his heartbeat. "Are you ready to spar?" he asked.

"Yes Master Owens," she replied. They'd been sparring several times a day ever since her revival, supposedly to help her improve her skills. But they both knew the real reason behind the matches; with Ariana having the Dead Man's shard in her brain, Kalibar had

60

ordered a thorough study of its capabilities. For, in addition to keeping her alive, the shard had an extraordinary number of automatic magical defenses programmed into it. Anyone attempting to attack her would trigger these defenses, and Master Owens' job was to catalog them...and attempt to find a way to defeat them. In doing so, Kalibar hoped to gain the upper hand against the Chosen, and against Xanos. Of course, her adoptive father had taken great care to ensure that no one – other than himself, Erasmus, Darius, Kyle, and Owens – knew the true source of her power. The Council would not be pleased to know that a Chosen existed among them.

"Good," Owens replied. "Grand Weaver Kalibar should be here soon," he added. Ariana nodded; her father had been attending her sparring matches recently, eager to learn how to combat her shard. He hadn't sparred with her yet though...and even the thought of facing Kalibar made her uneasy. "Let's get started, shall we?" Owens stated.

Ariana smiled back nervously, taking a step backward. Master Owens was the second-best Battle-Weaver in the Empire, with only Kalibar consistently able to defeat him. But even Owens' considerable talents had been sorely tested by Ariana's shard. He'd won all of their matches handily...up to the point of the finishing blow. It was then that the crystal in her forehead had unleashed a new surprise to counter him, each and every time.

"Ready?" Master Owens said, his eyes narrowing slightly. "Begin!"

Ariana tensed up, backpedaling away from her teacher. She saw gravity shields shimmer to life around Owens in multiple layers, saw another gravity field appear instantly to Owens' left. The Weaver slid rapidly toward it, a fireball appearing between his hands in front of his chest, shooting outward at her before she could so much as blink. Ariana felt her shard react, magic weaving impossibly fast in the center of her forehead. A dozen gravity shields appeared around her like the layers of an onion.

The fireball bounced harmlessly off of her shields, fiery *punk* splattering on the grass below.

Master Owens stopped sliding suddenly, flying straight up into the air. Ariana stopped backpedaling...then felt herself sliding

61

backward uncontrollably in the wet grass. She turned around just in time to see herself being sucked into a gravity sphere – filled with a massive burning glob of *punk*. She cried out, creating a gravity sphere of her own in front of her to counteract the pull of Owens' sphere.

Her sphere winked out of existence.

Ariana flew backward into the flaming sphere, throwing her arms in front of her face and closing her eyes. She screamed as tongues of fire surrounded her, fighting the sudden terror that threatened to overwhelm her. The heat of the flames was unbearable, and she gagged at the awful stench of burning flesh assaulting her nostrils. She grit her teeth, steeling herself as she forcibly lowered her arms. She opened her eyes, seeing her gravity shields still up, the burning *punk* orbiting around her harmlessly. She blinked, realizing that she could feel no actual heat coming from the flames. She felt her shard weave, saw Owens' gravity sphere vanish, the burning *punk* falling to the ground. The heat, the smell of burning flesh...it had all been in her head.

Ariana grit her teeth, feeling anger grow in her breast. She *hated* fire...and Master Owens knew it.

She turned her gaze upward, ignoring the black smoke rising from the burning *punk* on the ground around her. She saw Master Owens hovering some twenty feet above her head, studying her silently. Even from here she could see that he was completely relaxed, his posture one of utter confidence.

She had the sudden urge to wipe the floor with him.

Ariana crouched low, then leapt upward, her powerful legs sending her high into the air toward him. With her shard protecting her, she knew that she only had to collide with him. The shard would neutralize any foreign gravity shield it got near, leaving Owens completely unprotected.

But as she neared him, she saw her shields vanishing one-by-one, felt herself lurch to the side by some unseen force, missing Owens by a wide margin. She cried out, feeling herself spinning uncontrollably in the air, the world a jumble of green and blue rotating madly before her. She flailed her limbs wildly, then felt her left hip strike the ground with a terrible *crunch*, a horrid pain shooting down her leg. Her shoulder struck next, followed by her head, and stars exploded before her eyes. She cried out, curling into the fetal position on the wet grass.

Light burst forth into her mind's eye, magic weaving ferociously of its own accord.

And then everything *slowed*.

The stars in her eyes vanished instantly, her vision clearing. She looked upward, seeing Master Owens' descending toward her, his face twisted in horror, one hand reaching out toward her. She saw his black robes rippling gracefully, light scattering off of the edges of his gravity shields. She saw a single drop of water fall from his left boot, and was mesmerized by the rainbow of colors dancing off of it as it fell slowly toward her.

She stared at that single drop, watching as it overtook Owens, accelerating toward the earth while her teacher slowed his descent. It struck a single blade of grass at her feet, bending it all the way to the ground, then bursting into countless smaller drops, the blade of grass rebounding mightily. She watched as that verdant blade sprang upward, vibrating with the memory of its collision.

She felt her shard reacting, power arcing in her forehead, that part of her mind's eye over which she had no control. It wove much more slowly than usual, so that she could almost follow the patterns it created. She saw the air around her shimmer, saw layer after layer of gravity shields come to life around her, pushing her a few inches off of the grass.

Still, her shard wove.

She saw Owens land on the grass before her, now only a few feet away, the gravity shields a fraction of an inch below his black boots slowly crushing the countless blades of grass below. His knees bent slightly with the impact, his robes billowing upward around him. She reached out, her hand moving far faster than everything around her, and cried out a warning just as her shard finished its patterns, thrusting knots of magic automatically toward Owens.

His shields vanished.

Ariana watched as a huge sphere appeared around her teacher, stared in horror as the sides began to press inward toward him. She saw his black robes collapse inward, the cloth crushing against his limbs and body. She saw his eyes roll backward in his head, watched him slump forward, unconscious...even as the sphere around him continued to shrink. The sides closed in on him slowly, pushing his arms against his flanks, forcing his shoulders forward and inward.

Still, the sphere contracted.

Ariana's eyes widened with horror, and she tried to get up, to push herself off of the ground, but her left hip was useless. She felt her shard start to weave again, and clawed at her forehead with her fingernails, feeling pain lance through her skull.

Still, the sphere contracted.

She saw Owens' left elbow get shoved deeper into his side, heard a snapping sound as the ribs cracked underneath.

No!

Owens head was shoved downward and forward as the top and bottom of the gravity field contracted, his neck arching severely under that relentless pressure. She heard another crack as his right elbow dug into his right flank.

No, no, no!

Still the now-oval field around Owens shrank, and all Ariana could do was watch as her teacher was slowly crushed to death.

"Master Owens!" she cried.

And then it was done.

Chapter 5

"Try again," Lee ordered.

Kyle grimaced, stopping his magic stream to the cube he'd inscribed his first rune into. Or rather, his first *attempt* at a rune; he'd butchered the ring-shaped inscription at the beginning. It had to be a nearly perfect circle, not the squiggly mess that Kyle had managed. Streaming magic to the rune had resulted in nothing.

"It's hard," he protested.

"Quit whining," Lee scolded. "It'll be hard until it isn't." She pulled another brown cube out of the air, smacking it down on the table in front of him. Kyle sighed, then grabbed the small cube, leaning over it until his forehead was nearly touching the top facet. He closed his eyes, weaving the inscribing pattern, then sending the pattern outward carefully into the cube. He streamed magic into the pattern, moving the pattern – and the stream – in a tight circle downward, then upward. He shot his stream straight down, then back up, and then stopped.

He opened his eyes, lifting his head and staring questioningly at Lee.

"Go on," she ordered.

Kyle pushed the cube away from him, then streamed magic to it.

A massive jet of flame burst upward from the cube, its roar shattering the silence of the Archives. Kyle cried out, cutting his magic stream, and the flame slowly shrank, until it at petered out at last.

Kyle stared at Lee, then at the cube, swallowing in a dry throat. The once-brown cube was jet black.

"What did we learn?" Lee inquired, completely unfazed by Kyle's pyrotechnics.

"Uh," Kyle stammered. "Stream less magic next time?" Lee shook her head.

"Your runes are too thick," she corrected. "The thicker your wires, the easier it is for magic to flow through them. Thin wires resist magic flow."

"Got it," Kyle replied. It made sense; when he wove the fire pattern in his mind, the more magic he put into the pattern, the larger the flame. The more magic he streamed to it, the *hotter* the flame. It was, apparently, similar with runes.

"Again," Lee commanded. She conjured another cube, tossing it onto the table with a clatter. Kyle grabbed it, placing it in front of him as before. He leaned over it, weaving the inscribing pattern again. This time, he put far less magic into the pattern, knowing that this would make for a thinner wire. He inscribed the fire rune as before, then leaned back, pushing the cube a bit farther away from himself than before. Lee smirked.

"Okay," Kyle stated, rubbing his hands together. He streamed a small thread of magic to the cube. A tiny, wimpy excuse for a flame popped up a fraction of an inch from the cube's facet.

"Not bad," Lee conceded. Kyle broke into a smile, stopping his magic stream; the flame continued to burn for a long time before being snuffed out, undoubtedly feeding off of the magic the crystal around the rune had managed to store. The first flame must have burned through that stored magic quickly, extinguishing itself much sooner.

"It's getting easier," Kyle replied.

"I was talking about you figuring out to put less magic in the inscribing pattern, to make a thinner rune," Lee explained. "At least you're capable of *some* thought."

"Gee, thanks," Kyle grumbled.

"Most students aren't," Lee continued. "Usually have to hold their precious little hands all the way through, feeding them all the answers." She shook her head. "*That's* why I don't teach anymore."

"You're teaching me," Kyle countered. Lee gave him a wrinkled smirk.

"You're not giving me a reason to stop."

Kyle nodded, feeling proud of her endorsement. But he knew that he would continue to have to earn it; he wiped his sweaty palms on his white uniform, then took a deep breath in, letting it out slowly. Lee plucked another cube from the air, then set it in front of him. Kyle frowned, leaning over it and trying again. This time he put a little more magic into the inscribing pattern. When he was done, he pushed the cube away, streaming magic to it as before. A respectably-sized flame shot upward from the cube's surface.

"What are you doing wrong?" Lee asked. Kyle blinked, then frowned.

"It's working great," he protested, gesturing to the flaming cube.

"Oh really?" Lee shot back. Kyle frowned, stopping his magic stream, then waiting for the flame to wink out. He stared at the surface of the cube, realizing that it was stained black.

"Oops."

"You'll be real popular when your runics scald everyone who holds them," Lee stated wryly. "Put the rune deeper in the cube," she counseled. "Like this..."

She drew on a piece of paper, resulting in this:

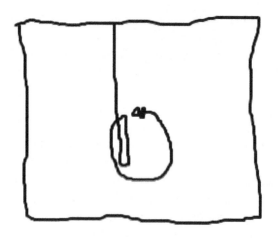

"Okay," Kyle replied. Lee produced yet another cube, and Kyle did as she instructed, creating a rune deeper within the cube, making a longer wire to the surface. Then he streamed magic to the cube. A small flame appeared, hovering slightly above the cube's surface. Only a small circle of black marred the surface.

"The longer it takes for magic to escape the surface after the rune is woven, the farther away the pattern will be executed from the rune," Lee explained. Kyle nodded, cutting off his magic stream.

"Got it," he replied. Lee snorted.

"No you don't," she replied. "But you will." She pulled yet another brown cube from thin air, placing it before him. "Again," she ordered.

Kyle sighed, grabbing the cube and leaning over it, weaving the inscribing pattern yet again.

* * *

Ariana lay on the wet grass of the Secula Magna campus, pain lancing down her left hip and leg as she struggled to get up. The world was still moving in slow motion, as if time had ground to a near-halt. She rolled onto her stomach, crying out as her hip crunched with the movement, shattered bone grating on bone. Not ten feet in front of her, Master Owens hovered unconscious in the middle of the shimmering oval her shard had created...and slowly, inexorably, it contracted around him. With her unnatural hearing, the sounds of her teacher's ribs cracking as his elbows sank into his ribcage were as loud as thunderclaps. Still the walls pressed inward, threatening to crush the life out of her gentle teacher.

"Master Owens!" she screamed. She wove magic frantically, creating a *pushing* gravity sphere around Owens to try to counteract the *pulling* field around him, but it was no use; her shard's gravity field would not be denied. She tried again, shoving as much magic as she could into the pattern.

Nothing happened.

She saw Owens' head arching downward and forward, so severely now that at any moment his neck would snap. She could hear his heart beating rapidly in his chest, heard his breathing stop as the gravity field's crushing force made breathing impossible. His heartbeat became fainter, until it was barely audible, even to her ears.

And then it stopped.

"No!" Ariana cried, covering her eyes with her hand and turning away. She slumped onto her belly on the wet grass below, burying her face in her hands. Great sobs wracked her thin frame, a feeling of utter hopelessness come over her. If she could've cried, if she had been able to make tears, she would have.

She felt her shard's magic stream stop suddenly, heard a dull *thump* as Master Owens' body fell to the ground before her.

Oh god, she thought, balling her hands into fists, gritting her teeth so hard she thought they might crack. She didn't dare open her eyes, knowing that the vision of her teacher's mangled corpse would haunt her memory for the rest of her life. *I'm so sorry.*

She thought of Owens' wife and daughter then, and cried.

Then she heard a *lub-dub.*

The sound of grass crunching beneath someone's foot reached her ears, so close to her that she froze.

Lub-dub.

Ariana paused, then opened her eyes, slowly raising her head.

Lub-dub.

She spotted a dark form laying in the grass...Master Owens' body lying on its back. She heard another footstep nearby, to her left, and turned her head slowly.

Lub-dub.

She saw a hint of black then, an inky boot slowly sinking down into the blades of grass beneath it. She raised her head further, tracing the boot upward to black pants, a black shirt with rows of glittering medals on the left breast, and then that familiar handsome face, two brown eyes staring back at her. Her eyes widened.

"Kalibar!"

Kalibar knelt down in slow-motion before her, his eyes filled with worry. His lips were moving slowly, and she realized that he was talking to her. Ariana turned her head, spotting two men in the black armor of the elite guard running in slow-motion toward Owens. They reached his body, sliding across the wet grass, droplets spraying upward from their boots as they did so. One of the guards reached out to feel Owens' neck, and turned to glance at Kalibar, nodding once.

Lub-dub.

And then time sped up.

"...are you okay?" she heard Kalibar asking. "Ariana!" he urged, shaking her shoulder. She turned to face him, and nodded.

"I'm okay," she answered. "Is he...?" she asked, turning back to Owens. A gravity sphere had appeared around the fallen Weaver, and the two men flew upward into the air, the gravity sphere carrying Owens behind them. They both zoomed toward the Tower in the distance. Kalibar watched them go, then turned back to Ariana.

"He's alive," he answered tersely. "I flew here as fast as I could."

"Will he be okay?" Ariana pressed, feeling fear grip her. Kalibar said nothing, his expression grim. He wrapped one arm around her shoulders, the other behind her knees, lifting her up off of the ground in one smooth motion. She tensed up, expecting to feel pain in her right hip, but to her surprise there was none. "I'm so sorry," she whispered, burying her face in Kalibar's chest. "I didn't mean to hurt him."

"I know honey."

Kalibar started carrying her back toward the cobblestone path nearby, the one leading back to the Tower. Ariana paused, then flexed her right hip experimentally, feeling no pain as she did so. It had likely already healed, as all of her injuries invariably did. She thought about telling Kalibar that he didn't need to carry her, but there was something comforting about being close to him. He'd been so busy running the Empire that he'd rarely had time to spend with her.

She nestled her head against his chest once more, staring up at his face. Kalibar noticed her gaze, and smiled down at her.

"Thank you," she murmured, closing her eyes. She took a deep, shaky breath in, then let it out slowly, feeling the tension seep out of her. Owens was alive, and that's all she cared about now. If it had been anyone else but Kalibar that had found them, her teacher would surely be dead. No one else could have beaten her shard.

Slowly, and silently, they made their way back home.

Chapter 6

Kalibar gazed down at Master Owens, who was propped upright in his hospital bed, sipping a glass of light green tea his nurse had just brought him. The old Weaver was in remarkably good spirits considering his injuries. With multiple broken ribs and a collapsed lung, Ariana's shard had nearly killed him. If Kalibar had come only a few seconds later...

"Master Owens!" he heard a voice cry. He glanced up, spotting Kyle running through the door into the room. The boy stopped before Owens' bed, looking terribly worried. Owens' nurse glanced at Kyle, then took the glass of tea away after Owens had finished it.

"That'll help with the pain," the nurse said. "Give it a few minutes," she instructed. Owens smiled ruefully at her.

"I'm no stranger to it," he replied, grimacing as he propped himself upright in his bed. Kalibar grinned at him.

"I remember," he stated. "You broke your leg at Tigus, during the border skirmishes."

"Not exactly a good memory," Owens replied with a chuckle. Then he grimaced, putting a hand on the left side of his chest. Kalibar glanced at Ariana, who was standing next to Kyle. She'd been staring at her feet the entire time they'd been visiting Owens, saying little. Kalibar saw Kyle grab her hand in his own, giving it a squeeze. She looked startled for a moment, then turned to Kyle, smiling weakly. It was good to see them supporting each other, Kalibar thought. Ariana needed all of the support she could get.

"If you'd had the good sense to have a *real* Battle Weaver to chaperone you," Erasmus cut in with a devilish grin, "...you'd never have gotten your sorry ass spanked." Owens raised an eyebrow at the Grand Runic.

"Didn't a *real* Battle-Weaver save you from Ibicus?" he countered. Erasmus snorted.

"As I recall, *my* invention killed Ibicus," he retorted. "At least I didn't get beat up by a *girl*," he added snidely. Then he glanced at Ariana, putting a hand up defensively. "Not that that's a bad thing," he stated hastily. But Ariana didn't seem amused. Owens turned to look at her.

"Come here Ariana," he beckoned, patting the bed beside him. Ariana hesitated, then obeyed, walking up to his bedside and sitting down dutifully. Owens grabbed her left hand in his own two hands. "I want you to know that what happened wasn't your fault," he stated gently. Ariana swallowed, then shook her head silently, lowering her gaze.

"He's right honey," Kalibar agreed.

"I'm sorry," she mumbled, still not making eye contact with her teacher. Owens sighed, patting her hand.

"I got...overzealous," he admitted, shaking his head ruefully. "I spent all of last night figuring out how I'd neutralize your shard's shields, and I finally came up with a solution. It worked," he added, "...but I shouldn't have used it while you were twenty feet in the air."

"You figured out how to neutralize her shields?" Erasmus asked, suddenly perking up. Owens nodded.

"Her shard generates a dozen shields automatically," Owens replied, "...when any nearby offensive pattern is woven. If I try to neutralize one of them, another is created in its place. So I created one gravity sphere around her shields, and put all the magic I had into it. It overwhelmed all of her weaker shields...her shard couldn't produce enough magic in the short term to keep up."

"That's what I did to save you," Kalibar revealed. He'd done much more than that, having to defend against Ariana's involuntary

73

assault on himself at the same time. His experience fighting the Dead Man – and attending Ariana's sparring matches – had come in handy.

"I should have realized that her shard would automatically protect her if her initial defenses were violated," Owens admitted. "If I'd thought it through, this never would have happened."

"That's for damn sure," Erasmus cut in. "If it hadn't been for Kalibar, you'd be a hell of a lot thinner right now."

"I owe you my life," Owens said, turning to Kalibar. Kalibar reached over and patted him on the shoulder. Erasmus snorted.

"Don't let it get to his head," he scoffed. "It's already overinflated as it is."

"Yes, well," Kalibar stated, glancing at Ariana. "Next time I'll be the one you spar."

"No," Ariana blurted out, shaking her head vehemently. "I'm not sparring again."

"Ariana..." Master Owens began, but Ariana stood up, pulling her hand from his.

"I can't."

"You'll have to," Kalibar countered firmly. Ariana froze, staring mutely at him. Kalibar ignored the part of him that wanted to comfort and protect her, forcing himself to keep his tone harsh. "Sooner or later Xanos is going to attack us again. *All* of his Chosen have your shard, and if someone like Ibicus attacks you again...or me, or Owens, or Kyle...you're going to be the only one who can stop them."

Ariana lowered her eyes to her feet, saying nothing.

"Ibicus would have killed you – and Owens, and Erasmus – if it hadn't been for Darius," Kalibar continued firmly. "If you don't learn to be as good, or better, than the Chosen, what hope do we have?"

"Kalibar," Erasmus warned, putting a hand on his shoulder. "You can't put that kind of pressure on her."

"If I don't," Kalibar countered, "...Xanos will."

"That's not fair," Erasmus insisted. "What could Ariana have done alone against a Void sphere? Or the Void Behemoth?"

"Maybe nothing," Kalibar replied, his voice softening. "But if we want the best chance at saving this Empire...and ourselves...we need everyone to do what they can."

Ariana sighed, raising her eyes to him.

"You're right," she murmured at last. Her expression nearly broke his heart.

"Ariana..." Erasmus began, but she cut him off.

"He's right," she repeated. "I'll do whatever it takes to stop Xanos," she added. "We all have to."

* * *

Kyle sat down in one of the many chairs surrounding the massive round table in the center of the War room, the chamber on the 40th floor the Council had used for their meetings ever since Xanos had first appeared. In addition to the large table, the room had communication orbs that allowed the Council – and Erasmus and Kalibar – to summon all levels of the military if needed. The orbs were not like telephones on Earth, in that they couldn't talk with anyone directly through them, but within minutes they could summon a messenger that could relay a message.

Kyle sighed, watching as Ariana pulled up a seat beside him. They'd been summoned to a Council meeting soon after they'd left Master Owens' bedside. Kalibar had brought Kyle and Ariana here to discuss a few matters with the Council. Mostly, they wanted to know about Kyle's absence...and Ampir.

"Good morning, ladies and gentlemen of the Council," Councilman Goran stated, sitting down in his own chair. He was an imposing figure with his jet-black hair slicked over his head, his black beard immaculately trimmed and speckled with gray. As the most senior Elitist in the Council, he'd inherited the mantle of Elder from the late Ibicus, gaining considerable influence and power.

"Councilman Goran," Kalibar greeted, walking up to his own seat with Erasmus at his side. They both sat.

"Your Excellencies," Goran replied. "Let's get to directly to business. What is the status of the Southwest Quarter?" Erasmus stood then, facing the Council.

"Construction of housing is almost complete," he answered, clearing his throat. "Those still living in temporary housing are being brought in gradually. Construction should be complete within the week."

"Excellent," Goran stated. "The Council appreciates our Grand Runic's tireless efforts," he added. Erasmus managed to force a smile, something that Kyle had never seen him do around Goran. Erasmus hated the man, mostly because Goran had made a fool out of the Grand Runic on countless occasions. Goran had warmed up to Erasmus – and Kalibar – ever so slightly since their escape from the Void spheres...and the Void Behemoth.

"What of the prisoners at Stridon Penitentiary?" Goran asked, turning back to Councilwoman Hess. She'd been tasked with organizing the return of escaped prisoners to the maximum-security prison, and to ensure its security once again.

"Eighty-six prisoners escaped," Hess replied. "Sixty-two were killed, twenty survived and were retrieved, and four are unaccounted for."

"And the prison itself?" Goran pressed. Hess glanced at Erasmus, who stood again.

"Entirely repaired," he replied. "My Runics installed additional security measures, as well as backup magic storage crystals in secret locations throughout the city." He grinned then. "I'll be damned if a Void sphere will drain them this time. I had the storage crystals and wiring insulated to prevent those things from sucking out magic so easily."

"And what of the evacuation tunnels?"

"Permanently sealed," Hess replied. "They're unusable now." Kalibar cleared his throat then, addressing the Council.

"I've created evacuation protocols for Stridon in conjunction with High Weaver Urson, the commanders of each of our legions, and our neighboring cities. We will be conducting drills within the next few days to familiarize the Council and lower government positions with the process."

"Our lives are in your capable hands," Goran stated. Kyle couldn't help smiling; Goran had learned firsthand of Kalibar's skill on the battlefield a week or so ago, having been saved by Kalibar more than once. On matters of warfare, Goran no longer doubted his Grand Weaver. "Which brings us to our next order of business," Goran continued. "The matter of Ampir."

Kyle glanced at Kalibar, feeling suddenly uneasy. This, he knew, was the *real* reason Goran had organized the meeting.

"We all know that this 'Sabin' believes that Ampir – *the* Ampir – is still alive, and is responsible for restoring Grand Weaver Kalibar's eyes," Goran stated. "And for doing all of the things we assumed Kyle's ring was responsible for," he added.

"More likely someone who is emulating him," Councilman Hewes, a scrawny middle-aged Runic, countered. "Unless you want to believe that a traitor who died two thousand years ago was resurrected to save us," he added dryly.

"He's Ampir," Kalibar interjected.

"How can you be so sure?" Councilman Hewes pressed.

"It's the only logical explanation," Kalibar explained. "Kyle's ring has been verified as originally belonging to Ampir. And as the inventor of teleportation two thousand years ago, only he could have instantly transported all of those citizens miles away from the Void Behemoth."

"He's got a point," Councilwoman Hess admitted.

"Perhaps," Hewes muttered.

"How many people did he save?" Goran inquired.

"Eight-hundred or so," Erasmus answered. "The death toll from the attack is unbelievably low."

"We owe Ampir – or whoever this is – an enormous debt," another Councilman stated.

"We can assume for now that the man – Ampir or otherwise – is powerful beyond our capacity to understand," Goran stated. "But we can't assume that he will continue to protect us from Xanos."

"Agreed," Kalibar said.

"Nevertheless," Goran continued, "...making contact with Ampir should be one of our highest priorities...if not our highest." He turned to Kyle then, his dark, piercing eyes making Kyle squirm. Kyle felt Ariana's cold hand squeeze his. "On that note, I'd like to welcome Kyle back to Stridon."

All eyes turned to Kyle then.

"It is our understanding," Goran stated, "...that Ampir sent you away for the last week, and that he's just brought you back to us. Is that correct?"

"Yes Councilman," Kyle confirmed.

"Tell us what you know about him," Goran ordered. Kyle squirmed in his chair again, feeling the weight of a dozen pairs of eyes staring at him. He shrugged.

"I don't know much," he lied. "He never talks to me," he added, which was mostly true.

"He hasn't said anything at all?" Goran pressed.

"He said he was Ampir," Kyle admitted. "And that he was going to take me back to Earth...ah, home," he added, kicking himself mentally for mentioning his home planet. But Goran just frowned.

"Urth...is that your hometown?" he asked. Kyle paused, then nodded. "Why do you suppose that Ampir is so interested in you?" Goran pressed.

"I wish I knew," Kyle answered. This hardly seemed to please the Elder Weaver.

"You must know *something*."

Kyle glanced at Kalibar, who returned his gaze silently, his expression neutral. Darius had made it clear that he wasn't to say anything about him.

"Give the kid a break," Erasmus piped in, crossing his arms in front of his impressive beard. "None of us knew about Ampir until Kalibar figured it out," he added.

"I can vouch for that," Kalibar agreed. "Kyle didn't even know who Ampir was – historically – until I told him. He's a mystery to all of us, Goran."

"I see," Goran grumbled. "So our Empire's fate lies in the hands of the man who allowed the Ancient Empire to be destroyed."

"That's crap," Erasmus spat. "There's no solid proof that Ampir betrayed the Ancients."

"The history books beg to differ," Goran countered icily.

"Only the ones *you* read," Erasmus retorted, giving the Elder Weaver a withering look. "Things are a little more complicated than you learned in elementary school, Goran."

"Our most distinguished historians..." Goran began, but Erasmus cut him off.

"Needed a scapegoat to blame for the fall of the Ancients," he interjected snidely. "So we wouldn't have to face the fact that our precious ancestors were beaten fair and square."

"Both," Kalibar stated suddenly, before Goran could counter Erasmus, "...theories have their supporters and detractors." He turned to Goran then. "I have to admit that I used to believe that Ampir was a traitor, as you do."

"And what do you believe now?" Goran inquired, sending an icy glare Erasmus's way.

"I believe that the truth may be more complicated," Kalibar stated diplomatically. Kyle saw Kalibar put a hand on Erasmus's leg, stopping the portly Runic from speaking up. "I also believe we may never know the truth," he added. "The fact is, we all know that history is created by the historian, and that it often does not accurately reflect reality."

"Granted," Hess agreed.

"In any case, this particular argument has been dividing historians for centuries, and I doubt we'll solve the mystery today," Kalibar stated with a sigh. "Suffice it to say that Ampir exists, and he gave me my eyes back, and he saved all of us from Xanos after Orik had Rivin and Bartholos assassinated. Whatever his past, none of us would be alive to accuse him today if he hadn't intervened."

The other members of the Council nodded at this, and even Goran had to agree. Erasmus, of course, was still itching for a fight, but wisely held his tongue...for once.

"But we must also remember that Ampir *didn't* help destroy the Void Behemoth, or the army that attacked us," Kalibar continued. "I submit that we concentrate on what *we* can do to defend ourselves against Xanos," he added. "And assume that Ampir will not help us again."

"But if we could just meet with him," Councilman Hewes protested.

"You're welcome to try to contact him," Kalibar interjected. "In the meantime, I believe our best chance for survival lies in the K-Array."

"Agreed," Goran stated. He turned to Erasmus then. "Care to debrief us?"

"We've discovered six new patterns," Erasmus declared, leaning forward eagerly. "The most promising are the killerpillar ray and the invisibility pattern."

"The invisibility pattern?"

"We found it yesterday afternoon," Erasmus clarified. "Derived from an Ardus," he added. "It's a small, furry animal with hooves," he clarified when met with Goran's blank stare. "It vanishes whenever it's threatened."

"Fascinating," Councilman Hewes murmured. "Think of the applications!"

"Oh I have," Erasmus said with a grin. "My Runics are already developing Battle-Weaver armor with cloaking technology."

"While that is extraordinary," Goran admitted, "...none of these patterns will be useful if we have more Chosen hidden in our midst." He was of course referring to Ibicus, whose mind had been taken over by one of Xanos's shards. No one had realized that they'd had a traitor among them...and no one could be sure of when Ibicus had been turned. It could have been days ago...or even years.

"Agreed," Kalibar replied. "Which is why these patterns are known to a select few people," he added. "Myself, Erasmus, a few Runics, and two of our elite guards."

"That's hardly reassuring," Goran muttered.

"It will have to do for now," Kalibar replied coolly. "Until we have a way to screen for these living Chosen."

The room became silent at that, each Councilman no doubt considering the implications of another Chosen secretly among them. Jax had been murdered in his sleep, and Kalibar had nearly met the same fate. What was to stop them all from succumbing to another traitor?

"We must continue to develop new technology," Kalibar stated at last, breaking the uncomfortable silence. "The K-Array remains our best chance of defending the Empire from Xanos." He glanced at Kyle then. "We cannot win this war with sheer power," he added grimly. "If we win, we will owe it to our ideas, and our ability to apply these to the defense of our great Empire."

Kyle felt the eyes of ever last person in the War room turn to him, and he lowered his gaze to the tabletop. He knew that they all expected him to come up with some other amazing idea...and he doubted that he would. The K-Array had been a fluke, a lucky guess.

But, to his dismay, there was not a single Councilman in that room who would deny that Kalibar was right.

Chapter 7

Sabin ignored the pain coursing through his body, a constant reminder of the strange illness that had nearly killed him long ago, when he'd been mortal. He focused on his avatar standing at the bottom of the huge Void chamber, controlling it with a fraction of his consciousness. The avatar stood holding a green shard to its forehead, inscribing countless microscopic runes into the shard.

It had taken a great deal of time for Sabin to master the skill necessary to control one body while dividing his concentration amongst his vast army of Chosen, but he'd had millennia to practice the art. He did not control every Chosen at the same time; this had proven, even for his augmented brain, impossible. Rather, he rapidly darted from Chosen to Chosen, accessing their senses and memories, and sending his commands to their brains. If he chose to, he could take over any Chosen's body completely, as he had done with Rivin's corpse over a month ago.

But his avatar, that ancient body tottering down the metallic platform, had no real mind of its own. With Sabin's body trapped in its eternal resting place, that body was his alone.

It hadn't always been this way, of course. He'd been mortal once.

Sabin withdrew his mind from Xanos suddenly, feeling the agony of his own body return with a vengeance. He endured the pain, focusing inward, into his own mind.

His memories of his mortal life were elusive, blurred by the passage of time and the limits of his finite brain. Certainly he would have recognized Darius as Ampir immediately if his memories of his early life had been better preserved. But he had learned how to store his own memories in the minds of his Chosen too late, and his recollection of that part of his past had been permanently damaged.

But he remembered some parts of his past...his mortal life. He'd long-ago learned how to store those memories in his Chosen, and often found himself sending a portion of his consciousness out to retrieve those memories, to relive each moment as if he were experiencing them for the first time.

What better time than now to do so, to reminisce?

He paused, then reached out to one of his oldest Chosen, one that had been locked in a Void crystal for nearly as long as he had. Sabin willed the primitive, long untouched memories from its mind, allowing a fraction of his enormous consciousness to experience them.

* * *

The courtyard is filled with the clamor of hundreds of Runic students rushing out from their lecture halls, enthusiastically making their way to one of the three restaurants serving lunch in the dorm complex nearby. A warm breeze carries the delicious smell of freshly cooked meats, rustling the leaves of the ornamental trees that decorate the large courtyard.

Sabin closes his eyes, taking a deep breath in through his nostrils, then lets it out. He looks down at the half-eaten meal before him, stabbing a piece of meat with his fork and putting it in his mouth. He'd finished giving his latest lecture only twenty minutes ago, coming to his favorite restaurant before the inevitable lunch-time rush.

He sips his glass of water, watching the young Runic students as they walk by, fresh-faced and energetic, and feels a pang of nostalgia for the old days. Twenty years ago, he'd been one of them, his life full of promise and possibility. Now he is in his mid-forties, locked into his career, his possibilities limited. The only promise he has left lies in his research and teaching. And, of course, his inventions.

He finds himself staring idly at the ring on his right middle finger, a black onyx band with a single diamond-shaped emerald in the center. A gift from the former Grand Runic, ten years ago, in recognition for Sabin's greatest invention: an earring that allowed anyone to understand, and be understood by, a person speaking a foreign language. It had been the natural product of his research into thought-activated runic technology...and selling the patent for it had made him a very wealthy man.

Sabin sighs, his eyes idly following a group of young women as they pass by the table he is sitting at. A few are quite pretty, and he has to be careful not to stare for too long. He is, after all, a distinguished professor of Runic Arts and an accomplished researcher, the preeminent expert not only on thought-activated runics, but also on his most recent focus: magic vacuity. He can't afford tarnishing that reputation by seeming like a lecherous old man.

It is a constant temptation, though.

He'd never taken a wife. Never had time for it, really...his work had seen to that. It is his one great regret, that he has only himself to come home to. A lonely existence.

He sighs again, tearing his eyes away from the group of women. He lowers his gaze to the food on his plate, feeling a strange tingling sensation shoot down his spine as he does so.

"Professor?"

Sabin jerks his head up from his plate, finding a young woman standing opposite him. She wears the black uniform of a Weaver student, and has long, wavy auburn hair that reaches all the way down to her lower back. Her features are strikingly...no, *painfully* beautiful, her skin pale and her gray eyes bright and expressive. He finds himself staring, his mouth half-open, and snaps it shut.

"Yes?" he asks, trying his best to sound casual. The young woman smiles apologetically, gesturing to the empty chair opposite him.

"May I sit?"

"Of course," he replies, gesturing to the chair. She obliges, flashing him another smile.

"I'm Vera," she greets, extending a hand across the table. Sabin reaches over and shakes it. "I really enjoyed your lecture," she adds. Sabin raises an eyebrow.

"I didn't realize I had an impostor in my class," he says with an easy grin. "What's a Weaver doing in an advanced Runic theory class?"

"I'm not actually enrolled in the class," Vera admits. "I wanted to see if the rumors were true," she adds with a mysterious smile. Sabin purses his lips.

"Rumors?" he inquires. "Hopefully nothing too scandalous."

"Not yet," she counters coyly, leaning forward. A lock of her thick auburn hair falls in front of her eyes, and she brushes it aside absently. For some reason Sabin finds this extraordinarily fetching. "I heard you were the best teacher in the Secula Magna," she explains. "And the world expert in magic vacuity."

"Well, you've been to my lecture," Sabin replies, leaning back in his chair. "Are the rumors true?"

"Mmm," she replies, cocking her head to the side slightly and eyeing him silently for a moment. "Perhaps."

"What else do you need to know to make your decision?" Sabin presses, his tone breezy. That earned him another mysterious smile.

"How about lunch?" she asks. Sabin gives her an apologetic smile.

"Ah, how rude of me," he states, flagging down a waiter. "What can I order for you?"

"Oh, you don't have to..." she begins, but Sabin cuts her off with one hand.

"I insist," he interjects. "We have rumors to feed." She cocks an eyebrow at this.

"What sorts of rumors?" she asks coyly. He feels a rush of adrenaline course through him, his heart pounding in his chest. He wills himself to remain calm, wondering how this girl – no doubt twenty years his junior – could have such an effect on him. He has a sudden mad desire to feed into this remarkable creature's flirty suggestions, to throw caution to the wind and see what wonderful things might happen.

"The kind with appetites," he replies smoothly. Vera grins.

"Well I've certainly got appetites."

"And I insist on feeding them," Sabin states. He catches the eye of a passing waiter, and Vera orders lunch. After the waiter leaves, Vera twirls a lock of her hair with one finger, staring at him silently. He finds himself profoundly uncomfortable under that gaze...and glad of it.

"Do *you* have appetites, professor?" Vera inquires at last, continuing to stare at him with those gray eyes. Sabin pauses, unsure of how to answer without getting himself into trouble.

"Doesn't everyone?" he counters at last.

"Mmm," Vera murmurs. The waiter returns with a plate full of food, and Vera grabs a piece of fruit, taking a bite out of it.

"So why magic vacuity?" Sabin presses, switching back to a safer subject. "Most students only care about thought-activated runics." Vera was certainly correct in her estimation of him; he *was* the world's expert on magic vacuity. He'd spent the last eight years of his life feeding that obsession, while continuing his research into thought-activated runics. With over a hundred patents to his name, including the one for the universal translator, he hardly needs the paltry salary of a professor. But he truly loves to teach, and he had maintained his ties to academia, hoping to inspire others to contribute to the magical sciences.

"I'm exploring the application of magic vacuity to Battle-Weaving," Vera answers. Sabin's eyebrows rise in surprise.

"You're a Battle-Weaver student?" he asks incredulously. Vera laughs, shaking her head.

"God no," she replies. "I'm not cut out for that," she adds without a hint of regret.

"What then?" he presses. "What do you want from life?"

"To get a job in academia," she answers without hesitation. "I want to do research, and I think magic vacuity has many applications to Battle-Weaving."

"Well you're right about that," Sabin agrees. "Magic vacuity is key in *any* magical endeavor." He smiles then. "So you're an academic at heart," he observes.

"Like you," Vera agrees, eating another piece of fruit. He watches her, then feels his heart start to race, a sudden kind of madness coming over him.

"It seems we have similar appetites," he murmurs. Immediately he regrets the bold implications of the statement, feeling a pang of fear come over him. But she only smiles at him with that mysterious way she has.

"Indeed," she replies.

Suddenly a young woman in a Weaver student uniform walks up to Vera, putting a hand on her shoulder.

"Come on, Vera," the woman urges. "We're going to be late for class."

Vera nods, standing up from the table and pushing her chair in. Sabin waves to her, and she waves back.

"See you around, professor," she promises.

And then she walks away.

Sabin follows her retreating form, his eyes drawn to her long legs and intriguing curves. He tears his gaze away, glancing about to see if anyone caught him staring, but no one seems to have. He stares down at his plate, feeling more than a little confused...yet somehow more alive than he's felt for years.

Maybe, just maybe, his life has some promise and possibility left after all.

* * *

Master Lee glared at Kyle from across the wooden table they always sat at in the Runic Archives, the scowl on her face making her appear even more ancient than she was. After the Council meeting, Kyle had returned to the Archives to finish the day's lessons with Lee. He'd inscribed so many runes that he'd long since lost count of how many. Lee had proven to be a brutal taskmaster, more similar to the Dead Man in her methods than she was to the late Master Banar. Minus the systematic psychological torture, of course.

"You're distracted," she observed testily. "What's wrong?"

"I'm just tired," Kyle mumbled. In truth, he was worried sick about Darius, and what might happen if...

"Bull," Lee retorted. "Don't lie to me again."

"I'll be fine," he muttered. Lee stared at him for a long moment, then sighed.

"Well if you won't open up to me," she growled, "...I expect you to perform as if nothing's wrong." Kyle blanched, then nodded silently.

"Now," Lee stated. "...what is the most important development in runic technology?"

"Runic logic," Kyle answered, verbatim from her previous lecture. Lee nodded.

"What does that mean?" she pressed. Kyle paused, wracking his brain, but came up with nothing. "It means the ability of runic items to make decisions," she concluded. She tapped on the cube in front of Kyle. "This is a fresh gem," she explained. "That's what we call crystals without any runes inscribed in them. I want you to demonstrate your understanding of Runic logic with it."

Kyle nodded silently.

"*If* this, *then* do this," Lee stated. "That is the simplest form of Runic logic." She sat back in her chair then. "For example: *if* the fire pattern is sensed nearby, *then* make a gravity shield to protect yourself."

"Got it," Kyle replied. Simple enough.

"You don't 'have it' until you've *done* it," Lee retorted. "Theory is useless without application. She pushed the cube toward Kyle. "Inscribe runes and link them to perform that logic."

Kyle stared at the cube in front of him, blanking on what he was supposed to do. After a long moment, he glanced up at Lee, who was staring silently at him. She leaned forward, propping her bony elbows on the table.

"Tell me what's wrong," she stated coldly, "...or I'll consider dropping you as my student."

Kyle paled.

"I'm worried what'll happen if Xanos attacks again," he admitted. It was true enough; he didn't need to mention that such a thing would only happen if Darius failed.

"He will," Lee replied bluntly.

"Gee, thanks," Kyle muttered. Lee snorted.

"Don't expect me to sugar-coat it, honey," she grumbled. "But it's not worth getting yourself worried sick over," she added. "There are an infinite number of possible futures to worry about, and only one of them will come true. Deal with the one. Trust me, life's better that way."

"I'm not worried about me," he clarified. "I'm worried about my friends."

"You think I don't worry?" Lee countered. "I don't give a damn about me," she added with a smirk. "I'm practically dead anyway. But I worry about my son."

"I'm really sorry," Kyle mumbled. "I can't concentrate today."

"Concentrate on now," Lee advised. "Take it from me, now is all you have. Now is all you'll ever have, a long stream of nows. And one day, *poof*...no more nows." She leaned back again. "Live while you're still alive, honey."

"I'll try," Kyle replied.

"Well lying in bed moping won't make you feel better," Lee retorted. "Idle minds invite madness. I'm going to give yours something to do." She pointed to the cube then. "*If* fire *then* make a shield. Go."

"I don't know how," Kyle protested.

"Figure it out," Lee retorted.

Kyle sighed, staring down at the cube. There was only one condition to meet – the presence of a fire – and the only way to sense magic was with a sensory rune. So he had to inscribe the fire pattern into the cube. But he couldn't use the pattern he'd used to inscribe the effector runes he'd practiced before. Like Kalibar and the late Master Banar had said, inscribing sensory runes required a special pattern – one that Kyle didn't know yet.

"I can't do it," Kyle stated. "I don't know how to make sensory runes." Master Lee smirked.

"That's more like it," she replied. "I'll show it to you." She showed Kyle the pattern a half-dozen times; it was far simpler than he'd expected. Within ten minutes or so, he'd mastered it.

"Now," Lee stated when they'd finished. "...continue with the exercise. *If* fire *then* gravity shield."

He lowered his forehead to the cube, closing his eyes and weaving the sensory pattern. He used it to create the fire rune, then stopped. He switched to the inscribing pattern, then drew the gravity shield pattern beside the fire pattern. Then he connected them with a thin line. When he was done, he let out a breath he hadn't realized he'd been holding. He glanced up at Lee then, who was leaning back in her chair, her eyes closed and her mouth open. She looked disturbingly dead.

He frowned at her, then realized she wasn't breathing.

"Master Lee!" he exclaimed, jumping up from his seat. Lee's eyes burst open, and she cackled shrilly.

"Thought I was dead, didn't you?" she asked between guffaws. "Got you!" Kyle glared at her, sliding the cube across the table toward her.

"I finished," he grumbled.

"Took you long enough," she opined. She snatched the cube up, staring at it intently. Then she frowned, glancing up at him. "Not bad," she admitted. Then she set the cube on the center of the tabletop, leaning back in her chair. "Now we test it. Weave the fire pattern."

Kyle complied, weaving the fire pattern in his mind's eye, then throwing it out in the air in front of him. A small blue sphere instantly appeared around the cube, and it jumped up from the tabletop, flying a few feet into the air. Then it fell, bouncing a few times before hovering a few inches above the table.

"Whoa," Kyle exclaimed. "What happened?"

"You tell me," Lee countered. Kyle frowned, staring at the cube. The lower fifth of the gravity shield was cut off, so it formed an

90

incomplete sphere. This lower edge was touching the table, so it was the shield that was forcing the cube to float. He said as much.

"Right," Lee confirmed. "I suppose Owens never told you that the gravity shield he taught you to weave wasn't a complete sphere."

"No, he did," Kyle countered.

"Well," Lee snorted. "At least he got *something* right. What would happen if you tried weaving a gravity shield that *was* a complete sphere around yourself?" Kyle thought about it; if he did that, then the lower edge of the gravity shield would intersect with the ground below his feet...and he'd pop up into the air, just that the cube had.

"I'd float above the ground," he concluded. Lee nodded.

"Your brain's working again," she observed.

"But what if I wanted to fly?" Kyle asked, suddenly concerned. "If I used the shield Owens taught me, someone from below could hit my feet."

"Exactly," Lee agreed. "Which is why Weavers cover their legs with their gravity shields when they're flying, and use the typical incomplete spheres when they fight on the ground."

"Huh."

Master Lee smiled, her cheeks crisscrossing with deep wrinkles as she did so. She produced another cube – out of thin air, as usual – and gave it to Kyle. "Well done. Do it again."

Kyle sighed, closing his eyes and leaning over the cube. But Lee pushed herself back from the table where she sat opposite him, standing up in that stooped manner she had.

"Practice on your own time," she grumbled, pushing her chair in. Kyle blinked.

"What?" he blurted out. "Why? What'd I do?" Master Lee rolled her eyes.

"You displayed competency," she answered. "Play with the runes," she added. "Change their size, make them thicker or thinner. Get a feel for them." She started walking toward the exit of the Archives, not even bothering to look back at him. "See you tomorrow."

"Thanks Master Lee," Kyle called out to her retreating posterior. Lee waved one hand, but didn't turn around.

And then she was gone.

Kyle sighed, grabbing the cube in front of him and putting it in his pocket. He stood up, turning around to follow Master Lee, then did a double-take. He'd almost forgotten to take the textbook Lee had left on the table for him...the one he was supposed to read tonight. It was quite thin, with a simple brown cover. On its surface were symbols that meant nothing to Kyle, but were apparently written in the language of the Empire. It was, distressingly enough, a book for toddlers...a picture book that would supposedly teach him how to read.

He grabbed the book, and walked out of the Archives.

Two elite guards materialized out of nowhere, walking in step on either side of Kyle. He flinched at first, then relaxed, remembering that they'd been there all along, practicing the invisibility pattern that Erasmus had discovered using the K-Array. The only time Kyle was truly alone was when he was in bed, and even then guards were stationed outside of his room throughout the night. It was a constant reminder of the fact that none of them were truly safe...that at any time, Xanos could attack.

The guards silently accompanied Kyle out of the Archives and down the riser to the lobby, where Kyle had agreed to meet with Ariana after finishing his lessons. He found her sitting in one of the many couches located along either wall of the massive room, her skin nearly blending into the perfect whiteness of the fabric. She was already following Kyle with her eyes, of course; ever since her resurrection, her senses had become so sharp it was almost eerie.

"Hey," Kyle greeted, watching Ariana stand up and walk toward him. She smiled.

"How were your lessons?" she asked. Kyle gave her a rueful smile. "Hard."

"How's Master Lee?" she pressed. Kyle shrugged.

"She's alright," he replied. "She's nice, but a little...brutal."

"Are you learning anything?" she asked. Kyle nodded.

"Yeah, you want to see?" he asked. She nodded, and Kyle took a small ceramic cup out of his pocket. At the bottom of the cup, there was a small brown crystal cube, one he'd placed there after inscribing a few patterns into the cube. It had been one of Master Lee's final exercises for him to complete.

"What does it do?" Ariana inquired. Kyle handed the cup to her.

"Stream magic to it."

Kyle saw Ariana concentrate. Within moments, the cube at the bottom of the cup glowed a faint blue, and the cup began to fill with water. Ariana's eyes widened, and she streamed magic until the cup was nearly full.

"Neat," she murmured.

"Touch the water," Kyle suggested. Ariana did so, and her eyebrows went up.

"It's hot!" she exclaimed. Kyle grinned.

"There's a water rune and a fire rune in the cube," he explained. "They're connected so the water rune activates first, then the fire rune. The fire rune is really thin, so it just heats the water instead of boiling it," he added. Ariana frowned.

"I don't get it," she admitted. "What do you mean by the rune being 'thin?'"

"Um, well," he began, but Ariana stopped him.

"It's okay," she interrupted. "Why don't you teach me later," she suggested. "Where its quieter."

Kyle nodded, remembering that Ariana hated being in crowds...and the lobby was very crowded. The stimulation from the sounds and sights sometimes overwhelmed her; she much preferred being in the relative peace of the outdoors.

"Want to go for a walk?"

"How about we go back to Kalibar's suite?" Ariana suggested. Kyle shrugged, not really caring where they went. As long as he was with her, life was good.

"Sure," he agreed. They made their way through the lobby and up the riser to Kalibar's suite. As they strode down the hallway toward the front door of the suite, they found Erasmus in the middle of the hallway.

"Kyle!" Erasmus exclaimed. "Good to see you," he added. "My mother was just telling me about your progress."

93

"Hi," Kyle greeted. Erasmus pushed open the door to the suite, and they all walked into the main room. Erasmus gestured for them to sit at one of the many tables there. Ariana sat in a chair beside Kyle, and Erasmus sat down opposite them.

"I wanted to talk to you about the Council meeting we had today," Erasmus stated.

"What about it?" Kyle asked.

"About what Goran said," Erasmus answered. "When he said there might be more Chosen hidden among us, waiting to attack again." He leaned forward, eyeing Kyle. "I came here to see if you had any ideas about how to approach the problem."

"Well," Kyle began, turning to Ariana, "...can't you sense Chosen when they're close?"

"I can tell if there's a Chosen nearby," Ariana explained. "...but only when Xanos is taking over their minds."

"So you wouldn't know if another butler was secretly spying for Xanos...not as long as Xanos didn't try to directly control him," Erasmus clarified. Ariana nodded.

"So we need some way to screen people for shards in their foreheads," Kyle deduced. Ariana stared at him for a moment, then shook her head.

"That wouldn't be good for me," she countered. "Nobody on the Council knows the true source of my abilities...and if they did..."

"Yeah," Kyle agreed. Then he stopped suddenly, his eyes widening.

"What?"

"I've got it!" he exclaimed, slamming his fist into his palm.

"Got what?"

"Why don't we put you near the K-Array," Kyle explained, "...and see what patterns are used to keep you...going?" Erasmus frowned.

"Why?"

"Well," Kyle explained, "...we could make a device that senses anyone using the same patterns Ariana's uses. If we put the device to a Chosen's forehead, it would light up."

"Wait, would that work?" Ariana asked, turning to Erasmus. The Grand Runic frowned, rubbing his chin, but Kyle nodded.

"It would," Kyle declared confidently. Erasmus's eyes brightened. "Damn right it would!" he exclaimed. "We could use it to screen everyone in the Tower," he added eagerly.

"As long as no one uses it on me," Ariana muttered darkly. "If the Council mistakes me for a Chosen, they'll try to kill me."

"Well, we could make it have a secret rune then," Kyle theorized. Something you can weave if you're near it, that will prevent it from lighting up."

"Hot damn!" Erasmus cried, practically leaping out of his chair and slapping the table with one hand. "Kyle, you're a genius! One day with my old lady and you're already running circles around those stuffy Tower academics," he added gleefully. "I'll make it myself...and I'll include that secret inhibitor rune Kyle offered."

"Thanks," Ariana said, giving Erasmus a relieved smile. The Grand Runic nodded, then turned to Kyle, a twinkle in his eyes.

"Any more ideas in that gourd of yours?" he asked. Kyle shook his head. "Well, I'd better get going," Erasmus added, standing up suddenly. "Thanks to you, I've got more work to do." He turned about and left then, the translucent door to Kalibar's suite closing behind him. Kyle watched him go, then turned to see Ariana staring at him.

"What's wrong?" she asked.

"What do you mean?"

"You're distracted," she replied. "You seem...down," she added. Kyle gave her a rueful smile.

"You sound like Master Lee," he mumbled. Ariana smiled, putting a hand on his.

"Tell me," she insisted. Kyle sighed, pulling his hand away...which made Ariana frown.

"I can't say," he mumbled. Ariana's frown deepened.

"You can't tell me?" she pressed. Kyle winced at the hurt in her voice.

"It's not that," he countered, "...it's just that I'm not supposed to tell anyone."

"You can tell me," she insisted, grabbing his hand again and giving it the gentlest of squeezes. This time he didn't pull away. "I promise I'll never tell anyone," she added firmly. Kyle glanced sidelong at her, feeling the sudden, overwhelming urge to confide in her. There was no doubt that she was telling the truth; when Ariana made a promise, her word was absolute.

"It's Ampir," he admitted, feeling his heart leap into his throat even as he spoke the words. He snapped his mouth shut so quickly his teeth clicked, suddenly horrified at what he might reveal.

"What about him?" she asked.

"Nothing," he mumbled, turning away from her. But Ariana put a cold hand on his cheek, gently but firmly turning him toward her again.

"Trust me," she pleaded.

Kyle stared into those brown, almond-shaped eyes, so lovely against that porcelain skin, and felt as if he'd fall into their depths. He yearned to come clean with her, to tell her everything. About Ampir, about Darius...*everything.*

"He found Xanos," he blurted out, feeling his heart hammer in his chest. Ariana took her hand off of his cheek, her eyes widening.

"He did?" she stated, drawing back from him. "Where?"

Kyle paused, then led Ariana to his bedroom. He peered behind the headboard, spotting the rolled-up map laying on the floor where he'd put it earlier, nearly invisible in the shadows. He tried to grab it, but it was a few inches too far away. He strained, trying to pull the bed back from the wall, but it was no use...the bed was impossibly heavy. He glanced back at Ariana, who grabbed the headboard with one hand, pulling the entire bed forward from the wall with ease.

"Thanks," Kyle mumbled.

He grabbed the map, and Ariana re-positioned the bed. He sat on the bed with her, unrolling the map in the middle of the bed. He grabbed the metallic bomb from within, placing it to one side.

"This is Stridon," he stated, pointing to a small dot on the west coast of a huge continent. He slid his finger across a broad ocean, to another continent further west. He stopped at its eastern shore, at the small red circle there. "This," he added, "...is where Xanos is."

"He's sure?" Ariana asked. Kyle nodded.

"Pretty sure," he confirmed. "Ampir's going to try to kill him," he added. Ariana's eyes widened.

"He is?"

"He is," he confirmed. Ariana broke into a huge grin, grabbing his hands in her own.

"That's great!" she exclaimed, pulling him in and giving him a rib-crushing hug. Luckily she disengaged quickly. "We'll finally be safe!"

"Yeah, maybe," he mumbled. She blinked, her smile slowly fading.

"Wait, what do you mean?" she pressed. Kyle shrugged, glancing at the clock on the wall nearest them. He'd learned to read numbers in Doma, enough that he could see it was already after five o'clock.

"He said if he didn't come back by tonight," Kyle admitted, "...that it would mean that he'd failed."

"What do you mean, failed?"

"That Xanos had killed him," Kyle clarified.

Ariana stared at him for a long moment, her mouth slightly open. She snapped it shut, then opened it again as if to say something. But no words came out. Finally, she shook her head, pulling back from him.

"So if he doesn't come back tonight," she mumbled, "...we're on our own."

Kyle nodded mutely.

Ariana stood up from the bed suddenly, walking away from him and putting a hand to her mouth. Kyle slid off the bed, walking to her and putting a hand on her shoulder.

"Ariana," he began, but she turned around suddenly, and he shrank back from her gaze. There was something in her eyes that made him suddenly afraid.

Of her.

"He *has* to win," she stated firmly, clenching her fists at her sides. Kyle took a step back reflexively, feeling his butt strike the edge of the table behind him.

"He will," he stated hastily.

"He *has* to," she repeated. "I can't go on like this," she added. "I can't keep waiting for Xanos to come back and destroy everything I care about!" She turned away then, clenching and unclenching her fists. Kyle paused, then approached her slowly. He hesitated, then reached out to touch her shoulder, half-expecting her to spin around and smack him clear across the room. But she didn't move.

"He will," he repeated, more confidently this time. And with a heck of a lot more confidence than he felt. Truth be told, he felt the same way as Ariana. With every hour that passed – and Darius still having not returned – he felt himself becoming more and more ill-at-ease. It seemed impossible that Darius could lose to Xanos, but if he did...

Ariana sighed, deflating somewhat. She turned around, leaning in and wrapping her arms around him, resting her head on his shoulder.

"I hope you're right," she murmured, her voice muffled by his shirt. He smiled, giving her a squeeze.

"I'm right," he insisted. For her sake, and for his own, Kyle desperately hoped that he *was* right. Ariana pulled away, brushing a strand of her dark brown hair from in front of her eyes. Despite himself, Kyle yawned.

"You're tired already?" Ariana asked. "It's not even six o'clock."

"I got two hours of sleep the night before last," he admitted. "And Master Lee had me wake up at five this morning."

"Why don't you sleep," Ariana offered.

"I don't know if I'll be able to."

"I'll have Jenkins get you a dreamweaver pillow," Ariana stated. Kyle nodded; sewn into the fibers of the pillowcase, dreamweaver silk would gently lull anyone to sleep. It was worth a shot. "I'll call him," she declared. She walked up to the crystalline communication orb resting on Kyle's nightstand to summon the butler.

"Wait," Kyle blurted out. "I can't leave you alone while I sleep," he protested. She paused, turning to glance at him questioningly. "I don't want you to worry alone," he clarified. He suddenly regretted telling her the truth, knowing that he'd ruined her evening...and her peace of mind.

"It's okay," she replied. "I worry about it every night," she admitted. "I've worried about it ever since we escaped the Arena."

She smiled ruefully. "The only difference is, now I can't get away from my own head by sleeping."

"Sorry," he mumbled. "I shouldn't have told you." But she shook her head.

"I'm glad you did," she countered. "I'd rather know the truth than have you feel like you need to keep things from me." She gave him another hug, then reached for the communication orb. "Let's get you that pillow." Kyle watched her activate the orb, unable to help himself from yawning again. When she was done, she stared at him with her lovely brown eyes, and he found himself staring back, his heart fluttering in his chest. Ariana frowned.

"What's wrong?" she asked. Kyle blinked.

"What do you mean?" he countered.

"Your heart," she answered, putting a hand on his chest. "It's beating really fast." Kyle slunk back from her hand.

"Uh," he stammered.

"You're blushing," she observed.

"I'm fine," he mumbled.

"Are you nervous?" she asked, giving him a look he couldn't read. Kyle tried to laugh nonchalantly...and failed. Ariana was about to say something more when they both heard the front door of the suite open suddenly. A moment later, Jenkins entered the bedroom, a pillow clutched in his arms. Kyle breathed a sigh of relief, eagerly taking the pillow from the blue-clad butler. Jenkins bowed before Kyle, unsuccessfully trying to stifle a yawn himself.

"Can I get you anything else, sir?" he inquired. Kyle shook his head, thanking Jenkins. The butler left, and Ariana gently prodded Kyle toward his bed. Kyle found himself yawning, the dreamweaver pillow already starting to exert its influence over him. He'd barely made it into his bed before his eyelids grew too heavy to keep open, and sleep claimed him.

Chapter 8

Sabin withdrew from the ancient memory he'd recalled. The all-too-familiar sensation of countless nerve endings screaming in pain greeted him, arms of fire encircling him in a burning embrace. It was indescribable, this torture that served as his eternal penance.

This was his prison, this body. The Hell he'd more than earned.

Sabin stopped that train of thought, refusing to allow himself to wallow in self-pity yet again. He knew all too well where that path led; he'd been down it many times before. Spending months, sometimes years bemoaning his fate, yearning for death.

Pathetic.

He tore his mind away from those thoughts, checking the internal clock he'd created within the network...a mere half-second had passed during his reverie.

If he'd had been able to sigh, he would have.

Ahhh, Ampir.

He was an enigma, that one, and always had been. And though his appearance had barely changed in the two thousand years since they'd last seen each other, Ampir had grown extraordinarily powerful, far exceeding Sabin's expectations. Even the runes he'd placed in that girl's bones had been absolutely incredible, sophisticated beyond anything Sabin had ever seen. But utterly useless against the power of the Void.

Sabin smiled inwardly, remembering the last time he'd seen Ampir as a mortal man. They had not parted on the best of terms. Sabin hesitated, then reached out again, to another Chosen he'd stored his memories within. His plans were progressing nicely. He could spare this indulgence now, another fraction of a second reliving the past, memories that he hadn't considered in centuries. A luxury, to reflect on one's own life. To relive each bittersweet moment in a way that no mortal ever could.

Now was the time to remember.

* * *

Central Square in Stridon is bustling with people as Sabin makes his way down the sidewalk, his gold-tipped cane clacking on the cement as he walks. A hovership zooms by a dozen feet above the rooftops around him, angling upward toward one of the three floating islands in the sky. Sabin looks upward at the floating island, or "skyland" as Renval had dubbed it. With five city blocks on each rocky surface, the skylands were an amazing invention, one of Renval's finest creations. The old Runic had certainly salvaged his family's name after his father had gone mad, babbling about alien planets. In fact, Renval was the only other inventor alive who had been awarded the same ring Sabin wore, the onyx band with its diamond-shaped emerald in the center. Renval's dream was to build an entire city in the sky – a bold goal, and one the brilliant man would no doubt achieve if he lived long enough.

Sabin lowers his gaze, watching the smaller hovercars zipping a mere foot above the wide city roads. He rarely used hovercars, much preferring to walk. He came by his best inventions when he walked, and despite an old knee injury that had necessitated his cane, he took these walks daily.

Now, however, instead of coming up with yet another idea for an invention, he finds himself thinking of Vera. He'd seen her often these last few weeks, and each visit had felt like the first. He was entirely smitten with her, and had nearly asked her out a week ago. The only thing that had stopped him was a conversation he'd had with his sister, asking her if it would be poor form to date a much younger student. His sister had stated quite definitively that such a scandal would ruin his reputation.

Sabin sighs, then jerks to a halt suddenly, nearly falling over. His left foot is numb and tingling, as if asleep. He stomps the foot on the ground to wake it, but the sensation persists. He looks around, realizing that he's blocking pedestrians from using the sidewalk, and moves to the side to sit on a bench to let them pass. The tingling in his foot intensifies, crawling up his calf. He massages his leg briskly, and the sensation subsides somewhat. He leans back on the bench, watching the crowd go by, his thoughts returning to Vera. If he'd only ignored his sister, he muses, he'd have a beautiful woman at his side.

And what a woman Vera was!

He pictures her as he saw her last, dressed in a simple summer dress, her gray eyes twinkling as she laughed at a joke he'd made. She laughed all the time, enjoying the simple pleasures of life with a passion he'd never known possible. It was infectious, that passion. It made him feel young again.

Sabin sighs again, watching as life speeds by around him. Everywhere he looks, couples walk hand-in-hand. Everyone has someone. Everyone except for him.

"Professor?"

Sabin jerks his head to the left, spotting a young woman walking down the street toward him. With her long auburn hair falling in thick curls around her, and those lovely gray eyes, his heart skips a beat.

"Vera!" he exclaims, standing up from the bench with a little difficulty. They hug, and she pulls away, smiling at him.

"Enjoying your walk?" she asks. Sabin nods.

"I was just taking a break," he replies. "My damn knee is acting up again."

"You're falling apart, professor," she quips, flashing him that miraculous smile.

102

"The rest of me works just fine," he says with a grin. Vera lets the comment pass without responding in kind, brushing away a lock of hair that had fallen in front of her eyes.

"Well, I have to run," she states, giving him an apologetic look. Sabin frowns. Something is...off...about her.

"What's wrong?" he asks.

"Nothing," she responds with a pained smile. "It's just...I'm meeting someone," she adds. Sabin feels an icy bolt of fear stab his innards.

"Business or pleasure?" he inquires, his voice deceptively casual. Again that pained smile.

"I'm seeing someone," she confesses, lowering her gaze. Sabin says nothing for a long moment, struggling to maintain his composure.

"Who's the lucky gentlemen?" he asks casually. She looks up at him.

"He's in the military," she admits. "He returned from deployment two weeks ago." Her voice starts to pick up pace. "He's a war hero," she adds.

"A soldier?" Sabin replies, unable to keep the disapproval from his voice. She's an academic, after all...a simple thug would hardly be able to provide the intellectual stimulation she craved.

"No, he's a Runic," she corrects. Sabin's eyebrows rise. "He's absolutely brilliant," she gushes, making Sabin go cold. She'd talked the same way about him only two weeks ago. "He can do things with magic that I've never even *imagined* before," she adds.

"And who is this fine young man?" Sabin asks, afraid that he already knows the answer. Vera smiles radiantly, unable to help herself.

"His name is Ampir."

* * *

Kyle groaned, rolling onto his back on his bed and staring up at the ceiling above. He heard the soft patter of rain drumming on his bedroom window, and the distant rumble of thunder. He rubbed his

103

eyes, glancing at the clock on his wall. It was nine o'clock in the morning. Fear shot through him, and he sat bolt upright, his heart pounding in his chest. He was late for class!

He leaped from his bed, scrambling out of his pajamas and into his white Runic uniform. He pulled on some socks, then his customary black gravity boots, then yanked his bedroom door open, bursting out into the main room of the suite. He froze then, seeing Kalibar and Erasmus sitting around a table, eating breakfast.

"Ah, good morning Kyle," Kalibar greeted, gesturing for him to join them at the table. "Come, have breakfast with us."

"Uh..." Kyle stammered. Erasmus turned to look at Kyle, his blue eyes twinkling.

"Ready for class so early?" he quipped. Then he chuckled. "No class today my little genius," he informed. "It's the weekend, remember?"

Kyle breathed a sigh of relief, walking up to the chair beside Kalibar and sitting down. He'd completely forgotten that it was the weekend; on Doma, weekends lasted three days, with four days left for the work week. Leisure was something taken quite seriously in the Empire.

"I trust you slept well?" Kalibar inquired. Kyle nodded.

"Jenkins got me a dreamweaver pillow," he replied. When had he gone to bed last night, six o'clock? He'd slept for fifteen hours! No wonder why he felt sleep-drunk.

"He certainly did," Kalibar replied with a chuckle. "I think we'll need a pillow with less dreamweaver silk," he added. Jenkins appeared suddenly, carrying a tray of steaming vegetables and what appeared to be chicken. The ever-dutiful butler placed the tray before Kyle, and he immediately felt his stomach growling. He dug in with zest, devouring the meal in minutes. When he was done, he gave a loud burp – as was the polite thing to do in the Empire after a good meal. A flash of lightning lit up the windows at the far end of the suite, followed by a rolling thunderclap.

"How can it be raining here?" Kyle asked, turning to look out of the window. "Isn't the Gate shield up?" The massive dome-shaped gravity shield that covered the campus should've kept the rain out, after all.

"It lets rain in," Erasmus replied. "And air. No one knows exactly how it works," he added. "We simply copied the Ancients' original design."

"Speaking of designs," Kalibar cut in, "Erasmus was telling me about your new idea," he added, leaning back in his chair and crossing his arms over his chest. "He's already used the K-Array to test Ariana. We've found a pattern it weaves constantly, and Erasmus is developing your screening tool."

"Cool," Kyle replied. Erasmus slapped his meaty palm on the tabletop.

"See, I told you he'd make a hell of a Runic," the Grand Runic declared. "And you didn't believe me!"

"You were right," Kalibar agreed. "You've become quite the inventor, Kyle," he added, putting an arm around Kyle's shoulders. "I'm proud of you, son."

"Thanks," Kyle replied, feeling a flush of pride. He'd never been particularly good at anything on Earth, being an average student and not great at sports. But here on Doma he'd found his niche.

"When's your speech in the Southwest Quarter?" Kalibar asked Erasmus.

"In an hour," the Grand Runic answered. "If the rain lets up. I'm making an appearance for the grand opening celebration," he explained to Kyle. "We're done rebuilding a major residential tower."

"Wow, that was quick," Kyle commented.

"That's the power of my Runics," Erasmus stated proudly. "They've been itching for a chance to show this city what they can do."

"They've more than succeeded," Kalibar said. "I suspect that with Kyle's inventions and the rebuilding of the city, we'll have more children applying to be Runic students than ever before."

"About time," Erasmus agreed. He sighed contentedly then, leaning back and patting his impressive belly. "You know, I could get used to this," he added. Kalibar raised an eyebrow.

"More of what?" he asked. Erasmus smirked.

"Not having your damn bodyguard around," he answered. "It's so peaceful without that meat-head constantly baiting me."

"Wait, did Darius come back yesterday?" Kyle asked, feeling a pang of fear. Kalibar shook his head.

"No, he's still vacationing," he replied.

"He's not back?" Kyle pressed, trying to keep the rising panic from his voice, and succeeding...barely.

"If he was, I'd know about it," Kalibar answered. "What's wrong?"

"Nothing," Kyle lied. There was no way he could tell them what was wrong...only Ariana knew. "Where's Ariana?"

"She's taking a walk about the campus."

"I need to talk to her," Kyle stated, rising out of his chair suddenly. Erasmus grinned.

"Ah, young love," he mused. He turned to Kalibar then. "It's about time you got yourself a girlfriend," he added with a lecherous wink. "Someone scandalously young and beautiful. Make all the guys jealous...you could have your pick of the Empire!"

"I don't have time for that," Kalibar replied dismissively. Erasmus snorted.

"*Everyone* has time for that," he retorted. "You'd better find someone before it's too late," he added. "You're not getting any younger, you know."

"Maybe you're right," Kalibar mused, tapping his goatee with one finger. Erasmus's jaw dropped.

"What?"

"Maybe you're right," Kalibar repeated. Then he sighed. "I've been avoiding it ever since Lena died." He shook his head then, staring off into the distance. "I don't even know how to meet women anymore. When I think of how much time I've wasted..."

"Bull," Erasmus interjected. "You're a damn national treasure, a father, and the finest Battle-Weaver in the Empire. You were just...padding your resume the last thirty years to attract the finest ladies."

Kalibar laughed out loud at that, and Erasmus chuckled. Kyle could only manage a weak smile, considering the circumstances. He was itching to find Ariana. Erasmus must have noticed his discomfort.

"Now see what we've done," he stated with a chuckle. "I think we burned his ears." He waved Kyle away. "Get out of here before we do any permanent psychological damage!"

Kyle nodded, bidding them both goodbye and nearly sprinting out of the suite. He made his way down to the lobby, to the double-doors of the lobby. He stopped short before the open doors, seeing dense sheets of rain pouring down from the heavens. The entire campus was covered in a muted gray, the occasional flash of lightning searing the heavens above. A cold wind bit his flesh, and he shivered, backing away from the double-doors. He certainly wasn't dressed for being out in the rain...he'd have to go all the way back up to his room if he wanted to change.

Then a flash of inspiration struck him, and Kyle wove magic, a gravity shield appearing around him. When Kyle stepped out into the deluge, he found himself completely dry. The rain ran down his shield in rippling torrents, however, making it difficult for him to see – like a car driving through the rain with the windshield wipers off. Still, he moved onward through the rain, his gravity boots splashing on the wet stone below. It wasn't long before the Tower was merely a tall shadow behind him, a darker shade of gray amongst more of the same. He paused, realizing that there was no way he was going to find Ariana this way...if he went any farther, he might not be able to find his way back. Ariana wouldn't have that problem, not with her amazingly keen senses.

Kyle nearly smacked himself in the forehead. Why not just call out to her? She'd be able to hear him from miles away, after all. He yelled out her name once, then again, shivering in the cold air despite the thick cloth of his uniform. He wove again, creating a small fire inside of his shields, and warmed his hands by it. He stayed where he was, calling her name out a third time, and then saw a shadow approaching him.

"Ariana?" he yelled, extinguishing the flame.

"Kyle!" a voice called out. The shadow grew more distinct as it drew near, and Kyle saw that it was indeed Ariana walking up to him.

107

She was completely drenched, her hair matted to her head, her black Weaver uniform soaked all the way through. She hardly seemed to notice the dreadful cold, nor the biting wind.

"What are you doing out here?" Kyle shouted over the din of the rain falling all around them.

"Just taking a walk," she shouted back. Kyle stared at her incredulously.

"It's freezing out here!" he protested. She just shrugged. "Come on," he insisted, "...let's go back inside."

"Drop your shield," she countered. He blinked.

"What?"

"Drop it," she repeated. He paused, then did as she asked, flinching at the inevitable downpour that would follow. But he remained utterly dry. He looked around, seeing a much larger gravity shield surrounding both of them, rain sliding down its edges in a 360-degree waterfall.

"How long have you been out here?"

"Since you went to sleep," Ariana admitted. "I needed to get away from the Tower," she explained. "I like the rain...the noise makes it hard to think."

Kyle shivered, creating another small flame in front of him. He placed his palms before it, feeling the heat soak into his cold flesh.

"You know about, uh..." he began, then stopped. He'd almost said *Darius* instead of Ampir.

"He didn't come back, did he," Ariana stated. Kyle shook his head. She turned away, putting a hand to her mouth.

"Sorry," he mumbled. She shook her head, turning back to face him. The raindrops dripping down her cheeks gave the illusion that she was crying...something she would never be able to do.

"What do we do now?" she asked. Kyle shrugged helplessly, not knowing what to say. Ariana sighed, a flash of lightning reflecting off of her porcelain skin. "Do we have a chance without him?"

He paused, then shook his head.

"We don't really know that he's dead," Ariana argued, running a hand through her wet hair.

"He said if he wasn't back, it would mean he was dead," Kyle countered. Then the reality of what he'd said struck him: Ampir was dead.

Darius was dead.

Kyle turned away from Ariana suddenly, swallowing down a sudden wave of nausea that had come over him. Darius was *dead*...his grandfather. His friend.

And now everyone he loved was going to die.

He felt lightheaded suddenly, and staggered away from Ariana, toward the perimeter of her gravity shield. He placed his palms on its shimmering surface, his head swimming.

"Kyle?"

He didn't answer, his heart starting to race. He felt something cold and wet touch his shoulder, and flinched away from it, spinning about to see Ariana staring at him.

"Kyle," she pressed, grabbing him by the upper arms firmly.

"He's dead, Ariana," he stated.

"Kyle, maybe he..."

"He's *dead*," Kyle interrupted. "We're *all* dead!"

With that, he tried to break away from Ariana's grasp, but she was too strong. Suddenly he felt as if he were suffocating, and tried again to break free from Ariana's grasp.

"I can't breathe," he gasped.

"Kyle!" she shouted, her fingers digging into his flesh. He felt something snap in his right arm, a horrible pain lancing through it. He cried out in agony, dropping instantly to his knees. Ariana gasped, kneeling before him and reaching out to him with both hands.

"Ow, what the hell?" he gasped, pushing her hands away with his left arm. He glanced down at his right arm, realizing that it was hanging at an impossible angle. He gaped at it in shock. "You broke my arm!"

"Oh my god!" Ariana exclaimed. "Did I really?" She reached down to his mangled arm, and Kyle fended her off with his good arm. She gasped then. "Oh my god, I broke your arm!"

"I know!" Kyle yelled, gritting his teeth against the pain. Ariana stepped backward, looking mortified. "You know, you're going to kill me one of these days," he grumbled. Another spasm of pain shot down his arm, and he cried out.

"I'm so sorry," Ariana blurted, reaching for Kyle, then stopping herself, wringing her hands helplessly. "I am so, so sorry Kyle!"

"It's okay," Kyle hissed through clenched teeth. "Just...don't touch me for a minute," he added as she started to reach for him again.

"Okay, okay," she replied. "What should I do?"

"I need to get back to the Tower," Kyle replied, attempting to get to his feet. The movement caused his right arm to shift, sending another wave of agony through him. He nearly blacked out, setting himself down slowly until he was sitting on the cobblestones below. He took a few deep, gulping breaths, squeezing his eyes shut.

"Right," Ariana agreed. "Can you get up slowly?"

"Let me sit here for a minute," he said, blowing out of pursed lips. The pain in his arm began to ease somewhat, and he nodded. "Okay, I'm gonna try again. Don't help!" he exclaimed as she reached for him. "I got it," he insisted. He collected himself, then rose slowly to his feet, grimacing at a sharp twinge of pain as he did so. He made it all the way up this time.

"Let's go," Ariana prompted. She walked forward, and Kyle followed, clutching his bad arm to his side to immobilize it. That worked; the pain was at least bearable now.

"Where are my bodyguards?" Kyle asked. Even though they were invisible, they should've followed him outside. He was never to venture outside without at least two elite guards with him at all times.

"They're up ahead," Ariana replied, pointing forward. Kyle peered through the storm beyond her gravity shield, but saw nothing. "They stayed back a ways," she added.

"You can see them?"

"I see the rain dripping off of them," she explained. "Come on, I'll bring you to them."

"Wait," Kyle interjected, stopping suddenly. Ariana turned to face him, her eyes filled with concern. Kyle paused, then let go of his grip on his injured arm. He hesitated, then flexed it gingerly, feeling a sharp jolt of pain as he did so. He gripped his arm again, grimacing against the pain, then clenched his teeth, letting go and flexing it again. The pain was intense, but not nearly as bad as it had been moments before.

"Kyle, be careful," Ariana cautioned. Kyle shook his head, rubbing his injured shoulder gingerly.

"It's not so bad now," he stated. Though his arm still throbbed terribly, he could move it now. He rotated his shoulder slowly throughout its range of motion. "Maybe it isn't broken after all," he admitted.

"I heard a snap," Ariana countered.

"Maybe you just dislocated it for a minute," Kyle reasoned. He reached over with his left hand, gently pressing on his right arm where Ariana had squeezed it. There was only a dull, gnawing ache now.

"Better?" Ariana asked, clearly relieved.

"A little," he agreed. "That really hurt, you know," he grumbled. It *still* hurt. Ariana lowered her gaze.

"I won't do it again," she promised. Kyle tried to glare at her, with little success.

"I don't heal like you do, you know," he warned.

"I know," she mumbled. "I'm really sorry," she added morosely.

"It's okay," he reassured. "I forgive you."

"Can I touch you now?" she asked. Kyle hesitated, then nodded. "Sure."

Ariana gave him a weak smile, then reached out to his shoulder – his left shoulder, thank goodness – putting a hand atop it. Kyle forced himself not to flinch, feeling her coldness even through his thick Runic shirt. She was exceedingly gentle this time.

"Hey, at least I stopped you from panicking," she ventured, giving his left shoulder the slightest of squeezes. Kyle glowered at her. She leaned in close, resting her head on his shoulder and wrapping her arms around him, giving him the gentlest of sideways hugs. "What are we going to do?" she asked.

"About what?" he asked.

"Xanos."

"I don't know," he admitted, feeling suddenly depressed. If Darius was truly dead, then what *could* they do? The answer, of course, was nothing.

"We have to do *something*," she insisted, pulling away from him. Kyle shrugged, feeling utterly helpless. He knew what *he* could do; with the spacetime bridge generator in his breastbone, he could teleport back to the safety of Earth...never to see Ariana, or anyone else on Doma, ever again.

And while he was safely away, they would all be killed.

"What can we do?" Kyle muttered. "We're no match for Xanos."

"What about the K-Array?" Ariana proposed. "We're learning new patterns every day." Kyle shook his head.

"It doesn't matter," he replied bitterly. Ariana frowned.

"What do you mean?"

"Xanos is Sabin," Kyle answered. Ariana blinked, then drew back from him.

"The old man?" she asked, her tone suddenly flat.

"*The* Sabin," Kyle countered. "The one who destroyed the Ancients."

Ariana's stared at Kyle for a moment, as if trying to process what he'd said. Then her mouth fell open, her eyes widening. She began to say something, then stopped, just staring at him. Finally, she shook her head.

"He's as old as Ampir," she proclaimed.

"Yeah."

"How can we win against him?" she asked. "We don't stand a chance!"

Kyle shrugged – then regretted it. His right arm throbbed with the motion, making him wince. They both knew that the only chance they'd had to beat Sabin had been Ampir...and that he had failed. She was right...there *was* no hope. If Darius had only left Kyle with a way to teleport his friends to Earth or Antara, he could've saved them...but Darius had left them with nothing.

Except...

"The bomb," Kyle mumbled. Ariana frowned at him.

"What?"

112

"Ampir gave me a bomb," he explained. "He told me to use it if he failed to kill Sabin."

"A bomb?"

"Yeah," Kyle replied. "It's supposed to blow up anything within 10 miles, in case Xanos...uh, Sabin...attacks again."

"You have it?"

"I do," Kyle confirmed. "It's in my room, inside the map." Ariana blinked, then her eyes widened.

"The map!" she exclaimed.

"What about it?"

"Come on," she answered, grabbing his hand and leading him back through the pouring rain, toward the Tower in the distance. "I have an idea."

* * *

Kyle rubbed his throbbing arm absently as he watched Ariana pull his large, ornate bed away from the wall. Then she walked behind the headboard to retrieve the rolled-up map from where he'd stowed it. She unrolled the map on the bed, glancing at the small black metal cylinder that had been placed within.

"Is that it?" she asked.

"That's it."

"It's so...small," she observed. Kyle shrugged.

"He said it'd blow up anything within 10 miles."

"How do we activate it?"

"I think you just tap one end," he answered. "But he said I was the only one who could arm it," he added. Ariana nodded, staring at the bomb for a long moment. Then she set it aside, turning back to the map.

"So Xanos is here," she stated, pointing to the red circle drawn on the map. Kyle nodded.

"Yep."

"So far away," she murmured. Kyle frowned at her.

"What are you thinking?"

113

"If Xanos attacks," she replied, "...and we use the bomb to protect ourselves, then it'll only save us once."

"That's what I told Ampir," Kyle agreed.

"But what if we use the bomb here?" she proposed, putting one pale finger on the map...right on the red circle. Kyle stared for a moment, then glanced up at her.

"On Xanos?" he asked.

"Right."

He stared back down at the map, mulling it over. If they could make it to Xanos's lair, then it might be possible to arm the bomb and run...

He felt his pulse quickening.

"That would do it," he stated. He broke out into a smile, suddenly gripped with a burst of hope. "Ariana, that's brilliant!"

"Right?" Ariana agreed.

"It *would* work," he proclaimed, slamming a fist into his palm. Then he froze. "Wait..."

"What?"

"That means *I* would have to go," he realized. "I'm the only one who can arm the bomb."

"Right."

"Right," Kyle mumbled, visibly deflating. Traveling to the heart of Xanos's lair to set a bomb there would hardly be a walk in the park. Chances were that Xanos had the area well-defended, after all...and what chance would he have against such an enemy?

"Well can't you just activate the bomb, then have Kalibar send a Weaver to fly it over there and drop it?" she asked. Kyle shook his head.

"It has a three-minute fuse," he countered. "We'd need to activate it right at his base."

"So you *have* to be there," she stated quietly, staring down at the map. Kyle nodded. She tapped her chin with one finger – much as Kalibar did when thinking – then nodded to herself.

"What?"

"So we'll go," she decided. Kyle blinked.

"Wait, what?"

114

"We'll go," she repeated. "If you're the only one who can do it, then you'll have to do it."

"But how?" he pressed. "Xanos will slaughter us before we ever get close."

"Maybe," she conceded. "But we have to try." Kyle shook his head.

"No," he stated firmly. "It won't work."

"It *has* to work," Ariana countered.

"It's too dangerous," Kyle protested.

"If we don't kill Xanos," she countered, "...we're all going to die." She crossed her arms over her chest. "This is the only way we'll have a chance."

Kyle opened his mouth to argue, then closed it. He could hardly dispute her point, after all. If they did nothing, death was certain. But to travel to another continent, to the heart of Xanos's lair...it was suicide.

Unless...

He put a hand to his chest then, over the device Darius had implanted in his breastbone. He *did* have a way out, if his life was threatened. He could teleport back to Earth at any time if he had to...and activate the bomb before he did so. He only had to get within 10 miles of Xanos's lair to destroy the self-proclaimed god, after all. But that meant he would never get to see Ariana or Kalibar...or any of his other friends on Doma...ever again.

But at least he could save them.

"I'll tell Kalibar," he stated suddenly.

"Wait, what?"

"I'll do it," he clarified, "...and Kalibar can get us there," he added, pointing to Xanos's lair on the map. Ariana stared at that finger for a moment, then shook her head.

"We can't tell him," she protested.

"Why not?"

"He'll never let us go," she explained. "He would never risk his children like that."

"But..."

"We can't tell Kalibar," she insisted firmly. "Even if he lets us go, he'll want to send a whole army of Battle-Weavers to protect us." She shook her head again, her long brown hair falling in front of her eyes. "Xanos will know we're coming, and he'll kill us all."

"So what," he stated, "...you want me to go alone?"

"No," she replied, putting a cool hand on his arm. "I'll go with you."

"But..."

"I can sense the Chosen," she interjected. "And I'm more dangerous than any Battle-Weaver," she added. "I don't sleep, so I can stand guard at night while you sleep."

"Ariana," he began, but she cut him off again.

"I'm going," she insisted.

"This is crazy," he protested. "It's too dangerous...it'll never work." He turned to the map. "Besides, how will we ever get across an entire ocean by ourselves?"

"There are big trading boats that go there all the time," she replied. "There's one that just got back here a few days ago." Kyle frowned at her.

"Wait, how do you know that?"

"I saw it," she answered. When Kyle stared at her blankly, she shrugged, lowering her gaze to the bedsheets. "I went past the Gate shield," she confessed.

"You did?" Kyle asked. "How?" It was a good question; Kalibar had forbidden either of them from leaving the campus of the Secula Magna, for fear of being kidnapped – or worse – like Kyle had been a short time ago. The Gate shield had been made from Ancient runic technology...not even Kalibar could get past it.

"My shard," Ariana replied, touching a fingertip to her forehead. "I tried walking through the Gate shield a week ago, and my shard protected me."

"Why did you do that?" Kyle demanded. She could have been hurt, after all...or even killed.

"I was getting sick of being trapped here," she admitted. "I felt like an animal in a cage, walking around the campus every night, over and over again." She turned away from Kyle then. "I just wanted to experience something new," she added. "You won't tell anyone, will you?"

"Of course not."

"Thanks," she said, looking much relieved.

"So you saw the boat?"

"Yes," she confirmed. "I can check the boat schedule tonight," she offered. "That way we'll know when the next ship is leaving."

"Wait, we can't go on the boat," he protested.

"Why not?"

"We'll get caught," he replied.

"We can board the boat at night," she countered. "They'll never see us."

"But what about when we're on the boat?" he pressed. "How long does it take to get to the other continent?"

"About a week," she admitted.

"We can't hide for that long," he protested. Then an idea struck him. "Or maybe we can." He smiled at her obvious confusion. "Remember our guards?"

"What about them?"

"They were practicing the invisibility pattern," he replied. "The one that the K-Array discovered. If we learned that pattern, we'd never get caught on the ship."

"You're right!" Ariana exclaimed. "Good idea Kyle," she added. "Okay…I'll check the boat schedule tonight, and you can learn the invisibility pattern. You're better at remembering patterns anyway."

"I'll ask Erasmus to show me the pattern," he offered.

"Good," she replied. She rolled up the map then, stowing the black cylindrical bomb inside, and placed it back in its hiding place behind Kyle's headboard. Kyle watched her, then sighed.

"I still don't like that we're not telling Kalibar," he admitted. "If we leave without telling him, he'll think we've been kidnapped…or killed."

"We can leave him a note," she offered. "Telling him that we're okay, but that we had to leave to do something."

"I guess," Kyle mumbled. But it still didn't feel right. Kalibar had risked his life on countless occasions to save them both, and had suffered Kyle's kidnapping – and Ariana's death – within the last week or so. It hardly seemed fair to do this to him. But what choice did they have? If they *didn't* do this, the Empire – and everyone in it – was surely doomed.

Ariana was right, he knew. The only way to stop Xanos was to kill him...and with Darius dead, Kyle was the only person on the planet who had even the slightest chance of doing that now.

Chapter 9

By the time Erasmus had gotten around to meeting with Kyle in the testing chamber adjacent to the Runic Archives, it had been well past noon. Despite it being a weekend, Kalibar and Erasmus were as busy as ever, attending countless meetings and giving speeches. He'd managed to catch Erasmus between meetings, and had asked the portly Grand Runic if he could see the K-Array. Erasmus had been overjoyed, eager to show Kyle the invention he'd helped to perfect. They'd gone down to the Runic Archives at once, arriving in the testing chamber where the K-Array had been placed, sitting on top of a plain white table.

The K-Array, it turned out, looked a bit like one of those machines at the store that printed receipts...except much larger. It was about the size of a washing machine, with spinning rolls hidden inside that moved a sheet of paper rapidly as a pattern was being sensed. Each time a sensory rune in the K-Array sensed a part of a pattern being woven, it would print that pattern fragment onto the paper. What came out was like a huge receipt, except with rows of symbols written on it. By linking the symbols together, Erasmus was able to recreate the pattern that had been sensed.

After demonstrating the K-Array a few times – while grinning like a boy opening presents on Christmas morning – Erasmus had agreed to teach Kyle the invisibility pattern. He'd handed Kyle a page with the symbol drawn out in standard Runic notation, just as Lee had for her lessons the other day. The pattern had been long and complicated, and Erasmus had made Kyle practice the pattern in the relative safety of the testing chamber a few times to make sure he'd gotten it right. After that, the old Runic had left to another meeting, leaving Kyle alone in the testing chamber...but not before destroying the drawing of the pattern, for security purposes.

Kyle sighed, walking out of the testing chamber and back into the Archives. He made his way into the hallway, walking toward the riser at the end of it. He'd agreed to meet Ariana back in his bedroom, and he rode the riser up to the 41st floor to do just that. He walked down the hallway, staring idly at the painted statues that lined the walls on either side. He'd passed by them almost every day since he'd starting living in Kalibar's suite. The statues were extraordinarily old, and were thought to be of Ancient Council members. His eye paused on one of the statues – of a man – and he slowed, then stopped in the middle of the hallway.

The statue looked awfully familiar.

He stared at its face, carved out of stone, remembering that he'd thought it had looked oddly familiar the first time he'd seen it...the first time he'd been in the Tower, in fact. And now he knew why. The squared jaw, the stern eyes, the nose...even the hair...was identical to the person it represented. Whoever had repainted the statue had gotten the colors wrong – they'd painted the eyes brown and the hair black – but even so, there was no doubt who it was.

Ampir.

Kyle felt a chill run through him, and he stared at the statue, remembering his last moments with Darius. There had been no real goodbyes, no fanfare before he'd left to battle Sabin. He hadn't wished Kyle luck, or even really talked that much.

He'd said nothing, really.

And that, to Kyle's dismay, was what he felt now as he stared at the man's ancient statue...nothing. He wanted to feel sadness, but he didn't. He couldn't. There was only a hollow feeling deep inside, a void in that place in Kyle's heart where his feelings for the bodyguard had been.

Kyle sighed, turning away from the statue and continuing down the hallway to Kalibar's suite. He unlocked the magical door with his mind, and the door opened of its own accord, letting him step inside. He found Ariana sitting on one of the couches in the main room of the suite.

"Hey," he greeted.

"Hi Kyle," Ariana replied, gesturing for Kyle to sit down next to her, which he did. "Did you learn the pattern?" Kyle nodded.

"You want to practice it?" he asked. Ariana nodded.

"Later," she agreed.

"We should do it now," Kyle countered. "I don't want you to get caught when you go out to the shipyard." Ariana considered this, then nodded.

"Good idea," she agreed. She stood then. "Come here first," she stated. Kyle got up, following Ariana to his bedroom. She crouched down before his bed, pulling a heavy-looking sack out from underneath and placing it on top of the bed. She reached inside, pulling out a silver breastplate.

"The Aegis," Kyle exclaimed. It was the Aegis of Athanasia, magical armor created by the Ancients. Over two thousand years old, it was enormously powerful, able to protect the wearer from nearly any manner of injury. Kalibar had given him the Aegis weeks ago, during the awards ceremony after his coronation as Grand Weaver.

"I got this too," Ariana stated, pulling a gray cloak out of the sack. It shimmered in the sunlight pouring in from the nearby window, its edges glowing silver, like the lining of a cloud.

"Your cloak!" Kyle exclaimed. She'd gotten it from Kalibar during the awards ceremony. He'd entirely forgotten about it.

"The Tempest cloak," she confirmed. "Kalibar said it would let me draw lightning from clouds, and I could never get hurt by falling if I wore it," she added. Kyle nodded; nearly every time Ariana got hurt in the last few weeks, it had been due to falling. The cloak would certainly come in handy.

Suddenly, Kyle had an idea.

"Hey, why don't we just fly there?"

"What?"

"Why don't we just fly to Sabin's lair?" he clarified. "You could wear my gravity boots and fly us there." He didn't know why he hadn't thought of that earlier; they could skip the boat entirely. "It wouldn't work," Ariana replied. Kyle frowned. "Why not?" he pressed. "You don't need to sleep," he argued. "You could fly us the whole way without stopping."

"I'd probably get lost," Ariana countered. "Especially if there was a storm. And even flying, it could take days to get there. I don't need to sleep or eat or drink, but you do."

"True," Kyle conceded.

"Come on," she urged. "If you teach me the invisibility pattern now, I won't have to wait until night to check the ship schedule."

"Okay," Kyle agreed. He wove the pattern in his mind's eye, casting it outward. At the same time, he attached a magic stream to keep the pattern going. He saw a faint blue sphere surrounding him.

"Oh..." Ariana murmured.

"Is it working?" he asked. He had no way to be sure; he hadn't thought to practice the pattern on something else (other than himself) while learning it. Ariana cocked her head to the side.

"Sort of," she replied. "It's kinda like I'm looking at you through a really strong magnifying glass..."

"Wait, let me try something," he urged. With every pattern he'd learned so far, the more magic he put in the pattern itself, the larger the area of effect...in this case, the larger the sphere surrounding him. Changing the amount of magic *streamed* to the pattern changed how intense the effect was. He tried increasing the magic stream.

"Whoa," Ariana blurted, blinking her eyes rapidly. "*Way* too strong."

"Oh," Kyle replied. He dialed back on the magic stream. "How about that?"

"Better," Ariana replied. "I can't see you anymore, but I can see the edges of the sphere." Kyle nodded, then realized she wouldn't be able to see the gesture. He decreased his magic stream a bit further.

"Perfect!" Ariana exclaimed. "Hold it there," she added. Kyle did so, trying to get a feel for how much magic he was streaming. Then he dropped the pattern.

"I'm gonna have to practice more," he admitted.

"Me too," she agreed. "But there's a problem."

"What?"

"Where the sphere touches the floor, it makes it look kinda weird."

"Hold on," he said. He wove the pattern again, sending it out to Ariana. She vanished instantly, but there was a strange bending of light near the borders of the sphere. He decreased his magic stream, and the effect vanished...but not at the floor. Where the sphere met the floor, it made the marble look warped...twisted and stretched. Ariana was right...while *she* was invisible, her invisibility was not.

"I see it," he admitted glumly.

"This isn't going to work," Ariana muttered glumly. Then Kyle snapped his fingers.

"We can fly!" he exclaimed. When Ariana gave him a confused look, he pointed to the gravity boots he always wore. "I can float us above the floor," he explained. "That way, the sphere won't touch it." He demonstrated, activating his boots to levitate a foot off of the floor. Then he wove the invisibility pattern.

"It's working!" Ariana exclaimed. "I can't see you at all now." Kyle dropped the pattern and lowered himself to the floor, smiling proudly.

"This might just work after all," he stated.

"Teach me the pattern," Ariana requested. "We can take turns practicing it until we both get it right."

* * *

The sunlight had long since stopped streaming through Kyle's bedroom window as noon came and went, and he stretched his legs out from where he sat on his bed. Ariana had taken quite a bit longer to learn the invisibility pattern than he had, having just mastered it after hours of practice. She knew that he'd learned it in a fraction of the time it had taken her, and before her death this would have frustrated her a great deal. But something had changed after her rebirth; she'd developed a seemingly unlimited amount of patience. Long after Kyle would've quit, she just practiced again and again until she got it right. Methodically, without stopping or resting. It was unnerving to watch...almost inhuman.

But in the end, she got it right. And in the process, they both learned a few other limitations of the pattern. Anything that passed into the invisibility sphere's influence vanished. If Kyle tried to pick something up, it vanished. When walking through narrow corridors, he had to be careful not to get too close to the walls, or they would end up appearing warped, like the floor had. Making the invisibility sphere as small as possible helped to limit these effects, but they would still need to be very careful.

Kyle yawned, stretching his arms up into the air, then dropping them to his sides. His stomach growled loudly, and Ariana looked at him from where she sat on the edge of his bed.

"You should go eat," she offered, sliding off the bed, and ushering him back into the main part of Kalibar's suite.

"Good idea," he replied. "What are you going to do?"

"Check the boat schedule," she replied. Kyle's brow furrowed.

"Now?"

"I'll be invisible," she replied.

"No you won't," he countered. "You don't have gravity boots on...the ground will look weird if you use the pattern."

"I mean I've got a disguise," she replied with a smile. "I'll just be another girl on the street."

"What disguise?"

"You'll see," she stated rather mysteriously. She said nothing more then, touching the communication orb nearest her, then walking to the front door to leave the suite. "I'll be back in a few hours."

"Good luck."

It was only moments after Ariana had left that Jenkins arrived. Kyle's stomach growled again, and he asked for his favorite dish: roasted duck. Jenkins bowed, leaving immediately to satisfy his young master's request, and Kyle's mouth watered with the thought of the delicious meal to come. He sat down on a nearby couch, stuffing his hands into his pockets. Something hard jabbed his fingertips, and he frowned, pulling out a small crystal cube. It was a fresh crystal, one that hadn't been inscribed yet.

He sighed, remembering the lesson with Lee earlier. He'd managed to create a gravity shield around the cube itself, which wasn't very useful. But if it created a gravity shield big enough for a *person...*

He placed the crystal on the table in front of him, bending over it and closing his eyes. He wove the inscribing pattern, then inscribed the gravity shield rune. This time he made the "wire" thicker, so magic could flow more easily through it, and make a larger sphere. When he'd finished, he slid the cube as far away from him as he could, then walked behind the couch. He streamed magic to it...and a large gravity shield appeared around the cube. The cube shot up into the air, the shield bouncing off of the ceiling and flying back down to the table. It bounced again, ricocheting up and down until it finally settled, floating a few feet above the table.

The front door opened suddenly, and Kyle quickly severed his magic stream, the cube falling with a clatter onto the tabletop. He was expecting Jenkins, but it wasn't the butler who walked through the door...it was Kalibar. The Grand Weaver looked imposing as ever in his jet-black uniform, his black gravity boots clicking sharply on the marble floor. When he saw Kyle, his customary strict expression softened into a warm smile.

"Ah, Kyle!" he exclaimed. "Have you eaten lunch?"

"Jenkins is getting me duck."

"I'll double that order," Kalibar decided. "I haven't had lunch yet either."

It wasn't long before Jenkins appeared with Kyle's meal, and he quickly ran off to fetch another for his Grand Weaver. Within a few minutes, Kyle and Kalibar were sitting at one of the tables, digging in to their respective meals. When they'd polished off their plates, Kalibar sat back in his chair, regarding Kyle silently for a long moment.

"What?" Kyle asked.

"Kyle, is something bothering you?" Kalibar inquired. Kyle blinked.

"What do you mean?"

"You're quieter than usual," Kalibar observed. "And you haven't smiled much today."

"I'm just tired," Kyle lied. Kalibar said nothing, continuing to stare at Kyle until the silence became extraordinarily uncomfortable. Then he leaned forward.

"You can tell me," he insisted gently. Kyle swallowed in a dry throat, lowering his gaze to the tabletop and saying nothing. Kalibar reached across the table, putting a hand on Kyle's. "You can tell me anything, son."

Kyle shook his head silently, resisting the urge to pull his hand away. He felt absolutely horrible lying to his adoptive father, especially after everything the man had done for him. He'd risked his life to save Kyle, after all. He'd defied the Dead Man, Xanos, and even the nearly unstoppable Void spheres. An image of Kalibar laying on a table, his arms and legs held by red-clad Death Weavers came to Kyle's mind. Of the Dead Man plunging his pale fingers into Kalibar's eye. Of Kalibar falling to the ground after his first eye had been plucked out, then staggering to his feet, pushing the Death Weavers surrounding him away.

He pictured Kalibar willingly climbing back onto that table. Laying down on his back so that the Dead Man could take the other eye.

Kyle felt a sudden, overwhelming shame come over him. He'd kept so many secrets from Kalibar, even though Kalibar had kept none from him. How terrible was he, that he was ready to betray Kalibar's trust by leaving him, by making him fear for Kyle's life yet again? What kind of son was he that he could keep so many secrets from the only person who had been there for him, time and time again, without reservation?

He felt Kalibar squeeze his hand gently.

"Tell me what's wrong, so I can help you."

Kyle looked up then, pulling his hand away and shaking his head from side to side.

"You can't help me," he replied miserably.

"I can try."

"It's no use," Kyle countered. "It's too late."

"Secrets are a lonely burden," Kalibar advised. "They only grow heavier and lonelier the longer you keep them, Kyle."

Kyle swallowed again, refusing to meet Kalibar's gaze. He felt the sudden, mad urge to tell him everything. *Everything.* About Ampir, about Darius...about his and Ariana's plan...everything. With Darius dead, and Sabin free to destroy the Empire, there wasn't any reason to keep Darius's secret any longer. But if he told Kalibar, he'd still be betraying Ariana.

"I would give my life for you, Kyle," Kalibar stated firmly.

Something inside Kyle broke.

"Ampir is dead," he blurted out, his voice cracking. He drew in a shuddering breath, then let it out slowly through clenched teeth.

"Excuse me?"

"He's dead," Kyle repeated, looking up at Kalibar's face at last. The old man looked shocked, his mouth agape.

"My god," Kalibar blurted out. "Are you sure?"

"I'm sure," he replied. "He went to kill Sabin," he added. "He found out where Sabin lives, and he went to kill him."

"What?" Kalibar pressed. "Ampir found *who?*"

"Sabin," Kyle answered. "He failed," he continued. "He couldn't beat him." Kalibar stared at Kyle in confusion.

"Sabin?"

"The Ancient," Kyle clarified. "He's the one behind everything," he added. "He's Xanos."

Kalibar stared at Kyle uncomprehendingly, his mouth opening, then closing.

Then his eyes widened.

He stood up suddenly, putting a hand over his mouth, his eyes wide but unseeing, staring far off into the distance. Then he lowered himself to the chair absently, sitting down with a thump.

"I'm sorry," Kyle mumbled. "He told me not to tell you."

Kalibar stirred suddenly, and he looked at Kyle as if he'd forgotten he was still there. He stood up, walking up to Kyle and putting a hand on Kyle's shoulder.

"Thank you," he stated. He paused then. "How long have you known?" he asked. Kyle shrugged.

"Ampir told me just before I came back here," he answered.

"I see."

"He made me promise not to tell," Kyle insisted. Kalibar smiled with his mouth but not his eyes.

"I would not have defied him either," the Grand Weaver admitted. "You did what you had to."

"Are you mad?"

"No," Kalibar stated firmly, shaking his head. "Not mad. Just...a little shell-shocked," he admitted. "It all makes sense now," he added.

"What do you mean?"

"Everything," Kalibar answered with a shrug. "Just...everything." He stared off into the distance again, as if in a trance, then shook himself out of it. "I should have figured it out."

"Why?"

"The Void crystals," he replied. "Sabin pioneered research into Void crystals back in Ancient times." He sighed then. "And he created the original Behemoths, after all."

"Yeah."

"So both he *and* Ampir managed to live this long," Kalibar murmured. "Two thousand years..." He shook his head. "And now Ampir is dead."

Kyle said nothing, letting his silence speak for itself.

"I suppose that's that," Kalibar muttered. He rubbed his eyes wearily, then ran his fingers through his hair, resting his elbows on the table. He suddenly looked much older than his sixty-odd years. He said nothing for a long time, staring at the table absently, a far-away look in his eyes. Then he sighed again, leaning back in his chair. He stared at Kyle then.

"What?" Kyle asked.

"I'm still confused," Kalibar admitted. "I don't understand why Ampir brought you here...why he gave you his ring, why he sent you his memories, why he protected you." Kyle shrugged, the urge to hide Ampir's true identity almost reflexive at this point. But he resisted the urge to lie; Kalibar deserved to know the truth.

"I'm his grandson."

Kalibar's jaw dropped.

Kyle lowered his gaze, feeling Kalibar's eyes on him.

"My dad on Earth," Kyle explained. "He's Ampir's son, like in the dreams. Ampir sent him to Earth."

"Kyle, that doesn't make any sense," Kalibar protested. "It's been two thousand years since..." He trailed off then, his mouth working silently. Then he turned to Kyle. "Time!" he exclaimed, slapping his forehead with one palm. "Of course, I'm such a fool!"

"What?"

"You were gone for a week, but that was only a few hours for you," Kalibar said to himself. "If a seventh of a day equals seven days here, that's forty-nine days here for every week...two thousand years divided by forty-nine...that's..." He frowned for a moment. "Forty-odd years." He turned to Kyle then. "How old is your father?"

"Forty-three."

"Of course!" Kalibar exclaimed, slamming one fist into his palm. "It all makes sense now...how didn't I see this earlier?" Kyle just stared at him, amazed that Kalibar's keen intellect had almost instantly deduced the answer...something Kyle would never have been able to do. Kalibar shook his head. "The dreams, your ring...your ability to see magic."

"Wait, how...?"

"Master Lee told Erasmus," Kalibar answered. "And Erasmus told me."

"I didn't mean to keep it a secret," Kyle stated apologetically. "I didn't even realize it until..." But Kalibar waved that away.

"I know," he replied. "You told me yourself that gravity shields were blue the first time you saw them, and like a fool I insisted they weren't. I should have been more observant. The answers were in front of me all along."

"You're not mad at me?"

"No, I'm not mad at you, Kyle." Kalibar replied. He smiled then. "Thank you for telling me the truth. I know it must have been hard for you, to keep such awful secrets."

Kyle nodded silently.

"Do you feel better now?"

"Yeah," Kyle answered. And it was true; he felt lighter somehow, as if a great weight had been lifted from his shoulders. But that relief was tempered by the knowledge that Sabin was out there, waiting to attack...and that there was no one left to protect them. Indeed, Kalibar's expression grew serious, and he drew in a deep breath, then let it out.

"Ampir is dead," he stated flatly. "How?"

"He found Sabin's lair," Kyle replied. "He said he was going to kill Sabin...that if he wasn't back in 24 hours, then he'd failed." He cleared his throat. "Died."

"Okay," Kalibar said. "We must assume Ampir is dead." He tapped his goatee with one finger. "We're on our own now."

"Yeah."

"If Sabin beat Ampir," Kalibar continued, "...then we have no chance of beating him with force. That means diplomacy is all we have." He shook his head. "Marcus – my mentor – told me that once. 'Violence is the recourse of a failed diplomat.'" He sighed. "Marcus never agreed with my emphasis on war," he admitted. "He said I used an army of thousands when one man would have sufficed."

"You're going to try to reason with Sabin?" Kyle asked incredulously. Kalibar shrugged.

"What other choice do I have?" he countered. "Erasmus and the Council believe that we can beat Sabin – Xanos – with patterns we derive from the K-Array. But the Ancients knew these patterns – and so many more – two thousand years ago. Sabin has had millennia to build his knowledge and power past anything we could ever match."

"Yeah," Kyle muttered. He sighed, his shoulders slumping. "I asked Ampir to bring you all to Earth," he admitted. "If he wasn't able to kill Sabin."

"You did?"

"I wanted to save you," Kyle confirmed.

"Thank you," Kalibar replied with a smile. "What did Ampir say?"

"He said if he failed, then..." He stopped, remembering exactly what he'd said.

They'll die.

"Yes?"

"He left me a weapon," Kyle stated, changing the subject. Kalibar's eyebrows rose.

"What kind of weapon?"

Kyle described the bomb to Kalibar, then told the Grand Weaver his and Ariana's plan to use it on Sabin's lair. Kalibar remained silent throughout, listening in his usual careful way. When Kyle had finished, he felt both relieved and guilty, knowing that Ariana would be furious at him for having revealed their plan...especially after she'd expressly told him not to. He dreaded her inevitable anger...and not just because of her physical strength. He admitted as much to Kalibar.

"Let me talk to her," Kalibar stated, rubbing his chin with one hand. "And Kyle," he added. "Thank you for being honest with me."

Kyle nodded.

"Is there anything else you want to say?" Kalibar asked. Kyle paused, knowing that he had one secret left. A secret he no longer had any reason to keep. About who Darius really was. But he shook his head, unable to fathom telling Kalibar. Ampir was dead, but in Kalibar's mind, Darius was still alive. It almost felt like, in telling Kalibar Darius's true identity, he would be killing him.

"No," he replied. And despite the lie, for the first time in weeks, he felt at peace. True, Sabin was still out there, but at least Kyle didn't feel so alone anymore. He had Kalibar on his side now. And whatever happened, good or bad...they would face it together.

"Where is Ariana?" Kalibar asked. Kyle paused, realizing that telling Kalibar the truth would betray Ariana yet again...revealing her ability to get through the Gate shield, and her violation of Kalibar's curfew. But he couldn't lie to Kalibar now.

"She's checking the boat schedule," he admitted. "She can get through the Gate shield with her shard," he added. Kalibar's eyebrows rose in surprise. Then he shook his head, chuckling quietly.

"Clever girl," he murmured. He smiled then, patting Kyle on the shoulder. "You're in deep trouble, you know."

"She's going to kill me," Kyle agreed. Kalibar laughed, but Kyle shook his head. "It's not funny," he complained. "She nearly broke my arm this morning!"

"I'll protect you," Kalibar promised. "Come on," he added, gesturing for Kyle to stand up. "I suspect Ariana will be back shortly." He sighed, rubbing his eyes wearily. "We have a lot to discuss."

Chapter 10

Sabin withdrew from his memories, letting his consciousness swim aimlessly through the innumerable minds of his Chosen, sampling their senses and memories as he went. A flash of sunlight peeking from behind a cloud, the faces of a thousand Death Weavers staring back at him...the crushing silence of one Chosen trapped in its Void crystal, staring endlessly, unblinkingly at the same patch of metal grating for the last five hundred years. Another Chosen's body, placed behind the giant crystalline eye of a Void Behemoth, staring silently at row after row of other Behemoths.

All waiting patiently to be mobilized.

Sabin felt something *tug* on his mind, and he withdrew from the stream, searching for the source of the psychic pull. He found it, throwing a portion of his mind to it...a Chosen nearly a thousand miles away. He *pushed* its mind to the side, taking over its brain. Almost immediately, he felt his own body fading away.

He opened his eyes.

He was standing in a grassy field next to a lone tree, the wind blowing through his hair. He looked down, seeing the Chosen's hands there...*his* hands now. He flexed the fingers, or tried to...a few seconds later, his hands obeyed him. At this distance from Xanos, there was a slight lag between intent and action. He'd gotten used to the delay long ago, but it made his Chosen somewhat vulnerable

133

while he was controlling them. This had not been an issue until Ampir – under the guise of Darius – had managed to kill so many of his Chosen while he was controlling them.

If it hadn't been for those seconds of lag, Ampir would not have found killing them so easy.

Sabin focused on his surroundings, spotting a man in golden armor standing next to a boy a few hundred feet away. No ordinary man could have heard them from this distance, but Sabin's Chosen were possessed of incredibly acute senses.

"I'm going after Sabin," the man in golden armor said. "If I'm not back in 24 hours, assume I'm dead."

Sabin felt the faint thrum of woven magic in his mind, and knew that the man – obviously Darius – had created a sound-dampening field around himself. The man continued to face Kyle – his back turned to Sabin – and he saw the boy nod once, then again. Darius handed the boy something.

And vanished.

Sabin paused for a moment, then withdrew his mind from the Chosen's, returning that portion of his consciousness to his own brain. He felt the immediate return of the endless agony of his tortured body, that horrible burning pain. He ignored this.

Ampir was coming, as expected. Everything was going according to plan.

He idly wondered what would happen if Ampir were to attack him, if the ancient Battle-Runic fought him here, in this very chamber. He hardly felt any fear at the prospect of battling his old acquaintance. Attacking his Chosen thousands of miles away was one thing, but facing him at the very center of his power, in a chamber he'd spent millennia perfecting, was tantamount to suicide. Here, he held the ultimate power – over magic itself. Here, there *was* no magic unless he allowed it. And the sheer enormity of *his* power – of a mind able to do a thousand things at once, in a chamber designed to thwart any would-be attacker – was unbeatable.

No one – not even the great Ampir – stood a chance.

He turned his mind back to the Chosen in this massive chamber, browsing the thousands of minds for a memory he'd avoided for a long, long, time. He hesitated briefly, wondering why he needed to do this now, to relive this particular memory.

He hesitated for a moment longer, then threw his consciousness into the mind of the Chosen, feeling his own body fade away.

* * *

Sabin feels the warm breeze dancing around him, carrying with it the sweet fragrance of nearby flowers. The laughter of children playing in the distance is followed by a surprised squeal, and more laughter. The kind of laughter that is the sole province of children; unreserved, joyful beyond measure.

Sabin opens his eyes, watching the children – two boys and a girl – chasing each other across the verdant grass of the park he'd decided to take a stroll through. His left foot had gone numb again, forcing him to sit on one of the many park benches available. It has been doing that on and off for months now, the numbness appearing in different areas, then vanishing. He smiles, vaguely remembering what it feels like to be so young. He wonders – for the umpteenth time – where all the time went. He turns his gaze to the children's parents, a young man and woman sitting on a bench across from him. Holding hands, still obviously in love.

He sighs, knowing full well where the time went. Right past him. He shifts his weight, taking off his shoe and rubbing his foot. He feels a familiar bitterness rising within him. Despite the months that had passed since Vera had...moved on, he hadn't been able to shake the thought that he'd let her get away. He *had* let her get away. He'd listened to his sister, and to his own doubts, and let his pride and reputation get in the way of his happiness.

He sighs again, the tingling sensation in his foot intensifying, pricking the bottom and side of his foot like dozens of tiny needles. He rubs his foot harder, cursing under his breath. His pride is all he has now, he knows. A lonely companion, that.

He leans back on the bench then, trying to ignore his foot. He spots another couple walking through the park, weaving deftly

135

around the frolicking children. As they draw closer, his heart leaps in his throat.

It's *her*.

Sabin feels fear grip him, and he bolts upright to leave before she spots him. But his left leg collapses under him, and he falls back onto the bench with a thud. He grimaces, clutching at his left calf, drawing a hissing breath through clenched teeth. The prickly sensation has spread nearly to his knee, and it's profoundly uncomfortable. He tries to rise again...but it's too late.

"Professor?" he hears that melodic voice ask.

He raises his eyes to meet hers, feeling his heart skip a beat. She is achingly beautiful, her gray eyes big and expressive, her lips full. Her hair flows in auburn waves down past her shoulders, all the way down to her buttocks. She is dressed in a simple white dress that hugs her curves tenderly. So perfect in that moment that his pain fades away. So perfect that he wants to weep.

Instead, he forces himself to smile, to feign surprise.

"Vera?" he asks, as if unsure. Another one of the constant stream of lies that makes polite conversation possible. She nods, extending a hand. He tries to rise to shake it, but his leg refuses to move, and he is unable to hide a grimace.

"Professor!" she exclaims, putting a hand on his shoulder. "Are you all right?" He nods.

"My knee is acting up," he lies. She steps back, wrapping her hand around the waist of the man standing beside her. The man Sabin has desperately been trying to ignore.

"Professor, this is Ampir," she introduces. Sabin forces himself to turn to the man, his heart sinking. Tall, young, and handsome, he is every bit the match for Vera. Short brown hair perfectly cropped, with the bluest eyes he has ever seen. Square, strong jaw, muscular shoulders and chest, tanned skin...everything that Sabin is not.

"Professor," Ampir greets, nodding slightly. Suitably polite, but efficient. The man had a reputation for not wasting words. Though Sabin had never met Ampir, *everyone* knew his reputation. A prodigy, teaching himself magic at the age of four. By six, weaving patterns no one had ever seen before. Graduating as a full Runic at ten years old, by far the youngest ever to do so. A Battle-Runic before he'd finished puberty. Unbeatable on the battlefield. Unbeatable in the classroom. A man of few words, but not because he was afraid to speak; because he rarely needed to.

And now...

"A shame I only know you by reputation," Sabin states, knowing that he will never win Vera's heart from this man.

"I enjoyed your research," Ampir replies. And Sabin can tell that he is telling the truth; he has no need of lies. Lies were for the weak, for losers. A way to save face, or to get something one was incapable of obtaining honestly. Ampir had a reputation for telling people exactly what he thought...and it usually wasn't flattering.

"I'm flattered," Sabin replies, and despite himself, he means it.

"How close are you to finding the 'void crystal?'" Ampir asks. Sabin sighs, hating that he feels intimidated by this man – still practically a boy, after all – and shrugs.

"The Secula Magna forbids vivisection, even of animals," he answers. "Until they allow me an exemption, I'm afraid I won't get any closer to finding it." Ampir considers this for a moment.

"Other governments are more lax," he replies at last.

"Yes, well," Sabin counters, a little too icily, "...my tenure is with the Secula Magna." But Ampir is unfazed.

"Your tenure is wherever you want it to be."

And that, Sabin knows, is true, though it irks him to admit it. He could get tenure instantaneously at any school in any country in the Empire, and even beyond it. His research is known far and wide, his reputation formidable...if not as awe-inspiring as Ampir's. He could easily continue his research unimpeded elsewhere.

But Stridon is his home.

Sabin says nothing for a long moment, finding himself staring at the ring on his right middle finger. The one he'd earned while the upstart young man in front of him hadn't even reached puberty yet. What right did Ampir have to question him, when he'd already earned the highest honor a Runic could be awarded?

"Oh come on Ampir," Vera scolds. "You're making the Professor uncomfortable." Ampir pauses, then nods at her. Turns back to Sabin.

"It was not my intention," he states. Sabin forces another smile. "Of course not," he replies. He turns to Vera then, his expression stony. "What reason would I have to be uncomfortable?" She stares at him silently, then lowers her gaze to her feet. Pulls on Ampir's arm.

"We should go," she urges, her eyes flicking back to Sabin's. He sees the hurt there, and immediately regrets his last comment. Now why had he gone and said that? But it was too late to take it back. His heart sinks, and he waves goodbye silently, knowing that she will not go out of her way to see him again.

It was over.

He closes his eyes, refusing to allow himself to watch her leave. He's tortured himself enough. It's time to move on.

He opens his eyes, leaning forward and pushing himself up from the bench. He half-expects his leg to fail him again, but the tingling has subsided somewhat. He stands with the help of his cane, and walks in the opposite direction of Vera and Ampir. Toward the riser at the edge of the floating island in the sky, the one he'd decided to visit today for the first time.

A marvel, this invention of Renval's.

He limps forward slowly, his cane clicking sharply on the cobblestones at his feet. He thinks of Ampir, of a man so powerful that he fears nothing. A man who says what he wants, does what he wants, and doesn't beg for permission. A man who sees what he wants and takes it without hesitation.

If only Sabin could have been that kind of man. If only he had trusted his feelings, and taken what Vera had offered when he'd had the chance. But he'd been weak. Unsure. Hobbled by an insecure mind and a slowly failing body. For all his riches and his reputation, he is still incapable of getting what he truly wants...incapable of conducting his research into the void crystal, and too hesitant in courting Vera. And now they are both dead ends.

He closes his eyes, feeling despair threaten to overcome him. He loathes the feeling, realizing how pathetic he has become. He thinks of Ampir, so young and unblemished by time, his future full of promise. Too young to understand how cruel life can be. How it will eventually wear him down, stealing his strength and his looks, ravaging his body and mind until there is nothing left but distant memories of better days.

Sabin shoves the thought aside, knowing full well it is the self-defeating product of a depressed mind. Thinking like that will only lead to a life filled with regrets. He'd had his fill of those already.

He clenches his jaw, his teeth threatening to crack with the pressure. His knuckles turn white where they grip his cane, and he stops in the middle of the cobblestone pathway, ignoring the people that are forced to walk around him.

No more regrets!

He starts walking again, faster now. He ignores the pain in his knee and the numbness in his foot, walking even faster just to spite them, refusing to let his body stop him this time. He stares straight ahead, ignoring the fragrance in the air, ignoring the sounds of laughter around him. He feels a sudden, exhilarating sense of power, of a momentary mastery over his body and mind, and he revels in it.

Ampir was right, as much as Sabin hates to admit it. His tenure *was* wherever he wanted it to be. He could have what he wanted, if he was willing. It's too late to win Vera's heart, but it isn't too late to learn from his mistake. In fact, losing Vera might end up being the best thing that ever happened to him.

From now on, he vows, *I will get what I want.*

Even if he has to take it.

* * *

Kyle sat on the edge of his bed, picking at his fingernails anxiously. It'd been over an hour since Kalibar had left the suite, canceling his next meeting to track Ariana down so that he could talk to her. Kyle wondered if Kalibar had found her, and for the umpteenth time, he imagined how Kalibar's conversation with her had gone. She would instantly know of Kyle's betrayal if Kalibar found her outside the Gate shield. And she would be furious.

He'd never betrayed Ariana before. Their relationship had always been one of complete trust. How would Ariana feel about him now that he'd done this to her?

Kyle pushed himself off of the edge of the bed, pacing back and forth across his bedroom floor. His gravity boots clicked sharply on the marble below, squeaking with each pivot he made. He cursed himself, wishing that he hadn't told Kalibar anything. Or that Kalibar hadn't come in for lunch right after Ariana had left. If Ariana had been there with him, he never would have broken down. But then he would have ended up betraying Kalibar.

There was a knock on the door, and then it opened. Kalibar stepped through, motioning for Kyle to follow him out of the bedroom. Kyle did so, stepping into the main suite. Kyle stopped dead in his tracks; Ariana was sitting on one of the couches, and she looked furious. It was all he could do to continue forward, silently obeying Kalibar's gesture for him to sit opposite Ariana. Kyle kept his eyes downcast, staring at his knees, but feeling Ariana's eyes boring into him. Kalibar sat down next to Ariana, facing Kyle.

"I told Ariana about our discussion," Kalibar stated. "And Ariana was kind enough to tell me her perspective," he added. "While I know it hasn't been easy for either of you, I do appreciate your honesty."

He paused for a moment, as if choosing his words carefully.

"I understand that what you did – what you planned to do – was with the best of intentions. As your father, I am – as I have always been – proud of the depth of your character, and your willingness to do right by the ones you love. I want you both to know that you can always be honest and open with me. That as a family, we *have* to be open and honest with each other."

"I also want you to trust that, no matter my particular weakness – my desire to protect you above all else – that I am capable of rising above this, of doing what is right." He sighed then. "I suppose it is every fathers' fear that his children will leave him, to go out into the world with all of its dangers, and that he will no longer be able to protect them."

Kalibar stopped then, turning to face Ariana, and Kyle looked up at the old man, unable to help a glance at her in the process. Her eyes were downcast, to his relief. Dark, brooding, and angry...but they were no longer on him.

"My duty to you – and to the Empire – is to protect you," Kalibar continued firmly. "But I recognize that this is no longer possible." He patted Ariana's knee gently, turning back to Kyle. "Ampir is dead. Sabin is too powerful for us to resist."

Kyle cleared his throat, but Kalibar stopped him from speaking with one outstretched palm.

"I have two options now," Kalibar stated. "Diplomacy is all that I can offer the Empire, personally. I will invite Sabin to discuss the terms of a truce."

"What!" Kyle blurted out. Ariana's eyes jerked up from the floor, and she stared at Kalibar incredulously.

"No!" she exclaimed, pulling away from Kalibar. "You can't give up!" But Kalibar shook his head.

"I'm not giving up," he insisted gently. "Please, hear me out. As I said, it is my duty to exercise all options in ensuring your safety – and that of my people," he continued. "I cannot ignore that my children offer a unique opportunity – the *only* other opportunity – to fulfill these obligations." Ariana blinked, turning to eye Kalibar questioningly. She did not, however, say anything.

"Kyle, you possess – and are the only person alive that can use – a weapon that has the potential to defeat Sabin," Kalibar stated. He turned to Ariana. "And Ariana, you alone have the ability to sense the Chosen, and possess their amazing power." He rubbed his palms together, taking a deep breath in, then letting it out. His jawline rippled, and Ariana put a hand on his shoulder.

"Father..." she began, but Kalibar stopped her.

"I must assume Sabin will destroy us," he interjected. "I must plan for diplomacy to fail." He looked at Ariana, then at Kyle. "The only way to ensure your safety is to destroy Sabin...and only you can do it." He sighed. "But traveling to the very center of Sabin's power is suicide."

"But..." Ariana began, but Kalibar cut her off.

"You cannot succeed," he stated firmly. "Ariana, you may have the shard of a Chosen, but you don't have the experience or the training of one." He shook his head. "The Dead Man – and any Chosen with similar skill – would easily destroy you...and that's without Sabin taking over."

He turned to Kyle.

"Kyle, you may have the only weapon able to destroy Sabin," Kalibar continued. "But neither I, nor Ariana, nor anyone else, would be capable of bringing you close enough to Sabin's lair to use it."

"You can't..." Ariana protested, but again Kalibar cut her off.

"I must," he countered. "Your welfare is my primary responsibility, and though in theory your plan is sound, in practice it is impractical." He shook his head. "I've led, and fought in, hundreds of battles. Ideas that seem brilliant on paper often fail on the battlefield. Sending two children to a foreign continent, across unfamiliar terrain, to a vague location on a map, is a daunting task in and of itself. Traveling into the heart of enemy territory – with absolutely no knowledge of the enemy's defenses – is pure folly."

Kyle lowered his gaze, feeling his cheeks flush with shame. He and Ariana had been ready to hop on a boat with a map and a bomb, without any real plan of what to do next. Kalibar was right; they were woefully unprepared.

"This would be true even of an enemy of similar ability as our own," Kalibar continued. "Our enemy is more powerful than Ampir. Do you really think you'll be able to walk right into Sabin's home and detonate a bomb there?"

To that, neither Kyle nor Ariana had an answer.

Kalibar gave a heavy sigh, putting an arm around Ariana's shoulders and gesturing for Kyle to sit next to him. Kyle slunk over to Kalibar's other side, and the old man draped an arm around Kyle's shoulders as well.

"I'm heartened that my children tried to come up with a plan to save the Empire," Kalibar stated. He smiled at them both, giving their shoulders a squeeze. "I'm proud of you both."

Ariana pulled away from Kalibar, standing up and facing him. "So we give up," she concluded angrily. When Kalibar didn't reply, she crossed her arms over her chest. "What about your speech?" she asked.

"What do you mean?"

"A week ago," she clarified. "When you were commemorating the new lobby," she added. "You said: 'I will give up my life to defend *your* right to be the captains of your own lives. I will die, as did those we commemorate, before I allow this Empire, this great nation and all it stands for, to perish.'"

Kalibar stared at Ariana for a long moment, then smiled ruefully. "I forgot about your new memory," he admitted. Ariana didn't smile back.

"You lied," she stated flatly.

"I did not."

"You lied!" Ariana retorted angrily. "You're going to surrender!"

"I said I would discuss the terms of a *truce*," Kalibar corrected. "I will insist that we be allowed our self-governance, in return for accepting Sabin's role as a consultant in developing the Empire."

"You can't," Ariana protested.

"I must."

"He killed my parents!" Ariana shouted, standing up from the couch and glaring down at Kalibar. "He burned my village to the ground!"

"He'll burn a thousand more," Kalibar countered quietly but firmly. "Leaving tens of thousands of children without homes," he added, shaking his head. "I have to try to avoid that."

"What if Sabin refuses?" Ariana pressed. "What if he refuses your truce?"

"Then we fight," Kalibar replied.

"Or drop the bomb," Kyle offered. Kalibar and Ariana turned to him. "If we're going to die anyway, we might as well try," he clarified.

143

"If it comes to that," Kalibar replied, turning to Kyle, "...then that is certainly an option." He shook his head then. "But only as a last resort. I will not risk your life if I can help it."

"So if Sabin won't cooperate, you'll let us use the bomb?" Ariana asked. Kalibar turned to her.

"Not you," he replied. "Kyle will go with a contingent of Battle-Weavers, activate the bomb, and be flown to safety while one of the Battle-Weavers sacrifices themselves deploying the bomb."

"But..." Ariana began.

"And then I will send you two far from the Empire, where Sabin will never find you."

"What?" Kyle blurted out.

"You can't!" Ariana protested.

"We won't leave you," Kyle agreed. Kalibar shook his head.

"I cannot risk your death, Ariana," he replied. "You are too important. If Kyle survives the mission, but the bomb fails to kill Sabin, Kyle will join you, and you both will go into hiding."

"No," Ariana stated firmly. "I'm not spending my life running from him anymore. I'm not spending every day looking over my shoulder, waiting for him to find me." She shook her head, her hands balled into tight fists at her sides. "I'm not going to stand there and watch Xanos kill everyone I love!"

"Ariana..."

"I watched my parents be murdered in front of me, and I couldn't do anything," she interjected. "I watched my village burn to the ground. I watched you get your eyes taken out," she added. "I watched Erasmus get stabbed," she continued, her voice wavering. "I watched Ibicus nearly kill Master Owens." She balled her left hand into a tight fist. "I watched as a man cut me open on my own bed, just watched as he *butchered* me, and I *died* watching."

She raised her fist up suddenly, slamming it down on a small end table beside the couch. The wood shattered with a loud *bang*, splinters flying in all directions onto the floor.

"I'm *done* watching!" Ariana declared.

Kyle and Kalibar stood there staring at her, no one saying anything. Ariana stared back at Kalibar for a long, uncomfortable

144

moment, her dark brown eyes smoldering. Then she spun about, storming to the front door. She yanked the door open with such force that its protective runes activated, showering her with pulses of bright blue light. A dozen gravity shields appeared around her, and a strobe-like series of blue flashes burst outward, ripping the magical door off of its hinges and sending it flying across the room. It smashed into one of the marble columns, gouging the thick stone, sending pieces of rubble scattering across the floor.

She walked out without a word.

Kyle stared at the ruins of the door, then glanced at Kalibar, who was staring silently at the empty doorway, looking old and suddenly haggard. Two elite guards rushed into the room, staring at the ruined door, then at the shattered end table strewn across the floor. Kalibar waved them away.

"Leave us," he stated. "I'm not hurt," he added. They paused, then saluted, leaving the suite. After they'd gone, Kalibar stood up from the couch, patting Kyle on the shoulder without looking at him, then walking toward the doorway, his shoulders slumped forward, his head bowed.

And that, Kyle knew, was a lie.

* * *

The torrential rain of the early morning gave way to scattered clouds, the sun burning through these to shine its warming rays on the puddles that the downpour had left behind. As the sun passed its peak, swinging ever westward over the campus of the Secula Magna, all evidence of the morning's rain had vanished. Now, as it fell gracefully behind the shadowy buildings rising toward the heavens in the distance, sprays of brilliant reds and purples shot across the sky.

It was, Kyle thought as he walked down the cobblestone path away from the Tower, like a painting come to life.

He sighed, looking down from the heavens, spotting Ariana's favorite tree in the distance. He'd left Kalibar's suite soon after Ariana had, taking the riser down to the lobby and walking out of

145

the Tower to find her. As he drew closer to the large tree, he saw a slender black form sitting by its trunk. It was Ariana, he knew. And if he'd spotted her, that meant she'd long since spotted him. He slowed his pace, feeling fear grip him. She'd been furious with Kalibar – more angry than he'd ever seen her before. There was no telling what she would do now. But he continued forward until he'd passed underneath the limbs of the tree, stopping before Ariana. She ignored him, sitting cross-legged with her back resting on the wide, smooth trunk, her eyes on the grass in front of her. He hesitated, then sat down next to her. Still she ignored him, neither blinking, nor even breathing. She was as much a statue as the one he'd seen of Ampir earlier.

"I'm sorry," he said at last.

Ariana said nothing.

"I'm sorry I told Kalibar," he continued, letting out a heavy sigh. "He...he knew something was wrong, and he asked me." He shook his head. "I thought about how he'd worry with us gone, thought about everything he's done for us."

Still, she didn't respond.

"I remembered what he did for me back in the Arena," Kyle said. "I couldn't lie to him, Ariana."

Nothing.

Kyle sighed again, picking up a small acorn-like nut from the ground and staring at it. Faint flashes of blue light – so slight as to be nearly invisible – pulsed on its surface. A seed, cut off from the tree that gave it life, the magic it wove the only sign of the life that existed within.

"I'm sorry I betrayed you," he muttered.

Ariana stirred then, turning her eyes toward him, strands of her dark brown hair blowing across her face in a sudden wind.

"I made you choose," she stated. Kyle blinked, staring back at her uncomprehendingly. "Between Kalibar and I," she clarified. "I forced you to betray one of us."

"Ariana..."

146

"It wasn't fair of me to ask," she interjected. "Not after what he did for you. For us." She turned away, staring down at her feet. "I'm still mad at you," she admitted.

"I know."

"I'm more mad at myself," she continued. "And at Kalibar."

"Because he wouldn't let you go with me?" Kyle asked. "To Sabin?" Ariana shook her head, turning her head away from him.

"What?" Kyle pressed.

Ariana said nothing.

"Talk to me," Kyle insisted. He hated that she was being so aloof. It'd always been so easy to talk to her in the past; now she was so distant that he wondered if she cared about him at all anymore.

"You really don't see it," she murmured at last, not turning around.

"See what?"

Ariana laughed then, a bitter, hopeless sound that burst from her lips. She turned to face him, her eyes filled with anger and hurt.

"Don't you see what he's asking me to do?" she demanded.

Kyle just stared at her.

"I'm supposed to run and hide while everyone I love dies," she declared acidly. "Spend years, or maybe even decades or more alone, watching my back, wondering when Sabin is going to find me, and do god-knows-what to me."

Kyle said nothing, swallowing through a sudden lump in his throat. He wanted to say something – *anything* – but he no words came. He hesitated, then put a hand on hers, saying nothing at all.

She leaned toward him then, resting her head on his right shoulder, her hair tickling his neck. She slipped her hand around his, squeezing it gently, and he squeezed hers back. They sat there silently under the tree, watching the sun set behind the tall buildings of the Southwest Quarter far in the distance. When the first stars began to wink down at them, Ariana stirred.

"It's not fair," she murmured. Kyle nodded, squeezing her hand. She brushed a few errant hairs from in front of her face, then turned to look at him. Her almond-shaped eyes were barely visible in the starlight, but he could almost *feel* the intensity of her gaze.

"What?" Kyle asked.

"I'm not running."

"What?"

"I'm not running," Ariana repeated. "I'm not going to do nothing while everyone I love is destroyed."

"Ariana..."

"No," she interrupted. "I won't do it." She squeezed his hand again. "I'm not afraid of dying anymore," she continued. "I'm afraid of living like this."

Kyle sighed, shaking his head and staring down at his feet. He knew how she felt; no matter their past victories over Sabin, the threat of utter annihilation was ever-present, a crushing weight that grew heavier to bear with every passing day.

"Come with me," Ariana urged, breaking Kyle from his reverie.

"What?"

"If we don't stop Sabin, he'll kill Kalibar, and he'll destroy the Empire," Ariana explained. "Even if I run and hide, Sabin will never die...and even if I wait centuries, he'll still be there." She shook her head. "The minute I reveal myself, he'll find me, and finish what he started." She stared into his eyes, taking his right hand in both of hers. "Come with me, so we can kill that bastard once and for all!"

"Ariana, it'll never work," Kyle protested.

"Maybe not," Ariana admitted. "Maybe we'll die. But if we don't, we're dead anyway." She lowered her gaze. "When the Dead Man murdered my parents, he was following Sabin's orders. Sabin killed Rivin and Bartholos, and he tried to kill Kalibar." She looked up, staring straight into his eyes, and touched her forehead with one finger. "And he killed me." She shook her head. "I'm not running anymore," she declared. "I'm going to find him, and I'm going to kill him...or die trying."

Kyle said nothing, but he rubbed his chest, remembering the spacetime bridge generator that Ampir had placed there. With a thought, he could return to Earth, where Sabin could never find him. He could escape with his life. But if he did, he would have to live with the guilt of knowing he'd abandoned his friends, leaving them

148

to die. And that even if they somehow managed to survive, he would never know for sure...and he would never be able to see them again. He dropped his hand, knowing that was something he could never do. Ariana was right...it wasn't fair of Kalibar to ask her to do the same. While it gave her the best chance of staying alive, it would hardly be a life worth living.

Kyle shook his head then, a rueful smile curling his lips.

"What?" Ariana asked.

"I was just thinking," Kyle answered. "Of the last thing...Ampir said to me before he left."

"What's that?"

"No regrets," Kyle murmured. He took a deep breath in, smelling the sweet aroma of the night air, of nearby wildflowers and recently cut grass. A soft, gentle breeze blew through his hair, and he closed his eyes, savoring the moment. Then he opened his eyes, and turned to Ariana.

"Okay," he declared at last. "Let's do it."

Chapter 11

"Take this," Ariana urged.

Kyle took a large leather backpack from Ariana, surprised by its weight. Ariana had handed it to him with one hand, as if it'd been empty. But it must have weighed forty pounds, if not more; he struggled to place it on his back. Ariana turned away to pack some underclothes into another bag, then turned to glance at him.

"Too heavy?" she asked. Kyle nodded ruefully. "Sorry," she apologized, grabbing the backpack back from him. She slung it casually over one slender shoulder, then finished packing the other pack. She was about to hand it to Kyle, then pulled it back. "I got it," she decided.

"I can carry it," Kyle protested, but Ariana ignored him, throwing the second pack over her other shoulder.

"You'll need food," Ariana said. "At least until we catch up with the boat."

"Wait, what do you mean, 'catch up?'"

"There are two boats scheduled to travel across the ocean," Ariana explained. "One left this morning, and the other leaves tomorrow morning."

"So we should board the ship tonight, before it leaves," Kyle reasoned. But Ariana shook her head.

"Once Kalibar realizes we're missing, he'll stop that boat," she countered. "He won't think to check the one that already left."

"Wait, we're taking the boat that left *twelve hours* ago?"

"We'll fly out to sea," she explained. "We can catch up to it, then board it."

"We'll never find it," Kyle countered.

"You forget my vision," Ariana replied.

"Right," Kyle conceded. "What's in those backpacks, anyway?"

"Your Aegis, and my Tempest cloak," she answered. "And some food, and a cup to put water in."

"We should wear disguises," Kyle reasoned. "If anyone recognizes us, they'll send us back home."

"Already thought of that," Ariana agreed. She sat on the bed then, setting her backpack down and taking off her boots. She peeled off her black Weaver shirt then, and Kyle turned away to give her privacy. "You can turn around," she added. "I'm wearing an undershirt, you know."

Kyle paused, then turned around, seeing that she was indeed wearing a dark gray undershirt. She smiled, slipping off of the bed and walking into the bathroom, closing the door behind her.

"Take off your clothes," she ordered, her voice muffled by the door. "Put on the ones I put on the bed." Kyle glanced at the bed, seeing a neatly folded pile of clothes there. He took off his shirt, glancing at his right arm as he did so. It was terribly bruised around his bicep, and it still ached slightly.

Kyle sighed, slipping on the shirt Ariana had given him. The material was rough, with muted gray and beige colors. It had numerous pockets sewn into it. He changed into the new pair of pants, then sat on the edge of the bed, waiting for Ariana to finish.

Minutes passed.

Kyle fidgeted, wondering what was taking her so long. He hesitated, then slipped down from the bed, walking over to the bathroom door.

"Ariana?" he called out. "You okay?" But there was no answer. He paused, then leaned against the door, putting his ear against it.

151

He heard a soft clicking sound beyond, and then the sound of water running for a moment. Then he heard nothing at all.

Suddenly the door opened, and Kyle took a step back, his eyes widening. Ariana had changed into gray and beige shirt and pants, very similar to his, with brown leather boots. But her hair was gone – most of it, that was. Once long enough to reach her waist, all that was left was a short pixie cut.

"Do you like it?" she asked.

"Uh, yeah," Kyle stammered. Her eyes narrowed, and he put up his hands defensively. "It's just...I have to get used to it, that's all." He smiled at her. "I do like it," he insisted.

"Thanks," she replied. "It's part of the disguise. Now we have to dye it."

"Wait, why do we need a disguise?" Kyle pressed. "We're going to be invisible."

"That might not work forever," she countered. "We can't afford to be recognized by anyone on the ship." She grabbed his hand then, pulling him toward the bathroom. "Come on," she urged. "We'll do yours first."

"My what?" he asked.

"Your hair, silly."

* * *

Kyle stared at the bathroom mirror in despair, running a hand through his hair. He hardly recognized himself after Ariana had finished with him. She'd cut his hair first – far too short, and hardly with the skill he'd become accustomed to at the hair salons back on Earth. Then she'd dyed it nearly blonde.

He looked, he thought in dismay, ridiculous.

"Can I use the mirror?" Ariana asked, gently pushing him to the side. Kyle nodded, stepping back and watching as Ariana wet her hair, then applied more dye to it. She'd chosen black dye, and it wasn't long before she'd finished. She rinsed off her hair, then dried it, being careful not to leave any dye on the towel. She combed her hair quickly, then turned to face Kyle.

"What do you think?" she asked.

"Wow."

With her short black hair and pale white skin, her big brown eyes were almost hypnotically beautiful, like pools of color against a stark snowy field. He found himself staring at her.

"You like it?"

"Uh," Kyle stammered. Ariana smiled widely, running a hand through her hair.

"You *do* like it," she observed. "You're blushing."

"Let's go," he mumbled, gesturing to the two backpacks on the bed. Ariana grabbed the backpacks and slung them over her shoulders with distressing ease. Kyle walked toward the bedroom door, but Ariana stopped him.

"Not that way," she stated. "We might be seen." Kyle turned to her with a frown.

"This is the only way," he protested. Ariana shook her head, leading him over to the large window beside his bed.

"We can get out this way," she countered. Kyle stared at the window, then shook his head.

"Not anymore," he reminded her. "Erasmus warded the windows so no assassins could get in."

"I know," Ariana replied. "I'll take care of it."

"How?" Kyle asked. "It'll set off an alarm if you try to break it."

"Step back," she requested, "...you make too much magic." Kyle complied, backing up until he was all the way on the other side of the bedroom, near the door. Ariana turned to the window, closing her eyes. A watermelon-sized gravity shield appeared to her left. At first it was only a faint blue, but the light quickly intensified as Ariana put more magic into the sphere. An impressive amount of magic; Kyle had never seen her create such a powerful sphere.

"What are you doing?" Kyle asked.

"Using up my magic."

The sphere continued to brighten, the blue hue of magic now visible on Ariana's forehead as well. In fact, Kyle realized that rays of blue light were coming from the walls, the floor, and the window, and were converging at her forehead.

153

"My shard has a Void crystal in it," Ariana reminded him. "When I get low on magic, it sucks magic in from around me."

"Right," Kyle murmured. That it was; it was sucking magic in rapidly enough to allow her to continue generating the powerful gravity sphere. He looked down, noticing that bright rays of light were coming from *him*. But while the rays coming from him stayed bright, those coming from everything else around Ariana began to dim as they were slowly drained of their power. It wasn't long before the lights winked out altogether.

"They're drained," Kyle declared. Ariana frowned, her gravity shield vanished abruptly.

"I can usually tell they're drained when I can't weave anymore," Ariana explained. "But you make so much magic that I couldn't tell."

"They're drained," Kyle repeated. "I can tell."

"Okay," Ariana replied, clearly unconvinced. But she walked up to the window, grabbing it and pulling it open. To Kyle's relief, no alarm sounded, and no bolt of lightning flew down from the heavens to annihilate her.

"Wow," Kyle breathed. "Good idea." Ariana smiled.

"Thanks," she replied. "Let's go."

"Wait," Kyle blurted out. He ran to his nightstand, opening one of the drawers there, revealing a few dozen small crystal cubes Lee had given him to practice with. He grabbed them all, stuffing them into his pockets. Then he walked back up to the window, gazing outward. The ground was over eight hundred feet below. A week ago, he would have been too terrified to consider climbing up onto the window ledge. In fact, a few weeks ago he'd nearly plummeted to his death from the Tower. But now he had his gravity boots. He activated them, levitating upward and out of the window, then turning around to extend a hand to Ariana.

"Grab my hand," he stated. She did so, and he pulled her in close. Once she was inside the stabilizing gravity fields that his boots generated, he barely needed to hold her up; she climbed onto his back, wrapping her arms around his shoulders. "Ready?" he asked.

"Ready."

Kyle streamed magic to his boots, flying away from the window, and wove the invisibility pattern just as he'd practiced it, seeing a faint blue haze surround him. It was doubtful that anyone would think to look up, and even less likely that anyone would see them in the darkness, but he wasn't about to take any chances. He felt Ariana tap him on the shoulder.

"The docks are that way," she stated, pointing to Kyle's right. He angled rightward, the huge expanse of the Secula Magna's campus stretching out underneath them. From way up here, the trees looked miniatures, and he could see the white roofs of the dormitories scattered across the campus. He accelerated, hearing the shriek of the cool night air blowing past them as they sped up. It wasn't long before he saw the tall black fence surrounding the campus, with the shimmering blue dome of the Gate shield before it. He brought them into a slow descent, aiming for a patch of grass a dozen feet in front of the shield, stopping a foot from the ground. He cut the magic stream to his boots, feeling himself lowering gently to the grass. Ariana let go of him, dropping to the ground.

"We've got to get you through the shield," Ariana stated.

"How do you do it?" Kyle asked. Ariana shrugged.

"I just walk through," she answered. "My shard does the rest." Then she hesitated. "I don't know if it'll protect *you* from the shield though." Kyle frowned, considering their options.

"Why don't you just suck the magic out of it?" he reasoned. "Like you did with the window?"

"It won't work," she replied. "The shield is powered by the city's underground magic storage crystals," she reminded. Kyle nodded; Erasmus had mentioned that during the Council meeting yesterday. The storage crystals were massive; it might take weeks or months to drain them.

"I'll wear the Aegis," he decided. "It should protect me if something goes wrong."

"Maybe," Ariana conceded. She took off the bigger backpack, rummaging through it until she found the Aegis. She handed it to him, and he put it on quickly. Despite its sturdy construction, it weighed almost nothing, and within seconds of putting it on, it shrank to accommodate his slender figure. Ariana stared at him, looking suddenly worried. "Are you sure you want to do this?"

"It's the only way," Kyle replied. But Ariana didn't seem convinced.

"Maybe this is a bad idea," she stated, glancing back toward the Tower far in the distance. "What if you get hurt?"

"I'll be fine," he insisted. He tried his best not to think of what would happen if he was wrong. "We have to clear the fence," he stated, pointing to the three-story tall fence that generated the Gate shield. "I can fly over it," he reasoned. "If you hold onto me, maybe your shard will protect me."

"Maybe," Ariana replied, clearly unconvinced.

"Come on," Kyle urged, presenting his back to her. She hesitated, then climbed up on him, and he activated his gravity boots. They floated gently upward, until they were a few feet above the fence, some forty feet above the ground. The faint blue outline of the Gate shield shimmered before him, and he took a deep breath in, letting it out slowly. He closed his eyes; images of himself being blown to bits came unbidden to his mind's eye, and he hesitated, fear gripping his innards.

Then he thought of the Void Behemoth descending through the heavens, the white-hot beam from its lone eye melting the entire city, of Kalibar and Erasmus bursting into flames as they tried in vain to escape. He remembered how Kalibar had given his eyes so that Kyle might live, a debt that Kyle had no way to repay.

Until now.

"Kyle?" he heard Ariana say.

Kyle opened his eyes, squeezing his hands into tight fists and glaring at the shimmering blue wall before him. He knew that if he didn't do this, if he didn't act now, he would never forgive himself.

No regrets.

He took a deep breath in, then gathered magic in his mind's eye, thrusting it at his boots.

* * *

Kyle's head exploded in a burst of light and ear-shredding sound, and suddenly he felt something strike him hard in the back. The world tilted crazily, the heavens and earth spinning madly around him. Then he felt something slam into the side of his head with terrible force, and his vision went black for a split second. He groaned, a white blur appearing above him. The blur came into focus, and he found that he was staring at Ariana's pale face, her eyes wide with fear. Her lips were moving, and he realized she was talking to him.

"Kyle!" she called out, lifting his head up...off of the ground, he realized. He was lying on the cool pavement of the road just outside of the Gate shield. "Kyle, are you okay?"

"I'm..." he began, then cleared his throat noisily. "I'm okay." Ariana broke out into a relieved smile.

"Oh thank god," she replied. She helped him get up into a sitting position, then lifted herself to her feet, pulling him up with her.

"What happened?" he asked, lifting his arm and rubbing the back of his head.

"There was an explosion when you went through the shield," she answered. "You flew through the air, then hit your head really hard on the road," she added. "Are you sure you're okay?"

"I'm wearing the Aegis, remember?" Kyle replied. "I'm fine." And he was, surprisingly enough. The Ancient armor had protected him. He glanced back at the three-story tall fence behind them. They were standing on a cement path that encircled the fence, some forty feet from the shimmering Gate shield. "Come on," Kyle urged, presenting his back to her again. She climbed on his back, and he wove magic, creating an invisibility sphere around them. Then he activated his boots, accelerating forward and upward into the night sky. A thousand stars twinkled at them from the infinite blackness of the heavens, the air cold and crisp. Ariana pointed to Kyle's right.

"The docks are a few miles that way."

Kyle nodded, and arced rightward, continuing to ascend. He glanced back over his shoulder, seeing the Tower standing miles away, the glittering crystalline pyramid at its peak shining like a diamond against the velvety blackness of the night.

"We're really doing this," Ariana murmured in his ear. Kyle said nothing, pushing even more magic at his boots, feeling them respond instantly. They were higher than the tallest buildings now, higher than Great Tower itself. He gazed at the maze-like city streets below, lit with a soft white glow by thousands of magic streetlamps. He'd never been this far up before; it was surreal, and a little daunting. At the same time, he felt a marvelous sense of freedom. He took them higher; beyond the vast stretch of buildings, he spotted the dark, glittering surface of the ocean, its churning waves sparkling dimly in the starlight.

As the city passed below them, the ocean grew bigger, until he couldn't tell where the ocean ended and the sky began. Kyle stared at that void, wondering what awaited them beyond that vast unknown. The infinite possibilities of his future stared back at him, terrifying and wondrous at the same time. For the first time in his life, *he* was choosing his path. For better or for worse.

He grabbed Ariana's hand with his own, aiming for that blackness where the ocean met the sky. Wherever it took them, and whatever his fate, he had Ariana with him. And no matter what happened, they would meet their fates together.

Chapter 12

Sabin pulled away from the memory he'd stored within his Chosen, returning that portion of his mind to his own brain. The eternal, bitter cold of the translucent crystal that surrounded his withered body was barely noticeable against the constant waves of fiery pain that rippled across his flesh. It was a reminder, that pain, of the tremendous sacrifice he'd made so that he would endure. The agony reminded him of the day he had been encased in this eternal prison, when his deteriorating body had failed him at last. When he'd finally succumbed to the pain, and wished only for death.

No more regrets.

That, he mused bitterly, had been a noble goal, one his younger self had striven to achieve after losing Vera. Such a noble sentiment, and one he'd utterly failed at. Only the dead were free from regrets.

He paused, then reached out for the Chosen that had watched as Ampir had spoken with Kyle on the lawn of the Secula Magna, seeing through the Chosen's eyes. Kyle was returning to the Tower after speaking with Ampir. Seconds had passed since Ampir had vanished...and it would likely be a long time still before Ampir arrived to meet him.

Sabin sighed inwardly, searching for another memory. Within seconds, he found the memory he was looking for, throwing a small portion of his consciousness into it, even as the rest of his enormous will prepared for Ampir's arrival.

* * *

The Council Chamber is filled with the hushed murmurs of the twelve Councilman seated around the massive, circular table, the sweet aroma of burning candles in the air. Sabin yawns, clasping his hands in front of him on the warm surface of the table, his crisp white robes contrasting starkly with the dark red wood.

He glances up at the men around him, all of them his age or older. The very eldest, the Elder Runic Samel, a man who had served on the Council for longer than Sabin had been alive, had decided to retire. Sabin leans back in his chair, rubbing his eyes tiredly and trying not to yawn again. The Council had called a late-night meeting to discuss Samel's retirement...and to vote for his replacement.

One of the Councilmen raises his hand, indicating that he has decided his vote. He pushes a folded piece of paper at the Councilman to his left, and the paper is passed along to the Elder Runic, who reads it silently, then folds it again and puts it down.

Sabin smiles, thinking of how far he's come in the last five years. Since he'd met Vera and Ampir in that park on Renval's floating island in the sky. From that day onward, he'd worked furiously, forging his future with a singularity of purpose that had surprised even him. He'd used his reputation to campaign successfully for mayor of Stridon, using his considerable resources and connections – and his willingness to devote the entirety of his being to his job – to usher in a golden era for the city. He'd become enormously popular, which had clinched him a nomination for a coveted spot on the Council.

And to his surprise, he'd won.

Sabin watches as the next Councilman raises his hand, folding his piece of paper and passing it along as before. Being the most junior of Councilmen, Sabin knows he will be the last to vote. He glances down at the blank sheet of paper before him, considering his options. He needs to write two names down, one for who will replace Samel as the Elder Councilman, and another for who will be chosen as the next Runic to be voted into the Council. For the first, Sabin knows he cannot put his own name; though it is his goal – his dream – to become Elder Runic, he has little chance to win the position now. He is the most junior member of the Council, regardless of his reputation. To write his own name down would be considered the ultimate in conceit.

He pauses, then scrawls down a name on the paper, folding the top of the sheet over it to hide it.

He sighs, stifling another yawn and leaning back in his chair. He has one more name to write, and in theory what he writes will be known only to the Elder Runic. But he has been in politics long enough to know that confidentiality is a lie, that men can never truly be entrusted with a secret. He must assume that everyone on the Council will discover his choice for the next Runic. The name he writes will have serious repercussions for the future.

Still, his pen hovers over the page, and he chews his lip, glancing up as the next Councilman raises his hand, folding his paper and sending it along. Sabin sighs, tapping his pen on the page, feeling an old bitterness – one he thought he'd long left behind – rise to the surface.

There is only one name he can write.

Still, he finds himself hesitating, unable to will his hand to write it. Another Councilman – three seats to his right – raises his hand. Sabin clenches his left hand under the table, his fingernails biting into his palm. He notices a sudden, prickly numbness in his left foot, a sensation he hasn't experienced in nearly five years.

The Councilman two seats away raises his hand.

Sabin glances down at his page, putting the tip of his pen to the stark white paper. A black dot appears, spreading outward slowly. He lifts the tip, staring at that inky spot, seeing the Councilman to his right shift his weight, then raise his hand.

He places the pen on the paper, gliding it across the surface with quick, clean strokes, then putting his pen down on the table. He raises his hand in the air, then stares at the paper for a split second

161

longer, at the name he scrawled there, before folding it and passing it along.

He leans back in his chair, folding his hands on his lap and watching as his paper is passed along to the Elder Runic, seated opposite him across the large circular table. The Elder unfolds his paper, then nods once, refolding it and placing it on top of the pile before him. Samel clears his throat, then stands, his eyes sweeping across the eleven seated Councilmen.

"We have a consensus," he declares, taking the stack of papers and shuffling them as he speaks. The Councilmen all breathe a sigh of relief, as does Sabin. If they hadn't reached a majority vote for each of the positions to fill, they would've had to start the process over again until they did. It is already after midnight, and everyone – Sabin included, is exhausted.

"For the position of Elder Runic," Samel declares, his voice still powerful and commanding despite his frail, elderly form, "...we have elected..."

A hush goes over the room, and Sabin knows all too well why. The choice of Elder Runic will greatly affect the balance of power in the Council, and by extension the entirety of the Empire.

"...Sabin."

Sabin stares at the Elder Runic in shock, his mouth falling open. He feels a strange numbness come over him, gooseflesh rising on his arms. His fellow Councilmen turn to look at him, and he closes his mouth abruptly, trying desperately to keep his expression calmly neutral.

They chose me?

He hardly believes his ears, staring in silence as the convened Councilmen start applauding, rising from their seats to give him their ovation. He stares down at the polished surface of the table, feeling a wave of giddiness wash over him, a pleasure he has not allowed himself for a very long time.

They chose me!

He stands then, barely noticing the numbness in his leg as he does so. He bows before his peers, placing his right hand on his chest in the gesture of acceptance, then sits back down. He suddenly feels like weeping, such is his amazement and joy. For this is his reward for his years of single-minded focus and dedication, the seemingly impossible goal he'd set for himself five years ago, as he limped down that cobblestone path away from Vera, away from the man who had taken her from him.

"Elder Runic Sabin," Samel states, nodding deferentially at Sabin, "...would you kindly declare the winner of the next seat on the Council?"

Sabin nods silently, watching as the former Elder Runic removes a folded piece of paper from the pile before him, unfolding it and staring at it before refolding it and passing it along. Sabin watches as it passes from hand to hand, until it is placed in his hands. He holds the folded paper for a moment, staring down at its stark surface.

Five years, he muses. That's how long it had taken him to create a new life for himself. A new fate. One where *he* was the architect of his future, instead of being a victim of the forces around him. It had taken the cruel words of a man whose name he still loathed to hear to realize who he was, and what he needed to become. The words of a man who had never allowed himself to be a victim of anyone.

"The newest member of the Council is..." he declares, his voice booming across the table. Sabin unfolds the paper slowly, seeing the familiar, precise strokes of his own writing there on the page. He doesn't even read the second name on the page, looking up at his fellow Councilman instead.

"Ampir."

* * *

The magic lanterns lining the docks of the Stridon marina cast a pale yellow glow on the churning seawater below, rippling waves crashing onto the shore with a spray of white foam. Far above, Kyle shivered in the cold night air, staring down at the shoreline as they passed by. He glanced at the huge shipping boat moored to the docks, then at the dozens of smaller vessels swaying gently in the water.

"That's the boat that's leaving tomorrow," Ariana shouted, pointing to the larger ship. Her voice was barely audible against the shrieking wind. "The one we're looking for looks just like it."

"Got it," Kyle shouted back. He shivered again, his teeth starting to chatter. He'd assumed that the Aegis he wore would have protected his entire body from the cold, but he'd apparently been wrong; he felt warm only where it covered him.

"You're shaking," Ariana observed. Kyle nodded, realizing that she probably didn't even realize how cold it was.

"I'm freezing," he shouted back. He wove magic, creating a gravity shield around them. The wind vanished; he wove again, creating a small flame in front of himself, feeling the welcome warmth it gave. He felt Ariana shift her weight on his back.

"Look," she stated, tapping on his shoulder. He glanced back, seeing the docks far away now. Hundreds of tiny lights shone like stars from the streets and buildings of Stridon, and the sight nearly took Kyle's breath away. He'd never realized just how big the city was. It stretched for miles along the shore, almost as far as the eye could see. Far in the distance, he could still make out the glittering pyramid atop the Great Tower.

"It's beautiful," Kyle murmured. He gazed at the city for a moment longer, then turned forward. "Where is the boat we're looking for?"

"Straight ahead," Ariana answered.

"Are you sure?" he asked skeptically. If the boat had been traveling since this morning, then it had certainly traveled a great distance out to sea. Searching for it would be like trying to find a needle in a haystack, unless they knew exactly where to look.

"I memorized the route on the shipping map," Ariana explained. They both gazed down at the endless stretch of water before them for a long moment. "Maybe we should go higher," Ariana reasoned. "It'll be easier to spot the boat that way."

Kyle complied, willing his boots to ascend, his gut sinking as they accelerated upward. He felt pressure building in his ears, and he held his nose and blew through it to equalize the pressure. Without any buildings or trees below them, it was impossible to gauge how high up they were, or how fast they were moving. It was also difficult to tell if they were moving forward in a straight line; if it hadn't been for the guarantee of a straight shot when activating only one crystal on his gravity boots, he could have been traveling in circles and not even know it.

"Do you see it yet?" Kyle asked. Ariana shook her head.

"Can you take us higher?"

"We're still going up," Kyle answered. He popped his ears again, then shivered. It was definitely getting colder, despite his fire and the insulating effect of the gravity shield. "I can't see anything," he admitted. Without the city lights, it was almost pitch black.

"I see everything," Ariana reassured. "Keep going." Kyle did so; the air was frigid now, and he was feeling a bit lightheaded. With the gravity shield completely insulating them from the wind, he had no idea how fast he was going anymore, just if they were speeding up or slowing down. He glanced backward, at the city. Or rather, where the city had been; now there was only blackness behind them. Blackness all around them, save for the enormous tapestry of stars above. He felt suddenly disoriented, as if he were hurtling through space uncontrollably, with no idea where he was going.

"You okay?" Ariana asked. "Your heart's beating faster."

"Yeah," he mumbled. He glanced backward, hoping to see that beacon of light atop the Great Tower, but there was only darkness. "I can't see the Tower anymore."

"It's there."

"You can see it?" he asked. He felt Ariana shift on his back.

"I can see it," she confirmed.

They flew forward and upward silently, the howling wind muted by the gravity shield around them. Kyle began shivering again, and he made the flame in front of him a little hotter.

"I think we're high enough now," Ariana opined.

"Yeah," Kyle agreed. He swept his gaze across the darkness below, hoping against hope to spot the shadowy form of a boat in the distance. But he saw nothing. "Do you see anything yet?" he asked.

"No."

"How far out do you think it is?"

"It's been sailing for a whole day," she reasoned. "It might take a while to catch up with it." Then he felt her body tense up against his back. "Wait," she exclaimed.

"What?"

"Slow down," she urged, patting his arm. He complied, decreasing his magic stream. "Can you drop us down?" she asked.

"Do you see it?" he asked, feeling his guts rise up as they started to descend.

"I see a line of waves," she replied, her eyes on the darkness below. She paused for a long moment, then squeezed his arm tightly. "I think they're from the boat!" She squeezed him again. "There it is! Bring us lower," she urged. Kyle complied, lowering them through the darkness. He still could only see black haziness below, despite the brilliance of the star-lit sky.

"Where is it?" Kyle asked.

"Maybe a mile away," she answered. "Can you see it?"

"No," Kyle admitted. "I can't see anything." He peered through the darkness, resisting the urge to create a light above their heads. He wasn't sure if the invisibility field would be able to nullify a powerful light source...and they'd be easily spotted from the boat if it couldn't. He noticed a subtle rippling as they continued to descend, and he blinked, wondering if his mind was playing tricks on him. But the rippling was definitely there...and it was growing ever more distinct. He spotted a gray-blue line below, a path of churning water in the endless ocean. He followed this outward, and saw the faintest of shadows in the distance.

"I see it!" Kyle exclaimed, squeezing Ariana's arm and pointing to the shadow.

"That's it," Ariana agreed. "We need to find a way onto it without getting caught."

"I'll get us lower," Kyle stated. "Maybe I can circle around it, to find a place to land." He paused then, glancing at the dancing flame in front of him. He cut the magic stream to it, and it abruptly vanished.

166

"We should hide out below-deck," Ariana reasoned. "There might be an empty room we can use."

"Maybe," Kyle replied, suddenly apprehensive. What if there *weren't* any rooms available...or any place for them to hide or sleep? He couldn't just fly above the ship forever, after all. It was freezing outside, and he would need to eat and sleep eventually. "Isn't this a trading ship?" he asked.

"It is," Ariana confirmed.

"There should be a cargo hold then," he stated. "We could hide there."

"Are you sure?"

"I don't think it'll be checked too often," he reasoned. "And it should have wide spaces, so our invisibility field won't hit any walls or floors and give us away."

"Good point."

They zoomed over the water, continuing to descend toward the water below. The shadowy form of the boat become more distinct as he flew them closer; it was similar to the boat they'd seen at the docks earlier, with a huge wooden deck and tall black sails jutting upward into the sky. A few tiny lights dotted its hull, leaving faint spotlights on the water below. Kyle was taken aback at just how far below them the boat was; despite having descended for minutes now, the boat was so far below them that it looked like a toy.

He cut back on his magic stream, slowing further while dropping sharply downward, ignoring the butterflies in his stomach at the sudden descent. They dropped through the air in an arc toward the rear of the boat, until they were only a hundred feet above and behind it. The massive deck of the ship extended outward before him, its tall black sails bowing outward with the wind. He scanned the deck, but there didn't appear to be any people on it. He adjusted his magic stream, leveling them out smoothly until they were a few dozen feet above the waves. The sharp tang of saltwater greeted his nostrils, and he took a deep breath in, instantly reminded of vacations at the beach back on Earth.

"Is there anyone on deck?" Kyle asked.

167

"No," Ariana answered. "There's a lookout on the mast though," she added, pointing to the huge wooden beam that the main sail came from. "Try bringing us along the side of the boat," she added. "I want to look in the porthole windows."

"Got it," Kyle replied. He accelerated forward and to the right, until he'd brought them alongside the right side of the ship. It was four stories tall from the top of the waves, with three rows of round windows extending along its length. He slowed down, passing by them one-by-one. Ariana peered into each, until Kyle had nearly reached the front of the ship. Tall waves rose from where the prow of the ship cut through the water, and Kyle rose upward to give them wide berth.

"Can you circle back to the left side?" Ariana requested. Kyle nodded, zooming forward a few dozen feet, then circling carefully around the front of the ship. It took all of his concentration to maintain the same speed as the ship while circling around it, and he breathed a sigh of relief when they'd made it to the other side. He slowed down slightly, allowing the ship to pass by as Ariana again scanned the rows of portholes.

"Okay," Ariana stated as they passed the last porthole. "I watched the sailors on the other ship earlier today, so I think I know how to get to the rooms below deck. The cargo hold should be somewhere around there."

"Where should we land?"

"There," she answered, pointing at the back of the boat. Above the deck, there was a two-story building of sorts. Kyle knew that it had a name, but he had no idea what that was. There was a door on the first story at the very rear of the ship. He flew them toward it until their feet were hovering over the wooden deck below, then lowered them carefully onto the deck, their feet barely making a sound as they touched down. Kyle walked up to the door, then paused, glancing at Ariana. She nodded once, and Kyle twisted the knob, then pushed it inward. A dark, narrow hallway greeted them, lit by a single lantern. A real lantern, Kyle noted, not the typical magical lanterns found throughout the Tower. Its flickering flames cast stark, shifting shadows that stretched down the hallway.

Ariana tapped Kyle's shoulder, then stepped in front of him, treading silently down the hall. Kyle followed close behind, then nearly jumped out of his skin as he heard a loud creak behind him. He spun about, his pulse pounding in his ears, but the hallway was empty. He realized that the entire boat was creaking as it rose and fell with the ocean's waves.

He felt a tap on his shoulder again, and turned around to see Ariana staring at him. He nodded, then followed her down the hallway again, until they came to a set of doors on the left. Ariana paused, putting her ear to one of the doors, then to the other. She nodded once, then opened the second door, motioning for him to follow. There was a cramped stairwell beyond, with stairs leading up and down. Ariana took the stairs downward into the belly of the ship. Again these were meagerly lit with oil lanterns; Kyle wondered why, seeing as how magic lanterns were so much better. They descended one story, then another, until they came to a door at the bottom. Ariana paused before it, then opened it up.

Kyle peered over Ariana's shoulder, seeing a much wider hallway beyond; it was more than wide enough to fit three cars side-by-side. Ariana led him down this, toward a set of double-doors at the rear wall. She stopped before the doors, grabbing the handles and pulling gently. The doors didn't budge.

"Locked," Ariana mouthed silently.

She leaned into the doors, peering at the inch or so gap between them. Then she closed her eyes, and a faint blue light appeared on her forehead. She grabbed the handles again, and pulled...and they swung open. Beyond was a massive, two-story room. Stacks of crates and barrels lined the walls, with pallets filled with cargo stacked nearly to the ceiling. Dust swirled in the gentle light cast by the lanterns on the walls, and Kyle stifled a sudden urge to sneeze. This, he realized, must be the ship's cargo hold.

They moved forward into the cargo hold, closing the double doors behind them. Ariana wove deftly between the veritable walls of barrels and pallets, Kyle following close behind. She stopped suddenly, and pointed up at a stack of crates that nearly went all the way up to the bare wooden beams of the ceiling two stories above.

She pointed to Kyle's gravity boots, then again pointed at the crates. Kyle nodded, turning his back to her, and she climbed on. He activated his boots, floating gently upward between the stacks of crates, until their heads were only a foot or two from the ceiling. Ariana pointed to the top of the crate stack, which was roughly ten feet square. Kyle nodded, bringing them over it, then dropping them gently atop it. She got off his back, forced to hunch over a little so that she wouldn't hit her head on the ceiling. She knelt down, dropping both backpacks onto the crates, then opened one of them, pulling out something wrapped in wax paper. She unfolded this, revealing a few pieces of duck.

"Here," she whispered, handing it to him. He grabbed it, feeling his stomach grumble. Using magic always seemed to give him a heck of an appetite; Ariana had no doubt heard his complaining gut with her amazing senses.

"Thanks," he whispered back. He chowed down, feeling the ship sway slightly beneath him. The wooden beams of the cargo hold creaked with the motion. "How many meals do we have?" he asked.

"There's only a few meals left," Ariana admitted. She grabbed a cup from the pack, magically filling it with water, then handing it to him. "We'll need to find more."

"Yeah," Kyle mumbled between bites of food. He felt the sudden urge to urinate, and glanced about the cargo hold. "How, um..." he trailed off, feeling his cheeks flush.

"How what?"

"I need to go to the bathroom," Kyle admitted.

"Oh, right," she replied. She glanced about, then made her way to the edge of the crates, peering down. "I'll get a barrel for you."

"A barrel?"

"I'll empty out one of the barrels," she reasoned. "You can pee in it, and stuff."

"Oh," Kyle mumbled. She knelt down, then swung her legs over the edge, dropping out of sight. Kyle walked to the edge, peering downward, and saw her weaving through the narrow gaps between cargo stacks. Soon she was out of sight.

Kyle sighed, sitting down. He put the cup of water to his lips, then thought better of drinking from it. The more he drank, the more often he'd have to pee.

Kyle heard the crates creak, then saw Ariana pull herself up into view with one hand. In the other was a large ceramic jug.

"Here," she whispered, handing it to him. "It was in one of the crates."

"Thanks," Kyle muttered, gazing at the jug dubiously. It would certainly do for peeing, but anything else would require exquisite aim. And lots of toilet paper. "Um, can you...?" Ariana stared blankly at him, and he blushed again, motioning for her to turn around. She smiled, turning away from him. He paused, then walked over to the other end of the crates, turning away from her and getting the jug into position. He paused again, then turned around. "I'm going down," he stated. When she didn't answer, he activated his gravity boots, jumping down the twenty-odd feet to the floor below. He glanced up at the stack of crates, then weaved through the narrow spaces of the cargo hold until he was well out of her line of sight. Then he hurriedly conducted his business.

That done, he stared at the jug for a long moment, not quite sure what to do with it.

"Dump it out a window," a voice whispered in his ear.

Kyle cried out, spinning around and nearly dropping the jug. He saw Ariana standing there.

"Geez!" he whispered harshly, putting a hand to his suddenly pounding heart. "You scared the crap out of me!"

"Sorry," she whispered back. "I knew you were done."

"You were *listening*?" he exclaimed. She put her finger to her lips.

"I can't help it," she whispered. She covered her ears with her hands, then uncovered them. "I could still hear everything."

"Great," Kyle muttered. Suddenly, the thought of pooping terrified him. Ariana seemed oblivious to his despair, leading him to the far wall of the hold. Together they forced one of the windows open, and Kyle emptied the jug's contents. That done, they made their way back up to the top of their tower of crates.

171

"You should sleep," Ariana recommended. Kyle nodded, stifling a sudden yawn. She was right; he was exhausted. It was almost certainly way past his bedtime, although there was no way to tell what time it was. But there wasn't anything to sleep on but the hard wooden tops of the crates. Ariana concentrated, and a faint rectangle of blue light appeared a foot above the crates at his side. He frowned, passing his hand over the rectangle, and raised his eyebrows in surprise when it pushed his hand up and away. It was a flat gravity field...something he'd never learned to weave. He was instantly jealous.

Ariana motioned for him to lay down.

Kyle yawned again, taking off his boots, then dropping carefully onto his side on the gravity field, half-expecting to fall straight through it onto the crates. But it held him easily, gently floating him a half-foot above. He sighed, rolling onto his back and staring up at Ariana. She smiled down at him, reaching out with one pale hand and touching his cheek. After their long flight over the ocean, her hand was icy cold, and he shivered with her touch. She drew her hand back, but he grabbed it with his own, squeezing it gently and smiling back at her.

"We did it," he whispered.

She nodded happily, looking radiant in the shadows, her eyes glittering in the faint light of the lanterns far below. He felt Ariana squeeze his hand gently. He squeezed back, staring at her silently. She looked different somehow, more vibrant. She was usually so reserved, even somber at times...especially since her death. Now she looked more lively than she ever had when she *was* alive, a bright smile on her face.

"We did," she whispered back, giving his hand another squeeze. Then she took off one of the backpacks, pulling out something fluffy and white and handing it to him. He recognized it immediately; it was the dreamweaver pillow Jenkins had left him.

"Thanks," he mouthed, tucking the pillow under his head. He yawned then, shifting his weight on the gravity field. His eyelids grew irresistibly heavy, and he closed them. He felt Ariana's hand squeeze his one more time, and then sleep claimed him.

Chapter 13

Kalibar stepped out of the large shower stall in his master bathroom, absently grabbing the towel Jenkins had left for him and patting drops of water from his bare skin. That done, he placed the towel back on the towel bar, then grabbed his bathrobe, slipping into it. The comforting softness of the fabric was a welcome reprieve from the coarse black uniform he'd worn all day. It was a simple luxury, but one he looked forward to every evening.

He sighed then, taking the sharp right turn from his bathroom into the bedroom. He walked up to his bed and sat down, rubbing his eyes and yawning.

It had been a long day.

He pulled down the blanket, then laid down on his bed, staring up at the ceiling. He glanced at his right hand, at the faint lines of blue light coming from the magical rings on his fingers. Every night, he reminded himself of what he'd been given, this gift of sight. Every night, he tried to remember what it had been like to be blind.

He took a deep breath, then let it out, shaking his head. A week ago, he'd watched as his world had been nearly destroyed around him, struggling against the petty politics of the Council. Now the Council – largely due to Goran's influence – had mostly ceased its bickering, banding together to rebuild the city and improve its defenses. Kyle's K-Array promised to revolutionize the magical sciences, providing more new patterns in a week than had been discovered in centuries. And he and Erasmus had been pardoned by the Council for their use of the Right of Dictatorship. Everything had been going so well...for once.

Kalibar sighed, feeling an all-too-familiar hopelessness come over him.

And now Ampir was dead.

There was little recourse now, he knew. If Xanos was truly Sabin – the Ancient traitor, the destroyer of the original Empire – then there would be no stopping him. The K-Array would not save them. Even Kyle's weapon – the bomb that Ampir had given the boy – had little chance of working. Sabin had defeated Ampir, after all; no weapon of Ampir's could be trusted to destroy the self-proclaimed god. No, the only thing that could stop Sabin now was the force of persuasion. Diplomacy.

And that, Kalibar knew, was a long shot.

He sighed again, rolling onto his side. Marcus would have told him to start with diplomacy, not end with it. Marcus had never agreed with Kalibar's vision for the Empire. Marcus had spent his career traveling beyond the Empire, to the various tribes that once existed beyond its borders. He'd lived with them, learned their customs, and gained their trust. And he'd gotten many of them to put down their weapons and join the Empire voluntarily, promising them a better life. And he'd given it to them.

Not all the tribes had been so convinced, however. Marcus had nearly been killed on several occasions, when he'd ventured into tribal territory that had resisted his influence. They'd shown Marcus exactly what they'd thought of his methods, raiding the Empire's border cities and burning them to the ground.

That had been right before Kalibar started training as a Battle-Weaver. Before his wife had killed herself.

Kalibar had spent *his* career using war as a means of peace. He'd seen what war could do, the horror of it. He knew that some people would never stop fighting, would never listen to reason. All of the tribes who had refused diplomacy met Kalibar on the battlefield. And they had all been conquered.

A generation of war that had ensured a united Empire. A peace that had reigned since the end of Kalibar's first term as Grand Weaver.

They'd called him a blood-thirsty imperialist, his opponents. Goran had been particularly vocal in criticizing him. Kalibar knew that the blood of countless men was on his hands, had to live with the knowledge that his decisions had caused so much suffering. But he'd justified it with the knowledge that millions more would have died had he not so acted.

And now, in a cruel twist of fate, *he* was the defiant one, facing an enemy far more powerful, an enemy that refused to let his people live as they saw fit. The Empire had been reduced to a lowly tribe, facing annihilation by a behemoth...literally and figuratively. And his only recourse now was diplomacy...the very tactic Marcus had pleaded with him to use.

Kalibar sighed, rolling onto his back and shaking his head.

Oh, what cruel irony, he mused. *If only Marcus could see me now.*

Still, he could not fully accept such an end for the Empire. Despite what he'd told Kyle and Ariana, a truce with Sabin was tantamount to allowing the man to run the Empire. Sabin would be a consultant only in name. With the ability to destroy the Empire at any time, he would have complete control.

It was no wonder that Kalibar couldn't let go of the idea of Kyle's bomb. A weapon that might – just *might* – be able to destroy Sabin was impossible for Kalibar to ignore. What if worked? What if, against all odds, Ampir's weapon had the capability to save the Empire?

What if, against all odds, his children were right?

He yawned then, despite himself, feeling the insidious magic of the dreamweaver pillow under his head exerting its influence on him. He was thankful for it, knowing that if it were not for that magic, he would never have been able to sleep tonight. He felt his concentration falter, his worries scattering like leaves in the wind, and he closed his eyes. Within seconds, he was asleep.

* * *

175

"Grand Weaver Kalibar!"

Kalibar groaned, opening his eyes and lifting his head off of his pillow. He squinted against the painfully bright light shining through his bedroom windows. He heard someone knock at his door.

"Grand Weaver Kalibar!" the voice repeated.

"One moment," Kalibar yelled out. He sat up, resisting the dreamweaver pillow's seductive call for him to go back to sleep, and got up from his bed, pulling his bathrobe tightly around him. He walked to the door, weaving the long, complex pattern that would unlock it. The door swung open, revealing one of his elite guards.

"Grand Weaver," the guard greeted, saluting crisply. Kalibar waved away the formality.

"At ease," he grumbled. "What is it?"

"Your children, sire," the guard answered. Then he hesitated, lowering his gaze. Kalibar frowned at him.

"Yes?"

"They're missing," the guard stated.

Kalibar stared at the man, feeling a chill run through him.

"What do you mean, they're missing?" he demanded.

"We did a routine check this morning," the guard clarified. "Neither of them were in their beds."

"Did you perform a search of the Tower?" Kalibar pressed, his tone sharp. The guard nodded.

"Already under way," he confirmed. "But sire, we have reason to believe they've left the Tower."

"Why?"

"Kyle's bedroom window was open," the guard explained. Kalibar stared at him uncomprehendingly.

"Open?" he asked. "How could it have been opened? They were warded!"

"They were apparently...drained," the guard explained, his tone apologetic.

"*Drained?*" Kalibar exclaimed. He felt another chill go through him, and saw the blood drain from the elite guard's face. Kalibar glanced down, realizing that his fists were clenched, the knuckles white. He forced them to relax, shoving down the panic that threatened to rise within him.

"Everything in Kyle's bedroom was drained," the guard continued, his voice trembling. "And we found...hair in the bathroom sink," he added. "We believe it was Ariana's."

"Her *hair*?" Kalibar asked incredulously. "Why...?" He cut the question off, his jaw snapping shut. His eyes narrowed. "What else did you find?"

"A pair of scissors by the sink," the guard replied. "And Kyle's Aegis is missing, and Ariana's Tempest cloak, sire." He paused, then took a deep breath in. "We believe they left under their own power, sire." Kalibar stared at the guard for a long moment, then nodded.

"Indeed," he muttered under his breath. "Continue searching the Tower," he ordered. "I want a dozen Battle-Weavers sweeping the campus." He paused. "And the docks," he added.

"The docks?" the guard inquired. "Sire, they couldn't have gotten past the Gate shield."

"Don't underestimate my children," Kalibar countered. "Get me the departure schedule for yesterday and today," he added. The guard nodded, saluting sharply, then turning on his heel and walking out of the suite. Kalibar watched him go, feeling his fear turning quickly to anger. The emotion surprised them, in that he had never felt this way toward his children before.

Then again, they had never defied him before.

Kalibar strode back into his bedroom, shutting the door behind him with a thought. He removed his bathrobe, reaching for the black Weaver uniform that was neatly folded on his nightstand. Kyle and Ariana had probably left last night; if they'd gotten past the Gate shield – which they almost certainly had – then they would have made their way to the docks, and maybe even onto one of the shipping frigates.

Kalibar put on his uniform, then found his gravity boots, pulling them on quickly. He activated the communication orb on his nightstand, then opened the bedroom door, striding back into the main suite, toward the front door. Within moments, a man in a red uniform appeared behind the one-way transparent door. Kalibar opened it, and the man – the Portmaster – saluted him.

"Good morning sire," the man stated.

"Good morning," Kalibar replied tersely. "I need all of the ships that have left or will leave for Verhan since yesterday," he stated, referring to the only city across the ocean that the Empire traded with.

"Only two ships were scheduled to depart this week," the Portmaster replied. "The *Explorer* left three hours ago, and the *Defiance* left yesterday morning."

"I want both ships stopped," Kalibar ordered. The Portmaster hesitated.

"There's no way to communicate with them," he protested. Kalibar smiled grimly.

"My Battle-Weavers will," he promised. Just then, a young man in black and silver armor appeared at Kalibar's door, pushing brusquely past the Portmaster. The man had long blond hair and striking green eyes, and saluted Kalibar with rapid efficiency.

"Grand Weaver," he stated, his tone crisp and terse.

"High Weaver Urson," Kalibar greeted, nodding at the man. Urson was his second in command, the commander of his Battle-Weavers...a highly talented man who had the misfortune of knowing it. "Send six Battle-Weavers to search the two ships that left for Verhan."

"Our target?" Urson inquired.

"My children," Kalibar answered. "Search the ships under the premise of harboring illegal cargo," he added. Urson nodded at once, pivoting sharply and leaving the suite, grabbing the Portmaster by the arm and dragging him out as well. Kalibar watched him go, marveling that the man had not asked anything more. If only all of his men were that efficient. He knew of only one other that was: Darius.

Where is *Darius?* Kalibar thought. The bodyguard was supposed to have returned yesterday. He doubted that Darius would have allowed Kyle and Ariana to get away with this stunt, but with him gone, the elite guards had been tasked to protect them.

My guards underestimated my children, he mused as he walked into the hallway, toward the riser in the distance. *And I overestimated them.*

* * *

Ariana stared down at Kyle, his face so peaceful as he slept. She'd found some blankets in another shipping crate, and had placed them underneath him, stopping the magic stream to the gravity field that had kept him afloat. He'd been so exhausted that he hadn't even stirred during the transition.

She sighed, then stared out across the cargo bay. She had eight hours until he woke, maybe nine. It was a long time to do nothing, and she already felt an urge to get up, to do something. She still had to find food for Kyle, after all.

The ship creaked as it swayed gently back and forth, the wind howling around it. She could hear footsteps on the deck above, the sound as crisp and clear to her ears as if they'd been walking next to her.

She turned to Kyle again, then leaned forward to kiss him on the cheek. He stirred slightly, then went still. She smiled, then stepped to the edge of the crates, easing herself down. Within moments, she'd reached the floor twenty feet below. She weaved silently through the cargo bay. She wasn't particularly worried about being caught...she would hear anyone approaching long before they could reach her. And with Kyle hidden atop the tower of crates, even if someone searched the cargo bay – unlikely at this time of night – they wouldn't find him.

She stopped before the double-doors exiting the cargo bay, then unlocked them, opening the doors and slipping through. She closed the doors behind her, peering down the wide hallway beyond. It was empty, as before. She made her way back up the stairway to the hallway above, stopping at the top to listen. She heard footsteps on deck above, louder this time. The wind continued to howl, waves crashing into the ship's hull. The clatter of metal striking metal...

Ariana's eyes narrowed, and she concentrated on the sound. Metal on metal...it sounded like pans clinking against each other

179

every time the ship swayed. Which meant that there was a kitchen somewhere on ship...and that meant food.

She turned her head, focusing on the sound. It seemed to be coming from below, to the right. She turned her head to the other side, confirming the location. Then she moved forward, locking on the sound. She reached the door leading to the rear of the deck, then opened it, slipping outside.

The icy wind shrieked in her ears, nearly drowning out every other sound. Sheets of rain fell on the deck, soaking her clothes and hair instantly.

She turned right, crouching low and moving forward across the deck. She knew that it was night-time, but to her eyes the ship was well-lit under the stars. She spotted the lookout high above, perched on the mast...fast asleep. She smiled, continuing forward, spotting another man in a raincoat patrolling the other end of the ship hundreds of feet away, his back turned to her. She continued forward, spotting another door to her right, on the side of the two-story structure. She made her way to it, opening it and slipping through. She closed the door silently behind her, peering through the darkness beyond, water dripping from her body. Another hallway, with a stairwell at the end. With the wind no longer shrieking in her ears, she could once again hear the sound of pans striking each other. They were closer now, maybe one story below.

More footsteps from above – two sets now. The muffled sound of men talking. Laughter, then silence.

Ariana made her way to the staircase, stepping silently down them. At the bottom she found another door, and opened it, finding herself in yet another hallway. This one, however, was well over a hundred feet long, with doors lining the sides. Oil lanterns flickered on the walls, sending shadows across the dark wood. She heard the sound of countless men snoring from the rooms all around her.

Ariana paused, wondering if she'd made a mistake. The kitchen was down the hall, to the left...but if even one of the men sleeping in the rooms around her woke up, she would be trapped in this hallway. A well-lit hallway, with only one exit that she knew of.

She bit her lip, considering her options. If she aborted the mission, Kyle would starve...so she had to continue. But doing so was risky, so she needed to take as much food as she could, so she wouldn't have to do this again. But if she stole a lot of food, the theft would be obvious, and might spur on a search of the ship to find the thieves...

She paused for a moment longer, then moved forward down the hallway. The wooden floor at her feet creaked under her weight, and she stopped, cursing silently.

One of the men's snoring stopped.

Ariana froze, locking on the man's location. One door behind her, to the left. Right in the way of the only exit.

She heard a thump, then footsteps approaching the door.

Ariana bolted forward, dashing down the hallway. She saw a fork in the hallway to the right, and turned down it, nearly slamming into a large door at the end of it. She grasped the knob and turned it, but it didn't budge. It was locked.

She heard a door in the hallway she'd come from opening.

She twisted the doorknob again, harder this time. There was a muffled snap, and she pushed the door open, rushing in and closing it behind her. She found herself in a large room, rows of stoves on one side, a large kitchen counter on the other. Pots and pans hung from hooks on the ceiling, clattering against each other with the rhythmic swaying of the ship.

She heard footsteps moving down the hallway behind her...moving away. She took a deep breath in, then exhaled, feeling the tension slowly leave her. Then she moved forward, scanning the kitchen for crates, or barrels...anything that could be used to store food. The kitchen was distressingly empty save for utensils and cooking equipment. But the food *had* to be somewhere nearby.

Ariana spotted a door at the other end of the kitchen, and walked toward it, hearing the pots clattering against each other as the ship tilted under her feet. She reached the door, finding it locked. She forced the lock, knowing that doing so would arouse suspicion. But there was no way she was going to make this trip again, and they still had the invisibility pattern if there was a search for stowaways.

She opened the door, and found a large storeroom beyond, with row upon row of barrels. She pulled the lid off of the one closest to her, seeing a few fish heads poking through a barrel filled with salt. A smile broke across her face, and she felt a burst of elation.

"Gotcha," she whispered.

She grabbed the barrel, heaving it upward without difficulty. She knew that it must weight hundreds of pounds, but the weight hardly strained her new body. She turned around, nudging the door open with her foot, then making her way across the kitchen again. She reached the door to the hallway, stopping before it and listening carefully.

No footsteps...only snoring and the creaking of the ship.

Still she paused, remembering the man who'd woken earlier. Had he returned to his room? Was he still awake, waiting for her to pass through the hallway again?

The ship swayed beneath her, accompanied by the loud creaking sound of wood grinding on wood.

An idea came to her suddenly; what if she only moved when the ship moved, hiding her footsteps with the creaking of the ship?

Ariana waited for the floor to tip in the opposite direction, then opened the door, slipping into the hallway just as the ship moaned around her. She stopped then, peering around the corner to the left, then the right, finding the hallway empty on both sides. She waited, then moved leftward as the ship swayed, the creaking of the floorboards melding with the sounds of the rest of the ship.

The snoring of dozens of men reached her ears from beyond their closed doors.

Still she pressed forward, patiently timing her movements with the ship, until she'd made it to the end of the hallway. She opened the door, climbing up the stairwell and making her way back outside, to the deck of the ship. The wind shrieked in her ears, whipping through her short hair as she scanned the deck, spotting the lookout -still sleeping, thank goodness – and no one else.

Then she heard someone cough to her left.

She jerked backward into the hallway, the door slamming shut in front of her. She cursed silently, crouching down in the corner.

There was another cough, followed by footsteps right outside of the door.

Ariana grabbed a thread of magic in her mind's eye, holding it there.

The footsteps stopped in front of the door, and she heard another cough, then the sound of liquid gurgling. The doorknob rattled, and then twisted.

The door swung inward!

Ariana felt a bolt of terror strike her, and she wove magic frantically into the invisibility pattern, throwing the pattern outward and streaming magic to it. This close to the wall, she would still be spotted easily, but it might just buy her some...

A man walked into the hallway past her, a bottle of brown liquid in one hand. He held the door open with one hand, water dripping from the sleeve of his coat, tilting his head back and bringing the bottle to his lips. He let go of the door, letting it slam behind him. Then he staggered forward, giving a loud belch as he stumbled toward the door to the stairwell beyond. He reached the door, throwing it open and leaving the hallway without ever looking back.

Ariana relaxed, ending her magic stream. She opened the door, slipping outside once again, scanning the deck. No one was nearby. She turned left, walking quickly across the slick wood until she reached the rear of the deck. She traced her way back to the hallway, descending two stories until she'd reached the wide hallway leading to the cargo bay. Then she froze.

The double-doors were open.

She stared at the open doors, at the cargo bay beyond, the barrel of fish clutched in her hands. She lowered the barrel to the ground, then stared at the doors.

The ship swayed under her feet, the double-doors swinging to the left, then the right.

She'd closed them. She *specifically* remembered closing them.

Ariana's eyes narrowed, and she listened carefully, ignoring the wind and the sounds of the doors slamming open and shut. She could barely hear the faint sound of breathing coming from the cargo hold.

Kyle!

Ariana lifted the barrel, striding forward through the double-doors and entering the cargo hold. She weaved through the towering stacks of crates and barrels, until she reached the one she'd left Kyle on. She heard him breathing, and felt the tension leave her shoulders. She lowered the barrel to the floor, then reached up to climb the tower, hooking her fingers into the small gaps between the crates. She pulled herself upward, making the climb easily. Within moments, she felt her hands grip the last stack. She pulled herself upward, and then froze.

The barrel of a gun was pointing right at her head.

Chapter 14

The utter silence of the Void greeted Sabin as he withdrew from his memories, followed by an intense, searing pain that crawled over his withered flesh. He sighed inwardly, recalling the easy freedom of his body as it once was, able to walk and speak, to truly live. Now he could only taste such freedom by proxy, by inhabiting his avatar, or his Chosen, or by reliving his memories. It was never the same; the greater part of his mind was always here, in the endless torture of his own ruined body. He could never escape it completely. It hadn't always been this way, of course. He'd been mortal for longer than any man should, prolonging his life far beyond its natural limit. He'd created his first Chosen decades before his body had finally succumbed to the ravages of time, refusing to resort to the same technology to achieve immortality himself.

If only he had.

Sabin pushed the thought away, knowing the futility of it. He'd wasted more time on that particular regret than any other. He of all people knew that the past was immutable, that it was absolute. None of his prior mistakes could be erased. And no matter how extraordinarily powerful he became, he would remain, as always, a slave to his past. Shackled by it.

And in this hollow, silent chamber, unable to move or speak, his only reprieve from his private hell was found in the memories of that past. And of course the memories of his Chosen. Fragmentary things, his Chosens' memories, the ones they'd formed themselves when they were alive. Difficult to access and interpret, but satisfying nonetheless. He often browsed through the millions of minds around him, sampling these memories. A necessary distraction from the overwhelming boredom of eternity.

Sabin felt the *tug* of a Chosen requesting his attention, and he gave a portion of his mind to it. A vision of a man in black armor flying above the ocean, a few miles from Stridon.

Ampir was coming.

Sabin smiled inwardly, withdrawing from the Chosen's mind. He had no doubt that Ampir would find the entrance to the Void tunnels. It was inevitable. Even as a mortal, Ampir had possessed a singularity of purpose that allowed him to excel at whatever it was he chose to focus on. He'd been an outstanding Runic, an even better Battle-Runic. And then, in politics, he'd found success once again.

It had been maddening.

And now Ampir was still alive after twenty centuries, free to roam the world as an immortal, with a body as robust as ever.

Sabin *pulled* on the countless threads of his divided consciousness suddenly, feeling his mind withdraw from each of the millions of Chosen scattered across the world. He felt his awareness shrink, felt the searing pain in his body intensify sharply, until it was almost unbearable. Still the pain grew, every nerve fiber in his shriveled body screaming in agony.

He let the invisible flames course over him, let them lick at his flesh. Let them consume him.

Then he reached out with his mind, rising above those flames, feeling his awareness expand across his vast network. The pain faded into the background, omnipresent but now bearable.

He was Xanos once more.

Sabin sighed inwardly, then devoted a sliver of his mind to sift through his Chosen, searching for another memory. The one that had changed everything.

* * *

The hovership slices smoothly through the crisp morning air, the surface of the ocean far below rippling endlessly. Sabin stares out of the many windows from inside its steel hull, feeling his body being gently but firmly pulled into the soft cushions of the couch beneath him. The gravity fields doing so are hardly necessary, given the incredible smoothness of the ride. Still, he finds the sensation comforting.

He yawns then, stretching his arms, then relaxing. He'd woken up earlier than usual today, wanting to prepare for his trip to the Empire's colonies across the ocean to the west. He'd spent his first few weeks as Elder Runic surveying the Empire, traveling to every major city. It was a tradition to do so, for both a new Elder Runic and a new Grand Runic and Grand Weaver. It allowed the Empire's citizens to see their leaders, and for those leaders to appreciate the enormity of the responsibility they'd been given.

Sabin rubs his bad knee absently, extending it gingerly. All the time he'd spent on his feet during his travels had made it act up again. He glances at the notebook on the fold-up table to his right, reading the title on the cover: "The Newly Liberated Colonies of Orja." He stares out of the window again, knowing that he will see the shore of that continent very soon. A recent discovery, Orja. Vast beyond measure, with all manner of exotic plant and animal life, inhabited by a strange, savage people. It was hard to believe that it had only been occupied by the Empire eight years ago. Before then, travel to Orja had been forbidden by its natives. Then the great plague came, leaving but a fraction of the natives alive in its wake.

That was when the Empire struck.

Sabin turns away from the notebook, spotting a hint of gray-brown beyond the blue. He feels a jolt of excitement, and shifts his weight in his seat. He has heard all sorts of stories about Orja, of wondrous magic and bizarre cultures. The researcher in him is delighted at the chance to experience these firsthand. That he only has a week to spend there is tragic; he must make the most of it.

He feels a slight pressure pushing him forward against the invisible restraints binding him to his seat, feels a subtle deceleration. The feeling intensifies slowly, and then stops. He feels the ship start to descend – straight down, in the manner of all hoverships – toward the landing pad that undoubtedly lies below. He grabs his notebook, making sure that he has a few pencils on him. Half of the notebook is empty after all, ready to be filled with his observations. If all goes well, this trip will yield more science than political capital.

The ship stops its descent abruptly, and Sabin feels the gravity fields pressing him into his chair fade away. He stands, stretching his sore knee, then nods at the Orjanian ambassador seated one row down from him. A few Battle-Weavers – part of Sabin's security detail – rise from their seats as well. The ambassador nods at Sabin, rising from his seat.

"We've arrived just east of the port of the largest coastal city in Orja," the ambassador explains. "It was the capitol of the dominant native government here, before the plague."

"Verhan," Sabin recounts, remembering the short passage on the city from his notebook. The ambassador nods.

"The bigger cities like Verhan were hit hardest," he informs. "Survivors fled the cities to the countryside, and only started returning after the plague died off. Some refuse to return. They claim the city is haunted."

"They're superstitious then," Sabin observes. The ambassador chuckles.

"They're goddamn savages," he corrects. "They mutilate themselves, worship plants." He smirks. "We can barely get them to wear clothes."

"Fascinating," Sabin murmurs. "I'd like to meet a few of them."

"Sure, if you want," the ambassador replies with a shrug. "Don't expect much."

Sabin nods, imagining what a native Orjanian might look like. He'd heard of their habit of cutting themselves, carving strange symbols in their flesh. Of their bizarre rituals. And most intriguing of all, their magic.

The side door of the hovership opens then, a warm breeze filling the cabin. Sabin takes a deep breath in, smelling the refreshing tang of salt in the air.

"After you," he tells the ambassador, gesturing toward the door. Sabin follows the man down the ramp extending from the ship to the white marble below, feeling the sun's hot rays warming his face and arms. The subtropical heat is refreshing compared to the more temperate climate back home. He turns to stare at the docks a few hundred yards away, marveling at the fact that they are also made of pure marble. It puts the shabby wooden docks of Stridon to shame.

"Remarkable architecture," Sabin observes. He turns in a slow circle, spotting a giant marble statue of a tree, some thirty feet tall. Every leaf is intricately carved, the furrowed bark so realistic that he would have thought it real, had it not been for the lack of color. Opposite the docks, a row of columns twenty feet tall supports a massive arch, also made of marble. Vines spiral up each column, their flowers of every color imaginable. He walks up to one of these columns, spotting large olive-green crystals shaped like leaves inset into the marble, with silver lines connecting them like branches.

"Those are peridot crystals," the ambassador explains. "The branches are made of steel."

"From the hematite ore," Sabin recalls from his briefing.

"Right," the ambassador replies. "Verhan has extraordinary deposits of hematite and peridot," he adds. "Although the primary export is diamonds, of course." He gestures for Sabin to follow him past the huge arch, into a wide street beyond. Tall buildings – three to eight stories – flank the street. Some are made of granite, others of brick and wood.

"How much are we exporting?" Sabin asks. The statistics hadn't been mentioned in the report he'd read. The ambassador grins.

"Twenty tons annually," he answers. Sabin's eyebrows go up.

"Of all three ores?" he asks. The ambassador shakes his head.

"Twenty tons of *diamonds*," he corrects. Sabin's jaw drops.

"You can't be serious!"

"Impressive, isn't it?" the ambassador replies. "That's five times the annual diamond production in the entire Empire."

"How is that possible?" Sabin presses. "The amount of manpower to mine that volume has to be..."

"Enormous," the ambassador agrees.

Sabin gives a low whistle, then glances at his surroundings. They've made it to an intersection in the street; there are rows of immaculate-looking buildings as far as the eye can see, in all four directions. Sabin can't help but notice that the streets are almost entirely empty.

"Where is everyone?" he asks.

"We've concentrated most of our people around the mines," the ambassador replies. "We don't have enough people from the Empire to populate Verhan yet...not even close. Place was like a ghost town after the plague. The city is huge...three times the square mileage of Stridon."

"I'd like to see one of the mines," Sabin declares. The ambassador nods.

"I thought you might," he says, stopping in the middle of the street. "Not much to see here anyway...not until night-time, when the soldiers come back to relax and have a good time. They throw a hell of a party, let me tell you."

"How about we go now?" Sabin presses.

"Sure," the ambassador replies. "We can come back here at sunset," he adds. "Show you the nightlife, if you're interested." He winks then. "We can even have you get to know a native or two, if you know what I mean." Sabin gives an obligatory smile. He knows exactly what the ambassador means...and has no intention of taking the man up on his offer. A few years ago, he might have been tempted. But now he is the Elder Runic, the third most powerful man in the Empire. Such indulgences are below the sanctity of his office.

"One thing at a time," he states noncommittally.

* * *

The hovership doesn't take long to bring Sabin and the ambassador from the white marble streets of Verhan to the lush,

190

rolling hills of the countryside. It is a beautiful sight, the untamed wilderness so markedly different than the manicured gardens of the Secula Magna's campus. He stares out of his window, spotting a wide dirt road cutting through the tall trees. Even from high above, he can see that it is well-used, marked with deep ruts from the vehicles that have traveled on it.

"We're almost there," the ambassador announces, leaning over to point out of Sabin's window. "See that clearing?"

Sabin follows the ambassador's finger, spotting a sandy break in the tree line ahead and to the left. As the hovership curves smoothly through the air toward it, he realizes he's staring at a massive, spiraling pit in the ground.

"That's the fourth-largest diamond mine in Orja," he informs. "Two miles in diameter, and a half-mile deep."

"Incredible," Sabin murmurs.

"Four tons of diamonds were mined from it last year," he adds. "The natives have Weavers that specialize in mining operations...we managed to win a few over two years ago. That alone tripled our output."

"I'd like to meet one of them," Sabin replies. The ambassador frowns.

"It'd be a bad idea to do that on site," he cautions. "The natives aren't too happy with those Weavers...call 'em traitors."

"Traitors?" Sabin asks. "Why?"

"Natives aren't too thrilled about having us here," the ambassador admits with a smirk. "You'll see."

The hovership slows, then stops, hovering a few hundred feet from the rightmost edge of the pit mine. They descend gently, until the aircraft is levitating a foot above the rocky ground. The ambassador stands, and a gravity shield immediately appears around him. The Battle-Weavers stand as well, activating their own shields. Sabin frowns.

"Why the shields?" he asks.

"Standard precautions," the ambassador answers. "The savages would like nothing better than to off a high-ranking government official." He nods at Sabin. "You brought your armor?"

"As requested," Sabin confirms. "Is it truly necessary?"

"I wouldn't go near the natives without it."

The hovership's ramp lowers itself to the ground, and the Battle-Weaver in front of the ambassador steps out, followed by the ambassador and Sabin. The other Battle-Weavers come in behind, then immediately position themselves to surround the two. A large, multilayered gravity shield appears around the entire company.

Damn, Sabin thinks. *You'd think we were entering a war zone.* His itinerary had requested he wear a nondescript, drab uniform over his armor. He'd been perplexed at the time, but now he understands; it makes him less of a target.

"Turn your communicator to receiving only," the ambassador orders. "No point in having them understand what we're saying.

"They don't speak Imperial Standard?" Sabin asks. The ambassador shakes his head.

"Not the ones working the mines," he replies. "The plague took out most of the educated people, the ones living in the cities. All that's left are country folk...dirty, dumb, and dangerous."

The Battle-Weavers lead them across the rocky terrain, toward the massive open pit mine. A hundred feet away, a line of shirtless men shuffle out of the mine, each carrying a bulging sack slung over their backs. The men are unlike anything Sabin has ever seen; they have dark brown skin, unheard of in the Empire. Most are shaved bald, and all – the men and the women – are covered in colorful tattoos from head to toe. Sabin stares at one of the women, following her as she shuffles toward them. Her head is bald, white and green tattoos forming intricate patterns across her temples. These extend in flowing curves down her neck, and explode into wondrous designs that leave not an inch of skin unmarked on the rest of her body. For she is shirtless as well.

"Like I said," the ambassador murmurs, having followed Sabin's gaze, "...I can have a couple of them brought to your room tonight." Sabin says nothing, disturbed by the woman's figure. She is dreadfully thin, her ribs prominent, her eyes sunken. Her flesh hangs from her bones like clothes on a line. She notices his stare, and turns away. Sabin glances at the ambassador, notices his hungry stare.

Sabin turns away, disgusted.

"Come on," the ambassador says. "I'll show you the mining process." They pass the line of natives, staying well clear of them. *All* of the natives are like the first woman, thin to the point of being skeletal, staring dully at the backs of the people in front of them. Very few even glance their way.

They reach the wide ramp traveling in a massive spiral down the pit, and stop a few feet from the edge. Sabin stares down at the endless spirals, his jaw dropping.

"I know, right?" the ambassador says with a grin. "Amazing, isn't it?" Sabin says nothing. Is unable to say anything. A strange sensation comes over him, a detached feeling. As if he is suddenly no longer there, as if this is happening to someone else.

There, in the countless miles of spiraling dirt pathway extending all the way down – a half mile – into the earth, two unbroken lines of humanity walk. One down, one up. Thousands...no, *tens* of thousands of men and women, all carrying a single bag slung over their backs.

All of them like the woman he'd seen. Dark skin, colorful tattoos. Nothing but skin and bones, their eyes dull, lifeless.

Broken.

Sabin turns away, swallowing back a sudden surge of a bile that gushes into his mouth. He stares at the ground, a wave of numbness passing over him. He swallows again, then looks at his hands, realizing they're balled into fists. Knuckles white. The ambassador stares at him, a confused look on his face.

"Sir?" he asks.

"I'm done here," Sabin declares, forcing the words from his throat. He refuses to look up at the ambassador, finds himself unable to do it. He is ashamed to be here, to be seen by these people.

"I thought you wanted..."

"I'm *done*," Sabin growls. He feels a spike of anger, raising his eyes from the ground and glaring at the ambassador. "Bring me back."

"But..."

"Now!"

"Yes sir," the ambassador stammers. The Battle-Weavers exchange nervous glances, but they respond immediately, leading the company back to the hovership. Sabin stares at each of the natives they pass, wanting to burn their faces into his memory. When they pass the last native, Sabin turns his eyes straight forward. He ignores the ambassador's questions, walking up the ramp to the hovership, then taking his seat. He feels the gravity fields suck him firmly into his seat, then stares at the notebook lying on the fold-up table to his right.

"The Newly Liberated Colonies of Orja."

He closes his eyes, resting his head on his seat-back.

Right.

Chapter 15

Ariana stared down the long barrel of the rifle pointed at her head, following it to the large, dirt-caked hand that held it. Beyond, she saw a square-jawed man with a short beard, a long scar running across the left side of his face.

The man stared down at her, leaning down until the butt of the rifle pressed against her forehead.

"Hello missy," the man growled.

Ariana stared at him mutely, her eyes wide with fear. The man above her smirked, obviously believing that she was afraid of him. But her fear was only for Kyle.

Where was he?

Ariana stayed where she was, clinging to the side of the tower of crates, some twenty feet above the floor below. She stared at the man with the gun silently.

"I suggest," the man growled, "...you get down." His smirk faded. "And don't even *think* about running," he added.

"Where's my friend?" Ariana asked, breaking her silence. She stayed right where she was, staring the man down defiantly.

If he hurt Kyle, she thought. Images of what she'd do to him came unbidden to her mind's eye.

"Up above," the man replied casually. "First Mate's got him now." He nudged Ariana's head with the gun. "Like I got you."

195

"Did you hurt him?" Ariana pressed, glaring at the man.

"Not yet," he replied. "Didn't give us a reason to," he added, narrowing his eyes. "Now I ain't a fan of asking twice," he growled, pressing the butt of the gun harder against her. She resisted the pressure for a moment, feeling her shard starting to wake from its slumber. She eased back, knowing what would happen to this man if she let it react. If she killed him – inadvertently or not – Kyle's life could be at risk.

She made her way down the stack of crates, her eyes never leaving the man's. When she reached the bottom, she saw the man climbing down the opposite end of the stack. He hopped down the last few feet, training his rifle on her once again.

"Found the other stowaway!" he called out, walking toward her, then motioning for her to turn around. She did so, walking toward the open double-doors in the distance. She heard footsteps coming down the staircase beyond, saw another man walking down the wide hallway toward her. He was short and heavyset, with a ruddy cherub face and a shock of red hair peeking out from his hat.

"That her?" the short man asked, staring at Ariana with disbelief. "She's just a little thing."

"Stowaway's a stowaway," the man with the gun countered. "We got orders."

"Put the damn gun down, Scar," the short man ordered. "She's not going to hurt anyone."

Oh how wrong you are, Ariana thought grimly.

"How do *you* know, Rusty?" the man behind her – Scar – retorted. "She ain't been Tested yet."

"She'll be Tested soon enough," Rusty replied, walking up to Ariana and reaching for her hand. She stepped back, then felt the cold butt of Scar's rifle on the back of her head. "Now now," Rusty said, shaking his head. "Don't make this harder for yourself, darling." He reached for her hand again, and she let him grab it this time. His eyebrows rose immediately.

"Damn," he exclaimed. "Her hand's cold as ice!"

"Probably been on deck," Scar reasoned.

"Poor gal," Rusty murmured, leaning in and putting a hand on her cheek. She shrunk back – as far as Scar's rifle let her. "Come on Scar, have a heart," he pleaded. "Let's get her to a fire to warm up." "She'll get to a fire soon enough," Scar growled. "She can join her friend in the First Mate's cabin."

"Come on then," Rusty coaxed, pulling on her hand, leading her toward the wide hallway beyond the double-doors. She paused, then let herself be led, with Scar following behind. Down the hallway they went, then up the stairwell, and across the upper hallway, until they exited onto the deck.

"Come on," Rusty urged, waving for Ariana to follow him around the corner, then across the long deck toward the front of the two-story structure. They turned the corner again, walking along the front of the structure. Ariana looked upward, seeing a long row of glass panels on the second story.

That must be the captain's bridge, she reasoned.

They came to another door, and led Ariana through a maze of corridors, then up a flight of stairs. She memorized the way, marking each hallway, each door in her mind. They eventually came to a door at the end of another hallway, and Rusty banged on it with his fist in a series of short raps. The door swung open, revealing a tall, muscular man with a fierce scowl. He was bald and clean-shaven, and dressed in a simple white t-shirt and shorts.

"Evening Grotes," Rusty greeted. The man in the doorway nodded back tiredly, then turned to Ariana, stifling a yawn.

"This the other stowaway?" Grotes asked. Rusty nodded. "Bring her in," Grotes ordered. "Put her with the other one."

"Yes sir," Scar replied. Ariana felt Scar grab her arm, yanking her from Rusty's grasp and pulling her into the room past Grotes. She found herself in a large room with expensive-looking rugs and fine wooden furniture. A fire crackled in the fireplace to the left, and at the far-right corner sat a large red couch. And lying on it...

"Kyle!" Ariana exclaimed.

* * *

197

Kyle groaned, opening his eyes. He found himself lying on a red couch, drool on the side of his mouth, his head resting on his dreamweaver pillow. He sat up, wiping the drool away, and looked around. He was in a small but luxurious room, and several strange men were standing near him...as well as a very familiar girl.

What the hell?

He stood from the couch, or tried to; a bald, muscular man stepped between them shoving Kyle back with one brawny arm. Kyle stumbled back onto the couch, glaring at the man.

"Sit your ass down," the man growled. He turned to Ariana, who stared back icily. "You, get on the couch next to him." Ariana just stood there staring at him, until the man behind her – a burly man with a long scar down the side of his face – shoved his rifle into the small of her back. She took the blow without moving or saying a word, her eyes still locked on the man who'd shoved Kyle.

"Touch him again," she warned, "...and I'll break your hands."

The bald man stared at Ariana, then sighed.

"She's got fire in her, doesn't she Grotes?" the man with the scar on his face declared. The bald man – Grotes – ignored him.

"Just get on the damn couch," Grotes ordered. Ariana glared at him, then finally walked – slowly – to the couch. She sat next to Kyle, grabbing his hand in her own.

"You okay?" she whispered. Kyle nodded.

"What happened?" he asked. The last thing he remembered, he'd fallen asleep on top of the crates, Ariana at his side.

"Shut up," Grotes ordered tiredly. He stood over them, rubbing his face for a moment, then pointing at Kyle. "How did you get on the *Defiance?*" Kyle stared at him blankly. "This ship," Grotes growled. Kyle paused, then glanced at Ariana. Grotes walked up and slammed his hand into the wall near Kyle's head with a terrible bang, glaring down at him. "I asked you a question," he growled.

"Last night," Kyle answered.

"That's when," Grotes retorted. "I asked *how.*"

"We snuck on," Ariana interjected. "We hid in barrels," she added. Grotes turned his glare to her.

"I wasn't asking you."

"She's telling the truth," Kyle insisted, squirming in his seat. He glanced over Grotes' shoulder, at the man with the rifle. Would a gravity shield stop a bullet? He had no idea. They couldn't hurt Ariana, but if they fired at him...

"Well that's just dandy," Grotes growled, stepping back and standing straight up. "Because you two just confessed to a crime." He smiled grimly. "Let's see if it's a felony." He turned to face the short, pudgy red-haired man. "Rusty, get me the orb."

"Yes sir," Rusty replied, leaving the room. Grotes turned back to Kyle and Ariana. He was about to say something when the door burst open.

"What's going on?" A voice demanded. Kyle leaned to the side, seeing an older man striding into the room. He was perhaps six feet tall, with short salt-and-pepper hair and a full beard, dressed in a blood-red uniform. Various medals glittered on his chest, and affixed to his belt was a sword on his left, and a pistol on his right. Everyone in the room stood a little straighter when the man entered, saluting him instantly.

"Captain!" they said in unison.

"I believe I asked a question," the captain stated wearily. He turned a quick eye on Kyle and Ariana, then turned to Grotes, clasping his hands behind his back and staring at him impatiently.

"Stowaways Captain," Grotes answered. "We found them hiding in the cargo bay."

"How did they get there?"

"They claim to have hidden in barrels Captain," Grotes replied. The Captain sighed.

"All barrels and crates were to be visually inspected and Tested per my order," the Captain stated. "You will instruct the inspection crew accordingly and dock their pay at your discretion."

"Yes Captain," Grotes replied. The Captain turned a weary eye on Kyle and Ariana.

"Have they been Tested?" he asked.

"Not yet," Grotes replied. "Rusty is on it." The Captain nodded curtly.

"Carry on," he replied.

"If they Test positive?" Grotes asked. The Captain glanced back at Kyle and Ariana.

"Drain them, shoot them, and throw them overboard."

"Yes Captain."

"I will return," the Captain informed, turning about sharply and walking out of the room. The door closed behind him with a *click*.

Kyle swallowed in a dry throat, his heart pounding in his chest.

"What's this Test?" Ariana asked, staring at the man with the rifle, who glared at her.

"We didn't give you permission to talk," he growled.

"You'll find out soon enough," Grotes answered, pulling up a chair and sitting down on it. He crossed his arms and leaned back, stifling another yawn. Then he turned to Ariana. "The Test," he stated, "...is for magic." He gave them a tight smile. "You make it, you die."

"What?" Kyle blurted out. "Why?"

"You sound worried," Grotes commented, raising an eyebrow.

"And if we don't make magic?" Ariana interjected. Grotes turned to her.

"That's up to the Captain."

Kyle turned to Ariana, feeling his pulse quicken. She stared back at him, squeezing his hand – hard. The muscles of her jaw tightened, and her eyes darted to the man with the gun, the barrel still aimed right at them. Kyle knew what she was thinking...whether or not to fight back. With Kyle's magic and her incredible strength and speed, these sailors wouldn't stand a chance against them. But then they'd have to leave the ship, and their mission would be in peril.

The door to the room opened, and Rusty walked through. In one hand was a small, clear crystalline orb, about the size of an orange. It was instantaneously familiar...a Finder stone.

The door opened again, and the Captain walked through.

"Let us commence," the Captain ordered, pointing at Kyle. "Test him first." Rusty paused, then walked toward, the Finder stone in hand. Kyle squeezed Ariana's hand, leaning to whisper in her ear.

"Remember the window in the Tower?"

Ariana frowned, then nodded slightly. She squeezed his hand once, hopefully indicating that she understood what he meant. She'd drained the magically-warded window in the Tower using her shard previously; if she could do something similar to the Finder stone...

"No talking," Grotes grumbled. Kyle glanced at the Finder stone; it glittered in the soft yellow light of the lanterns.

"Take the orb son," Rusty instructed, stopping before him. He extended the orb out toward Kyle, who stared at it mutely.

"Why are you stalling, boy?" Grotes asked. He turned to the Captain. "Think he's weaving?"

"It doesn't matter," the Captain replied, his piercing eyes locking on Kyle's. "Magic has no power here."

Kyle stared at the orb, feeling his mouth go dry. He glanced at Ariana again, who was sitting as still as a statue. Streaks of blue light began to pull into her forehead...all of them coming from *him*. He turned back to the Captain, wondering at what he'd said.

Magic has no power here?

"Take the damn orb, boy!" Grotes commanded, standing up from his chair suddenly. The Captain reached for the pistol at his right hip, unholstering it.

"I will take your refusal as an admission of guilt," he stated casually. He raised the pistol, aiming it at Kyle's forehead.

"No, don't!" Kyle cried.

"Take it," Rusty urged.

Kyle stared at the orb, then at the two guns aimed at him. Blue rays were still streaking from his body to Ariana...much more faintly now, but still there. He paused, then reached for the orb, feeling sweat pour down his flanks. He swallowed in a dry throat, then reached out for a thread of magic in his mind, to weave a gravity shield.

Rusty dropped the orb into his hands.

"Open your eyes boy," he heard Grotes order. Kyle obeyed, seeing the First Mate standing next to the Captain. He glanced down at the Finder stone.

It was clear!

"Test the girl," the Captain ordered, training his pistol on Ariana's forehead. Ariana reached immediately for the Finder stone, taking it from Kyle's hands. She held it in front of her, her eyes never leaving the Captain. Again, the crystal remained clear; Ariana had drained all of the magic from her body and stored it in her shard.

"I'll take that," Rusty stated, retrieving the Finder stone. The Captain lowered his pistol, placing it back in its holster. He turned to Kyle.

"Why are you on my ship?" he asked. Kyle blinked, glancing at Ariana, then back at the Captain. His mind raced, trying to come up with an excuse. Why hadn't they created a cover story *before* reaching the ship? He felt Ariana pat his hand.

"We're trying to escape..." Ariana began, but the Captain cut her off with a gesture.

"I asked *him*," he interjected. "Speak boy."

"Uh..." Kyle mumbled. He stared blankly at the Captain.

"What's wrong with him?" Grotes asked Ariana. "Is he slow?" Ariana paused, then nodded.

"He is," she confirmed. Kyle blinked, then turned to her incredulously. He was *slow*? She just patted him on top of the head, staring at him piteously. "He got hit in the head when he was younger," she explained.

"That explains a lot," Grotes muttered, turning to the Captain. "He must not have understood the Test, thought he was going to be shot."

"Indeed," the Captain murmured. He stared at Kyle for a long moment, then turned back to Ariana. "Continue."

"We were trying to escape Stridon," Ariana explained. "To get away before the city was attacked again."

"Understandable," the Captain replied. "But illegal. And my country will refuse you entry without the proper immigration paperwork. You will be returned to Stridon."

"You can't!" Ariana exclaimed. The Captain raised one eyebrow.

"I can and will," he countered. "I will complete my return to Verhan, and you will remain in this ship until the next shipment to Stridon. You will be returned to your parents at that time."

202

"I don't have any," Ariana shot back. Grotes rolled his eyes.

"Great, an orphan," he muttered.

"Then you will be returned to your authorities for processing," the Captain decided.

"You don't understand," Ariana complained. "My parents were murdered," she added. "By Weavers." She spat the last word out, as if it were a curse word. The Captain stared at Ariana for a long moment.

"Go on."

"I come from Mortown," she continued. "A group of Weavers attacked my village in the middle of the night, killing almost everyone." She lowered her gaze. "They burned my home to the ground, then took me underground as a prisoner."

"I heard of these raids," Grotes admitted. "It was the talk of the bars two months ago, on my last trip here. Some sort of cult, they said."

"Death Weavers," Ariana agreed. "They held me for over a year before I escaped." She turned to Kyle. "He was the only other survivor from my town...I brought him with me when I escaped." She smiled, squeezing his hand. "I've been taking care of him ever since."

Kyle tried his very hardest not to glare at her.

"Continue," the Captain prompted.

"We made it to Stridon," she said. "But the...authorities, they treated us like criminals. Held us, kept questioning us about the Death Weavers, as if we were hiding some secret about them." She paused, taking a deep, shaky breath in, then letting it out. "When the...attack came, we managed to escape, but I knew it was just a matter of time before they found us again."

"Thus your plan," the Captain deduced. Ariana nodded.

"I knew we had no future in the Empire," she muttered. "They don't care about people like us," she added, turning to Kyle and running a hand over his scalp. "People who don't make magic."

"That," the Captain stated crisply, rubbing his chin with one hand, "is more true than you can ever know, child." He regarded Ariana and Kyle for a long moment, then sighed. "Regarding your illegal departure from Stridon, and your illegal entry onto the *Defiance*, that I will forgive." He turned to Grotes. "Rent them a room," he ordered. "They will pay in full through daily manual labor." He turned back to Ariana. "No days off, no special treatment. You will excel in both obedience and effort, or I will withdraw my offer."

"Yes sir," Ariana replied.

"Yes *Captain*," the Captain corrected. "As regards your desire to emigrate, I will discuss the matter with Verhan authorities when we arrive at port."

"Captain," Grotes interjected, pointing to a tabletop nearby. Kyle saw two very familiar backpacks sitting there. "We found contraband in their bags." He reached into one bag, pulling out one of Kyle's gravity boots. "They've got crystals in them."

"Test them."

Rusty brought the Finder stone to the boots, then the Aegis, and Ariana's Tempest cloak. To Kyle's relief, the stone remained clear with each. Ariana's shard had drained them as well.

"Return them to our guests," the Captain ordered.

"Yes sir."

"That will be all," The Captain stated. He turned about sharply then, and walked out of the room, the door closing behind him.

Kyle let out a breath he hadn't realized he'd been holding.

"Rusty," Grotes grumbled, gesturing for Ariana and Kyle to stand up. "Show these two to their rooms."

"Yes sir," Rusty replied. He grabbed their backpacks, then gestured for Ariana and Kyle to follow him. They left the First Mate's quarters, traveling through a maze of hallways and down several flights of stairs before arriving in a long hallway with doors on either side. Rusty stopped before one of the doors, opening it and ushering them through. Kyle found himself in a cramped room – smaller than his bathroom at the Tower – with a bunk bed on the far wall.

"Key is hanging on the hook," Rusty informed. He smiled then, dropping their backpacks on the floor. "Glad to have you aboard."

"Thanks," Ariana replied. Rusty's smile broadened, and he nodded, then walked out of the room, the door shutting behind him.

As soon as it closed, Ariana grabbed the key from the hook, locking the door.

"I'm *slow*?" Kyle hissed, glaring at Ariana. She shrugged innocently.

"You were taking too long," she countered. "I just went with Grotes."

"You pat my head like I was a moron!" he complained. Ariana's lips twitched, then broadened into a smile, and she put a cool hand on top of his head, ruffling his hair.

"You're so *cute*," she cooed. Kyle stepped out of her reach.

"Now I have to act dumb all the time," he groused. Ariana smirked.

"Act?"

"Oooh, you're asking for it," Kyle warned, pointing a finger at her. Ariana laughed, batting it away, then sliding in and hugging him.

"I'm just kidding," she murmured, giving him a gentle squeeze. She pulled away, staring at him with her adorable eyes. "I'm just glad we're okay now." Kyle hesitated, then smiled back.

"Yeah, me too," he agreed. "So I guess we're part of the crew now."

"Yeah."

"We'll do whatever they say until we get close to port, then head off on our own," he said. "You should keep us drained, just in case they decide to test us again."

"Agreed."

"We should ask when we're supposed to arrive, then jump ship the night before," he added. He reached down to one of the backpacks, pulling out the rolled-up map and unrolling it. He searched the map carefully. "Verhan is here," he observed, pointing to a dot on the eastern coast of the continent opposite the Empire. Ariana's eyebrows went up.

"How can you read that?" she asked.

"Master Lee gave me a book," he replied, remembering the toddler's book he'd been given. No need for her to know that little detail. "I've been practicing."

"So if Verhan is there, then we'll be..." Ariana paused, measuring with her fingers. "Maybe three hundred miles away from Sabin."

"Not bad," Kyle replied, stifling another yawn.

"You should get some more sleep," Ariana counseled. "Which bunk do you want?"

"I'll take bottom." He rolled onto the bed, rather dismayed at its firmness. It was hardly the plush, comfortable mattress he'd gotten accustomed to in Kalibar's suite. "Hey," he called out. "That flat gravity field you made, the one I slept on."

"Yeah?"

"Can you teach me how to do that?" he asked.

"Now?"

"If that's okay," Kyle replied. He'd been thinking about it ever since Ariana had woven it. The potential applications were enormous...far more useful than a sphere.

"Sure," Ariana agreed. She motioned for him to scoot over, and she laid down beside him. She traced the pattern in the air above them.

"It's like the gravity sphere, mostly," she admitted.

"Do it again," he requested. She complied, tracing the pattern in the air. He committed the pattern to memory, then reached into his pocket, pulling out a fresh crystalline cube. He inscribed the pattern carefully into the cube.

"What are you doing?" she asked.

"Recording it," he answered. "This way I won't forget."

He streamed a measly thread of magic to the cube, and sure enough, a small blue square appeared above it. He felt a slight breeze against his hand.

"Got it," he stated. "Thanks," he added. He yawned a third time, then stuffed the cube back into his pocket. Ariana smiled.

"Time for bed, sleepy-head." she whispered, leaning in and kissing his cheek. "Goodnight."

"Goodnight."

He closed his eyes then, and soon fell fast asleep.

Chapter 16

The morning sun greeted the moist wooden planks of the *Defiance's* massive deck, rising above dark, rolling clouds near the horizon to shine its rays on the ship. A flock of seagulls flew overhead, circling high above the rippling sails, calling out to the sailors hard at work below. Men swept the drying deck, checked and re-checked the cannons, and cleaned every surface of the ship's exterior. It was a sight to see, this frenzied activity, and Kyle would have enjoyed it much more if he hadn't been so dang sick.

He groaned, closing his eyes and leaning against the window he was cleaning, swallowing down yet another wave of nausea as the ship rolled to one side. He waited for it to pass, then used the cloth in his right hand to scrub vigorously at the white, salty residue that had been baked onto one of the dozens of windows on the cabin, the two-story structure at the back of the ship that housed the bridge. A few sailors had erected a makeshift scaffold on the second story, so that Kyle could clean the wall of huge windows that looked into the ship's bridge. The ship dipped suddenly, and Kyle grit his teeth against another wave of nausea.

"Shee-it, someone ain't got their sea legs yet," a man behind Kyle observed, clapping a hand on his back. It was Slim, one of the sailors Kyle and Ariana had been introduced to that morning. Slim was only a little taller than Kyle, but freakishly thin. He must have been in his early forties, with long, curly black hair that looked like it hadn't been washed this year. Neither, apparently, had his mouth.

"I'll be fine," Kyle mumbled, scrubbing the last of the grit from the window. He dragged himself over to the next window, lugging a bucket of soapy water with him. The ship swayed again, nearly causing him to stumble off of the scaffolding. Slim caught him just in time, yanking him back from the edge.

"Now now," Slim groused, "...no need to kill yourself. Things ain't *that* bad." He reached into his pocket, then handed Kyle something brown and stringy. It looked suspiciously like a root.

"What is it?"

"Gutroot," Slim answered. "So you don't puke on me." He grinned, revealing two missing front teeth. "Go on, chew it...or I'll let you take a dive next time."

"Gee thanks," Kyle grumbled, breaking off a piece and putting it in his mouth. It tasted awfully bitter. Slim picked up his own bucket, dropping it beside Kyle and scrubbing the window next to him. The man made quick work of his window, cleaning the entire thing in the amount of time it took Kyle to clean a mere quarter.

"Better hurry Guts," Slim advised. "Captain's going to be on the bridge soon." Slim gave another grin. "Gets all pissy when things ain't clean." Kyle frowned.

"Guts?"

"That's your name boy," Slim explained. "Unless you like what everyone else calls you." Kyle frowned.

"What's that?" he asked.

"Retard."

"Well great," Kyle muttered. He briefly entertained strangling Ariana for telling everyone he was slow. Not that that would particularly affect her.

"Some of the boys think that's too long," Slim admitted. "They call you 'Tard', but I think it sounds too much like 'Turd' and that name's already taken. Wouldn't want folks to get confused."

"I'll take Guts," Kyle grumbled, feeling the blood rush to his cheeks. Slim gave another dentally-challenged grin.

"Figured you would."

Kyle rolled his eyes, scrubbing harder and faster. He chewed the gutroot vigorously, desperately hoping that it would work. Slim went on to the next window, making quick work of it. The man hadn't stopped since he'd woken Kyle up this morning. None of the crew had. The Captain ran a tight ship.

Within a few minutes, Kyle realized that he wasn't feeling so nauseous anymore. In fact, he barely registered the movement of the ship at all now. This allowed him to fully concentrate on his work, and he set about his task with renewed vigor.

"Come on Guts," Slim shouted gleefully as they neared the end of the long row of windows. "My momma can work faster than you!"

"Then get her out here," Kyle shot back, feeling rather fed up with the man's constant taunting. Slim grinned.

"I would," he replied. "But she's dead!" He cackled, moving on to the next window, scrubbing even faster. "Faster Guts!" he cried. "Captain's coming any minute now!" Kyle scrubbed like a madman, his shoulders burning with the effort, sweat pouring down his arms and forehead. He ignored the pain, breathing through it. Within minutes, they were done, and Slim dropped his bucket, tossing his cloth into it and slapping Kyle on the back.

"All right Guts, time to take all this shit down," he ordered, sitting down at the edge of the scaffolding, then swinging his legs over. He hung there like a monkey on a branch, then dropped down to the deck below. Kyle did the same, albeit much more slowly, falling the six or so feet to the deck and falling onto his butt. Slim cackled, offering Kyle a hand and pulling him up.

"You splat like a Turd," he observed. "Maybe that *should* be your name." Kyle rolled his eyes at him. "Come on Guts!" He walked up to the scaffolding, dismantling it piece by piece. Kyle took each piece, stacking it in a tall crate. When they were done, Slim grabbed a dolly and tied the crate to it. They made their way down to the cargo hold, opening a trap door in the deck and going down a ramp to get there. When they opened the double-doors to the cargo hold, they found Ariana standing there with Rusty, who was breathing heavily, sweat glistening on his forehead.

"Hey Rusty," Slim greeted, grinning at the hefty man. "Whoa big guy, you're sweating like a whore in church!" Rusty ignored the comment, gesturing to Ariana.

"Slim, this is Ariana." Slim regarded Ariana for a moment, his grin never faltering.

"Damn," he swore. "You born in a cave?"

"She's got anemia," Rusty explained.

"You're Ghost," Slim declared. Ariana raised an eyebrow.

"Ghost?"

"You're white as one, ain't you?" Slim asked.

"Okay..." Ariana replied, glancing at Kyle, who shrugged helplessly. Rusty wiped his sweaty forehead with the back of his hand.

"You guys all set with the scaffolding?" he asked. Slim nodded. "You need help rotating?"

"Sure," Rusty answered. He put a hand on Ariana's shoulder. "Though I have to say, Ariana – er, Ghost – here is quite the worker." He shook his head in amazement. "She's twice as strong as she looks, and she hasn't stopped a single second till now!"

"Wish I could say the same about Guts here," Slim said, slapping Kyle on the back again. "He's slower than snot." Kyle glared at the man, while Ariana stared at Kyle, mouthing "Guts," with a questioning expression. Kyle ignored her.

"We have to move all of the crates with the orange marks from the center to the edges of the ship," Rusty explained to Ariana. "And take the crates at the edges – the ones marked blue – and put them in the center."

"Why?" Ariana asked. Kyle agreed; it seemed like a heck of a lot of work for no reason.

"Well that's a long story," Rusty answered. "See, where we come from – Verhan – they don't allow magic." Ariana's eyebrows rose.

"Why not?"

"Back in what you call Ancient times," Rusty replied, "...your Empire invaded Verhan's cities and demolished their government. They murdered millions of natives, then made the survivors into slaves to work the mines." He shook his head. "They sucked the mines dry, shipping precious stones back to the Empire for their Runics."

"*What?*" Kyle blurted out. "That's a lie!" Slim smirked. "Aw hell, they didn't teach you that in school?" he remarked. He turned to Rusty. "Must've skipped over the part where their ancestors got into the genocidal slave-driver business." He shook his head. "Ain't that precious."

"Yes, well," Rusty muttered. "It's no lie. Eventually the natives freed the slaves and won back their freedom. People from the Empire mated with the natives, diluting their blood and creating our ancestors. Eventually our ancestors rebuilt the government and its cities." He scratched his beard. "After...everything that happened, our ancestors decided to forbid the use of magic."

"But why?" Ariana asked.

"Magic annihilated our people," Rusty replied. "Twice."

"But doesn't not making magic leave you vulnerable to those that do?" Ariana pressed. Rusty smiled.

"You would think," he agreed. "But we discovered a technology that neutralizes magic. If anyone tried to attack our cities, they would have to do so without it."

"Wait, how can you neutralize magic?" Kyle asked. Slim frowned at him.

"You're awfully quick for being slow, Guts."

"He's smart enough," Ariana interjected. "He has a hard time talking sometimes, that's all."

"Oh," Rusty replied. "Well, I can't really tell you that," he admitted. "You'd have to ask the Captain." He shrugged. "Anyway, no magic is allowed in Verhan. Not in things, not in people."

"What happens to people that are born able to make magic?" Ariana asked.

"I'm not sure," Rusty answered. "Come on," he added. "We'd better get going on moving this cargo." He walked up to one ten-foot stack of crates, crouching down before it. "Each stack is on a metal pallet with wheels that lock," he informed. "We unlock the wheels, then push the stacks."

"Isn't that dangerous?" Kyle asked. "What if it tips over?" Slim grinned.

"Why you think we're having *you* do it?" he countered. Rusty rolled his eyes.

"It's dangerous, yes," Rusty admitted, bending over to unlock each wheel. "Take it slow and they won't tip over." He gestured at the stack. "All the marked crates – the ones we need to move – are shorter and lighter than the stationary ones." Rusty and Slim got to one side of the crate stack, then pushed hard. The stack slowly rolled, and they moved it a dozen feet before stopping.

"Now," Slim stated, "...we take a stack from the edges and put it here," he added, pointing to where the stack had just been.

"So why do all this again?" Ariana asked.

"To suck the magic out," Slim answered. Rusty nodded.

"The Captain does business with the Empire," he explained. "We ship gemstones to your government, in return for a variety of crops and other goods. Problem is, your goods – your whole *city* – is contaminated by magic." He wiped a few beads of sweat from his forehead. "Since magic is forbidden in Verhan, we have to make sure all that magic is leeched out before we get to port."

"Or else," Slim agreed.

"What happens if they find magic?" Kyle asked.

"Best-case scenario," Rusty answered, "...they confiscate and destroy the contaminated cargo, and fine the Captain." He cleared his throat then. "Worst-case, they hang the Captain and the crew."

"Whoa," Kyle murmured.

"That's why he wanted you two Tested," Rusty explained. "If you'd made magic, you would've contaminated the entire ship, and he would've been done for." He gave them a pained look. "That's why he said he'd, you know..."

"Shoot us and throw us in the ocean?" Ariana asked.

"Right."

"Great," Ariana muttered.

"So anyway," Rusty continued, looking rather flustered, "...we Test all cargo ahead of time, and mark the stacks that Test positive for magic. Then we put as many as we can as close to the hull of the ship as possible, and if we can't fit them all there, we rotate them every day."

"But why?" Kyle pressed.

"The ocean," Slim answered. "Slurps the magic right outta stuff."

Rusty nodded.

"The deep ocean has no magic," he informed. "So it slowly sucks magic out of anything near it. The *Defiance's* hull has metal beams designed to conduct magic, so any contaminated crates near it will leak magic to the hull, which will carry it out into the ocean."

"Ohhh," Kyle murmured. "Got it." He had to give the Captain credit; that was actually pretty clever.

"All right ladies, enough yapping," Slim groused, gesturing for Kyle and Ariana to follow him to another stack of crates. "These things ain't gonna move themselves."

* * *

Kalibar sighed, closing the book he'd been reading and tilting his head back to rest his aching neck. He slid the book across the table he was sitting at, staring absently across the room, at the row upon row of bookshelves in the Runic Archives. Then he sighed again, glancing down at the book's ornate cover.

A Brief History of Verhan, it read.

He'd come down to the Archives soon after talking with High Weaver Urson about getting his children back. He didn't know why he'd had the sudden compulsion to come here, to be surrounded by books. He found it comforting, he supposed. To be steeped in knowledge, to escape, for a moment, into someone else's mind. But it was telling that every book he'd chosen to skim through was dedicated to that continent on the other side of the ocean: Orja. Liberated by the Ancients a mere decade before the fall of the old Empire, only the easternmost coast had been mapped, its native peoples and cultures poorly understood.

Now was no different. They'd rediscovered Orja by accident, recovering ancient texts about the continent a few years ago. Ships had been sent to Orja, to the coordinates recorded in those books...some of which Kalibar had just spent the last few hours perusing. They'd found the bustling city of Verhan, much larger than Stridon. A city without magic.

Kalibar heard footsteps approaching, and turned to see a stooped old woman walk into the Archives. It was Master Lee, Erasmus's mother. He smiled wearily at her.

"Good afternoon, Lee," he greeted. She smiled back.

"Kalibar," she replied. She glanced down at the books scattered on the surface of Kalibar's table. "Reading up on Orja I see."

"Yes," he admitted. "Hardly pleasure reading," he added ruefully. She walked up to the chair opposite him.

"This seat taken?" she inquired. He shook his head, and she sat down, leaning her skinny, wrinkled elbows on the tabletop. He stared at her desiccated flesh with dismay. When he'd first met Erasmus as a young man, Lee had been quite the beautiful woman. Time had been cruel to her, draining her of that beauty. And yet, Kalibar knew that beneath her aged flesh was the same mind as that gorgeous woman he'd once marveled to look at, no doubt horrified by what it had become. That was the fate of everyone who had the misfortune of growing old; Kalibar had started to feel the same dismay about his own reflection years ago.

"You're depressed," Lee observed, giving Kalibar a wrinkly smirk. Kalibar sighed; Lee had always been frighteningly observant. Erasmus hadn't gotten away with much when he was younger.

"Indeed," he murmured. When she just sat there staring at him, he gave her a rueful smile. "You're trying to get me to talk," he observed. Lee grinned.

"Now if only my son were so observant," she said, giving a dry, rasping chuckle. "You can tell me your darkest secrets, you know," she added. "I'll be dead before I can spill my guts to anyone."

"Only because you'd never tell anyone else," Kalibar countered. And it was true; Lee was, like Erasmus, utterly trustworthy. He paused, glancing down at the books he'd been perusing, then wove magic in his mind's eye, creating a sound-dampening field around them. Lee's eyebrows rose slightly, but she said nothing. "Kyle and Ariana are missing," he admitted.

214

"Taken?" Lee asked instantly. Kalibar shook his head.

"They left Stridon for Orja," he corrected. "We have reason to believe Xanos is located there."

"Why'd they leave?" she asked. Kalibar hesitated, then lowered his gaze to the tabletop.

"Ampir is dead."

Lee stared at Kalibar for a long moment, her expression unreadable. Then she sighed, leaning back in her chair.

"I see," she murmured. "So why Orja?" Kalibar glanced at the shimmering blue surface of the sound-dampening field surrounding them, then shook his head.

"We're not secure here," he warned. And it was true; as good as the field was, it was still possible to eavesdrop through. Lee smirked.

"We are now," she countered, retrieving a small crystal from thin air, as was her way. She activated it, and a half-dozen faint blue spheres surrounded them in layers instantly. Kalibar couldn't help but smile. Lee would never admit to it, and few realized it, but she was very likely the most skilled Runic in the Empire...even better than Erasmus and the late Jax. "Tell me," she prompted.

Kalibar sighed, then relayed his last conversation with Kyle and Ariana, about their plan to travel to Orja. And of Ariana's...reaction. Lee listened silently throughout, saying not a word until he was finished...and for a long moment afterward. Finally, she sighed.

"Kalibar," she stated, breaking the silence. "I love you like my own son. Sometimes more."

"Thank..." Kalibar began.

"You're an idiot," she interrupted. Kalibar's mouth snapped shut, and he stared at her incredulously.

"Okay..."

"You told your daughter to let everyone she loves die or be enslaved while she hides from Sabin for eternity."

"I agree it's cruel," Kalibar countered. "But attacking Sabin would be suicide."

"Isn't Ariana already dead?" Lee asked.

"Well yes, but..."

"So you told her to choose between being afraid for the rest of her potentially infinite life, or defying you?" Lee pressed.

Kalibar grimaced, shifting his weight in his chair.

"Right," Lee grumbled.

"I don't have the luxury of protecting her feelings," Kalibar protested. "With Ampir dead, nothing will stop Xanos from annihilating us. You know as well as I do that he won't settle for anything less than complete control of the Empire."

"I don't disagree," Lee replied. "He acts like a man who values his vision for humanity more than he values humanity itself." She sighed. "Tyrants can justify murdering millions as long as it's for a good cause." Kalibar raised an eyebrow at that.

"Isn't that what I did?" he mused. "I destroyed the tribes to create a unified Empire." Lee shook her head.

"You didn't attack the tribes first," she countered. "And you didn't attack Xanos first." She sighed. "Xanos should be powerful enough to not *need* to kill everyone just to get his way."

"I've often thought the same thing," Kalibar agreed. "If I were Xanos, I would have stayed hidden, controlling the Empire through the living Chosen."

"But he didn't," Lee stated. "Why?"

"Someone was killing his Chosen," Kalibar reasoned. "He was trying to flush out Ampir."

"And that," Lee replied, "...was worth more to him than the thousands of souls he attacked in the Southwest Quarter." She leaned forward, propping her elbows on the table again. "That's the kind of man we're dealing with."

"Mmm."

"He destroyed the old Empire," Lee continued. "And he's clearly willing to destroy this one. He can always start over, try again."

"And he will," Kalibar agreed, staring off into the distance at nothing in particular. "Unless we stop him."

"You derided your children's plan," Lee stated. "Do you have a better one?" Kalibar sighed, knowing she already knew the answer. He'd come down here to read these books for a reason.

"No."

"Well then," she replied, standing up from her chair and pushing it up to the table. Its wooden legs screeched against the floor. The half-dozen magical fields around them vanished abruptly. "I'll leave you to it." She turned about then, walking away from him, toward the exit at the far end of the room.

"Thank you, Lee," Kalibar called out to her. She waved one skinny arm without turning around.

"Didn't tell you anything you didn't already know."

He heard the sound of a door opening and closing, and then there was silence. Kalibar rubbed his eyes, then stood up himself, stretching his aching back. He thought back to the speech he'd given to commemorate the deaths of his Battle-Weavers and elite guards in the lobby over a week ago, the one Ariana had quoted back to him:

I will give up my life to defend your right to be the captains of your own lives. I will die, as did those we commemorate, before I allow this Empire, this great nation and all it stands for, to perish.

He sighed, staring at the books scattered on the table before him for a long time, lost in thought.

* * *

By the time Kyle and Ariana had finished their work in the cargo bay and climbed the ramp to the deck of the *Defiance*, the sky was a bright purple-blue with the long rays cast by the setting sun dipping below the horizon. Kyle wiped the sweat off of his forehead with the back of his hand, still trying to catch his breath from the back-breaking work of rotating the crates. Slim and Rusty were equally sweaty, and even Slim's mouth was tired, to everyone's relief. Ariana, to both Slim and Rusty's amazement, wasn't sweating one bit. In fact, she looked positively radiant in the dying sunlight, her skin like porcelain, her short black hair rippling in the crisp ocean breeze. Kyle was enormously grateful for her help in the cargo bay earlier; long after he'd utterly exhausted himself, she'd picked up the slack, using her enormous strength to push the crates by herself while he just pretended to push.

The strong breeze felt marvelous on Kyle's hot, sweaty skin, and he closed his eyes for a moment to enjoy it. Then he glanced at Rusty and Slim.

"What now?" he asked.

"Now we eat," Rusty answered. Kyle's stomach growled immediately; they'd snacked a bit while working in the cargo hold, but Kyle hadn't had a full meal since breakfast.

"Don't we eat downstairs?" Ariana asked. They'd had breakfast and lunch in the mess hall below deck earlier. Rusty shook his head.

"You're eating with the officers tonight," Rusty corrected. "The Captain and Grotes want to speak with you."

"What do they want with a bunch of kids?" Slim asked.

"Don't know," Rusty replied with a shrug. "I was just told to bring them to the Captain's quarters for dinner." He gestured for Kyle and Ariana to follow him to the two-story cabin, and they navigated through the corridors and stairwells until they arrived before the door to the Captain's quarters. The door itself was impressively ornate, with intricate designs carved into its red-hued wood. Rusty knocked on the door three times, then waited. A few moments later, the door opened, revealing Grotes. The First Mate opened the door wide, gesturing for Kyle and Ariana to come in.

Kyle stepped past Grotes, finding himself in a large room. The floors were made of glossy dark cherry, and fine paintings hung on the walls. A gilded fireplace burned merrily on the far wall, with a miniature model of the *Defiance* resting on the mantle. A long, ornate wooden table sat in the center of the room. The Captain sat at the head of this table, dressed in his fine red uniform. A steaming silver platter lay before him on the table, and three more were at the empty chairs near him. Grotes sat down on a chair near the Captain, and gestured for Kyle and Ariana to sit opposite him.

"Sit," the Captain ordered. Kyle and Ariana did so, and Kyle felt Ariana's hand grasp his under the table. He gave it a squeeze. The Captain removed the lid from his platter, revealing a delicious-appearing steak. Kyle and Ariana did the same with their platters, and Kyle's mouth began watering as the aroma of sizzling meat reached his nostrils. Grotes and the Captain began eating, and Kyle joined them, devouring his meal with unfettered glee.

"You're not eating," Grotes observed between bites, staring at Ariana. Ariana shrugged. "I don't eat much," she admitted. The Captain frowned. "No wonder you're anemic," he declared. "I insist that you eat; a body cannot withstand the violence of a day's work without food to replenish it."

"I hear you put the men to shame today," Grotes chimed in, nodding at Ariana. "Impressive."

"Thank you sir," Ariana mumbled. She cut off a tiny piece of meat, putting it in her mouth and chewing slowly. This seemed to satisfy the Captain, who returned to finishing his own meal. When he was done, he covered his platter with its silver lid. It was instantly whisked away by a servant that Kyle hadn't even realized was there.

"So," the Captain stated suddenly, gazing at Ariana. "You say you were held for questioning, but escaped during the attack on Stridon?" Ariana nodded. "Is it true that the city was attacked by a giant flying machine?" he inquired.

"Yes Captain," Ariana answered.

"And that this machine," he continued, "...destroyed several city blocks in less than a minute?"

"Yes."

"Intriguing," he murmured, rubbing his chin. "And what is the nature of this 'Xanos' I've been hearing about?"

"Nobody knows for sure," Ariana lied. Kyle noticed that she was still chewing the same piece of meat she'd started with. "They say he's like a god."

"Yes, well," the Captain stated. "In my experience, which is considerable, there are no gods. Only men deluding others...and sometimes themselves." When Ariana didn't respond, the Captain frowned. "Your countrymen are under the impression that Xanos will succeed in destroying the Empire."

Ariana glanced at Kyle, who kept his eyes on his plate.

219

"You can imagine this scenario to be of extreme interest to *my* government," the Captain stated.

"Because then you wouldn't be able to trade?" Ariana asked. The Captain gave her a tight smile.

"Consider the possibilities," he replied. "One: the Empire survives its assault. Surely it will be profoundly weakened. This would make it an attractive target for my people."

"You mean, to attack?" Kyle asked. The Captain turned to him. "Correct."

"But aren't you allies?" Ariana pressed.

"Neutral, actually," the Captain replied. "But that is always subject to change, given the right opportunity." He cleared his throat. "Possibility two: the Empire falls, and Xanos eyes Verhan as his next potential conquest. This could be disastrous for us." He took a sip of whatever liquid was in his cup. "Possibility three: we ally with Xanos to ensure the destruction of the Empire while protecting ourselves."

"He'd turn on you," Ariana warned. The Captain nodded.

"I suspect so," he agreed. "Thus far, the only scenario in our favor is for the Empire to destroy Xanos...whether we invade afterward or not." He took another sip of his drink. "So logically, it would be best for us to ally with the Empire against Xanos."

"Really?" Ariana asked. "You're going to do that?" Grotes chuckled.

"Fat chance," he replied.

"Why not?" Kyle asked, forgetting that he was supposed to play dumb. The Captain turned to him.

"My government has an unfortunate history with the Empire," he answered. "Or rather, the Empire preceding yours. My people would never agree to an alliance."

"Did the Ancients really enslave your people?" Ariana asked. The Captain nodded.

"Our native ancestors, yes," he confirmed. "They've been bred out of existence for the most part."

"I can't believe it," Kyle muttered. The Captain raised an eyebrow at him.

"Believe it, boy," he replied. "Your precious ancestors were morally bankrupt men hiding behind a veil of righteousness." He leaned forward. "And as you have seen, your current government is little better."

Kyle was about to reply when he felt Ariana squeeze his wrist – hard. He glanced at her, and she shook her head imperceptibly.

"Even the fact that I trade with your Empire is looked down upon by my people," the Captain continued. Grotes smirked.

"That's one way to put it," he stated. "Last time we docked in Verhan, a mob tried to set fire to the ship."

"Indeed," the Captain agreed. "Which is why I pay the Verhanian guards so handsomely for their protection." He sighed. "But I digress. If the Empire falls – and I believe it will – my people may be next."

"Why are you telling us this?" Ariana inquired. The Captain lifted his cup, bringing it to his lips for a long moment, then lowering it to the tabletop.

"Because, my dear," he replied. "You will be questioned extensively by the authorities in Verhan – especially if you request amnesty there." He drummed his fingers on his cup. "The answers you provide may prove very lucrative for me."

"I don't get it," Kyle stated.

"Hardly surprising," Grotes commented. Kyle blushed despite himself, and lowered his gaze to his lap.

"If the people of Verhan become convinced that Xanos is a threat to them, they'll panic. The rich will be desperate for runic technology to protect themselves."

"But isn't magic illegal?" Kyle asked.

"Indeed," the Captain replied. "But the rich can afford to worry less about laws, and runic items *can* be smuggled. One simply has to remove magic from the item so that it passes Testing at customs, and disguise it."

"You mean by rotating the cargo like we did today?" Ariana asked.

"That works for items with residual magic," the Captain answered. "For a well-charged runic item that would take weeks to work." He smiled. "I have a much quicker solution."

"Like what?" Ariana pressed.

"That is none of your concern," he replied. "Suffice it to say that any man with the capability to smuggle runic technology from the Empire will become extraordinarily wealthy...as long as we convince the populace that the end is near." He smirked. "Fear makes for very effective marketing."

"And that's where you come in," Ariana deduced. The Captain nodded.

"This is my proposal," he declared. "In exchange for safe passage to Verhan and a generous payment to certain officials to guarantee your citizenship papers, you will provide information regarding the Empire's inevitable demise, and hint at Xanos's plan to conquer Verhan next."

"Okay," Ariana said. "But why would they believe us? We're just kids."

"You were a prisoner of the Death Weavers," he replied. "You can say you overheard the plans to attack Verhan. And if you're earnest enough, your youth may work in your favor." He turned to Grotes. "That is where my First Mate comes in."

"We'll be rehearsing your interrogations tomorrow," Grotes stated. "And every day after, until we get to port."

"When is that?" Kyle piped in. Ariana nodded; they still needed to figure out when they should escape the ship.

"Five days," Grotes answered.

"Do we have a deal?" the Captain asked. Ariana glanced at Kyle, who nodded. It hardly mattered what deal they made, seeing as how they had no intention of staying with the ship long enough to get questioned. Ariana turned to the Captain.

"We'll do it."

"A wise decision," the Captain replied. He stood up from his chair then, motioning for Kyle and Ariana to do the same. "Leave us now," he ordered. "You may join the festivities on deck."

"Festivities?" Kyle asked.

"A birthday celebration for one of the sailors."

With that, Grotes ushered them out of the Captain's quarters and into the hallway. Rusty was waiting for them, and led them back down to the first floor of the cabin. When they reached the deck, the sun had finished setting. Thousands of stars winked down on them from above, the cool ocean breeze blowing through their hair. Kyle heard music playing and sailors singing in the distance; a few dozen men were clustered near the front of the ship, lit from below by a half-dozen lanterns placed on the deck. Some were dancing merrily, while others were playing their instruments, and still others were clapping in time to the music.

"Come on!" Rusty urged, leading them across the deck toward the men. They reached the rest of the crew, and Kyle saw Slim jump up from where he was sitting, a mostly-empty flask in his hand.

"Guts!" Slim cried, stumbling forward and throwing a scrawny arm over Kyle's shoulders. His breath stank of alcohol. "Have a drink kid," he slurred, pressing the mouth of the flask to Kyle's lips. Kyle pushed the flask away gently, shaking his head.

"I can't," he protested. Slim made a face.

"You drink water, don'cha?" he countered. "Same thing," he added, shoving the flask at Kyle. Kyle pushed it away again.

"It makes me puke," Kyle explained. Slim shrugged.

"Makes *everyone* puke," he declared, taking another swig. "That's," he added while pointing one finger at Kyle's nose, "...how you know you've had enough."

"It's all right Slim," Rusty interjected, gently pulling Slim away. Slim turned his bloodshot eyes to Ariana.

"Hey bee-yootiful," he leered, putting a hand on Ariana's shoulder. Ariana put her hand on top of his, and squeezed. Slim dropped like a stone, howling in pain. He clutched his hand to his belly, curling up into the fetal position on the deck.

"I'm taken," Ariana declared, grabbing Kyle's hand and stepping over Slim. A few of the sailors had clearly been watching, and they all burst out laughing. Rusty ignored Slim, bringing Kyle and Ariana near the sailors playing their instruments.

223

"You know any sailing songs?" Rusty shouted over the music. They both shook their heads. "Listen!" The crowd of sailors waited a few beats, then burst out into song.

"O, the sea's a kinder maiden,
Than any girl back home...
Wherever prow should meet her,
She'll leave a trail of foam.

If yer lost in her waters,
Or sinkin' to your doom...
To find them other seamen,
Keep an eye out for her spume!"

There was a loud cheer, and the sailors raised their flasks in the air, chanting the next verse with abandon:

"If ever you be pining...
For what you had on land...
Just drown your mates in spirits,
They're sure to lend a hand.

An' lift your spirits up 'til,
Yer so merry you'll explode...
So cast away yer worries,
They'll gladly share the load!"

There was another cheer, followed by laughter. Kyle grinned at Ariana, and she smiled back. The sailors were having so much fun it was impossible *not* to smile. Even Slim was back on his feet, joining the singing with abandon. The song went on for an impressive number of verses, until at last it ended, and everyone took a hearty swig from their flasks. Kyle gazed at the sailors, realizing that all of them – to a man – were horribly drunk. He felt Ariana tug at his hand, and he turned to her. She smiled at him, gesturing for him to follow her. He allowed himself to be led away from the crowd, back toward the cabin at the other end of the *Defiance*. The music and cheering faded away as they walked, until it was barely audible over the crashing waves all around them.

Ariana turned, leading him to the side of the ship. She stopped before the railing at the edge, staring down at the inky waves below. "It's beautiful, isn't it?" she murmured. She stood there for a long moment, then smiled. "I've never been on a boat before this."

"Really?"

"Really," Ariana replied. "My parents took me to Stridon once, when I was younger. I wanted to see the ocean, but we spent too much time seeing the sights downtown, and in the Tower." She sighed. "I never got to see it with them."

Kyle heard the sound of men singing in the distance, the music starting anew. He found himself staring at Ariana, her eyes hauntingly dark against her pale skin, her black pixie hair rippling in the wind. He had the sudden mad urge to kiss her, and he leaned in and did just that, kissing her cheek. She turned in surprise, staring at him for a long moment. Then she grabbed his ears oh-so-gently, pulling him in and kissing him right on the lips. Kyle felt a strange tingling sensation all over his body, and barely realized when she pulled away. She leaned her head on his shoulder then, staring at the waves for a long time, then lifting her eyes to the stars above. They were positively splendid, unlike anything Kyle had ever seen on Earth. Thousands of stars shining brighter than the north star, their silvery light reflecting off of the churning waves below.

Kyle stared at that awesome vista, feeling the cool breeze in his hair, and Ariana's hair tickling his neck. The deck shifted gently and rhythmically under his feet, the sounds of laughter and singing in the air. He smiled, closing his eyes, enjoying every bit of it.

This night, this moment...it was perfect.

Chapter 17

Kyle groaned, feeling a hand grab his shoulder and shake it. He pushed the hand away, rolling onto his side and pulling the blankets over his head. The hand returned, shaking him again.

"Kyle!" a voice hissed in his ear.

"Go away," he mumbled. The hand shook him again, harder this time.

"Kyle, wake up!"

He sighed, rolling onto his back and rubbing the sleep out of his eyes. Then he lowered his hands, seeing Ariana staring down at him. She looked worried.

"What's wrong?" he asked.

"I heard something," she answered. Kyle sat up, and Ariana sat down on the edge of the bed beside him. "Something beyond the ship."

"What was it?"

"I don't know," she admitted. "But a little while later, I heard someone shouting up on deck." She stared at their bedroom door, which was closed and locked. "I wanted to check it out, but I didn't want to leave you here."

"I'll go with you," he mumbled, hardly looking forward to the prospect of leaving his warm, comfy bed. Ariana reached down and grabbed his boots for him. He sighed, throwing off his covers and slipping on his gravity boots. Then he walked to the door. He opened it, peering out into the hallway beyond. It was deserted.

"Let's go upstairs, to the deck," Ariana proposed. Kyle nodded, and they left the room, walking down the corridor. They'd made it halfway across when Ariana stopped suddenly, staring off into space.

"What?" Kyle asked.

Ariana threw herself at him, shoving him sideways. His fell onto his back on the wooden floor below, Ariana landing on top of him. She pressed him firmly downward, covering his body with her own.

"What the..." he gasped.

The leftmost wall of the hallway exploded with a deafening *boom*, wooden shrapnel flying in all directions. Kyle threw his arms in front of his face just in time, his forearms stinging as pieces of wood struck them. Moments later, he felt an icy wetness rush up his back, so incredibly cold that it took his breath away.

"Kyle!" Ariana yelled, her eyes wide with horror. Kyle lowered his arms, his jaw going slack. A massive hole had been ripped into the left wall of the hallway, ice-cold water gushing in. The water was forming a rapidly growing pool on the floor, soaking through their clothes. Kyle pushed himself off of the floor, wincing at a sharp pain in his left forearm. He looked down, seeing a few sharp slivers of wood sticking through his bloodied skin.

"Kyle, are you hurt?" Ariana asked.

"I'm fine," he replied. The doors lining the hallway opened, men dashing out of their rooms barely clothed.

"Everyone on deck!" one of the men shouted. The men made a mad dash for the stairwell at the far end of the corridor, their feet splashing in the steadily rising water covering the floor. One of them slammed into Kyle's shoulder as they ran past, nearly knocking him over. Ariana pulled him away from the wreckage, but he resisted.

"We've got to get out of here!" she urged.

"The map!" he countered, pointing back to their room...or what remained of it. The door had been taken right off of its hinges, the door frame around it shattered. The last of the men ran up the stairwell, leaving the hallway empty. Kyle walked up to the shattered doorway, but when he looked through the door frame, he saw that

227

the floor had been almost entirely demolished by whatever had struck it. Only a deep hole remained, lined by the jagged ends of broken floorboards.

"Stay here," Kyle ordered, making sure no one was around to see him, then activating his gravity boots and levitating a foot off of the ground. He streamed magic into his boots then, flying through the shattered doorway into the room. He hovered over the gaping hole in the floor, spotting a backpack hanging by its strap on one of the hooks nailed to the wall. He grabbed it, searching for the second backpack...but it was nowhere to be seen. He flew back to Ariana, handing the backpack to her. There was another *boom*, and the entire ship seemed to shudder. He heard someone yelling in the distance, and barely had time to cut his magic stream to his boots and their gravity shields before whoever it was could see him using magic. The icy water below lapped at his ankles, chilling him to the bone.

"Come on!" a voice shouted. Kyle spun about, seeing Rusty running toward them. The heavyset sailor pointed to the door at the far end of the hallway, where everyone else had gone. "Go, go!"

"What's going on?" Kyle asked. He followed Rusty's advice, his boots kicking up freezing seawater onto his pants. Ariana was right beside him, her bare feet cutting through the water with ease.

"Don't talk, *move!*" Rusty yelled, pushing them both forward. The man's face was beet red, his eyes bloodshot from the night before. Without warning, a rapid-fire volley of explosions rocked the ship, the very walls vibrating with the violence of it. The ship lurched to the left, and Kyle slid leftward, slamming his shoulder into the wall. Then the ship tilted to the right, and he fell away from the wall, landing on his right side in the bone-chilling water. The shock of it took his breath away, and he found himself swallowing reflexively as his face dipped into the icy seawater. He pushed himself quickly to his feet, seeing Rusty scrambling to do the same behind him. Only Ariana remained on her feet, and she lifted Rusty from the floor with one hand.

Suddenly the wall behind them exploded, debris flying in all directions. Kyle turned his face away just in time, something sharp striking the back of his head, knocking him forward. He landed on his hands and knees, hearing a horrid cracking sound behind him. He turned about, seeing a new hole in the ship. The hallway steadily tilted to the right, throwing them all into the rightmost wall.

"Go go go!" Rusty screamed. The man was huddled against the wall, clutching his chest with one hand. Blood trickled from between his fingers, forming dark red trails down his forearm. He waved them away with his other hand. "Save yourselves!"

"Come on!" Ariana cried, grabbing Rusty under the shoulder and hauling him up onto his feet. Rusty's face turned pale, and his eyes rolled up into the back of his head. He slumped forward, and would have landed on his face in the water if Ariana hadn't caught him. She stared at Rusty, then looked up at Kyle. "We have to get him out of here," she yelled over the sound of gushing water.

"Carry him!" Kyle yelled back, gesturing for her to follow him. She slung Rusty over one shoulder, then trudged forward, following Kyle down the hallway toward the stairwell. Another volley of ear-splitting *booms* wracked the ship, and again the hallway tilted crazily to the left. Kyle was thrown into the wall again, grunting as his already tender shoulder slammed into the wood. The hallway tilted the other way, and he stumbled to the right, tripping over his own feet and landing face-first into the frigid water. His entire body went rigid, his throat spasming shut as his face entered the water. He tried to push himself upward, but his arms were so weak and stiff that he couldn't. He grit his teeth, ignoring the bitter cold and the burning in his lungs, and heaved downward on the floor with his hands as hard as he could, his face rising up above the water.

Air!

He gulped air into his lungs greedily, then locked his elbows and slid his knees underneath him, kneeling there for a moment. He felt a cold hand grab his arm and lift him to his feet. It was Ariana!

"You okay?" she asked. Kyle nodded mutely, his teeth chattering uncontrollably, and he crossed his arms over his chest in a vain attempt to keep warm.

"Keep going," Ariana urged, now at his side. Even carrying Rusty, she was still moving much faster than he was. Kyle tried to keep up, but his legs felt so incredibly weak and slow, every step requiring enormous effort. He fell behind, his entire body shaking now.

"I can't," Kyle gasped, stumbling forward in the ever-rising water. It was nearly up to his knees now. He stopped, closing his eyes and hugging his arms to his chest. He grit his teeth, then pulled a strand of magic into his mind's eye, throwing it at his boots. He lifted up out of the water, hovering a foot above it.

"Kyle," Ariana warned, stopping and grabbing his arm. "They'll see you using magic!"

"Let them," Kyle retorted. He flew down the flooded corridor, gesturing for Ariana to follow. "Come on!"

With his gravity boots activated, Kyle passed Ariana, reaching the end of the hallway in seconds, passing through the doorway there to the stairwell beyond. He flew up it, finding the closed door at the top. He glanced back, seeing Ariana running up the stairs behind him, Rusty still draped over her shoulder. He cut off his magic stream, descending until his boots touched the floor. He felt the floorboards shudder as another *boom* sounded in the distance. He opened the door with difficulty, his hands slow and clumsy with the cold.

"Come on," he urged, waving Ariana through. She jogged up the stairs and went through the door, Kyle following behind. They ran down another long hallway, this one mercifully dry. There was something *off* about it, however; Kyle realized that the entire hallway was tilted a few degrees to the left.

An awful cracking sound echoed down the hallway, followed by muffled screams in the distance.

"Kyle," Ariana blurted out suddenly, tapping him on the shoulder. She lowered Rusty to the ground, putting a hand on his chest.

"What?"

"I can't hear his heart," Ariana replied, her voice rising in panic. "It's not beating, Kyle!" Kyle felt a chill run through him, and dropped to his hands and knees at Rusty's side, putting two fingers to his neck like his parents had taught him. He held them there for a long moment.

No pulse.

Kyle clasped his hands together over Rusty's chest, locking his elbows and shoving downward. He pumped hard and fast, feeling something pop under his palms as he did so.

"Kyle, what are you doing?"

"CPR," Kyle replied. He continued the chest compressions, feeling his own heart hammering in his chest. He remembered what his parents – both of them emergency doctors – had taught him.

Nine, ten, eleven, twelve...

Sweat began beading up on his forehead, dripping down over his eyebrows and into his eyes.

Twenty-eight, twenty-nine...thirty!

He scrambled to Rusty's head, leaning over and tilting the man's chin back. He hesitated for a split second, then leaned in, placing his mouth over Rusty's, ignoring his instinctive revulsion. He gave two breaths.

"What do I do?" Ariana asked. Kyle resumed chest compressions, pointing to Rusty's mouth.

"When I count to thirty, give him two more breaths," Kyle instructed. Ariana made a face. "Just do it," Kyle urged. "Eleven, twelve, thirteen..." His arms were already starting to burn, and he realized he was bending his elbows, using his arms. He locked them again, focusing on bending at the waist like his parents had taught him. "Twenty-nine...thirty. Go!"

Ariana did as she was instructed, giving Rusty two breaths. Then Kyle continued CPR. His hands slipped on Rusty's chest, and Kyle nearly fell over. His hands were slick with dark red blood; he wiped them on Rusty's pants, then continued compressions.

"Ten, eleven, twelve..."

"Kyle," Ariana called out.

"Sixteen, seventeen..."

"Kyle!" Ariana nearly shouted. Kyle turned to look at Ariana, and saw her shaking her head. "He's not coming back."

"You don't understand," Kyle retorted. "We can save him!" He closed his eyes, continuing counting his compressions, ignoring the sweat pouring from him. He felt Ariana's hand on his shoulder.

"Kyle, look."

He opened his eyes, following Ariana's finger to Rusty's chest. A pool of blood had formed there, immersing Kyle's hands all the way to the wrists. He jerked his hands up from Rusty's chest, staring at his soaked fingers, then at Rusty. The man was as pale as Ariana, his eyes staring lifelessly upward, his mouth slightly open.

He was dead.

Kyle staggered to his feet, holding his hands in front of him. He felt awfully lightheaded suddenly, and his legs buckled underneath him. He felt cool arms catch him from behind, then lower him slowly to the floor.

"Kyle?"

"I'm fine," he assured her, still feeling woozy. "Just...give me a minute." He stared at Rusty, swallowing past a lump in his throat.

If I'd just used magic earlier, he thought, *he'd still be alive.*

"Kyle," Ariana urged, shaking his shoulder. Kyle said nothing, looking down at his own bloodied hands.

Rusty was dead because of *him.*

The floor below him shuddered, the sounds of men shouting coming from beyond the door at the end of the hallway.

"We need to get going," Ariana urged, grabbing Kyle's arm and hauling him upward. Kyle got his legs under him, and rose shakily to his feet. "Come on," she said, pulling him forward. Kyle turned to look down at Rusty one more time. He expected to feel sad, but he only felt exhausted...numb. He turned away from the man, following Ariana's lead. They reached the door at the end, and Ariana threw it open, sprinting through. Kyle ran after her as fast as his wobbly legs could take him, and found himself outside under the inky black night sky, on the massive deck of the *Defiance.* Dozens of men were on deck, running frantically toward the left side of the ship...toward the cannons. Kyle spotted the Captain standing on deck, behind the men at the cannons.

"Run the powder boys ragged!" the Captain barked. "I want grape shot on their damn quarterdeck!" He raised his hand in the air. "On my signal, carronade on their hull!" He paused, letting the ship sway for a moment, then lowered his arm sharply. *"Fire!"*

The men at one cannon – the largest and shortest – pulled a rope, and the cannon fired with an ear-shattering explosion, the deck vibrating powerfully under Kyle's feet. The entire left side of the ship rose as the deck tilted, and Kyle caught himself before he stumbled backward. He focused beyond the cannons, at the roiling ocean. Then he eyes widened, his jaw dropping open.

There was a ship there in the distance, flanking the *Defiance*. Its huge black sails fluttered in the howling wind, cannons lining its side in a single row. As he watched, those cannons flashed.

Bam-bam-bam-bam!

"Brace!" the Captain screamed, dropping to the deck. There was a high-pitched whistling sound; it got louder and louder, until it seemed like it was right on top of them. Suddenly the deck exploded around Kyle, debris flying up into the air. He felt himself flying backward, felt his back strike something hard, the air blasting out of his lungs. A sharp pain lanced through his ears, and he howled in pain, curling his knees to his chest and covering his ears with his hands. Thick black smoke rose all around him, and he sucked air into his lungs, choking on the thick, oily fumes. He coughed uncontrollably, his eyes burning and thick with tears. He groaned, rolling onto his hands and knees, then staggered to his feet.

A shadowy form limped through the thick smoke toward Kyle, and he took a step back until he realized it was a sailor. The man looked dazed, his left ear torn clean off, blood spilling down the side of his neck. Kyle turned around, and saw another man standing perfectly still, staring dumbly at his right arm...or what was left of it. His hand had been amputated, his wrist reduced to tattered, bloody flesh.

Kyle spun about in a slow circle, feeling numb with shock. Everywhere he looked, there was carnage.

"Kyle!"

He turned around, seeing another shadow moving quickly toward him. The smoke parted, revealing a familiar pale face.

"Ariana!" he cried.

She ran up to Kyle, grabbing him by the shoulders, her eyes wide with fear. Kyle stared past her, at the shattered deck of the *Defiance*.

The polished wooden planks had shattered, leaving huge, gaping holes with blackened, flaming edges across the entire mid-deck. As the smoke began to clear, Kyle spotted the Captain rising to his feet, barking orders and gesturing wildly. A few men rose to their feet around him, sprinting to the cannons and pushing aside their dead and dying crew-mates to man them.

And in the distance, at the front-most mast of the *Defiance*, the sails were on fire.

"Kyle, we have to get out of here!" Ariana yelled.

Kyle heard another round of cannon-fire, and again that high-pitched whistling sound. Ariana shouted, throwing herself at him, and they fell to the deck. Kyle smashed his head against the hard wood, stars exploding in his eyes. He fought back the immediate urge to vomit, gritting his teeth against the bitter bile surging up into his mouth.

Another explosion rocked the ship, shards of wood and metal flying past them. Kyle *pulled* magic into his mind's eye, weaving rapidly. A shimmering blue aura appeared around them, debris ricocheting off of it. Men screamed in the distance.

"Foremast down!" came a panicked shout.

There was a terrible cracking sound, and Kyle glanced upward, spotting the mast at the front of the ship. The base of it had shattered, the remaining massive wooden beam slowly falling backward toward them. Kyle pushed Ariana off of him frantically, then scrambled to his feet.

"Run!" he screamed.

He grabbed her by the arm, yanking her out of the path of the falling beam. The mast descended toward them, its massive sails rippling sinuously in the wind, the thick white fabric engulfed in flames. Its cross-beams crashed into the next mast, snapping it in half. Kyle felt Ariana take over, grabbing him around the waist and leaping through the air. The foremast barely missed them, clipping the edge of his gravity shield. The shield shoved back against the foremast, catapulting them forward. They fell to the deck, hovering a foot above it. The flaming sails and rigging descended in slow-

234

motion all around them, draping over the shield and leaving them in near-darkness.

The heat from the burning sails was immediate and intense, and Ariana's shard reacted immediately, snuffing out the inferno and cooling the air within the gravity shield. She pushed herself off of him, nullifying his shield and grabbing the charred fabric with both hands, then pulling outward. The sinews in her neck and arms strained, and there was a loud ripping sound as the thick fabric tore. Light spilled in from the widening hole, and Ariana stood up, lending Kyle a hand. He grasped it, hauling himself up onto his feet.

"We have to get out of here," Ariana shouted. Kyle shook his head.

"Look," he yelled, pointing at the huge sail, a third of it now engulfed in flames. Its surface rippled and bulged in a dozen places, with muffled screams coming from the sections that were burning. "They're burning alive!"

"We need to save ourselves," Ariana protested.

"No," Kyle insisted.

"Kyle, our mission..."

"I let Rusty die," Kyle interrupted, his tone sharp. "I could have protected him. I won't let these people die too." He turned back to the burning sail. "I'm going to get that sail off them." The *boom* of the *Defiance's* cannons rippled through the air, and the ship lurched to the right.

"Fine," Ariana replied. "Make water and drop it on them." Kyle shook his head.

"It'll take too long." He dropped through the hole in the sail, crawling underneath until he was completely covered. Then he stood, pushing the heavy fabric up with his hands.

"What are you doing?" he heard Ariana ask. He ignored her, weaving magic in his mind's eye, creating a gravity shield around himself. Then he paused, taking a deep breath in; he let it out slowly, then streamed magic to his boots.

Suddenly he felt himself burst upward, the sail tenting over his gravity shield as he rose through the air. He streamed even more magic to his boots, his gut dropping as he accelerated upward, taking the sail with him. He glanced down past his feet, seeing the huge sail hanging down all around him, the rigging attaching the sail to the fallen mast's crossbeam uncoiling rapidly on the deck. He decreased the magic stream just as the rigging and sail went taught, right before he was jerked to a halt. The sudden, crushing deceleration took the breath right out of his lungs, and he gasped for air, stars floating in the periphery of his vision. He grit his teeth, ignoring the burning in his chest, and stared down at the now-taught rigging bolted to the cross-beams below.

He had to get the sail free from the mast, or it would just fall back down on the crew below...

Kyle took a deep breath in, then shoved as much magic into his gravity boots as he could. The sail and rigging strained below him, the cross-beams far below starting to bend under the steadily increasing tension, arcing upward from the deck. He *pulled* as much magic into his mind as he could, throwing it at his boots. The cross-beams creaked, arcing even higher, until they snapped off of the fallen mast. He burst upward in the air with gut-wrenching speed, his guts dropping to his feet as he hurtled through space. The burning sail and dangling rigging came with him, soaring high above the *Defiance's* remaining sails.

Kyle cut back sharply on his magic stream, turning to the left and flying away from the *Defiance's* ruined deck. The dark blue waters of the ocean were below him now, barely visible in the darkness. He waited another few seconds, then stopped abruptly in mid-air, the fluttering sail and rigging continuing forward past him like a giant flying jellyfish.

As he watched, the sail flew forward and downward, black smoke rising from the still-burning fabric. Still it fell, until it crashed into the ocean, the flames snuffed out in a burst of steam.

He turned to the *Defiance*, watching as the sailors who'd been trapped underneath the burning sail rolled on the deck to snuff out the fire licking at their clothes. Watched as they all stood up, their eyes on the sail floating in the ocean. As they raised their eyes to the heavens, looking at *him*.

Kyle flew back over the *Defiance*, descending slowly through the air toward the deck below. He dropped down right next to Ariana, his black gravity boots striking the deck with a dull thud. The Captain, his fine red uniform smudged with dirt and soot, walked up to them, his expression incredulous.

"The hell?" the Captain blurted out.

Kyle turned to the man, eyeing the pistol at his waist, and pushed a little more magic into his gravity shield.

"You're a damn Weaver?" the Captain exclaimed. Kyle hesitated, then nodded. "How did..." the Captain began, but he stopped himself, turning to his flabbergasted crew. "Quit gawking and get to the cannons!" he barked, grabbing one of the sailors by the collar and yanking him toward one of the unmanned cannons. "Tell the pilot to give me a hard starboard," the Captain ordered, sending another sailor toward the bridge. "We run or we die!"

The *Defiance* slowly turned right, angling away from the warship, which also began turning right, trailing behind them. Its port cannon – at the front of the warship – fired, sending a cannonball upward and outward. Kyle backpedaled, watching as the huge iron ball arced in the air toward them.

"Brace!" the Captain yelled.

The sailors dropped to the deck, but the cannonball overshot the *Defiance* entirely, splashing in the ocean beyond. The Captain pointed toward the back of his ship.

"Get to the stern chaser!" he barked. "Slow them down!" He turned to Kyle then. "You lied to me," he accused.

"He saved your men," Ariana countered angrily. "You should be thanking him!"

"I was about to," the Captain retorted, eyeing her suspiciously. "I suppose you're a Weaver as well?" Ariana paused, then nodded. The Captain sighed. "So your whole story was a fabrication." Another nod.

"The warship is gaining on us fast, Cap'n," a sailor warned, pointing to the rear of the ship. The Captain turned to look, then swore.

"We'll never outrun a Quadra-class warship without full sails!"

237

"We can help," Kyle declared. "Ariana, if we could make a big enough flat gravity field, we could pull air into that sail," he added, pointing to the one intact mast. Wind that passed through the gravity field would be shoved into the sail, making the ship retreat much more quickly. But Ariana shook her head.

"We have to take out that warship first," she countered. The Captain snorted.

"That's a Quadra-class warship with a crew of two hundred armed men," he retorted. "I don't care if you're a Weaver," he added. "I guarantee you they have a Neutralizer just like I do."

"A what?" Kyle asked.

"A Neutralizer," the Captain repeated. He reached into his pocket, retrieving a silver amulet. In the center was a small white crystal. "It'll drain the magic out of you."

"*That's* why you said magic wouldn't work around you," Kyle realized. The gemstone looked like a Void crystal. The Captain smiled grimly.

"It takes a while to reset after each use," he explained. "But one use is all it'll take." He shook his head. "You won't stand a chance."

Ariana wavered, glancing at Kyle. He knew what she was thinking; without magic, she would be useless. The Neutralizer would incapacitate her...but it might not work as well against him. When it came to making magic, no one could beat him.

"We'll see about that," Kyle replied, nodding at Ariana. "I'll top you off," he said, streaming magic to her shard. When he was done, he turned to the warship in the distance. "I'll fly us to the ship," he decided. "Stay close to me. If they use the Neutralizer, I'll revive you."

"Got it," Ariana replied. Kyle turned to the Captain.

"I'll be back," he promised. The Captain snorted.

"No you won't," he countered. "But thank you."

Kyle nodded back, then turned to Ariana.

"Get on my back," he ordered. She complied, and he streamed magic to his gravity boots, rising above the deck of the *Defiance*. The Captain stared up at them.

"You're both dead," he grumbled. Ariana smirked.

"You're right, I am," she replied. "But so are they."

* * *

Kyle streamed magic to his gravity boots, feeling Ariana's arms tighten around his chest as he rose up into the air, Ariana on his back. The deck of the *Defiance* shrank below his boots, the open ocean rippling all around the ship.

"Ready?" Kyle asked. He felt Ariana give him a squeeze.

"Ready."

He took a deep breath in, then flew toward the warship in the distance, taking a curved path toward the enemy ship. He felt a subtle vibration, and saw a gravity shield appear around them. He pushed more magic at his boots, picking up speed quickly, the ocean flying by a few dozen feet below. He aimed toward the back of the warship, scanning it carefully. Sailors swarmed to-and-fro across the huge deck, cannons flashing as they fired at the *Defiance*.

"They've spotted us," Ariana warned. She was right; Kyle spotted a few sailors pointing up in their direction, gesticulating wildly. "They've got guns," Ariana added. Muzzles flashed, the *pop, pop* of gunfire reaching Kyle's ears moments later. He dodged to the side, aiming for the rear deck of the ship, where there was cover behind a two-story structure and no sailors. He took a sudden, deep descent toward it, decelerating rapidly, and landed on the deck, Ariana dropping down from his back.

"Shield yourself," Ariana stated, her gravity shield vanishing. "I'm not sure what my crystal is going to do when they start attacking."

"Got it," Kyle replied. He wove quickly, a gravity shield appearing around him. "We need to overpower them as quickly as possible," he added. "Before they can use that Neutralizer."

"Right," Ariana agreed.

"Stay close to me just in case they do use it," Kyle stated. Ariana nodded.

"On my count," she stated. "One, two...three!"

Ariana ran in front of Kyle, turning the corner around the two-story structure and sprinting toward the front of the ship. Kyle ran after her, increasing the magic stream to his shields. A sailor spotted them, shouting something Kyle couldn't make out. More sailors ran toward them, rifles in hand.

And Ariana sprinted right at them.

She moved with unnatural speed, ignoring the volley of gunfire as the enemy sailors took aim and fired at them. She leaped at the closest sailor, grabbing him and tossing him to the side, right off the edge of the ship.

Another sailor shot at Ariana, almost point-blank, and gravity shields sprang to life around her, the bullet ricocheting off harmlessly. She rammed him, and he bounced off of her gravity shields, flying through the air and slamming into a mast.

"Get her!"

Another sailor shot at Ariana, and she ran up to him, grabbing his rifle and snapping it in two, then whipping the butt of the rifle across his temple. It collided with his skull in a spray of blood, and he fell to the ground, his limbs spasming, then going still.

Jesus!

Kyle heard bullets whiz by him, and swore again, ducking low and following behind Ariana. He wove magic, throwing it outward at a sailor; a flat gravity field appeared to one side of the man, sucking him into it. The sailor flew through the air, landing headfirst onto the deck. Kyle saw Ariana burst toward a group of nearby sailors, grabbing them one-by-one and flinging them over the edge of the boat.

Then Kyle saw blue light streaking from Ariana's body – and his own – converging toward a man behind a line of sailors toward the middle of the ship. A man holding a large white sphere.

"Ariana!" Kyle warned. "The Neutralizer!"

Ariana pivoted, sprinting toward the line of sailors, a ball of fire appearing before her. Kyle ran out from behind cover, sprinting after her, pouring magic into his gravity shield. Ariana's fireball shot outward at the line of sailors, and they dodged out of the way, leaving the man with the Neutralizer exposed. Ariana ran straight toward the man, blue light *pulling* from her.

And then she dropped to the deck like a rag doll, skidding across the wooden planks.

"Ariana!" Kyle cried, rushing toward her.

The sailors regrouped, rushing toward Ariana, aiming their rifles down at her motionless body. Kyle swore, weaving magic as he sprinted across the deck, sending a gravity field outward at the soldiers. Two of them were flung to the side, slamming into a mast and falling to the deck. The others trained their rifles on *him*, the muzzles flashing as they fired. Kyle ducked reflexively, hearing the bullets *whiz* by. But still he ran, only twenty feet from Ariana now.

Rays of blue light flowed from him, converging on the Neutralizer.

Kyle felt his magic draining, his magic stream to his gravity shields faltering. One of the sailors fired their rifle, and Kyle felt his right shoulder jerk backward. He nearly lost his balance, stumbling toward Ariana, nearly losing his magic stream to his shield completely.

Pain lanced through his shoulder, blood seeping from a hole in his shirt there.

Kyle grit his teeth, running up to Ariana's side. The sailors backpedaled, their rifles still trained on him. He knelt before her, *pulling* magic into his mind's eye.

Bam, bam bam!

The sailors fired, and Ariana's body jerked once, then again, holes appearing in her chest.

No!

Kyle wove frantically, creating another gravity shield around himself and Ariana, then let go of his own shield. He scooped her up into his arms, backing away from the sailors.

Bam!

Kyle felt something slam into his upper chest, and he lurched backward, the breath knocked out of him. He stumbled, barely keeping his balance, and stared down, seeing a bullet lying on the ground at his feet. It must have penetrated his gravity shield...slowing just enough not to kill him.

Jesus!

"Shoot them!" he heard the man with the Neutralizer cry. No more magic was flowing into it; it was expended its power...for now. The soldiers advanced, their muzzles firing in rapid succession. Kyle felt a stinging sensation in his thigh, then saw Ariana's head jerk to the side, a hole appearing in her left temple.

"Stop it!" Kyle shouted, backing away. Another gunshot echoed through the air, and he saw blood spray from his left shoulder. He stumbled, falling onto his back on the deck, Ariana landing on top of him. The sailors strode toward him, more quickly now, reloading their weapons.

"Kill those fucking Weavers!"

Kyle grit his teeth, pain shooting through both shoulders, his chest burning.

Bam!

Ariana's head jerked again, another hole appearing in her skull.

"Stop it!" Kyle yelled, clutching Ariana to his chest, covering her head with his hands. More shots fired, and he felt a sharp pain in his left hand, then his knee. "God *damn* it!" he swore, feeling anger rise up within his breast.

Still the sailors advanced, reloading quickly. One of them fired, Ariana's body jerking again as another bullet struck her in the back. Kyle clenched his jaw so hard his teeth nearly cracked.

"I said *STOP!*"

He *tore* magic from his skull, a thick cord of power appearing in his mind's eye. His head exploded in pain, his vision blackening. He screamed, wrapping the cords into a massive, pulsing knot, and threw it outward, thrusting a torrent of magic at it.

An enormous dome of blinding blue light appeared all around him, covering nearly half of the width of the warship. The sailors flew backward instantly, the air sucking outward in all directions, blasting everyone on board the ship. All sound stopped as the air was sucked out of the dome.

And then the dome vanished.

Air sucked back into the void instantly, a shockwave slamming into the ship. The mast in front of Kyle *exploded*, the deck all around him rippling like the surface of the ocean. Then the deck shattered, pieces of wood flying upward all around him. A muffled *boom* struck his ears, and even through his gravity shield the sound was deafening. Sailors flew high into the air, bodies flinging dozens of feet upward and outward, falling toward the ocean beyond the ship. The ships cannons blew clean off the ship, a few of them exploding in a rain of shrapnel.

And then, in a matter of seconds, it was over.

Kyle's vision slowly cleared, and he looked around him, his jaw dropping.

The ship was *decimated*.

He and Ariana were laying on a small island of intact deck, a crater four stories deep and over fifty feet wide surrounding them. The warship's main mast had blown right off, the two-story structure at the back of the ship in ruins. Not a single sailor remained on deck.

Not alive, anyway.

Kyle laid there, his ears ringing, staring at the devastation. Then he lowered his gaze to Ariana, at her bullet-riddled body. He streamed magic to her forehead, seeing her limbs jerk as he did so, her eyes fluttering open. As he watched, her wounds began to close, hunks of metal pushing out of her skull and landing on the deck with a *clink*.

She blinked, then pushed herself off of him, rising to her feet. She turned in a slow circle, her mouth forming a perfect "O."

"Did I do that, she asked, "...or did you do that?"

"I did that," Kyle replied. She turned to him, staring at him in disbelief.

"How?" she pressed. Kyle smiled grimly, putting pressure on the shallow wound on his right shoulder.

"They pissed me off."

Ariana stared at him for a moment longer, then gazed at the ruins of the warship, shaking her head in disbelief.

"Holy shit, Kyle."

"Yeah," he muttered, pushing himself to his feet. Ariana turned to him again.

"Remind me not to get you mad."

"Don't get me mad," he stated.

She gazed at the massive crater surrounding them, at the shattered masts. At the dismembered remains of sailors strewn across the deck, and in the shattered rooms exposed in the crater below.

"I won't," she replied.

Chapter 18

Sabin sighed inwardly as he broke away from his Chosen's mind, feeling a familiar bitterness come over him. It always amazed him how powerful negative memories were, how they maintained their hold over him. Two thousand years, and the shame he felt was no less vivid, no less painful. Long after his good memories had faded, the bad ones lived on.

It was no wonder that he had been shaped by them, these singular, tragic moments in his past. They, more than anything else, had made him who he was today.

He paused, then reached out to the Chosen again, searching for yet another memory. He found it easily, having visited it innumerable times...whenever he wavered in his resolve, or found himself doubting the importance of his grand plan.

The most painful memories were often the most valuable.

* * *

Sabin folds his arms over his chest, staring at the polished surface of Grand Runic Nespo's desk. Nespo, a tall, muscular man with jet-black hair, is a man he'd only spoken to in private a handful of times. The last time was to congratulate Sabin on his appointment as Elder Runic. At fifty, Nespo is one of the youngest Grand Runics in recent history. He looks considerably younger, with a rugged handsomeness that could be winsome or intimidating depending on his mood. Right now, it is the former.

"I understand your concerns," Nespo states at last, leaning back in his chair. "Really, I do."

"Do you?" Sabin counters, looking up from the table. He tries to keep his voice calm. "Four hundred thousand natives, Nespo. Working those mines sixteen hours a day, every day. Have you *seen* the working conditions there?"

"I have."

"They're starving!" Sabin exclaims. "Living in their own filth, dying of easily preventable infections."

"There is no modernized sewer system..." Nespo began.

"They're slaves, Nespo!" Sabin interrupts. "They're worse than slaves. They're..." He pauses, unable to think of the right word. "They're *shit*. Expendable. Worthless." He shakes his head. "We're the *Empire*, Nero. We stand for freedom, justice...the sanctity of human life." Sabin pauses, remembering the other mines he'd visited, after he'd recovered from the first. He'd spent a week exposing himself to the realities of those mines, and the concentration camps. Systematic enslavement and torture, all in the name of the glorious Empire.

It had been the single worst experience of his life.

"Sabin..."

"How can we dare to take other countries to task for their human rights violations when we commit crimes far worse than they?"

"Sabin, *please*," Nespo insists. "Give me a chance to explain." Sabin bites his tongue, then nods. Nespo sighs, leaning back in his chair and steepling his hands.

"The conditions at the mines are deplorable," he agrees. "I cannot condone them personally. But the mines are not ours, and the miners are not under our jurisdiction."

"What do you mean?"

"The Orjanian mines are owned by private companies," Nespo explains. Companies created and maintained in Orja, by citizens of Verhan, not the Empire."

"What?" Sabin asks, taken aback. "Every soldier I saw was wearing Imperial armor. Speaking Imperial Standard."

"All employees of the mining companies," Nespo continues, "...are required to forfeit their citizenship to the Empire as a term of employment. Therefore we have no jurisdiction over them, and they are not bound by our laws."

"That's ludicrous!"

"It is the law," Nespo counters calmly. "The mining companies therefore are subject to the laws of Verhan."

"Verhan has no government," Sabin protests. "It was wiped out by the plague." Nespo shrugs.

"And that," he replies, "...is why everything they are doing – no matter how unseemly it is to you or I – is perfectly legal."

"It can't be," Sabin retorts. "Verhan and the entire eastern seaboard are colonies of the Empire," he exclaims. "They're not a foreign power at all."

"They *were* our colonies," Nespo counters. "The Council – and my predecessor – voted to revoke colonial status."

"So that we could keep our hands clean," Sabin deduces. "...while our diamond industry benefits from rock-bottom trade prices with Orja." He shakes his head at Nespo, dumbstruck. Nespo merely nods.

"That was the strategy, yes."

"And you're okay with that?" Sabin asks incredulously. Nespo shrugs.

"I am merely continuing a lawful, established trade relationship with a very generous and strategically necessary foreign power," he replies. "A relationship agreed upon by the Council, my predecessor, and the Grand Weaver."

Sabin stares at Nespo, speechless. Nespo stands from his chair, walking to the large window in his office, offering an impressive view of the cityscape beyond the Secula Magna's verdant campus.

"Do you realize what this has made possible?" he asks. He gestures at the window. "The hovercars that carry you around the city? The hovership you flied in? Renval's floating islands?" He shook his head. "We never would have been able to make these advancements without that trade relationship."

"At what price?" Sabin counters. "Nespo, there are *children* working and dying at those mines!"

"Our military *depends* on trade with Orja," Nespo continues, unfazed. "Do you think our enemies have any qualms about doing whatever they can to gain an advantage over us?" He spreads his arms out wide. "If we hadn't stepped in, someone else would have...and that would have endangered the Empire."

"So it's okay because someone else would have done it?" Sabin asks incredulously. "That's your justification?"

"I don't blame you for your naivete," Nespo replies, walking back to his chair and sitting down. "You're just an academic, after all. You've never had a chance to understand the harsh realities of the world."

Sabin stares at Nespo as if he's been slapped across the face.

"You haven't traveled the world, you haven't seen how very common this sort of thing is," Nespo continues. "I can tell you that nearly every government does it. Those that don't cannot survive." He shakes his head. "We insulate the citizens of the Empire from these realities. They are privileged to never know of them, but I can tell you they enjoy the fruits of these operations every day."

"It isn't right," Sabin insists.

"I understand how you feel," Nespo insists. "Really, I do. It's common to feel this way when you first learn the truth...when the veil of innocence is lifted. The world is a cruel, dark place, Sabin. Our citizens have the best standard of living in the world, and for that we should be grateful." He smiled. "That is a true accomplishment, one you should be proud of."

"Not when we pay for it with our souls!"

"Nevertheless," Nespo states calmly, "The operations are lawful, trade with Orja is necessary to our survival, and it will continue as is

248

for the time being." He sighs. "I hope that conditions at the mines will improve, but that isn't up to us."

"It *is* up to us," Sabin retorts. "Demand change. Threaten to stop trade unless conditions improve."

"That's an idea," Nespo replies noncommittally. "I'll bring it up during the next Council meeting."

"You're patronizing me," Sabin accuses. Nespo sighs.

"Sabin, what do you want me to say?"

"I want you to publicly denounce the working conditions in Orja," Sabin replies. "I want you to enact legislation that forces those companies to treat the natives like goddamn human beings!"

"The Council will not accept that."

"I don't believe it," Sabin retorted. "I *can't* believe that."

"Sabin, this situation has become far more complicated than you seem to understand," Nespo stated earnestly. "Remember that the natives murder our...former citizens every day. They associate those companies with the Empire-"

"Can't imagine why," Sabin interjects sarcastically. Nero's eyes harden.

"You're proposing giving freedom and power to people that want us dead," he states, his voice suddenly too calm.

"They'll never stop wanting us dead until we treat them like human beings!"

Nespo stares at Sabin for a long moment, then leans back in his chair, folding his arms across his chest.

"All right," he replies. "Thank you for your suggestions. Is there anything else you wanted to discuss?"

Sabin stares at Nespo incredulously, realizing he's just been dismissed. He says nothing for a long moment, feeling an impotent rage building within him. He suddenly wants to hurt Nespo, to wipe that smug look right off of the bastard's face.

"So everyone on the Council knows the truth about Orja," he states.

"Correct."

"Even Ampir?" Sabin presses. Ampir is still the newest Councilman, mere weeks into his appointment. But already he holds tremendous influence, by virtue not only of his formidable power, but also the fact that he rarely speaks. When he does, everyone listens. Nespo regards Sabin silently for a few seconds, his expression unreadable.

"Ampir is...young," he answers. "Idealistic. He still sees things in black and white, not shades of gray." He shook his head. "He's not ready for these...unfortunate realities."

"You mean he's not corrupt enough yet," Sabin retorts. Nespo's jawline ripples, and his voice goes cold.

"Regardless of your opinion – or mine, for that matter – the Orjanian operations are classified," he warns. "Ampir does not yet have the clearance to view them, and you do not have the authority to inform him."

"How convenient."

"Ampir is an anomaly," Nespo continues, drumming his fingers on the desktop. "As it is, he's the Empire's single greatest asset...an assurance of continued national security." He turns to stare out of the window, at the cityscape in the distance. "But it's unsafe to have so much power concentrated in one person," he muses. "If Ampir were to decide that he no longer supported the Empire, he would represent a grave threat – the greatest single threat – to our nation." Nespo turns back to Sabin. "I can't let that happen."

"If he knew, he wouldn't attack the Empire," Sabin counters. "He'd force you to stop selling our souls for profit."

"As I said, that information is classified," Nespo replies. "If you said anything to him – or anyone else for that matter – I would have no choice but to charge you with treason."

Sabin stands up then, placing his palms on Nespo's desk and leaning forward to stare him right in the eye. He gives the Grand Runic a tight smile.

"I would consider that," he replies, "...the greatest accomplishment of my life."

* * *

250

Kyle and Ariana landed on the deck of the *Defiance*, a few feet from where the Captain stood. In the distance, the warship stood dead in the water, debris floating in the ocean all around it. Ariana separated from Kyle, and they faced the Captain, who was staring at them in disbelief.

"You don't have to worry about that warship anymore," Kyle stated. He rubbed his chest, the bruise there still smarting. Luckily the bullets that had struck his shoulders had only grazed them.

"I see that," the Captain replied, glancing at the ruined warship. "I can't believe it, but I see it."

"We're safe now," Ariana declared, smiling at the Captain. But the Captain shook his head.

"I'm afraid not," he countered grimly. "With two masts down, we're dead in the water."

Kyle looked up at the remaining mast. The lower portions of the sails were badly burnt, but the rest of them were whole.

"I can push wind into those sails," he offered, pointing to the three sails on the rear mast.

"That may be," the Captain conceded. "But it won't do any good when we're sinking to the bottom of the ocean." He sighed heavily. "There aren't enough lifeboats for all of my men," he added. "And most of them can't swim."

"I can give your men gravity shields," Kyle suggested, feeling the dozen quartz cubes in his pockets...the ones he'd gotten from Master Lee. He retrieved one, quickly inscribing the gravity shield pattern into it. "Take this," he said, handing the cube to the Captain.

"What good will that do?" the Captain asked. "We're not under attack anymore."

"Give them to the men that can't swim," Kyle replied. "They'll float on the water until we find a way to rescue them."

The Captain nodded, taking the cube and placing it in the breast pocket of his uniform. Kyle streamed magic to the cube until it was full, and immediately a blue gravity shield appeared around him.

"How many of those do you have?" the Captain asked.

"About a dozen."

"Give them to Grotes," he ordered. "He'll redistribute them." Kyle nodded, sprinting across the deck to the scowling First Mate. He inscribed another cube, handing it to the man.

"Take this," Kyle instructed. The brawny man frowned at the cube.

"What the hell is this?"

"It'll put gravity shields around your men that can't swim," Kyle explained. "If they fall in the water, they'll float." He inscribed the other cubes quickly, handing them all to Grotes. "Give them out, then bring each man to me."

Grotes nodded, doing as Kyle ordered. Sailors lined up in front of Kyle, and he filled their cubes one-by-one, gravity shields appearing around each man. When he was done, Kyle returned to the Captain, who was talking to Grotes.

"The floor below-deck is half-flooded," Grotes was saying. "...and filling fast. I'd say we have a half-hour till we're sunk."

"Damn," the Captain swore. He lowered his head, staring at his feet. Then he looked up at Grotes. "Get as many of the men to the lifeboats," he ordered, his voice subdued. "I'll stay with a skeleton crew while you escape."

"Captain!" Grotes protested.

"That's an order, First Mate," the Captain stated icily. "Consider it my last." Grotes stared at the Captain for a long moment, then saluted sharply, his eyes moist.

"Yes Captain."

He sprinted off, and the Captain turned to Kyle.

"Thank you for your help," he said, waving Kyle away. "Go with the others...you are no longer required."

"But..."

"Go!" the Captain shouted, waving Kyle away. Kyle stared mutely at the man, then turned around, looking across the deck of the *Defiance*. The once-immaculate ship was battered almost beyond recognition. The rear of the deck was nearly level with the ocean beyond, the front of the ship rising steadily up into the air. Kyle turned to the crew members running for the remaining lifeboats on the right side of the ship, feeling hopelessness come over him.

It was over, he realized. The only option left was to run.

Or was it?

Kyle turned to the Captain.

"Where is the leak?" he asked. The Captain frowned.

"What are you talking about?"

"The *leak*," Kyle repeated. "Where are we taking on water?"

"It has to be the hull," the Captain replied. "Rear port-side."

"We still might have a chance," Kyle declared. "I just need a few men...and a hammer, and some wood...and nails."

"I can get you those," the Captain replied. "What are you thinking?"

"Just get me what I need," Kyle replied.

"Alright," the Captain agreed. "Guns! Slim! Get your asses over here!" he shouted. A short man with impressively large biceps ran up to the Captain, as did Slim. They saluted sharply. "Get hammers, wood, and nails," the Captain instructed. He pointed at Kyle. "Whatever he says, you do. Understand?" Both men glanced at Kyle, then nodded.

"Come on," Kyle said, running toward the cabin at the rear of the ship. "Follow me until we get to the water, then wait until my signal." Both men nodded again, and Kyle led them through to the cabin. He opened the door to the hallway beyond, sprinting down the stairwell he'd come through only a short time before. He came to the bottom of the stairs, and found the last set of stairs to be submerged in water. The entire hallway beyond was flooded.

"Stay here," he ordered. "Where's the wood?"

"Cargo hold," Slim replied. "Damn Guts, you're really a Weaver?"

"When the water goes down, get as much wood as you can," Kyle instructed, ignoring Slim's question. "My room is the...eleventh door on the right."

"Eleventh door on the right," Slim repeated. Kyle nodded.

"When you hear me yelling, go to my room. There's a hole there into the hull. Go to the hole and wait for me to help you down."

"Got it," Guns replied. Slim frowned.

"What you up to, Guts?"

"You'll see," Kyle answered. He wove magic then, generating a gravity shield...but not the usual kind. He created one spherical gravity sphere pushing outward, then a slightly smaller one pushing inward. The result was like a gravity shield, but there was no gap allowing air in and out. He felt his boots rise above the floor as the lower pole of the shield pushed up against the ground. He activated his gravity boots, then flew forward over the rippling water beyond the landing. He took a deep breath, then shot downward, plunging through the water.

The seawater parted around his gravity shield, quickly rising to waist-height around him. The air trapped around him made him buoyant, forcing him back upward. He streamed more magic into his boots, forcing himself downward, until water completely engulfed him. He was immediately plunged into murky darkness, the hallway beyond blurry and indistinct. He wove magic, creating a small light beyond his gravity shield, bathing the hallway in a pale glow. Then he plowed forward through the water, counting the doors on the right as he went.

One, two, three, four...

He continued down the hallway, spotting two large holes in the left wall where cannons had struck earlier.

Nine, ten...eleven!

He spotted the partially open door to the right, and pushed through the water, the edge of his gravity shield forcing the door all the way open. He found his room just as he had left it, a large, gaping hole in the floor. He descended through it, bringing his magical light with him. Below, he found a huge room with vertical wooden planks running from a wide horizontal beam far below, curving upward on either side. Wide, thick horizontal beams crisscrossed the vertical walls, no doubt for support. This, he realized, must be the hull.

Kyle scanned the curved walls of the hull carefully. The warship's cannons had struck on the left side...toward his room's door. He turned to face the left wall of the hull, scanning from left to right. If he could find the breaks in the hull...

He spotted two of them, nearly five feet in diameter each, spaced about twenty feet apart. They were a few feet above the floor of the hull. He used his gravity boots to move up to the right one, then closed his eyes, gathering magic in his mind. He wove rapidly, then carefully threw the pattern outward. A flat gravity field appeared a fraction of an inch beyond the outer surface of the hole. Kyle felt a slight tug pulling him toward the field, and he zoomed to the left until he was in front of the other hole. He repeated the pattern, creating another gravity field. Then he backed away to the other end of the hull, streaming more magic into each of the fields.

He saw the two gravity fields flash a brighter blue, but that was it. He frowned, then took a deep breath in, feeling a little lightheaded all of a sudden. There was only so much air inside of his shield; was he running out already?

Suddenly he felt a sharp tug, and he jerked forward from the wall behind him. He pumped magic into his gravity boots reflexively, resisting the pull. Sweat poured down his forehead and into his eyes, making them sting. He ignored the discomfort, concentrating on maintaining his magic streams – one to each hole, one to his gravity boots, one to his light, and the last to his gravity shield. He sucked in another deep breath, his fingertips starting to tingle. He felt panic grip him...he was running out of air!

Kyle closed his eyes, forcing himself to slow down his breathing. *You have to do this,* he told himself. *People are counting on you.*

He opened his eyes, ignoring the tingling in his hands, and streamed more magic to the two holes in the hull, sweating with the effort. He glanced up at the hole in the ceiling of the hull...the one leading to his room. It was impossible to see whether or not his plan was working, if the water level in the ship was decreasing.

He continued to maintain all four streams, feeling sweat dripping down his flanks now, his heart hammering rapidly in his chest. His head felt like it was swimming, and it was taking more and more effort to keep focused. His entire body was tingling now, his breath coming in short gasps. He closed his eyes, wiping the sweat from his forehead, then glanced up at the ceiling again...and blinked.

He couldn't see the hole anymore.

He stared upward blankly, then scanned the ceiling again, very carefully, but the hole still wasn't there. It was gone.

What the...

Then it came to him. He couldn't see the hole because he wasn't looking at the ceiling anymore. He was staring at the surface of the water...it had dropped below the level of the ceiling!

Kyle whooped out with joy, cutting the magic stream to his gravity boots. The air in his shield made him shoot upward like a bullet through the water, bursting to the surface not ten feet above. He cut his stream to his gravity shield, and immediately fell into the water. The ice-cold seawater soaked through his clothes instantly, sending a terrible shock through him, and nearly made him lose control of his gravity streams. He cried out, then tried desperately to suck air into his lungs. But the frigid water made his throat seize up, and he could barely breathe at all. He clawed at the water, trying desperately to keep his head above it. Black spots floated across his vision, his chest burning.

Boots!

He gasped, fumbling for a thread of magic. He found one, then shot it toward his boots. He rose quickly out of the water, nearly hitting his head on the ceiling above. Water dripped down his arms and legs, splattering on the quickly receding waterline. He took deep, gulping breaths, the black spots fading from his vision. The tingling in his fingertips faded slowly.

"Guts!" he heard a voice shout from above, the sound echoing through the now half-filled hull. He looked up, spotting Slim and Guns peering down through the hole.

"It's almost empty!" Kyle shouted back, glancing back down at the waterline. "Get your stuff ready," he ordered. "I'll bring you both down when it's empty."

"What do we do?"

"There's two holes in the hull," Kyle explained, his teeth chattering. He hugged his arms to his chest. "We need to patch them up before I run out of magic."

"Got it." Slim frowned then. "How much time we got kid?" Kyle paused, mulling it over. Once he got all of the water out, he could drastically decrease the amount of magic he was streaming to each gravity field. He only needed to keep the ocean out, after all...and he didn't want to suck Slim and Guns through the holes.

"Ten minutes maybe," Kyle estimated. He glanced down; the hull was nearly empty now. In fact, the water line was below the holes now; no more water was being sucked out. He cut back on the two magic streams carefully, until water started pouring back in. He increased the streams slightly, then waved at Slim and Guns.

"Move back," he urged. Then he flew up through the hole, hovering above it. Both men stared at him, their jaws slack. "Drop the wood through the hole," Kyle instructed. They both nodded, then ran out into the damp hallway, to two large heaps of wooden boards. They grabbed an armful at a time, lugging the wood to the hole and dropping it through. It wasn't long before all of the wood had been tossed down to the hull.

"How you gonna get us down there?" Slim asked. Kyle extended a hand.

"Grab your hammer and nails," he replied. "Then grab on to me. I won't let you fall."

"If you say so kid," Slim muttered. He reached down for his hammer, tucking it in his pants, then grabbed a large bag of nails. He reached out to Kyle, and was immediately sucked in by the gravity boots' stabilization fields. Kyle dropped quickly through the hole in the floor, flying up to the leftmost breach. The water line was right below it...there was nothing for Slim to stand on.

"Set me down on that cross-beam," Slim ordered, pointing to one of the thick, wide wooden support beams running horizontally across the hull. There was one right below the hole, immersed in a few inches of water. Kyle complied, setting Slim down there. Slim clung to the next highest cross-beam with one hand, handing Kyle his bag of nails. "Take these, and hand them out when I tell you." He pointed down at one of the long planks of wood floating on the water. "Get me that, but get Guns here first."

Kyle nodded, flying back up the hole to his bedroom. He carried Guns to the support beam, on the other side of the hull breach. Slim asked for a piece of wood, and Kyle retrieved one. Slim held it on one end, Guns on the other, crossing the very bottom of the hole.

Kyle gave both a nail on request, and they made quick work of securing it to the hull. They repeated the process, nailing the next plank to the one below to force them as close together as possible, then securing it to the hull. And so it went, until the entire hole was covered.

"That'll do it," Slim stated. "Feet are frozen," he added ruefully, lifting one foot out of the water and shaking it. He turned to Guns. "Shimmy on to the next one."

The two sailors did just that, patching the hole the same way they had the first time. By the time they were done, Kyle was nearly out of magic, only maintaining his streams with the greatest of effort.

"Drop the left one," Slim told Kyle. "But be ready to put it back up." Kyle nodded, slowly decreasing that magic stream. To his dismay, water wept around the top, but even when he cut his magic stream, the patch otherwise held. He repeated the process for the right one, and got a similar result. Slim grinned, punching Guns on the shoulder.

"Well ain't that the purdiest thing you ever saw!" Slim declared. He turned to Kyle. "Now get me on deck so they can amputate my feet."

"Hold up," Guns stated. "What's that?" he asked, pointing down. Kyle followed his finger, spotting something lying at the bottom of the deck. He flew over to it, realizing that it was the backpack that had gone missing. He picked it up, slinging it over his shoulders, then brought Guns and Slim back up through the hole in the ceiling. They made their way to the stairs, both Slim and Guns limping – and complaining about their frozen feet – the whole time, but in a good-natured sort of way. They reached the end of the upper hallway, and opened the door to step out onto the deck of the *Defiance*. The Captain and Grotes were both standing at the right of the ship, directing sailors into the lifeboats.

"Hold up!" Slim shouted, limping toward the Captain. "Bring 'em back on deck!" The Captain and Grotes turned, staring at Slim.

"Explain," the Captain ordered.

"Guts here drained the water right outta the ship," Slim declared, wrapping an arm around Kyle's shoulders. "Guns 'n me patched the hull. We're afloat!"

"You drained the entire ship?" Grotes exclaimed in disbelief. He glanced across the deck to the ocean, then turned to the Captain. "We *are* riding higher, Captain." The Captain nodded, glancing toward the rear of the *Defiance*. The warship was a little farther away than before.

"Put a hold on lowering the lifeboats," he shouted. He turned to Grotes. "Keep putting the crew in the lifeboats," he told the First Mate. "Hold them there until we're sure we're not taking on more water."

"Yes Captain."

The Captain turned to Kyle, putting a hand on his shoulder.

"You, my young friend," he stated, "...just saved every soul on this ship." He smiled then...an expression that looked out-of-place on the surly Captain's face. "Thank you."

Chapter 19

Kalibar yawned, sitting up in his bed. He glanced at his clock, discovering with dismay that it was only five o'clock in the morning. He'd gone to bed late the previous night...or more accurately, earlier this morning. He'd canceled most of his meetings yesterday, spending the majority of his day and night reading in the Runic Archives. Then he'd come here, to his bedroom, to continue reading.

About Orja. About Verhan.

Very little historical information survived regarding the enigmatic continent and its capitol city. Apparently even the Ancients had been mostly ignorant of the place. Only the coastline of the continent – rumored to be even larger than their own – had been explored. Verhan and its surrounding cities had been accepted as colonies of the Empire in the last decade of the Ancients' reign. Renowned for its legendary diamond mines, Verhan had offered a lucrative boon to the Ancient Empire, in exchange for inclusion into the most powerful and influential government in the world. After the Ancients had been destroyed by Sabin's armies, Verhan – indeed, all of Orja – had been all but forgotten.

Kalibar sighed, stretching his neck from side to side. He considered going back to sleep, but decided against it. He'd spent hours lying in bed staring at the ceiling before finally sleeping, his mind continuing to race long after he'd stopped reading. Now he found himself doing the same, and he knew that there was no chance of him falling back to sleep. Luckily, he was more than accustomed to sleep deprivation. A good night's sleep was not a luxury Grand Weavers typically enjoyed.

He sat up again, swinging his legs over the edge of his bed, then standing up. He stretched his arms, then his back, feeling none of the stiffness and soreness he'd grown accustomed to for the past ten years. He hadn't felt it since that night, about two weeks ago, when he'd been given back his eyes. He suspected that Ampir had done much more than just give him his sight back – and the ability to see magic.

Kalibar yawned again, walking the short distance to his master bathroom. He stood before the sink, staring at his reflection in the mirror. Brown eyes stared back, crow's feet sprouting from the corners, shallow horizontal lines crossing his forehead. His white hair, not yet washed or combed, sprung in wild tufts from his scalp. He raised his chin up, noting with dismay the wrinkles in his neck.

He looked *old.*

He sighed, turning away from the mirror. He seldom engaged in such foolishness, contemplating his appearance. Probably because he still felt as though he were in his thirties, young and full of life, an infinity of days ahead of him. His reflection told the depressing truth: time was ever marching forward, and his body was slowly betraying him. He recalled the first time he'd spotted a bit of gray in his beard, the shock that had been. The first wrinkles. Of tugging on his skin, trying to flatten those wrinkles out, only to watch them spring back again when he let go. The realization that, though he felt no different than he always had, he was getting older.

Vain, that, to never expect it could happen to *him.*

Kalibar stepped forward into the shower stall, then heard a chime coming from his bedroom. He turned about, walking back to his bed, spotting the communication orb on his nightstand glowing faintly. He grabbed his bathrobe, putting it on hastily and walking quickly into his main suite, toward the front entrance. He saw High Weaver Urson standing behind the transparent front door, dressed in his usual black and silver uniform. Kalibar rushed to open the door.

"Grand Weaver," Urson greeted tersely, saluting sharply.

"At ease," Kalibar ordered. "What's going on?"

"Your children were not on the second ship that left port today, the *Explorer*," Urson replied. "A group of Battle-Weavers flew on the *Defiance's* route. We found the remains of a Verhanian military warship along that route."

"Go on."

"We found and questioned the few remaining survivors. They claim they had orders to intercept the *Defiance*, destroy its cargo, and apprehend its captain, who has been found guilty of smuggling illegal goods into Verhan and bribing customs officials."

"So what happened?"

"The warship attacked, the *Defiance* was crippled," Urson explained. "Then a girl and a boy attacked the warship and destroyed it using magic." He hesitated. "They matched your children's' descriptions," he added, "...accounting for their likely disguises."

"*What?*" Kalibar exclaimed. "They destroyed an entire *ship?*"

"Yes sire," Urson replied. "The *Defiance* managed to escape with only a mizzen-mast left standing, and multiple confirmed hits to its hull."

"But your men haven't found it yet?"

"No," Urson confirmed.

"Thank you Urson," Kalibar said. He hesitated, then put a hand on Urson's shoulder. "Don't let word get out that my children destroyed that warship," he instructed. "The last thing we need now is an international incident."

"Yes Grand Weaver."

Urson saluted, then left the suite as quickly as he had come. After the door had shut behind the High Weaver, Kalibar closed his eyes, taking a deep breath in and letting it out slowly. His heart was still pounding in his chest.

They're alive.

He turned away from the door, walking to one of his couches and sitting down. He put his face in his hands for a long moment, then leaned back in the couch, staring up at the crystalline ceiling above. Kyle and Ariana were alive. The *Defiance* had been crippled, and still had not been found, but it had escaped the warship. And even if it had taken too much damage and sunk, Kyle had brought his gravity boots. They were safe. They *had* to be safe.

Unless...

They were still in international waters, wanted criminals almost certainly being hunted by a fleet of Verhanian warships. In an all-but-incapacitated cargo ship.

Kalibar stood up from the couch, feeling suddenly restless. He turned about, looking at the suite all around him. The spotless granite floors, the marble columns extending all the way to the sloping transparent roof above. Riches everywhere he looked, the trappings of an emperor. Any man who first set eyes on this room would be struck with awe, but to Kalibar these luxuries were mere distractions. Functionless, useless. Priceless to others, but to him, worthless.

He closed his eyes, picturing his children out there in the ocean somewhere, standing on the deck of a crippled ship. Alone.

He opened his eyes, staring at the finery around him. He imagined the Void Behemoth's fiery gaze melting the stone, setting fire to the furniture. Melting flesh to the bone. Imagined Erasmus, Owens, Lee, the Council...everyone screaming in agony as they burned.

Kalibar sighed heavily, feeling the weight of millions of lives on his shoulders, all of them looking to him to save them.

And what could he do? What could he possibly do?

Defeat was inevitable. Either he sacrificed the ideals of the Empire – freedom, self-determination, cultivation of the inherent excellence of Man – and allowed Sabin to rule, or he upheld those ideals and watched helplessly as the Empire burned. As his friends, his people, and even his children were taken from him.

He was Kalibar, the greatest Battle-Weaver of his generation, perhaps the most celebrated Grand Weaver of the new Empire. The most powerful mortal Weaver in the known world. And yet, for all of his accomplishments – a lifetime of sacrifice for the Empire – he will die helpless. No matter what his decision, he will watch his world, and everything he has fought for, be destroyed.

He has already failed.

Kalibar lowered his gaze to his feet, thinking back to his mansion in Bellingham. How simple life had been then, until a young boy had appeared at his doorstep, mere inches from death. He remembered the wonder in Kyle's eyes as he'd seen magic for the first time. The same wonder when he'd walked into the Great Tower, mesmerized by the inverted lobby. Even now, Kalibar smiled at the memory.

Yes, his life had been simpler in Bellingham, but it had been empty as well. He'd filled his life with duties instead of people. He'd played it safe.

He thought back to Kyle's dreams, about Ampir, the greatest Battle-Runic of all time. Beloved of the Ancient Empire, yet even he did not stop it from being destroyed. He'd chosen his son over all else, and that son had survived. And two thousand years later, Ampir's grandson had returned to this, the new Empire. Kyle's was a life made possible only by the destruction of the Ancients, the end result of Ampir's impossible decision.

Now that boy, Ampir's legacy, was somewhere far away, making his way toward the very man who had destroyed the Ancients. Ampir's grandson, alive only at the expense of the old Empire, was risking his life to save the new one.

And here Kalibar stood, the man whose sole responsibility was to protect the Empire, doing nothing.

* * *

Kyle stabbed his fork into the steaming fish on his plate, eagerly bringing the well-seasoned meat to his mouth. He devoured it with the bare minimum of chewing, swallowing it nearly whole. Then he dipped into the fish again, desperate to sate his incredible hunger. He'd never been so hungry in his life; he knew that it was on account of the incredible amount of magic he'd used only an hour ago. He polished off his plate in minutes, and despite the fact that it'd been heaping with food, he was not nearly satisfied. He looked up, seeing the Captain, Grotes, and Ariana staring at him from across the table.

"I have never seen a man, nor a boy, so ravenous in my life," the Captain declared. "Get our hero another plate," he ordered a nearby servant. Within moments, a fresh plate appeared before Kyle, and he dove into it with unfettered delight.

"You aren't eating," Grotes told Ariana, who had insisted on not being given a plate. Of course she'd been given one anyway, much to her obvious consternation.

"I don't eat," she stated for the third time. This did not sit well with Grotes, who frowned at her.

"Everyone eats, girl," he grumbled.

"How long until we get to Verhan?" she asked, changing the subject. Grotes glanced at the Captain, who cleared his throat.

"That has become a complicated question," the Captain answered. Ariana frowned.

"What do you mean?"

"The warship that attacked us," the Captain explained, "...was a Verhanian military vessel." He paused, rapping his knuckles on the table. "It appears I am no longer welcome in Verhan."

"Wait," Kyle blurted out between gulps of food. "What do you mean?"

"Besides the fact that we've destroyed a Verhanian warship," the Captain replied, "...and employed Weavers to do so, no less, I must assume that the warship attacked us on orders."

"But why?"

"Well," the Captain replied, rubbing his chin for a moment. "We have, from time to time, engaged in practices that have been...less than lawful."

"You're *criminals?*" Ariana exclaimed, her eyes widening. Grotes put both hands up defensively.

"Hold on," he interjected. "We've shipped depleted runics to wealthy patrons back in Verhan from time to time, that's all."

"So you let us attack the *good* guys?" Ariana exclaimed incredulously. She turned to Kyle. "I don't believe this!"

"The only reason you're still alive is because you did that," Grotes retorted. "They would've killed you without a second thought. You're undocumented Weavers being illegally smuggled into the country."

"Great," Ariana muttered.

"And this won't be the last attack," the Captain piped in. "One doesn't send a single warship to intercept another ship in the deep ocean. I guarantee there are other warships patrolling our route...and that the odds of meeting one will increase the closer we sail to Orja."

"So unless you're willing to defend us again," Grotes stated, "...we're all dead men."

Ariana turned to Kyle, who stared at the tabletop, drumming his fingers on its polished surface. Then he snapped his fingers, looking up.

"We could make the ship invisible," he declared. All three pairs of eyes stared at him blankly.

"Invisible," Grotes stated slowly. "The entire ship."

"Well why not?" Kyle asked. He turned to Ariana. "We could use the invisibility pattern to hide it from the other warships."

"Kyle, there's no way we could make a field that large," Ariana protested.

"Why not?" Kyle countered. "It's just a matter of how much magic we use...and I make a lot." And that was an understatement; Kyle made even more magic than Kalibar now. It was one thing Kyle did better than anyone else.

"But I don't," Ariana reminded him. "And you have to sleep sometime. We can't keep a field that large going all day and night."

"We can if we make a runic to do it for us," Kyle insisted. He turned back to the Captain, feeling the same burst of excitement he'd felt when he'd first told Master Banar about the K-Array. "Do you have any large crystals?" he asked.

"We're carrying quartz blocks," the Captain replied. "In various colors. We sell them to high-end optics manufacturers to make tinted lenses."

"Can I see them?" Kyle pressed. The Captain nodded.

"Of course," he replied. "What are you planning?"

266

"Quartz stores magic pretty well," Kyle stated. "If I can get a big enough crystal, it should be able to hold enough magic to power the invisibility field while I'm sleeping."

"I'll bring you down to the cargo hold after we finish eating," Grotes offered. Kyle remembered his still-grumbling belly, and dug in to his food, making quick work of it. He thought about asking for a third plate, but decided against it. He looked up to find the others having long since finished their own meals. They were looking at him with funny expressions on their faces.

"What?" he asked.

"Never seen a boy your size eat like that," Grotes admitted. "You sure you're done?" Kyle nodded, wiping his mouth with his napkin.

"So now what?" he asked. The Captain sighed.

"Now we change course," he replied. "We'll seek amnesty northeast of Verhan, in the Shimmering Isle." Grotes nodded.

"Our cargo should more than pay our way," he agreed. "And they don't extradite to Verhan."

"Wait," Ariana interjected. "We need to get to Verhan!"

"That's out of the question," the Captain retorted. "We'd never make it to port alive."

"But..."

"We appreciate your help," Grotes interrupted. "We really do. But we can't risk the lives of every man on this ship just to get you there."

"So what are we supposed to do?" she pressed. The Captain raised one eyebrow.

"Why do you need to get to Verhan?" he asked. Ariana glanced at Kyle, who cleared his throat. He thought about lying, but there really wasn't any point.

"We don't," Kyle admitted. "We need to get somewhere nearby."

"Can you be more specific?" Grotes pressed. Kyle paused, then nodded at Ariana. She glowered at him, but reached down to the one of the backpacks at her feet, retrieving the rolled-up map. Grotes and the Captain cleared the dishes near her, and she unrolled the map on the tabletop. She pointed to the small red circle northwest of Verhan.

"That's where we need to go," she told them.

"Let me see that," the Captain said, slipping on a pair of reading glasses and peering at the map. He frowned, jerking his eyes up to look at Kyle, then Ariana. "That's the Barrens," he declared.

"The Barrens?" Kyle asked. The Captain stared at Kyle for a long moment. Then he leaned back in his chair.

"You're telling me," he stated, "...that you need to get to the Barrens, and you don't even know what it is?"

"We need to get to wherever this is," Ariana replied, tapping her index finger on the red circle. "That's all you need to know."

"Well that isn't all *you* need to know," the Captain declared, his tone suddenly sharp. "...because going anywhere *close* to the Barrens is suicide."

"Why?" Kyle asked.

"The Barrens," the Captain replied, "...is surrounded by the Barren forest, which is inhabited by a tribe of extraordinarily dangerous savages." He sat back in his chair. "I'll give you both credit, you're skilled Weavers. But I can guarantee they're much, much better."

"Wait, they're Weavers?" Kyle asked. The Captain nodded. "I thought magic was forbidden in Verhan."

"It is," the Captain agreed. "But we're not about to tell the Barren tribes that. Our military won't go near their forest, not with all the Neutralizers in Orja."

"I don't get it," Kyle said. "If you can neutralize any magic, why can't you go near the forest?"

"Neutralizers don't work on them," Grotes explained. "And don't ask why, 'cause nobody knows." He crossed his arms over his chest. "But we do know this: they will kill anyone that enters their territory. It doesn't matter how powerful you think you are...you go to the Barrens, you die."

"Who are these people?" Ariana asked. The Captain rubbed his chin.

"No one is quite sure," he admitted. "Our anthropologists suggest they're descendants of the original tribes that lived around the Barrens before the first Empire massacred our ancestors." He

268

gave Ariana a tight smile. "Even your Ancients failed to conquer those tribes...and they were much better Weavers than any alive today."

"How do we get there?" Ariana pressed. The Captain and Grotes glanced at each other, then back at her.

"I don't think you're hearing us right," Grotes muttered. Ariana leaned over the table, unfazed.

"What do you care?" she retorted. "It's our funeral. Just tell us where to go."

The Captain stared at her for a long time, drumming his fingers on the table agitatedly. Then he shifted in his seat, crossing his arms over his chest.

"The Barrens is northwest of Verhan, on the mainland," he stated, pointing at the red circle on the map. "We're going to the Shimmering Isle, which is an island city north of Verhan, and twenty miles from the coast. If you go due west from the Shimmering Isle when we hit port," he continued, tracing his finger from a small set of islands west to the coastline, "...you'll be about one hundred-fifty miles from the Barrens."

"But how do we find the Barrens after we get to the coast?" Kyle asked. The Captain frowned at him.

"Ideally you'd have a compass and a detailed topographical map," he replied. "Which this," he added, pointing at the map, "...is not."

"Well that's no help," Kyle grumbled. Grotes smirked.

"The Barrens are at the foot of a mountain range," he stated. "The Barren forest is south of the tallest mountain. You can't miss it."

"What does the mountain look like?" Ariana asked.

"Like a damn mountain," Grotes replied. "You can't miss it."

Ariana glanced at Kyle, who nodded. It wasn't what they'd planned, but it was better than nothing. At least they knew where to go now. But they hadn't counted on the Barren tribes. If these people were as dangerous as the Captain and Grotes believed them to be, how were Ariana and Kyle possibly going to get past them?

"Drop us off at the Shimmering Isle then," Ariana stated. The Captain shrugged.

"Very well," he replied. "I will do as you ask. But I do believe that you, young girl, were absolutely right." Ariana blinked.

"About what?"

"It's your funeral," he answered.

* * *

The morning sun rose above the horizon as Kyle stared at the twenty-odd translucent cubes sitting on the wooden deck of the *Defiance*, casting the ship in an orange glow. The deck rose upward under his feet as the ship sailed over a particularly large wave, making him feel a bit queasy. He reached into one of the many pockets in his shirt, retrieving the gutroot Slim had given him the day before, and bit off a piece, chewing it vigorously.

"What now?" Ariana asked. She was standing a few feet away, as were Slim and a few other sailors Kyle didn't recognize.

"First I need to inscribe the invisibility rune in one of these blocks," Kyle answered, gesturing at the quartz cubes. Each was roughly the size of a basketball, and was incredibly heavy, hence the sailors. "I'll need to experiment until I get the size of the field right." He glanced at Slim. "It might take a while."

"Go to it Guts," Slim stated. "We're yours for as long as you need us." Kyle nodded, then got to it. The thicker the threads of the rune, the larger the field would be. He started inscribing the invisibility pattern, making the threads thicker than he'd ever made them before. When he was done, he stood back, then streamed magic to the cube. When he looked up from it, he saw the faint blue of the invisibility field some thirty feet away. Beyond that, sailors turned to stare, their eyes wide with wonder.

"Too small," Kyle muttered, cutting off his magic stream. He tried inscribing again, using the same crystal, making the threads twice as thick as before. He streamed magic again, and saw the blue field some eighty feet away...about halfway to the ship's prow. He turned around, seeing the field extending halfway again, to the rear of the ship...as well as the first field. "Well then," he murmured.

"What's wrong?" Ariana asked. Kyle cut off his magic stream.

"I'm burning through magic pretty quickly even at this size," Kyle replied. "I don't think any of these cubes will be big enough to power a full-sized field for very long." He focused on the quartz crystal again, now with two runes inscribed in it. He created a third rune, this with threads three times the thickness of the first. When he streamed magic to it, three fields appeared: the first two, and a third field that extended a few feet past the prow of the ship...and from the rear as well. He turned his gaze upward to the mizzen-mast – the rearmost mast of the ship, the only one still standing – and found the field easily extending above it.

"Got it," he declared, cutting off his magic stream. It'd taken a formidable amount of magic to power the three fields; he stood, walking to another quartz cube, crouching before it. He recreated the third field, then tested it, again making sure that the resulting field encompassed the ship...which it did. He stood up, staring at the cube for a long moment.

"What're you thinking, Guts?" Slim asked.

"I need to figure out if the field is warping light correctly," he answered. "Too much or too little, and people will notice."

"Why don't you fly beyond the field, and see what it looks like," Ariana offered. Kyle nodded.

"Can you power the cube while I do that?" he asked.

"Sure."

Kyle streamed magic to his boots, rising upward and forward from the deck. He soared past the prow – and the edge of the field – turning around as he did so. He saw the ocean before him...and nothing else.

So far, so good.

He continued to fly backward, rising up as he did so. It was then that he noticed a rim of color outlining the massive sphere of the gravity field; while the center of the field was perfectly invisible, the edges were well, sort of like looking into a magnifying glass. The ocean was distorted. He sighed, flying back toward the ship. When he passed the edge of the invisibility field, the *Defiance* blinked into existence before him. He flew down beside Ariana.

"How is it?" she asked.

"It's close," he replied. "A little too weak, I think. I'll tweak it using another cube."

"It uses a lot of magic," Ariana warned. "I don't know how much longer I could've powered it for."

"I know," Kyle muttered. He'd have to figure out a solution to that. But getting the field right came first. He squatted over the cube, staring at it. He knew how to make the invisibility field larger, but Master Lee had never taught him how to manipulate the *strength* of a runic. He'd learned how to make a flame larger or smaller, and even how to make it float higher or lower, but not *hotter*. He'd never gotten far enough in his lessons to learn that. Which meant he had no idea how to make the invisibility field stronger.

Well, he was just going to have to figure it out for himself.

He frowned, thinking it through. The thickness of the thread corresponded to the amount of magic he put into a pattern while weaving. The greater the distance of the rune from the surface of the cube, the farther away the pattern was woven – just as when he tossed magic outward great distances with his mind. So what determined how much magic was streamed to the rune?

Then he had an idea; every rune had a thread attaching it to the surface of the mineral, one that wasn't technically part of the pattern. What if he made *that* thread thicker or thinner? He found the thread, and widened it ever-so-slightly. Then he stood up.

"Let's try it now," he stated. Ariana shook her head.

"I don't have enough magic."

"I'll stream some to you," Kyle offered. He pushed magic toward her, until she held up one hand.

"Okay, go ahead."

Kyle nodded, flying upward and forward once again. He passed the invisibility field quickly, and kept going until he was far away. When he finally turned to look back at the ship, he saw nothing at all...just the rolling ocean under the perfect blue sky – and the faint blue of the field's magic. Then his eye caught a strange irregularity in the ocean waves, a subtle rippling effect at the edges. It was barely visible, only evident because he knew where to look. A consequence of the field passing through the ocean, no doubt. It would have to do.

He flew back to the ship, landing beside Ariana once again. He smiled at her.

"It's good," he declared. "We're invisible." Slim whooped, clapping Kyle on the shoulder.

"Damn Guts," he exclaimed. "You saved our butts once, and now you've gone and done it again!" He grinned. "Shoulda called you 'Brains,' eh?"

"We still have to figure out a way to power it," Ariana interjected. "I almost ran out of magic again, and that was only a minute or two."

"Let me think," Kyle replied. He tapped his chin with his finger, staring at the cubes in front of him. One cube was hardly enough to maintain the field for very long, and there were no larger cubes available. Once he filled a cube with magic, it would power the rune immediately, so it wasn't like he could make a dozen identical runics and fill them all with magic for use later. They could conserve magic by only using the field when an enemy was spotted, but for that he would need a way to be able to turn the invisibility field on and off, like a light switch. Or a way to store extra magic for the runic, like popping new batteries into a flashlight to keep it going.

Suddenly he had an idea!

"I've got it," he declared, snapping his fingers. A wonderfully giddy sensation came over him. "Slide that cube..." he ordered, pointing to a fresh cube a foot away, "...within an inch of this one."

"What you thinking, Guts?" Slim asked.

"You'll see," Kyle answered. Slim and Guns lugged the cube next to Kyle's. Kyle streamed magic to the fresh cube for a long moment, pushing as much magic as he could into it. Then he stepped back. "Now, slide the cubes together, so they're touching." Again, Slim and Guns obeyed.

A pale blue sphere appeared around the ship.

"There we are," Kyle declared, unable to help himself from grinning. "Now pull them apart." They did so, and the field immediately vanished.

"What's going on?" Slim asked.

"I filled the empty cube with magic," Kyle answered. "When it touched the cube with the rune, magic flowed to it, powering the invisibility field." He turned to Ariana. "I can fill all of these cubes with magic, and all we have to do is touch the runic to them to activate the invisibility field...and pull the runic away to turn it off."

"Wow," Ariana murmured.

"We may not have enough magic to power the field 24 hours a day," Kyle continued, "...but if you stay on lookout, with your eyesight you should be able to spot any possible enemies, and turn on the field before they spot us."

"And I'm strong enough to move the cubes," she reasoned. She stared at Kyle, a smile growing on her lips. "Kyle, that's brilliant!"

"Damn Guts," Slim swore, shaking his head. "You're one hell of a Weaver!"

"No, I'm not a Weaver," Kyle replied proudly. "I'm a Runic."

Chapter 20

The sun rose slowly above the tree line of the Barren forest, its bright rays lighting on the rocky terrain ahead. Sabin paused to enjoy the sight, seen through one of his Chosen's eyes. Then he focused his attention on the rest of his Chosen, rapidly updating himself on the state of the world.

Kyle had made it back to the Great Tower after his talk with Ampir. He was with the girl now, getting prepared for bed. Kalibar was in a late-night meeting with the Council. Ampir was still coming for him, flying above the ocean, now nearly at Orja's shore.

Sabin sighed inwardly, ignored the searing agony of his flesh, concentrating on the task at hand. He returned his focus to his avatar, still slaving over the shard hovering before its grotesque head. It was nearly complete, the shard. Another hour or two of work remained. There was little else to do now but wait.

He paused, then reached out to another Chosen trapped in its Void crystal, selecting yet another memory to relive.

* * *

Sabin opens his eyes.

The perfect blackness of his bedroom greets him, all light deflected by the room's magic, per his request. He cannot sleep any other way; the slightest light or sound never fails to wake him.

He hears a creaking sound close by.

Sabin freezes, feeling his pulse quicken. The noise had come from just outside his bedroom door, by the sound of it. No one is allowed in his suite, without his consent, not unless there is an emergency. He hears no alarm, no indication that such an emergency is taking place. There shouldn't be...there *couldn't* be...anyone in his suite.

There is another creaking sound, as if weight is being shifted on the wooden floorboards beyond the closed door.

Sabin activates one of the lamps by his bed, setting it to glow almost imperceptibly. Too faint a light for anyone beyond his door to see, but enough for him to make out the outlines of his room. His bedroom, at least, is empty. His heart hammers in his chest, and he contemplates activating his silent alarm, one that would bring a dozen elite guards to his room within less than a minute. He hesitates, knowing that he has powerful defensive wards scattered about his room, many of them well hidden. Some of them he'd made himself.

Light appears from beyond the bedroom door, faint rays shining through the gaps between the door and the door frame.

Sabin bolts upright in his bed, immediately streaming magic to the silent alarm, activating it. He activates the half-dozen rings on his fingers, the amulet around his neck, the earring in his left earlobe. The runics flare to life, surrounding him in layer upon layer of form-fitting gravity shields. He levitates up from the bed until his is standing on thin air a foot above it, at the same time willing the door of his magically sealed safe open. His walking cane flies from the safe into his left hand; a runic weapon of extraordinary power, no one but him realizes its true abilities.

The door bursts open!

"Stay back!" Sabin cries, squinting against the sudden bright light, holding his staff before him. "By order of the Elder Runic!"

A shadow appears in the doorway, a man.

"Guards!" Sabin shouts. He activates the silent alarm again, wondering why his elite guards haven't arrived yet. He watches as the man in the doorway steps forward, makes out a dull, black metallic boot. He follows the boot upward, his eyes slowly adjusting to the light.

His eyes widen in recognition.

"Ampir!" he exclaims, lowering his staff. The man in the doorway takes another step forward, and Sabin confirms that it is indeed his fellow Councilman, dressed in his Battle-Runic armor. Sabin frowns, lowering himself until his feet touch the mattress. "What are you doing here?"

Ampir says nothing, taking another step forward.

"Wait," Sabin states, holding up his left hand. "Don't come any closer. I haven't deactivated my wards yet..."

Ampir strides forward, and then all hell breaks loose. A half-dozen wards activate at once, bursts of white-hot energy slamming into Ampir from all directions. Sabin cries out, shielding his eyes with his forearm. More lights flash as his wards continue to fire loudly, popping and shrieking as they discharge their deadly attacks. He cringes at the ear-splitting sounds, turning his head away and bringing his hands to his ears.

And then the lights and noises stop.

Sabin slowly lowers his forearm from his eyes, turning to face the doorway...and sees Ampir standing at the foot of his bed...unharmed.

"What..." Sabin begins, then lurches forward as his staff is ripped from his hands by an unseen force, flying past Ampir and clattering on the floor. His amulet and his rings slip off, flying forward, all of his runics leaving him of their own accord. Within seconds, he has nothing left but his bedclothes.

Ampir faces Sabin silently for a long moment, his mirrored visor reflecting Sabin's dumbstruck expression. Then he turns away, back toward the bedroom door.

"He's yours," he calls out.

Suddenly a half-dozen men rush into the bedroom, surrounding Sabin's bed. Elite guards all of them. Sabin stares at them incredulously, unable to speak even as they grab his wrists, yanking him down face-first onto the bed. He feels hands on his ankles and legs, feels someone's knee grind into his lower back.

He howls in pain.

"Don't move," he hears a voice growl in his ear. "You move, you die!"

"Okay, okay!" Sabin exclaims, going limp on the bed. He grits his teeth against the pain in his lower back. "What the hell is going on here?"

"You know damn well what's going on," the guard accuses. Sabin feels someone cross his wrists together, then feels something cold and hard slide onto them.

"Like hell I do," Sabin retorts. He lifts his head up from the bed, seeing Ampir standing there in the doorway, his back turned. "Ampir!" Sabin shouts. "Ampir, what's happening? Why are they doing this to me?"

"You," the guard at his ear growls, grabbing the back of Sabin's head and shoving his face into the mattress, "...are wanted for conspiring to commit murder." Sabin struggles to breath, his mouth and nose smothered by the thick blankets below.

"That's not...true!" he gasps. "That's a lie!" He twists his head to the side, stealing a quick breath before the guard forces his face back into the bedding.

"Shut up," the guard orders. "Where's the damn patch?"

Sabin feels something cool and wet on the back of his neck, followed by an immediate, overwhelming urge to sleep. He resists, twisting his head to the side again.

"Ampir," he cries out. "Ampir, I didn't do it!"

And then his eyelids grow impossibly heavy, far too heavy to keep open. He gives in at last, letting the darkness take him.

* * *

Thick, dark clouds hung low in the sky, splashes of purple and red painting their underbellies. In the distance, the sun was starting to awaken, rising beyond the tall evergreen trees of the forest to the east.

The first trees that Kyle had seen in nearly a week.

A warm breeze blew through his hair as he stood on the battered deck of the *Defiance*, his hands on the railing at the side of the ship. He looked down, seeing a long pier far below, with many smaller boats docked alongside it. Beyond the docks stood a short stone wall rising up from the water...and beyond that, the sprawling island city called the Shimmering Isle.

Kyle yawned, still sleepy from being woken up only a half-hour ago by the sounds of the ship docking. He'd come to the starboard side of the ship – that was the right side, he'd learned – to watch as the crew anchored the ship and installed the gangplank, a wide ramp angling down toward the pier below. He'd learned quite a bit about boats from Slim and the other sailors in the three days since the Verhanian warship had attacked. The invisibility field had kept them safe from further harm, and with Kyle and Ariana's help, the ship's two masts had been mostly repaired. Well, mostly Ariana's help. With her limitless endurance and inability to sleep, she had worked around the clock to repair the *Defiance*. While the deck was still riddled with small holes, and the wood was still charred, the bulk of the damage had been patched over.

Their help had made them instant celebrities among the sailors, and even Grotes and the Captain treated Kyle and Ariana like heroes. Which in a small way, Kyle supposed they were.

He smiled, turning to see Ariana standing next to him. She was watching the sunrise with him, her pale skin glowing a faint red like the clouds above her. She noticed him watching her, and smiled back at him, then turned her gaze back at the land before them.

The Shimmering Isle, a haven for pirates, other criminals, and unscrupulous businessmen. It was quite a beautiful city, filled with two to three story-tall houses of every imaginable color. Beyond these rose a small mountain, with lush forests surrounding its base. It was quite tropical, as was the weather; it was early morning, yet Kyle was already sweating in his light shirt and pants.

Kyle heard footsteps approaching from behind, and he turned about to see Grotes there. The First Mate nodded at them both.

"We're almost finished docking," Grotes informed them. "The Captain and I need to meet with Immigration authorities before we're allowed beyond the city borders."

"How long will that take?" Kyle asked.

"A few hours," Grotes answered. "The office won't be open for another hour or so. Enough cargo survived to buy citizenship and housing for the crew." He smiled then – a rare expression on the man. "Thank you, both of you. None of us would be here if it hadn't been for you."

Kyle nodded silently at the First Mate, not quite sure what to say. Neither, apparently, did Ariana.

"You can stay on the ship," Grotes offered, "...or you can go with some of the crew to the pub for a bit, until we're finished."

"Can't we just fly out now?" Kyle asked. He was eager to get going, even though he was dreading reaching the Barren forest, especially after what the Captain had told them about the place.

"Give me some time to get some things together," Grotes countered. "You'll need a local map, and supplies."

"Okay," Ariana agreed.

"Hey Ghost, Guts!" a voice called out. Kyle turned to see Slim and a few other sailors walking up to them. Slim flashed a devilish grin. "You coming to the pub with us? My money's so hot, it's gonna burn my pants right off!"

"Better do more 'n that," another sailor cackled.

"Uh, sure," Kyle replied, glancing at Ariana, who nodded.

"I'll meet you two at the pub later then," Grotes stated. "Did you drain yourselves of magic like I told you to?"

"Yep," Kyle confirmed. They'd just done it this morning, filling as many of the big quartz cubes as they could so they could recharge later.

"Good," Grotes replied. "That'll make getting through security a lot simpler." He turned to Slim and the others. "Have fun boys," he stated. "But don't cause too much trouble. We're gonna be staying a while."

"You got it," Slim promised. "Come on you two," he added, gesturing for Kyle and Ariana to follow him. "Paradise is just around the corner!"

Kyle and Ariana exchanged shrugs, and followed Slim and the gang across the deck to the gangplank, a wide ramp angling down toward the pier below. They made their way across the long pier to the shore beyond, where they were met by stern-looking men dressed in thick leather armor. The leather was studded with crystals of various colors, and Kyle sensed magic in them...and in the men themselves. These, he realized, must be guards...and Weavers to boot. Apparently the Shimmering Isle was more accepting toward magic than Verhan. Slim spoke with one of them, and then they were all asked to raise their arms up for a pat-down. Finding no weapons – and no detectable magic in Kyle or Ariana – they were allowed past the security checkpoint and into the city.

The cobblestone streets of the Shimmering Isle were broad and well-kept, as were the colorful shops that flanked them. Kyle was surprised; for a city so accepting of the criminal element, everything was quite orderly and clean. There were, he noted, guards posted on nearly every block, Weavers just like the ones at the security checkpoint. Their presence made Kyle a little nervous, given that he regenerated his magic so quickly. He wouldn't be able to stay in the city for very long before Ariana would have to drain him again, and draining him meant she'd have to weave magic. With so many Weaver guards all around them, it could prove difficult for her do to so without getting caught. Kyle leaned in to whisper in Ariana's ear.

"We should leave as soon as possible."

"Okay," she whispered back. Then she smiled. "You don't have to whisper in my ear," she added. Kyle nodded, realizing of course that she was right. She could probably hear him blinking from this distance. Then he had a sobering thought; how many times had he farted when she was nearby, taking extraordinary pains to remain as stealthy as possible? She'd probably heard him doing it every time. Every single time. No, not probably...*definitely*.

"Look," Ariana said, pointing down the street. There, a block away, was a three-story gray stone building, a large banner hanging above the front door. Kyle couldn't read it, but the drawing of two frothy mugs was unmistakable.

"Come on boys," Slim cried. "To cheap booze and expensive women!"

"Only expensive for *you*," Guns shot back, flexing a massive bicep. Everyone laughed, and the group made their way to the pub entrance, filing through. The pungent aroma of cigar smoke struck Kyle as he entered, and he wrinkled his nose, trying not to cough. The inside of the pub was smoky, loud, and dark...and noisy. For being so early in the morning, there were a surprising number of patrons at the bar. Slim and the gang asked a rather pretty waitress for a table, and she led them to a corner of the pub, to a large round table. They all took their seats.

"What can I get for you boys?" the waitress asked.

"Beers all around to start," Slim replied. Then he grinned. "And you for dessert."

"Sorry, I'm not on the menu," the waitress replied, not missing a beat. "And for you two?" she asked, nodding at Kyle and Ariana.

"Uh, just water," Kyle replied.

"I'm good," Ariana mumbled.

A few moments later, everyone but Kyle and Ariana had beers in hand. And almost as quickly, those beers were emptied, and a second round was asked for. Slim regaled the group with a slightly embellished version of his and Guns' heroic patching of the hull, to the delight of the crew. That led to others recounting their own harrowing tales of the warship's attack. By the time their waitress had brought a fourth round, the mood had become somber as the men remembered those who died. Slim gave a touching, if quite drunk, tribute to Rusty that left everyone's eyes moist – especially Kyle's. Even their waitress stopped to listen, as did half of the patrons in the bar. Then food was brought, and Kyle ate heartily with the others. When he was sated, the waitress whisked his plate away, and the men ordered yet another round of beers.

Kyle felt a tap on his shoulder, and turned about to see Grotes standing behind him.

"Let's go back to the ship," the First Mate said. Kyle stood from his chair, as did Ariana, and they bid a very intoxicated Slim and the others farewell. Then they left the bar, traveling back across the pier to the *Defiance*. Once on deck, Grotes handed Kyle a heavy backpack.

"This should have everything you'll need for the next few days," he said. "Food, knives, canteens, first aid kits, a compass. And a topographical map," he added. "If you fly due west, the coast should only be twenty miles away. Then go northwest until you see a mountain range. One mountain is much taller than the rest...that's Mount Grimore."

"The one we fly toward," Kyle said. Grotes nodded.

"You'll approach its southern end," he stated. "They'll be a large forest there...that's the Barren forest."

"And the entrance to the Barrens?" Ariana asked.

"No one's lived to map it," Grotes admitted. He paused then. "Mind telling me what you're looking for there?" Ariana glanced at Kyle, then shook her head.

"We can't say," she replied apologetically. "No offense," she added. Grotes shrugged.

"Alright, well, if you change your mind, the Captain and I set aside funds for you both," he informed. "Enough to buy some land and a house." Ariana's eyes widened, as did Kyle's. An entire *house*? It was far too generous, and Kyle found himself dumbstruck, having no idea what to say.

"Thank you Grotes," Ariana said at last, reaching in and giving the First Mate a hug. She drew back then. "You know, you're not such a bad guy, for a pirate." Grotes smirked.

"Pirates steal," he corrected. "Technically, I'm a smuggler."

"Well you're not such a bad guy...for a bad guy," Ariana corrected. Grotes gave a grudging smile.

"This ship and my crew wouldn't be here without you two," he said. "You're both braver than most men will ever hope to be. Take my advice...don't throw your lives away."

Kyle glanced at Ariana, who said nothing for a long moment. Then she hugged Grotes again. Grotes sighed, then extended a hand to Kyle, who shook it.

"Good luck," Grotes stated.

Kyle slung the backpack over his shoulders, grunting at the weight. Ariana took it from him, slinging it over her own shoulders with ease, then took his hand, leading him toward the rear cabin and back to their room. Or rather, the room a few doors down from where theirs had been. Ariana retrieved the other two backpacks, emptying the contents of Grotes' backpack into both of them. Then they both went to the corner of the room, where they'd put the quartz cubes they'd drained their magic into earlier. They charged up, then made their way back up to the deck.

"Alright," Kyle stated, taking a deep breath in and letting it out slowly. "Ready?" Ariana nodded.

"Ready."

"I'll make us invisible while we fly," Kyle offered. Ariana approached him from behind, wrapping her cool, slender arms around his shoulders. Then Kyle frowned. "Oops, I need the compass."

"Oh, here," Ariana replied, handing it to him. He glanced down at it, not recognizing any of the characters written on it. But one of the compass's letters was red, while the rest were black. That had to be north. He glanced at the sun – which he knew rose in the east, on Doma as well as Earth – and confirmed that the red letter was indeed north.

"All right, here goes..." Kyle muttered. He streamed magic to his gravity boots, and they lifted off of the deck of the *Defiance*. Kyle wove magic, and an invisibility field surrounded them both. He saw Grotes standing on port side of the deck, next to a few sailors, and waved goodbye. Then he blushed, realizing that the man couldn't see him.

"Oh Kyle," Ariana murmured. "You're so *cute*."

"Yeah yeah," Kyle grumbled. "I guess I am a little slow."

"Only when it doesn't count," she replied, resting her chin on his shoulder. They both watched as the *Defiance* grew smaller and smaller below them, then turned to the west, seeing the Shimmering Isle before them. The city's buildings were like toys now, the people walking on the streets like ants. Kyle kept rising upward until they

284

were as high as the small mountain on the island, then streamed magic to his boots, accelerating forward.

"Look," Ariana said, pointing down as they passed over the city. "It's Slim!" Kyle looked down, but only saw a bunch of buildings, with tiny people walking about.

"I can't see that far," Kyle reminded her.

"Oh, right," she said. There was a short silence, and then Kyle felt her stir on his back. "I'm forgetting what it's like to be normal." The way she said it, she seemed disturbed by the prospect.

"It's okay," Kyle replied. "Normal is overrated."

They flew in silence then, watching as the city passed by underneath them, followed by rolling, densely forested hills. Kyle streamed more magic into his boots, feeling an immediate burst of speed. Faster they went, until the wind was howling in Kyle's ears, the landscape whizzing by beneath them. A few minutes later, they saw the far side of the island, with the rocky coast giving way to the ocean.

"What are we going to do about the Barren forest?" Kyle yelled over the wind.

"I don't know," Ariana yelled back. "I'm hoping my shard will take care of that."

"We need a plan," Kyle shouted. Hoping for the best wasn't going to be good enough.

"Let's drop down by the shore when we reach land," Ariana proposed. "We should think it through before we go any further."

"Okay."

Kyle pushed even more magic into his gravity boots, making them burst forward even faster above the rippling ocean. He'd rarely had the chance to fly while having a full supply of magic. At full strength, he could reach incredible speeds with hardly any effort at all. He felt a thrill as he accelerated, pushing himself to his limits, the wind screaming past them as they shot across the ocean far below. After what felt like ten minutes, he could barely make out a coastline in the distance.

"Look!" he shouted. Ariana squeezed his shoulder. Kyle flexed his mental muscle, pushing steadily more magic into his boots, the ocean zipping by underneath him. It wasn't long before they were descending toward the coast. Waves crashed onto the shore below, lapping at the yellow sand. Beyond the beach was a lush forest. Kyle was surprised; he'd expected to find another town or city here, with a pier to dock ships at. But there wasn't a building – or any people – to be seen.

Ariana tapped Kyle's shoulder, and he saw her pointing at a large, flat sandy area on the beach. He slowed his flight down gradually, lowering them toward it. They touched down on the beach gently, Kyle's boots sinking into the fine sand. Ariana got off of Kyle's back, which he was incredibly thankful for; without the gravity boots supporting her weight, she – and the backpacks – were far too heavy for him to carry for long.

"That was quick," Ariana said, smiling at Kyle. "That was twenty miles, right?" Kyle nodded. "At this rate, we could make it to the Barrens today."

"I don't know," Kyle replied uneasily. While it was certainly true – they'd taken less than ten minutes to fly the last twenty miles – he was hardly looking forward to reaching the Barren forest, and its dreaded Weavers.

"You're right, we need a plan," Ariana agreed, ignoring Kyle's obvious unease. "Our goal is to reach Sabin's lair without being seen, drop the bomb, and leave before it blows."

"And make it past the Barrens," Kyle reminded her.

"Right."

"Well, we'll have to stay invisible if we don't want to be seen," Kyle reasoned. "When we fly, when we sleep...we can't afford to be caught by a Chosen."

"I can keep us invisible while you sleep," Ariana offered. Kyle nodded.

"But what are we going to do about the tribes?" Kyle pressed. Ariana shrugged.

"If we're invisible, maybe they won't even see us."

"But what if they do?" he countered. "We have to plan for the worst, not the best."

"Okay," Ariana agreed. "Well, my shard will probably protect me from any of their Weavers. But it won't protect you."

"True," Kyle muttered. He felt terrible to admit it, but he was far less worried about Ariana at this point than himself. She was practically invincible, after all...as long as they didn't run into a Chosen.

"Your Aegis should protect you," she stated.

"Maybe not," Kyle countered. "These Weavers beat the Ancients, remember?"

Ariana stared off into space for a long moment, neither blinking nor breathing. She looked disturbingly like a statue, until she finally turned her gaze back to him. "So what do we do?" Kyle thought about it for a moment, tapping his chin with his fingertip.

"What if we drain ourselves of most of our magic," he proposed, "...and pretend to be helpless children? Maybe they wouldn't attack us then." Ariana raised an eyebrow at that.

"But if they do," she countered, "...we'll be completely helpless. You won't be able to use your gravity boots to escape. They'll kill us on the spot."

"Right, stupid idea," Kyle admitted sheepishly. Ariana smiled.

"Don't worry about it, just keep thinking," she urged. "You're good at coming up with ideas."

"Okay," Kyle agreed. He felt emboldened by Ariana's praise, and began to pace, thinking it through. Their goal was to detonate the bomb at Sabin's lair, which was apparently in or near a place called the Barrens. So they had to get through the Barren forest to get there. Or did they? Darius had said that Sabin's lair was about eight miles in diameter, and Kyle's bomb had a blast diameter of ten miles. That didn't leave too much room for error in placing the bomb. That meant they had to be absolutely sure they were near the center of Sabin's lair before they activated it. If they guessed wrong – or worse, left it to chance – they could end up wasting their one hope of destroying Sabin and saving the Empire.

Kyle tapped his chin with one finger, continuing to pace. What if they simply flew *above* the Barren forest, using the invisibility field to avoid the tribes altogether? It might be their only chance to get to the Barrens alive. He said as much to Ariana.

"I don't know," she replied, clearly unconvinced. "The tribal Weavers might be able to detect us. And the closer we get to Sabin's hideout, the more Chosen there might be," she added. "If they have the same senses I do, they might be able to sense us coming."

"How?" Kyle asked. "You can't see me when I'm using the invisibility field."

"But I can hear you," she reminded him. "Your heartbeat, your breathing."

"What if I seal myself in a gravity shield?" He asked. "That would prevent any sound from getting out. I used one to fix the *Defiance's* hull a few days ago."

"But you won't be able to breath for very long in it."

"True," Kyle admitted. "But isn't the same true if we go through the forest on foot? They'll be able to hear us then too."

"It's less likely," Ariana replied. "When I was in the Tower, or out on the streets in Stridon, the noise made it impossible to hear any one particular person very well. If the forest has a lot of ambient sound, we might not be heard."

"And what if it's quiet?" Kyle countered.

"Well, the tribal Weavers live there," Ariana reasoned. "It wouldn't be surprising to hear people moving through the forest."

"I don't know," Kyle muttered. "If we walk, the invisibility field will contact the ground and give us away." He pondered for a moment, then snapped his fingers. "What if we fly just above the treetops? Then we'll still have the sounds of the forest to help camouflage us."

"I don't know..."

"I can seal us in a gravity shield," he continued, "...and when the air runs out, I can release the shield, then make another one. That way we'll be mostly silent."

"That might work," Ariana admitted. "And even if we're forced to go through the forest on foot, I'll be able to hear and see anyone before they ever have a chance to notice us," she added. "Either way, they'll never even know we're there."

"But what if we're wrong?" Kyle asked. "What if they *do* find us?"

"Then I'll fend them off while you fly away," she answered. "They won't be able to win against my shard."

"You don't know that for sure," Kyle countered. "And I wouldn't just abandon you and run off like that."

"I can take care of myself," Ariana reminded him, removing her hand from his shoulder. "And you're the only person who can activate Ampir's bomb, so we *have* to keep you alive, no matter what."

"I still don't like it," Kyle muttered. But he had to admit that she was right. Without him, the mission was impossible...it would fail. He had to stay alive long enough to make it to Sabin's lair, even if that meant putting Ariana at risk. He hated the thought of leaving her – and of having to go on alone – but if it came to that, he'd have to do it. If he didn't, everyone else he loved on Doma would die.

"I know," Ariana said, leaning in and giving him a peck on the cheek. "Neither do I," she added. They both turned to look past the yellow sand of the beach, at the forest beyond. The trees were unlike those he'd become accustomed to near Stridon; they were taller, and much more lush. Dense undergrowth blanketed the ground, thick vines hanging from the tree limbs, nearly reaching the forest floor.

"Well, I guess we'd better get to it," he sighed. He pulled the compass Grotes had given him out of his pocket, finding northwest. Then Ariana wrapped her arms around him from behind, and he streamed magic to his gravity boots, lifting off of the sandy shore and into the blue sky above.

Chapter 21

Sabin stared at the shimmering facets of the green shard through his avatar's eyes, cupping it in one hand. He traced the microscopic network of runes within, double-checking, then triple-checking his work.

It was, of course, flawless.

He pulled his mind back from his avatar then, allowing his consciousness to swim amongst the millions of Chosen that comprised his extended brain. Thousands of Behemoths, hundreds of Void Behemoths. Fleets of flying ships, each piloted by a Chosen's disembodied brain. An army of elite Chosen, the Void Chosen.

The work of twenty lifetimes, an army more powerful than any that had ever been built before. No enemy could withstand it. Even Ampir would be useless against such a force; Sabin's army was scattered across the world, and even if Ampir had the capability of eventually destroying it, Sabin could rain destruction on the planet before Ampir would ever be able to save it.

He who had the power to destroy something, controlled it utterly.

Sabin had no intention of resorting to such drastic measures. Indeed, before Ampir's arrival, he hadn't expected to ever require the use of his secret army. But he'd learned long ago the importance of power. How vital it was in ensuring that no one would ever be able to repeat the injustices that had nearly destroyed him.

No tyrant would take advantage of humanity again, taking from the weak to benefit the strong.

He cast his mind outward then, to one of his Chosen, suddenly eager to remember. He'd met countless tyrants across the centuries, but the first had taught him the most.

* * *

Sabin opens his eyes.

He feels something cold and hard pressing against his face, and he lifts his head up, realizing that he is laying on his side on a gray stone floor. He grunts, rolling onto his hands and knees, wincing as he bends his left knee. Then he pushes himself to his feet.

All around him are dull gray stone walls, ten feet to a side. There are no windows, no doors. On one corner there is a small, round hole in the floor, barely large enough to fit his fist into. He walks up to it, kneeling before it. The rim of the hole is stained, the pungent odor of urine and feces rising from it.

He stands up, backing away.

Sabin turns in a slow circle, then glances upward, seeing the ceiling some ten feet above his head, also made of gray stone. A single lantern hangs in one corner, its lone flame casting a yellow light down on the cold stone floor below. The room is utterly quiet; he hears no sound save for his own breathing. But that is not the only thing that's missing.

There is, he realizes as he searches his mind's eye, no magic.

He glances up at the lantern on the ceiling again, concentrating on it. No magic emanates from it. There is no magic in the walls, or the floor. No magic in his mind. No magic at all.

He fights down a sudden bolt of panic.

He remembers waking up in his bed now, remembers the guards storming his room. Remembers one of them shouting in his ear, accusing him of some terrible crime. And then...

He can't remember.

He makes another slow turn, taking in the starkness of his small room. He knows where he is, though he has never seen this room before. There is only one place in Stridon with rooms like these, rooms designed to be inescapable. He'd heard of them, but had never seen one. Rooms designed to slowly suck the magic out of their occupants, rendering them utterly helpless. State-of-the-art cells in the most advanced prison ever built.

Stridon Penitentiary.

Sabin feels his legs start to wobble, and lowers himself to the ground, feeling the cold stone floor on his buttocks. He looks down at himself, realizing that he is dressed only in an undershirt and his underwear, his pale, scrawny legs splayed out before him. A wave of nausea comes over him, and his gut lurches, sour fluid rushing into his mouth. He swallows it back down, shuddering at the awful taste, and nearly retches again.

Then he hears a screeching sound from above.

He scrambles to his feet, jerking his gaze upward. A thin groove appears in the ceiling, slowly lengthening, forming a long line in the stone. Another line appears parallel to the first, a few feet to the left. Then two more lines appear perpendicular to the others, forming a large square.

Sabin backs away slowly, his eyes locked on that square. There is a loud *thump*, and then the square starts to lower itself into the room.

Sabin feels his back strike the cold stone of the wall behind him, and he presses himself against it, staring at the stone slab descending from the ceiling. His bare foot lands on something moist, and he looks down, seeing his heel next to the hole in the floor. He grimaces, scraping his heel on the stone, then stepping to the side.

Two feet appear, standing on the stone square as it lowers itself. White boots, followed by stark white pants. A perfectly pressed white shirt. And then, a face.

Sabin's eyes widen, and he steps forward from the wall, his jaw dropping. He recognizes the man descending into the room through the hole left by the stone square immediately, his heart leaping into his throat.

Nespo!

The platform the Grand Runic stands on slows its descent, meeting the floor with a dull *thud*. Nespo stares at Sabin for a long moment, then steps off of the platform onto the floor. The stone platform rises up of its own accord, fusing with the ceiling above.

"Good morning, Sabin," Nespo greets.

"Nespo!" Sabin cries, rushing up to the man. Nespo holds out one hand, and Sabin stops in his tracks. Layer upon layer of gravity shields appear around the Grand Runic.

"Stand where you are."

"Nespo, what the hell is going on?" Sabin asks. "Your guards attacked me last night...they're accusing me of murder!"

"So I've heard," Nespo replies calmly

"You don't understand," he states. "I haven't murdered anyone. You have to-"

"I don't *have* to do anything," Nespo interrupts coldly. "Particularly for the man who conspired to assassinate me."

Sabin's eyes widen, and he takes a step back.

"Wait, *what?*" he exclaimed. "Nespo, I didn't..."

"I think you did, Nespo interjects. "The accomplice you hired ratted you out. In exchange for immunity, of course. He was more than happy to provide the letters you wrote him detailing your little plan."

"Letters?" Sabin exclaims. "What letters? What accomplice?" He shakes his head angrily. "Nespo, I swear I don't know what you're talking about!"

"The evidence is overwhelming," Nespo states calmly. "The letters were written in your hand. The signatures you so stupidly signed them with are yours. Even now, the Grand Court is reviewing the documents."

"Nespo, whatever you found, it wasn't me," Sabin insists. "I didn't hire anybody, I didn't send any letters!" He steps forward, pressing his palms against Nespo's outermost gravity shield. "I'm innocent, damn it!"

"Innocent?" Nespo retorts, raising one eyebrow. He pulls a folded-up piece of paper from his pocket, unfolding it and holding it out from behind his gravity shields. Sabin stares at it.

We must act quickly. The longer we wait, the greater our likelihood of being discovered. The tyrant must die. It cannot be traced to me, or our efforts are in vain. With luck, I will be sitting in Nespo's office, ordained with his power, within the month.

You will be richly rewarded for your efforts.

- S

Sabin's mouth falls open, his eyes widening. The letter is in his handwriting, there is no denying it. But he never wrote it.

"I didn't write that," Sabin protests. "Nespo, I didn't write that, it's a forgery!"

"Your accomplice gave us this," Nespo retorts. "Along with many, many others."

"Nespo, I swear I didn't write those," Sabin protests. "Someone else must have done it, forged my handwriting and my signature. I'm being framed!"

Nespo folds the paper into a small rectangle, then deposits it back in his pocket. Sabin feels a slight vibration, and the stone platform descends from the ceiling again, lowering itself to the floor beside Nespo. The Grand Runic lowers his gaze to Sabin's right hand, and Sabin stares at it himself, seeing his ring there, on his middle finger. The onyx ring with the diamond-shaped emerald.

"It wasn't enough, was it," Nespo murmurs, his eyes flicking back up to Sabin's. "You had to have more." He steps onto the stone platform then, and it immediately begins to rise.

"Nespo," Sabin cries. "Nespo, wait!"

"Your trial is in two days," Nespo declares as he rises slowly through the air, toward the hole in the ceiling. "When you are found guilty, you will be sentenced to public execution." He folds his arms over his chest, his stark white clothes practically glowing in the light from the lantern above. He stares down at Sabin as he ascends, his expression stony. "They'll cut off your fingers, then your toes. Then your limbs, piece by piece, cauterizing every wound. When they finally cut you open and burn your intestines, you'll be begging for death. And everyone you care about will be present to bear witness...all of your friends, your colleagues, even your family."

"Nespo!" Sabin shouts, rushing forward to grab onto the edge of the platform. He is thrown backward by an invisible force, slamming his back against the stone wall. He crumples onto the floor, gasping for breath as Nespo continues to rise. The Grand Runic stares impassively at Sabin, the corner of his mouth twisting into a slight smirk.

"Consider this," he stated, extending both arms out to his sides. "...the greatest accomplishment of your life."

* * *

The twelve Councilman, Kalibar, and Erasmus sat around the circular table in the center of the War room for the third hour of meetings that day. Kalibar stretched his legs under the table, shifting his weight from one buttock to the other to try to keep his legs from falling asleep. He glanced at Erasmus, who was clearly having trouble keeping his entire body from falling asleep, and tapped the Grand Runic's leg with his foot. Erasmus jerked awake, glancing at Kalibar, then immediately pretending to be engrossed in Councilman Hewes' speech.

"...and so a five percent global tax increase is the only realistic option we have left," Hewes concluded. Councilman Goran shook his head.

"I cannot endorse that," he stated firmly, crossing his arms over his chest. "And neither will our citizens...not after their fortunes evaporated with the attack on Stridon Central Bank."

"Then how do you propose we pay for rebuilding the Southwest Quarter?" Hewes demanded. "We're suffering from the largest deficit in twenty years..."

"I am well aware of the state of our budget," Goran interrupted. "We'll pay for it by raising the cost of the properties we rebuilt."

"Some of the Quarter's residents won't be able to afford a rent increase," Hewes retorted. "You'd be effectively kicking them out of their homes right after we celebrated their return!"

"A tax increase won't do the same?" Goran countered.

Just then, the front door of the War room opened. Kalibar twisted around in his chair, spotting High Weaver Urson standing at the entrance.

"My apologies, Councilmen," Urson stated. He walked up to Kalibar's side, leaning in. "I have news," he whispered. Kalibar nodded, pushing himself away from the table, then rising to his feet. He turned to face the Council.

"I'll be back," he stated. Goran and the other Councilmen nodded, and Erasmus stared at Kalibar questioningly. Kalibar ignored the look, turning about and following Urson out of the room. They made their way to Kalibar's suite. Kalibar unlocked the magic door, then ushered Urson in, closing it behind them. Urson turned to face Kalibar, his expression – as usual – impossible to read.

"We found the *Defiance*," Urson declared. Kalibar felt a chill run down his spine, and he struggled to maintain his outward calm. The *Defiance* had been crippled in international waters, with Verhanian warships searching for it. There were only two possibilities: either the ship had been rescued, or it had been destroyed...and Kyle and Ariana with it.

"And?"

"Docked at an island called the Shimmering Isle, eighty miles north of Verhan," Urson replied. "A neutral territory without extradition to Verhan. It docked today. The captain and crew are alive."

"And my children?" Kalibar pressed, trying his best to hide his sudden frustration. *Get on with it,* he thought.

"Missing."

"*Missing?*" Kalibar exclaimed incredulously. Urson nodded.

"The island's officials are refusing access to the captain and the crew," Urson stated apologetically. "We haven't been allowed to interrogate them."

"Get access," Kalibar ordered. "Bribe them. You have clearance to mobilize whatever funds you require."

"Yes sire."

"Find my children, Urson," Kalibar urged, putting a hand on the man's shoulder. "Make it happen." Urson nodded crisply.

"Will that be all?"

"Yes," Kalibar answered. "Get to it." Urson saluted, then turned about, leaving the suite. The door shut slowly and silently behind him, leaving Kalibar alone in his room. He stared at the door for a long moment, then lowered his gaze to the floor.

They're alive, he thought, a wave of relief washing over him. He felt lightheaded suddenly, and walked over to one of his couches, sitting down on it and leaning back into the plush cushions. Somehow, the *Defiance* had escaped, sailing across hundreds of miles of open ocean in a few days despite being all but crippled. It was an impossible feat, one that could only have been achieved with magic.

And that meant his children had been aboard to save the ship.

Kalibar sighed, leaning forward and resting his elbows on his thighs. He rubbed his face with his hands, then stared at the tabletop before him.

My children are alive, he thought. *And they've made it to Orja.*

He smiled despite himself, shaking his head and chuckling quietly. He hadn't given them enough credit, it appeared. He should have realized that Ariana's incredible talents would keep them both safe. With her shard protecting her, not even a fleet of warships stood a chance.

Still, against one of Sabin's Chosen, she would be utterly helpless.

Kalibar sighed, standing up from the couch. He began to pace, his boots clicking on the granite floor below with every step. Then he stopped suddenly, pivoting about and walking to his bedroom. His eyes went to the desk in the corner, where he'd put the stack of books from the Archives. Or rather, to the roll of paper next to them. He walked up to it, unrolling it and placing it on the bed. It was a huge map of Orja, the most current one they had. His predecessor, Grand Weaver Rivin, had gotten it as a gift from the King of Verhan. He traced his finger over the Orjanian coast, finding Verhan there. He went north, finding a small series of islands off of the coast. One was labeled "Shimmering Isle." He paused, staring at it.

Kyle said Ampir had given him a map...

Kalibar cursed under his breath, wishing that he'd taken a look at that map when he'd had the chance. He had no idea where Sabin's lair was...no idea where Kyle and Ariana were going. And, as Erasmus had recently admitted to him, Kyle had specifically asked to learn the invisibility pattern before running away. Which meant that if Kyle and Ariana were using the pattern, his Battle-Weavers would never be able to find them...even if they knew where they were going. His Battle-Weavers could be standing a hundred feet away from the two, and they wouldn't even know it.

But I would, Kalibar thought.

He – and *only* he – had the ability to see magic. While sensing magic normally required the subject to be close by, Kalibar could sense magic as far as his eyes could see. He *would* be able to see the invisibility field surrounding Kyle and Ariana. That made him the only person who could possibly find them.

Kalibar stared at the map for a moment longer, then stood up straight, taking a deep breath in, then letting it out.

"Alright," he muttered, turning away from the map and walking up to his nightstand. He streamed magic to the communication orb there, then walked out of the bedroom, back into his suite. He stopped a few feet from the translucent front door, then closed his eyes, taking another deep breath in.

Alright.

* * *

"You're doing *what?*" Erasmus exclaimed, staring at Kalibar in disbelief. Kalibar sighed, sitting down on one of Erasmus's chairs around a large table in the Grand Runic's suite, meeting his bewildered gaze. Kalibar had gone back to the Council meeting soon after talking with Urson, and when the meeting had finally adjourned, he'd asked Erasmus to speak with him here.

"I've made up my mind," Kalibar stated firmly. Erasmus continued to stare at Kalibar, shaking his head slowly.

"You're out of your mind!" the portly Runic exclaimed. "You're out of your damn mind," he added emphatically.

"I'm going after them," Kalibar insisted.

"You're the goddamn leader of the free world!" Erasmus retorted heatedly. "You can't just pack up and leave to get your children!"

"I'm not 'getting' my children," Kalibar countered calmly.

"Is that so?" Erasmus stated, putting his hands on his hips. "Then what the hell *are* you doing?"

"I'm going with them."

Erasmus stared at Kalibar for a long moment, his eyebrows furrowing.

"You're going with them?" Erasmus asked. "What does that even *mean?*"

"My duty," Kalibar replied, "...is to protect the Empire."

"Exactly," Erasmus agreed. "Which means you need to stay here and lead the damn country with me."

"Erasmus, please...hear me out," Kalibar insisted. Erasmus rolled his eyes, then gestured for Kalibar to continue. "My duty is to protect the Empire," Kalibar repeated, "...but my position as Grand Weaver prevents me from doing just that."

Erasmus started to say something, but in a rare moment of self-control, he stopped himself.

"Kyle and Ariana are in possession of the one weapon that has the capability of destroying Sabin," Kalibar stated. Erasmus nodded, having already been told about Ampir's death, Xanos's true identity, and Kyle's bomb. "They're bringing it to Sabin so they can activate it."

"I got that," Erasmus grumbled impatiently.

"As far as I know," Kalibar continued, "...I am the most skilled Battle-Weaver in the Empire, and the only Weaver with experience...and success...in fighting the Chosen."

"Granted."

"If Kyle and Ariana fail to destroy Sabin, the Empire will either be destroyed, or it will be subjugated. There is no other likely outcome."

"But you know damn well they'll never make it," Erasmus complained. "You said yourself that it's a fool's errand!"

"I did," Kalibar agreed. "But it is the best – and only – chance that we have left." He sighed then, lowering his gaze. "And so, in order to serve my people to the best of my ability, and to save my children, I must step down as Grand Weaver."

"This is madness," Erasmus protested, running both hands over his bald pate. He started to pace. "You know who's going to take over if you step down," he added darkly. Kalibar tried to hide a smirk, but failed.

"Goran isn't so bad," he soothed. Erasmus stopped pacing, turning to glare at him.

"Not that bad?" he exclaimed indignantly. "I hate that bastard and you know it!" He started pacing again. "Ever since that conniving, two-faced son-of-a..."

"Erasmus," Kalibar interrupted gently. "It's only temporary."

"Easy for *you* to say," Erasmus retorted, throwing his hands up into the air. "You get to go on some hare-brained adventure with your kids while I'm stuck with that pompous, arrogant..."

"It'll be a week at most," Kalibar stated, cutting his friend off. "I'll claim a week of vacation, and appoint Goran as acting Grand Weaver until I return."

"*If* you return," Erasmus muttered darkly. Kalibar nodded.

"If I return," he agreed. "If not, then Goran will replace me permanently."

"Which is exactly what's going to happen, by the way," Erasmus stated, crossing his arms over his chest. "This is a suicide mission and you damn well know it," he accused.

"Perhaps so," Kalibar admitted. "If you have any better ideas, I'd be happy to hear them." Erasmus snorted.

"You know I don't," he grumbled. He sighed then, lowering his hands to his sides, then walking up to the couch and sitting down beside Kalibar. He turned to look at Kalibar for a long moment, then gave his old friend a weak smile. "You'd better make it back," he warned. He put a hand on Kalibar's shoulder then. "I wouldn't know what to do without you."

"You did fine while I was holed up in Bellingham," Kalibar countered, returning Erasmus's smile. Erasmus chuckled.

"Never expected you to turn into a shut-in," he admitted. "You were really pathetic for a few years there, you know." Kalibar laughed, then nodded reluctantly.

"I was, wasn't I?"

"Hell yes you were," Erasmus replied with a grin. "Down in your dank basement in Boringham, wasting your life away on hopeless projects. If I'd had your looks, I'd have spent my retirement drinking wine and chasing women."

"In all fairness, I *did* drink a fair bit of wine."

"Not enough," Erasmus retorted. "If you'd had enough, you'd have a damn village filled with illegitimate children by now!"

"I think I would've enjoyed that particular project," Kalibar admitted with a grin. Erasmus laughed, and so did Kalibar. But when the laughter died down, Erasmus sighed, standing up from the couch and facing Kalibar. Kalibar stood as well.

"Good luck old friend," Erasmus said. He stepped forward then, wrapping his arms around Kalibar, giving him a hug. Then he stepped back, holding Kalibar's shoulders at arm's length. "If anyone can do it, you can."

"Thank you," Kalibar replied. Erasmus smiled then, but his eyes were sad, moisture lining his lower lids.

"You'd better come back, you old bastard," he warned, his voice cracking. "You're my best friend, you know."

"I know," Kalibar replied, feeling his own eyes grow moist. "I love you too, old buddy."

"Yeah, well," Erasmus muttered, clearing his throat and blinking rapidly. "We'd better go tell the Council about your vacation." He chuckled then, despite himself. "The worst timed vacation in history, by the way."

"I never did take a vacation in my first term," Kalibar countered. "I'd say I'm long overdue."

"One of these days," Erasmus groused, "...you'll have to take a *real* vacation." Kalibar smiled.

"All right," he replied. "If I make it back alive, I promise I'll take a real vacation."

"With a date," Erasmus insisted, giving a lecherous wink. Kalibar smirked.

"Fair enough."

"Now I know you're hoping to die," Erasmus said with a chuckle. Kalibar shook his head.

"No, I think it's about time I settled down," Kalibar countered. "Not having a woman in my life is one regret I don't want to go to my deathbed with."

"You obviously haven't been married for a while," Erasmus quipped. Kalibar grinned.

"I should tell your wife you said that."

"Do it after you come back," he said with a wink. Then he sighed. "Come on then old friend," he urged, turning toward the front door of his suite and pulling Kalibar toward it. "Let's get to it."

Chapter 22

The sun chased Kyle and Ariana as they flew northwest through the warm, humid air, well above the horizon now. The wind howled in Kyle ears as they pressed ever forward, the landscape whipping by beneath them. Kyle had no idea how long they'd been flying for, but it must have been at least a couple of hours. They'd stopped a few times so that he could rest, and to check their position on the topographical map that Grotes had given them. By comparing nearby landmarks – a hill here, a lake there – they'd been able to track their progress rather accurately. The First Mate had been right; without that map, they would definitely have gotten lost.

Kyle frowned, peering beyond the treetops whizzing by a hundred feet below. There, in the distance, were a cluster of mountains rising up into the sky. Trees grew at their bases, growing sparse and stunted the higher the elevation, until there was only bare gray rock all the way up to the mountain peaks. These were capped with snow, which seemed impossible given the sweat pouring from Kyle's body. Down here, it was oppressively tropical.

One mountain stood head and shoulders above the rest, however. It had to be Mount Grimore. It was exactly as Grotes had described: impossible to miss. Ever since Ariana had spotted it – long before Kyle, of course – they hadn't had to recheck their map. The mountain was their guide now, to the dark forest that surrounded its massive base.

The Barren forest.

Kyle stared at that forest, unable to make out much. Thick white mist surrounded it, making it impossible to see very far in. Not to mention that they were still miles away.

"Slow down," Ariana yelled in Kyle's ear, her voice cutting through the shrill screaming of the wind around them. He complied, gradually decreasing his magic stream to his gravity boots. The wind grew quieter as they slowed.

"That's got to be it," Kyle said, pointing to the mist-shrouded forest. "Not sure why they call it the 'Barren' forest," he added. It was the exact opposite of barren, actually. The trees were tall and lush, and from what he could see, the undergrowth was dense, with bushes and ferns sprouting from every inch of mossy ground. It was a veritable rain forest, like the ones Kyle had seen in his biology textbook back on Earth.

"You should make your gravity shield now," Ariana suggested. "A completely closed one, so no one can hear us."

"Good idea," Kyle agreed. He wove magic, and a spherical shield appeared around them.

"Maybe a little bigger," Ariana suggested. "So you can fit more air in."

"Oh, right," Kyle mumbled. He stopped his stream to the first shield, creating a second – much larger – one. It extended about four feet above and below them, glowing a faint blue to Kyle's eyes. "We're almost there," he added. The edge of the forest was only a few hundred yards away now. "We should fly over the trees slowly, so we don't make too much noise." While his gravity shield blocked any noise that *he* might hear, blasting through the sky at a hundred miles per hour would make quite a racket outside of the shield. Going slow would take a lot longer, but they'd be less likely to be detected that way.

"Good idea," Ariana agreed. "Let's go over our plan again."

"Refresh the gravity shield every few minutes to get more air," Kyle stated, having already gone over it many times before. "Stay above the treetops. Fly as fast as I can back to the Shimmering Isle if you tell me to run."

"And don't come to get me," Ariana added. Kyle sighed, then nodded.

"I won't."

"Seriously Kyle," Ariana insisted. "The Empire can't afford you risking yourself."

"You sound like Kalibar now," Kyle grumbled.

"I'll take that as a compliment."

Kyle continued to fly them toward the tree line, now only fifty feet away. He slowed even further, until they were going maybe ten miles an hour, and brought them down to just above the treetops...far enough above to ensure that his gravity shield didn't accidentally hit a tree branch. They flew over the forest, peering down into the dark, misty depths. The forest floor was practically invisible, even from here, the mist too thick to see through.

"Can you see anything?" Kyle asked. Ariana shook her head.

"Not really."

They continued forward, looking straight down, past his boots. The mist around the treetops directly below was a faint blue color, and he couldn't make out much of anything beyond it. The mist faded to white all around them, swirling with the wind of their passage.

"If we can't see anything, how are we going to know when we're at Sabin's lair?" Kyle pressed. From what Grotes had mentioned, the Barren forest led to the Barrens, at the foot of Mount Grimore. That was where Ampir's map had said Sabin would be, but he didn't know anything more specific than that.

"I don't know," Ariana admitted. "Didn't Ampir say it was in one of those Void rooms?"

"Yeah," Kyle replied. A Void room far larger than the Dead Man's had been. Kyle had assumed that it was underground, like the Dead Man's, but now he wasn't so certain. And if it *was* underground, there was no guarantee that they'd be able to find the entrance leading to it. Not to mention that it was almost certainly guarded by Chosen...or worse. "What if we can't find it?" he asked.

305

Ariana said nothing for a long moment. Then she stiffened.

"What's wrong?" Kyle asked. Ariana put a finger to her lips. Then her eyes unfocused, and she stared off into space. Kyle wanted to ask her again, but he kept his mouth shut. Finally, after a long moment, she relaxed.

"There are Chosen nearby," she declared.

"What?" Kyle blurted out, feeling the hairs on the back of his neck rise. "Where?"

"I don't know," she admitted. Then she shook her head. "I don't think they notice us."

"How do you know?"

"I can hear their thoughts," she replied. "Only bits and pieces. It's hard to describe...but I don't think it's Sabin controlling them, like when I heard Ibicus's thoughts." Kyle nodded, remembering Ariana telling him of how she'd sensed what Ibicus was going to say before he said it, when Sabin had taken over the Councilman's hidden shard.

"What're they thinking?"

"I think they're communicating with each other," Ariana murmured. "Sharing thoughts through their shards." She shook her head. "I didn't know they could do that."

"We never saw more than one Chosen at a time."

"We're getting farther away from them," Ariana observed. "I can barely sense them now."

"Good," Kyle stated. His heart was pounding in his chest at the mere thought of running into one of the Chosen here...and he was feeling a little lightheaded.

"You're breathing too fast," Ariana stated suddenly. "I think you're running out of air."

"Right," Kyle muttered. He cut the stream to his gravity shield, and immediately felt a rush of fresh air whipping through his hair. He took a few deep breaths in, then recreated the shield. He felt immediately refreshed. "Thanks."

"No problem."

They continued onward in silence for a time, the unending sameness of the misty forest treetops having an almost hypnotic quality as the minutes passed. Kyle felt his mind start to wander, for some reason picturing the forest around Crescent Lake. How they'd trekked in that forest, Darius, Kalibar, and him, until they'd walked out into that beautiful clearing. A tall, glittering waterfall cascading down into a shallow lake, it had been one of the most beautiful places Kyle had ever seen. He remembered learning magic with Kalibar, then swallowing the feathergrass potion and leaping through the air with unfettered glee. And then spending the night laying in his bedroll, staring at the stars twinkling against the inky black sky, the forest around them shrouded in perfect darkness. His eyes slowly closing as sleep overtook him after a long day's...

"Kyle," Ariana urged, squeezing his shoulder. Kyle jerked his head upward, realizing he'd been zoning out. "Pull up...we're dropping."

Kyle glanced downward, realizing that they were only a few feet above the trees now. He streamed more magic into his boots, rising upward again. He canceled his gravity shield for a moment to refresh his air, then recreated it. They continued onward for a while, watching as the trees passed. Kyle glanced back over his shoulder, seeing an infinite expanse of misty treetops behind them...and a faint trail of blue-tinted mist marking their path, a faint blue line in the whiteness.

"Kyle, we're dropping again," Ariana said. Kyle blinked, turning around, and realized that she was right – again. He streamed more magic into his boots, surprised to find it a little difficult to do so. They'd been traveling for some time, and he'd been having to keep multiple magic streams going. Maybe he was using up his magic more quickly than he could replenish it.

"I'm running a little low on magic," Kyle admitted, concentrating on maintaining his magic streams. It was, he found, getting harder and harder to do so. He cleared his throat, trying to keep the alarm out of his voice. "I'm running out."

"I'll stream you some," Ariana offered. She paused for a moment, then stiffened. "Kyle, I'm running out too!"

"Wait, how are *you* running out?" Kyle asked, feeling a pang of fear in his gut. "You haven't been weaving."

"I don't know," Ariana answered. "Kyle, I can't stream you anything. How much do you have left?"

"Not much," he replied, his heart starting to hammer in his chest. He didn't have much left at all...and he was losing what little remained impossibly fast. "We have to go back," he exclaimed.

"Wait, we have crystals in the bags," Ariana remembered. Kyle felt her shifting her weight on his back, then felt her put something cool and slick into his right hand. He looked down, seeing a quartz cube there. He tried to pull magic from it, but it was empty.

"That one's empty," he complained. She rummaged in the backpacks, then handed him another, with similar results. "I need one with magic in it!" he exclaimed.

"I know," Ariana retorted. "I'm trying to find one." More rummaging. "They're all empty!"

"*What?*" Kyle blurted out. "I just filled them this morning!"

"Well they're empty now!"

"I'm turning around," Kyle declared, shifting his magic stream to his boots. They swung around in a U-shape, flying in the opposite direction. Kyle pumped more magic into his boots, though it required a great deal of effort to do so. They began to speed up, the trees whizzing by below them.

"Kyle!" he heard Ariana shout, her body tensing up. "No, oh no please don't!"

"What?" Kyle demanded.

"My shard," she replied. "It's almost empty!"

"I'll go faster," Kyle said, pushing even more magic into his boots.

"No, my shard, when it's empty, it's going to drain your magic," Ariana protested. "You have to let me go!"

"What? No!"

"You *have* to," Ariana retorted. "I'll be fine."

"You *won't* be fine," Kyle countered. "You won't have any magic!"

"I'm going," Ariana insisted. He felt her grip on him loosening. "Kyle, drop the gravity shield."

"No!"

308

"Kyle, do it," Ariana insisted, her voice icy calm. "Do it now."
Kyle felt her arms slipping from his torso, and he panicked, grabbing her wrists and holding them to his chest.

"Ariana, don't!"

"Kyle, *let me go.*"

He felt his magic stream falter then, felt them drop suddenly toward the treetops below. He strained, pushing as much magic as he could into his boots, feeling his other streams – to his gravity shield and his invisibility field – die out.

"Kyle!"

Ariana's eyelids fluttered, then closed, and she went limp. Rays of blue light began to pull from his body, converging on her shard. He felt what little remained of his magic draining rapidly. They continued to drop through the air, accelerating toward the treetops, now only a few feet away. Kyle squeezed his eyes shut, gritting his teeth and yanking on the last remaining wisps of magic in his mind's eye, pushing them toward his boots...knowing that it wouldn't be enough.

He felt something smack his left foot, then his right leg, and opened his eyes, seeing them skimming the treetops, branching slapping at their legs. Downward they dropped, Kyle's gravity boots dying out, the stabilization fields around them vanishing. Kyle felt Ariana's full weight on his back, felt him rotating, his legs swinging up into the air in front of him. Something very hard struck his butt, and he felt Ariana's arms jerk him backward suddenly. Her grip loosened, one hand falling away. Then a branch struck him in the chest, knocking the wind right out of him. He spun to the side, his left hip striking another branch, the world tilting crazily around him. He felt Ariana's other arm slip away, and then he was falling through thick white fog. He screamed, spinning madly through space, feeling countless branches beating at his body. He threw his arms over his face, then felt something slam into his back. Air burst from his lungs, and he gasped, lowering his arms to his chest. He stared wide-eyed at the sea of green leaves above him, stars swimming at the edges of his vision, hard ground pressing into his back.

I'm alive, he realized.

He laid there, sucking air into his lungs, staring upward. A tangle of tree branches swayed gently far above, leaves rustling in a sudden breeze. Beyond that, he could see the clear blue sky.

I'm alive!

He grunted, rolling onto his side, then pushing himself up into a sitting position. His tested his arms and legs, finding them sore but intact. He was covered in broken twigs, and several wrist-thick branches were strewn around him on the forest floor. They must have broken his fall, striking his Aegis. Even without magic, the armor had saved him.

Then he frowned, rising to his feet. He spun around in a circle, his eyes darting from tree to tree. Where was Ariana? She'd fallen away from him earlier, but she had to be close by. He focused, scanning the trees overhead for broken branches, finding some nearby...right above a large bush. He sprinted toward it, and soon found a pale leg sticking out of it.

Ariana!

He pulled her leg, leaning his back into it, and she slid out, leaves and broken twigs covering her body. Her eyes stared outward lifelessly, her body limp.

"Ariana!" Kyle cried. He leaned over her, grabbing her by the shoulders and shaking her. "Ariana, wake up!" But it was no use; she laid there on the forest floor, unresponsive. Kyle shook her again, and slapped gently at her face, but she just laid there.

She needs magic.

He closed his eyes, searching for the slightest hint of magic in his mind's eye, and found some there...but barely. Not enough magic to wake her for long. He needed more.

Then Kyle saw one of her backpacks on the ground near the bush he'd pulled her from and ran to it, carrying it back to her. He rummaged through it, finding a few small crystal cubes inside, the ones Master Lee had given him. He tried *pulling* magic from them, but it was useless...they were empty. He distinctly remembering filling them earlier that morning, back on the *Defiance*; where had all the magic gone? And why wasn't he making any more?

Leaves rustled behind him.

310

Kyle spun around, crouching low and scanning the forest, his eyes darting from tree to tree. He saw nothing. He glanced down at Ariana, finding her in the same position she'd been in earlier.

Again, the rustling.

Kyle spun around in a slow circle, searching the dense underbrush for the source of the sound, his heart hammering in his chest.

They're coming, he thought, goosebumps rising on his arms. *We have to get out of here!*

He glanced back at the bush Ariana had fallen into, then grabbed her by the ankles, pulling her toward it. Then he backed into it, pushing branches aside until he was nearly surrounded by the bush. He reached out, grabbing Ariana's ankles again and dragging her inside with him. He kept inching backward, pulling her foot by foot, until they were a few feet in. He could barely see anything past the countless twigs of the dense bush.

He waited, sweat dripping down his flanks, his pulse bounding in his ears.

The forest was silent.

He glanced down at Ariana, laying on the ground beside him. With her eyes partially open, her skin deathly pale, she looked like a corpse. He had a sudden pang of fear; how long could she last without magic, before she started to...

He closed his eyes, feeling a wave of nausea come over him.

There was another rustling sound, only a few feet beyond the bush.

Kyle's shoulders tensed, and he held his breath, staying perfectly still. Sweat dripped into his eyes, making them sting, and he ignored the pain, not daring to reach up to wipe his eyes. He squinted, peering through the branches, trying to see past them. He couldn't see a thing.

Maybe it's an animal, he thought, letting his breath out slowly, then taking a breath in. *Maybe it's just a harmless...*

There was a whizzing sound, and then he felt a sharp pain in the back of his shoulder.

"What the..." he blurted out, grabbing at his shoulder. He felt something sticking out of it, and yanked it out.

It was dart.

He swore, rushing forward out of the bush, tossing the dart to the ground. He *pulled* magic into his mind's eye again, turning around in a quick circle, his eyes darting from tree to tree. But he saw nothing.

Then he heard leaves rustling behind him.

Kyle turned around, weaving magic into a tight knot in his mind's eyes. He saw a man with jet-black skin rushing toward him, a vicious-looking machete in his hand. The man raised the machete high in the air, then swung it down, right at Kyle's head!

Kyle shoved his pattern outward.

A gravity shield burst to life around him, and his attacker struck it full-on, flying backward high into the air. He fell into a large bush some twenty feet away with a dull *thump*.

"Lob mi joc!" he heard someone shout from behind.

Kyle spun around, seeing another black-skinned man running toward him, a spear in his hand. The man stopped a dozen feet away, eyeing Kyle warily.

"Get away!" Kyle shouted, reaching into his mind's eye again. He felt magic there, but barely. He wouldn't be able to defend himself for much longer. The man with the spear just stared at him, crouched low, the tip of his spear pointed at Kyle.

Then the world began to spin.

Kyle stumbled to the side, barely keeping his balance. He righted himself, feeling a sudden wave of nausea, and swallowed back a surge of bile.

"Ik tom qua," he heard the man call out.

The world began to spin faster, and Kyle stumbled again, falling to his hands and knees on the packed dirt below. Another wave of nausea came over him, and he retched, closing his eyes. Still the world spun, and he fell onto his side, retching again.

"Cov Petra," he heard a different voice say.

"Rasli cov," the man growled, shoving Kyle's chest, then pointing to the base of the hill. He stared fiercely at Kyle, and Kyle lowered his gaze, feeling sweat trickle down his armpits to his flanks. He swallowed, staring at the ground.

I'm going to die, he realized. *They're going to kill me.*

The man in front of him stared at him for a moment longer, then turned about, striding up to the base of the hill, to a large bush there. He dropped to his hands and knees, crawling into the bush, and disappeared. Kyle felt something hit his back a third time, and he caught his balance this time, twisting around to find another man – dressed the same as the first, but with long black hair and a beard – glaring at him. The man gestured for Kyle to move forward, toward the bush.

"Rasli cov!" he yelled. "Rasli cov!"

Kyle glanced at Ariana's body, still lying on the plank, then turned around, taking a deep breath in, then stepping forward. He made his way toward the bush at the base of the hill, stopping before it. The man behind him kicked him in the back of the legs, dropping him onto his knees in the dirt. The man gestured toward the bush again, making crawling motions with his hands. Kyle nodded, lowering himself onto his belly. With his hands still bound, he had to bow his head down, pushing the prickly branches aside with his head. They scraped at his scalp and ears, and he ignored the discomfort, pushing forward. He'd crawled a few feet when his hands dipped into a hole in the dirt. He paused, lifting his bound wrists to feel around the perimeter of the hole. It was a few feet in diameter, at most.

"Rasli cov," the man behind him urged.

Kyle continued forward into the hole, which was at a 45-degree angle down into the hillside. It soon became almost pitch-black, the edges of the hole barely visible. Still he continued, sneezing at the musty odor of the dirt kicked up by his elbows. Then his hands struck something cool and hard...it felt like metal. He heard a click, followed by a screeching sound from beyond. Then a sliver of light appeared before him, and he realized he was laying in front of a round metal door. The door swung outward away from him, letting more light in.

"Cov," the man behind him ordered.

Kyle grabbed the edge of the door frame – also metal – and pulled himself forward, using his legs to push himself through. He grunted as his head and chest swung forward and down, and he fell onto his forearms on a dark wooden floor below. He felt hands grab him, pulling him all the way through the doorway and up onto his feet. It was the man he'd seen crawl into the bush first, the one with the machete.

"Cov," the man said, pointing ahead. Kyle paused, getting his bearings. He was in a small room, the floor made of wide, dark brown wooden boards. The walls were constructed of larger beams of the same material, with gray stone columns at each corner. The ceiling was surprisingly tall, maybe eight feet, and made of large, crisscrossing wooden beams. The tribesman ahead of him slapped him on the shoulder, pointing again toward the far side of the room, toward an archway there. Kyle heard a scraping sound, and saw two dark legs dangle out of the tunnel. It was the second tribesman, the one who'd been behind him. He dropped to the floor, then reached his arms back into the tunnel, pulling two pale legs through. He gave one jerk, then another, and a limp body fell from the tunnel onto the floor with a loud *thud*. It was, Kyle realized, Ariana.

"Cov!" the first tribesman barked, slapping Kyle on the shoulder, harder this time. Kyle nodded, glancing one last time at Ariana before walking across the room to the archway on the other side. He stepped through, the other men following behind him, and found himself in a wide hallway. The walls and ceiling were constructed of the same material as the room before. There were three doorways on either side, each with a long piece of black cloth hanging from a rod near the ceiling. At the end of the hallway was a real door – made of black strips of wood – and it was to this that the tribesmen ushered Kyle. Machete – that's what Slim would have named him – pushed ahead of Kyle and strode up to the door, knocking on it with a rapid series of taps. It opened, and Kyle was led through.

He found himself in a small room, perhaps ten feet square. The walls, floor, and ceiling were all made of thin strips of the same black, woody material he'd seen on the door. In the center of the room was a woman sitting cross-legged on the bare floor, her eyes closed. She was wearing a black uniform that looked like it was made of the same stuff as the walls; it covered her from her feet all the way up to her neck. It was remarkably form-fitting, so much so that Kyle found himself looking away to one side, his cheeks flushing; the woman was quite beautiful, with the same dark skin as the tribesmen, black eyebrows arching over her closed eyes. She too had tattoos covering her, crawling up the sides of her neck and temples in intricate patterns. But she also had thin, raised scars that extended from the sides of her neck upward, splitting into multiple scars that crawled across her temples like the bones of a bat's wing. She had thick black hair pulled into a ponytail, a few loose strands falling across her face. Her skintight black uniform made it quite clear that she was rather astoundingly feminine, with proportions above and below that threatened to burst free of the fabric that confined them.

He heard a clicking sound, and turned to find Machete closing the door behind them. The tribesman motioned for Kyle to turn back around to face the woman, and he did so, trying unsuccessfully not to stare.

Then he felt cold steel on the back of his neck.

He flinched, and tried to turn around, but the other tribesman – the one with the long hair and beard – reached up and forcibly twisted his head back to face the woman sitting on the floor.

She opened her eyes, focusing on Kyle.

"Lee yog no?" she asked, her dark eyes never leaving him. Kyle shrugged helplessly.

"I can't understand you," he said. He reached into his mind's eye, finding a little magic there, and send some to his earring. The woman uncrossed her legs, then stood up in one graceful motion. She was surprisingly tall and slender, and once again Kyle found himself staring. She walked up to him, stopping a few feet away.

"You say he used magic in the forest?" she asked, putting a hand to the side of his face. Her uniform extended to her fingertips, the black material rough against his skin. Kyle swallowed in a dry throat, staring down at his bare feet. He realized that he wasn't wearing his boots. "He has magic even now."

Kyle kept his gaze downward, considering his options. Ariana had to be just outside. Whoever this woman was, she was probably a better Weaver than him. He'd have no chance against her in a fair fight, but Ariana certainly would. If he could launch a surprise attack and get to Ariana, then stream magic to her...

"We found these," the hairy tribesman said, handing the woman a large tan sack. She took it, pulling out his gravity boots. She stared at them for a long moment, turning away from Kyle and walking back into the center of the room. He saw a faint blue light appear at her forehead, saw it shoot toward the crystals in his boots.

"Simple," the woman murmured. "But elegant." She set the boots on the floor next to her, then reached into the sack again, pulling out Kyle's Aegis. This she stared at for a much longer time, silently turning it over and over in her hands. Then she placed in on the floor, turning to face Kyle.

"Where did you get this?" she asked, gesturing at the Aegis.

Kyle said nothing. If he spoke, she would understand him now, and she'd realize that he could understand *her*.

She repeated the question, in a different language – the earring's interpretation was the same, but her lips moved differently – but still he said nothing.

"Either he doesn't understand us," Machete stated, "...or he won't answer."

The woman stared at Kyle for a long, uncomfortable moment. Then she nodded at Machete.

"Take him outside," she stated. "Burn the girl's body. I'll finish this boy."

Kyle felt hands grab him from behind, and he lunged forward out of their grasp, shaking his head.

"No, wait!" he cried. The woman arched an eyebrow.

"You *can* understand us," she murmured. "Speak again."

"What do you mean?" Kyle asked. The woman frowned.

"I can understand you," she stated. "But your lips do not form the words I hear. How is this possible?" Kyle grimaced, realizing he'd been tricked.

"My earring," he muttered. "It's a universal translator."

318

She stared at him for a long moment, and he found it hard to look back at her. She was painfully attractive, in an exotic sort of way. She pointed back to the Aegis.

"This is yours?"

"It is," he confirmed. She seemed taken aback by this.

"You made it?"

"Uh, no," Kyle admitted. "It's two thousand years old, it was made by powerful Runics."

"Who would give such a thing to a boy?" she demanded. Kyle shrugged.

"It was a gift."

"This is common where you come from?" she pressed, again pointing to the Aegis. Kyle shook his head.

"No, it's very rare," he admitted. "My boots are common there," he added. She seemed relieved by this.

"Your boots are simple," she agreed. Then she cocked her head at him. "Where do you come from?"

"The Empire."

"Where is that?" she inquired.

"East, across the ocean."

"Why are you here?"

Kyle blinked, taken aback by the sudden change of subject. He felt the cold edge of Machete's blade against the back of his neck, felt it press harder into his flesh. He swallowed in a suddenly dry throat. What could he say? If he told them a lie, they'd know it. He was terrible at lying, especially in the heat of the moment. But if he told them the truth, they might kill him anyway.

"We were looking for something," he answered at last. The woman's eyes narrowed.

"What?"

"My, uh, friend," he stammered. "She wanted to meet someone in the Barrens."

"Your friend?" she pressed. "The dead girl?"

"She's not dead," Kyle corrected. "I mean, she's...well, she *looks* dead, but she's not. Not really."

"She is dead," the woman countered. "Tavek says she has no pulse," she added, pointing to the bearded tribesman.

"She doesn't have a pulse," Kyle agreed. "She lives on magic." The woman frowned, then crossed her arms under her bosom.

"Show me," she ordered, nodding at Tavek.

"Yes Petra," Tavek replied. He turned and opened the door, walking out of the room and closing it immediately behind him. A few moments later, the door opened again, and Tavek walked in, Ariana draped over his shoulder. He dropped Ariana gently down onto the floor, then stepped back. The woman – Petra – knelt down over Ariana, putting her fingers to Ariana's throat. Then she stood.

"This girl is dead," she declared. But Kyle barely heard her. For he saw faint tendrils of blue light leaking from the woman's scalp, pulling down toward Ariana's forehead.

She's still alive, he realized, his pulse quickening. Just a little more magic, and she would awaken...and then Petra wouldn't stand a chance.

"How can you say she is alive?" Petra demanded. Then Ariana's eyes twitched, fluttering open.

Petra swore, backing away from Ariana, her eyes widening. Kyle paused, then slowly stepped toward Ariana, feeling Machete's blade still at his neck. He put his hands up, trying to look as innocent as possible. A few feet away, Ariana groaned, her left leg jerking once. Then her arms spasmed. Her eyes widened, and then she turned her head to the side, staring right at Kyle.

"Kyle!" she exclaimed.

"Ariana..." Kyle replied, dashing forward toward her. He heard Machete yell, felt strong hands grab onto his shoulders, yanking him backward. He froze. "Okay, okay! I won't move."

"Kyle, what's going on?" Ariana asked, pushing herself up to sit on the floor. "What happened?" Tavek walked up to her, jabbing his spear toward her chest.

"Don't move!" he exclaimed, glaring at her. Ariana glared at him, then grabbed the point of his spear in one hand, shoving it back. Tavek flew backward, slamming into the wall behind him, his spear

320

falling to the floor with a clatter. He landed in a heap on the floor, groaning in pain.

"Stop!" Petra ordered. Ariana glared at Tavek, then turned to Machete, who was striding toward her. He stopped in his tracks, glancing at Petra. "Leave her be," Petra stated. Ariana turned to Kyle. "Where are we?" she asked. "Who are these people?"

"I think they're the Barren tribes," Kyle answered. "We lost our magic somehow, and we fell into the forest. These people captured us and brought us here."

"You trespassed on our land," Petra countered coldly. "You're lucky that I've let you live this long." She glanced at Ariana. "I sense magic in her," she observed. "Tell her I will examine her."

"She wants to examine you," Kyle told Ariana. "She's a Weaver," he added.

"I know," Ariana replied. "I can understand her." Kyle blinked, taken aback. How could Ariana understand Petra? Ariana didn't have an earring like Kyle, after all. He was about to ask when Ariana stopped him with one outstretched hand, shaking her head. "Does she understand me?"

"What is she saying?" Petra asked.

"She's asking if you can understand her," Kyle replied. He couldn't very well lie, after all...if Petra *could* understand Ariana, he'd be caught red-handed. Although it was clear from Petra's tone that she probably couldn't. Ariana's shard must have a universal translator of sorts in it, he realized. It only appeared to work one-way, however, allowing her to understand everyone, but not the other way around.

"I cannot," Petra answered.

"Tell her that if anyone attacks us again, it'll be the last thing they do," Ariana stated, glaring at Petra. Kyle glanced at Petra, then back at Ariana. Escalating the situation hardly seemed like a good idea. They could always fight Petra if they had to...but so far they hadn't really been harmed.

"She's says it's okay to examine her," Kyle lied, nodding at Petra. Ariana's eyes widened, and she glared at him, but Petra was already walking up to her. The tribeswoman stared at her intently, then reached out, pressing her fingers onto the side of Ariana's neck. Ariana stiffened, but didn't resist.

"She has no pulse," Petra observed with disbelief, dropping her hand to her side. She twisted her torso to look at Kyle, her profile so remarkable that Kyle couldn't help but gawk. He blushed, turning away; looking at this woman was like looking at the sun...impossible to do for long without dire consequences. "You told the truth."

"I did," Kyle agreed, hoping Ariana didn't notice the source of his embarrassment.

"She is between life and death?" Petra pressed. Kyle nodded, turning to Ariana. It was better that Petra didn't know that Ariana could understand her without him translating. "She's asking if you're uh...between life and death."

"I am," Ariana confirmed. Kyle translated for her. Petra's brows furrowed.

"How is she kept like this?" she asked. Kyle glanced at Ariana, who nodded slightly.

"She has a...crystal," Kyle answered, pointing to his forehead. "In here, under the skin. It keeps her alive."

Petra took a sharp breath in, backing away from Ariana quickly. Her eyes widened, her jaw going slack.

"She is an Immortal!" she exclaimed. Tavek – having struggled to his feet and reclaimed his spear – stared at Ariana in disbelief, as did Machete. "She is from below?" Petra pressed. "From the Void?"

"You know about the Void?" Kyle asked, taken aback. Petra nodded.

"The Immortals are born from it," she stated. "Deep in the earth, in the cave of our ancestors below the mountain."

"You know where these caves are?" Kyle pressed, his heart skipping a beat. She had to mean Mount Grimore...and the caves, the Void, might lead them right to Sabin!

"Of course."

"We came to take her there," Kyle stated, feeling a sudden burst of hope. If these people knew where the entrance to Sabin's lair was, they could lead Kyle and Ariana right to it. "Can you help us?"

"If she is truly an Immortal," Petra agreed. She frowned then. "The Barrens do not remove magic from the Immortals," she added. "How is it that she was drained?"

"I don't know," Kyle replied, his mind racing to come up with a reason, but finding none. "She was...uh...born just a few weeks ago, and lost her memory."

"I see," Petra murmured. To Kyle's dismay, she didn't seem convinced. She turned to face Kyle. "If she is an Immortal, of course I will help her return to her kind. But she must prove herself first."

"Ask her how," Ariana stated.

"How?" he asked.

"We will take her to the mouth of the cave, and she must walk into it and retrieve a Void crystal from within. Only an Immortal can do this."

"What cave?" Ariana asked. Kyle translated for her.

"A cave distant from the one that leads to the Void," Petra replied. "Those who walk into it share the same fate as those who attempt to enter the Void."

"What happens, exactly?" Kyle pressed.

"Anyone who walks into the cave dies within minutes. Only an Immortal can survive. If you return, you will have proven your nature. If you don't, you will be dead."

Kyle glanced at Ariana, who stared back at him. If anyone who ventured into the caves died except for the Immortals – or rather, the Chosen – then what would happen when *he* tried to go into them? He still had to detonate the bomb as close to Sabin as possible...and the only way to be sure was to detonate the bomb in the cave. There was no way to know how far from the cave entrance Sabin's lair was, after all. It couldn't possibly be more than five miles, though – half the diameter of the bomb's blast. Or could it?

"Why does everyone who goes into the caves die?" Kyle asked Petra. She shrugged.

"No one knows," she admitted. "Those who have tried, their skin turns red. They lose their mind, and soon after they fall asleep.

Sometimes they fall to the ground and their arms and legs shake. Then they die."

"Oh," Kyle mumbled. He caught Ariana looking at him; she was clearly thinking the same thing he was: if Kyle couldn't go into the cave without dying, how could they possibly go forward with their plan?

"And if I refuse?" Ariana pressed. Again, Kyle translated for her.

"Then you will be left in the Barren forest," Petra answered. "Your magic will be drained, and you will be dead. Your friend," she added, turning to Kyle, "...will also be put to death for trespassing on our land."

Kyle swallowed in a suddenly dry throat, glancing at Ariana.

"Sounds like an easy task," Ariana opined. "We could use her help. If something goes wrong and they attack us, we'll have to kill them."

Kyle nodded silently, swallowed in a dry throat. He turned back to Petra.

"I guess we don't have a choice," he muttered. Petra nodded.

"Then you agree," she stated. Ariana nodded, and so did Kyle. "Very well," Petra said. "I will bring you to the mouth of the cave for her test."

Chapter 23

Sabin rests his back against the cold stone wall of his cell, sitting down on the floor, his legs splayed out in front of him. He stares off into space, ignoring the box of food that had been dropped unceremoniously in front of him a half-hour ago. His stomach complains bitterly, but the thought of eating makes him nauseous.

Guilty.

The trial had been a sham, of course. He'd been appointed a lawyer, competent but without talent. With the incredible volume of fabricated evidence Nespo's attorney had revealed, no amount of skill could have saved Sabin. Any suggestion of Nespo having framed Sabin was deemed so improbable that no one had believed it.

Sabin lowers his gaze to his hands, staring at the ring on his right middle finger. They'd taken everything else from him. His clothes, his land. His home. Even his patents had been acquired by the government. They'd taken everything, forever tarnishing his reputation. In one fell swoop, Nespo had nullified Sabin's entire life, robbing him of every accomplishment. The Grand Runic had destroyed Sabin's legacy, and very soon, would take his life.

Sabin stares at his ring, the black onyx with the diamond-shaped emerald. It is the only possession he'd been allowed to keep. A reminder of what he'd been, before Nespo had set him up. A reminder of how far he's fallen.

And now none of that matters. Because tomorrow, he will face death. He will be executed, his limbs removed ounce by ounce, his body mutilated until there is nothing left. He'd seen it once before, this type of execution. Or rather, he'd seen part of it; he'd had to leave soon after it had started, unable to stomach the horrible screams of the man who'd been sentenced. The idea that it is going to happen to *him* tomorrow is unreal. Impossible. And yet he knows that he will have to face it.

Tomorrow, he will die.

Sabin's eyes scan the room for the umpteenth time since he'd been returned to it after his trial, pointlessly searching for a way to escape. Without magic, there is nothing he can do. There is no way to reach the ceiling ten feet above, where the only exit of the cell is. An exit that, when closed off, is fused to the stone ceiling around it.

He returns his gaze to his hands, staring at his fingers. Imagines himself standing in the courtyard in Stridon square, surrounded by Battle-Weavers, tied upright to a cross made of sturdy wooden beams. Imagines the rough ropes binding his wrists and ankles to those beams, the executioner grabbing his index finger, pressing a serrated knife at the crease of his last knuckle.

He closes his eyes, imagining that blade moving up and down slowly, sawing through his flesh. The grating sound it would make as the metal struck bone. The pain. Watching as his fingertip fell to the ground, rolling on the street below while the remaining stump squirted blood, until the red-hot brand was pressed into it.

Sabin shudders then, his pulse quickening, and opens his eyes, staring at his finger. A low moan escapes his lips, and rises in pitch. His mind continues to work despite itself, imagining the executioner taking one finger after the other. Then his wrists. His forearms. His elbows.

Oh god oh god oh god...

Sabin clenches his hands, his knuckles going white. He's breathing faster now, the air growing thin around him. He feels a

326

terrible pain in his chest, and pulls his legs under him, lurching to his feet. He staggers forward, staring up at the ceiling, at the exit.

"Help!" he shouts, clutching his chest with his hands. The pressure there is incredible, like nothing he has ever experienced. He feels tremendously lightheaded all of a sudden, his face burning hot. His legs give out beneath him, and he falls to his knees on the unforgiving stone floor. Pain shoots up his legs, and he cries out, landing on his palms.

The cell spins around him.

"Help!" he shouts, rolling onto his side, then onto his back. He clings to consciousness desperately, every muscle in his body clenching. The pressure in his chest remains, making it almost impossible to breath.

I'm having a heart attack, he realizes, squeezing his eyes shut. He feels sweat trickling down his flanks, feels heat rising from him despite the cold stone at his back. And yet, for all his shouting, no one is coming to help him.

It is only then that Sabin realizes the absurdity of his thoughts.

"I'm having a heart attack," he murmurs, his voice hollow-sounding as it echoes throughout his cell. His lips twitch, then curl into a smirk. He laughs then, an abrupt, barking sound.

I'm having a heart attack!

Elation courses over him.

He closes his eyes, lifting his hands from his chest and laying them out to his sides. His smirk widens into a grin, and he laughs again.

Take me now, he urges silently. *Give that bastard one last middle finger.*

He waits.

But the pressure in his chest gradually subsides, his pulse slowing. His eyes snap open, and he feels a bolt of panic.

No!

He stares down at his chest, then balls his right hand into a fist, slamming it into the center of his chest.

"No, god damn it!" he shouts, raising his fist and slamming it into his chest again. Over and over his strikes himself, each dull thump echoing off of the stone walls. "No, no, no!"

327

He stops then, feeling a painful throbbing in his chest. He waits, hoping to feel that pressure again, that horrible squeezing sensation. But it's gone. He takes a deep breath in, clenching his fists.

"*Shit!*" he screams at the top of his lungs. He staggers to his feet, clutching his hair with both hands, pulling as hard as he can. He screams again, feeling hair ripping out of his scalp, the sudden stinging pain making his eyes water. He steps backward, feeling his spine strike the wall behind him. He lets go of his hair, seeing clumps of it fall gently to the ground. He stares at his hands, curling his fingers into claws, and grabs at his own throat, digging his fingertips into his flesh. He feels his windpipe there, and grips it tightly.

He sucks air into his lungs, hyperventilating now, psyching himself up. He squeezes his eyes shut, swallowing once, then again. *One good pull,* he commands himself. *Do it.*

He opens his eyes, then closes them again, shifting his weight from foot to foot. *Do it you miserable bastard. You goddamn worthless coward!*

He feels his grip loosening, and he shakes his head, letting out a guttural roar. He grasps his neck more firmly, sliding his fingers up around his Adam's apple, taking in another round of short, quick breaths.

Come on come on come on...

Then he imagines himself with his windpipe crushed, unable to breath, unable to speak. Slowly drowning in a sea of air, the life ebbing out of him. His resolve waivers.

"Damn it!" he shouts, letting go of his neck and slamming the meat of his fist into the wall behind him. *I can't even kill myself!* He drops his face into his hands, sliding his back down the wall behind him, feeling his buttocks strike the floor. A muffled sob escapes his lips, and quickly turns into bitter laughter.

Oh don't you worry, he tells himself. *Someone else will be happy to do it for you real soon.*

He closes his eyes, resting his head back on the wall behind him. He feeling his pulse slowing, sweat dribbling down his flanks. Then he opens his eyes.

A man is standing in the center of the cell.

Sabin blinks, not believing his eyes. Then he rises to his feet, his jaw dropping.

There, in front of him, stands a tall man in jet black armor, his eyes hidden beneath a curved, mirrored visor.

"Ampir!" Sabin cries.

"Sabin," Ampir replies, nodding slightly. He pauses for a moment. "Catch you at a bad time?"

"How..." Sabin begins, then clears his throat. "How did you get in here?" He glances up at the ceiling, seeing only smooth, unbroken stone and the flickering lantern there. He suddenly wonders if he is going mad, if Ampir is just a figment of his delusional mind.

"I could ask you the same question," Ampir replies coolly.

"I didn't do it, Ampir," Sabin states, stepping forward and grabbing Ampir by the shoulders. To his surprise, no gravity shields appear around the Battle-Runic. "I'm innocent, you have to believe me!"

"Right."

"It's *true*," Sabin insists. He drops to his knees then, ignoring the painful hardness of the floor, sliding his hands down to Ampir's armored wrists. "I'm begging you," he pleads, feeling tears well up in his eyes. "You have to believe me!"

"Get up," Ampir growls, his tone disgusted. He yanks Sabin to his feet.

"I was framed..." Sabin begins, but Ampir cuts him off.

"I know."

"It was Nespo," Sabin continues. "He...what?"

"I know," Ampir repeats. Sabin stares at him for a long, silent moment, his mouth agape. Then he snaps it shut, his teeth clicking. "You *know*?"

"After you were charged, Vera couldn't believe Nespo's allegations," Ampir states. "She said you weren't capable of murder. She insisted that I investigate." His lips twitched then. "She was...persuasive."

"What did you do?"

"I eavesdropped on Nespo," Ampir answers. "Neutralized his wards and stood in his room without him knowing it. Listened to every conversation."

"And?"

"As you said," Ampir confirms. "...you were framed."

"You know!" Sabin exclaims, breaking out into a smile. "Oh thank god..." He feels a rush of excitement, his heart hammering in his chest. "You have to help me," he insists. "You have to get me out of here!"

"Why did he do it?" Ampir presses. Sabin blinks, then frowns. "What?"

Ampir just stands there, saying nothing.

"Oh..." Sabin stammers. "He...I went to Orja," he answers. "For my initiation tour. I was expecting to see another province of the Empire, but..." He shakes his head then. "Ampir, you can't imagine what I saw."

"Try me."

"The Empire is using the natives as slaves," Sabin states. "Hundreds of thousands of men and women...even children...living in squalor, worked literally to death. They're free labor for the diamond mines. Our men beat the natives to death on a whim. They bring the women back to Verhan to take turns...using them."

"Go on."

"The Council voted unanimously to make the Orjanian colonies legally separate from the Empire," Sabin explains. "So that they could deliberately remove their authority to prosecute their own citizens – former citizens – for crimes against humanity."

"And you confronted Nespo," Ampir states. Sabin nods. "I did."

"Idiot," Ampir mutters. Sabin stares at the man, his mouth agape. "What?"

"You're an idiot," Ampir repeats.

"How can you..."

"You're here, aren't you?" Ampir interrupts, gesturing with one arm at the cell surrounding them. "What were you expecting to happen?"

"I wasn't expecting our Grand Runic to be a slave-trading tyrant," Sabin retorts indignantly. "I wasn't *expecting* him to frame his Elder Runic for murder!"

"He's corrupt," Ampir explains, as if it were obvious all along.

"How was I supposed to know that?" Sabin retorts. Ampir rolls his eyes.

"He's a politician."

"So am I," Sabin retorts. "But I'm not corrupt." And it's true. He never had to resort to that, and never would.

"You're naïve."

"How can you be so damn..." Sabin begins, then stops himself, taking a deep breath in, then letting it out. "I was just trying to do the right thing."

"Think strategically," Ampir retorts. "Politics is war. Your colleagues are your enemies. Blindly charging at a more powerful enemy is suicide."

"Maybe so," Sabin concedes. "But I had to do *something*."

"All you did was almost get yourself killed."

Sabin lowers his gaze, unable to refute the obvious truth. He'd acted on impulse, doing exactly as Ampir said...threatening Nespo without really thinking about what he was doing. He should have gone straight to Ampir first. There was no need to go out on his own, making himself a target.

Then Sabin jerks his head back up, staring at his own reflection in Ampir's visor.

"Almost?" he asks. "I *almost* got myself killed? What does that..."

"I'm getting you out of here," Ampir interrupts. Sabin's eyes widen, and he lets out a single, barking laugh, clutching at Ampir's arms. He laughs again, his eyes filling with tears, and he embraces the silent Battle-Runic. Then he pushes himself back, staring into that mirrored visor.

"Thank you," Sabin says, his voice cracking. "Thank you Ampir!"

"Don't mention it," Ampir replies. "Seriously, don't."

"My lips are sealed," Sabin promises. Then he frowns, staring up at the ceiling again. "How are we going to escape?"

"The same way I got in," Ampir answers. Sabin's eyebrows knit together.

"How *did* you get in here?" he asks. Ampir smirks, and Sabin feels a slight vibration in his skull. He feels his eyelids growing heavy, the urge to sleep overwhelming. He slumps into Ampir's arms.

"I blinked," Ampir replies.

* * *

Kalibar squinted against the fading sunlight, using one hand as a visor to shield his eyes as he stared out of the window of the carriage that raced across the highway leading toward his estate in Bellingham. It wasn't the usual horse-drawn carriage he'd used during his retirement; it was a levitating carriage without a horse, steered by the dozen elite guards levitating all around it. It was capable of taking him from Stridon all the way to his mansion in Bellingham in a few hours, a trip that would've taken three full days by horse-drawn carriage. He'd undertaken the trip a few hours after notifying the Council of his decision to take his vacation.

That had not gone well.

Councilman Goran had led the impassioned revolt against the very idea of Kalibar leaving, citing the terrible timing, what with the recent attack on the city. How could Kalibar even *think* of taking time off for leisure at a time like this? Not to mention what the citizens of Stridon might think, knowing their esteemed leader was off vacationing while Xanos lurked in every shadow, ready to strike. Kalibar had listened patiently, having expected such a reaction. When Goran had finished, Kalibar had simply replied that he felt he was leaving the Empire in excellent hands, what with Goran taking over the office of Grand Weaver temporarily. That silenced Goran – to refute it would be to refute his own abilities, something the man was loathe to do – and to the rest, Kalibar said that he planned on spending his vacation pondering the proper strategy for dealing with Xanos once and for all. This, he'd proposed, was something he simply could not do effectively while shouldering the many burdens of his office.

Surprisingly, that had worked.

The carriage slowed, then came to a stop before the grand front doors of Kalibar's mansion, parking on the dark brown cobblestone driveway. An elite guard opened the carriage door for Kalibar, and Kalibar stepped down, his black boots clicking on the stone below. He nodded at his guards, then walked up to the front double-doors of his retirement home, hardly surprised when the doors opened before he'd even reached them. Out stepped his property manager, a short, studious man wearing glasses and a gray suit. The man's name was Reo, and he had proven to be a most trustworthy and capable man in the six years that Kalibar had known him.

"Welcome back Master," Reo greeted. "Grand Weaver," he corrected immediately, with obvious embarrassment. Kalibar smiled.

"Good to be back Reo," he replied. He noticed his elite guards fanning out around him, some walking into the mansion while others made their way into the front yard. They were ensuring the mansion's security, of course. Not that it was likely to be necessary; when Kalibar had started his second term as Grand Weaver, the mansion had undergone a complete security overhaul. He'd nearly been assassinated here only a month or so ago, after all. "How is your family?"

"Quite well," Reo answered. "Carla and the boys went fishing today at the pond."

"Glad to hear it," Kalibar replied. "Any outstanding issues with the property?"

"No Master," Reo answered. "Everything is running smoothly."

"And my accounts?" Kalibar pressed. His fortune – a considerable one at that – was also managed by Reo, along with a team of gifted accountants and lawyers. Reo sighed.

"Your investments suffered with the recent attack on Stridon," he admitted. "But you'll find that they are still quite healthy. The market is recovering slowly."

"Indeed," Kalibar murmured, only half-listening. He was rich beyond the wildest dreams of his youth, wealthy enough not to care about money anymore. It was only a tool now, a means to an end. He'd mentioned it to Reo purely to make the property manager feel that his efforts were acknowledged, so that he would feel fulfilled in his role. That was what most people wanted, after all...to be acknowledged. "Well done Reo," he said, putting a hand on the man's shoulder. "I don't know what I'd do without you."

"It was nothing," Reo replied. But the man was clearly pleased. "Is there anything you'll be requiring for your vacation?"

"I will be spending it in my laboratory," Kalibar answered. Reo nodded.

"The usual rules, sire?" he inquired. Kalibar nodded. He'd spent much of his retirement here in his laboratory in the basement, reading and experimenting with magic. He'd been known to spend days, if not weeks, holed up in there, emerging only for meals and his evening exercise. Reo knew exactly what Kalibar wanted: no interruptions, no visitors, no questions asked.

"I'll prepare my own meals," Kalibar informed the man. "No one is to disturb me for any reason."

"As you wish," Reo replied, bowing deeply. "Will there be anything else?"

"No."

Reo turned about and left, and Kalibar stepped into the foyer of his mansion and looked around. The mansion was just as he'd left it, with yellow-painted walls and elaborate white crown-molding where the walls met the ceiling some twelve feet above. A wide staircase led up to the second floor, the two archways flanking it leading further into the first floor. It was instantly familiar, but somehow foreign. While it was still his house, it no longer felt like *home*. Even his suite back in the Tower felt strangely empty without Kyle and Ariana there...and without Darius.

Where *was* Darius, anyway? The bodyguard had left for his vacation days ago, and had never returned. It was unlike the man to be late, or at least it had been. Darius had proven unreliable during the attack on the Tower a little over two weeks ago as well. Kalibar hated to think that he'd have to demote the man, given that he still owed Darius his life...several times over, in fact. He would have to have a talk with Darius when the bodyguard returned.

Kalibar sighed then, snapping out of his reverie and striding across the foyer. He walked through the left archway, continuing down a long hallway until he came to a door near the end, on the left. He spotted a faint blue tint to it, evidence of its magical nature. With a thought, he wove the pattern to unlock the door, and it swung open without him having to touch it. Beyond, there was a narrow staircase that led down to the basement...to his laboratory. He paused before it, wondering how many times in the last six years he'd made this same journey, walking down this stairwell to spend countless hours below. He felt a pang of regret, and wondered how much of his life he'd wasted down there, distracting himself from truly living. All those years of research, and nothing to show for it.

He sighed again, then stepped through the doorway and made his way down the stairwell. It turned left, then left again, ending before enough magically sealed door. Kalibar opened this as he'd done for the first, and walked into his laboratory.

The first thing that struck him was the smell. He'd forbidden anyone from entering his laboratory since he'd had it built in the mansion's basement over six years ago, including the cleaning staff. As a result, a fine layer of dust had settled over everything, leaving a musty smell in the air. He looked around, spotting the familiar rows of tables with various gemstones neatly categorized by type on each, a reminder of the last project he'd worked on here, the very day Darius had brought Kyle to his door, in fact. He'd been trying to recreate Sabin's research into magic vacuity, methodically filling various gemstones with magic, then measuring the rate of flow between them and an empty reference gem...a diamond. That particular experiment had been done before – every Runic student had to perform it – but Kalibar had taken it a step further, draining *himself*, then measuring how quickly he could drain magic from each filled gemstone, and comparing it to the reference diamond. He'd found that the magic vacuity of his brain was a hundredfold greater than that of an empty diamond.

Which, according to classical magicodynamics, was impossible.

Kalibar walked up to one of the tables, passing his fingers over a large chunk of hematite. How he'd wracked his brain to reconcile his findings with everything else he'd known about magic! He'd spent weeks running his experiment over and over again, with the same results. He'd assumed his experiment was flawed somehow, and had all but abandoned the experiment by the time Kyle had come into his life. He'd taken solace in the fact that the great Sabin himself had failed to uncover his theoretical "void mineral," dying before ever managing to isolate it.

But of course, Sabin hadn't died. And he *had* discovered the void mineral...

Kalibar closed his eyes, picturing the Void sphere. Sabin's masterful invention, so elegantly simple yet so deadly. Able to drain magic out of everything around it, then use that magic to destroy those it drained. It had even, for a single moment back in the Tower lobby, managed to drain Kalibar's will to live.

Kalibar opened his eyes, and stared at the gems on the table in front of him, his mind starting to churn. The Void sphere somehow managed to suck in magic at great distances, something regular gemstones could not do. Normally, even an empty diamond would not pull any measurable magic from a full gem that was more than a foot away. The greater the distance between gems, the less magic would be exchanged...to double the distance would decrease the magic exchange by eight times. But the Void sphere had drained magic from objects throughout the entire lobby...a massive room indeed. The question was...how?

Kalibar stared *through* the table, his mind in full gear now, ticking through the possibilities.

The more empty a gem was, the greater the vacuity of that gem...in other words, the more strongly it would drain magic from objects around it. A truly empty gem – completely empty, something nearly impossible to achieve unless dipping it into the deep ocean for long periods of time – had nearly infinite magic vacuity. If one could maintain a crystal at near-absolute zero magic, that crystal's vacuity would remain enormously high, exponentially higher than if it had even a tiny amount of magic left in it.

Kalibar realized his eyes were stinging, he'd held them open for so long. He blinked, then put a hand up to his right earlobe. It still ached a bit from having it pierced earlier today; he'd had a universal translator placed there, a handy device to have when traveling to foreign lands. He fiddled with it absently, staring off into space again. The Void sphere had sucked magic in, then used magic to power its gravity fields. But Kalibar distinctly remembered its magic-draining ability rapidly waning right before it activated those fields. What if the sphere had been sucking in magic, then *using* that magic to power some invisible process? What if it had been draining *itself* of magic at the same time it had been draining everything else, using it all up to keep itself at near-absolute zero?

Goosebumps rose on the backs of Kalibar's forearms.

What if the mind did the same thing?

He stepped back from the table then, staring at the gems there. He spotted a fist-sized diamond at the end, and walked up to it, filling it with magic until a pale blue glow emanated from its surface. Then he backed up, until he was some fifteen feet away. He stared at the diamond for a long moment, then *pulled* at its magic with his mind.

A thin blue line shot out from it, right at his forehead.

"My god," he breathed, his pulse quickening. He felt the hairs on the back of his neck stand on end. "I'll be damned."

All minerals theoretically reached near-infinite vacuity at absolute zero magic. Getting a mineral to lose almost all of its magic was enormously difficult...and far more so the greater its magic vacuity. Which meant that the easiest mineral to get to near-zero wouldn't be the one with the *highest* magic vacuity...it would be the one with the *lowest*.

"I'll be *damned*," Kalibar swore, shaking his head slowly. Then he laughed. He turned away from the table, laughing again, then sprinted back through the doorway he'd come from, taking the stairs three at a time. He burst through the door at the top, running down the hallways until he reached the large foyer.

"Reo!" he cried, feeling an elation he hadn't experienced in years. "Reo!"

337

His property manager burst through one of the foyer's many doors, looking quite harried. He was followed rapidly by half a dozen elite guards.

"Grand Weaver," one of them exclaimed. "Are you all right?"

"All right?" Kalibar retorted with a grin. "I'm *fantastic!*" He grabbed Reo's shoulders with both hands, shaking the poor man a bit. "Get me a pen and a letter at once!"

"Yes Master," Reo stated immediately, looking quite bewildered. But he did as he was commanded, leaving quickly and returning moments later with the requested items. Kalibar took these, placing the letter on the wall nearest him, and wrote quickly. Reo stared at him for a long moment, stealing nervous glances at the elite guards.

"May I ask what has happened?" he inquired meekly. Kalibar ignored the question until he was done writing, and folded the paper, handing it to one of his elite guards.

"You are to take this letter to Grand Runic Erasmus immediately," he ordered. "No eyes but his will read it."

"Yes, Grand Weaver," the guard replied, saluting sharply, then leaving at once. Kalibar watched him go, feeling suddenly so happy that he could kiss someone.

"Master, are you all right?" Reo asked. "What happened?"

"You know of Sabin?" Kalibar asked. Reo nodded.

"The Ancient traitor, I presume?" he asked. Kalibar nodded.

"Also one of the most creative minds in the history of magic," he added.

"What of him?"

"I saw his glorious mind, for a moment," Kalibar answered. "As I was following in his footsteps."

Reo just stared at him, clearly bewildered. Kalibar sighed, suddenly wishing he'd never left the Tower...that he could run to Erasmus and tell him what he'd discovered in person. What he wouldn't give to see his old friend's face when he read his letter! The man would be overjoyed...and furious that Kalibar – a Weaver, no less – had thought of it first.

"My experiments are going well," he explained. Then he cleared his throat. "I suppose I should get back to them."

"Yes Master, Grand Weaver," Reo stated, backing up, then turning away and escaping the foyer. Kalibar watched him go, then made his way back down to his laboratory, standing before his rows of gem-topped tables once again. He'd come down here for a reason, after all...as an excuse to vanish for a week without anyone asking questions, and without anyone looking for him. It was vital that no one knew what he was really up to...flying on a suicide mission to help his children finish what Ampir had started.

He took a deep breath in, then let it out slowly, feeling his elation slowly wane. Then he strode across the lab to one of the sinks at one end, staring at himself in the mirror above it. Short white hair, brown eyes with crow's feet radiating out from the sides, a narrow nose, and a firm, square jaw. He supposed he looked the part of a Grand Weaver, still handsome despite his years. He'd been lucky in many ways, to be possessed of an agile mind and a strong will, to say nothing of his looks. He'd resisted any pride in these qualities of his, knowing that they were a circumstance of his birth, and had little to do with any accomplishment of his own.

He took a straight razor from his pocket, raising it to his scalp, pausing at his hairline. He took another deep breath, then got to work.

Chapter 24

Kyle crawled out of the musty tunnel toward the forest surrounding Petra's home inside of the hill, sneezing as the dust kicked up by his passage tickled his nostrils. He saw sunlight shining through the thin branches of the bush that hid the tunnel's entrance, and crawled up to it, lowering his head and closing his eyes as he pushed his way through. The branches scratched at his face and ears, but he ignored them, continuing onward until he was standing on the forest floor. Sunlight cascaded through the lush forest canopy, a slight breeze rustling the green leaves. Kyle noticed for the first time that the leaves did not glow, undoubtedly due to a lack of magic. Tavek and Machete were standing before him; they'd crawled through the tunnel ahead of him, so that he wouldn't get any foolish notions of trying to escape.

Kyle heard a scraping noise behind him, and saw Ariana emerging from the tunnel, followed by Petra. The tribal Weaver had allowed Ariana to borrow a black uniform similar to the one she herself wore, and it clung to Ariana tightly. Apparently the material – whatever it was – insulated against magic loss. There was a hood of sorts hanging from the back of the uniform at Ariana's neck, and she pulled it up over her head. It was a bit like a ninja mask, covering everything but her eyebrows and her eyes. It was quite effective, Kyle realized; he could only see the faintest blue glow leaking from around her eyes.

"This way," Petra ordered, striding forward past Tavek and Machete. She didn't bother to pull her hood over her head, letting it hang on her upper back. Kyle glanced at the hood, then found his gaze sliding down Petra's back, to her shapely posterior. He felt something hit him on the shoulder, and jerked his gaze away, realizing that Ariana was glaring at him.

"I'll go first," she grumbled, stepping in front of Kyle and effectively blocking his view. He felt his cheeks flush, and he followed behind Ariana, staring at the ground in shame. It was at least the second time Ariana had caught him gawking, and yet despite her ire he found himself unable to help himself.

"The cave is near," Petra declared, slinging a backpack she was carrying over her shoulder. "You will stay with me while Ariana is tested."

"Can I tell her?" Kyle asked. Petra nodded. He relayed the information to Ariana, who seemed a bit distracted.

"Got it," she mumbled.

"So she won't lose magic in that suit?" Kyle asked Petra. He was worried that she would run out of magic during the test.

"She will, but slowly," Petra replied. "The suit she wears was mine when I was younger. It is made of the same material as the room you met me in."

"So that room was insulated too," Kyle deduced. Petra nodded, stepping around a large fallen tree trunk.

"Without insulation, weaving magic is impossible for all but the Joined," she explained. "And apparently you." Kyle's brow furrowed.

"The Joined?"

"If she passes the test," Petra stated coolly, "...you will have earned the right to know more."

They walked in silence then. The forest was silent save for their footsteps, the sun's rays streaming through the gaps in the leaves above their heads. Kyle stared up at the sky for a moment, then frowned.

341

"How come I can see the sun?" he asked. Petra stared at him. "I mean, there was mist all around the treetops when we were flying above the forest."

"The trees make the mist," she replied. "Sun comes in, but it doesn't come out."

"Doesn't that take magic?" Kyle pressed.

"Yes."

"But..." he began.

"If she passes the test," Petra repeated, "...you will have earned the right to know more."

Kyle sighed, continuing forward silently. Petra guided the party around the tree trunks, weaving through the forest with practiced ease. The ground began to angle upward slightly, making the going a bit more difficult for Kyle's sore muscles. He'd been banged up quite a bit on the *Defiance* during the warship's attack, not to mention during his free-fall into the forest. His left hip was particularly bruised, giving him a sharp pain with every step, forcing him to limp. If Petra noticed, she certainly didn't act like it; she maintained her quick, steady pace. He grit his teeth, refusing to let her see him struggle. He didn't want her to think of him as weak, after all.

Eventually the forest floor leveled out, the trees becoming more sparse as they continued forward. It took only a few minutes – and a few hundred painful steps – later that they came to a sheer rock wall. It was, Kyle realized as his eye drew upward, the base of a mountain.

"Mount Grimore," Kyle breathed. Petra shook her head.

"This is a hill," she corrected. "Mount Grimore is much farther away." She turned left, walking alongside the sheer rock wall, and everyone else followed, Kyle still at her side. "The cave is near."

After another few minutes, Kyle saw that Petra was right; they came to a large hole in the wall, twice as tall as a man and at least ten feet wide. The cave beyond was shrouded in darkness, the sun's rays not daring to venture too far within. Petra steered everyone far clear of the cave's entrance, stopping some thirty feet away. The tribal Weaver turned to Ariana then.

"This is the cave you must enter," she stated solemnly. "Immortals have been seen entering this cave and leaving with Void minerals."

"So I'm supposed to just walk in there, grab a white stone, and bring it back," Ariana muttered. Kyle translated.

"Correct," Petra replied.

"Easy enough," Ariana stated. She strode forward toward the mouth of the cave, her feet crunching on the fallen leaves and twigs littering the forest floor. She stopped before the cave entrance, pivoting about suddenly and looking at Petra.

"What happens if I fail?" she asked. Kyle hesitated, holding Ariana's gaze for a moment, the hair on his neck rising on end. He felt Petra's eyes on him, and he turned to her, using his earring to translate.

"Then you will be dead," Petra answered without skipping a beat. "And your friend," she added coldly, putting a hand on Kyle's shoulder, "...will join you."

* * *

Ariana stepped forward through the gaping maw of the cave's entrance, feeling a chill run through her as she did so. It was not the cold that got to her – she hardly noticed variations in temperature anymore – but the idea of being underground. Over a year trapped beneath the earth, never seeing the sun, had taken its toll on her, and now she found herself suddenly afraid of being trapped again. She glanced over her shoulder, spotting Kyle and that woman standing there watching her. She turned back, facing the darkness of the cave, and continued forward, her boots crunching on the small stones littering the cave floor. It was dark, but with her augmented eyes, the cave's walls and ceiling were plainly visible. Dark gray stone all around, covered in a heavy layer of dust. The air felt heavier here somehow, and she felt a slight pressure in her ears. She forced herself to yawn, and her ears popped, the pressure equalizing. She continued forward slowly, her eyes scanning the tunnel ahead.

The first thing she noticed were the bodies.

There were easily dozens of small corpses a few yards into the cave, most of them birds. Their little bodies lay strewn on the ground in front of her, most having decomposed some time ago. She dropped down to one knee, examining what looked like a freshly dead sparrow. It was intact save for a small hole in its skull. A hole that led to a hollowed-out cranium.

The brain was missing.

Ariana frowned, finding another bird, this one slightly more decomposed. She grabbed a small stone, then used it to roll the corpse over onto its belly, and found a similar hole in its skull. Again, the skull was empty while the rest of the body was essentially intact.

Well that's strange, she thought.

She rose to her feet, stepping over the corpses and continuing forward through the cave. There were far fewer corpses as she went along, the bodies becoming more and more sporadic until there were none at all. The cavern grew narrower, forming a cramped tunnel, the walls only five or so feet apart now. The uneven ceiling drew lower and lower, until it was not even two feet above her head. It felt like the cave was closing in on her, like the earth was getting ready to swallow her whole.

Stop it, she chastised herself. *Just get in and get out.*

She moved faster, feeling the suit Petra had given her hugging her body tightly, so much so that it was a little uncomfortable. She couldn't help but remember what Petra had said about it...that the uniform had been hers when she was a girl.

Not a girl anymore, she muttered to herself.

She sighed then, quickening her pace. Petra was certainly not a girl anymore, that was for sure. She was a woman, something Ariana would never become. And Ariana hadn't been the only one to notice that; Kyle had clearly noticed too.

He noticed all right, she thought darkly. *He couldn't stop noticing.*

Ariana felt anger rising within her, and shoved the feeling down, clenching her fists. Then she heard a loud snap, felt something cave in under her left foot. She stopped cold, staring down at the ground. She'd stepped on something whitish-yellow, something round. She lifted her foot up, realizing what it was.

344

A skull.

She stared at it for a moment, expecting to feel some sort of surprise or revulsion, but felt neither. Just mild curiosity. She stepped back, then knelt down on the cavern floor, peering at the broken dome of the skull. It was, like everything else here, covered in a thick layer of dust, nearly invisible until she'd stepped on it. She scanned the floor around the skull, spotting the spinal column a few feet away, and a half-shattered rib cage. Some sort of rusted tool laid on the ground near the skeleton's hand; Ariana reached for it, picking it up. Dust cascaded down from it as she did so, revealing a rusted mining pick.

They must have been mining Void crystals, she realized. And if they'd been successful before they'd died, there should be crystals still on them. She shifted her weight, using one hand to brush the dust off of the rest of the skeleton. Other than a few pieces of rotted leather – and some metallic earrings with the gemstones curiously missing – there was no trace of Void minerals. Disappointed, she rose to her feet, stepping around the skeleton and continuing forward. She brushed dust from the front of her uniform as she walked deeper into the cave, grimacing at the flatness there. It'd been obvious what Kyle had been staring at back there, in the forest. And in the room where they'd first met Petra. Ariana stared down at her chest, feeling suddenly inadequate.

Damn hussy flaunting her damn...

She quickened her pace, ignoring the steadily narrowing tunnel, the walls now only three feet apart, barely wide enough to accommodate her shoulders. The floor began to dip downward, at first slightly, then more sharply, until it was nearly at a forty-five-degree angle. Her foot slipped on a few pebbles, and she nearly fell back onto her butt. She caught herself, cursing quietly, her voice echoing off of the narrow tunnel.

He stared at her butt too, she thought darkly, continuing forward and downward. She kept her eyes on the ground, avoiding any more loose rocks. *Her suit was so tight I bet he could see her pores.*

Something moved near her foot, snapping her out of her thoughts. She skid to a stop, bracing her hands against the rocky walls on either side, and peered down at her own feet. She saw something small and white next to her right foot, about as big as a coin. She leaned over to get a better look; it was some sort of insect, she realized. It had a round, segmented body with a tiny head, little antennae waving about in the air. It was entirely white, translucent even, except for its tiny head, which was black. It paid her no mind, crawling past her, back toward the cave entrance. She straightened up, continuing forward, but keeping her eyes on the downward-sloping cavern floor.

She spotted something round ahead, nestled up against the left wall, and made her way to it.

Another skull, she discovered. A human skull. This one was whole, thanks to her not stepping on it. She crouched before it, brushing the dust from the smooth, white surface, then picking it up. It was nearly intact, save for a small hole in its right temple. The edges of the hole were smooth, and it was just big enough to fit her index finger in.

Strange, she thought.

She put the skull back down, then resumed her slow march forward, and was relieved when the floor leveled out, no longer a forty-five-degree slope. Her relief soon evaporated, however; about thirty feet ahead, she saw the narrow tunnel end abruptly. She felt a sudden pang of fear, and if her heart were still beating it would have hammered in her chest. If this was the end of the line, and there were no Void minerals left in this cave...

She briefly entertained running back out of the cave, and using her shard to blow Petra and her two escorts to bits. But mostly Petra.

They'll kill Kyle, she reminded herself. And as much as she disliked the woman, Petra *had* been reasonable...had given Ariana a chance. It wasn't the woman's fault that she looked the way she did, although she could at least *try* to cover herself up a bit.

Ariana slowed as she came to the end of the cave, and stared at the rocky wall in front of her, feeling her heart sink. This was it...the cave went no further. She turned in a slow circle, scanning the floor and walls for the slightest hint of a white stone, then spotted something on the floor to her right. Her spirit soared for a split

346

second, until she realized that it wasn't a Void crystal. It was another one of those white beetle-like insects crawling on the floor.

Damn it, she swore silently. The insect crawled away from her, toward the rightmost wall.

Then in vanished.

Ariana blinked, then dropped to her knees, peering at the cavern floor where the insect had been. She realized that her vision had faded a little, the cavern darker than it had been only a few minutes ago. No light could possibly get this far in to the cave, she knew. It was only due to the remarkable magic of her shard that she could see anything at all. She placed her hands on the floor, tracing her fingers over the path the beetle had taken...and felt her fingers slip off into nothingness.

Huh.

She pulled her hand back, then put it out again, feeling the same, sudden drop-off. She paused, then put her whole arm through, and realized that there was a hole in the side of the floor, where it met the wall. A good-sized hole at that. It was probably large enough for her to fit through.

She felt a glimmer of hope.

Ariana withdrew her arm, then turned around, facing away from the hole and dropping onto her belly on the cool stone floor. She slid backward, her legs slipping through the hole, then her hips. She got stuck there, and wiggled a bit, feeling stone scraping her buttocks. Then she pushed, and her hips popped through. She felt her legs dangle in space below, and swung them forward, her feet striking something hard – a rock wall. She swung one leg backward, and struck another wall behind her, maybe three feet from the first.

It's a chasm, she realized. *Maybe if I can brace myself...*

She slid down through the hole, all the way up to her shoulders, where she got stuck again. She paused, scissoring her legs, bracing one foot on the front wall below, the other on the back wall. Then she relaxed her shoulders, putting her arms up over her head and sliding her shoulders through the hole. She slipped through, using her hands and her feet stop herself from falling, her head passing through the hole. She hung there for a moment, staring down into the darkness. The walls sandwiching her extending downward as far as she could see, the gap between them a nearly straight vertical drop. If she braced her feet against the wall in front of her, and her hands and back on the rear wall...

She tried it, letting go of the lip of the hole with one hand, then the other. Her heart leaped into her throat as she dropped a foot or two, her feet slipping on the wall in front of her. Panicking, she pushed outward hard with her legs, pressing her back against the rear wall.

Her fall slowed, then stopped.

She hung there for a long moment, suspended between the two walls, staring downward. She had no idea how far down this chasm went; if she'd fallen too far, she'd have been in deep trouble. Her body could recover from any injury, but if her uniform tore, she'd bleed magic quickly...and that would be that.

She took a deep breath in, then slid one foot down, then the other, inching down the gap between the walls. This time, her boots held true, and she didn't slip as she descended further into the darkness. She noticed a faint sound in the distance, coming from below; it sounded like running water. Maybe there was an underground stream or pool below her. Her hand brushed up against something, and she froze; there, crawling on the wall before her, was another one of those white, translucent bugs. In fact, there were several of them. A few were crawling up the wall, while one was climbing down, a small black twig in its mouth.

She continued downward, being careful not to squish the bugs with her hands or feet as she went. She glanced upward, and realized she could no longer see the hole she'd come through. It was impossible to be sure of how far she'd traveled, but she guessed it might be fifty feet or so. The farther down she went, the more bugs she saw crawling up and down the walls. Thankfully they skittered out of the way of her hands and feet as she descended, otherwise she wouldn't have been able to avoid killing them. Picking up a human skull was one thing, but squishing bugs was *gross*.

Wait, Ariana thought. *How can these bugs be alive?*

She stared at one of the insects, watching it carrying another small black twig down the wall before her. How could it live in this cave when everything else died? She thought back to the corpses littering the entrance to the cavern, and remembered what Petra had said. Anything that dared to venture into the cave would go mad, then seize, and die. Except, apparently, these bugs. And herself, of course.

Strange.

She tore her gaze away from the dozen or so bugs, glancing downward. To her surprise, she thought she could see something far below, a hint of a rocky floor.

Is it...?

She moved down, faster now, more confident in her ability to scale the narrow chasm. Yes, there was definitely rock below...about twenty feet down. She felt a burst of excitement, and had to force herself to maintain her methodical pace, being careful not to slip. She descended toward the floor, until her feet were only a few feet above it. Then she pulled her arms and legs in, falling the last few feet to the floor below...and stepping on a whole lot of bugs as she did so.

"Ew, gross," she whispered to herself, wrinkling her nose. She grimaced, lifting one foot up, seeing a mass of flattened white bugs there, their legs still squirming madly. She felt a wave of nausea come over her, and she scraped the soles of her boots against a bare section of wall one at a time, until they were reasonably clean. Then she looked about, getting her bearings.

The two vertical walls extended all the way to the floor on either side, with a third sheer wall in front of her. She turned about, and saw another wall, making an enclosed rectangle. Nearly enclosed; there was a slight gap between the forth wall and the floor, over a foot high. She noticed more white bugs crawling through that gap. Maybe if she flattened herself on the ground, she could crawl under it.

Ariana tried it, lowering herself slowly onto her belly, waiting for the bugs to sense her and get out of the way before resting her body on the cool stone. She peered under the gap, and saw that it was a tunnel only a few feet long, leading to a much larger chamber beyond. She pulled herself forward, using her knees and elbows to crawl under the gap, and barely fit through, her head and buttocks scraping against the stone above. She took a great deal of satisfaction in knowing that Petra would never have been able to fit through the gap, given her ridiculous proportions.

Ariana crawled out from under the ledge, then got to her feet. Then her jaw dropped.

Before her was a massive underground cavern – nearly as large as the Arena stadium had been – with black walls climbing over a hundred feet in the air to the craggy ceiling above. To her surprise, she saw a shaft of light shining through a carriage-sized hole in the center of the ceiling, a hole through which a steady stream of water cascaded down in a glittering waterfall to the cavern floor below. The waterfall fed a subterranean lake in the center of the cavern, which was surrounded by a wide perimeter of what appeared to be black stone.

She stepped forward, careful to avoid stepping on any more bugs. That grew increasingly difficult, seeing as how the cavern floor here was practically swarming with them. They scurried around her feet, hundreds of them. She held back a wave of disgust, steeling herself against her natural aversion to the things; she had a mission to complete, and Kyle's life was at stake.

She continued forward carefully, peering at the very edges of the pond, where the water met the surrounding rock. There were more white things there, lots of them, densely clustered at the water's edge. At first Ariana thought they were more bugs, but she soon realized that they weren't moving. She got closer, and discovered that they were clusters of translucent white bubbles sticking to the rocks like barnacles, each the size of a marble. As she drew closer, she realized that there were long, black, stringy things protruding from each of the bubbles. She walked up to a cluster of these at the edge of the pool, and crouched down, getting a closer look. They looked like thin vines growing from the bubbles, their short roots encased in the spheres. She traced the vines across the floor, and realized they were fanning out from the edge of the pool, extending all the way to the rocky walls of the chamber. In fact, the entire floor – and walls – were completely covered with the vines, so thick with them that no rock was visible beneath them. The vines continued upward along those walls, all the way up to the hole in the ceiling over a hundred feet up.

She lowered her gaze, staring at the white bubbles where the roots lay encased. There were bugs crawling all over them; some of the bugs had little pieces of the vines in their mouths. She followed one of these bugs with her eyes, tracking it as it crawled over the white bubbles along the edge of the deep pool of water. It stopped before a long, slime-covered tubular structure that extended up from the depths of the pool, a white, translucent hose with wart-like bumps encasing it. As Ariana watched, the hose pulsed, and a few of the warts expanded, blowing up like little balloons. These slipped off the surface of the tube, landing on top of the other bubbles sticking to the rocks below.

Gross, she thought.

The beetle she'd been following crawled right up to the end of the tube, and dropped the little fragment of vine onto a series of long hairs that extended out from the mouth of the thing. Ariana noticed that there were many other little bits of vine on these hairs, as well as what looked like little pieces of bone, and a feather. Suddenly the hairs pulled in, retracting into the mouth of the tube, and the tube spasmed. Then the hairs slowly came out again...but now they were clean.

They're feeding it, she realized.

She crept closer to the edge of the pool, being careful not to step on any of the bugs swarming below here, or the white bubbles. Then she crouched again, tracing the squirming tube down below the surface of the water. It was long – incredibly long, she realized, extending all the way down to the center of the pond. She stood, trying to see where it ended. Then she froze, her eyes widening. There, at the very bottom of the pond, was...something. Something *big*.

She took a step back.

It was a bug...a *massive* bug lying in the center of the pond, at the bottom some thirty feet below the surface. It looked similar to the little bugs on the surface, with smooth, translucent white skin. But it was many, many times bigger, easily fifty feet long, with long segmented legs that clung to the rocky bottom. Long tubular appendages fanned outward from the sides of its body, six on a side, draping across the pond floor until they emerged at the shore, just like the one Ariana had been watching. And all of those appendages were being fed by the little bugs, spasming as they swallowed the offerings whole.

She stared at that massive body, seeing little holes above the base of each appendage. As she watched, a cloud of fine white particles shot out of each of them into the water, slowly settling to the bottom. The massive creature was surrounded in a bed of the white particles, a layer of white sandy material a few feet deep.

Ariana's eyes traveled back to the edge of the pond, catching something twinkling on the dark gray rock a few inches below the water there. She paused, then walked forward toward it, stepping around the white bubbles – and staying far clear of the tube. She stopped a few inches before the water's edge, crouching down low and peering at the twinkling object she'd seen. It was a crystal, growing outward from the rock around it.

A white crystal.

Her heart leaped in her chest, her eyes widening. It was a Void crystal...it had to be! And it wasn't the only one...not even close. The entire perimeter of the pond was covered in masses of the white crystals. The only reason she hadn't noticed them earlier was because she'd thought they were just more of the white bubbles.

Ariana reached down with one hand, dipping her fingers into the water, and pulled at the Void crystal. It was anchored firmly to the rock, and didn't budge. She grabbed the very base of it, and squeezed harder, using her considerable strength to try and break it off. She felt it crack, and withdrew a chunk of the crystal from the water.

Gotcha!

She stood then, glancing at the huge creature at the bottom of the lake, then turning around, stepping carefully around the bubbles caking the rocky floor. She cleared the perimeter of the lake, and made her way back toward the small opening in the rock wall she'd come through earlier, dodging bugs as she went. She was about twenty feet away from it when she heard a splashing sound behind her.

She glanced over her shoulder, and saw a huge white dome rising from the water.

Crap!

She turned forward, breaking out into a run, the Void crystal clutched in her right hand. Clusters of white bugs were crushed under her feet as she sprinted, sticking to the bottom of her feet. She heard a gushing sound, saw a shallow film of water rush around her feet, carrying hundreds of bugs along with it.

Oh crap oh crap...

She reached the gap in the wall, lunging forward onto her belly and reaching under it with her hands, pulling herself along the now-wet ground. She got her head underneath, and had to turn it to the side to fit it in. Her shoulders passed under, then the small of her back. She felt another wave of ice-cold water rush around her, soaking the front of her uniform, followed by a *thump* behind her. She reached out with her hands again, pulling herself further forward, feeling her buttocks get wedged under the rock. She pulled harder, but didn't get anywhere.

She was stuck!

"Oh come *on!*" she yelled, gritting her teeth. She pulled even harder, sucking her butt in and straining. Then she jolted forward, hearing a loud ripping sound as she did so, her legs passing under the ledge. She pulled herself through quickly, until she was back in the narrow vertical gap between the two rock walls. She scrambled to her feet, feeling a slight draft on her back, and felt along her left buttock with one hand. There was bare skin there...she'd torn her uniform. Badly.

I'm going to start losing magic, she realized, a cold bolt of fear shooting through her. She pushed that fear away, trying to think. If she could patch over the hole, it should be all right. Maybe she could hold it together with one hand while...

A mass of small white bugs swarmed under the ledge around her, spilling over her feet. Then they were crawling up her legs, hundreds of them, so many that she couldn't see her feet at all anymore!

"Get *off!*" she cried, reaching down and wiping the bugs from her legs. Some fell off, while others clung to her hands, crawling up her arms. She backed up, slamming her shoulder blades against the rock wall behind her, and shook her arms violently, then scraped her arms against the wall behind her. Dozens of bugs fell from her arms, but countless more continued to swarm up her legs, coating her uniform in a sea of white.

Run you idiot!

She tucked the Void crystal down the front of her uniform, then reached up with her arms, pressing them against either wall. She hauled herself upward, trying to ignore the bugs crawling up her legs and onto her lower belly, concentrating on placing her feet on either wall. She pulled herself upward, one side at a time, ascending the narrow gap.

The bugs streamed up her body, up to her chest now. She felt tiny little legs on her neck, and fought back a wave of revulsion. She was intensely grateful for the uniform covering her flesh...still, it took everything she had not to stop and brush the bugs from her neck. She felt one crawl over her right ear, and shuddered.

Come on, she urged herself. *Focus!*

She continued upward, one foot at a time, pulling herself toward the hole in the ceiling she knew had to be above her. Then her left foot slipped on the wall, her sole slick with the gooey remains of the bugs she'd crushed underfoot. She slid down a few feet, then managed to catch herself. She cursed, scraping one foot, then the other, on the rock walls. Her legs were entirely covered in bugs now. Thousands of them were still spilling into the narrow chasm, crawling up the two walls in a horrid frenzy.

All coming for her.

She grit her teeth, pulling herself upward again and again, feeling the bugs on her cheeks now, on her *lips*, even crawling up the back of her scalp. She could feel them through the thin fabric of the mask covering her head and face. One crawled over her left eye, and she closed it, cursing aloud again. She shook her head, but it was no use...the bug clung to her eyelid, digging its little legs into her flesh. She forced herself to ignore it, going faster now, hitting her stride. Waves of bugs swarmed up the walls around her, and she felt them squishing under her palms as she went, coating her hands in sticky goo. She had to stop to scrape her palms rapidly against each wall just so that they wouldn't slip.

Where is that damn hole, she growled silently, looking up into the darkness. Another beetle crawled over her other eye, forcing her to close that one too. She pursed her lips, fighting back another wave of disgust, and continued upward blindly. She felt one of the bugs crawl onto the exposed bridge of her nose, then squeeze itself *under* her mask, crawling over her forehead. That made her stop, bracing herself between the walls with one arm and both legs, while reaching under her mask and yanking the little bugger out. She flung it downward, then swiped more bugs off of her face before resuming her ascent.

Ariana kept her eyes upward, and spotted the ceiling some thirty feet above, barely visible in the darkness. She pulled herself toward it, resisting the urge to go faster. All it would take was one slip-up to send her all the way back down. She tested every handhold and foothold, ignoring the bugs swarming over her body. She paused every few yards to swipe more bugs from her face, then resumed climbing, until she'd reached the top at last.

Yes!

She paused, then lifted her legs upward, planting her feet a little bit higher on either wall. Then she let go with one hand, then the other, carefully straightening her legs and reaching up through the hole with her arms. Gripping the edges of the floor above, she pulled upward, letting her feet dangle free. She made it about halfway up, and then her arms began to wobble.

What the...

She paused, resting on her elbows, then tried again...but her arms felt terribly weak, and she slumped back onto her elbows. She rested there again, trying to process what was happening. The tunnel around her began to darken slowly, until she could barely make out the outline of the rocky walls.

Come on, she urged herself.

She bent her legs, then placed her feet as high up on the two walls below as she could. Then she straightened her legs, pushing up on the floor with her hands at the same time. Her arms started to wobble again, and her feet slipped on the walls below, forcing her to fall onto her armpits on the floor with a dull *thump.* She stayed there for a moment, feeling bugs swarming over every inch of her body, crawling under her mask once again. This time, she didn't bother to swipe them away. She was too damn tired to care.

Just rest for a minute, she told herself, closing her eyes. *God I'm tired.* It made perfect sense, of course...she hadn't slept in weeks. *I'm finally going to sleep,* she mused. She needed it, after everything she'd been through. She deserved it.

But if she slept now, she'd fall down through the hole...and that woman would kill Kyle.

She opened her eyes, groaning as she placed her palms on the rocky floor around her. She tried to push upward, managing to lift one leg up onto the floor above, then the other. She cleared the hole, falling onto her stomach on the floor of the tunnel. Countless tiny legs crawled across the skin of her neck and back under her uniform, making her shudder.

If you don't get up, she told herself, *Kyle will die.*

She felt the bugs crawl over the exposed skin of her left buttock, then realized what was happening – she was losing magic. She barely had enough to move her arms and legs now, and it would only get worse the longer she waited. In another minute, she might not have any magic left at all...and then she'd lay here for eternity, these awful bugs slowly tearing the flesh from her bones so they could feed it to that monster in the pond.

No!

She grit her teeth, fighting the crushing fatigue that threatened to overwhelm her, and collected herself, hauling upward with everything she had. She managed to get up onto her hands and knees, then pushed herself to her feet, steadying herself by placing her hands on the rock wall on either side of her.

Magic...

She felt the hardness of the Void crystal she'd taken pressing against the skin of her upper chest, and pulled the neck of her mask up, ignoring the bugs swarming down the front of her uniform as she did so. She grabbed the crystal, pressing it against her forehead.

Come on...

She *pulled* at the crystal, waiting to feel magic flowing into her mind's eye...but there was nothing. She tried again, straining to pull magic from the crystal, but it was utterly empty.

Damn it!

She grit her teeth, putting the crystal back, then forcing herself to walk forward, brushing bugs off of her as she went. She could feel them crawling under her uniform, and resisted the urge to smoosh them. The floor of the tunnel began to angle upward, and she leaned forward, putting one foot in front of the other. Then she felt something pinch her left temple...hard. An incredible pain lanced through her head, and she cried out, stumbling to her knees, her hands on either side of her head.

Her shard reacted, magic weaving unbidden in her mind's eye.

She felt her hair rise on end, and then a burst of white-hot sparks surged all around her. The pain in her temple vanished instantly, and the bugs on her uniform dropped immediately to the ground. Ariana stared at them, blinking away the spots in her eyes. Then she rose to her feet...or tried to. Her legs wobbled, and she nearly fell back onto her knees.

"Oh come on!" she cried, taking a step forward. Her legs were like rubber, barely able to hold her weight. Her shard must have used up most of its magic killing those damn bugs! Or not so dead; she saw the pile of bugs begin to squirm as the things came to, crawling up her legs again. She cursed, taking another step forward, then another up the 45-degree incline.

You're so close, she thought. *Just keep moving...*

She hobbled forward and upward, feeling the bugs swarm up her body, even the ones inside of her uniform coming back to life. She felt a sudden terror overcome her, knowing that if just one of those bugs decided to bite her again, her shard would almost certainly discharge the rest of its magic to defend her.

And there would be nothing she could do about it.

She whimpered, taking another step forward, then another. Her feet began to drag on the rocky floor with each step, and she felt her left leg wobble dangerously below her. She tried to lift it, and her right leg gave out, dropping her to her hands and knees.

No no no...

She crawled up the incline, inch by inch, picturing Kyle waiting for her at the mouth of the cave, smiling at her in the sunlight. She started to cry then, great sobs wracking her steadily weakening body. Her head began to swim sickeningly, her vision darkening, her fingers going numb.

No no, please no...

She fell onto her belly, the cold stone inviting her to rest there, to put her head down and sleep. She reached forward with one hand, grasping a rocky outcropping and pulling herself forward. She felt the incline start to level off, and knew that she was no more than a hundred feet from the cave entrance now. She tried to yell out, to call for help, but no words came. She felt her head dropping downward, the muscles of her neck no longer strong enough to hold it up. She rested her cheek on the cold stone, feeling her eyelids starting to close.

No, don't...

She barely felt the biting pain at her left temple before oblivion claimed her.

Chapter 25

The eternal silence of the Void met Sabin as he withdrew from his memories, followed immediately by the full force of his unending pain. He welcomed it, letting the invisible fire envelope him, letting it eat at his flesh.

He deserved it.

Sabin thought back to the memory he'd re-experienced, remembering the hope, the joy he'd felt when Ampir had arrived to save him from Nespo's trap. And to think that it had been Vera who had convinced Ampir to question Nespo. That she had come to his rescue, quite literally saving his life.

He withdrew the rest of his consciousness from his vast network, retreating into his own mind. The pain intensified a hundredfold, and he screamed silently, feeling as if his flesh were melting from his bones. On and on it went, this agony. Minute after minute, until he lost track of time. Until time had no meaning anymore. Until there was only pain.

His penance.

At last he thrust his consciousness outward, his mind expanding across the Void, across the *world*, his pain lessening with every Chosen whose mind he overtook. Larger and larger his mind grew, until he was Xanos once more.

He gazed across his domain through the eyes of dozens of his Chosen, empires on nearly every continent in the world. Governments mankind thought of as their own creations, constructs of their mortal wills. It was necessary, this deceit. For all their searching for a higher power to lead them, their incessant clamoring for immortal God to guide them and give their lives purpose, mankind ultimately loathed a visible god. A tangible god.

And Sabin knew that, ultimately, mankind was corrupt. Leadership bred corruption, resulting in the creation and preservation of power at the expense of the governed. But it was a lie that absolute power led to corruption; a being with absolute power would not need corruption to maintain it. Only those with limited power required deceit to maintain that power. And man was, by definition, limited.

Xanos, however, was not.

Sabin observed his empires for a long moment, then pulled away, his visions of Doma's many lands winking out instantly. He turned his attention to yet another Chosen trapped in its Void crystal within the massive chamber they shared. He reached out to it, recalling the last words he'd heard Ampir say after he'd rescued Sabin from his prison cell. He'd pointed at Sabin's ring, then said five fateful words.

Do what you're best at.

He'd certainly done that.

Sabin reached into the Chosen's mind, feeling darkness come over him.

* * *

The air is cool and dry, with a musty tang that permeates every inch of the massive underground mining chamber. Liberated from the Empire's corrupt mining company only a week ago, the huge diamond mine has been converted into the center of operations for the Orjanian Resistance, a few thousand men and women dedicated to fighting back against the oppression of the Imperialists. Underground, the Resistance is invisible to the enemy, able to work in secrecy. And they are well-protected; with their ability to destroy the mine at any moment – and therefore its vast cache of diamonds – it is virtually guaranteed that the Empire will not make a direct attack against them.

The underground chamber, one of many man-made caverns hollowed out by generations of Orjanian miners, is linked to other chambers by long, winding tunnels. Magic lights hang overhead, casting a pale yellow glow across the rocky floor and walls. Hundreds of men and women toil in the chamber, carrying equipment to and fro, supplying food and water, and performing all of the other tasks needed to keep the Resistance thriving.

Sabin smiles from his vantage point in one corner of the chamber, his arms draped over the armrests of his chair, his feet propped up on a wooden table in front of him. He watches the men and women around him work, marvels at their energy, their drive. *Ours is a sacred mission*, he muses. *We fight for our freedom.*

He turns away from the spectacle, dropping his feet onto the rocky floor and concentrating on the papers laying on the table before him. A series of quick sketches, drawn hastily with a thick piece of charcoal, of his newest invention. He finds it much easier to create new ideas with such a blunt instrument; unable to draw any real detail, it forces him to think in broad strokes, to avoid plunging into minutia too soon.

He glances up from the paper, spotting two men carrying a heavy-looking sheet of black metal toward him. They drop the metal onto a stack on similarly-sized sheets, then walk away to retrieve another one. To Sabin's left, a group of men sit along a wooden table some forty feet long, each hunched over a glittering diamond. After a moment, they each pass their diamond to the person at their left, then hunch over again. Sabin smiles, feeling a swell of pride in seeing them at work. Not only the men at the table, but *all* of the people working in this chamber. They are all here for the same reason: to bring Sabin's visions to life.

Sabin continues to watch, remarking on how much his life has changed in the last year. After his escape from prison, Ampir had flown him to a neutral territory in Orja, not yet occupied by the Empire. Sabin shook his head, remembering that flight in the starlit sky, the world zipping by in a blur below them. He'd never imagined traveling at such speed, would not have believed it possible had he not experienced it himself. After they'd arrived in Orja, Ampir had put a hand on Sabin's shoulder.

"Do what you're best at," he'd said. And then he'd flown away.

Sabin glances down at his right hand, at the black and green ring there. A symbol of his greatest contributions to the Empire, it is a constant reminder of what he *is* best at...creation. And what incredible things he has created in the last year! Thought-activated weapons more sophisticated than any possessed by the Imperial army. Armor that made the soldiers of the Resistance one-man armies, able to withstand the best that the Empire's Battle-Weavers could throw at them. Sabin's inventions had turned a weak, fledgling group of revolutionaries into one of the most powerful forces in the world. They'd descended on the Orjanian mines like vengeful ghosts, winning back their land and sending the Empire's corrupt mining companies fleeing back to Verhan.

"Good morning, Sabin," he hears a voice say. Sabin snaps out of his reverie, looking up to find a tall, burly man with short black hair standing opposite him. The man's countenance is fierce, his jaw square. He holds himself with utter confidence, and for good reason; he is Gunthar, the leader of the Resistance.

"Good morning sir," Sabin replies, standing up from his chair and saluting. Gunthar waves away the formality.

"Sit, sit," he urges, and Sabin complies. Gunthar sits down on a chair opposite Sabin, gesturing at the men and women busily working on creating Sabin's newest inventions.

"Are my men working to your satisfaction?" he inquires. Sabin nods.

"Beyond expectation," he answers. And it's true; bolstered by their repeated victories, the men and women of the Resistance seem imbued with limitless energy, working day and night on Sabin's creations. They are not infected by the complacency of the Empire, believing that they are too powerful to fail.

"My Runics are sufficient?" Gunthar presses. Sabin pauses, then nods. Most of the Runics – the men sitting around the long table with the diamonds – are relatively unskilled, and none can hold a candle to his own skill. Sabin had devised a way around this deficiency, tasking each Runic to place specific runes in a gem, then pass it to the next Runic, who would inscribe different runes, and so on down the line. That way, no Runic needed to understand the entire device, only their small contribution to it.

"For the time being," Sabin answers. He devotes each morning to training them, but most are not gifted students. Gunthar, of course, already knows this.

"We'll recruit more," the leader promises. He glances at the Runics. "Ingenious, to have them work this way," he adds. "Your Empire was stupid to cast you away."

"Not mine anymore," Sabin counters. "Orja is my home now."

"Of course," Gunthar agrees. "And the Resistance is lucky to have you," he adds with a smile. "How are your projects progressing?"

"Very well," Sabin answers. "We have three hundred units of the latest version of the invisi-suit in quality testing now," he adds. Suits of armor with advanced defensive runics, they also allow the wearer to become absolutely invisible – in multiple spectra of light – as well as completely silent. It had allowed for decisive victories against the Imperial military. Sabin had created new versions of the suit with each major battle, anticipating that the Empire's Weavers and Runics might reverse-engineer the technology and learn how to neutralize it. Each new version used a novel mechanism of promoting invisibility, making the Empire's efforts worthless.

"Excellent," Gunthar replies.

"I've also developed something I call the Imploder," Sabin continues. "A gem that shoots out of a miniature, hand-held cannon, and consumes all of its magic in a fraction of a second, creating an enormously powerful gravity field to pull in and crush anything around it."

"Won't the enemy Weavers have runes to neutralize this?"

"They will, many of them," Sabin agrees. "But they take time to sense the gravity field and activate a response. The Imploder discharges so quickly that those closest to it will be killed, and those farther away will expend much of their magic neutralizing its effects."

"Interesting."

"I've also been developing a new set of armor," Sabin states. "I've been working on the prototype myself," he adds.

"What does it do?" Gunthar inquires.

"It automatically sizes itself to the wearer," Sabin explains. "And uses thought-based technology to sense when the wearer is in danger. It neutralizes any potential damage – whether by heat, cold, electricity, blunt force trauma, or penetrating trauma – and neutralizes its own weight, leaving the wearer extremely mobile."

"How close to completion are you?"

"A few months," Sabin admits. "It's quite sophisticated, the most complicated invention I've ever created."

"And you can mass-produce it?" Gunthar presses. Sabin frowns.

"Maybe one every few days," he answers. "But anyone who wore it would become a one-man army."

"Tell me what I can do to help, and you will have it," Gunthar promises. "What are you calling this armor?"

"The Aegis of Athanasia," Sabin replies. Gunthar frowns.

"Athanasia?"

"My mother's name," Sabin admits, feeling rather foolish suddenly. But Gunthar nods.

"A good name," he agrees. "Will this Aegis protect us against Ampir?"

Sabin blinks, struck by the abrupt change in subject. He shakes his head.

"Ampir is not a problem," he replies, and not for the first time. Ever since Gunthar had learned of the legendary Battle-Runic, he'd been almost obsessed with the possibility that the Empire might send Ampir to end the Resistance. Ampir had promised Sabin he would not do so, as long as the Resistance remained in Orja.

"Any man who could destroy us is a problem," Gunthar counters. "And from what I'm told, he *can* destroy us."

"He will not."

"Is he capable of it?" Gunthar presses. Sabin pauses, then shrugs.

"I've never seen him in battle," he admits. Gunthar seems displeased at the answer.

"You knew him," the man states. "What do you think?"

"I think," Sabin answers, lowering his gaze and folding his arms across his chest. "...that whoever Ampir chooses to defeat, is defeated."

"Even against you?"

Sabin sighs, running one hand through his hair. He looks up at Gunthar, and finds the man staring at him intensely.

"He's beyond me," Sabin confesses at last. "He's beyond everyone. I don't worry about Ampir because it's pointless. If he wanted to destroy us, we would be destroyed."

Gunthar stares at Sabin for a long time, then turns his head, tracking the men bringing the large metal plates into the cavern. He turns back to Sabin, his jawline rippling.

"No man is invincible," he proclaims. Sabin nods.

"I agree."

"Then out-think him," Gunthar orders. "Create a weapon powerful enough to free us from the Empire's corruption once and for all." He stands then, stepping around the table and stopping at Sabin's side. He puts one heavy hand on Sabin's shoulder. "If anyone can save us, it's you, Sabin."

"I'll do everything I can," Sabin promises.

"You always do," Gunthar replies. "Thank you Sabin."

With that, the man lets go of Sabin's shoulder, striding down the cavern toward one of the tunnels beyond. Sabin watches him go, then sighs, staring back down at the charcoal drawings laying on the table before him. His latest creation, existing in his mind, and in substantially cruder form, on paper. A vehicle of sorts, piloted by several Weavers, with weapons and defenses that would make it ideal for defending the Resistance's newly acquired territories. Sabin stares at the drawing, at the two thick legs supporting a broad body, two arms bolted on either side. His eyes lift to the domed head of the vehicle, a hollow cabin that will serve as a control room for the pilots.

It needs to be big, he thinks. *It needs to be a symbol.*

The Empire will strike back at the Resistance, that is certain. Two mines had already been reclaimed by the Resistance, constituting a devastating blow to the Empire's mining operations. A massive assault is coming...it's just a matter of time. The Resistance doesn't just need to win...it needs to send a message to the Council, to Nespo. One that will make it unmistakably clear what the Resistance stands for.

Sabin stares at the drawing, then glances to his right, spotting his black ring on his middle finger, the green diamond-shaped crystal glittering in the light from overhead. The right corner of his mouth twitches, then curls up into a smirk. He picks up a stick of charcoal, then draws a diamond-shaped eye on the vehicle's domed head. He stares at this for a long moment, then leans back in his chair, folding his arms over his chest. He feels a sudden giddy satisfaction, and allows himself the indulgence.

"There's our symbol," he murmurs to himself. It's perfect, really. He closes his eyes, imagining how Nespo will react when he hears of it. A final gesture, reminding the corrupt Grand Runic exacting what finger Sabin had worn the ring on.

Sabin chuckles to himself.

The greatest accomplishment of his life, indeed.

* * *

Captain Barram leaned back in his plush, oversized leather chair, setting his boots atop an equally oversized wooden desk. It was the same desk he'd had in his quarters on the *Defiance*, and indeed the same desk his father had once sat at when the old man – rest his righteous soul – had served as governor of a small city west of Verhan. It was extraordinarily well-made, the desk, sturdy yet decorated with elegant curves and various grains of wood in spectacular patterns. Everything it contained, both on and within, was well over fifty years old. His father's journals, old maps, a collection of old books on philosophy, a few others on various theories of governance. Captain Barram's father had been a virtuous man, always of the inclination to work toward his own improvement as well as the betterment of his fellows.

If ever he was raised from the dead to see me, Barram mused, *he would die again of shame.*

He pretended that the prospect didn't bother him, but inwardly he knew it did. His father had set impossibly high standards, standards no man but himself could have met. As such, Barram had rejected his father, joining the Verhanian navy to escape his father's control. A few years at war had shown Barram the truth about mankind...and it had been far removed from the noble views espoused by his father.

Black and white only at the ends, Barram thought, *with an infinity of gray in between.*

He fidgeted, ill at ease for reasons he couldn't put his finger on. He'd been thinking a lot about his father recently, after the near-sinking of the *Defiance.* Perhaps his brush with mortality had done it; his father had died in a duel, defending his honor against some slander or other. He got to keep his honor, but not his life.

Barram sighed, looking about his spacious office, one of two in his new home in the Shimmering Isle. He'd purchased the house just this morning, and his crew had seen to it that Barram's things were brought in to furnish it. With eight bedrooms and six baths, he had a long way to go before it was fully furnished, but there would be ample time for that.

He turned his gaze back to his desk, his eye drawn to one of the books there. *On the Inherent Virtues of Man,* the binding read. He smirked. Not because he thought that Man was not virtuous...indeed, he'd witnessed more virtue in the last few days than most men had the opportunity to witness in a lifetime. And a surprising amount from two children. No, he smirked because of what that virtue had won.

A perfectly legal military vessel, conducting a state-sanctioned and entirely justified attack on a smuggler's ship, destroyed by men and women – and children – acting virtuously.

He took his boots off of his desk, lowering his feet to the floor with a *thump.* He leaned over the desk, grabbing the book and flipping through the pages. Then he set it down, suddenly too tired to read it.

Virtue was a matter of perspective, of course. That was something his father had never understood. He'd been an academic, devouring books by other academics, building a worldview without ever having truly viewed the world. And he'd placed all of his self-worth in his beliefs, quite literally dying for them. That had been his father's final, unintended lesson to him, the most valuable lesson of all.

Beliefs are more often wrong when they're strong, he recited to himself. It was a mantra of his, one that had served him well. Had allowed him to see through the smoke and mirrors of society, and of his own mind, to grasp the true nature of the world.

That it was all just a matter of perspective.

There was a series of knocks on the door.

"Come in," Barram called out. The knocking had been in the proper rhythm, notifying him that a member of his crew was on the other side. The door opened, and a young woman stepped into his office, accompanied by one of his former sailors. The woman was tall, slender, and quite lovely. She had long, wavy black hair that fell in waves to the small of her back, and bronze skin. A native of Meros, a nearby island. She was just the kind of woman he found irresistible.

"Company for tonight, Cap'n," the sailor offered, gesturing toward the woman. Barram stared at her for a long moment, allowing his gaze to linger over her figure, then waved her away.

"I will entertain her in another hour," he replied. The sailor nodded, pulling the girl out of the office, and closing the door behind him. Barram watched them go, then sighed. He hadn't really felt like entertaining company...or in this case, being entertained...up until he'd seen her. He briefly thought about inviting her back now, but resisted the urge. Ardor, like all appetites, grew more urgent and powerful when denied. To give in to it at last, to resist until the final moment, was the true path to ecstasy. Instant gratification, in all aspects of life, led to misery.

The Captain drummed his fingers on the top of his desk, picturing the girl in his mind's eye, letting his desire grow.

There was a shout in the distance, followed by the sound of glass shattering outside.

Barram shot upright in his chair, his left hand automatically landing on the butt of his revolver. He withdrew the gun from its holster, forcing himself to remain seated in his chair. There were no windows in his office; he'd been loath to have people see him while he worked. As a consequence, he couldn't see out. He waited for a knock on his door, for one of his guards to notify him of what was happening.

No one came.

Barram stared at the door, his revolver held under his desk in his left hand, the barrel pointed at the center of the door. He felt his ire rising; he'd paid a lot of money to ensure that the city guard – all skilled Weavers – would protect his home.

They should have come by now, he thought, feeling the hairs on the back of his neck rise.

There was another shout from beyond the office door, followed by a loud *thump*. The paintings on the walls rattled.

Time to go.

Barram swiveled in his chair, glancing down at a rug on the floor. Beneath it was a trapdoor leading to escape tunnels beneath the property. A necessity in a city filled with criminals. He glanced back at the door to his office – still closed – then stood up from his chair, walking toward the rug.

He heard the door burst open.

Barram dropped to squat behind the desk, turning around and aiming his revolver at the doorway. He saw someone standing there, silhouetted in the bright light of the hallway. A figure in a dark brown cloak, face hidden behind a loose hood.

Barram aimed for the head, then squeezed the trigger.

His hand jerked to the left at the last minute, his knuckles slamming into one of the heavy wooden legs of his chair. The gun fired far left of its target, and it was all Barram could do to keep his grip on it. He scrambled backward across the floor toward the trapdoor, aiming his revolver at the cloaked figure in the doorway.

The gun jerked forward, flying out of Barram's hand and striking the floor with a clatter. It slid across the floor, stopping at the figure's feet.

"Damn Weaver," Barram growled, reaching inside his uniform, feeling something heavy and smooth in an inside pocket. It was his Neutralizer. He found a shallow depression in its surface, and pressed it with one finger, feeling a *click*. "Time to die," he muttered under his breath. Then he rose to his feet, unsheathing the sword at his right hip and vaulting over his desk, sending books flying onto the floor. He leaped at the cloaked figure, swinging his sword at the Weaver's neck. The man stepped back, putting his left arm *outward*, right in the path of his sword.

Fool, Barram thought with grim satisfaction.

His blade met the Weaver's forearm, slashing through it with a spray of blood. The Weaver stepped *forward* then, instead of backward like he should have, and kicked Barram right in the shin. Barram grunted, his knee locking, his upper body lurching forward. The Weaver pivoted, slamming his elbow into Barram's left temple. He cried out, his head exploding in pain, feeling himself falling to the side, his vision blackening. He felt his shoulder hit the floor, then his head, tiny lights bursting across his field of vision. Slowly, his vision began to return.

He heard someone moaning, and realized it was *him*.

He felt the floor vibrate under him, heard a *thump, thump* as footsteps approached. Two worn brown boots stood in front of his head, little drops of blood spattering on the floor beside them. Barram raised his eyes up, following the boots to that simple brown cloak, to the face hidden under its hood.

"Well done," Barram gasped, wincing at the sudden pounding in his head. He squinted against the pain. "Can I ask why you've come to kill me?"

Not that it matters, his mind scolded. *I won't care when I'm dead.*

"Wrong question," the Weaver replied. The voice was smooth, and slightly deep, with an accent he'd heard before; this man was from the Empire. Barram blinked, then realized the Weaver was holding his gun...and that the barrel was pointing right at him.

"Enlighten me," he grumbled, rolling onto his back. The motion made him suddenly and horribly nauseated, and he vomited, his head pounding with the pressure. When he was finished, he spit the acid from his mouth, wiping his lips with his sleeve. He looked up, and saw the Weaver standing there. The man pulled up his left sleeve, revealing a long gash in his left forearm...all the way to the pearly white bone. The Weaver lifted this wound to his forehead, closing his eyes.

What the hell...

The Weaver lowered his arm, then knelt down before Barram, avoiding the pool of vomit on the floor, and turned the revolver around...

Handing it right back to Barram.

Barram stared at the revolver, then at the Weaver, feeling utterly confused. Still, he took it, and to his surprise, the Weaver let go of the weapon. Barram pointed the revolver at the man's chest, his eyebrows furrowing.

"You can't be that stupid," he protested. The Weaver stood slowly, offering his left hand to Barram. Barram ignored the offer, until he realized that the wound on the Weaver's forearm was healing...right in front of his eyes.

"Who *are* you?" he asked, his jaw going slack. The Weaver said nothing, but grabbed the sides of his hood, pulling it away from his head. He revealed a bald scalp, with stern brown eyes below strong white eyebrows. The man was smooth-shaven, maybe fifty. And he did not look the least bit afraid.

"That," the man replied, "...is a better question." He gestured with his left hand, offering it again to Barram, who stared at it mutely. "I want to talk to you," the Weaver added. "It will be more comfortable for both of us if you're upright."

Barram clenched his teeth, pointing his revolver at the Weaver's chest.

"Give me one reason why I shouldn't kill you right now," he growled. The Weaver smiled.

371

"I didn't kill you," he answered. Barram paused, then nodded grudgingly.

"You didn't," he agreed. But he didn't lower his gun. "Why?"

"I came to talk, not fight."

"Oh really," Barram countered, gesturing at himself. The corner of the Weaver's lips twitched.

"As I recall, you tried to shoot me."

"You trespassed on my property," Barram shot back. "And killed my guards."

"Oh, they're not dead," the man corrected. "Merely sleeping on the job. But as to the former charge, I admit I am guilty...but only because you make yourself so difficult to access."

"I prefer it that way," Barram retorted.

"I inferred," the Weaver replied. "But clearly your security measures are inadequate. Consider the service I've done you in revealing their flaws; all I ask in return is conversation."

"Conversation," Barram repeated. "You mean *information*."

"Information then."

Barram grunted, then shifted his weight onto his left elbow, raising himself into a sitting position. The motion made his stomach lurch, and he stifled the urge to vomit again.

"What did you strike me with, a brick?" he grumbled.

"My elbow," the Weaver corrected. When Barram glared at him, the man shrugged. "You drained my magic and tried to kill me."

"I did do that," Barram admitted. He leaned forward to try and stand up, but his head swam with the effort, and he remained seated on the floor.

"Let me help you," the Weaver offered. Barram shook his head.

"The room spins if I move my head."

"Not a problem," the Weaver replied. Suddenly Barram felt himself rising up from the floor, and then his chair rolled across the floor until it was under him. He was lowered onto his plush seat, and the chair rolled slowly forward until it was behind the desk once more.

Barram stared at the Weaver, his jaw slack.

"How did you..."

372

"Weave magic after you drained me?" the Weaver interjected. "You'll find I'm more resourceful than your typical Weaver." He smiled then, sitting on the edge of Barram's desk and crossing his arms over his chest. "Something I apparently have in common with my children."

"Your what?"

"My children," the Weaver repeated, eyeing Barram with those shrewd brown eyes. The man's intensity was unnerving, the utter confidence he exuded even more so. This was clearly no ordinary Weaver; he carried himself with the poise of a man accustomed to command. Barram had seen that look before, in his own father, but in this man the effect was tenfold.

"I don't understand," Barram admitted.

"You haven't forgotten them already, have you?" the Weaver asked. "If my sources are correct, you owe them a great deal."

"You mean..."

"Kyle and Ariana," the Weaver interrupted. Barram stared at him for a long moment.

"You're..."

"Their father, yes."

"Right," Barram muttered, shifting in his chair. "I find it odd that they never mentioned you."

"I should hope not."

"Point of fact," Barram continued, "...I believe the girl informed me her father had been murdered."

"He was," the Weaver agreed. "Her hometown was raided by a group of cultists calling themselves 'Death Weavers.' They murdered Ariana's parents, and enslaved her for over a year. I helped to rescue her, and adopted her...as well as Kyle."

"I see," Barram murmured. Ariana *had* told him that very story, minus the part about this man adopting her. Still, he was hesitant to believe this man. "Describe them."

"Very well," the Weaver replied. "Ariana is pale, slender, with dark hair and brown eyes. She is quiet, possessed of incredible strength and stamina, and never seems to eat or sleep. She is practical, and is quite good at thinking on her feet."

"And the boy?"

"Kyle is curious, inquisitive, and creative," the Weaver replied instantly. "He tends to be a little unsure of himself, though he is brave beyond measure when put to the test. He is easily flustered in a crisis, however...I suspect Ariana masterminded your escape from the Verhanian warship."

"Incorrect," Barram replied. "Kyle single-handedly saved my ship and my crew, and destroyed a Verhanian warship. He's remarkably resourceful for his age." Still, it was clear that, whoever this man was, he knew Kyle and Ariana well enough. The Weaver's eyebrows rose.

"Really?" he murmured. He smiled then, a genuine, wistful smile. "What I wouldn't give to have witnessed that."

"What do you want?" Barram demanded.

"I want to know where my children are."

"Why?" Barram pressed.

"Because they're in grave danger," the Weaver answered. "I need to find them before they reach their destination."

"And where exactly is that?" Barram inquired.

"They never showed me the map," the Weaver admitted. "The one they were following. But I believe they're headed for a mine or cave complex somewhere on the mainland."

"I saw the map," Barram confessed. "They're headed for the Barrens."

"And where is that?"

"I can provide a map," Barram answered. Then he smirked. "As long as you agree to make this your final unannounced visit."

"Agreed."

"Very well then." Barram pointed to one of the bookshelves on the left wall of his office. "Top drawer, second from the right." The Weaver walked to the drawer, and retrieved a rolled-up map from it. He unfurled it, and studied it carefully. Then he brought it to Barram, pointing right at the Barrens.

"Here?"

"Correct," Barram confirmed. "You know how to read Verhanian script," he observed.

374

"I know how to read most major languages," the man replied.

"Who *are* you?"

"One day," the Weaver answered, "...I might just come back and tell you." Barram chuckled then, shaking his head.

"I'm afraid I'll have to live with my ignorance then," he replied.

"Why is that?"

"If you're traveling to the Barrens," Barram replied, "...I'm quite certain that neither I, nor anyone else, will ever see you again."

Chapter 26

Kyle watched as Ariana's slender, black-clad form was swallowed whole by the impenetrable darkness of the cave not thirty feet from where he stood. No longer able to see her, he felt suddenly helpless; throughout their long journey here, they'd always had each other to rely on when the going got tough. Now she was alone, with no one to help her. And if she failed in her mission...

He felt Petra's hand resting on his shoulder, and stole a glance at the woman, finding her staring back at him.

"Who is she to you?" she inquired.

"My friend," Kyle answered. For some reason, he was embarrassed to tell this woman that Ariana was his girlfriend. The answer didn't seem to satisfy Petra.

"How did you meet?" she pressed.

"In a cave," Kyle answered. "We were both prisoners, and we escaped together." He paused then, realizing he was doing a terrible job of relaying their story. He started over, explaining how Ariana's family had been killed, how she'd been taken captive. He left out the fact that a Chosen had been responsible, of course. Then he told of his own capture, and their harrowing escape. When he was done, Petra turned to the cave entrance, saying nothing for a long moment. Kyle's eyes took the opportunity – quite of their own accord – to sneak a glance at her physique. He barely had time to turn his gaze away when Petra turned back to him.

"How did she come to be reborn as an Immortal?"

Kyle considered the question for a moment, realizing that how he answered it could matter a great deal. Clearly these people worshiped the Chosen, so telling them that Ariana wasn't technically one of them could be disastrous.

"After we escaped," he answered, "...there was a war between the Chosen and the people who'd captured us. Ariana was killed, but one of the Cho...uh, the Immortals turned her into one of them." Kyle paused then, realizing he'd have to find some way to tell Ariana of his lies in case they questioned her later.

"She was not reborn in the Barrens?" Petra asked. Kyle shook his head.

"She's never been there," he confirmed. "Not yet, anyway."

"Why is she here?" Petra pressed. Kyle considered the question for a moment. Then he shrugged.

"I don't know," he lied. "All I know is she wants to meet her creator."

"The Immortals feel compelled to return to their home," Petra deduced. "Interesting." The way she said it, he wasn't entirely sure she was convinced of what he'd said. The woman was incredibly hard to read. They both said nothing for a long time, seconds passing by, then minutes, the sound of leaves hissing in the wind the only noise breaking the silence. Kyle felt more uncomfortable with each passing minute, remembering what Petra had told Ariana before she'd gone into the cave.

If Ariana failed, she would die...and Kyle would join her.

His pulse quickened then, and he felt a tremendous unease come over him.

"How is it that you can make magic in the Barrens?" Petra asked.

"I make a lot of magic," he answered. Petra considered this silently, staring at the cave entrance. A minute passed, and Kyle fidgeted.

"So you live here?" Kyle asked, if only to break the silence. Petra just stared at him, making him feel like a complete fool. But he found remaining silent impossible. "Do you have a family?"

"My people are my family," she answered coolly.

"You mean them?" Kyle pressed, glancing back at Tavek and Machete, or whatever his name was.

"Including them."

"How'd you learn how to weave?" he asked. Again, Petra just stared back at him, her expression unreadable. "I mean..."

"If your friend returns," she interrupted, "...I may answer your questions."

"Right," Kyle mumbled, staring down at the ground. He felt Petra's eyes on him.

"You're afraid of death," she observed. "If it comes today," she continued, "...it will be quick and painless."

"Well that makes me feel better," he muttered under his breath. He looked back to the cave entrance, hoping to spot Ariana emerging from the darkness, but no such luck. How long had it been...ten minutes? Fifteen? Without a phone or a watch, time was more abstract.

What are you going to do if she doesn't come back?

He stared at the cave entrance, considering his options. He could use magic to try to kill Petra, but she was clearly a more skilled Weaver, and while he still had *some* magic, the Barrens had drained most of it. He did have the bomb Darius had given him; he supposed he could use it to threaten Petra, saying it would destroy her and her people if she tried to kill him. But then she'd just kill him before he could arm it. And if she called his bluff – which she just might, given that she probably wouldn't believe the bomb was real – then what would he do? If he activated it, he would certainly die, as would Ariana. He had no magic here, after all, and there would be no way he could escape the blast radius in time.

Unless...

He put a hand to his breastbone then, remembering the device Darius had placed within. A teleportation device, one that would send him back to Earth with a thought. If Ariana didn't return, and

Petra was going to kill him, he could activate the device, and return safely to Earth.

But then Sabin would win, and the Empire would fall.

Of course, there was a possibility that, if he armed the bomb and teleported to safety afterward, the blast radius would reach Sabin and kill him. It would kill Petra and her people as well, not to mention Ariana. Kyle would be responsible for murdering the girl he loved...but the Empire would be saved. Kalibar, Erasmus...everyone he cared about would live.

Sweat trickled down his forehead, stinging his eyes.

Then again, if Ariana *didn't* return, it probably meant she'd been drained of magic, and since no one could venture into the cave without dying, she'd be as good as dead anyway. And Petra and her people had no problem killing children, so they weren't exactly innocents, were they? But to massacre them all...

Come on, Ariana...

Tavek stirred, folding his arms over his bare chest.

"She's been gone a long time," he observed.

"We lose nothing in waiting but time," Petra countered, not even looking at the man. Tavek nodded, saying nothing more. It was clear that Petra was their leader, or that she at least outranked them. Kyle supposed it was because she was a Weaver, and Tavek was not. Kyle stole another glance at Petra, at the thin scars traveling up the sides of her neck all the way to her temples. He struggled to remain silent, but found it impossible.

"How did you get those?" Kyle asked. Petra turned to him.

"Get what?"

"Your scars," he clarified. "How did you get them?"

"I earned them," she replied.

"How?"

"By excelling as a Weaver."

"So they, uh...cut you?" he pressed. That hardly seemed like a reward worth earning. Petra nodded.

"Another Joined did."

"Joined?" Kyle asked. Petra stared at him for a long moment, then turned her gaze back to the cave. He felt a sudden frustration at her aloofness. "I answered *your* questions," he muttered, then immediately regretted the remark. Petra turned back to him, and – he could hardly believe his eyes! – actually smiled.

"Fair enough," she conceded. "But to understand, you will need to know this first. My people revere magic, but the Barrens robs us of it. The most skilled Weavers of each generation are tested, one against the other, and whoever is proven best earns the privilege of becoming one of the Joined."

"Okay..."

"There is a plant," she continued. "...that grows from deep within the earth. A black vine that rises through holes in the ground. Its bark is black, and it is from this that my uniform," she stated, gesturing at herself – which naturally made Kyle look, and blush – "...was made."

"So the bark insulates magic?" Kyle pressed. Petra nodded. Kyle thought about that for a moment, then frowned. "But what does that have to do with your scars?"

"We call the vine the Reaper vine," Petra answered. "The Joined are those who place Reaper vines within their flesh."

"By making cuts in your skin," Kyle deduced, staring at Petra's scars. "So there are vines under there?" The thought disturbed him.

"Yes," Petra confirmed.

"But why?"

"The Reaper vines produce magic," she explained. "But with their bark, the Barrens cannot drain them of it very easily. My vines," she stated, pointing to her right temple, "...store magic so I can weave, even without my uniform."

"Why not just uh, carry some vines in a bag or something?"

"The Reaper vine only produces magic when alive," she answered. "And the vines must be close to my brain to transfer their magic without that magic being drained by the Barrens."

"Oh," Kyle mumbled. Then he furrowed his brow. "But why the vines?" he asked. "I mean, couldn't you just wear your uniform and make magic that way?" Not that he minded her wearing her uniform.

"My uniform slows the loss of magic," Petra answered, "...but it doesn't stop it. If I don't weave, I lose magic faster than I can produce it. If I weave, I will quickly drain what magic I have left. As a Joined, my vines produce large amounts of magic, and I have no fear of running out."

"But how does the vine survive in your body?" Kyle pressed. "Doesn't it need sunlight or something?"

"When outside, yes," Petra agreed. "But when a young vine is placed in flesh, it consumes this instead."

"Wait, the vine is *eating* you?" Kyle exclaimed. He found the idea extraordinarily hard to believe; Petra had an abundance of flesh, albeit in very specific locations. But she nodded.

"Slowly," she confirmed. "It grows within me, plunging its roots into my flesh, and then my bones, deeper with every day. One day, it will invade my brain, and I will die."

"Wait, *what?*" Kyle blurted out. Petra smirked.

"Now you understand the origin of its name."

"Can't you just take it out?"

"No," she answered. "It has become a part of me."

"How long does it take?" Kyle pressed. "To, uh, you know..."

"Perhaps another decade or two."

"But you're so young!" And it was true; she looked like she was in her twenties.

"A sacrifice for my people," she explained. "It is why the Joined are revered. We give our lives to protect them."

Kyle shook his head, wondering how someone could do that to themselves, knowing that they would die young just to be able to weave magic in this place. A steep price to pay for the ability to use magic; he wondered if he would ever be willing to make that sacrifice.

"Your friend has not returned," Petra observed, changing the subject. Kyle glanced at her, then at the mouth of the cave, realizing that she was right. It had been quite a long time now. Kyle felt fear grip his innards; where was she?

"She'll come back," he promised. But Petra was unswayed.

"I do not have more time to wait," she stated coldly, turning away from the mouth of the cave. She nodded at Tavek and Machete. "I have a meeting with Isha. See things through here," she ordered.

Tavek nodded, walking up to Kyle and raising the point of his spear to Kyle's chest. Machete hesitated.

"What if he uses magic?" he stated nervously. Petra slid the strap of her backpack off of her shoulder, reaching in to retrieve something. It was a small white crystal...a Void crystal.

Terror gripped Kyle's heart.

Before he could react, blue rays shot out from him, converging on the stone. Within moments, the rays faded. What little remained of his magic had been drained.

Petra placed the stone back in her backpack, slinging the pack over her shoulder and turning to look at Kyle one last time. Her expression was cold, not a hint of emotion on her face.

"Tova sho."

She strode away, weaving through the trees until she was no longer visible in the distance, leaving Kyle alone with the two armed men. Tavek stared at Kyle silently, his spear still pointed at Kyle's chest. Machete grabbed for his axe, striding toward Kyle menacingly.

A cold sweat trickled down his sides, and he took a step backward, raising his hands in front of him. Tavek and Machete stepped forward, and Tavek pressed the sharp point of his spear into Kyle's chest. Kyle yelped, backpedaling rapidly.

"Wait!" he cried, glancing behind him. He saw the mouth of the cave there, some twenty feet away, with near-vertical rock walls surrounding it. Machete and Tavek continued forward slowly, their weapons trained on him.

Kyle continued to back up, realizing that there was no place to run. Tavek and Machete were blocking his way forward, and to the sides. There was no way he'd be able to run away from them without being cut down...and even if he *did* manage to slip past them, the men looked to be in incredible shape. They would almost certainly run him down and kill him.

Come on, he urged himself, reaching into his mind's eye, searching for a thread of magic. *Just one pattern...*

But there was nothing.

He continued to back up, until the cave was only ten feet away. Tavek and Machete hesitated then, and Tavek's eyes narrowed.

"Jop!" he yelled.

They're afraid of the cave, he realized, glancing behind him. *They know it will kill them.*

"Jop urot!" Tavek barked as Kyle continued to backpedal, now only five feet from the cave entrance. "Cov nur sop! Bak tor nat wa?"

Anyone who goes into the cave dies, Kyle recalled, his heart hammering in his chest. He glanced back, seeing the gaping maw of the cave ready to swallow him whole. *But there's no magic there.* If there was, he'd be able to see it, after all. He noticed the corpses of many small animals scattered on the cave floor some twenty to thirty feet in. *Whatever killed them wasn't magic.*

He remembered Petra's words then: *"Those who try, their skin turns red. They go crazy, then fall asleep. Sometimes their arms and legs shake. Then they die."*

So it wasn't some beast that killed them, Kyle deduced. Which meant that whatever it was must be invisible, all around them...but not magical.

The air!

Kyle turned back to Tavek and Machete, stopping a mere yard from the cave entrance. Both men had stopped, and were staring at Kyle incredulously.

"Lokas ur orot?" Machete exclaimed. "Nav vuy ruan!" Tavek raised his spear above his shoulder with one hand, as if ready to throw it.

Kyle took a deep breath in, then bolted toward the cave.

"Jop urot!" he heard Tavek scream.

Kyle sprinted as fast as he could, leaping over the corpses of the animals underfoot, then continuing onward toward the cave. He heard shouting behind him, followed by a whistling sound by his left ear. Tavek's spear whizzed past him, bouncing off of the rock wall to the side of the cave.

Oh shit oh shit...

He dodged to the right, running right into the cave, taking one last deep breath before plunging into darkness. He slowed, now utterly blind, reaching out with his hands on either side to feel the rocky walls of the cave closing in. He felt his lungs starting to burn, already struggling to continue to hold the breath he'd taken. He ignored the discomfort, then felt his boot cave into something with a loud *crunch*. He nearly toppled over, only barely managing to keep his balance. He felt lightheaded now, his lungs burning terribly, the urge to take a breath in becoming more and more urgent.

I'm going to die, he realized. *I'm actually going to die.*

And then his foot struck something hard, and he toppled headfirst toward the ground, barely able to get his hands in front of him before he landed...on something soft.

Kyle grimaced, pushing himself up onto his hands and knees, his lungs on fire now. He felt the ground with his hands, his fingers slipping over hard, cool rock, then coming up onto something soft...very soft. It felt like skin, although it was very cold. He slid his hands forward, feeling the lip of a slightly rough fabric...and then something that felt like a leg. His heart leaped into his throat.

Ariana!

He crawled backward, feeling shoulders, then a neck, then...something squirming, under his fingertips. He frowned, knowing that this was where her head was supposed to be. He raked his fingers across the writhing mass, and felt whatever it was fall away, felt a soft nose underneath.

It *was* Ariana!

Kyle slid his arms back more, finding her arms, then her hands. He grabbed at her wrists, then pulled, feeling her slide back a foot. His lungs complained bitterly, the urge to breath nearly unbearable now. He had to take a breath, and soon. There was no way he was going to be able to get Ariana out of here fast enough, though...he had to go back.

Kyle let go of Ariana's wrists, turning about and bracing his hands on the rocky walls on either side of him. He sprinted forward then, feeling his head started to swim. His heart was nearly pounding out of his chest, his entire body slick with sweat. He felt a short breath burst from his lips, and stopped himself from breathing in only with the greatest of effort.

Come on come on...

He ran faster, feeling as if he was getting lighter and lighter. His lips began to tremble, and he felt breath escaping through them, his body betraying him. He grit his teeth, terror gripping him.

No!

In the distance, he saw a hint of light splashing against the rocky wall, not even fifty feet away. His throat spasmed, and he felt the overwhelming urge to breath come over him.

Come on!

He stumbled then, the world starting to spin around him, and barely kept his balance, staggering toward the light before him. The light grew brighter and brighter, and at last he burst out of the cave. He opened his mouth, sucking air into his tortured lungs, his legs giving out beneath him. He fell to the ground on his hands and knees, gasping for air, the world spinning around him.

"Yaruv!"

He looked up, spotting Tavek and Machete standing not a dozen feet away. Machete still had his axe, but Tavek hadn't retrieved his spear. They were both staring at him, their eyes wide, their jaws slack. Kyle rose to his feet, clutching his burning chest.

"Ariana!" he cried, pointing to the cave. "Ariana's in there! We need to get her out!"

"Ariana?" Tavek replied, pointing to the cave. Kyle nodded.

"She's there," he repeated.

"Ariana com cov," Tavek told Machete, who shook his head.

"I'm going to get her," Kyle stated, stepping backward toward the cave. Tavek and Machete just stared at him. Kyle took another step backward, then took a few deep breaths, forcing himself to hyperventilate. He'd used the trick back on Earth, when he'd wanted to swim a whole lap in the swimming pool at his grandparents' house underwater.

"Com cov!" Tavek shouted.

Kyle took one last breath in, holding it. Then he turned back toward the cave, running into it. He half-expected the two men to stop him, but they just watched him go. Kyle made it through the cave entrance, stepping around the corpses littering the floor and making his way deeper into the tunnel beyond. He moved faster than he had before, more confident now. He went at a steady pace, using one outstretched hand to feel along the left wall. He continued forward, feeling the walls on either side narrowing. He slowed his pace, knowing that Ariana was somewhere nearby. Then he felt his boot strike something soft, and he caught himself before he tripped, crouching down and feeling around with his hands.

It was Ariana!

He found her wrists, and tugged on them, feeling her slide backward a little. He paused, then dropped one wrist, turning back toward the cave entrance and walking forward, pulling her along with him. She was heavier than he'd expected, forcing him to yank her forward one or two feet at a time, then rest in-between. He felt his lungs starting to burn, and he paused.

Get out, he told himself. *You can always come back.*

He dropped her wrist, then sprinted back the way he'd come, feeling the burn in his lungs steadily increasing. It wasn't long before he saw the faint light of the cave entrance ahead; he increased his pace, running toward it. The mouth of the cave greeted him and he burst through it, finding Tavek and Machete waiting for him on the other side. They were both staring at him, their mouths agape.

Kyle ignored them, getting a good ten feet from the cave, then hyperventilating again. Once he felt his lips starting to tingle, he took a deep breath in and held it, running back into the cave. This time he reached Ariana a little sooner, sparing no time in grabbing her wrist and hauling her back. He'd made it halfway back when he had to run outside for another breather. On the third trip in, he reached Ariana's side with surprising quickness, and managed to drag her to within ten feet of the cave's entrance before running out.

Tavek and Machete stared at Kyle, then at Ariana.

"Juvak Ariana!" Tavek shouted, pointed at Ariana. Kyle turned to look at her, and frowned, seeing something moving around her head. Something white. He held his breath, running up to her and staring down at her. There were white things covering her head, crawling over her. They looked like bugs.

"Oh!" Kyle gasped, crouching down and sweeping the things off with his hand, grimacing as he did so. The bugs flew away with each swipe, revealing her masked face. Her eyes were staring lifelessly outward. Kyle looked down at her body, and realized that the surface of her entire uniform was moving, as if hundreds of bugs were crawling underneath.

"Oh!" he cried again. He hesitated, then peeled back the neck of her uniform, exposing a mass of white bugs underneath. He recoiled in disgust, then grabbed her wrist, hauling her away from the cave entrance. He was surprised to find Tavek and Machete running up to help him, grabbing her limbs and bringing her well clear of the cave. They lowered her onto the ground, and Kyle peeled back the neck of her uniform again, exposing the bugs for them to see.

"Juvak," Tavek exclaimed. He turned to Machete. "Cov tog Petra," he urged. Machete nodded, leaping to his feet and sprinting into the forest the way Petra had gone. Kyle watched him go, then turned back to Ariana, sweeping bugs from her neck. More emerged from her uniform, crawling toward her head, toward her temple.

"What the..." Kyle began, then stopped in mid-sentence. He stared at Ariana's temple, seeing a hole in her uniform there. He grabbed at her mask, peeling it off of her head, revealing her pale face. There, at her temple, a mass of bugs lay squirming. He brushed them aside, then had to peel off the remaining bugs that clung to her flesh, revealing a small hole in her temple. He stared at the hole, seeing the stark white of her skull exposed within. Even that was partially eaten away.

"Oh, god!" Kyle exclaimed. He felt something crawling up his arms, and jumped to his feet. swiping bugs off of his forearms. "Quick, get them off of her!" He crouched down again, lifting the edge of the uniform at her neck again, swiping away bugs as they scurried out. A few clung to his hands, crawling up his arms again, and he swiped them away. Then he heard footsteps approaching, and he looked up, seeing Machete and Petra running toward them. Petra stopped beside Ariana, pushing Kyle away.

"Ruav es ounav," she ordered. Kyle stared at her uncomprehendingly. A small ray of blue light shot out from her forehead to his right ear. "Stand back," she ordered. "Take the boy away." She gestured for Tavek and Machete to leave with Kyle. "I need to undress her!" Both men nodded, and they grabbed Kyle's arms, hauling him away from Ariana and Petra and back into the forest. Kyle glanced back, seeing Petra peeling back Ariana's uniform, a wave of white bugs gushing out all over her. He turned away from the sight, feeling suddenly queasy. Tavek and Machete led him far away, walking silently through the forest for several minutes before stopping. The two men sat down then, and gestured for Kyle to do the same.

They sat, waiting. Tavek and Machete spoke to each other in hushed tones, too quietly for Kyle to hear what they were saying. Several minutes passed, and then Kyle heard footsteps coming toward them. He turned around, and saw Petra walking toward them...with Ariana walking at her side!

"Ariana!" he cried, jumping to his feet and running toward her. He crashed into her, wrapping his arms around her and squeezing her as tightly as he could. "Oh, thank god you're okay! I thought you were..."

"Dead?" she asked, smiling at him. "I'm alright," she added, glancing at Petra, then back at Kyle. "What happened?"

"You don't remember?" Kyle asked. Ariana shook her head.

"The last thing I remember is walking into the cave," she admitted. "After that, everything gets hazy."

"You were gone for a really long time," Kyle stated. "Petra left, and then Tavek and uh, the other guy," he added, gesturing at the two men, "...tried to kill me, so I ran into the cave after you."

"He almost did our job for us," Machete muttered. He turned to Petra. "He ran into the cave for over a minute. He held his breath and lived."

"Fascinating," Petra murmured. "And how did you think to do that?" Kyle shrugged.

"There wasn't any magic in the cave, so I assumed the it was the air that was poisonous," he replied. Petra arched one eyebrow.

"Well done."

Kyle nodded, then glanced at Ariana. She was giving him a strange look.

"What?" he asked her.

"You ran into the cave to save me?"

"Yeah," he answered. "You were lying on the floor, covered in those bugs," he added. "I dragged you out."

"Kyle, you could've died!"

"Well I couldn't let you die," Kyle retorted rather defensively. He'd saved her life after all...she should be grateful, not scolding him! But she was clearly pissed.

"Kyle, you can't risk your life like that," she scolded. "You're too important."

"You're important too," he countered.

"Not as important as you," she insisted. Kyle stared at her, then lowered his gaze to his feet, realizing that she was right. He was the only one who could activate Ampir's bomb, the only one who could save the Empire. If he had died in there...

"Sorry," he mumbled. He felt Ariana's hand on his shoulder, and looked up at her.

"My sweet Kyle," she murmured, leaning in and kissing him on the cheek. "Thank you." He blushed, then glanced at Petra, who was watching them with a rather amused expression on her face. Kyle blushed harder.

"I'd ask you what she said," Petra stated, "...but I think I get the idea."

"So what now?" Kyle asked. Petra turned about, walking away from them. She gestured for them to follow.

"Now we go home," she answered, lifting up one hand and opening it, revealing a small white crystal within. Kyle blinked, then glanced at Ariana, who just smiled back at him. Tavek and Machete flanked Petra, and Kyle and Ariana followed behind. Kyle found his eyes naturally resting on Petra's posterior, and jerked his gaze upward, not wanting to get caught by Ariana again. To his dismay, Ariana pinched his arm, then walked in front of him, blocking his view. Kyle sighed, then looked at Ariana's posterior, finding a great big tear in her uniform exposing the upper part of her left butt cheek. Then he remembered when he'd first fallen onto her in the cave, how his hand had touched exposed skin above her leg.

"Uh..." Kyle began.

"Figures you'd look," Ariana shot back. Kyle blushed yet again, fixing his eyes firmly on the ground ahead of him. He'd never imagined that his eyes could get him into so much trouble. It was as if the world had suddenly been filled with visual landmines...mines that pulled his gaze toward them constantly with their formidable magnetism. How could he possibly be expected to safely navigate around such effective and deadly weapons?

"I saved that butt you know," Kyle muttered under his breath.

"I can hear you," Ariana reminded him. Kyle sighed, shoving his hands in his pockets and trudging across the forest floor behind Ariana and the others, keeping his eyes – and his thoughts – to himself.

Chapter 27

The infinite blackness of space opens up above Sabin as he steps into the massive underground cavern where his Behemoths have been assembled and stored. Originally the largest cavern in the mine, the Resistance had deepened and widened it to accommodate the massive bulk of Sabin's twelve Behemoths, and had demolished the domed ceiling far above, revealing the starlit sky.

Sabin stares at his creations – his masterpieces – and smiles.

It had taken the better part of two years to create them all, with men working day and night to assemble them. They are massive, each of them standing hundreds of feet tall when fully erect. The relatively limited space of the cavern had necessitated building them in a bent-over position, their arms and legs planted on the ground, their domed heads bowing to the floor. But in an hour, they would stand tall below the huge hole in the domed ceiling above, and would fly upward through it into the night sky.

"They're beautiful, aren't they?" a man beside Sabin asks. Sabin turns to see one of his Runics, a younger man named Witt, staring at the Behemoths. Witt had become Sabin's best pupil over the last few years, and while hardly a match for the sheer talent of the Empire's Runic students, he was more than competent. Sabin had come to think of the man as something like a son.

"They certainly are," Sabin agrees, putting an arm around Witt's shoulders. "What I wouldn't give to see them in action," he adds wistfully.

"I know."

"By sunrise," Sabin declares, "...Verhan will be ours." That had been the plan all along, one that Gunthar had created. The Behemoths had evolved into much more than mere defensive vehicles to guard the mines; Sabin had, under Gunthar's orders, outfitted the enormous runic machines with powerful siege weaponry, the most impressive of which was a state-of-the-art magical cannon set it its single, diamond-shaped eye. Able to melt steel and stone in seconds, Sabin had even created complex algorithms to ensure that the beam would be difficult to deflect by gravity fields, making the Empire's main defenses useless against it. And each Behemoth was equipped with an upgrade to the stealth technology he'd created for the Resistance's troops earlier, allowing each monstrosity to become invisible until the moment of attack.

Verhan, the capitol city of the fallen Orjanian government, would soon be delivered into the hands of the Resistance.

"Right," he hears Witt reply. There is something odd about the man's tone, and Sabin frowns, turning to look at him.

"Is something wrong?"

"No," Witt replies, too quickly. Sabin's frown deepens, and he turns to the man.

"You can tell me, Witt," he insists, giving the Runic a warm smile. In addition to being Witt's teacher, he'd become something of a confidant to the younger man, helping to guide him through the usual travails of early adulthood. It was a role he'd never thought he'd enjoy, much less cherish. Being a mentor had given Sabin a sense of connection that had been sorely lacking in his mostly solitary life.

Looking at Witt, Sabin suddenly regrets never having become a father.

"It's nothing," Witt insists, but he appears troubled. Sabin gestures toward one of the tunnels leading away from the massive chamber.

"Follow me," he urges, pulling Witt into the tunnel and walking alongside him. They navigate the winding, rocky tunnel for a few minutes, until they reach a small, dark chamber. Hollowed out long ago by eager miners, it is a dead end...and no one has any reason to be here but them. Sabin turns to Witt then.

"What is it?" he asks. "Come on, I know something is bothering you." Witt holds Sabin's gaze for a moment, then lowers his chin to his chest, staring at the ground.

"I can't tell you," he confesses. Sabin frowns, taken aback.

"Why not?"

"I've been ordered not to," Witt answers, his eyes still downcast. Sabin stares at the man for a long moment, feeling a creeping doubt come over him. His relationship with Witt had been one of complete openness, a friendship free of lies or secrets...or so he'd thought.

"I see," Sabin replies. He doesn't ask who ordered Witt to be silent...he doesn't need to. Only Gunthar has the authority to hold such sway over the man. Sabin feels anger rise in his breast, and pushes it downward, trying to see it from Witt's perspective. "I'm sorry you've been put in this position," he adds, putting a hand on Witt's shoulder. "It must be difficult for you." Witt swallows, then nods, looking up at Sabin at last.

"It is," he agrees. Sabin is struck by how pale the man is. "I'm sorry," Witt adds, and it is immediately apparent that he means it. Sabin sighs.

"While I admit I'm curious as to what you've been ordered to withhold from me," he states, "...I would not risk any harm to you or to our relationship by insisting that you break your silence." He smiles at Witt, patting him on the shoulder. "Come on," he adds, gesturing back down the tunnel. "We should be celebrating!"

"They're not going to Verhan," Witt blurts out suddenly.

"What?"

"They're not going to Verhan," Witt repeats, more quietly this time. Again, Sabin stares at him for a long moment.

"What do you mean?" he finally asks. "Who isn't going to Verhan?"

"Nobody is," Witt answers in a whisper. "The Behemoths, our Weavers...nobody."

"But we're launching the Behemoths today," Sabin protests, gesturing down the tunnel. "Gunthar himself is coming to see them off!"

"They're launching," Witt agrees, "...but they're not going to Verhan."

"But..."

"They're going to Stridon," Witt interjects.

"*What?*"

"Gunthar's sending the Behemoths to Stridon," Witt clarifies. "And half of our Weavers."

Sabin stares at Witt, his mouth open. Speechless.

"Don't let Gunthar know I told you," Witt pleads, glancing down the hallway behind Sabin. "He ordered us not to." Sabin stares at Witt, then nods.

"Uh, yes, of course," he mumbles. Then he shakes his head in disbelief. "They're going to *Stridon?*"

"Right."

"But why would..." Sabin begins, then stops, feeling a chill run down his spine. He draws in a sharp breath, realization setting in. "My god," he whispers. "He's going to attack the Empire!"

"We're going to win the war," Witt proclaims, a smile breaking across his face. "We're going to beat the Empire once and for all!"

"No," Sabin retorts. "No we won't." He pulls away from Witt's hand, turning around to face the man. "If we attack Stridon, we're going to *lose* the war."

"What?" Witt exclaims, taken aback. "But we've got the Behemoths...we've got you!"

"And the Empire has Ampir," Sabin counters, covering his face with his hands. He feels despair threaten to overcome him, but it is quickly replaced by anger.

The damn fool!

He lowers his hands, turning away from Witt and striding back down the tunnel the way they'd come. He hears Witt's footsteps following behind him.

"Sabin, wait!"

That damn, stupid, idiotic...

"Sabin!"

He feels Witt's hand on his shoulder, and jerks away from it angrily. He walks faster through the tunnel, his footsteps echoing off of the stone walls.

"Sabin, wait!"

He feels Witt's hand on him again, and spins around, grasping Witt by the temples.

"We're dead," he states acidly, glaring at Witt. "Do you understand me? If we attack Stridon, we're *done*." Witt stares back at him, his face pale.

"But..."

"Gunthar's a fool," Sabin proclaims, letting go of Witt and turning away, continuing down the tunnel. "And if I don't stop him, the Resistance – and everything we've fought for – will be for nothing."

* * *

The blackened wood of Petra's magically insulated room under the hill surrounded Kyle, magic lanterns casting a soft glow over the monochromatic floor, walls, and ceiling. He shifted his weight from one side to the other as he sat on the hard floor, stealing a glance at Ariana, who was sitting beside him. They'd both returned to the tribal home under the hill an hour ago, and Kyle had spent the majority of that time eating lunch while Petra repaired Ariana's uniform. Then he'd been brought to this room, and had found Ariana and Petra sitting on the floor.

Kyle smiled at Ariana, who smiled back, but pointed to her teeth, then at Kyle. Kyle frowned, sweeping his teeth with his tongue, and realized he had a piece of meat stuck there. He picked it out with one finger; his lunch had been mostly vegetables, with a few pieces of meat intermixed. It'd reminded him of his Vietnamese grandparents' cooking, bringing back memories of happier times playing in their backyard, and swimming in their pool in the summertime.

Kyle sighed, turning to look at Petra. She was sitting cross-legged in the center of the room opposite Kyle and Ariana, examining the white crystal Ariana had managed to retrieve from the cave.

"This is a perfect specimen," Petra declared, looking at Ariana. "You're sure you don't remember how far into the cave it was?" Ariana shook her head; her memory of her time in the cave had been drained from her, along with her magic. Petra sighed, putting the crystal down. "If we could hold our breaths long enough, we could retrieve more of these."

"Why do you need them?" Kyle asked.

"They allow us to use magic in the Barrens," Petra answered.

"Wait, don't your vines to that?"

"Yes," Petra confirmed. "But that is for weaving. Runic devices don't work in the Barrens...unless you make them from these," she added, pointing to the crystal. "This stone is what drains magic in the Barrens; our ancestors knew that vast amounts of this Void mineral lay beneath this forest, and beneath Mount Grimore."

"It's not draining anything now," Kyle observed. Indeed, there was no blue light at all around it, nor was any magic being sucked into it.

"True," Petra replied. "It only drains magic if it uses magic. If I inscribed the light pattern into it, it would weave that pattern until completely empty of magic, then start draining magic from everything around it to continue weaving."

"Like Ariana's shard," Kyle deduced. Petra arched an eyebrow at him, turning to Ariana.

"Her what?"

"Uh, the thing that makes her an Immortal," Kyle explained. "Maybe that's how she drains magic when she's low on it."

"Perhaps."

"So," Ariana stated suddenly, eyeing Petra. "When are you taking us to the Immortals?" Petra frowned, turning a questioning eye on Kyle.

"She wants to know when we're going to the real cave," Kyle translated. "To the other Immortals."

"Tomorrow," Petra answered. "Today we rest." She smiled at Kyle then, an expression that looked odd on her somehow, but only served to magnify her already considerable beauty. "And I promised that I would answer your questions." She stood up then, gesturing for them to do the same. "Come, we'll go outside with the others."

"The others?" Kyle asked, standing up. Ariana stood as well, and Petra led them out of the room and through the narrow hallway, to the room at the entrance to the home. She crawled through the tunnel toward forest first, and Ariana went afterward, mercilessly denying Kyle a rather magnificent view. Kyle followed after Ariana, crawling through the narrow tunnel until he emerged on the side of the hill. The sun had swung overhead to the west, and to Kyle's practiced eye it was about three o'clock in the afternoon now. When he lowered his gaze, he realized that they were not alone. In fact, they were far from it.

Standing before him, at the base of the hill, were dozens of men and women, all dressed like Machete and Tavek. All were covered in tattoos from head to toe, with various weapons clutched in their hands or strapped to their backs. Kyle spotted Tavek among them; the man walked up to Petra, gesturing at the crowd.

"As you requested," he stated. Petra nodded, then turned to Kyle.

"Come," she urged, grabbing his hand. "I will introduce you." Kyle hesitated, resisting her pull.

"Who are they?" he asked, staring at the forty-odd people surrounding them. None of them looked particularly inviting.

"My family," Petra answered. Kyle did a double take.

"*All* of them?"

"All of them," she confirmed. She pulled him forward then, and he followed her to an older man and woman standing at the front of the crowd. They looked to be in their fifties, with graying hair and fine wrinkles on their faces, but they were remarkably fit, in better shape than most people half their age. The woman looked remarkably like Petra, with similar...attributes.

"These are your guests?" the woman asked.

"Yes mother," Petra replied. "This is Kyle," she introduced, putting a hand on Kyle's shoulder. "And this," she added, gesturing for Ariana to step up, "...is Ariana."

"Welcome," Petra's mother greeted, smiling at them both. Petra's father did the same. "They're outsiders," Petra's mother observed, glancing questioningly at Petra.

"They are worthy," Petra replied. Both her mother and father seemed to accept that, and they turned to gesture at the rest of the crowd.

"These are our children and their children," Petra's mother explained. "Everyone, this is Kyle and Ariana; they are worthy." Everyone waved or mumbled greetings. A short, broad-shouldered man with a spear on his back strode up to Kyle, extending a hand. Kyle shook it, and the man grinned at him.

"You understand me?" he asked. Kyle nodded.

"Uh, yeah."

"Damn," the man said with a grin. "Too bad, we can't make fun of you." Kyle blinked, then turned to Petra, who rolled her eyes.

"That's Otto," she said. "Ignore everything he says." Otto gave Petra a wounded look.

"Aw come on sis," he complained. "I'm family!" Then he turned to Kyle, leaning in conspiratorially. "She's pretty hot, huh?" he whispered rather loudly. Kyle blushed, absolutely mortified. "You know, if she weren't my sister..."

"Otto," Petra's mother scolded rather wearily. "Please." Otto grinned, winking at Kyle, then turned to his mother, his expression changing to one of shocked indignation.

"Aw come on, Mom," he complained. "I was just trying to find some common ground here!" He turned to Petra. "Poor kid must be out of his mind being around you all the time," he told her, much to Kyle's horror. He turned to Kyle, grinning like a fox. "I know I was."

"Otto," a deep voice interjected. Kyle and Otto turned to see Petra's father staring at Otto. Otto nodded once, managing to steal one last wink at Kyle before turning around and walking back into the crowd.

398

"Welcome kid," he called out, waving his hand. Petra's mother sighed, turning a sympathetic eye on Kyle.

"Try to ignore him," she soothed, reaching up and patting his hand. "Everyone else does."

"Heard that!" Otto cried. True to her word, she ignored him.

"Have you eaten?" Petra's mom asked. Kyle nodded, but she hardly looked convinced. She grabbed Kyle's upper arm, *tsk*ing disapprovingly. "You're skin and bones," she declared, turning to Ariana. "Both of you," she added. "Come, we'll make you a meal."

"Uh, I'm not..." Kyle began, but she'd already turned away, and was heading back into the crowd, pulling him behind her.

"You too," she insisted, pointing at Ariana, who glanced at Petra.

"She doesn't eat," Petra stated. Kyle felt her mother stop suddenly, and nearly ran into her.

"What do you mean she doesn't eat?" she asked, her tone incredulous. Petra paused, then put a hand on Ariana's slender shoulder.

"She's an Immortal, mother."

Petra's mother stared at Petra, then Ariana, her mouth agape. Then she came to, snapping her jaw shut with a click. She dropped down to one knee then, bowing her head at Ariana.

"An Immortal!" she proclaimed, her voice cutting through the din of the crowd. All eyes turned to Petra's mother, then to Ariana, and then *everyone* dropped to one knee, bowing before her. Even Petra stood back from Ariana, then prostrated herself before her.

Ariana stared at Petra, then at the crowd, looking horrified.

"Stand up," she blurted out. "Please!" Everyone stared at her, and Kyle translated quickly. Within seconds, the crowd did as she requested, including Petra. Still, every eye was on her, and everyone was silent. Ariana turned to Petra. "Please, tell them not to do that," she insisted, with Kyle translating. Petra nodded, turning to her family.

"She wishes to be treated as a mortal," she explained. That caused a stir, and it was clear that Petra's family was taken aback by this request. It was Petra's father that stepped forward, extending a hand to Ariana.

"Welcome," he greeted, shaking her hand, then reaching in and giving her a hug. That got a gasp out of the crowd, and Petra's mother looked particularly horrified. But her husband ignored her, letting go of Ariana and smiling at her. "We are honored to meet you, and to have you as our guest."

"Thank you," Ariana replied with a smile, looking quite relieved. Kyle saw Otto walk up to her then.

"You don't eat?" he asked. Ariana shook her head, and Otto frowned, putting a hand to his chin. "That's weird. Can you cook?"

"A little," Ariana answered, gesturing by putting her index finger and thumb close together when Otto couldn't understand her. Otto broke out into a grin, clapping her on the shoulder.

"We can be friends," he determined. "Hey everyone, she can cook!"

"Wait..." Ariana protested, but Otto ignored her, ushering her into the crowd. Petra's mother pulled Kyle alongside, and everyone parted for them. Petra took the lead, alongside her parents, with Ariana and Kyle walking next, and the rest of the family trailing behind.

"Where are we going?" Kyle asked.

"To my parents' home," Petra answered. "My family lives there."

"Why don't you live with them?" he asked.

"I'm Joined," she replied. "I must live alone."

"But why?" Kyle pressed.

"It is my responsibility to protect my people," she explained. "I train daily in weaving so that I will be prepared for any threat. I cannot afford to be distracted."

"So you live alone?" Kyle pressed. Petra nodded. "But what about them?" he added, pointing to Tavek and Machete.

"They were hunting when they found you."

"So you really live alone," he repeated. "Don't you get, uh, lonely?" She raised an eyebrow at him, and he blushed despite himself; he hadn't meant it *that* way!

"I have my family," she replied, gesturing to the people trailing behind them. "I see them once a week."

"So you're by yourself pretty much all the time?"

"Yes."

Kyle imagined what it would be like to be alone all the time, spending every day training, having no one to talk to most of the time. He couldn't imagine living such an empty life.

"Don't you ever wish you could be, you know..." he began, then trailed off. Petra smiled.

"Normal?" she finished for him. He blushed again.

"Yeah."

"Yes," she answered. "I do." She turned away then, remaining silent for some time, until Kyle began to worry that he'd hurt her feelings. Then she turned back to him. "Life doesn't always give me what I want," she stated, gesturing to the men and women behind her. "But my sacrifices give my family a chance to have the life *they* want."

"I guess so," Kyle mumbled. He supposed that he was making a similar choice, having risked his own life on several occasions to save his friends. "I think I'd do the same."

"You went into the cave to save your friend," Petra replied, putting a hand on his shoulder. "You already have."

Kyle heard a shout, and turned to see two men running toward them from the left. They were dressed much like Tavek and Machete, with loincloths and weapons, but not much else. Petra stopped in her tracks, putting a hand out to stop Kyle and Ariana.

"Petra!" one of the men cried. He ran up to Petra, stopping before her. "Petra, we found two bodies south of here, a mile away."

"Who?" she asked.

"Rul and Tok," he replied.

"How long dead?" she pressed, her voice tense.

"Less than an hour."

"How were they killed?" she asked.

"With their own weapons."

"Were there any tracks?"

"Many," he replied. "All by the killer. They made false trails, all ended in dead ends." Petra nodded.

"A skilled opponent," she murmured. "Take me to the bodies."

The man nodded, and he and his partner led Petra through the forest, with everyone – even Petra's huge family – following behind. Within ten or so minutes, they came upon two bodies lying motionless on the forest floor. They were both men; one was lying across a fallen log, two arrows in his chest. The other was splayed across the ground, his spear jutting out of the left side of his chest. Blood soaked the ground around them, the air thick with the awful smell of it. Tiny insects buzzed around the bodies, forming shifting clouds over the deceased.

Petra walked up to the body on the log, examining it for a long time. Then she went to the man's back, staring at the arrowhead protruding there. She snapped the head off of the arrow, then gripped the shaft from the other side, slowly pulling the arrow from the man's chest. She stared at its length for a long moment, then walked to the second body, kneeling down before it. Kyle felt a hand on his shoulder. He turned to see Petra's mother at his side.

"Are you all right?" she asked. He stared at her uncomprehendingly, then realized she was concerned about him seeing the bodies.

"Yeah," he answered. "I've seen it before."

"Who would do such a thing?" she wondered, shaking her head at the carnage.

"Are they...family?" Kyle asked. She shook her head.

"A different family, but the same tribe," she corrected. "Good boys, both of them."

Petra stood suddenly, leaving the bodies and striding up to her mother and father, still holding the blood-streaked arrow in her hand.

"They were killed by a Weaver," she declared. Her mother glanced at her father.

"How do you know?" he asked.

"Rul has a full quiver," she explained, pointing to the man draped over the log. "Except for this arrow," she added, holding it up, "...which is of the same make."

"So someone shot him with his own arrow," Petra's mother deduced. Petra nodded, running a finger down the arrow's length.

"The shaft is curved," she continued. "And the fletching," she added, pointing to the three triangular pieces at the back of the arrow, "...has been pulled in the same direction as the curve."

"Which means?" her father asked.

"Rul shot this arrow at the murderer," Petra answered, "...and the murderer used a gravity field to arc it back to Rul, striking him in the heart."

"But how?" Kyle asked. Everyone turned to him. "Only the Joined can use magic here," he explained.

"Or a Weaver with a Reaper suit," Petra replied, gesturing at her own uniform.

"Outsiders have no Reaper vines to make a suit," Petra's father protested. "Only a Joined could have done this."

"The tribes are at peace," Petra countered. "And Rul would not have shot an arrow at one of the Joined." She turned back to the body on the log. "It takes incredible skill to pull an arrow through the air and strike a man in the heart like that. Only myself and perhaps one other Joined could have done it."

"What about an Immortal?" one of Petra's other family members asked, a tall, thin man. All eyes went to Ariana then.

"Immortals have never harmed us," Petra countered. "And Rul would not have attacked an Immortal, except by accident."

"I agree," Petra's father declared. "Even when attacked by mistake, the Immortals have spared us. They have no fear of being harmed by our weapons."

"So it was an outsider," Petra's mother concluded. "An outsider who can weave magic in the Barrens." She looked suddenly pale, and stared at her daughter, who tossed the arrow onto the ground, then knelt down to wipe her bloodied hands on tufts of grass. She stood back up, facing her family.

"Go home," she ordered. "My wards will protect you there. I will find the murderer, and I will kill them."

"Yes Petra," her father replied. He turned about, grabbing his wife by the hand, and gestured for the rest of his family to follow him back through the woods, the way they'd come. Kyle began to follow along, but realized that Ariana hadn't moved, still standing near Petra. He stopped.

"You coming?" he asked. Ariana turned to Petra.

"I want to help," she said. Petra hesitated, then nodded.

"Thank you."

"I'll help too," Kyle stated. Ariana shook her head.

"It's too dangerous," she countered. "Go with the others."

"But..."

"She's right," Petra agreed.

"Hey," Kyle protested, "...I can weave too, you know."

"You don't have much magic," Petra retorted.

Kyle sighed, realizing he wasn't going to win this argument. He turned back toward where the rest of the family had gone, and realized that they'd already vanished into the woods. Petra gestured for him to go.

"Go," she ordered. "Run and catch up with-"

There was a burst of blue light, and Petra shot backward through the air.

"Kyle!" he heard Ariana shout. Then he flew back into him, throwing him toward the ground. He landed on his back, Ariana lying on top of him. He wove magic frantically, a blue gravity shield appearing around them both. Kyle turned to Petra, saw her levitating in mid-air some ten feet above the ground. She lowered herself to the forest floor, crouching down low, her eyes scanning the forest rapidly.

"Petra!" Ariana cried.

"Protect Kyle!" Petra ordered. She stood then, rising to her full height. "Come out, coward! Show yourself!"

Kyle saw something flicker in his peripheral vision, and turned to see the spear pull itself out of Rul's body, then launch itself through the air...directly at Petra.

"Watch out!" he warned.

The spear shot toward her with terrifying speed, and Petra barely had time to turn her head to even see it. Kyle felt his heart leap in his throat, and he knew then that she was about to die.

404

Suddenly a large gravity sphere appeared around Petra, and she leaped to the side, the spear missing her left flank by inches. The gravity sphere contracted rapidly, making the spear spin around her body in a half-circle, shooting outward the way it'd come.

Yes!

Then the spear arced again, shooting right back toward her!

Petra's eyes widened, and she dodged to the side, her feet hovering inches above the forest floor. The spear followed her, picking up speed as it went. She burst to the other side without warning, reversing direction, but the spear locked on her position again, shooting right at her.

Then she slammed sidelong into a tree trunk with a sickening *thump*. She bounced off, then fell to the forest floor.

"Petra!" Ariana cried.

The spear flew right into the center of her chest.

Kyle closed his eyes, turning away at the last minute. He heard a massive explosion, a shockwave slamming into his gravity shield. A spray of dirt and small stones pelted the shields, trees flying outward from where Petra had been standing, thick trunks snapping like twigs, a few branches ricocheting off of his shield. Ariana pushed herself off of him, rising to her feet and pulling Kyle up to his.

"Kyle!" she shouted. "Are you okay?"

"Yeah," he answered. Then he turned his head, and saw Petra floating a few feet above the ground, the jagged ends of severed tree trunks all around her. She descended, touching down on the forest floor. Kyle stared at her breastbone, realizing that there wasn't a single mark on it. Or on anything near it, he was relieved to see.

"Not bad," a deep, masculine voice called out, somewhere to their right. Kyle and Ariana turned toward the sound, spotting a dark shape dropping down from the trees, his descent slowing at the last minute so that he landed on the ground without a sound. The man stood there for a moment, then strode toward them. He was tall, and covered from head to toe in black mud. Even his face was covered, only his eyes visible through that earthen mask. He stopped ten feet in front of them, turning to Petra, then back to Kyle and Ariana.

"Who are you?" Petra demanded. The stranger ignored her question, staring at Kyle and Ariana. Petra strode forward then, pointing at the stranger. "You're a dead man," she promised, her tone ice cold.

"Then there's no point in killing me, is there?" he replied calmly, not even looking at her. Petra stopped, gravity shields bursting to life around her.

"You think this is a joke?" she exclaimed.

"No."

"You'll pay for murdering Rul and Tok," she threatened. He turned his gaze to her then.

"They paid for attempting to murder me."

"You're trespassing on our land!" she exclaimed. "All outsiders should know that the penalty for this is death."

"They're trespassing," the stranger countered, pointing to Kyle and Ariana. "Yet they still live." He began walking toward them again, and Ariana moved to stand in front of Kyle.

"Don't you even *think* about hurting them," Petra warned.

"I won't," the man replied. "I think they'll attest to that," he added. He smiled then. "Hello, by the way," he added, nodding at Kyle and Ariana. "I have to say I'm impressed...you made it much farther than I expected."

"What?" Kyle asked.

"Do we know you?" Ariana pressed.

"I certainly hope so," the man replied with a smirk. "After all, I *am* your father."

Chapter 28

Kyle stared at man before him, his mouth agape.

"*Kalibar?*" he asked incredulously. The man didn't look anything like him. Which might have been due to him being covered in mud, but still, he could hardly believe it.

"Indeed," the man confirmed. Kyle's eyes widened, and he felt his heart skip a beat. It *was* Kalibar's voice! Ariana nullified Kyle's gravity shield, running up to the man and throwing her arms around him, ignoring the mud covering him.

"Daddy!" she cried, giving him a big hug. By the way Kalibar's eyes popped out, she'd forgotten to temper her enormous strength. She pulled back, no doubt sensing his discomfort, and apologized profusely.

"I think you broke a rib," Kalibar gasped, clutching his right side. Ariana's eyes widened in horror, and Kalibar grimaced. "Don't worry," he added, "...it'll heal in a minute."

"Is it really you?" Kyle asked, still not daring to believe. He took a step forward, peering at the man. Even through the mud, it was clear that he didn't have any hair, or a goatee for that matter. Without them, he was hardly recognizable as the Grand Weaver of the Empire.

"I'd take off this mud and prove it," Kalibar replied, "...but your friend over there might kill me if I did." Kyle glanced at Petra, whose

407

eyes darted back and forth between the three of them, then frowned at Kalibar.

"What's with the mud?" he asked.

"Remember back at the Tower?" Kalibar asked. "When we covered ourselves with mud to protect ourselves from the Void spheres?" Kyle nodded; they'd discovered that the mud insulated them a bit from the deadly spheres, preventing magic from being rapidly drained. In fact, he himself had been the one to come up with the idea. He nearly slapped himself in the forehead, realizing that he could've done the same thing here, and might have been able to weave more magic if he had. Of course, there was no way he could have known about the dangers of the Barrens ahead of time.

"Oh *man*," Kyle groaned. Kalibar chuckled, walking up and putting a muddy hand on his shoulder.

"It's all right," he consoled. "A momentary lapse. From what I hear, you've been remarkably resourceful otherwise. The good Captain had wonderful things to say about you."

"The Captain?" Kyle exclaimed. "You met him?" Kalibar nodded.

"I did indeed," he confirmed. "It took a bit of...convincing, but he was quite helpful in assisting me to find you."

"What are you doing here?" Ariana asked. "I'm not going back," she added firmly. "Not until I..."

"You're right," Kalibar interjected. Ariana stared at him.

"What?"

"I didn't come here to stop you," he explained. "I came to help."

Both Kyle and Ariana stared at Kalibar silently for a long moment, barely able to believe their ears.

"Really?" Ariana asked at last. Kalibar chuckled.

"I've found," he replied, putting an arm around her shoulder, "...not for the first time, that my children are sometimes wiser than I."

"Enough," Kyle heard a voice order. He turned, seeing Petra glaring at them. Or rather, at Kalibar. "You may be their father, and they are welcome guests here," she continued. "But you are not."

"Please, let me explain," Kalibar began, but Petra cut him off with a gesture.

"Let *me* explain," she retorted coldly. "You murdered two of my people. By law, this is punishable by death. I am responsible for upholding the law."

"I understand..." Kalibar began, but again, Petra cut him off.

"Then there is nothing more to discuss." She stepped back then, gesturing at Kyle and Ariana. "Step aside, children." Kyle stayed where he was, and Ariana did the same. Kalibar sighed.

"Kyle, Ariana, why don't you step aside for a moment," he requested. "It seems your friend and I have a disagreement to resolve." He turned to Petra. "I want you to know that those two men..."

"Rul and Tok!" Petra interrupted.

"I want you to know that Rul and Tok attacked me first, without provocation," Kalibar stated. "To them, I was an unarmed man. I had limited magic to defend myself, as I do now. Had I been possessed of my full strength, I would not have had to kill them."

"Enough talk," Petra ordered.

"Very well," Kalibar replied calmly. He stood before Petra with his arms at his sides, looking unnervingly vulnerable. Kyle backed away, pulling Ariana with him. A bolt of fear shot through him.

"Don't do it, Petra," he pleaded. Petra glanced at him.

"I know this is your father," she replied. "But I must uphold our laws."

"I'm not worried about him," Kyle countered. "I'm worried about *you*."

"Your concern is misplaced," Petra promised.

"No, he's right," Ariana insisted. "You really don't want to fight him." Kyle saw Petra hesitate for a moment.

"And why is that?"

"He's the best Battle-Weaver in the world," Ariana answered. Petra turned to Kalibar, eyeing him for a long moment. Then she bent her knees slightly, her eyes hardening.

"We'll see about that," she muttered. "Get back!"

Kyle obeyed, backing up even further, but Ariana stayed where she was. Kalibar turned to her.

"It's all right," he told her. "You don't need to help me."

"But you don't have much magic," Ariana protested. Kalibar turned to Petra.

"She's correct," he stated. "You have much more magic than I...this is hardly an even fight."

"I don't care," Petra replied. "This isn't a duel," she added coldly. "It's an execution."

"By all means then," Kalibar replied coolly, extending his arms to the sides. "Execute."

And then he vanished into thin air.

Petra stepped back, blue light flashing from her forehead, and a powerful wind slammed into the ground where Kalibar had been. Dirt and leaves flew upward from the ground, circling around in a mad frenzy. Then the wind stopped suddenly, the dirt and leaves falling to the ground. Kyle saw a faint swirl of leaves, as if something invisible was pushing them to the side.

Petra's eyes locked on that movement, and her eyes narrowed. Kyle felt the hairs on his arms and neck rise, and then there was a flash of pure white light as a bolt of lightning shot down from the sky, slamming into the ground with an ear-splitting *boom*.

Right where Kalibar had been.

Kyle squinted against the flash of light, spotting Kalibar appearing out of thin air to the side of the lightning bolt, a fireball shooting from him and flying toward Petra with incredible speed. Her eyes widened, and she lurched backward, creating a gravity field around herself just in time. The fireball arced around her, then shot back at Kalibar. Just as quickly, it turned around again, swinging right back at her. This time, however, Petra was ready; a ball of water appeared before her, and she shot it out at the fireball. They collided in a hiss of steam, extinguishing the fireball instantly.

A blackened ball of *punk* dropped to the forest floor.

"Well done," Kalibar stated. "You learn quickly."

"Stop talking to me like a student," Petra ordered, glaring at him. Kalibar raised an eyebrow.

"Stop talking to me like an equal," he retorted calmly. Petra's eyes narrowed, and the broken-off tree trunks resting on the ground around her lifted up into the air, coalescing so that the trunks – some over thirty feet long – came together like the spokes on a wheel. That wheel began to spin, quickly picking up pace. The whole thing began to move forward then, slamming into nearby trees as it went, viciously severing their trunks in a spray of wooden shards. It accelerated rapidly...heading straight for Kalibar.

"Kalibar!" Kyle cried.

The Grand Weaver stood there as the spinning wheel of death approached him – just stood there! – until it was nearly on top of him. Without warning, the earth around him exploded, a geyser of dirt bursting up into the air. The spinning wheel slammed into the ground where he stood, sending huge chunks of dirt flying into the air right at Kyle and Ariana. Kyle cried out, throwing more magic at his gravity shield. The dirt splashed off of the shield, falling harmlessly to the ground.

Kyle lowered his arms, staring at Kalibar. Or rather, at the empty space where he'd been only seconds ago. The Grand Weaver was nowhere to be seen. Kyle scanned the forest, spotting the scattered trunks that had made up Petra's whirling weapon earlier, terrified that he might find his adoptive father's body strewn among them. But he saw nothing.

"Not bad," he heard a voice say.

Kyle turned toward the source of the voice, finding Kalibar – alive and whole! – standing right where he had been earlier...straddling a man-sized hole in the ground directly below him. He stepped away from this, giving Petra a nod.

"You've got talent," Kalibar continued. "But a suggestion, if you will. Don't use a cannon..."

Petra shouted, a large rock beside her lifting upward and forward, throwing itself at Kalibar. Kalibar stepped aside, a thin ray of retina-searing light shooting outward from him, aiming right at Petra's face. She cried out, throwing up her arms and squeezing her eyes shut, stumbling backward. A few layers of gravity shields appeared around her, bending the light away from her face. She blinked rapidly, another boulder launching itself at Kalibar, but it flew wide of its mark.

"...when an arrow will do," Kalibar finished. Then he pointed up, above Petra's head. "Watch out."

Petra looked up.

A large tree branch hovered inches above her head, having fallen from a tree overhead. Petra stared at it for a split second, then realized that her gravity shields had disappeared. She grimaced, and the tree limb flew to the side, tumbling to the ground.

"Clever," she muttered. "but...ow!" She arched her back, crying out in pain and surprise, then turned around. There, hovering in the air behind her, was an arrow from Rul's quiver. A small bit of blood shone on the tip of the arrowhead.

"As I said," Kalibar stated calmly. Petra spun around, knocking the arrow away and glaring at him. Her fists clenched, then unclenched, her jaw rippling.

"Why didn't you kill me?" she demanded.

"I didn't want to," Kalibar answered. Petra shook her head.

"I wanted to kill *you*," she retorted. "You should have killed me."

"You still can kill me if you like," Kalibar offered. "I don't have any magic left." Petra stared at him.

"What?"

"I don't have any magic left," Kalibar repeated. "Therefore, if you wish to kill me, you'll find it easy to do so now."

"You used the last of your magic to spare me?" Petra asked incredulously. "That's..."

"Generous?"

"Stupid," Petra retorted. "Why would you do that?"

"You've earned the trust of my children," Kalibar replied, gesturing to Kyle and Ariana, "...and I trust their judgment implicitly. You must be of fine character to have won them over. I only ask that you give me a chance to prove that I am as well."

Petra stared silently at Kalibar, then turned her gaze to Kyle and Ariana. She lowered her chin then, staring at the ground for a while, before turning back to Kalibar.

"I won't be able to forgive myself for killing a man who spared my life," she stated at last. "As much as I want to," she added darkly. She turned to Kyle and Ariana. "Come here," she ordered, gesturing for them to step forward. Kyle glanced at Ariana, then strode forward across the now-shattered patch of forest. Petra's magic had devastated the area, a testament to her raw power. That she could perform such feats despite the constant vacuum of the Barrens was formidable indeed.

"Thank you," Kalibar stated, bowing slightly to Petra. "Now, if you would, I'd like to get this mud off of me."

"Of course," Petra replied. A stream of water appeared above Kalibar's head, splashing down on him. Kalibar went rigid as it coursed over him, taking a sharp breath in and clenching his fists. Within a few moments, the mud had been mostly rinsed away; Kyle was shocked to find Kalibar completely bald, his goatee gone, dressed only in a simple – and thoroughly soaked – brown cloak, pants, and boots. He was shivering violently.

"Thank you," Kalibar grumbled, glaring at Petra, "...for not making it solid ice." She smiled sweetly back at him.

"My pleasure."

"I suppose I deserve that," Kalibar admitted. Petra said nothing, turning about and striding away from them. Kyle noticed a small hole in her uniform, right in the small of her back.

"Follow me," Petra commanded, continuing forward with her customary graceful stride. Ariana pointedly stepped in front of Kyle, blocking his view once again. Kyle glanced at Kalibar, and was vindicated to see the older man taking notice of Petra's remarkable form. Kalibar noticed Kyle noticing him noticing, and cleared his throat, pointedly keeping his eyes straight ahead...and out of such perilous territory.

"Well then," Kyle heard Kalibar mutter under his breath. "This should be interesting."

* * *

413

The sun rode low in the late afternoon sky, its waning rays peeking between the treetops. A warm breeze rustled the leaves overhead, then faded away, leaving the Barren forest eerily still. Kyle fidgeted, picking at his fingernails, and glanced at Ariana. They were sitting outside, some twenty feet from the entrance to Petra's parents' house. It was a home unlike any that Kyle had ever seen, a building three stories tall, built between two massive rock walls at the base of a large hill. Its walls were lined with the black bark of the Reaper vine, allowing the defensive wards inside to hold their magic against the almighty greed of the Barrens. Kyle had, for some reason, imagined that the tribe would live in tree-houses or simple huts. Instead, he found their architecture rustic but remarkably well-made.

"They're taking forever," Kyle muttered, glancing back at the large door at the entrance to the house.

"I know," Ariana agreed, looking as worried as he felt. Petra had taken Kalibar into her family's home over an hour ago. While Petra had agreed not to kill Kalibar, she was only the enforcer of the law; her parents, being the highest authority in her tribe, had ultimate say over Kalibar's fate. Kyle had questioned whether that was a good idea...after all, without magic, Kalibar would be helpless if Petra's family decided to put him to death. But Kalibar had asked Kyle to trust him, and had gone with Petra willingly. Kyle and Ariana had been forced to stay outside.

And so they waited.

"I hope he's okay," Kyle muttered. He felt Ariana's arm slip around his shoulders, and he gave her a weak smile. "I still can't believe he's here."

"I know."

Kyle sighed, forcing himself to stop picking at his fingernails. He hated this feeling – of being utterly helpless – while his loved ones faced danger alone.

"Can you hear anything?" he asked hopefully, recalling her amazing senses. Ariana shook her head.

"I think the house is shielded," she answered. "I can't hear anything from inside."

"Oh."

"If they decide to...execute Kalibar," Ariana said, "...we need a plan."

"Right," Kyle agreed.

"They won't be able to kill me," Ariana reasoned. "Unless I run out of magic." Kyle nodded.

"I could cover myself with mud like Kalibar did," he proposed. "That way, I'd be able to store up some magic and stream it to you if you were running out."

"Then I could save Kalibar, and we could escape," Ariana agreed. Kyle felt a surge of hope...until he thought of something.

"Unless they decide to kill him now," he countered darkly. Just the thought of it made him feel sick, and he resumed picking at his nails. The edge of one nail broke, and started to bleed. Ariana said nothing for a long moment. Then she withdrew her arm from Kyle's shoulders.

"If they kill him," she stated, her eyes dark, "...it'll be the last thing they do."

Kyle stared at her wordlessly, unnerved by the utter certainty of her words. But then he imagined these people murdering Kalibar, and felt anger grow within him. He clenched his fists, staring at the house in the distance.

"Agreed," he stated.

Suddenly, the door to the house opened, and Petra stepped through the doorway, walking down the wide path toward them.

"Where's Kalibar?" Kyle asked, rising to his feet. Ariana stood as well, and strode toward Petra, her fists clenched. Kyle sprinted after her down the wide path, until they reached Petra.

"Where is he?" Ariana demanded, her tone cold. Petra stopped before them.

"Come inside," Petra replied. "It is done."

"*What* is done?" Ariana pressed.

"Please," Petra insisted. "Come inside." She turned away from them, walking back down the path toward the house. Ariana glanced at Kyle, then followed behind Petra. Kyle took the rear, feeling his

415

pulse quicken. He wiped his sweaty palms against his pants, suddenly having no desire to go into that house.

What if they really killed him, he thought. *What if they...*

Petra stopped before the front door, opening it and gesturing for Kyle and Ariana to step through. Ariana paused at the threshold, then continued forward, and Kyle followed her. The doorway opened up into a large foyer, with a staircase rising up to the second floor to their left, and a wide corridor to the right. Unlike the walls of the house outside, the interior walls were made of stone and light brown wood. Petra led them both down the corridor, to a large room beyond. It was there that Petra's family was gathered, many standing, while others sat on couches and chairs neatly arranged around a crackling stone fireplace. Kyle noticed Ariana's father speaking with another man near the fireplace, and his eyes widened.

"Kalibar!" he cried.

Kyle sprinted toward the Grand Weaver, but Ariana had him beat, outpacing him easily. She ran up to Kalibar, throwing her arms around him. Somehow Kalibar managed to keep his balance as she slammed into him, wrapping his arms around her in return. Then he stepped back, greeting Kyle with open arms.

"You're alive!" Kyle exclaimed, hugging the man. Kalibar chuckled, returning the embrace, then disengaging. He smiled down at Kyle, ruffling his hair affectionately.

"I am indeed," he replied. "I'm sorry I worried you," he added. "The meeting took longer than I expected."

"What happened?" Kyle pressed. Petra's father turned to him.

"The family has found Kalibar guilty of killing Rul and Tok," he answered. Kyle blinked, taken aback.

"Wait, what?" he exclaimed. "But..."

"However," Petra's father continued, putting a hand on Kalibar's shoulder, "...your father spared my daughter's life, proving that he is a man of mercy. He also entrusted his life to her after she promised not to kill him, removing his ability to defend himself. This proves that he is a trustworthy man." Petra's father smiled. "Men who can't be trusted seldom put their trust in others."

"So wait," Kyle interjected. "What does this mean? They're not going to kill you?"

"Correct," Kalibar confirmed. "However, I have been sentenced," Kalibar added. "I am to instruct Petra in Battle-Weaving, so that she may better defend her family and the other tribes."

"Oh," Ariana said. "That's great!" Then she frowned. "But what about our...um..."

"We'll discuss that later," Kalibar interrupted. "The family is throwing a celebration, and we're invited as honored guests."

"A celebration?" Kyle asked. "What for?"

"We have an Immortal in our midst," Petra's father answered. "And we celebrate our daughter's life, and the generosity of the man who spared her." He grabbed Kalibar's hand then, leading the Grand Weaver back toward the foyer. "Come on," he urged. "I'll show you to the rooftop." Kalibar let himself be pulled along, and Kyle and Ariana followed close behind. They went up the stairs to the second floor, and then the third, walking down a short hallway to a door at the end. Petra's father opened the door, revealing a rooftop terrace. Kyle followed Ariana through the doorway and into the warm night air, marveling at the size of the terrace. It was at least forty feet long and twenty wide, with a short wooden fence surrounding its perimeter. Stone bowl-shaped things topped the fence at regular intervals, flames leaping up from their depths. All around them were sounds of the forest...birds chirping, leaves hissing in the wind, and a sweet grasshopper-like cadence behind it all.

"Come, sit," Petra's father urged, gesturing to one of many round tables lined up on the terrace. He pulled a seat out for Kalibar, and then for Kyle and Ariana, and they sat down. Kyle was surprised when Petra's father didn't sit on the fourth – and final – chair, remaining standing instead. "The food is almost done," he explained. "You must be starving."

"I know I am," Kalibar admitted with a rueful grin. "Thank you for your hospitality."

"Thank you for your mercy," Petra's father replied. He left then, walking back into the house. Kalibar watched him go, then turned to Kyle and Ariana, taking a deep breath in, then letting it out.

"Well then," he declared, smiling at them both. "How have you two been?" Kyle and Ariana exchanged glances; so much had happened to them since they'd left the Tower! How could they possibly explain their unlikely adventure?

"Uh, busy," Kyle answered, glancing again at Ariana, who smiled.

"It's been a lot," she added. "You want me to tell the story, or you?" she asked Kyle. Kyle shrugged.

"You start," he decided. "I'll fill in the gaps."

Kyle heard the door behind them open and close, and twisted around, looking over his shoulder. Petra was there, in her usual outfit; she walked up to their table, pulling back the empty seat and sitting down. She smiled at Kyle and Ariana – making Kyle blush, for she'd caught him with his gaze a bit farther south than it should have been – and then pointedly ignored Kalibar.

"Did I interrupt something?" she inquired. Kalibar cleared his throat.

"They were just about to tell me their story," he replied. "Of how they managed to get this far."

"Please," Petra said, "...I'd like to hear it."

Ariana began, telling Kalibar how she and Kyle had escaped the Tower that night, and how they'd managed to get through the Gate shield. She described their flight to the *Defiance*, their capture, and the harrowing battle with the warship. And how Kyle had managed to defeat the warship and save the *Defiance*. They gave a brief recap of flying over the forest, and their capture by Petra. By the time Ariana finished telling what little she remembered of the cave, Petra's father – and a few other relatives – had arrived with steaming plates of food in tow. Petra's father served each of them, except for Ariana of course. Then the rest of the family sat at the other tables, until the terrace was bustling with lively conversation.

"What a remarkable journey," Kalibar exclaimed. "I'm so proud of both of you." Kyle smiled, flushing with pride.

"Thanks," he said. "Now tell us about how you got here."

418

"Yeah," Ariana agreed. "If you're gone, then who's running the..."

"Ahem," Kalibar interrupted, giving Ariana a look. Her jaw snapped shut with a click, and she glanced at Petra. "I'd be happy to tell my story," he added quickly, "...but I'm afraid you wouldn't be able to hear it over my stomach growling." He dug into his food them, forking a sizable chunk of yummy-smelling meat into his mouth. Kyle did the same, surprised at how mouth-wateringly delicious it was.

"Wow that's good," he mumbled, forking another piece into his mouth. Petra smiled at him.

"Tell my father," she urged. "He's very proud of his cooking."

"He has every right to be," Kalibar declared. "This is exquisite...and I'm no stranger to good food."

"Are you a master chef as well then?" Petra asked him. "Should I have my father take lessons from you?"

"Hardly," Kalibar retorted with a chuckle. "I don't have a mind for cooking."

"But you have one for teaching?" she asked coolly.

"I do," Kalibar confirmed. "And I find the most important part of being a teacher is respecting one's student."

"And what if the reverse isn't true?"

"That makes it difficult," Kalibar replied with a slight smirk. He raised a chunk of meat to his lips, and held it there, his eyes twinkling. "But there's nothing I enjoy more than a good challenge."

"Not all challenges are surmountable," Petra retorted, taking a bite from her own plate. Kalibar raised one eyebrow.

"I never said I had to win to enjoy it," he countered.

Petra arched an eyebrow, then resumed eating, ignoring Kalibar's quiet chuckle. They sat in silence for a while, everyone focusing on their meal. After a few minutes, Kalibar had finished his meal...despite the fact that everyone else was barely half done. Kyle found it best to keep his eyes on his plate, seeing as how Petra was seated opposite him. If he looked at her, his eyes would invariably wander into dangerous territory, and Ariana would be sure to notice.

"I find it remarkable that this wood insulates against the Barren forest," Kalibar stated suddenly, gesturing at the black walls of the house's exterior. "I take it your suit is made of the same material?"

"It is," Petra answered, not looking up from her plate.

"That explains how you can survive here," Kalibar told Ariana. "What tree does it grow from?"

"It doesn't," Petra replied. When Kalibar didn't say anything, she looked up from her plate. "It's from a vine."

"The Reaper vine," Kyle piped in. Petra raised an eyebrow at him, and he blushed. "What?"

"Where does it come from?" Kalibar pressed.

"The ground," Petra quipped.

"A valuable plant indeed," Kalibar observed, ignoring her glib reply. "I wonder if I could study some live samples?"

"They're very difficult to come by," Petra replied. "Most of the vines we find are already dead. The only living vines my tribe has now are inside of me."

"That'll do," he replied. Petra's eyes widened for a moment, but she regained her composure quickly, leaning back in her chair and crossing her arms over her chest.

"I thought a teacher such as yourself would treat his student with more respect," she stated coolly. Kalibar hardly seemed dismayed by her tone.

"Speaking of which," he replied, "...if I'm going to teach you, I'll need to be able to weave outdoors. A suit like yours would be quite helpful."

"Only the Joined can wear it," Petra retorted. Kalibar glanced at Ariana, raising one eyebrow. "And Immortals," Petra added.

"Quite alright," Kalibar stated with a smile. "I seem to get by well enough with dirt."

"I think you've been crawling in it for too long," Petra retorted. "It's seeped into your mind." She finished her food then, standing up from her chair and nodding at Kyle and Ariana. "Good night," she stated crisply. Then she turned and left, making her way back indoors. Kyle watched her go, then turned to see Kalibar watching her go. Kalibar snapped out of his trance, realizing that Kyle and

420

Ariana were looking at him...and that Ariana was rolling her eyes. He cleared his throat.

"Well then," he said, pushing himself away from the table, the legs of his chair screeching on the floor. Just then, Petra's mother stopped by their table, and asked if she could sit down. All three immediately said yes, and she took a seat, smiling apologetically at Kalibar.

"Did you enjoy your meals?" she asked. Everyone nodded enthusiastically, except for Ariana.

"It was exquisite," Kalibar replied.

"Oh good," she stated, clearly pleased. "I hope Petra was...pleasant tonight," she added tentatively. Kalibar smiled.

"She was," he assured. "You have a lovely daughter."

"Oh I know," Petra's mother agreed. "And a stubborn one," she added ruefully. "Everything she does, she excels at. She's been the best Weaver of all the tribes for years now...I don't know if she's very happy about being beaten."

"She seems to be taking it well," Kalibar observed. He smiled at her, patting the back of her hand. "Thank you. For everything."

"You're welcome," she replied. Then she stood, making her way back to her own table. Kalibar sighed, glancing at his two children wearily.

"How about we go for a walk?" he proposed. Kyle nodded, and so did Ariana. They stood from the table, attempting to take their own plates, but they were stopped at once, the plates whisked away by Petra's family. Kalibar went to Petra's parents' table to express his amazement at her father's cooking, and then all three went downstairs, and out of the front door. The starlit sky greeted them as they strode across the wide path away from the house, tiny points of light peeking between the leaves high above their heads.

"I have to admit," Kalibar stated, breaking the silence. "I never expected today to end like this."

"Tell me about it," Kyle agreed, smiling up at his father. "I still can't believe you're actually here."

"We have a job to do," Kalibar stated, putting an arm around Kyle's shoulders, and around Ariana's. "A job that only we can do."

421

He sighed then. "But this," he added, gesturing back at the house in the distance, "...may complicate things." Kyle frowned.

"How's that?"

"Sabin's lair is somewhere around here, correct?" Kalibar asked. Kyle nodded. "And the blast radius of Ampir's bomb, what is it again?"

"Ten miles," Kyle replied. "Uh, a ten mile *diameter*," he corrected. Kalibar nodded.

"That's what I thought," he replied. "Which means that if Sabin's lair is within five miles of this house..." He stopped then, lowering his gaze to the ground. Kyle's eyes widened.

"They'll be killed!" he exclaimed in horror. Kalibar frowned, letting go of Ariana and putting a finger to his lips. Then he sighed again.

"We may have to have them evacuate," he stated. "The question is...if they knew we were going to kill the Immortals – and potentially destroy their home and perhaps even their forest – how would they respond?"

"Not well," Ariana replied.

"Yet we cannot in good conscience let them die," Kalibar continued. "So we have to find a way to get them to evacuate themselves – and the rest of the tribes – without telling them the truth."

"How the heck are we going to do that?" Kyle pressed. Kalibar gave him a wry smile.

"I suspect I'll be spending most of the night pondering that very question."

They walked in silence then for a while, until the path had faded away, leaving nothing but endless forest floor before them. Kalibar stopped then, glancing back the way they'd come.

"I suppose we'd better be getting back," he said. He turned about, beginning the long walk back to the house, and Kyle followed along. But Ariana stayed where she was, her eyes on Kyle.

"What?" Kyle asked.

"Can I talk to you for a little bit?" she asked him. Kalibar raised an eyebrow.

"I'll leave you to it," he said. He continued onward, waving with one hand. "Don't take too long." Kyle nodded, and both he and Ariana watched Kalibar go. When the old man had long since been swallowed whole by darkness of the forest, Ariana turned to Kyle.

"Kyle," she began, her expression suddenly serious. "I need to talk to you about something." Kyle blinked, then frowned.

"Sure, anything," he replied. "What's wrong?"

"It's just..." she started, then stopped, looking like she was searching for the right words. "I've been thinking a lot lately."

"About what?"

"About...us," she answered. Kyle smiled.

"Me too," he replied. She shook her head.

"No, I mean...it's just that..." She trailed off then, turning away from him, her pale face looking radiant in the starlight. Then she turned back to him, taking a deep breath in, then letting it out slowly. Then she shook her head. "Never mind."

"What?"

"Nothing," Ariana mumbled.

"But you were just going to..."

"Forget about it," Ariana insisted, grabbing his hand and pulling him back toward the path. "Come on, let's go home." But Kyle resisted.

"Tell me," he insisted. "What's wrong?"

Ariana hesitated, lowering her gaze to her feet. She took a deep breath in, then let it out.

"It's about us," she said at last. Kyle frowned.

"What about us?"

Ariana looked up at him, her expression unreadable. Then she swallowed visibly.

"It's about *me*," she corrected. She shook her head. "I don't think I'm right for you, Kyle."

"What?" Kyle blurted out. "What do you mean? Of course you are!"

"No," Ariana retorted firmly. "I'm not." Kyle opened his mouth to respond, and Ariana put a finger to his lips. "I'm dead, Kyle."

423

"I don't care about that."

"Not now," she conceded. "But you will."

"Ariana..."

"I'll never get any older, Kyle," she continued. "I can't have kids, or...anything," she added. Kyle shook his head.

"I don't care," he retorted. "It doesn't matter."

"Doesn't it?" she pressed. She put a hand on his shoulder. "Kyle, I can't be what you'll want me to be."

Kyle frowned, staring at her silently for a moment.

"What is *that* supposed to mean?" he asked.

Ariana lowered her gaze, saying nothing, her hand slipping off of his shoulder. Kyle grabbed her hands in his own, and leaning in to kiss her on the forehead. Then he hugged her. At first she just stood there, not moving. Then he felt her hug him back.

"It's not fair" she mumbled. Kyle pulled back.

"What?"

"This," she muttered, gesturing at herself. Then she brought a hand up to her forehead. "And this." She sighed, shaking her head. "Even if I kill Xanos, he'll still have destroyed my past." She looked up at him. "And my future."

"Ariana, that's not true," Kyle insisted. Ariana turned away, staring off into the forest, utterly still. In that moment, she looked like a statue, her shoulders not rising and falling with breath, her eyes unblinking. Kyle stared at her, unsure of what to say. After a long moment, she turned back to him, giving him a weak smile.

"Thank you for saving me back there," she stated. "In the cave."

"No problem," Kyle replied.

"I love you," Ariana stated suddenly, reaching out and squeezing his hand. Kyle turned to her, his heart skipping a beat.

"Huh?"

"I love you," she repeated. She stopped, pulling him up to her and giving him a kiss on the lips. Then she pulled away. He blinked, touching his lips with his fingertips, then staring at her.

"I love you too," he replied.

"I know."

She turned back toward the house then, pulling Kyle along with her. She walked slowly, gazing up at the stars, her hand cool and her grip firm. They'd gotten within a hundred feet of the house when she leaned the side of her head against Kyle's cheek, letting go of his hand and wrapping an arm around his waist.

"I'm glad I can't forget anything," she stated.

"Hmm?"

She rubbed the small of his back, continuing forward.

"I'll always have my memories," she murmured. "No matter what happens."

"We'll make good ones then," Kyle decided. Ariana turned to him, a smile on her lips.

"Yeah."

They made their way back toward the house without another word, following the wide path hand-in-hand, the pale starlight casting the forest in a gentle glow. It was, Kyle realized, one of the most serene nights he'd ever experienced. In spite of the horrors he'd faced that day, the night had ended with him surrounded by those he loved the most, along with the hope that he might just end up succeeding in this impossible mission after all.

Chapter 29

Sabin stands in the small hollowed-out space in the mines that serves as Gunthar's office, his arms crossed over his chest as he stares down at the leader of the Resistance. Gunthar remains seated, as he has throughout their brief meeting. Despite Sabin's fury, and despite the accusations Sabin has leveled at him, Gunthar appears calm.

"I understand your concerns," Gunthar states, breaking the silence. Sabin raises his eyebrows.

"Really?" he asks. "Then you'll call off the attack?"

"No."

"*What?*" Sabin exclaims. He stares at Gunthar incredulously. "How can you..."

"Because I am the leader of this government," Gunthar interjects coolly. "And because I am not as stupid as you apparently think I am."

"I never said..."

"You didn't need to," Gunthar interrupts. He steeples his hands together, staring at Sabin silently, until Sabin squirms under his unblinking gaze. "I happen to be more resourceful than you think."

"What do you mean?"

"Your concern about Ampir is well-founded," Gunthar replies. "I've seen the blueprints for his armor...they're very impressive."

"Blueprints?" Sabin asks. "What blueprints?"

"Your government..."

"Former government," Sabin corrects. Gunthar's jaw ripples at the interruption.

"Your *former* government wasn't stupid enough to let Ampir keep his armor a secret from them," he explains. "They forced him to submit blueprints for his armor for military intelligence."

"Uh huh," Sabin mutters. "And you really believe he gave accurate blueprints? You can't be *that* naïve."

"I do," Gunthar retorts. "And I happen to have a contact in your Empire that received a very large reward for providing me with those blueprints."

"So?"

"So after you finished designing the Behemoths, I had a second team of Runics use those blueprints to add some...modifications to your original design."

"You what?" Sabin exclaims. "You couldn't have," he protests. "I know every inch of those machines!" But Gunthar only smirks.

"Apparently not," he replies. Sabin can only stare at the man, his mind spinning with the ramifications of Gunthar's betrayal. Finally, he finds his tongue.

"You can't attack the Empire," he protests. "My entire family lives there!" And it's true; his sister, her children, and his mother live in Stridon, along with almost everyone he's ever cared about.

Including Vera.

"And that," Gunthar replies, "...is why the Empire is, and always will be, your country." He sighs then, staring at the rock wall to his side. "At least until it is destroyed."

"Why?" Sabin asks. "The Resistance is almost finished with its mission! Verhan is ours for the taking...we can reclaim our land, free our people! Send the Behemoths to Verhan instead, like we planned!"

"You're not thinking of the long game," Gunthar retorts. "As long as the Empire exists, it will never stop threatening my people. A victory at Verhan would only encourage the Empire to mount a massive counterattack, to destroy the government that dared to rise

427

up against it. The only way to be free from the Empire's tyranny and corruption is to destroy it once and for all."

"This is madness," Sabin declares, throwing up his hands. "Millions of innocent people live in Stridon, people that had nothing to do with any of this! If you kill all of them, you'll be no better than the Empire!"

"Sabin," Gunthar says with a sigh. "You're an idealist. I understand this must be difficult for you. Don't get me wrong, I do appreciate everything you've done for us...I really do."

"What are you saying?"

"The Empire is doomed," Gunthar answers. "My Behemoths and airships will launch tonight, and arrive at your Empire this evening. Stridon and eleven other major cities will be destroyed, and the Imperialists will be crushed." He shrugs then. "After which your extraordinarily valuable services will no longer be required."

"You can't be serious," Sabin protests. "I'm as much a part of the Resistance as anyone else here! You wouldn't even *have* the Behemoths if it weren't for me!" He throws up his hands. "And now you're just going to let me go?"

"Goodness no," Gunthar retorts. "I wouldn't think of doing such a thing with a man as valuable as yourself." There is a knock on the door then. "Ah, right on time," Gunthar declares. "Come in."

The door opens, and two guards – Gunthar's personal Weavers – walk through, Witt standing between them. The young man looks terrified, his eyes glued to the floor.

"Witt," Sabin greets. "What's wrong? Are you alright?"

"Oh, he's fine," Gunthar says. Then he nods at the guards. Witt jerks forward suddenly, arching his back, his eyes widening. He cries out, and then the front of his shirt bulges outward in the middle of his chest. A maroon stain appears there, spreading rapidly, and the front of his shirt rips, revealing the bloodstained tip of a blade. The blade retracts, and one of the guards shoves Witt forward. The young Runic falls toward the ground, his head slamming against the rock wall on the way down. He collapses in a heap, a bloody puddle growing around his limp body.

"Witt!" Sabin cries, bursting out of his seat and kneeling at Witt's side.

"Ah well," Gunthar murmurs. "I suppose I spoke too soon."

"You killed him!" Sabin gasps in horror. He turns to Gunthar, shaking his head in disbelief. "Why?"

"I ordered him not to reveal my plans," Gunthar replies. "He disobeyed said order. That is treason, and the punishment for treason is death." He gestured down at Witt's body. "And that is what death looks like."

"He was just a boy," Sabin protests. "You're a monster!"

"He was a man," Gunthar counters. "And I treated him like one until he betrayed me. And now, because of his betrayal, I have to deal with you."

"Deal with me?" Sabin asks, his eyes widening. He rises to his feet, backing away from Witt's corpse, feeling his back strike the cold stone wall behind him. He glances at Gunthar, then back at the guards, his heart pounding in his chest.

"Relax," Gunthar urges, his voice soothing. "I'm not going to kill you. I am a man of the law, not a despot like your Grand Runic Nespo. The only crime you're guilty of is the involuntary acquisition of classified information...and, given your defiant outbursts, insubordination."

"Not a despot?" Sabin declares incredulously, pointing at Witt's lifeless body. "You murdered my best student in cold blood!"

"I had him executed as the law requires," Gunthar retorts calmly. "Keep in mind that he was well aware of the law – and the consequences of breaking it – before he ever chose to." He nods at the guards then. "Take him away," he orders. "Place him in prison until his sentencing." He grimaced then, gesturing at Witt's body. "And get somebody to clean up this mess." The guards turn on Sabin, grabbing his arms and pulling him away from Gunthar, out of the small office. Sabin resists, digging his heels into the stone floor.

"Wait," he pleads. "What if you're wrong? What if you don't kill Ampir? He'll come after you!"

"Oh I don't think so," Gunthar retorts. "My army has been instructed to make it very clear who designed and constructed their

Behemoths." He smiles. "Very clever, to put your symbol on each of them. If they fail, Ampir won't be coming after me...he'll be coming for you."

"You son of a bitch!"

"You'll be interested to know," Gunthar adds as Sabin is pulled forcibly down the hallway away from him, "...that I will be having one team specifically target Ampir's wife and child. Such a simple strategy, yet so effective." He raises one hand, chopping it downward in a straight line. "Divide," he murmurs, "...and conquer."

* * *

Kyle felt something tapping at his shoulder, and he opened his eyes, blinking against the bright sunlight streaming through his bedroom window. He rubbed the crust from his eyes, and saw Ariana standing at his bedside, her hand on his shoulder.

"Come on," she urged. "Get up." By her tone, it wasn't the first time she'd said it.

"Oh, hey," Kyle mumbled. He propped himself up in bed, squinting at her. "What's up?"

"We need to go," she replied, grabbing his wrist and pulling him out of bed. "Get dressed and meet me downstairs, okay?"

"Okay."

"Don't forget the bomb," she reminded him. "And hurry," she added, turning about and walking out of his room. He watched her go, then yawned, stretching his arms over his head and dropping them to his lap.

"Alrighty then," he muttered.

He swung his legs over the side of the bed, hopping off and getting dressed. He checked the backpack he'd stowed in the corner of the room, finding the bomb safely tucked within. He shoved it in his pocket, then made his way through the wide hallways of Petra's parents' house, eventually reaching the large staircase to the first floor. When he took a turn into the main room – the one the family had congregated in yesterday – he found it completely empty. A coffee table in front of one of the couches lay shattered on the floor, split right down the middle. Splinters were strewn across the family room in front of it.

"What the..." he began, then felt a hand on his shoulder. He turned around, seeing Ariana there. He gestured at the broken table. "What happened here?"

"I'll tell you, but don't say anything," she replied. Kyle nodded. "I spent all night thinking about what Kalibar said," she continued.

"About what?"

"Don't say anything," she reminded him. "I was thinking about how the bomb might end up killing Petra's family, and the other tribes. Most of the family was here this morning," she continued, gesturing at the large family room. "So I sat on the couch there, and was talking with Petra's mother. Then I stood up and pretended to be possessed by Xanos."

"You..."

"Shush," Ariana scolded, making Kyle grimace. "I said that something big was coming, and that the tribes were in danger. The Immortals must return to their creator, and the tribes had to evacuate, or they would surely be destroyed."

"Oh," Kyle blurted, his eyes widening. "Oh!"

"Kalibar translated for me. I wasn't getting the response I wanted, so I pretended to pass out, and fell into the table."

"*You* broke it?" he asked. Ariana nodded.

"With my face," she replied rather proudly. "It was very convincing."

"I'll say," Kyle muttered, staring at the shattered furniture.

"Anyway, Kalibar played along. The whole family got spooked, and they've been packing up and traveling to the other tribes to warn them ever since."

"Ariana, that's..." Kyle began, then stopped himself, shaking his head. It was absolutely *brilliant*, is what it was!

"I know," she replied with a smile. She pulled him away from the room then, back toward the foyer. "Come on, we'd better get going."

"Where?"

"Petra's going to take us to the cave like she promised," she explained. "Kalibar's waiting with her outside."

"She isn't evacuating?"

"No," Ariana confirmed. "I told them the Immortals had to return to their creator, remember?"

"Right," he replied. "Wow."

"I know, right?"

Kyle shook his head in wonder; Ariana had always been clever, but this was a stroke of pure genius. Unable to say so, he hugged her, then let her lead him out the front door and onto the path beyond. A hundred or so feet ahead, they found Kalibar talking with Petra. The Grand Weaver was once again covered from head to toe in mud; Petra had been serious about not letting him have a Reaper suit...not that any of hers would've fit him.

"The tribes shouldn't all evacuate to one place," Kalibar was saying. "I think they should spread out at the edges of the forest, just in case this is a trap."

"A trap?" Petra replied, clearly unconvinced. "The Immortals would not harm us."

"Yes, well," Kalibar muttered. "I don't trust them." Then he saw Ariana approaching, and smiled. "Except for this one, of course."

"Hi dad," Ariana greeted. "I told him," she added, gesturing at Kyle. Petra frowned.

"What did she say?"

"Kyle knows what happened," Kalibar answered. He turned to Ariana then. "You're *sure* you're alright?"

"I'm fine," Ariana insisted. Kalibar turned to Petra.

"And you're sure you still want to do this?"

"I gave my word," Petra declared. "I will take Ariana to her creator." She turned then, striding away from them and into the forest, gesturing for them to follow her. Kyle glanced at Kalibar, who appeared rather preoccupied with Petra's retreating form. He smiled, thinking back to what the old man had said so long ago, when Kyle had first met him...that men never outgrew their fascination with such things. He glanced at Ariana, who had clearly located the source of Kalibar's curiosity, and appeared rather exasperated with it. Perhaps women never outgrew their frustration at men's fascination with their particulars either.

"How far away is the cave?" Kalibar inquired, catching up with Petra and walking at her side.

"Up the mountain," she replied.

"What distance?" Kalibar pressed.

"I haven't measured it," came the deadpan reply.

"Is it filled with the same gas as the cave Ariana went into?" Kalibar asked. They'd concluded that there must be a poisonous gas throughout the cave, after Kyle's success in navigating it while holding his breath. Petra nodded.

"Anyone who goes inside dies in the same way," she confirmed.

"That could complicate things," Kalibar murmured. "We'll have to create a large gravity sphere to trap air inside before going in."

"A good idea," Petra opined. Kalibar raised an eyebrow at her, and she frowned. "What?"

"I wasn't expecting praise," Kalibar replied with a mischievous grin. "I'm speechless."

"That was my intention," Petra shot back, giving him a little smirk. Kalibar chuckled, and Kyle caught Ariana glancing at him. Kyle frowned, and Ariana cocked her head at Kalibar and Petra, arching an eyebrow. Kyle shrugged.

"You hardly have to speak to leave me that way," Kalibar replied smoothly, keeping his eyes straight forward. Petra's eyes widened, and she glared at him. Kyle thought he saw her cheeks turn a little pink, but it was hard to tell with her dark skin.

"Not speaking might be best for you," she grumbled, increasing her pace. This had the unintended effect of leaving Kalibar behind, giving him an unfettered view of hers.

"What is that around your neck?" Kalibar asked. Petra didn't slow down, forcing Kalibar – and everyone else – to speed up just to keep up with her. Petra ignored the question at first, but when Kalibar let the question hang in the air, she stopped, turning around. Kyle frowned; he couldn't see anything around Petra's neck. Then he realized that there were small bumps under her uniform, in the shape of a necklace. He'd never even noticed it, having spent far more time observing matters immediately below.

433

"A necklace," she answered, turning around and resuming her quick pace. "A diamond necklace," she clarified. "My grandfather gave it to me before he passed."

"I see," Kalibar replied. They walked in silence for a few moments, and to Petra's obvious annoyance, Kalibar kept up with her easily. "What do you know about this cave?" he asked, wisely changing the subject.

"It was the main entrance to my ancestors' caves over two thousand years ago," she answered grudgingly. "The only caves in the world that carry the Void crystals...and the Reaper Queens."

"The what?"

"Sacred creatures," Petra answered. "In a way, they are the mother of all the Barrens," she added. "That is why the caves were so sacred to my ancestors. They guarded the caves from anyone who tried to steal their treasures. Many tried to defeat them, but none succeeded."

"Interesting," Kalibar replied. "I've read reports from that time...they discussed a tribe of forest-dwelling Weavers defending such a cave."

"My ancestors were the best Weavers in the world," Petra declared proudly. Then she deflated somewhat. "At least until the Outsider came."

"The Outsider?"

"A man," Petra confirmed. "My ancestors took him in, and he lived among them for many years."

"What happened then?"

"The Outsider discovered the key to eternal life," Petra replied. "He gave this to my ancestors, plunging stones into their heads to make them the first of the Immortals."

"My god," Kalibar breathed. "It was Sabin!" Kyle felt a chill run down his spine, and he turned to Ariana, who looked similarly disturbed. It made perfect sense, of course; Sabin had made his lair here, after all. Still, the thought that Sabin himself had lived here, among these tribes, was mind-boggling.

"Sabin?" Petra asked.

"A man from my country," Kalibar explained. "He was a brilliant researcher and Runic." He shook his head. "No one knew where he went after he...after he left the country. I suppose it makes sense that he traveled here."

"Yes, well," Petra stated. "The Outsider – Sabin – took my ancestors' best Weavers and made them all into Immortals, and then they vanished into the caves."

"What happened to them?" Kalibar pressed. Petra shrugged.

"No one knows," she admitted. "The entrance to the caves was filled with water, and then poison air. My ancestors tried to get in, but those who did died. With their best Weavers gone, they lost much of their knowledge of weaving, and the tribes have never been the same since." She slapped a bug that landed on the back of her neck. "We see the Immortals now and again, but they never speak to us, and most of them are not from our people."

"That's terrible," Kalibar murmured. "I'm sorry."

"It's the past," Petra said matter-of-factly. "My people hope that one day our ancestors – the first Immortals – will return to us, and teach us the old ways."

"That's why you revere them," Kalibar deduced. Petra nodded.

"They are our past," she explained. "We guard these woods and the caves as they did, and wait for them to consider us worthy of their knowledge and wisdom."

They walked in silence then, Petra's body language clearly indicating that she was done talking. Minutes passed, the crunching of their boots on the dead leaves and twigs underfoot forming a mind-numbing rhythm as they navigated through the forest. Eventually the forest floor began to angle upward, gradually at first, then more sharply. Kyle's legs, as accustomed as they had become to being put through their paces, began to burn. He soon found himself struggling to keep up with the others.

"You okay?" Ariana asked. Kyle nodded, sweat trickling down his forehead.

"I'm," he gasped, "...fine."

"Want me to carry you?" she offered. Kyle stared at her incredulously, then shook his head.

435

"S'okay," he replied, trudging forward and upward. Ariana folded her arms over her chest, keeping pace with him with annoying ease. "What, you don't want to look weak in front of your girlfriend?" she pressed. Kyle gave her a look.

"You don't...care about that," he replied.

"I wasn't talking about me," Ariana retorted. "She can't even see you, you know."

"What are you..." Kyle began, and then he realized Ariana was talking about Petra. He blushed furiously, and turned away. He could feel Ariana's eyes on him.

"Relax, she can't understand me," Ariana muttered. "And besides, they're too far away to hear." It was true; they'd gone about thirty to forty feet ahead, up a path through the trees that climbed leftward.

"She's not my girlfriend," Kyle retorted, feeling his cheeks grow hotter. He silently cursed his traitorous body. "*You* are."

"Uh huh," Ariana mumbled. He stumbled then, and she caught him before he landed flat on his face. "Here, at least lean on me," she urged. Kyle did so gladly, realizing that Kalibar and Petra had stopped to wait for them. It still amazed him that Kalibar had kept himself in such incredible shape, despite his age. The old man was keeping up with Petra – and hardly even breaking a sweat. Neither was Petra, for that matter...but she had quite obviously spent a great deal of effort in developing the appropriate muscles for the task.

"Are you all right Kyle?" Kalibar inquired as they caught up. Kyle nodded, wiping the sweat from his brow. Kalibar turned, looking up the path they were following. It leveled out in the distance, leading to a rock wall some twenty feet high. To the right of the wall was a small stream that cascaded down as a waterfall onto the rocks below.

"Petra, if you could fly us up over that wall?" Kalibar requested. Petra nodded. They both walked up to the rocky wall, and shot up through the air and over it, landing on the ground above. Petra came down, bringing Kyle next, and then Ariana. They faced the small stream then, seeing a row of flat-faced boulders sticking out above the water.

436

"Why don't we just use magic to fly all the way to the top?" Kyle asked, using the sudden break to catch his breath. He did have a little magic stored up, after all.

"We need to conserve magic," Kalibar replied. He turned to Petra then. "...seeing as how I don't have a Reaper suit. Unless of course you want to provide the magic?"

"We walk," Petra replied. When Kalibar raised an eyebrow at her, she put her hands on her hips. "Using my Reaper vines has its consequences," she added, as if that explained it.

"Very well," Kalibar replied. "Let's go."

They crossed the stream one at a time, with Petra leading. They all held hands in an unbroken chain, ensuring that if someone fell into the water, they wouldn't be swept down the waterfall. Luckily the precaution proved unnecessary, as they crossed without incident. The path climbed ever higher beyond.

"Oh man," Kyle complained, staring upward with dismay. He turned to look down the way they'd come, and saw a steep drop to the forest far below. He felt woozy for a moment, and stepped well clear of the edge. He hadn't realized just how far up they'd traveled. The trees around them were noticeably shorter than the ones below, with moss and lichen growing on the rocks in abundance. It was also a bit colder, the wind sending a chill through him.

"You'll have a break ahead," Petra promised, starting up the path, Kalibar following close behind. "We'll be crossing the Spine of Grimore soon."

"What's that?" Kyle asked, trekking up the path. He seriously considered taking Ariana up on her offer to carry him, but his pride would not allow it. No matter how many times his pride had caused him to suffer in the past, for some reason he still catered to it. It was, he realized, a rather abusive relationship.

"A narrow path from here to Grimore's peak," Petra answered.

"We're almost up the mountain?"

"No," Petra replied. "We're still near the base."

"Oh *man*," Kyle complained. He heard Petra laugh...for the first time, he realized.

"The cave is also near the base," she consoled. "We're getting close."

They continued upward silently from there, the path becoming so steep that even Kalibar and Petra were having a hard time of it. Kyle found himself relying more and more on Ariana to help him up, which she did with silent ease. Still, Petra refused to use her magic, relying on sheer muscle to ascend the mountain. It was obvious that this wasn't her first time; the relative ease with which she climbed certainly explained the impressive proportions of her lower half. Kyle had to reign in his admiration in that regard, especially with Ariana watching him like a hawk.

"Almost," Kyle mumbled to himself, pulling himself upward one lunging step at a time. "...there." He glanced down, and immediately regretted it. It was an almost sheer drop below, at least a hundred feet to the nearest ledge. He turned away, clinging to the face of the mountain with all of his might, pressing himself against the cool rock.

"You okay?" Ariana asked.

"If I fall," Kyle grumbled, "...I'm flying the rest of the way up."

"You have magic?" Ariana pressed, clearly surprised. Kyle nodded.

"A little," he confirmed. In fact, he had quite a bit more magic now than before; it seemed that the higher they went, the less powerful the drain on his magic was.

At long last, to Kyle's utter delight and relief, they reached the top.

"Oh thank god," Kyle gasped, crawling onto the gloriously flat surface beyond. He had half a mind to kiss the ground.

"His first time up a mountain?" he heard Petra ask wryly. He looked up, seeing all three of them standing there staring at him. He groaned, rising shakily to his hands and knees, then to his feet, stepping far clear of the edge he'd just scaled.

"It is," Kyle answered defensively. He brushed off bits of rock and dust from the front of his shirt, then looked forward.

His jaw dropped.

438

Before him was a rocky path that extended forward an incredible distance, easily a half-mile. The path was narrow, only wide enough for two or three people to stand side-by-side before it dropped off on either side. And what a drop it was...a near-vertical drop all the way down to the mist-covered forest thousands of feet below. This, Kyle realized, was the Spine of Grimore. At its end, far in the distance, the enormous bulk of Mount Grimore stood, its sharp peak piercing the cloudy sky.

"You're doing very well, Kyle," Kalibar stated, giving him an approving nod. "That was a difficult climb, even for me."

"We should walk single-file," Petra suggested, facing the Spine of Grimore. "And be careful...the wind can get very powerful here."

Everyone did as she suggested, Petra going first, then Kalibar, with Kyle and Ariana taking the rear. They strode forward, the rocky path narrowing as they stepped onto the Spine. Without warning, a blast of air shrieked up from Kyle's right, a vertical wall of dense gray mist shooting upward into the sky. Within seconds, the wind died down, the wall of mist slowly dissipating high above their heads.

"What was *that?*" Kyle exclaimed.

"Wind," came Petra's terse reply. "It carries clouds up the sides of the spine."

"Strange," Kalibar said. "From up here, the entire forest looks like it's covered in mist, but there wasn't any mist when we were walking through the forest to get here." Kyle nodded; he'd noticed the same thing earlier. Petra had promised to tell him about it later.

"No one knows why," Petra admitted.

"They do keep prying eyes from seeing in," Kalibar murmured, his eyes on the forest below. "I wonder..."

"Guys," Ariana interrupted, stopping suddenly. She was staring forward, and Kyle followed her gaze. There, about a hundred feet ahead, another burst of mist was shooting up both sides of the narrow spine. Tendrils of the white fog pulled inward, forming a gray wall there.

"What is it?" Kyle asked.

Then a dark shape appeared in the center of the fog.

"Get behind me," Kalibar warned, stepping in front of Petra.

439

A shadow appeared out of the mist, a tall figure in a long black cloak, its face hidden in a hood. It stepped toward them, stopping a few feet in front of the wall of fog, unmoving. Kyle could see only its hands emerging from the long sleeves of its cloak; its skin was as black as night.

"It's a Chosen," Ariana warned, taking a step back. Kyle's breath caught in his throat, and he froze, goosebumps rising on his arms. *They found us!*

"It's an Immortal?" Petra asked, turning to Ariana, who nodded. "I will talk to it," she stated. She stepped in front of Kalibar, striding toward the Chosen.

"Petra, wait!" Kalibar cried, grabbing her shoulder. But she pulled away from his grasp, continuing forward.

"Welcome," Petra called out to the Chosen. "We have an Immortal girl here," she added. "We've come to take her home."

"Petra!" Kalibar warned.

The Chosen stood there as Petra walked toward it, its cloak rippling in the howling wind rushing up either side of the mountain.

Then it raised one hand toward her.

A burst of white light shot outward at Petra, slamming into her. She flew backward, colliding with the ground, smoke rising from her shoulder.

"Petra!" Kalibar cried, flying forward. He reached Petra's side, a gravity shield appearing around them. The Chosen stepped forward, raising its hand again, a ball of fire shooting outward at Kalibar...just as Kalibar's shields vanished. Kalibar flew upward, Petra in his arms, the fireball missing them by mere inches. Kalibar counterattacked, a bolt of lightning shooting down from the heavens, slamming into the Chosen.

Or rather, its shields. A dozen appeared in layers around the being, the lightning bolt scattering harmlessly over their surface.

Kalibar flew backward and downward, landing in front of Ariana and Kyle, setting Petra down. Then he stepped forward, standing tall against the Chosen.

"Leave," he ordered, his tone one of utter confidence. "Or die."

The Chosen burst forward, its cloak rippling fiercely behind it. Kalibar stayed where he was, more layers of gravity shields appearing around him. A barrage of fireballs appeared before him, shooting outward at the Chosen in rapid succession. At the same time, the Chosen's gravity shields – all of them – vanished at once.

"Wrong choice," Kalibar growled.

The fireballs flew at incredible speed, aiming unerringly at the quickly-approaching Chosen. But at the last minute, the Chosen dodged to the side, moving so quickly that it was a blur. Then it leaped into the air, flying right at Kalibar. Kalibar's shields began to wink out, and the Grand Weaver took a step backward.

"Kalibar!" Kyle warned.

He saw Ariana burst forward then, moving with unnatural speed across the Spine of Grimore. She leaned over as she ran, picking up a large rock in one hand, then leaping *over* Kalibar, hurtling high into the air above the Grand Weaver's head. She tossed the rock at the Chosen while they were both still in mid-air, and it veered out of the way at the last minute, shoved aside by a gravity field. At the same time, the Chosen threw a massive fireball right at Ariana.

No!

Ariana created a gravity sphere to her right, and it pulled her out of the way of the Chosen's fireball at the last minute. She created another gravity field near the fireball – now far behind her – and it reversed direction, flying right back at the Chosen. A single gravity shield appeared around the cloaked figure at the last minute, the fireball smashing into it harmlessly. But the impact pushed the Chosen backward, and it fell to the ground, landing on its feet, its gravity shield shimmering faint blue against the fog wall behind it.

Ariana landed twenty feet from the Chosen, and burst forward, rushing it. She slammed into it, shields appearing automatically around her. Their shields collided, bursts of light shooting outward from both of them as their shards reacted. They flew apart, the Chosen backpedaling rapidly, Ariana sliding toward Kalibar, somehow managing to stay on her feet.

The Chosen stopped, regaining its balance. Its hood fell back, revealing a man's face. His skin was black, darker even than Petra's.

Tattoos crawled up the sides of his head, and like Petra, scars fanned out like the bones in a bat's wing at his temples. And in the center of his forehead, a green, diamond-shaped crystal glittered in the sunlight.

"A Joined!" Kyle heard Petra gasp. She rose to her feet, staring wide-eyed at the Chosen. "One of the Ancestors!" She strode forward, past Kalibar and Ariana.

"Stay back!" Kalibar ordered. But Petra ignored him.

"I am Joined, like you!" Petra declared, walking toward the Chosen. "We are your descendants...the people of the Barren forest," she added. "We come in peace."

The Chosen stood there, its cloak rippling in the wind.

"Please," Petra pleaded. "We mean you no harm." She stopped just past Ariana, still far away from him. "We've waited centuries to meet you," she added. "To learn from you."

Still, the Chosen stood there, saying nothing.

"Petra, get back," Kalibar warned.

Then the Chosen burst forward, a ray of eye-searing light shooting outward from its palm at Petra.

"Petra!" Kalibar cried.

Ariana burst forward with inhuman speed, intercepting the beam right before it struck Petra. A dozen shields appeared around her instantly, the beam reflecting off of her outermost shield's surface. She sprinted at the Chosen, a ball of fire appearing before her.

Then her shields vanished, her fireball blowing right back at her face.

Ariana screamed, her face and chest bursting into flames. A burst of light shot out from the Chosen, slamming into Ariana and hurtling her backward. She fell to the ground, rolling to a stop twenty feet from where Kyle stood, engulfed in fire.

"*Ariana!*" Kyle shouted. He wove rapidly, creating a waterfall above her, snuffing out the flames. Steam rose from her body, hissing angrily. Kyle and Kalibar ran to her side.

"Ariana, are you okay?" Kalibar blurted out. A gravity shield appeared around all three of them. Kyle rolled Ariana onto her back, ash falling from her mask and left shoulder, revealing burnt, blackened skin. Ariana gasped, clutched at her chest, her breath coming in short gasps.

"Ariana!" Kyle gasped. Half of her face was horribly burnt, her hair gone, her scalp charred. She stared at her hands with one good eye, at her charred fingertips, and screamed.

In the distance, the Chosen strode toward them, mist shooting upward on either side of him. His black eyes dropped to Ariana, and he smirked.

Kyle glared at him, rising to his feet. He grit his teeth, his hands clenched into fists at his sides.

You son-of-a-bitch.

Kalibar stepped in front of Kyle and Ariana, facing the approaching Chosen. A barrage of bright white missiles shot outward at the Chosen, who flew forward suddenly, slamming *into* the missiles. They scattered before him harmlessly, and he shot forward at incredible speed, flying right at Kalibar. Kalibar's shields flickered, then vanished, just as the Chosen slammed into him.

"Kalibar!" Petra cried.

Kalibar flew backward, rolling across the narrow path. He came to a stop on his back, his eyes wide open, gasping for air.

The Chosen flew past Kyle and Petra, landing before Kalibar, then walking slowly toward the Grand Weaver.

You goddamn son-of-a-bitch!

"No!" Kyle shouted, rising to his feet. The Chosen ignored him, striding toward Kalibar, who was still gasping for air, helpless on the ground. Petra burst forward, but Kyle stopped her with one outstretched arm.

"Kyle..." she began, but Kyle cut her off.

"Get back," he ordered. "Get everyone as far away from me as you can." Then he turned to the Chosen. "Hey!" he shouted. Still, the Chosen ignored him.

Fine then.

Kyle *pulled* magic into his mind's eye, weaving rapidly. He threw the pattern outward, right at the Chosen, then threw a large amount of magic into his magic stream. A bright blue gravity field appeared to one side of the Chosen. It burst to the side instantly, hurtling off of the side of the narrow spine of rock, falling toward the forest thousands of feet below.

Kyle glared at Petra, who was still standing near him.

"I said get *back*," he ordered, his tone cold. Petra's eyes widened, and she nodded silently, rushing to Kalibar's side and helping the Grand Weaver to his feet. She ran toward Ariana, who was already healing, her skin mending rapidly, her hair already starting to regrow...but to its original, full length. She got Ariana to her feet, sprinting away from Kyle, toward the far end of the Spine of Grimore.

The Chosen rose through the air to the left of the Spine, cutting Petra and the others off. It landed on the narrow path, its jaw rippling.

"Back toward me!" Kyle shouted.

Petra skid to a stop, turning about and running back toward him. The Chosen flew up into the air, landing between them and Kyle. A burst of flames shot out at Petra, Ariana, and Kalibar, and Petra created a gravity shield just in time, the flames parting before its shimmering blue surface.

"Leave them *alone!*" Kyle shouted. He activated his gravity boots, lifting upward into the air. He *tore* magic from his skull, feeling huge cords of it pull inward into his mind's eye. Pain shot through his skull, agony unlike anything he had ever felt. He ignored this, weaving quickly, throwing out pattern after pattern, then *shoving* a massive torrent of magic into them.

A huge ball of *punk* appeared before him, as large as a house. Air rushed inward toward it, nearly tearing Kyle's clothes from his body. The *punk* burst into flames, and Kyle created a gravity field in front of it, tossing the massive fireball outward and downward at incredible speed...right at the Chosen. It slammed into the Chosen's shields, splashing across the ground, flaming gobs of it falling to the forest far below on either side of the Spine. The *punk* stuck to the Chosen's shields, burning so hotly that Kyle could feel the heat on his face even from far above.

Kyle wove again, *yanking* even more magic into his mind's eye, then weaving the gravity field pattern. He threw it at the Chosen, pouring as much magic as he could into it.

A huge gravity sphere appeared around the Chosen, *punk* flying inward toward the cloaked figure, air sucking violently into the sphere. The flames grew brighter and hotter; the Chosen's gravity shields were no match for the sheer power of Kyle's gravity sphere, and *punk* sucked inward *past* its shields, *punk* adhering to its body. Flames engulfed the Chosen instantly, burning hotter and hotter.

Its mouth opened in a silent scream, no sound able to escape Kyle's gravity sphere.

The Chosen wove magic, blue light appearing at its shard. Again and again it wove, but it was no use; neither it or its shard could generate enough magic to neutralize the overwhelming power of Kyle's gravity sphere. Flames licked greedily at its cloak, at its very flesh, consuming it rapidly.

And then crystal on the Chosen's forehead flashed bright green...and the Chosen vanished.

Kyle blinked, cutting off the magic stream to his gravity sphere. A large section of the Spine of Grimore below him continued to burn, consuming the *punk*. Heat rose from the flames, the air rippling above the path. Kyle descended toward the edge of the flames closest to Kalibar, Ariana and Petra, his boots touching the ground. The others walked up behind him, staring at the fire.

Or rather, *through* it.

For there, standing at the other end of the huge swath of burning *punk*, was the Chosen, its forehead glowing like a miniature green sun.

How...

The Chosen faced them, its cloak in tatters. The flesh on its face was almost entirely gone, its charred skull and jawbone exposed. Its left eye had melted away, its right eye staring through the flames at them.

And then the *punk* exploded into dust, the wind on either side of the Spine of Grimore whisking it upward and away.

445

"Get behind me!" Kalibar ordered, pulling Ariana and Kyle back. The Chosen levitated forward toward them, its lone eye unblinking. Ariana ignored Kalibar, sprinting toward the Chosen. Petra followed, flying above the Spine, gravity shields appearing around her. Petra wove magic, rocks and boulders rising from the sides of the path around her, then shooting forward at the Chosen. Fireballs flew from Ariana, shooting right at the charred figure.

...who vanished again.

The rocks and fireballs flew through the spot where the Chosen had been.

"Guys!" Kyle shouted, staring behind him. There, hovering over the path, was the Chosen. He felt his blood go cold, the hair on the nape of his neck rising on end.

It can teleport!

Ariana skid to a halt, turning about and running back toward the Chosen. She leaped into the air, flying above Kyle and Kalibar's heads, careening toward the cloaked figure.

Then her gravity shields vanished, and she burst into flames, shooting backward through the air and landing on the narrow path behind Kyle.

"Ariana!" Kyle cried. Ariana rolled on the ground, snuffing out the flames, then got to her feet. Petra shot through the air toward the Chosen, bolts of lightning shooting outward toward the Chosen...but struck its shields harmlessly. She stopped abruptly in mid-air, a gravity sphere appearing around her.

Then it began to shrink.

"Petra!" Kalibar cried. "Kyle, give me magic!" Kyle complied, streaming magic to the Grand Weaver. But the Chosen burst forward, slamming into Kalibar, shoving him across the narrow path...and into Ariana, who caught him. The sphere around Petra continued to shrink, shoving her head downward and forcing her into the fetal position in mid-air.

No!

Kyle clenched his fists, *pulling* magic into his mind's eye and weaving rapidly. A powerful gravity field appeared around the Chosen, sucking inward. But the Chosen vanished again, appearing outside of the sphere...and the sphere around Petra continued to shrink.

The Chosen stared up at Petra, its shard glowing brightly, what remained of its lips curling into a smirk.

"You cannot defeat Me," its voice boomed, guttural and raspy. "Without Ampir, you are nothing."

"Run!" Kalibar shouted, rushing up to Kyle's side. "I'll save Petra. Go!" But Kyle shook his head.

"I'm not running," he stated.

"Kyle..." Kalibar began, putting a hand on Kyle's shoulder. Kyle pulled away.

"I said *no*," he declared. He turned back toward the Chosen. "I'm done running."

The Chosen lowered its gaze from Petra, staring at Kyle with its single eye, its smirk never faltering.

"How brave," it declared. "Perhaps the Dead Man was right about you after all." It cocked its head to one side. "You'll make an excellent Chosen."

"I'll die first," Kyle retorted. The Chosen chuckled.

"Naturally."

Kyle felt Kalibar grab his shoulder again, felt himself being pulled backward. He resisted, staring at the Chosen. He felt a strange calmness come over him. His eyes went to the Chosen's glowing shard, noting the faint blue light there, evidence of the Chosen's magic. But no ray of light went *to* the shard. Sabin was controlling the Chosen from a distance, that much was clear...but whatever signals Sabin was sending to it couldn't be magical in nature. That meant the signals had to be something else.

Electromagnetic.

It was the only possibility...a signal that could travel miles, and was invisible. Perhaps radio waves, or something similar. A special frequency that could send information to and from the Chosen.

"I think I'll kill her first," the Chosen declared, returning its gaze up to Petra. The sphere around her started to shrink again...but Kyle ignored him.

Radio waves were electromagnetic...just like light.

Like *light*.

Kyle smirked at the Chosen, pulling magic into his mind's eye, weaving quickly. A tight knot pulsed there, and he threw it outward at the Chosen, attaching a weak magic stream.

The light around the Chosen warped.

"Kyle!" he heard Kalibar shout.

Kyle focused, streaming more magic to the invisibility pattern, watching as the light around the Chosen warped more and more powerfully. Then the Chosen vanished.

"What are you..."

Kyle poured even more magic into the stream, and the Chosen reappeared suddenly, the diamond-shaped crystal on its forehead glowing bright green.

Then it winked out.

The Chosen's eye widened, its jaw dropping. The sphere around Petra vanished, and she fell toward the ground. Ariana caught her easily, lowering her to the ground.

"Time to die, asshole," Kyle growled.

He wove again, *pulling* huge cords of magic into his mind's eye and thrusting the pattern outward. A powerful gravity sphere appeared around the Chosen, sucking air violently into it. Kyle wove again, creating a gravity shield around Kalibar, Petra, and Ariana, protecting them from the powerful vacuum. The Chosen collapsed into the fetal position, hovering in the center of the sphere. Kyle continued the magic stream to his invisibility pattern, blocking Sabin from resuming control.

The Chosen resisted, raising its arms to the sides, the tattered arms of its cloak sliding up its forearms. Bone-white crystals were embedded in the black flesh of its forearms.

Kyle's breath caught in his throat.

Rays of blue light shot outward from him, converging on the white crystals.

"Kyle!" Kalibar shouted.

Kyle stared at those blue rays, feeling his mind draining of magic. Ariana dropped like a rag-doll beside him.

"Petra, give me magic!" Kalibar shouted. Petra complied, and suddenly dozens of rocks lifted up into the air around them. They were immediately sucked inward by Kyle's gravity sphere, converging on the Chosen. The blue rays entering its Void crystals dimmed instantly, the magical vacuum insulated by the depleted stone.

"Revive Ariana," Kyle ordered. Petra nodded, kneeling down and streaming magic into Ariana's forehead. Kyle pulled more magic into his mind's eye, streaming it to Kalibar. "Finish that thing!"

And then Kyle saw the gravity shield around him vanish.

The Chosen burst forward through the gravity sphere, slamming headlong into Kyle. Pain exploded across Kyle's chest and he felt himself flying backward through the air. He slammed back-first into the hard rock below, the air blasting from his lungs. He lost control of his magic streams, his vision blackening for a moment, stars floating in the periphery of his vision.

Then an ungodly green glow pierced the darkness.

Kyle's vision returned, and he saw the Chosen standing over him, its shard shining brightly. It smirked.

"Impressive," its raspy voice boomed.

And then it gripped Kyle's face in one hand, slamming the back of his head into the ground.

* * *

"Kyle!" Kalibar shouted, watching in horror as the Chosen gripped his son's face, slamming his head into the ground. Kyle's arms jerked, then went still, his eyes rolling back into his skull. Kalibar rushed forward, but felt powerful hands grip him, shoving him backward.

"Run," Ariana ordered, pushing Kalibar back down the Spine of Grimore, the way they'd come. "I'll give you some time."

"No," Kalibar retorted. "He'll kill you!" But Ariana shook her head.

449

"I'm already dead," she stated firmly. She shoved him down the path, then turned around, running along the narrow Spine, straight for the Chosen.

"No!" Kalibar shouted, sprinting after her. He saw a wall of faint blue light appear before him, and he slammed into it, stumbling backward. "Ariana!"

"Let her go," he heard Petra say, feeling her hand on his shoulder. He pulled away, shaking his head.

"I can't," he retorted. "I won't!"

"She's gone," Petra stated, her voice cold. "And it'll be for nothing if you don't come with me *right now*."

Kalibar hesitated, turning back to see Ariana sprinting right at the Chosen. She roared, blue light flashing, a dozen gravity shields bursting into being around her. She charged right at the Chosen with incredible speed...

And then her gravity shields vanished.

The Chosen moved so quickly that it was a blur, its right arm shooting out and catching Ariana by the throat, stopping her cold. Her legs swung out in front of her, carried by her incredible momentum, until she was almost lying horizontal in the air. Then the Chosen swung its arm downward, pushing her straight into the rock below by the neck. She hit the ground with a sickening crunch.

"Ariana!" Kalibar screamed.

"Come *on!*" Petra shouted, gripping him by the shoulders and spinning him around forcibly. She pulled him back across the Spine, and he stumbled along after her, his eyes blurry with tears. His legs felt like rubber, threatening to give out from under him. Petra grunted, wrapping an arm around his waist and pulling him bodily forward. Kalibar looked back over his shoulder, seeing the Chosen standing there, some fifty feet away, staring down at Ariana's body. Her legs twitched, and then her arms came up, wrapping around the Chosen's dark forearm even as its hand clutched at her neck.

She gripped his dark arm, the muscles of her forearm rippling as she squeezed.

The Chosen smirked, blue light pulling from Ariana's forehead into the Void crystals on its forearm. Her eyes widened, and she

450

struggled against the Chosen's iron grip, flailing her legs helplessly. Her struggles became weaker, her legs barely moving, her eyes rolling up into the back of her skull.

And then she went limp.

"No!" Kalibar shouted, even as he was pulled away. He saw the Chosen pick Ariana up, again by the throat. Its forearm tensed, its fingers squeezing Ariana's windpipe. Kalibar heard a sickening *crunch*.

And then the Chosen held her over the edge of the Spine, and let her go.

Ariana fell, striking the steeply-angled surface of the path's edge, then plummeted into the sheer vertical drop beyond. A gust of mist shot upward around her falling body, engulfing her as it roared upward above the Spine, shooting high into the air.

"Oh god," Kalibar gasped, his legs failing. He stumbled to the ground, landing on his hands and knees.

"Get up!" Petra shouted, hooking her arm under his armpits and yanking upward.

And then a gust of wind shot upward from her left, making her lurch to the right. She lost her footing, stumbling to the side, her foot slipping on the steep decline. She cried out, sliding downward toward the sheer drop mere inches away. Kalibar lunged for her, landing on his stomach on the hard rock, the air blasting from his lungs. He reached out desperately with one hand, grabbing Petra's ankle right before she slipped off the edge. He felt himself get yanked toward her, and dug his feet into the ground, reaching out with his other hand and gripping her leg with both hands.

"Let go," Petra shouted, twisting around to glare at him.

"I won't," Kalibar retorted. Then he grimaced. "The Chosen drained my magic," he added. "I've got nothing left."

"Well I do," Petra countered.

Kalibar nodded grudgingly, letting go of her. She fell down the mountainside, vanishing into the mist below.

The Chosen ignored them, kneeling before Kyle's motionless body. Kalibar hesitated, then got to his feet, striding up to the Chosen and stopping before it.

"Hello, Sabin," he stated coldly. The Chosen glanced up at him with its lone eye.

"Kalibar," it replied.

"Come to murder an old man and his son?" Kalibar asked, his tone casual. But his heart was hammering in his chest, and he knew very well that this Chosen could hear every beat.

"Just an old man," the Chosen replied.

"So you can rule the Empire," Kalibar stated. "The very Empire you destroyed." The Chosen smirked.

"History is a tapestry of guesses and lies," it retorted. "Your entire world is a myth."

"What?"

"You talk about your Empire as if Man created it," the Chosen stated.

"We *did* create it," Kalibar countered. The Chosen chuckled in that deep, raspy voice.

"How ironic," he mused. "You defend – to the death – a government that owes its entire existence to Me."

Kalibar stared at the Chosen, his mind going blank. He took a step back.

"What?"

"Two hundred and thirty-eight years ago," the Chosen declared. "My Chosen united the savages of your lands, by My will. And by *My* will, the Ancient Empire was recreated, brick by brick, stone by stone. Every building, every street, so that if a man were brought from the Ancient Empire to the new one, he would not notice the difference."

"You're lying," Kalibar retorted.

"Your entire system of government," the Chosen continued. "Shaped by My hand. And in every generation, my Chosen have walked among you, hidden in plain sight, guiding the Empire under My command."

"That's a lie!" Kalibar declared, clenching his fists. But he felt doubt creeping in, and the Chosen chuckled again.

"I admire you Kalibar," it said. "Your dedication to your ideals is absolute. You are exactly the citizen I dreamed of creating, a man cast in the same mold as my mortal self."

"You're lying," Kalibar muttered, but even he didn't believe it now. That part of his mind, ever logical and calculating, ticked away at Sabin's claims, and they were all not only plausible, but likely.

"Mankind will never believe in a god they can see," the Chosen stated, rising to its feet and reaching out to place a hand on Kalibar's chest. Kalibar tried to take a step back, but his body would not obey him, his muscles suddenly locked in a rigid state. "You are proof of that. You yourself believe in the Empire that I created, yet now that you see Me, you resist my vision."

"I believe in mankind," Kalibar retorted. "You don't."

The Chosen smiled, gripped the front of Kalibar's shirt with one hand, then lifting him off of the ground. He turned, letting Kalibar's feet dangle over the edge of the Spine.

"I believe in Me."

Kalibar saw motion in the periphery of his vision, and glanced past the Chosen, seeing Kyle's eyes flutter open. The boy rolled onto his side, his eyes locking on Kalibar's.

I'm sorry, son.

Kyle grimaced, then reached into his pants pocket, retrieving a small black cylinder.

"Run," he croaked.

"Kyle!" Kalibar shouted, his heart leaping into his throat. If Kyle activated the bomb, the boy was as good as dead. "No, don't!"

The Chosen turned to face Kyle, who slipped the cylinder back into his pocket.

"It will be more merciful if the boy doesn't witness your death," it decided, swinging Kalibar back over the narrow Spine, then setting him down.

"What?" Kalibar blurted out. The Chosen strode away from him, toward Kyle, who was trying to rise to his feet. "No!"

But the Chosen ignored him, walking right up to Kyle and grabbing him by the jaw with one hand. Kyle gripped the Chosen's arm with both hands, his eyes widening in terror, muffled screams coming from behind the Chosen's dark hand. The Chosen swept one leg out behind Kyle's, tripping him and pushing him straight onto his back on the narrow ledge below.

"No!" Kalibar screamed. He tried to move, to run after them, but his muscles were still locked in position. He could only watch as the Chosen pressed Kyle into the ground, his hand still around the boy's mouth and jaw. Then he saw the Chosen reach into its charred cloak, pulling out a long, tapered green crystal.

No!

The Chosen leaned over Kyle, bringing the pointed end of the green crystal to Kyle's forehead, and pressing it into his skin. Kyle thrashed underneath the cloaked man, gripping his dark forearm. Kalibar heard Kyle screaming, heard the primal terror in his voice.

"*No!*" Kalibar screamed, willing his body to move. He strained his muscles, sweat pouring down every inch of his skin, his heart nearly bounding out of his chest. But still, he couldn't move.

The Chosen pressed down, Kyle's skin indenting under the pressure, and the green crystal pierced the boy's flesh, sliding downward a quarter-inch before stopping. Kyle cried out, kicking the Chosen and slamming his fists into the man's face, but the Chosen didn't so much as blink.

"Kyle!" Kalibar shouted. "Kyle, do it now!" But Kyle kept flailing, screaming as the Chosen continued to press down on the crystal. There was a sudden, sickening crunch, and Kyle let out a horrible, piercing shriek that went straight to Kalibar's soul. Kalibar wailed, his eyes filling with tears, feeling more helpless than he'd ever felt in his life. His breath came in great gulps, and he steadied himself, slowing his breathing, then taking a deep breath in.

"Kyle, do it NOW!" he screamed.

He saw Kyle stop, saw the green crystal sink deeper into the boy's skull. Kyle's eyelids fluttered, his right hand dropping from the Chosen's forearm, landing on his front pants pocket. Kyle's hand twitched, and he fumbled for the pocket's opening, reaching in and pulling out a short black cylinder. Kyle moaned as the crystal slipped ever deeper, his legs twitching grotesquely. He clung to the cylinder, his chest rising and falling rapidly, vomit pouring up and out of his mouth.

Oh god, Kalibar thought, closing his eyes. Tears squeezed out from between his eyelids, streaming down his cheeks. He opened his eyes, forcing himself to look, though ever fiber in his being screamed at him not to.

Kyle's eyes rolled into the back of his head, his thumb hovering over one end of the black cylinder.

And then he pressed it.

Kalibar saw the end of the cylinder extend, saw a faint red light appear there, smooth silver metal shimmering underneath. Then Kyle's entire body convulsed, and the cylinder fell from his hand, rolling down the side of the path and falling into the abyss.

My boy, Kalibar thought. *My sweet, sweet boy...*

And then there was a brilliant flash of light, like a thousand suns exploding at once. Kalibar cried out, squeezing his eyes shut, and suddenly his limbs came back to life. He nearly collapsed, catching himself at the last minute and rising back to his feet, shielding his eyes with one hand. He peeked out between his fingers, seeing the Chosen shielding its eyes from the assault. The light vanished suddenly, and a dark shape hurtled through the sky right at the Chosen.

It was Petra!

She shot toward the ungodly creature, a half-dozen gravity shields appearing around her. The Chosen stood up, turning away from Kyle and smirking at her. She shouted, ramming straight into the thing. But her shields vanished at the last minute, and the Chosen grabbed her out of the air by the neck, holding her a foot above the path. She struggled, kicking her legs wildly, bursts of light slamming into the Chosen's shields. But the Chosen continued to squeeze her neck, and her flailing slowed, then stopped, her eyes rolling into the back of her head.

Then he threw her backward, tossing her through the air...right at Kalibar.

Kalibar's eyes widened, and he backpedaled frantically on the narrow ridge, but he was too slow. Petra hurtled right at him,

slamming into him and knocking him off of his feet. He fell
backward and to the side, landing on his back on the steeply-angled
edge of the path, Petra laying limply on top of him. He grabbed
onto her with one arm wrapped around her waist, feeling himself
sliding headfirst down the slope. He dug his heels into the rock,
reaching out with his other hand and grabbing at the loose stone,
but he continued to slide, falling faster and faster. He felt the rocks
scraping his back disappear, felt the sickening lurch of free-fall grip
his stomach. He plummeted through the mist, the sheer vertical rock
wall of the Spine of Grimore speeding past him.

So this is how it ends, he thought.

He looked down at Petra then, at her lovely face, those slim
eyebrows arching over her closed eyes. Her full lips.

What could have been, he mused.

Then he spotted the faint U-shaped bulge at her neckline,
underneath her uniform.

The necklace!

He reached for her neck with one hand, slipping his fingers
under the tight cloth of her uniform, sliding his whole hand down,
until he felt the warm metal of her necklace between his fingers. He
pulled on it, feeling the chain snap. He withdrew his hand, seeing
the necklace there, dozens of tiny diamonds on a golden
chain...glowing the faintest of blues.

Yes!

Kalibar felt his heels strike the rock wall before him, and tumbled
through the air violently, nearly losing his grip on Petra. He clung to
her, pressing the necklace against his forehead.

He *pulled.*

Magic seeped into his mind's eye, and he twisted it into a tight
knot, flinging the pattern outward and attaching a magic stream to
it. He felt the wind ripping through his cloak stop, felt his descent
starting to slow. He concentrated, pulling more magic from the
necklace, straining with the effort. The diamonds were so small that
they held precious little magic; he was still falling far too quickly. He
arched his neck back, seeing the mist-shrouded forest coming up on
them...and fast.

Come on!

He closed his eyes, pushing himself even harder, yanking as much magic as he could out of the necklace and streaming it outward. Again his descent slowed...but they were still falling at a deadly pace. The forest rose up meet them, the treetops only a few dozen yards below now. His heart sank as realization dawned on him.

They weren't going to make it.

Kalibar pulled the last threads of magic out of Petra's necklace, letting go of the other pattern and weaving a new one. He thrust it outward at Petra, right as the first tree branch slammed into his back. A horrible pain ripped through his back and into his belly, and then he felt himself strike another branch, the world spinning crazily around him. A kaleidoscope of brown, green, and blue spun around him, branch after branch beating at his arms and chest.

And then he slammed into the ground.

* * *

Petra groaned, then opened her eyes...and immediately regretted it. Painfully bright light assaulted her, and she squeezed her eyes shut, turning her head to the side and covering her face with her one hand. The motion made her horribly nauseous, and she resisted the urge to puke. She kept perfectly still then, too afraid to try moving again. She tried to remember where she was, but she couldn't. Even the effort to do so was overwhelming.

She was laying on the ground, that much she did know.

Petra grit her teeth, then tried to move her head again, more slowly this time. She rolled onto her belly, her head spinning with the effort. She fought back another wave of nausea, clenching her teeth and staying perfectly still, waiting for the feeling to pass. And it did...slowly. Equally slowly, she pulled her arms and legs under her, then pushed herself up onto her hands and knees.

And promptly vomited.

Her head pounded, the pain so incredible that she cried out, dropping to the ground and rolling onto her right side, feeling a sharp, stabbing pain in her right flank. She nearly threw up again, clutching her spinning head in both hands, tears welling up in her eyes. She moaned, hoping, *praying* for the pain to stop.

Then she heard a voice.

Petra froze, ignoring her pounding skull, opening her eyes. The light was painfully bright, lancing through her eyeballs into her skull. She grit her teeth, blinking against the light, her eyes slowly adjusting. She saw trees in front of her, and the forest floor below, broken tree branches scattered across it.

She heard the voice again.

It was nearby, that much she could tell. Coming from her left. It seemed urgent. Petra closed her eyes, turning slowly until she was on her back, then rolling onto her left side. She ignored the pain and nausea, opening her eyes, and saw someone lying there next to her. A man, his back propped up against a thick tree trunk. He was saying something.

"Vens ibis al," he gasped.

Petra stared at him, at his lips. He was looking right at her. He looked familiar somehow.

"Vens ibis *al*," he repeated. Petra stared at him, at his eyes, his nose...his lips...and then she remembered.

"Kalibar!" she cried.

"Petra," he gasped. She realized that his breaths were coming in short gasps, his face terribly pale. She frowned, pushing herself up – very carefully – into a sitting position.

"Kalibar, what's wrong?"

He grimaced, then raised one hand – it was covered in blood, she realized – and pointed below his chest. She followed his finger, staring at his abdomen.

Her eyes widened.

"Kalibar!" she gasped, recoiling in horror. Something very large was sticking out of the center of his abdomen. It was the sharp end of a broken tree branch, as thick around as her calf, and covered in bright red blood. Her hand went to her mouth, and she shook her head. "Oh Kalibar," she repeated, staring at the branch. Blood oozed around it, spilling down his brown cloak and forming an ever-widening puddle around him.

"Petra," he murmured, closing his eyes, then opening them again. "Vens ibis *al.*" She stared at him mutely, then shook her head.

"I can't understand you!"

He grunted, then lifted his hand up to his ear, touching the yellow earring there. Then his hand slumped back down to his side. Petra stared at the earring for a moment, then cursed. Of course...she'd forgotten about his earring! She reached into the stream of magic within her, finding a faint trickle of magic there. She diverted it to Kalibar's earring.

"Try it now," she urged, pointing at his ear.

"Magic," he gasped. "Vens ibis, ne thul tist," he added, pointing to the large branch protruding from his abdomen. Petra frowned, then grabbed onto the end of the stick.

"Like this?"

"Es, es, es!" he gasped, shaking his head side to side. Petra let go of the stick, and Kalibar moaned, his head slumping back against the ground. His eyes fluttered, then closed. "Vens ibis al," he mumbled. Petra crawled over his limp body, ignoring the pain in her head, until she was right over him. She reached into her magic stream, finding little magic left. She felt the *others* at the edge of her mind, the Reaper vines with their promise of boundless power. She paused, then *pulled* at them. She felt an all-too-familiar pain in her skull, and throughout the rest of her body, her bones starting to ache. She ignored the pain, knowing it was the price she paid for her request.

A moment later, magic flowed into her, filling her mind with power. She concentrated, taking a large stream of it and sending it outward at Kalibar's earring.

"Magic," he gasped, his voice barely audible now. His skin was becoming deathly pale, almost as pale as Ariana's. Petra shook her head, feeling panic rising in her breast.

"Magic what?" she asked, holding his head in her hands. His skin was cold, like a corpse's.

"Magic," he mumbled.

"Magic *what?*" she almost screamed. He opened his eyes, then closed them again. Petra felt terror grip her, and she slapped his cheek with one hand, her heart thumping in her chest. "Come on, tell me!"

"Give me," he gasped.

And then he stopped.

Petra hesitated, then slapped his face again, harder this time. His head rolled to the side, his eyes open but unseeing.

"No," she said, rolling his head back toward her. "No, no!" She stared at him in horror, tears welling up in her eyes. She took his head in her hands, then slipped the fingers of her right hand down to his neck, at the great vessel there.

Nothing.

"Kalibar!" she shouted, shaking him now, grabbing him by the shoulders and shaking him. "Kalibar!" She shook him again, then leaned over him until her forehead was touching his.

Give him magic!

She closed her eyes, feeling the river of magic within her, sending it gushing outward at Kalibar's forehead. She felt the magic leave her, felt it flow like water breaching a dam. She let it go, let it pour from her into him, until there was nothing left. Then she pushed herself up, staring at him, her fingers still on the side of his neck.

No pulse.

"Come on!" she urged. She lowered herself to him again, closing her eyes and reaching out to the *others* within her. She *pulled* magic from them, feeling that awful aching in her bones. The pain was worse this time, becoming sharp, as if knives were being thrust into her head and limbs. She knew what that meant; the vines were consuming her, digging their roots ever deeper into her bones.

She ignored the pain, continuing to *pull*, and felt magic flood her mind. She poured it into Kalibar as quickly as she could, filling him with it. She started to sense his mind resisting the flow, and knew that his mind was nearly full. Still she poured, until she could do so no more.

Petra opened her eyes, pushing herself up from Kalibar's cool, pale skin. She placed her fingertips on his neck, feeling for the throb of blood within. She waited, her lower lip starting to tremble, her vision blurring with moisture.

Nothing.

It was then that she started to cry, great sobs wracking her body. Tears streamed down her cheeks, and she laid across Kalibar, cradling his head to her bosom.

"Kalibar, please..." she pleaded, knowing that it was too late.

He was already dead.

Chapter 30

The wrought-iron bars of Sabin's prison cell extend from the stone floor all the way up to the irregular ceiling above, each spaced five inches apart from the one beside it. Sabin rests his back against the cool rock wall opposite those bars, at the far end of his cell, his legs splayed on in front of him on the dusty stone floor. There is no bed in the cell, only a small hole in the ground for a toilet. He'd been locked in this cell since Witt's execution yesterday. Night had come, and the Behemoths had launched, making their way toward the Empire. He'd felt the vibrations in the floor of his cell when they'd gone. That had been at least twelve hours ago.

Which meant they'd already reached the Empire, and very likely had destroyed it.

Sabin takes a deep breath in, then lets it out slowly, staring beyond the gaps between the bars, at the two guards sitting in chairs nearby pretending to watch him. It's obvious that they have no fear of him escaping...and for good reason. There's no way to escape.

Sabin closes his eyes, seeing Witt's body lying on the floor in a pool of his own blood, then opens them again. He stares at those guards, imagining himself weaving magic to burst through those prison bars. Imagines himself slaughtering those cocky, arrogant guards. He closes his eyes again, picturing himself wrapping his hands around Gunthar's throat, and squeezing.

He opens his eyes, realizing that his hands are curled into claws before him. He hears the guards laughing, and drops his hands to his lap.

Pricks.

He lowers his gaze to his feet, ignoring the guards' laughter. He feels his rage seeping out of him, knowing that he'll never have his revenge. The world doesn't work that way, he knows all too well. There is no higher power to ensure that justice will prevail.

The strong win at the expense of the weak, he muses. *The weak suffer at the whim of the strong.*

He closes his eyes, picturing Nespo's face as he'd last seen the man. So calm, so serene as he'd ascended toward the hole in the ceiling of Sabin's prison cell.

Men who crave power over people get it, Sabin thinks. *And they're the last people who should have it.*

He chuckles then, quietly, his lips twisting into a smirk. How ironic that he should find himself in the exact same position as he was over two years ago, in some prison cell at the whim of a despot. He'd traveled across the ocean, to another damn continent, working tirelessly for the exact cause he'd been imprisoned for, only to be imprisoned by the very people he'd liberated.

If only Ampir had let me die.

Sabin closes his eyes again, feeling despair come over him. To think that Ampir had seen it so many years ago. How naïve Sabin was. How weak and pathetic. Even back on the floating island, when Sabin had first met the man, he'd exposed Sabin's powerlessness in advocating for his line of research. Not to mention his indecisiveness with Vera.

Vera.

He feels shame then, a horrible, crushing shame. He imagines her dying, that lovely fire in her eyes winking out, leaving a cold, lifeless corpse behind. The thought is so excruciatingly painful that he has the sudden urge to kill himself. To smash his head against the rock wall behind him, to tear out his own throat. But he knows from experience that he is too much of a coward to follow through with it.

Instead, he sits there, doing nothing.

Minutes pass, and Sabin finds himself staring up at the ceiling, at a small white crystal embedded into the rock there. Gunthar had commented on it when he'd first had Sabin thrown into the cell. A mysterious crystal, a Runic device crafted by the Orjanian tribes of the north forest, at the base of Mount Grimore. Within minutes, it had completely drained Sabin of his magic, rendering him utterly helpless. The Empire would never have believed that such a device could exist, that a single crystal the size of a small fruit could have done such an incredible thing.

And yet it had...and continued to do so. It's no wonder that the guards don't fear him escaping.

Sabin stares at that crystal, knowing that the tribes who had created it were the only Orjanians who had managed to successfully stave off the Empire's initial assault on Orja. The Empire had lost so badly to the "primitive" tribes that they'd never ventured near Mount Grimore again.

Sabin is taken by the sudden urge to meet these people, to learn from them. He shakes his head bitterly, knowing that that is what Ampir had told him to do after he'd freed Sabin from prison.

Do what you're best at.

Creating massive war machines for a tyrant hadn't been what Ampir had meant, of course. Sabin's strength had always been his research.

Not that it matters now.

Sabin sighs, feeling suddenly and overwhelmingly exhausted, he slumps down onto his side on the floor, curling up into a fetal position. He hears the guards making snide remarks, but doesn't care. His pride is pointless now. There's no way to escape, and he knows all too well that Gunthar will never let him go. Sabin is too valuable. Too dangerous. Despite Gunthar's promise not to kill him, Sabin knows that is just another lie. Men like Gunthar and Nespo – men with power – can never be trusted. There is no other way for this to end but for Gunthar to execute him.

Sabin feels a subtle vibration in the stone floor, sees a fine layer of dust fall from the ceiling, swirling in the torchlight coming from beyond his cell. Then he feels a second vibration – much stronger this time – followed by a shower of dust from the ceiling.

Boom.

The muffled sound echoes through the hallway outside of his cell, and this time his guards *do* notice, standing up from their chairs and walking out of Sabin's field of view.

Boom.

The floor shakes again, more dust and tiny pebbles falling from the ceiling above Sabin's head. He feels the dust strike his head and shoulders, and pushes himself up from the floor, sneezing violently. He hears his guards' footsteps echoing down the hall, getting fainter and fainter.

Boom.

And then nothing.

Sabin stands there, staring out between the bars of his cell, at the empty chairs his guards had been stationed at. He walks up to the bars, pressing his forehead against the cool, rusted iron. Waiting.

He hears shouting far in the distance. A moment later, muffled screams echo off of the stone walls.

He backs away from the prison bars, feeling a chill run down his spine. There is more shouting, following by a loud cracking sound. More screams echo through the tunnels, followed by silence.

Minutes pass.

Sabin hears footsteps then, faintly. Hears a voice in the distance.

"This way, here..."

There is a shout, and another scream, very close now. Sabin sees something fly through the air just outside of his cell, crashing through the two chairs sitting there, then slamming into the wall with a sickening *thud.* It drops to the ground limply, and Sabin stares at it, realizing it's one of his guards.

Dead.

He hears another shout, and then footsteps approaching, much louder now. He takes a step back, then another, feeling his back strike the stone wall behind him. A man walks into view, just beyond his cell. A very familiar man. A very frightened looking man.

Gunthar.

The tyrant stares at Sabin, then points straight at him.

"There," he states. A few seconds passed, and then another man comes into view. A man in black, metallic armor, with a reflective visor hiding his eyes. Sabin's eyes widen.

"Ampir!" he exclaims, stepping forward from the wall. It *is* the legendary Battle-Runic! Ampir turns to look at him, his expression utterly flat. He says nothing.

"He's the one you want," Gunthar declares, continuing to point at Sabin. "He made the Behemoths, he had them sent to Stridon against my orders!"

"*What?*" Sabin blurts out incredulously. His eyes shift from Gunthar back to Ampir, righteous indignation rising in his breast. "That's a lie! I wanted to send them to Verhan! *You're* the one who tricked me!"

"I just wanted Verhan back for my people," Gunthar retorts furiously, turning to Ampir. "He insisted on having his petty revenge against Nespo!"

Sabin is about to reply when Ampir raises his hand. Both men's mouths snap shut. The wrought iron bars of Sabin's cell bend outward from the middle, the stone they are embedded in cracking loudly, hunks of rock falling to the ground. Ampir steps forward through the now-wide gap between them, entering Sabin's cell. Sabin sees Gunthar glance upward at the white crystal in the ceiling, then quickly look down.

"Ampir, he's lying to you," Sabin insists, but Ampir merely stares back at him, his expression, as always, unreadable. "The Tower, is it...?" he begins, and finds he can't finish the sentence.

"Destroyed," Ampir replies. Sabin stares at him in disbelief, taking a step back, his jaw going slack.

Destroyed!

He feels his legs go weak, feels them start to wobble underneath him. He slides down onto his buttocks on the floor, shaking his head mutely, unable to even look at Ampir.

"Don't pretend you didn't want it!" Gunthar accuses, but Ampir raises his hand again, and Gunthar's jaw snaps shut. Sabin raises his head, staring into his own reflection in Ampir's visor. He feels utter

466

exhaustion come over him, so powerful that his head drops again, his chin resting on his chest.

"I just wanted to help these people," Sabin mumbles. "I never wanted to hurt the Empire."

"Bullshit," Gunthar retorts. "You even had your friends in Stridon give you the blueprints for Ampir's armor so you could kill him!" He turns to Ampir again. "He specifically told my Weavers – without my knowledge – to kill your wife!"

Ampir stands there, perfectly still for nearly a minute, then turns away from Sabin, staring at Gunthar. His gauntleted hands curl into fists.

"What?" he asks. Gunthar stands taller, pointing at Sabin.

"That traitor," he declares, "...told my men to target your wife and son, to distract you so you'd be easier to kill." Ampir stares at the man mutely, then turns back to Sabin. Sabin feels his guts twist with fear, and he stares back at Ampir, his lips trembling. He starts to speak, then stops. He clears his throat, then tries again.

"Vera," he states, feeling dread creep over him. "...is she...?"

"Dead," Ampir mutters.

Something inside Sabin breaks.

"Oh, no," he pleads, tears welling up in his eyes. "Oh no, no...please, no..."

"You lying piece of..." Gunthar begins, crossing through the bars of the cell and striding toward Sabin. Ampir's left fist shoots out, slamming into Gunthar's temple with a loud crack. The man flies headlong into the side wall of the cell, his skull ricocheting violently off of the hard stone, then falling in a heap onto the floor.

Dead.

Sabin stares at Gunthar's unmoving body, at the man's eyes staring lifelessly outward. Then he raises his gaze to Ampir's visor. He feels a calmness come over him.

"Kill me," he states. There is no pleading, no fear in his voice. He pictures Vera as he'd last seen her, so vibrant and full of life. Her sweet laugh, the way the sun shone on the long curls of her auburn hair.

467

Ampir turns back to him, saying nothing. Blood drips from his left fist onto the floor.

"Kill me," Sabin repeats calmly, even confidently. "I want to die now."

Still, Ampir says nothing.

"Please," Sabin pleads. "I'm ready." Ampir just stares at him, and Sabin rises to his feet suddenly, balling his hands into fists and staring back defiantly. "It's true," he declares. "Everything Gunthar said. *I* ordered the Behemoths to go to Stridon. *I* ordered them to kill Vera!" He flinches then, expecting Ampir's fist to shoot out and crush his skull, as it had for Gunthar. But Ampir just stares down at him, saying nothing.

Then he turns his back to Sabin, walking out of the cell.

"Ampir?" Sabin cries, walking after him. "Ampir!" The man ignores him, stepping through the bars of the cell. "Ampir, wait!"

And then Ampir vanishes into thin air.

* * *

The pain was everything.

Kyle no longer felt the ground beneath him, no longer saw the dark Chosen leaning over him, pressing that green shard into his forehead. He didn't hear Kalibar screaming anymore, couldn't even feel his own arms and legs. They were gone. Everything was gone.

Except for the pain.

It shot through his forehead, radiating through to the back of his skull, a pulsing agony that refused to end. If he could have wished for death, if his brain had been capable of forming such a thought, he would have.

Something appeared then, not in his vision but in his mind's eye. It was bright, humming with twisting, churning power, a maelstrom of magic in the center of his mind. He felt the threads of magic within it, sensed them starting to weave. Magic tied itself into impossibly complex patterns within him, weaving with dizzying speed.

And then the light went out.

Kyle felt the pain in his skull surge, felt something pulling at his forehead. He saw a burst of light – with his eyes now – a rich blue sky with feathery clouds suspended high above. He saw the glittering green facets of the shard hovering above his own forehead, its tapered peak streaked with red. He stared at it, feeling his arms and legs return to him. Beyond the green shard, he saw the Chosen above him, rising to its feet, its remaining eye opening wide. It took a step back, its black cloak rippling in the wind.

The horrible pain in Kyle's head start to fade, quickly replaced by an intense burning in his chest, and an overwhelming hunger for air. He gasped, inhaling deeply, then felt thick chunks suck into his windpipe. He choked, turning to the side and hacking violently. Gobs of vomit flew out of his mouth, splattering on the rocky ledge beside him. He drew in another breath, coughing again.

And then there was ecstasy.

An incredible force slammed into his consciousness, an immense power that pulsed in his mind's eye, coursing through his bones. Blue light exploded around and through the Chosen, engulfing it instantly. Its rippling black cloak disintegrated, its flesh melting to the bone. Its eyes widened, blue light bursting from its sockets and from its gaping mouth.

And then it exploded.

The blue light intensified, becoming so bright that it was all-encompassing, filling Kyle's mind to the exclusion of everything else. No thought was possible, no sensation left to him but utter rapture.

And then it stopped.

The blue light vanished, the ecstasy fading as quickly as it had come. Kyle laid there on the cold hard rock of the Spine of Grimore, his eyes wide, his skin slick with sweat. He felt his heart hammering in his chest, the great vessels of his neck pulsing with each beat. He heard the *crunch, crunch* of heavy footsteps approaching.

He groaned, rolling onto his side, feeling the sharp edge of a rock digging into his side. Staring past the toes of his boots, he saw a pair of jet-black boots standing there. He followed the boots up with his eyes, seeing black armored legs, then a black armored chest.

Blue light coursed over the surface of the metallic armor, weaving random, tiny patterns there.

Goosebumps rose on his arms, a chill running down his spine.

His gaze continued to rise, noting a black armored chestplate, the sun's rays reflecting dully from the inky metal. And above this, a strong, square jaw, smooth shaven, the skin gently bronzed. Above this, a mirror-like visor, short brown hair rippling in the howling wind.

What the...

The man standing before him reached down with one gauntleted hand, his fingers extended toward Kyle. Kyle reached out without thinking, and the man grabbed his wrist. Kyle felt himself lifting off of the hard stone of the Spine, rising slowly to his feet. He stood there then, staring at his own reflection in that mirrored visor, his eyes wide and his jaw slack. Then he rushed forward, slamming into the man and wrapping his arms around him.

"Darius!" Kyle cried, burying his face in the man's chest. He felt Darius give him a squeeze.

"Hey kid," Darius greeted.

Chapter 31

Petra knelt on the packed dirt of the forest floor, one arm circled around Kalibar's back, the other hand cradling his head against her chest. She held him there, feeling tears trickle down her cheeks. Despite the fact that she'd only met him yesterday, he'd proven himself to be a good man. A brave man. And a good father.

And she had watched him die...*let* him die...while he begged her for help.

Petra inhaled deeply, grimacing at the pain in her ribs, then let the air out. She let Kalibar's head go, setting it gently back onto the large tree trunk behind him. She leaned back, wiping her cheeks with the back of her hand. Her eyes dropped to his abdomen, to the blood-soaked brown cloak, and the severed tree branch that...

She drew a sharp breath in, rising to her feet and backing away.

The branch was in Kalibar's lap.

She stared at the branch, then at Kalibar's brown cloak, seeing the gaping hole in the cloth over his belly, the mass of maroon clots adhered to his flesh there. Then she lifted her gaze to his face...and realized that his eyes were open. Not just open...they were staring right at her!

"You look terrible," Kalibar stated casually, a slight smile on his lips. Petra's eyes widened, and she took another step backward.

"How..."

"Thank you for the, ah, pleasant awakening," he added, glancing at her bosom for a split second, then raising his eyes back to hers. She blinked, then looked downward, feeling her cheeks flush. Kalibar looked down at his own belly, brushing away the clots there and exposing perfectly intact skin. "I'm guessing you gave me magic," he deduced.

"You were dead!" Petra blurted out. Kalibar nodded.

"I suppose I was," he agreed. "Almost." He grunted, propping himself further up on the tree trunk. "Thank you for saving my life, by the way."

"You can't be alive," Petra protested, staring at the healed wound. "I watched you die!"

"Yes, well," Kalibar replied. "It just so happens that a very powerful man placed runes in my bones," he added. "...that heal any major injuries as long as I have magic."

Petra stared at him mutely for a moment. Then she shook her head.

"That's not possible," she declared. Kalibar chuckled.

"You've never met Ampir," Kalibar countered with a wry smile. The smile quickly vanished, however, replaced by horror. "Kyle!" he exclaimed.

"What?" Petra asked. Kalibar grimaced, pushing himself up to his feet. He swayed a little, then righted himself.

"How long have we been here?" he demanded, his tone suddenly sharp.

"Two minutes, maybe three?" Petra ventured, taken aback by his sudden change.

"We need to get out of here," Kalibar said, his voice hard. "*Now.*" He grabbed her hand. "Fly us out of here!"

"What?" she asked. "Why?"

"Someone set off a bomb," Kalibar answered. "And we've got about two minutes to fly five miles, or we're dead." He got behind her and wrapped his arms around her waist, which made her eyes widen. "Go!" he ordered.

Petra let magic flow into her mind's eye, shaping it and pouring it outward. She rose up from the ground, feeling Kalibar's weight

472

pulling down on her. She increased her magic stream, shooting higher into the air. She dodged tree limbs as she rose, quickly clearing the treetops and bursting into the clear blue sky.

"There!" Kalibar shouted over the shrieking wind. He pointed outward, toward a small mountain northwest of Mount Grimore...Mount Kress. "If we can get behind that, it should shield us from the blast." Petra changed direction abruptly, feeling the blood drain from her head as she did so, her vision blackening. She clenched the muscles in her legs, resisting the urge to slow down, and zoomed upward and forward toward the smaller mountain. Faster and faster she went, pouring more and more magic into her stream, the wind tearing through her hair.

"Faster!" Kalibar urged.

Petra grimaced, reaching for the *others* within her mind, and bracing herself for the inevitable pain that was the price of their gift. She felt magic gush into her mind, and threw it immediately at her magic stream, ignoring the aching in her bones...and the knowledge that every time she used the Reaper vines, it brought her closer to her untimely death.

They zoomed high above the treetops, and Petra felt Kalibar tightening his grip on her waist. She created a gravity shield around them both, instantly nullifying the roaring wind, and ensuring that if Kalibar let go, he would merely fall onto the lower dome of the shield. Mount Kress grew rapidly before them; Petra had never in her life attempted to fly this quickly. She felt her magic draining rapidly, and begged the *others* for more.

"Faster, faster!" Kalibar yelled. "We're almost there!" And they were...the base of the mountain was only a half-mile away now. "Circle around to the back," Kalibar instructed. Petra complied, curving slightly rightward, arcing toward the side of the mountain, then reversing direction to curve leftward around its base. She felt Kalibar twist around behind her. "A few more seconds," he stated. "Slow down, we're almost behind it..."

Petra gladly decreased her magic stream, feeling the sudden pull of her deceleration. She continued circling around the base of the mountain, only a hundred or so feet from the treetops climbing the rocky surface. She felt Kalibar squeeze her torso.

"Okay," he stated. "Land us."

Petra did so, dropping them between a gap in the trees on the mountainside. When their feet struck the ground, Kalibar disengaged from Petra, walking a few steps away. She saw his knees wobble, and then he fell to the ground.

* * *

Kalibar barely heard Petra calling his name as he stumbled away from her, his legs feeling like rubber beneath him. They gave out suddenly, and he dropped to the ground. His body felt numb, as if he were in a dream. No...a nightmare.

"...you okay?" he heard Petra ask. She walked up in front of him, squatting down and putting a hand on his shoulder. He turned away, unable to face her.

Kyle!

He closed his eyes, remembering the Chosen standing over his son, the green shard piercing through the poor boy's forehead. The way Kyle had struggled, the fear in his voice. Kalibar put his head in his hands, taking deep, shaking breaths.

I can't do this, he thought. He pictured Ariana, tossed off of the Spine of Grimore like a rag doll, her eyes unseeing, her throat crushed. He began to rock back and forth. *I can't do this!*

"Kalibar, are you hurt?" he heard Petra press. Her voice was rising, panic-stricken. He ignored her, trying to rise to his feet to walk away. He didn't want to be near her now. Didn't want to be near *anyone.* He managed to get to his feet, and took a few steps before his legs gave out again. He felt a sharp pain in his buttocks as they struck the ground, but it was nothing to him. He heard Petra run up to him, saw her kneeling before him, cupping the sides of his face in her hands.

"Kalibar!" she exclaimed, staring into his eyes. He tried to turn away, but she held him tightly. "What's wrong? Tell me," she pleaded. He swallowed, feeling tears trickling down his cheeks. He took a deep breath in, and started to speak, but his voice cracked, and it took everything he had not to break down and weep in front of her. He closed his eyes, steeling himself.

"They're gone," he muttered.

"Who?" Petra asked. Then her eyes widened. "Wait, where's Kyle and Ariana?" she exclaimed with sudden alarm. Kalibar shook his head.

"Gone."

"What do you mean, gone?" she pressed. He tried to turn away again, but she held his head firmly in her palms, forcing him to look at her.

"The Chosen," he muttered, an image of the black-cloaked creature kneeling over Kyle coming unbidden to his mind. "He...turned Kyle."

"What Chosen?" Petra asked, clearly baffled. Kalibar stared at her.

"You don't remember?"

"No," Petra replied. "What happened?" But Kalibar shook his head.

"I can't," he muttered, "I can't do this."

"What *happened?*"

Kalibar felt anger then, a hot spike of rage that burst up from deep within him. He reached up, grabbing her wrists and pulling them off of his face. Petra jerked backward.

"He killed them!" he shouted, his heart hammering in his chest. He let go of her wrists. "Sabin sent one of his Chosen after us. He snapped Ariana's neck and threw her off the mountain, turned Kyle into one of his slaves, and nearly killed us!" He stood there, feeling suddenly empty. "He *did* kill me."

"Wait," Petra exclaimed. "Ariana can't die, she's an Immortal!" She shook him. "Where is she? If I give her magic..."

"The bomb," Kalibar interjected bitterly. "If we'd gone to find her it would've killed us all." And as true as that statement was, he still felt like he'd abandoned her.

I should have died trying to find her, he realized. *I should have had Petra fly away and stayed with my little girl.*

475

Shame came over him, so heavy that he felt it would crush him.

"What bomb?" Petra pressed. "I don't understand."

"Ky-" he began, the stopped himself. "The Chosen activated a bomb to kill us," he lied. "I've seen them before. They destroy everything within a five mile radius."

"You said they take five minutes to explode?" Petra asked. Kalibar nodded. She frowned, then got to her feet. "I don't understand," she added. "It's been almost ten minutes, and I haven't heard any explosions."

Kalibar stared at her mutely.

"You said five minutes, right?" Petra pressed. Kalibar nodded. She extended a hand down to him, and he took it, letting her pull him to his feet. "Kalibar, neither of your children is dead," she insisted.

"If the bomb doesn't go off, we might be able to find Ariana," he realized, feeling a burst of hope. But it quickly faded. "But Kyle is beyond us."

"Why? Petra asked. "He'll be an Immortal just like Ariana."

"Not like Ariana," Kalibar countered. "Ariana's...different."

"Then we'll start with her," Petra concluded. Kalibar hesitated.

"If we're wrong, and the bomb goes off, it'll kill us both," he warned. "And the Chosen might still be out there." He shook his head. "I'll search for Ariana, but you should stay here. I can't risk your life too."

"You need me," Petra retorted. "And *I* decide who I risk my life for."

"Petra..."

"Kyle and Ariana need us," she interrupted. "And I'm going to help them." She stood back then, putting her hands on her hips. "You can come along if you want."

476

Chapter 32

Kyle felt Darius pushing him away gently, and finally unwrapped his arms from around the bodyguard's armored body. He stepped back, hardly knowing what to feel. On the one hand, he felt profound relief. On the other, he was utterly confused.

"I thought you were dead!" he exclaimed, finding his voice. Darius smirked.

"Not yet," he replied. The air around his left hand shimmered, and suddenly a long black cylinder appeared, hovering over his left hand. It was the bomb, its activated end still glowing red. Darius tapped the end with his thumb, and it stopping glowing, retreating back into the cylinder. Then he lifted his right hand to the side, palm up. A dark form rose from beyond the edge of the Spine, levitating upward until it was level with Darius.

"Ariana!" Kyle cried. It *was* Ariana, hovering upright in the air, her spine arched backward, her head tipping back so that her unseeing eyes faced the sky above. Darius lifted his right hand to her forehead, and a pulse of brilliant blue light burst from his gauntlet, bathing her in its glow. Her eyes shot open, her limbs tensing, and she drew in a deep, gasping breath. Her windpipe, crushed by the Chosen's deadly grip, re-expanded and straightened out in front of Kyle's eyes. Darius guided her to the narrow ledge between himself and Kyle, and lowered her onto it. Ariana turned to Kyle, then back to Darius, looking absolutely thunderstruck.

"You!" she exclaimed, backing away from Darius. "You're supposed to be dead!" Darius said nothing, and Ariana turned to Kyle. "Kyle!" she gasped, running forward and embracing him...and nearly crushing his ribs in the process. "You're okay!"

"I'm fine," Kyle gasped. Ariana immediately relaxed her vise-like grip on him, giving him a quick kiss on the lips, then pulling away. Kyle smiled back; still, he put a hand to his forehead, shuddering at the memory of the Chosen's shard piercing through his skull. To his relief, he felt only smooth, unbroken skin there. Ariana frowned.

"What happened?" she asked. Then she turned back to Darius. "Where's Kalibar and Petra?"

"Uh," Kyle stammered, glancing up at Darius.

They're fine, he heard a deep, resonant voice in his mind say.

"They're fine," Kyle parroted, trying to sound reassuring. Then he paused; he had no idea where the two were. One minute Kalibar had been shouting for him to activate the bomb, and the next, he'd been gone.

"I heard him," Ariana replied. "Where are they?" she pressed.

Safe.

Ariana stared back at Darius, clearly dissatisfied with this answer.

"You're supposed to be dead," she accused, putting her hands on her hips. She turned back to Kyle. "You said if he didn't come back in one day, then Sabin had killed him!"

"That's what Darius told me," Kyle stated rather defensively. Ariana stared back at him, a strange look on her face.

"Darius told you?" she asked. Kyle's eyes widened in horror, and he took a step back, glancing up at Darius...who was shaking his head slowly.

"I mean..." he stammered.

"*Darius* told you?" Ariana repeated, turning to face Darius. She inspected him for a long moment, and then her eyes widened, her jaw dropping. "Oh my..."

And then a cord of blue shot out from her forehead into Darius, and she immediately collapsed onto the ground.

"Ariana!" Kyle exclaimed. Darius sighed, his visor flashing bright white, then vanishing. The bodyguard stared at Kyle, continuing to shake his head.

"Seriously?" he asked.

"I'm sorry," Kyle blurted out. "It just slipped out..."

"Put it back in," Darius growled. "...and keep it there." Kyle nodded, feeling his cheeks burning. He glanced down at Ariana, who was still lying unconscious on the ground.

"Is she going to remember?" he asked. Darius shook his head. Kyle breathed a sigh of relief, then frowned at the man. "Are you going to wake her up?"

"That depends," Darius grumbled.

"Sorry," Kyle mumbled. "You *are* supposed to be dead," he added. As happy as he was to see his grandfather, he was more than a little irritated that the man had only now decided to show up. "You said if you didn't come back in one day, Sabin had killed you!"

"Wrong," Darius retorted.

"No," Kyle insisted. "That *is* what you said."

"I said *assume* I was dead," Darius countered calmly, folding his arms over his chest. Kyle felt righteous indignation rise within his breast.

"You said you were going to try to kill him!" he accused.

"I said I was going after him," Darius corrected. "Which I am."

"But...!" Kyle began, then stood there, fuming at the man. He'd been certain that Darius had said he was going to kill Sabin, but now he wasn't sure. Even so, Kyle still had the undeniable feeling that he'd been tricked somehow.

"You're welcome," Darius said. Kyle blinked.

"What?"

Darius glanced at Kyle's forehead, and then at Ariana.

"Right. Thanks," Kyle muttered. As usual, Darius had somehow managed to infuriate him within minutes of saving his life. There was no doubt about it...the man was surely gifted.

"Let's go," Darius stated, stepping over Ariana and past Kyle. He stopped before the shattered section of the Spine of Grimore, the fifty or so feet of the path that had been destroyed by the Chosen. Mount Grimore's massive peak stood tall in the distance.

"Go where?" Kyle asked.

"There," Darius replied, gesturing beyond the Spine. Kyle stared at the gulf between them and the remainder of the Spine.

"What are we going to do?"

"We're going to deal with Sabin," Darius answered. "Once and for all."

* * *

The sun beat down upon Ariana's head and shoulders as she made her way across the narrow path winding up the face of Mount Grimore. The trees around them – if they could even be called trees – were barely as tall as she was, with thick, gnarled branches. Moss hugged the rocks around her, huddling against the steadily cooling air. Ariana noticed Kyle shivering beside her, and she grabbed his hand, holding it in her own. She wished – not for the first time – that her body produced heat, so that she could huddle beside him and warm him up.

She looked forward then, at Ampir's black-armored back. The man hadn't said a word since she'd awoken. She'd found herself lying down before the legendary Battle-Runic on the Spine of Grimore, between him and Kyle. She still couldn't believe that Ampir was really alive, really *here*...and that he was going to bring them straight to Sabin's doorstep.

How many times had she dreamed of this day? How many times over the last year, lying awake in bed at night in the Arena, had she imagined herself living this moment? Killing the Dead Man – and Xanos – had been her dark fantasy ever since they'd killed her parents. And though she'd brought Kyle here, plotting to kill Sabin once and for all, she'd never really allowed herself to believe that they could actually succeed. It had always been a long shot, one last desperate attempt to save everyone she loved – and to get revenge on the evil that had quite literally destroyed her life.

But now, with Ampir, they actually had a chance.

The path leveled off gradually, the steep rock slope giving way to a wide path that curved ever-so-slightly to the left. Vertical rock walls rose over a hundred feet above their heads on either side of the path; if it hadn't been for the noon sun being directly overhead, they would surely have been blanketed in the shadows thrown by those imposing walls. Ampir continued to lead them down this path, not even hesitating as he strode into the canyon. Ariana saw Kyle hesitate, slowing as the canyon walls rose around them.

"What's wrong?" she asked.

"I don't know," he replied. She saw him stare at the canyon walls uneasily. She could hear his heart beating faster in his chest. "It reminds me of Crescent Lake," he added after a moment.

"What do you mean?"

"Me and uh, Darius, went to go get some food in the woods," Kyle answered. "We went to a place kinda like this, with cliffs. The Death Weavers attacked us there."

"Oh," Ariana replied. They continued silently around the gentle left curve of the canyon, until the path straightened out. The path beyond climbed at a shallow angle upward, the massive peak of the mountain visible high above in the distance.

...stand back...

Ariana stopped cold in her tracks, forcing Kyle to stop with her. She spun around, staring the way they'd come, and saw only the empty path behind her.

"What?" she heard Kyle ask. She turned forward again, shaking her head.

"Thought I heard something," she replied. She glanced over her should again, then resumed walking.

...coming...

She spun around again, seeing nothing but the empty path. She turned back to Kyle, feeling a chill run through her.

"I *know* I just heard something," she insisted. Kyle frowned.

"Heard what?" he pressed. "I didn't hear anything." He turned to Ampir, who was still walking ahead of them. "Did you hear anything?" But Ampir didn't answer. Kyle turned back to Ariana. "He said he didn't hear anything."

481

"No he didn't," Ariana protested. "He didn't say anything." Kyle blushed, and she narrowed her eyes at him. "What's going on?"

"He's sends me thoughts," Kyle admitted. Ariana blinked.

"Has he been talking to you the entire time?" she asked. Kyle hesitated, and Ariana glared at him. "You've been talking behind my back?" she accused.

"No," Kyle protested. "He hasn't said anything but that." Ariana continued to glare at him. "Honest," he insisted.

"Well I heard something," she muttered. Still, she resumed walking, quickening her pace to catch up with Ampir.

...them pass...

She slowed, then stopped again.

"Did you hear something again?" Kyle asked. Ariana paused, then shook her head, feeling another chill run down her spine. The voice had been stronger this time, much more clear than before. So much so that she realized that she hadn't really *heard* anything.

It'd been in her head.

"Stop," Ariana blurted out. She turned to Ampir, who was still walking. "Stop!" she cried, running up to him. Ampir slowed, then stopped, turning to face her. "There's a Chosen nearby!"

Ampir stared at her – or at least it seemed that way, as his eyes were unseeable behind that visor – then turned around, continuing forward. Ariana stared at him incredulously, then turned to Kyle, who looked suddenly very pale.

"What?" she asked. Kyle swallowed, his Adam's apple moving up and down with the motion.

"He knows," Kyle answered. He paused for a moment, then looked upward. "He says they're up there."

Ariana turned her gaze upward, to the tops of the cliffs looming on either side of them, well over a hundred feet above. With her incredible vision, it didn't take her long to spot the dark shapes standing at the edge of the cliff. Figures clad in black cloaks, their faces obscured by the shadows cast by the dark hoods over their heads. Hundreds of them, standing shoulder-to-shoulder at the edge of both cliffs, all the way down the length of the canyon.

Not hundreds of them. *Thousands* of them.

Ariana felt terror grip her, and she took a step backward, staring up at those countless faces staring back down at her. She could *feel* them, the Chosen.

...your ground...

...them pass...

She shook her head, taking another step back.

"Ariana?" Kyle asked.

"I can't," she stated, shaking her head again. She felt fear clutch at her, wrapping its dark tentacles around her heart and squeezing it. She knew that feeling, knew it all too well. She'd felt the exact same feeling around the Dead Man, when she'd been mortal. "I can't do this." Kyle grabbed her hands in his own.

"It's okay," he said. "We've got him now," he added, nodding at Ampir's retreating form. Kyle smiled at her. "We've got Ampir." Ariana stared at Ampir, then back at the countless Chosen looming over them. She closed her eyes, taking a deep breath in, then letting it out. She pictured the *Defiance*, its sails engulfed in flames, its crew set to flee. Pictured the mouth of the cave Petra had tested her in. She'd gone through so much, and had gotten so far.

Remember your mission, she thought.

She opened her eyes, turning her gaze upward to glare at the Chosen, her jaw clenched tight. She pictured her parents' house engulfed in flames, screams echoing through the night air.

I'm going to make you pay, she promised, wondering if they could hear *her* thoughts.

"Let's go," she said, slipping one hand out of Kyle's and striding forward. Kyle walked beside her, and they once again caught up to Ampir. The path continued forward for a while, until they came to another left turn. Beyond this, the canyon fanned out, growing much wider. The path continued upward at a gentle incline, the canyon walls rising high above. Countless Chosen continued to line the tops of the walls, standing motionless, their black cloaks rippling in the wind. Huge statues rose high above the hundred-foot cliff walls on either side, each easily three times as tall as the canyon itself, their stout legs and feet embedded into the rock. With their thick torsos, their wide-spaced arms, and their domed heads, it was all-too-obvious what they represented.

"Behemoths," Ariana heard Kyle whisper. She felt him tense up, heard his heart beating quicker.

"They're just statues," Ariana countered, trying to sound reassuring. She stared up at one of those domed heads, spotting the white diamond-shaped crystalline eye there. Eerily enough, it looked like the statue was looking right at her. A trick of their design, no doubt, in order to cast fear into anyone who dared venture here.

"I don't think so," Kyle countered in a harsh whisper. Ariana glanced back up at the statue, and saw that it did indeed look like it was still watching her. She frowned, continuing forward, following Ampir down the long path upward.

The statue's head *shifted*, dust and small pebbles falling from the canyon wall around it, that lone eye tracking her as she went.

Ariana's throat tightened, and she quickened her pace, catching up to Ampir and walking alongside him, with Kyle at her left and Ampir at her right. She looked up at another statue, then another, and saw their massive heads following them as they passed.

"Ampir?" she asked, grabbing onto the silent Battle-Runic's left arm. He said nothing, but he didn't pull away either. He continued forward up the path, ignoring the Chosen and the statues around him. Ariana tried to do the same, keeping her eyes forward, but she could still hear the disjointed fragments of the Chosen's thoughts in her mind, like a crowd quietly whispering all around her.

It made her skin crawl.

The path continued upward and forward, until it began to level off. As it did so, it revealed a sudden end to the canyon, a massive rocky hill rising in a dome high above the canyon walls around it. Beyond and above this dome, the steep mountainside shot upward high into the sky, forming Mount Grimore's peak hundreds of feet above.

Ariana stared at that peak, then lowered her gaze back to the path. It led to a giant hole in the center of the dome, the gaping maw of a cave. Ariana felt a chill run through her, and realized beyond any

484

doubt that this must be the cave Petra had told them about. The one she'd been leading them toward before the Chosen had attacked.

The entrance to Sabin's lair.

Ampir led them toward it, the *crunch, crunch* of his black boots on the scattered pebbles underfoot never wavering in their steady rhythm. Ariana could feel the eyes of the Behemoths and the Chosen staring down at them, countless silent sentinels watching their every move.

If they wanted to attack, she thought, *they already would've.*

So why hadn't they?

The end of the wide path drew near, the mouth of the cave now only some fifty feet away. The entrance to the massive domed hill was at least fifty feet high and a hundred feet wide, large enough to send an army of men through. She felt Kyle squeezing her hand, and she turned to him. His face was awfully flushed, and he was taking deep, gulping breaths.

"What's wrong?" Ariana asked. Kyle stopped walking, and let go of her hand, bending over and resting his palms on his thighs. He shook his head.

"Can't...breathe," he gasped.

"Ampir!" Ariana warned, pulling on the Battle-Runic's arm. Ampir stopped, turning to face Kyle. Then he turned back to the cave entrance. Ariana felt a powerful *thrumming* in her mind's eye, and suddenly the air around them burst into a fine cloud of black dust. The dust fell slowly to the ground, and Kyle's complexion began to clear, his breath coming much easier.

"Thanks," Kyle mumbled.

"What happened?" Ariana asked. Kyle stood straight up, grabbing her hand in his own.

"He says it's carbon dioxide," Kyle answered. "The cave is filled with it."

"What's carbon...whatever you said?" Ariana pressed.

"Poison gas," Kyle explained. "I think it was in the other cave too," he added. "Ampir turned it into oxygen and carbon," he added. "That's the black dust."

"Oh," Ariana said, not really understanding. "So it's safe now?"
Kyle nodded.

"I think so."

Ampir turned forward again, continuing his steady stride into the mouth of the domed cave. The shadows cast by the gaping maw swallowed him whole, his footsteps echoing throughout the cavern beyond. Kyle and Ariana glanced at each other, then followed behind the man, hand-in-hand.

* * *

Kyle felt a chill as he stepped out of the sunlight streaming into the wide canyon, crossing over into the shadows thrown by the gray and brown stone arch that marked the entrance to Sabin's lair. He shivered, squeezing Ariana's hand as they passed through. She squeezed him back, giving him a weak smile. He knew what they were both thinking.

This was it.

Kyle sneezed as he breathed in the musty air of the cave, black dust still hanging in the air, swirling in the gentle breeze blowing out of the cave entrance and back into the canyon. The cave was enormous, even taller and wider than the entrance had been. It was also pitch black, the sunlight making it only a few yards in. Ampir continued to walk forward into that utter blackness, only visible due to the blue magic of his armor's runes. Though Kyle could see the magic even in the darkness, that magic cast no actual light on Ampir's surroundings. Every step forward was like walking into the abyss of space, a leap of faith that there would be more ground beyond. Kyle didn't dare slow down or stop, knowing that Ampir would almost certainly leave them behind if he did. But with each step Kyle took, fear grew in his heart, tightening its grip on him. He squeezed Ariana's hand – *hard* – and was about to create a magical light when Ampir stopped.

Kyle felt a powerful vibration in his skull then, reverberating through his bones. He saw blue light burst from his limbs, outlining them in the pitch blackness. The light vanished, and suddenly Kyle felt the bitter chill of the cold mountain air vanish, replaced by a comfortable warmth. He even felt lighter somehow, and the aching in his legs and back from the climb up the mountain were gone. He heard Ariana take a sharp breath in, and felt something cool and hard in his right hand, where her hand had been seconds ago. He let go, taking a step back.

A light appeared from high above, a single white globe some thirty feet above their heads. Kyle squinted against the sudden brightness, blinking rapidly, then opened his eyes wider as they adjusted.

They were standing in a tunnel over a hundred feet wide, the walls curving upward to the roughly-hewn ceiling above. Ampir was standing before Kyle and Ariana, facing them. Kyle turned to Ariana, and then blinked, staring at her in disbelief. Where she'd moments ago been covered from head to toe in her Reaper uniform, now she was clad in black, metallic armor. Her armor looked awfully similar to Ampir's, though much simpler in its appearance, and with no blue runes flashing on its surface. He realized that Ariana was staring back at him with a similar expression. He looked down, and saw that he too was wearing black metal armor, identical to Ariana's. He gasped, staring at his hands. They were covered in metal gauntlets, but he couldn't feel the weight of them; it was as if he weren't wearing anything at all. He touched his armored belly, and was surprised to feel the cool metal of it under his fingertips.

"What the..." he began, then raised his fingers to his face. He could feel the warm skin of his lips and cheek as if his hands were bare...as if they weren't covered in thick metal! He saw Ariana do the same, bringing her right gauntlet to her face, her eyes widening in disbelief.

"I can feel everything!" she exclaimed. She turned to Ampir then. "What is this?"

Battle-Runic armor, Kyle heard Ampir's voice in his mind say. He glanced at Ariana, then relayed the message.

"Like his?" she asked, pointing at Ampir, who gave a wry smirk.

Not even close.

"He says..." Kyle began.

"I think I get it," Ariana interrupted. She flexed and extended her fingers, staring at them in wonder. Kyle saw Ampir turn around, resuming his trek deeper into the massive underground tunnel.

Forward.

"Come on," Kyle urged, grabbing Ariana's gauntleted hand. He felt the cool metal surrounding her fingers, and once again marveled at the sensation. If he closed his eyes, he'd have no idea that he was wearing a suit of armor at all. Indeed, each step he took was oddly effortless, almost as if his suit was reading his mind, performing each motion without the need of his muscles.

"Oh wow," he heard Ariana exclaim, and turned to see her smiling as she walked. She shook her head at him. "Are you *feeling* this?"

"I know, right?" Kyle replied, grinning back at her. "I feel like Ampir!"

No you don't.

"Yeah, yeah," Kyle grumbled. Ariana looked at him questioningly. "He says I don't," he muttered, feeling his cheeks heat up. Ariana laughed, bumping her shoulder into his lightly. He felt absolutely none of the impact, though he could feel the metal on the skin of his shoulder. Which was strange, because he was still wearing a shirt. He saw Ariana frown, and saw her put a hand to her belly, her eyes widening.

"Are we *naked* under here?" she exclaimed. Kyle mirrored her frown, putting a hand to his own belly, feeling cool metal over the skin of his bellybutton. Kyle waited for Ampir to answer, but the Battle-Runic said nothing. Ariana turned to Kyle, who ran a hand down his own torso. While his hand felt the smooth metal of his armor, the skin of his chest and belly felt the metal of his gauntlets. It was a very strange sensation.

"Uh..." Kyle mumbled, his cheeks burning. "I guess so." Ariana seemed none too pleased with this answer, and immediately covered her unmentionables with her hands. Which was, of course, entirely unnecessary.

The floor of the tunnel dipped suddenly, slanting downward at a slight angle. Ampir's light followed them from far above, allowing them to see a hundred or so feet in all directions. Kyle stared at the ceiling far above, at the long, broad stalactites hanging down from it. Drops of water fell from the tips of the stalactites onto the rock below, making the ground slick with moisture. Kyle's feet, encased in his Battle-Runic armor, didn't slip once.

"Look," Ariana whispered. She pointed forward and to the right, at the upper portion of the tunnel wall ahead of them. Kyle followed her finger, spotting something dark and spindly on the face of the gray and brown stone. It was long, its surface shiny and black, and it hugged the tunnel wall like a twisting vein, its end tapering to a point. Kyle looked at the left wall, and saw a few more of the things, twisting and branching across it.

"What are those?" Kyle asked.

"I don't know," Ariana replied. As they continued forward, the branches grew steadily thicker, and there were many more of them. They were easily thicker than Kyle's torso now, and looked like smooth tree branches clinging to the walls and ceiling.

"Weird," Kyle murmured.

"Watch out," Ariana warned, pointing down. Kyle looked at the floor, realizing that he'd nearly stepped on a similar black branch that clung to the ground to his left. He veered away from it, only to find more of the branches on the ground ahead. He stepped around them, but it wasn't long before the branches became so dense that the floor was barely visible beneath them. In fact, the entire tunnel was covered with them now, the walls, ceiling, and floor. They resembled thick black tubes here, row after row extending along the length of the tunnel, no longer branching out.

"What *are* these?" Kyle asked Ampir, who appeared entirely unconcerned by the thick black cords, as he was walking right on them. Kyle hesitated, then stepped on one of the things, and was surprised to find that it was rock-hard.

"They look like Reaper vines," Ariana answered. "Don't they?"

"Kinda," Kyle admitted. He saw Ariana crouch down and peer at the things. Then she stood back up.

"They *are*," she confirmed. "They have the same bark."

"They're huge," Kyle muttered. The vines in Petra's flesh had been as small as veins; these were as big around as tree trunks. "I wonder if they're alive," he added.

"If they are," Ariana replied, "...they must make a ton of magic."

"Yeah."

The tunnel continued downward at a steeper angle, the rocky walls no longer visible underneath the massive Reaper vines. They walked down the tunnel without talking, the *clunking* of their boots echoing dully off of the walls. After a few minutes, the tunnel started to broaden, then abruptly opened up into a much larger cavern, whose surface was entirely covered with more black vines.

Ampir stopped suddenly, putting one hand up. Ariana and Kyle stopped behind him, and watched as his light continued forward far above their heads, growing brighter and brighter as it went. Suddenly it split into a dozen small globes, each as bright as the original, that shot out in all directions, lighting up the entire cavern. The cavern was enormous, larger than a football stadium. In the center of the cavern was a huge lake, its black surface absolutely still. Reaper vines converged on the lake on all sides, plunging into its depths; more vines crawled up the curved walls to the domed ceiling a hundred feet above their heads.

"What now?" Ariana asked. Kyle frowned, scanning the cavern, and realized that Ariana had a point. The cavern appeared to be a dead end; the only way in, and the only way out, was the tunnel they'd just come from. He turned to Ampir, who was still facing the lake. The man stepped forward, striding up to the edge of the lake, then paused, staring down at it. He crouched down, then reached out with his right hand, dipping his gauntleted fingers into the dark waters. Ripples shot outward with the disturbance, then faded away, leaving the surface of the lake still once again.

Kyle felt a vibration in his feet, and saw fine ripples form around the periphery of the lake. The vibrations intensified, the ripples growing larger and larger. A low bass sound echoed throughout the chamber, so deep and powerful that Kyle could feel it in his chest, his lungs vibrating like a drum. The surface of the lake began to ripple so violently that fine droplets of water shot up from its

490

surface, all across the lake, forming a thick mist directly above its churning waters.

Everyone but Ampir took a step backward.

The center of the lake heaved upward then, a huge black dome rising above its surface. The thing was enormous, nearly fifty feet in diameter. Water streamed down its edges to the churning lake below with roar of a waterfall. Kyle took another step back, his hackles rising. He felt Ariana's hand grip his, and squeeze hard; with his Battle-Runic armor, he could feel the enormous pressure of her grip, but there was no pain.

She looked terrified.

"He's here!" she yelled, her voice barely audible. Kyle's breath caught in his throat.

There, hovering above the roiling waters of the lake, was a monstrosity unlike anything he had ever seen. The slick black dome was only the top of it; below that were pale, bloated human heads, their necks embedded into the smooth black surface of the thing, lining its perimeter in a single horizontal row. Each head faced outward, a green diamond-shaped crystal embedded in its forehead, its swollen eyelids closed. Below them, a row of thin black spikes glistened menacingly, water dripping from their deadly points. Pure white crystals plunged downward from the bottom of the monstrosity, their facets gleaming in the light from above.

"Kyle!" Ariana warned, gripping his hand even tighter. She took a step back, then another.

The massive hovering disc began to rotate, the heads spinning slowly, water flying from the sharp spikes to spray across the lake below. Then the rotation slowed, until it stopped, a single head facing them.

Its eyes opened.

"AMPIR," it said, its pale lips moving grotesquely, water spilling from its mouth. Its voice was impossibly deep, resonating throughout the cavern and chilling Kyle to the bone. He felt it in his mind as much as he heard it with his ears, and there was only one thing he felt as he heard it.

Terror.

491

Ampir stood before the thing, the runes on his armor flashing blue in random patterns, his feet planted firmly on the ground, his arms at his sides.

"Sabin," he replied calmly.

The disembodied head stared down at Ampir, then turned its gaze to Kyle, then Ariana. Kyle shrank under its baleful glare, and it took everything he had not to turn and run.

"WELCOME," the head boomed, that single word forcing the lake below to ripple violently.

"Doesn't feel that way," Ampir replied coolly. The head glanced at Kyle and Ariana again.

"YOU COME ALONE."

"Wrong," Ampir retorted. He folded his arms across his broad chest. "Now if you don't put away your toys, I'm going to break them," he warned. "And then you won't be able to play with them anymore."

The head stared at him, its lips curling into a smirk. But it said nothing, its eyes closing. Then the entire monstrosity fell out of the air, slamming into the lake's surface with an ear-splitting *boom*. Water shot upward from the impact, sending a dark tidal wave forward toward them. Kyle cried out, letting go of Ariana's hand and turning to run. He felt cool water strike his back, felt the extreme force of its weight, but he did not budge from where he stood. Water shot forward around him, rising up to his knees, then slowly retreating back into the surface of the lake. Kyle paused, then turned around, facing the lake once again, just in time to see the slick black dome sinking beneath its surface. It stopped just before being fully immersed, and then started to move forward toward them. It stopped at the edge of the lake, its edge touching the black Reaper vines at the shore.

The churning waters calmed slowly, until its surface was only faintly rippling.

"Come on," Ampir stated, stepping forward onto the dome. He walked up to its center, then turned and gestured for Kyle and Ariana to join him. Kyle hesitated, glancing at Ariana – who looked equally reticent – then grabbed her hand, stepping forward. Ariana walked at his side, and they both stepped from the Reaper vine floor to the slick surface of the dome. Kyle expected his feet to slip, but again, his armor prevented it. He strode up the shallow dome easily, stopping at Ampir's side.

Then the dome began to descend into the water.

Kyle stepped back, grabbing onto Ampir's upper arm, and stared down at the water rushing up over the submerging dome toward them. The water receded suddenly, starting to rotate around the dome, forming a huge whirlpool around them. They continued to descend, the dome dropping below the lake's surface, walls of spinning water forming around it. They descended through that spiraling tunnel, the roar of the whirlpool deafening around them. Kyle looked upward, and saw the watery tunnel collapsing far above them, water gushing in from the sides to refill the void.

And then a black, Reaper vine-lined tunnel appeared around them, below the water.

Kyle did a double-take, then turned his gaze upward, seeing the water of the lake above him. It was as if the entire body of water had been suspended in the air by an invisible floor; the whirlpool collapsed entirely above their heads, the lake bottom reforming. Below it, this tunnel continued straight downward.

"What's holding it up?" Kyle asked, letting go of Ampir's arm.

"Magic," Ampir answered.

"You don't say," Kyle mumbled. The dome descended steadily, the lake's bottom receding above. It passed beyond the reach of Ampir's lights – still glowing above their heads – and vanished in the darkness. Ariana squeezed Kyle's hand.

"I can feel him," she whispered. Kyle nodded, squeezing hers back. He didn't have to ask who. Ariana's eyes unfocused, her grip relaxing. Then she snapped out of her trance, turning to Ampir. "He's everywhere," she added, a mix of awe and fear in her voice. She brought her hands to her temples, closing her eyes.

"What's wrong?" Kyle asked. Ariana shook her head, opening her eyes.

"I can't keep up," she replied. "He's thinking so many things at once, in so many different places." She squeezed her eyes shut again, and grimaced. "I wish I could turn it off."

The tunnel began to widen as they continued downward, the walls still completely covered in thick Reaper vines. The dome slowed its descent, until it was barely moving. A sheer wall of the vines stood in front of them, and it was before this that the dome stopped. Ampir strode forward immediately, toward the edge of the dome, and Kyle and Ariana followed quickly behind. They stopped at the edge, and Kyle looked down, seeing the floor some twenty feet below. Or what seemed to be the floor; it was mostly white, with black specks moving about randomly on its irregular surface. He felt Ariana grip his arm.

"I don't like this," she said, her voice tense. Ampir ignored her, leaping off of the edge of the dome. He dropped through the air toward the ground, and suddenly the floor below him formed a black circle, the white and black specks retracting to reveal Reaper vines covering the floor below. Ampir landed on the vines, then turned to look up at Ariana and Kyle.

"Come on," Kyle urged, bending his knees to jump. Ariana pulled him back, shaking her head, her eyes locked on the floor below.

"I can't," she protested, her voice rising in fear. She stepped back from the edge of the dome.

"What's wrong?" he asked.

"Those...things," she answered, pointing to the white section of the floor. Kyle's eyebrows furrowed.

"What things?"

"The *bugs*," she replied. Kyle stared at her in confusion, then took a closer look at the floor. He saw the same irregular white surface, black specks moving all over it. At first he thought the specks were what Ariana was talking about, but then he realized that he was mistaken. The white wasn't the floor...it was the bodies of millions upon millions of bugs crawling *on* the floor. Round, white-bodied bugs with tiny black heads crawling all over each other, forming a thick layer on top of the Reaper vines Ampir was standing on.

494

"Oh," Kyle gasped. He knew where he'd seen those bugs before...crawling all over Ariana in the cave he'd rescued her from.

Come down.

Kyle looked at Ampir, still standing below, the white bugs giving him a wide berth. Kyle squeezed Ariana's hand.

"We have to jump," he stated firmly. Ariana shook her head vehemently.

"No."

"They won't hurt you," Kyle insisted.

"*No,*" Ariana repeated. She backed up another step. Then she lurched forward without warning, toppling off of the edge of the dome and falling down to the floor twenty feet below. She landed flat on her back with a loud *thump*, not two feet from where Ampir stood. The bugs had parted under her just in time, leaving a few feet of bared Reaper vines around her. She scrambled to her feet, giving out a loud shriek and clutching onto Ampir's arm, pressing against his side. She stared in wide-eyed horror at the mass of bugs swarming on the floor around her.

Kyle took a steadying breath, then jumped off of the edge of the dome, feeling his stomach lurch as he fell toward the ground. He saw the bugs part under him, and then his feet slammed into the ground. He felt the force of the impact, but no pain, his knees barely bending. Ariana immediately disengaged from Ampir, rushing to Kyle's side and clinging to him with her incredible strength. Then she glared at Ampir.

"You did that!" she accused. Ampir smirked.

"They won't bug you," he replied. Kyle would've smiled at the terrible pun, but Ariana was looking at him. He restrained himself, then realized that Ampir had spoken with his normal voice – Darius's voice – instead of speaking telepathically. He glanced at Ariana, but she hardly seemed to notice, her eyes still glued to the writhing floor.

There was a sudden rush of air, and Kyle turned around, seeing the huge domed...thing...rising upward. It gained speed rapidly, shooting up into the tunnel in the ceiling far above, vanishing into the shadows there.

Let's go.

"Okay," Kyle replied. Then he realized Ampir hadn't spoken aloud.

"Okay what?" Ariana asked. Ampir walked forward, to where the domed thing had been, and away from the sheer wall in front of Kyle and Ariana. The bugs avoided Ampir expertly, scurrying away from his feet before they had a chance to be crushed underneath. Kyle stepped forward as well, and the bugs treated him similarly. He heard Ariana take a deep breath in, and she stepped forward, still clinging to his arm. After a few dozen steps, she relaxed her grip a bit, clearly realizing that the bugs weren't going after her. Still, she stayed close to Kyle.

They came to a steep ramp angling down to a lower level of the cavern, and continued down it. The bugs parted before them, and Kyle noticed that their numbers were starting to dwindle as they went forward. The Reaper vines below were fading to a dark brown, the thick cords splitting into numerous smaller ones. A few yards ahead, a thick, white, gooey-looking substance covered these thinner cords, which transitioned from brown to a translucent white color. They looked like roots.

"What *is* that?" Ariana asked, staring at the slimy goop. Ampir said nothing, but the dozen lights levitating above his head expanded outward, brightening as they did so. Kyle saw more goo-covered Reaper vine roots in the distance, and then his eye caught something glinting at the edge of the wide circle of illumination Ampir's magical glowing orbs cast. Ampir stepped right into the goo, ignoring the squelching sound it made as it sucked at his boots, and Kyle followed suit, grimacing as he went. He could feel the slick, cool slime on the bottom of his feet, even through his boots, due to their strange magic. The sensation was revolting.

They trudged forward, and Kyle kept his attention on the glinting object in the distance. It was a facet of a white crystal jutting out of the goop, he realized. There were lots of them, each about the size of a man's fist, sitting in dense clusters between pockets of goo. Beyond this, there was an unbroken arc of white crystals. And perhaps five feet beyond this, Kyle saw rippling water...the edge of a pool. He followed Ampir to where the goo ended and the crystals began; the Battle-Runic stopped there, crouching down and staring, the crystals reflected in his visor. Kyle followed suit, not quite sure what he was doing; he saw fine white hair-like appendages sprouting from the Reaper vine roots and embedding themselves into tiny cracks in the crystals.

Ampir stood abruptly, lifting his head to gaze across the water beyond.

"What?" Kyle asked. Ampir said nothing, but his lights shot forward above the water, growing almost painfully bright. Kyle squinted, raising one hand to shield his eyes.

He heard Ariana gasp.

The light dimmed slightly, and Kyle lowered his hand, staring out across the water. It was another lake, he realized...and much larger than even the first had been. It formed a circle in the floor of the massive cavern, and along its shore were countless clusters of white crystals...and a ring of the goo-covered roots, and beyond that, the endlessly crawling white bugs.

"Look!" Ariana exclaimed. She pointed down at the surface of the lake. Kyle stared at it, not seeing anything.

"What?" he asked.

"Under the water," she clarified. Kyle frowned, refocusing below the rippling surface of the lake, into the depths below. The lake bottom angled steeply downward, and Kyle realized that there were white crystals clinging to the rock there. Huge white crystals, each easily as big and tall as a man. He followed these deeper into the lake, making out the vague outlines of more huge crystals. And then...a shadow. An *enormous* shadow.

It moved.

"Whoa!" Kyle blurted out, lurching backward. "What the heck is that?"

Let's go.

Ampir turned right, striding quickly across the goo-covered roots, circling around the shore. Kyle followed close behind, pulling Ariana along with him, their boots making awful sucking sounds in the goo as they went. At length they reached a tunnel on the other end of the cavern, and they entered it, leaving the cavern – and the bugs – behind.

Ampir led the way, walking further into the dark tunnel. Most of his lights vanished overhead, leaving a few to illuminate the way. The tunnel was small compared to those that came before, maybe twenty feet high and ten feet across. Like the others, however, it was covered in Reaper vines. Even with the lights overhead, they could only see a few dozen feet in front of them. The lights cast long shadows across the Reaper vines, shadows that shifted eerily as the lights moved forward. The tunnel began to angle downward, slightly at first, then more steeply. After a few minutes, they came to a fork in the tunnel.

"Which way do..." Ariana began, but Ampir strode into the rightmost tunnel without hesitation. She glanced at Kyle, who shrugged. How the man knew which way to go was beyond him. "Are you sure this is the right way?" Ariana called out after Ampir. He said nothing, of course. Ariana turned to Kyle. "Did he say anything?"

"Nope," Kyle replied. Ariana looked peeved, but there was little either of them could do about it. Wherever Ampir went, they had to follow. They did so silently, this new tunnel taking them on a winding downward slope. Eventually they came to another fork, and Ampir chose the rightmost one again. Kyle felt Ariana squeeze his hand as they went ever deeper into the earth, her gait slowing.

"What's wrong?" he asked.

"I can feel him," Ariana answered. "It's stronger now," she added. "Louder. Before it was just fragments of thoughts, but now..." She trailed off, her eyes unfocusing.

"What?"

"He's everywhere," she replied, snapping to. She paused for a long moment, then shook her head. "It's like being in a noisy crowd," she described. "I can hear what he's thinking, but he's thinking so many things at once that I can't understand any of it."

"Are you okay?" Kyle asked, giving her hand a squeeze.

"No," she answered. She stared at him then, her brown eyes wide against her pale skin. She suddenly looked terrified. "I don't like this," she continued. "I think he's more powerful than we thought. A *lot* more powerful." She turned to Ampir, then, still striding through the tunnel ahead of them. If the Battle-Runic had heard them talking, he didn't show it.

"We've got Ampir," Kyle reassured, noticing the direction of Ariana's gaze. She hardly seemed comforted by the fact.

"He's only one man," she countered. "Sabin's...he's *big*. I don't think he's even human anymore."

"Sometimes I think the same thing about him," Kyle replied wryly, nodding at Ampir. Ariana didn't smile. Kyle sighed, putting an arm around her shoulders. "We have to trust him," he insisted.

"Why?" Ariana asked. Kyle gave her a tight smile.

"We don't have a choice."

Chapter 33

Sabin withdrew from the minds of the seventy-eight Chosen embedded in the domed death machine that guarded the entrance of his lair, unable to help himself from smiling inwardly. If he could have laughed, he would have.

Twenty centuries, and Ampir hadn't changed a bit.

He felt almost giddy, a sensation he hadn't experienced in an eternity...one he'd almost forgotten even existed. This was the moment he'd been waiting for ever since Ampir had been revealed. The moment to share his masterpiece with the only other person alive who could possibly understand it, and appreciate it. The culmination of millennia of effort, the creation of a mind beyond description, a consciousness greater than anything the world had ever seen.

And to share his grand plan for the ultimate ascension of Man! A path to a nobler race, one no longer so consumed with personal gain at the expense of their fellows. To a people connected to each other in a way that would make their brute, selfish tendencies impossible. To be connected as *he* was connected; to understand humanity as *he* understood it.

Sabin ignored the eternal agony of his flesh, knowing that the fruits of his labors were more than worth the sacrifice of his suffering. He scanned his Chosen, sensing Ampir and the two children entering the hive of one of his oldest Queens. A creature even older than himself...and the inspiration for his grand plan, and indeed his very existence.

He turned to another Chosen then, casting a sliver of his consciousness to it. He had a sudden desire to experience a memory he'd revisited many times before. One of his last fully preserved memories as a mortal, and one of the happiest times of his life.

* * *

Sabin barely notices the musty air of his underground laboratory, a single, large room built into the side of a hill. He sits before a long wooden table, upon which are rows of glass jars. He grabs one of them, pulling it toward himself, and stares at it intently. A single insect is inside, crawling madly along the side of the jar. A white, round-bodied insect with a small, jet-black head...and the one species he has been studying almost exclusively for the last three years.

The Reapers, he calls them.

Sabin observes the insect for a moment longer, then pushes the jar away, grabbing another one. This is filled with tiny, needle-shaped crystals, a quarter of the length of an eyelash. Painstakingly extracted from the brains of the reapers he has collected, they are an absolute marvel of natural runic technology. Of course, he never would have realized this had he not, on a whim, created a powerful lens using gravity fields to magnify the crystals. He'd discovered their microscopic runes then, all two hundred and forty-six of them, packed into that tiny space.

He stares at the crystals, then turns to a stack of papers on the table to his right, his notes on those very runes. A page for each one of them, with a symbol written in standard Runic notation, and his observations after weaving each. More pages on the connections and interactions between the runes. A veritable encyclopedia of information, over two thousand pages long, written about something smaller than a grain of rice.

He sighs then, rubbing his eyes for a moment, then gazing across his simple laboratory. It is hard for him to believe that it's been five years – to the day – since he'd escaped from that prison cell in the Orjanian mine. Since the worst day of his life.

Sabin stands up from his chair, grimacing at the steady, burning pain running from the side of his left forearm down to the last two fingers of his left hand. A remnant of the last two weeks, when the pain had consumed his entire arm. His attacks were much more severe now, and were lasting far longer than they had before. And now, even when they finally abated, they never did so entirely, always leaving a slight burning sensation behind. A little weakness, a little numbness.

He was running out of time.

The door to his lab opens, a young woman stepping through. She is tall, slender, and breathtakingly beautiful, with skin as black as night and long dark hair that springs wildly from her head in tight curls. With only a loincloth covering her, her breasts bare, she is a marvel to behold. She walks up to Sabin, leaning over to give him a soft, lingering kiss on the cheek.

"Morning love," she greets, her sultry voice sending shivers down his spine, her scent intoxicating. Sabin smiles.

"Morning," he replies. He still can't believe his luck, that he has found such a woman. Smart, confident, and sexy, she is perfect for him. They'd met a few years ago, and married soon after.

Finally, for the first time in his life, he was truly happy.

"Going to work?" she inquires. Sabin nods.

"For a bit," he confirms. She straightens up.

"Take your time my love," she says. "I'll help you relax when you come home," she adds with a slight smile. She waves at him, then walks out of the lab, closing the door behind her. Sabin stares at her retreating form, finding himself contemplating far more pleasant things than his research. Then he shakes his head to clear it, gazing at the stack of papers before him. He sighs.

Time to get to work.

He stands with some difficulty, walking to the front door and stepping through. The forest opens up before him, a magnificent tapestry of green and brown, with a brilliant blue sky above. He feels the sun strike him instantly with its warming rays, and it feels wonderful. He closes his eyes, savoring the sensation.

"Good morning," a man's voice bellows, and Sabin opens his eyes, spotting a tall, black-skinned man waving to him some twenty feet away. Nearly naked, his body covered in black tattoos, and carrying a long spear, he is someone Sabin would never have expected himself to associate with.

"Good morning, Calef," Sabin replies, waving back. The son of the eldest Joined, Calef is next in line to undergo the ritual to place the Reaper vines within his flesh. He is also an extraordinarily gifted Weaver; while lacking in the academic rigor expected of students in the Secula Magna, the man possesses an intuition for magic that would have been the envy of the Empire's great instructors.

"Your wife was looking for you," Calef states. Sabin nods.

"She found me," he replies, continuing forward.

Sabin shakes his head, marveling at how he'd ended up here, in one of the most remote jungles in the world, accepted and even beloved of a tribe of what were widely considered to be deadly, xenophobic savages.

He had his cowardice to thank for that. After escaping from his prison cell, he'd blamed himself bitterly for the destruction of the Empire, and Vera's murder. He'd attempted suicide – again – and failed again. Then he'd wandered the countryside, living like an animal, using his magic to hunt small animals and create shelter. He'd entered into madness then, vowing to live the rest of his life alone. To never allow his good intentions to destroy the lives of those he loved, and to never love another enough to care if they were destroyed.

Those had been dark times. Times best forgotten.

Eventually, however, his better nature had returned to him, the loneliness of such an existence prompting him to yearn for the company of others. He'd remembered his dream then, to study amongst the legendary Weavers of the Barren tribes, to learn of their strange magic and culture. He'd traveled northwest to find them, and find them he had. They'd almost killed him outright, and would have had it not been for the very invention that had earned him renown across the late Empire: his universal translator. Amazed by this technology, they'd taken him in, and had grown to trust him. And, in the last few years, he'd learned as much from them as they had from him.

Sabin stretches his arms to his sides, then walks forward through the forest, his boots crunching on the fallen twigs and leaves. He walks with a bad limp, a reminder of a particularly bad bout of his peculiar disease a year ago. He'd lost all use of his left leg then, and the pain – as if his entire leg had been immersed in boiling water – had been unbearable. If it had not been for the narcotic herbs his wife had administered to him, Sabin would have certainly found the courage to end his life then. The pain had eventually faded, but his leg had never fully recovered.

He limps along, and it isn't long before he finds himself coming up to a sheer cliff wall, and the mouth of a cave. The trees around the cave are without leaves, the shrubs nearly picked clean of theirs as well. Twelve feet high and ten feet wide, the mouth of the cave is shrouded in darkness, the bodies of small animals and birds strewn across its entrance. Most have been stripped bare of their flesh, leaving only bones behind.

The work of the Reapers.

Sabin enters the cave, a small runic device in the necklace he wears converting the deadly carbon dioxide filling the cavern to oxygen and carbon dust. He continues forward, traveling down the long, narrow tunnel as he has so many times in the past, until he comes to the end of it. He spots a narrow hole in the ground, and lowers himself through it, dropping down into the narrow vertical shaft below. The magical boots he wears slow his fall, and it is well that they do; the shaft is over a hundred feet deep, sandwiched between two sheer rock walls. He reaches the bottom, and drops to his belly, sliding under a narrow gap between the wall and the floor. He reaches the large cavern beyond, and rises to his feet. And though he's been here hundreds of times in the last three years, he can't help but smile.

Before him is a massive underground cavern, its floor, walls, and ceiling crawling with black, spindly Reaper vines. A large pond sits in the middle of the cavern, a ring of white crystals surrounding lining its perimeter. The roots of the Reaper vines are embedded in these crystals, and a layer of slimy organic material oozes from these roots, protecting and nurturing them. Beyond this are a veritable army of Reapers, the same small bugs he had back in his lab. They ignore him, well aware after years of daily visits that he poses no threat to them. Or more importantly, to their Queen.

He steps forward, up to the edge of the subterranean pond, staring down into it. A much larger Reaper, at least two feet long and possessed of six tentacles that floated lazily in the still water, sat at the bottom of the pond.

The Reaper Queen.

He stares down at the thing, smiling to himself. It itself has no eyes, no ears, but he knows very well that it is aware of him. That, in fact, it *can* see him, through the millions of Reapers crawling in this chamber. For, through the tiny crystals embedded in their brains, the Reapers send their thoughts and sensations back to their Queen. And through these crystals, the Queen has utter control over the simple minds of her brood.

What a revelation that knowledge had been!

Sabin stares down at the Queen for a moment longer, then turns his gaze upward, at the Reaper vines crawling up the rock walls to the small hole in the center of the domed ceiling above, through which a small stream cascades into a waterfall down to the pond below. Then he looks down, grabbing a small hunk of white crystal from the edge of the pond, staring at its glittering facets.

The Void mineral, found at last.

Another revelation, that. The same mineral he'd seen in Gunthar's prison cell, the one that had drained Sabin of his magic, the simple white crystal had proven to be the very substance he'd been searching for for years. To think that the answer to one of the most important questions in magic theory had been waiting here, in this cavern, all along. Waiting for him to find it.

Even after three years, it still gives him goosebumps.

He turns back to the bottom of the lake, watching as Reapers come to the edge of the pond, bits of leaves and animal tissue in their little mouths, probably brain tissue. They dive into the water, using their little legs to swim to the bottom, to the hollow ends of the Queen's tentacles. They feed their Queen, who extracts the Void mineral from the brain tissue and excretes it into the pond, saturating the water over time. The Void crystals form on the irregular rocky edges of the pond bottom, and at its shores, supplying the Reaper vines' roots. The Reaper vines, in turn, use the Void mineral to grow and power their incredible capacity to absorb and discharge magic. Where the Reaper vines grow, magic is drained from the surrounding environment...thus the unique magic-stealing property of the Barrens.

An ecosystem like no other on Doma.

Sabin turns to one of the Reaper vines, studying its smooth, black bark. Another amazing substance, the bark is the only material he knows of that is a complete insulator of magic. He'd fashioned the black cloak he wore from the substance, to limit the loss of magic from his flesh. Similarly, the Reapers chew on the bark and digest it, depositing the black insulating substance into the flesh around their heads. This, he knows from his experiments, is critical for their survival. Or rather, their immortality. For most of the Reapers in this cavern are no longer truly alive; they are undead, kept animate only by the tiny crystals embedded in their brains, and the extraordinary runes within. Without the insulation around these crystals, they would lose magic from the surrounding Reaper vines – whose appetite for magic is nearly insatiable – and they would quickly die.

He'd tested that theory, stripping the insulation from the Reapers in his lab, and watching as they slowly stopped moving. Streaming magic to them reanimated them instantly. Killing a Reaper that was still alive – and not yet undead – resulted in it entering the undead state, no longer needing food or water.

Fascinating.

Sabin grimaces as the pain in his left forearm flares up, rubbing it briskly with his right hand. It's no use, of course. He reaches into his pants pocket, retrieving a clump of leaves from it, and pops them into his mouth, chewing vigorously. The bitter taste of the narcotic within numbs his tongue, and he swallows, already starting to feel the pain in his forearm abating. He feels a wave of nausea, and ignores it, knowing that it will pass soon. A Reaper crawls onto his boot, then stops, seemingly to stare at him. Sabin stares back, his head swimming slightly as the narcotic kicks in.

Immortality.

He sighs, running a hand through his thinning hair. All white now, seemingly overnight. Though in his mind he is still a young man, his body tells him the truth. With every betrayal, it shows him that his time is running out.

He stares at the Reaper, then gently brushes it from his boot, turning away from the pond and its silent Queen.

That the Queen is sentient, even intelligent, is almost certain. While her brood is undead, she is alive, guiding her children with her wisdom, for the protection and betterment of the colony. There is no dissent, no possibility of civil war or strife. The Queen lives for her children, and her children obey the Queen.

If only humanity could be so wise...so unified and peaceful.

Sabin walks back the way he came, sliding under the gap between the floor and the wall above, then flying upward through the narrow shaft to the tunnel above. He limps back to the entrance of the cave, feeling the sunlight bathe his cool skin as he emerges from its shadows. He barely feels it, his mind too preoccupied to notice its gentle warmth.

Immortality, he muses.

The thought of it sends a shiver down his spine. The Reapers – even the undead ones – are mostly autonomous, he believes. The Queen *can* control them, but it would be far more efficient if she didn't need to do so constantly. No, they *had* to be autonomous. Which meant they were immortal, and possessed of their own minds.

He thinks back to his two thousand pages of notes on the tiny crystals that granted the Reapers their never-ending lives, and feels a burst of motivation strike him. If it is possible to grant immortality to a simple insect, then it might just be possible to do so for a human

507

being. And perhaps even to allow two people to communicate their thoughts to each other, to understand each other in a way never possible before. A society of men and women, able to know each other in this way, would be incapable of the atrocities of Nespo and Gunthar.

Sabin limps back into the woods toward his laboratory, walking faster now, feeling the weight of Time on his shoulders. There is so much work left to be done, and so little time left to do it. He can no longer afford to kill time. For it is slowly – but surely – killing him.

* * *

The muted shriek of the wind blowing past Petra's gravity shield assaulted Kalibar's ears as they flew through the air toward the Spine of Grimore, their feet only a few yards above the treetops of the Barren forest. The ever-present white mist hanging there swirled into the vacuum created by their passage, leaving a contrail behind them. Kalibar hung on to Petra's back, his arms around her shoulders, acutely aware of her body pressed against his. He shifted his weight, feeling growing discomfort at the sensation. It had been a long, long time since he'd been this close to a woman...and he'd never been this close to a woman like Petra.

The curse of men, he thought wryly, *that I would think of such a thing at a time like this.*

It wasn't long before they neared the bottom of the Spine, an almost vertical rock wall extending from the base of the mountain to the ledge they'd faced the Chosen on. Kalibar closed his eyes, trying to recall which side of the Spine Ariana had fallen from. The Chosen had been facing Mount Grimore's peak, and had been holding Ariana with its right hand...which meant that they should see the peak to their right, and fly to the leftmost end of the Spine.

"Over there," Kalibar yelled, pointing to that very spot. Petra complied, flying above the treetops toward it. Kalibar scanned the wall of the Spine, searching the occasional rocky outcroppings for Ariana's body, but saw nothing. "Set us below the trees," he ordered. They reached the sheer cliff wall, then descended through the

508

swirling mist to the forest floor below. Kalibar disengaged from Petra then, turning in a slow circle, searching the forest floor and the tree branches above for any signs of Ariana's black uniform.

Nothing.

Kalibar caught Petra staring upward, and frowned at her.

"What's wrong?" he asked.

"I'm keeping an eye out for Chosen," she replied, lowering her gaze to look at him. "If we see one, we run."

"Agreed."

"We should look for broken branches on the ground," Petra proposed. Kalibar nodded. It made sense; Ariana would have snapped off quite a few branches from the dense foliage above on her way down. They got to it, walking along the edge of the sheer rock wall of the Spine's base, keeping their eyes peeled. They walked silently for several minutes, until Petra stopped, turning her head to stare at Kalibar. He stopped as well, frowning at her.

"What is it?" he asked.

"How did we end up at the bottom of the Spine before?" she asked. "I don't remember."

"You attacked the Chosen," Kalibar answered. "After you faked your own death." He paused then. "You took your time, you know."

"I would defend myself," Petra replied a bit tersely, "...if I remembered anything." Kalibar had to give her that.

"The Chosen knocked you out cold, then threw you at me. We fell off of the edge of the Spine."

"What happened then?" she asked. Kalibar paused, feeling suddenly uncomfortable. He turned away from her, continuing to scan the surroundings as he walked. He felt her hand on his shoulder. "Tell me," she pressed. He sighed.

"I didn't have much magic left," he admitted. "I...sensed magic coming from your necklace, and used it to slow our fall. But there wasn't enough magic in it."

Petra blinked, putting a hand to her upper chest, clearly realizing that her necklace was no longer there.

"Where is it?" she asked, appearing alarmed.

509

"Probably somewhere near where we landed," he answered. "I must have dropped it after being impaled."

"You're being fresh," Petra noted, glaring at him. Her glare wavered, however, and she nodded at him. "My grandfather would have been happy to know that his gift saved my life."

"Indeed," Kalibar murmured. Petra frowned then.

"I didn't get badly injured from the fall," she realized, stopping suddenly and turning to face him. He stopped as well. "But you did."

"Well, yes," Kalibar replied, suddenly feeling uncomfortable again. Petra stared at him, then folded her arms under her breasts. Kalibar kept his eyes on hers only by virtue of his considerable will.

"How?" she pressed.

"I knew I didn't have enough magic to save both of us," he admitted. "So at the last moment, I created a large gravity shield around you. It slowed your fall."

Petra's eyes widened, and her mouth fell open. She stared at him for a long, silent moment, then snapped her jaw shut with a click.

"You saved me," she stated bluntly.

"I did."

"Because you knew you could heal if I woke?" she pressed. Kalibar shrugged.

"To be honest, I'd forgotten about that," he admitted sheepishly. Petra arched one eyebrow.

"So you sacrificed yourself to save me," she repeated. Kalibar paused, then nodded.

"Yes, I suppose I did."

"Why?"

"I don't know," Kalibar admitted, rubbing the back of his head. It still felt strange to not feel any hair there. "I didn't have time to think it through. I just did it."

"Yesterday you spared my life, trusting me not to kill you," Petra stated, her tone strangely flat. "And today you saved my life at the expense of your own."

Kalibar said nothing, but he felt his cheeks grow warm, a sensation that he hadn't felt in a long, long time. He found himself unable to meet her gaze, and turned away, staring off at nothing in particular.

"You flirted with me last night," she accused, putting her hands on her hips. Kalibar sighed.

"True," he admitted. "Not well, I admit. It's been a...long time since I've...well..." He trailed off then, and Petra arched her eyebrow again.

"How long?" she asked.

"A *long* time," Kalibar admitted. "Over thirty years." Not counting what had happened at the Arena, of course. Kalibar grimaced, pushing the thought out of his mind.

Petra stared at him, her eyebrows rising.

"I was married once," Kalibar explained, resuming his walk forward. Petra strode quickly to catch up. "My wife lost my son in labor, and she...blamed me. She killed herself, and that was that."

"I'm sorry," Petra murmured. Now it was her turn to look away, although it was impossible to tell if she was blushing. Kalibar sighed; it was peculiar that some wounds never fully healed. Even after decades, the memory still had a terrible power over him.

"It was a long time ago," he muttered.

"And you haven't been with a woman since?" she asked, her tone incredulous. Kalibar cleared his throat.

"I kept myself busy," he countered, more defensively than he would have liked. Petra smirked.

"You must have."

"Focusing on my career," Kalibar clarified with a wry smirk.

"Becoming a warrior?" she guessed. Kalibar nodded.

"That and...other things."

"So you were like me," she observed. "You lived alone, and devoted your life to learning magic."

"For a long time, yes," he agreed. Petra mulled this over, then glanced at him sidelong as they walked.

"Do you regret it?" she asked.

"Sometimes," he admitted. "Mine has been a lonely life." He turned away from her. "I suppose I never realized that until I met Kyle and Ariana." He felt Petra's hand on his shoulder.

511

"I'm sorry."

"Me too," Kalibar replied.

"We'll find them," Petra promised.

And then her head jerked up and to the left, and her eyes widened.

"Run!" she cried.

She grabbed Kalibar's hands, turning around and draping them over her shoulders, then bolted up into the air, flying upward around the tree branches. Within seconds, they burst through the white mist bathing the treetops, accelerating into the blue sky. Petra shot high into the air, aiming toward the smaller mountain they'd come from – Mount Kress.

"What's wrong?" Kalibar shouted over the shrieking of the wind.

"Behind you!" Petra shouted back. Kalibar twisted around, peering over his shoulder. He saw dozens of black shapes flying through the air over the Spine of Grimore, toward the peak of the mountain beyond. At first he thought they were birds, but then he realized they were men in rippling black cloaks.

Chosen.

"I don't think they saw us," Kalibar exclaimed. None of the Chosen seemed to be flying after them.

"We'll wait for them to pass," Petra stated. "We'll circle back for Ariana later."

"Agreed," Kalibar replied. As eager as he was to find Ariana, he knew that facing so many Chosen was tantamount to suicide. He turned forward, relaxing against Petra, and allowed himself to be carried away.

I'll come for you, he promised silently.

And then he felt something slam into him from behind.

Kalibar heard Petra shout, felt himself tear away from her back. The world spun crazily around him, the wind shrieking as he tumbled through the air. He reached into his mind's eye instinctively, and found it utterly devoid of magic.

Panic seized him.

Suddenly he felt something slam into his back, felt arms wrapping around his torso. He looked down, seeing black-clad arms hugging him from behind.

Petra!

The spinning stopped, and then they were flying through the air above the treetops, weaving from side to side. Kalibar looked over his shoulder, spotting two cloaked figures flying after them, not a hundred feet away...and gaining fast.

Chosen, he realized. They'd been spotted after all!

He cursed under his breath, then gripped Petra's hand.

"Stream magic to me!" he shouted over the howling wind. He felt Petra flinch, then felt a vibration in his skull as magic poured into him.

And then he felt it drain away.

He cursed again, turning back to look at the Chosen. They were a dozen feet away now, a stream of blue light traveling from Petra and Kalibar to the exposed white crystals in one of the Chosen's forearms. He heard Petra swear, then realized they were falling toward the mist-shrouded treetops below...and fast.

"Pull up!" he shouted.

"I can't!" Petra yelled back. He felt his left foot get yanked backward as it struck a tree branch, felt his head lurching forward and downward.

"Gravity shields!" he cried.

His foot struck another branch, and then he was cartwheeling through the air, the world a spinning kaleidoscope of blue and green. He saw gravity shields appear around him, heard the sharp *crack* of branches snapping. Then the awful sensation of free-fall took him, followed by a sickening crunch, and a scream.

Chapter 34

Ampir's magical light sent white rays down and across the twisting, black tunnel that Kyle had followed down into the bowels of the earth, Ariana at his side. They'd long since gone silent, lulled into a kind of hypnosis by the never-ending maze of tunnels they'd passed through. Ampir had led them from one forking path to the next, until Kyle had lost count of how many times the tunnel had split. His only focus now was staying close to Ampir; without his grandfather, there would be no hope of him ever making it out of these tunnels. Even Ariana's incredible memory might not prove worthy of the task.

Still onward and downward the tunnels went.

The air was cool here, even frigid, but though he could feel the cold, his Battle-Runic armor kept him quite comfortable overall. Their footsteps echoed through the tunnels in a mind-numbing cadence, and Kyle found himself counting their steps until the numbers got too big, then starting over again.

One-oh-one, one-oh-two...

Then he blinked, realizing that something had changed.

He looked around as he walked, realizing that the tunnel had gotten much larger, so wide now that all three of them could have walked side-by-side with room to spare. In the distance, at the edge of Ampir's light, he saw a huge glittering ring nearly as wide around as the tunnel itself. He heard a *clunk*, and then another, and looked down, realizing that he was stepping onto a metallic platform that angled upward, then leveled off some seven or eight feet above the Reaper vine-covered floor. It was only wide enough to accommodate him and Ariana single-file, and he was forced to let go of her hand. She motioned for him to walk ahead of her, and he did so.

They continued forward, and it soon became apparent what the glittering ring ahead was. A ring of white crystals jutting out from the tunnel walls, ceiling, and floor, forming a tube that extended as far as the eye could see. Each crystal was over three feet wide at the base, and seven feet long, tapering to a razor-sharp point. Each crystal pointed toward the center of the tunnel, leaving just enough room for Ampir to pass through without stooping.

Kyle felt a chill run down his spine; he slowed, then stopped, feeling Ariana bump into him from behind.

"What's wrong?" Ariana asked. Of course she couldn't know; the Dead Man had never shown her the Void. But Kyle knew what it meant. What it *had* to mean.

Sabin was near.

"This is the Void," he whispered back. He explained how the Dead Man had brought him to a similar place back in the Arena. Ariana stared at the huge crystals all around her.

"What do all these crystals do?" she pressed.

"Drain magic," Kyle answered. Ariana seemed to accept that, continuing forward behind him. Then she stopped suddenly, with a sharp intake of breath.

"He sees us!" she whispered harshly.

"What?"

"Sabin's watching us," she clarified, putting a hand on his shoulder. She scanned the crystal-studded tunnel with her eyes. "I can *feel* him watching us." Kyle tensed up, peering up and down the narrow tunnel, but saw no one. The Void crystals refracted the rays of Ampir's hovering light, sending a brilliant kaleidoscope of shifting white shapes across the tunnel.

"How?" Kyle asked. Then he saw Ariana turn to one of the crystals beside her, and stop cold, her eyes narrowing. She leaned in a little, peering into the crystal, then lurched backward as if she'd been struck. "What's wrong?" he asked.

"Look," Ariana replied, pointing at the Void crystal. She looked terribly shaken. Kyle turned to the crystal, seeing its white, translucent glittering facets.

"I don't see anything," he admitted.

"Look deeper."

He did so, refocusing his eyes, and stepping to the side a little so he wasn't looking at the crystal dead on. He stared at the base, seeing the shadowy darkness there, then followed that darkness up to a foot before the crystal began to taper. He saw...*something* there.

"What is that?" he asked. He shifted to the side, seeing the shadow shift as the crystal's facets refracted the light. The movement gave shape to the shadow, defining two legs bent back at the knees at the base of the Void crystal. Kyle shifted his weight again, and followed the legs up to an emaciated torso, two thin arms by its sides, and a head tilted back at an impossible angle. He saw a face there, pale and sunken, a white diamond-shaped crystal embedded in its forehead.

With eyes staring right at him.

Kyle lurched backward, feeling the sharp point of the Void crystal behind him jutting into the small of his back. He turned and ran forward down the metal walkway toward Ampir, who had stopped and was watching them. Kyle ran up to the Battle-Runic, rubbing the spot where the Void crystal had poked him, and felt only cool metal there. His armor had allowed him to feel the sharpness of the crystal's point, but it had protected him.

"There's Chosen in the crystals!" Kyle exclaimed. He turned to another crystal, then another, seeing more contorted bodies within, their eyes facing inward toward the center of the chamber. "They're everywhere!"

"Yep," Ampir replied. The man turned away from Kyle and Ariana then, resuming his walk down the narrow platform. Kyle

516

watched him go, then sprinted to catch up with him, Ariana following close behind.

"Jesus," Kyle swore, staying as close as possible to Ampir's back. Ariana frowned at him.

"What?"

"Uh," Kyle began, realizing what he'd said. There was no way he was going to be able to explain *that* to her...certainly not now. "Nothing."

"They're alive," Ariana whispered in horror, staring at the crystals as they passed. "All of them." She swallowed then. "Like me." She put a hand on Kyle's shoulder from behind, pressing up against him. He wanted to say something to comfort her, but no words came. He imagined her trapped in one of those crystals, unable to move, a prisoner for eternity...and shuddered. The idea that Sabin had done this to his Chosen, had sentenced them to this horrifying fate, a fate worse than death...it was unthinkable.

Kyle walked behind Ampir silently, his eyes glued to Ampir's back, trying hard not to let his eyes stray to the countless Void crystals around him. Onward they went, their footsteps *clanging* on the metal platform below, the sound echoing through the long tunnel. Minutes passed, and still the tunnel stretched forward and slightly downward, a never-ending straight-shot into the bowels of Hell.

Kyle felt his eyes wandering to the side, fixating on the Void crystals as he passed them by. How many had they passed already? Thousands? Tens of thousands? All of them with Chosen, each very likely as powerful as the Dead Man. And the Dead Man alone could have faced the armies of the Empire and defeated them. Even with Ampir, what chance could they have against thousands of Chosen? Or even millions?

Suddenly, Ampir stopped.

Kyle bumped into the man's broad back, and Ariana in turned bumped into him. Kyle leaned to the side, peeking past Ampir's shoulder, and felt his body go cold. He heard Ariana gasp behind him, felt her hand grip his shoulder.

There, not ten feet from Ampir, an old man stood on the metal platform, hunched over a wooden cane. Not just old...ancient. His

517

thin, white hair hardly covered his pale, wrinkled and spotted skull, two cataract-glazed eyes peering from under drooping lids. His skin was thin as paper, and deeply wrinkled, his mouth twisted into a sickening grin. His breath hissed from the yellowed, broken stumps of what teeth remained.

"Welcome, Ampir," the old man rasped, resting both of his hands on his cane. His revolting smile curled into a smirk. "You're late."

* * *

Kyle backed up a step, feeling Ariana press against his back, her hands clutching at his shoulders, fingers digging into the armor there. Her strength was enormous, the pressure beyond description, but he felt no pain.

"Kyle..." he heard her whisper harshly in his ear. He could feel the panic in her voice. She pulled him backward a step, away from Ampir.

"Sabin," Ampir replied coolly.

"I expected you days ago," Sabin croaked in that leathery voice.

"Been busy," Ampir stated.

"Quite," Sabin murmured. "Visiting my Chosen all over the world. A remarkable discovery, your ability to teleport."

He vanished.

Kyle blinked, staring at the space where Sabin had been.

"I have to thank you for showing it to me," he heard a voice behind him say. He spun around, and saw Sabin standing behind them, not five feet from Ariana. She backed up into Kyle, pushing him backward as well. Sabin vanished again, and reappeared in front of Ampir. He smiled again. "It wasn't hard to extract the pattern from the useless noise you tried to hide it with. You'll find my mind is far more powerful than it once was."

"Congratulations," Ampir replied, his tone flat. "I figured it out when I was twelve."

"That's how you rescued me from Nespo's prison," Sabin deduced.

518

"My mistake."

"Yes, well," Sabin replied. "I've since learned not to be anyone's fool." He sighed then, tapping the butt of his cane on the platform below. "I still regret that Vera had to die for me to learn that lesson," he admitted, lowering his gaze. "I'm sorry, Ampir."

"I know."

Sabin turned around then, standing at the end of the platform. Beyond it, the tunnel extended as the eye could see. The Void crystals were longer, however, extending so far into the tunnel that their sharp points formed a channel barely more than a foot in diameter. He gestured at the crystals with one gnarled hand.

"Welcome to my home," he stated, turning around to face them again. He smiled apologetically. "I know it's not much to look at, but I don't get company often."

"I'll renovate it for you," Ampir offered coolly. Sabin laughed, a barking, wheezing sound that ended with a rattle in his throat.

"Always the warrior," he observed. "Solving your problems with violence."

"You're one to talk."

"I suppose I deserve that," Sabin admitted ruefully. He turned his sharp eyes on Kyle then, making Kyle lower his own gaze. "Sorry about the boy," he added. "I was merely attempting to extract information from him." He turned back to Ampir. "Although I admit I still don't understand your devotion to these children."

"He's Vera's grandson," Ampir stated.

Sabin stared at Ampir, then at Kyle, his eyes widening. He took a step back then, his mouth falling open, then snapping shut. He regained his composure quickly, returning his gaze to Ampir.

"Impossible," he retorted.

"He is," Ampir insisted.

"How?"

"Long story," Ampir replied. Sabin stared at Kyle for a long moment, studying him. Then his eyes widened.

"I see it," he murmured. "He has her eyes." He straightened his back then, as much as his twisted spine would allow. "I regret every wrong I've committed against you," he stated firmly. "I will never

519

again raise a hand against you, and I will see to it that anyone who does will wish they had never been born."

Kyle stared back at the ancient man, hardly able to comprehend what was happening.

"He can fight his own battles," Ampir countered.

"He will never need to," Sabin retorted. "I failed to protect Vera. I won't make that mistake with him." He turned to Ariana then. "And her...what is her significance?"

"She's Kyle's girlfriend," Ampir answered. Sabin arched one eyebrow.

"Is that so," he murmured. "I regret any pain I might have caused you by harming her," he added, nodding at Kyle. Ariana's grip on Kyle's shoulders intensified.

"No," she blurted out. Sabin turned to her. "No," she repeated furiously. "You don't get to apologize for what you did to me." Sabin said nothing, turning back to Ampir. Ariana's eyes widened. "Don't ignore me!" she shouted. "Look at me!"

Sabin turned to her, his expression suddenly flat.

"You murdered my parents!" Ariana accused, stepping forward suddenly. "You murdered *me*!" Kyle put his arms around her, trying to hold her back, but she was far too strong. She pushed past him, and was about to squeeze past Ampir when Ampir held up one hand, turning to face her.

"Stop," he commanded.

Ariana froze.

Sabin sighed, leaning on his cane with both hands again.

"I've helped – and hurt – a great many people in my life," he admitted. "Sometimes the greater good demands a lesser evil." He smiled sadly at Ariana. "Perhaps one day you will understand that."

Ariana opened her mouth to reply, but Ampir stopped her with one hand on her shoulder. Then he turned back to Sabin.

"I'm here," he said, removing his hand from Ariana's shoulder. "Where are you?"

Sabin's smile faded, and he stared at Ampir for a long, silent moment. Then he chuckled, the low, grating sound issuing forth from between his rotted teeth.

"Ever observant," he murmured, the corner of his mouth twisting into a smirk. "I've actually been looking forward to seeing you with my own eyes," he admitted. He turned around then, his stooped back facing them. He stepped to the edge of the platform, and suddenly the Void crystals beyond retracted, creating a wide tunnel ahead. Sabin turned back to face Ampir, gesturing at the tunnel. "This way," he rasped. Then he stepped off the edge of the platform. His feet dangled above the deadly peaks of the Void crystals below, his body levitating above them. Slowly he flew backward through the tunnel, still facing them.

Ampir paused, then strode up to the edge of the platform, the crystal-lined tunnel beyond reflecting off of his visor. Then he stepped off the platform, levitating forward just as Sabin had. Ampir gestured for Kyle and Ariana to follow.

Kyle hesitated, then followed Ariana as she stepped up to the edge of the platform. She stared down at the glittering spikes below, then turned to Kyle.

"Together?" she asked, holding out her hand. Kyle paused, then grabbed it.

"Together," he agreed.

They turned to face the edge of the platform.

"On three," Ariana said, bending her knees a little. "One...two...three!"

They jumped off of the platform, falling toward the vicious tips of the Void crystals. They stopped in mid-air a foot above the crystals, levitating above them. Then they floated forward through the tunnel, Ampir and Sabin a few feet ahead. Kyle saw Sabin drop down suddenly, and moments later, Ampir did the same. He tensed up, holding on to Ariana's hand. The floor ahead of them opened into a vertical, crystal-lined shaft.

"Watch out," he warned. "I think we're gonna-"

They dropped.

Ariana screamed, and Kyle felt his breath lock in his throat, his stomach flipping as he entered into free fall. Void crystals zipped past them from all sides as they plunged downward. Faster and faster they fell, until the points of the crystals were a blur, air rushing up all around them. Suddenly the tunnel ended, opening up into an enormous cavern. They dropped into that empty space, their limbs flailing, their screams echoing through the air.

This is it, he realized, his guts twisting with horror. *We're going to die.*

And then he felt his descent slowing, felt the G-forces pulling on his body as decelerated. He looked down seeing a floor hundreds of feet below, utterly saturated with softly glowing white Void crystals, their tapered ends pointing upward at him. He noticed a flash of green to his left, and turned to see a large ring of green crystals there. The green crystals surrounded the base of a huge, translucent white cylinder easily fifty feet in diameter. He followed the cylinder upward, saw it rising hundreds of feet to meet the ceiling above. Void crystals, some over a hundred feet long, hung from the ceiling, surrounded by normal-sized crystals. The entire chamber was bathed in a soft white glow emitted from each and every one of the crystals.

And in each and every one of the millions upon millions of crystals, a Chosen lay contorted within, its eyes facing into the cavern.

"My god," he heard Ariana gasp.

He saw Ampir and Sabin floating below, and he continued to decelerate until he was floating alongside Ampir. Sabin levitated before them, the massive crystalline cylinder a mere fifty feet behind him.

"Welcome," Sabin stated, spreading his arms out wide. "...to my masterpiece." He lowered his hands. "You are the first to see it since its completion."

"I'm touched," Ampir grumbled.

"Yes, well," Sabin murmured. They began to move forward through the air then, Sabin still facing them, until they were only ten or so feet away from the huge cylinder behind Sabin. He smiled. "You wanted to meet me..."

He floated off to one side.

Ariana was the first to gasp, her fingers squeezing Kyle's hand. Kyle shifted his eyes from Sabin's stooped form, looking at the cylinder before him. He saw a darkness there, deep within, and squinted, peering inside. A soft glow appeared within the cylinder, illuminating the shadow.

It was Kyle's turn to gasp.

There, suspended in the center of the translucent cylinder, was a body. It was gruesomely thin, its arms and legs not much more than skin and bone. Its flesh sank into the spaces between its ribs, pale, purple veins crawling across its paper-thin skin. The rope-like tendons of its neck jutted out, leading to a wrinkled, sunken face. A sparse white beard surrounded its grotesque mouth, frozen in a toothless snarl. Thin white hair capped its skull.

And there, within its sunken sockets, two eyes stared outward at them.

Kyle stared at the man suspended in the cylinder, goosebumps rising on his arms. Sabin sighed.

"As you can see," he stated, his eyes on Ampir. "...I didn't age as gracefully as you."

"You look like shit," Ampir declared. Sabin chuckled.

"You always did have a way with words."

Ampir stared at Sabin's true body for a long, silent moment, then shook his head.

"Why?"

"Necessity," Sabin's avatar explained. "As a mortal, I was afflicted by a disease of the brain..."

"You don't say," Ampir interjected. Sabin grimaced.

"...that led to me being incapable of moving. Trapped in my own body, as it were. Even immortality could not change that. My only recourse was to use this," he continued, gesturing at his stooped, ancient form, "...and the bodies of my Chosen to continue my work."

"Your work?"

"Originally it was to create this," he replied, gesturing at the huge chamber. "At first I only wanted to create my Chosen, and guide them to continue my research. Over time I realized the limitations of my consciousness, the limitation of *any* single consciousness." He turned around in the air, facing his own emaciated body. "Then came my epiphany: I could take over the minds of my Chosen to control their bodies...why not also use their minds as my own? Why

523

not use their minds to create the greatest single consciousness ever to exist?"

"They're your slaves," Ampir observed. Sabin shrugged.

"Servants to a cause," he corrected. "A sacrifice of a few to ensure a great future for the many."

"Ironic that *you* should say that," Ampir grumbled.

"Yes, I am aware that Nespo used the same justification," Sabin replied evenly. Ampir shook his head, then gestured at the millions of Void crystals lining the chamber.

"This is beyond Nespo," he retorted. "Beyond Gunthar. They never trapped millions of people in stone prisons, imprisoning them for eternity while raping their minds."

"I guarantee you," Sabin responded coolly, "...that I have suffered, and do suffer, more than any of them." He gestured to his true body. "I do not ask them to do anything that I haven't done. They sacrifice themselves as I do, to see that their descendants have a life greater than their own." He stared at Ampir disapprovingly. "What parent would not make the same sacrifice for their children?"

"You didn't give them a choice."

"A few gave themselves willingly," Sabin countered. "But yes, most were...drafted into service. And most are only half-aware, as if in a dream."

"That doesn't make it right."

"That," Sabin retorted sharply, "...is a matter of perspective."

"You should worry about my perspective," Ampir shot back.

"Oh, I doubt that," Sabin murmured. "My mind can think a thousand thoughts for every one you have. I've already considered every possible way for this meeting to conclude, and I've planned accordingly." He smiled grotesquely. "I'm not afraid of you anymore, Ampir."

"You should be."

"I didn't bring you here to fight you," Sabin countered. "I brought you here to share my work with you." He smiled. "We're two of a kind Ampir...no one else can understand us. No one else has lived twenty centuries, seen empires rise and fall, entire civilizations be born, then die. No one else understands Man for

524

what he is, and what he can be. With my guidance, and yours, Man will grow beyond his limitations, and achieve true transcendence."

"They don't need you," Ampir retorted. "Or me."

"Oh but they do," Sabin argued. "Without a god to guide them, they're nothing but savages, blindly living one generation to the next, repeating the same mistakes over and over again, never learning, never caring what came before." He shook his head. "Ask any man about history, and you'll see how ignorant they are. They have no concept of what came before. In a few generations, no one will remember that they even existed."

"You haven't seen what they can do."

"I have eyes everywhere," Sabin retorted. "I can see every continent in the world at the same time, every government. I created half of them."

"Let them go, Sabin."

"I can't do that," Sabin replied.

"Then I will."

Sabin stared at Ampir silently for a moment, then gave him a tight smile.

"I should remind you that you're two hundred feet above the ground," he stated, his voice deceptively mild. "And that I can drain you of magic instantaneously, at any time." He shook his head. "No one can weave magic in this chamber," he declared. "Except me."

"Try me," Ampir shot back. Sabin shrugged.

"So be it."

The blue light of the gravity fields surrounding them vanished. Kyle felt his heart leap into his throat, and gripped Ariana's hand tightly, expecting to plunge down to the vicious-looking spikes below.

But nothing happened.

"Impressive," Sabin murmured. "Let me guess...your armor insulates against magic loss, and you've woven gravity fields inside of them?"

Ampir smirked.

"Your armor must have the same insulating material the Reaper vines have," Sabin deduced. "No wonder your armor is black."

"It wasn't always," Ampir stated. Sabin's eyebrows knit together.

"Yes, now that I think of it," he murmured. "Your original armor was gold." He gave a twisted smile. "That's why they called you the 'golden warrior' of the Empire." He chuckled then. "You do have a sense of irony, don't you? Disguising yourself as yourself." The smile faded. "Why did you change your armor?"

"I fought against Verhan during their 'liberation,' remember?" Ampir answered. Sabin nodded.

"I do," he agreed. "I always wondered why the Empire couldn't defeat the Barren tribes when they had you on their side."

"They didn't," Ampir countered. "I refused to fight the tribes."

"But you discovered the Reaper bark," Sabin deduced. "And applied it to your armor." He nodded. "Very clever."

"It's over, Sabin," Ampir stated. He gestured at the Void crystals all around them. "Free these people. Let them rest. Humanity doesn't need to be controlled. Help them find their own way."

"I tried that once," Sabin retorted. "It failed."

"Let them fail," Ampir shot back. "It's the only way they'll grow."

"No," Sabin stated, his tone sharp. "*Not* the only way. I've guided humanity to heights of civilization they haven't even imagined since the fall of the Empire. I've created civilizations across the globe, on every continent."

"They would have done it themselves."

"Not like this," Sabin retorted. "The world has been at peace for over two hundred years," he added. "No major nations have gone to war with each other. There is no slavery. There are no despots, no demagogues." He shook his head. "All this would be impossible if humanity were allowed to govern themselves. Men with power gain more at the expense of the powerless, taking advantage of the ignorance and rage of the very people they abuse, redirecting it for their benefit. It's in their nature."

Ampir put a hand on Kyle's shoulder.

"I've seen what humanity can accomplish without you. Without me," he argued.

"So have I," Sabin countered. "And without me, they would resume the cycle of corruption and violence. I am the only one who can bring order and justice to this world...*true* justice."

526

"It's over," Ampir stated. "If you don't end this, I will."

Sabin stared at Ampir, then started to laugh. Great, rasping bellows echoed throughout the massive chamber, his thin lips stretched wide over his rotted teeth and gums. He ended with a wheezing chuckle, shaking his head.

"You can't," he proclaimed. "And even if you could, you won't."

"Try me," Ampir growled.

"You won't," Sabin repeated, "...because if you do, everything you've fought for will be lost." He smiled. "You *can't*, because only I can weave magic. You can't attack me here."

"I won't need to."

"It's pointless to argue," Sabin stated. "If you kill me, my Chosen – millions of them – will rise at once, and they have orders to destroy every city of every country in the world. Thousands of Behemoths will descend from the skies, and they will erase Man from the face of the planet."

"You really do care about them," Ampir grumbled. Sabin shrugged.

"I do," he replied. "Think of it as an...insurance policy. Ensuring my safety is the best way to protect them."

"By threatening to destroy them."

"It will never come to that, will it, Ampir?" Sabin mused. "I'll tell you what; I'm willing to let you have your Empire, if you want it. I'll withdraw my Chosen from it, and they will not attack again."

"You're right," Ampir agreed. "They won't." He reached into the recesses of his armor then, and pulled out a familiar black cylinder. It was the bomb Kyle had carried all the way from the Empire.

"What is that?" Sabin asked.

"The most powerful weapon of all," Ampir replied. He touched one end of the cylinder, and it flashed red, extending outward to reveal silver metal beneath. Then he tapped the *other* end, and it too flashed red, extending outward. He tossed it up into the air, and it hovered there for a moment. Then the cylinder split in half, each end shooting in the opposite direction, connected by a brilliant line of red light. The entire thing began to spin, forming a red circle in front of Sabin, spinning faster and faster, until it was a blur.

"Am I supposed to be afraid?" Sabin asked wryly. "What kind of weapon is this?" Ampir smirked.

"Information."

The red circle began to rotate on its vertical axis, picking up speed until it formed a perfect red sphere before them, over twenty feet in diameter. Bright red dots appeared on the surface of the sphere, followed by thin red lines. They were, Kyle realized, the outlines of Doma's continents. And the tiny red dots were speckled across all of them. Millions of red dots.

"What is this?" Sabin demanded, staring at the globe. The hologram gave the illusion of slowly rotating, like a planet in space.

"The location of every Chosen outside of this cave complex," Ampir replied. "Or, more precisely, their shards."

Sabin stared at the globe, his eyes widening.

"How did you get this?"

"You just gave it to me," Ampir answered. He draped an arm over Ariana's shoulder then. "Through her."

"*What?*"

"I made some modifications to the Dead Man's shard after I killed him," Ampir explained. "It listens in to your network, but only from a short distance." He stared up at the spinning globe, the red lights reflecting off of his visor. "When she was close to your Chosen, she could hear your commands to them. Now that she's close to you, I have access to your entire network through her." He gave Sabin a tight smile. "Thanks for inviting her in, by the way."

"Clever," Sabin conceded. "But useless. I've just changed the way I communicate with my Chosen." He smiled. "My mind can think a thousand thoughts at once," he added. "You don't stand a chance against me."

"Too late," Ampir retorted.

"Too late for what?"

"I'm revoking your insurance policy."

And then, almost as one, the red dots on the globe vanished.

Chapter 35

Kalibar heard someone moaning.

He ignored the sound, far too tired to pay it much mind. He was sleepy, so sleepy. It was a blissful feeling, really. It reminded him of when he'd been a boy. Of snuggling into his warm, comfortable bed after a day filled with adventure, of spending time with his father on the lake. So tired that he felt like sinking into his pillow, drunk with the ecstasy of falling into his dreams.

It was heaven, this feeling.

He heard the moan come again, and felt mildly irritated by it. He was, after all, trying to sleep. He wished it would just go away, but he was too tired to make the supreme effort of asking. He sighed inwardly, feeling as if he were floating on a cloud. His arms and legs felt heavy to the point of being immovable. Not that it mattered...he had no desire to move them.

Again, the moaning.

He felt his irritation return, stronger this time. It cut through him, jarring him from that profound sense of peace, and he had the sudden urge to lash out at whoever was disturbing him. He felt a sharp pain in his neck, followed by shooting pains in his arms and legs, and he heard the moaning come again.

It was only then that he realized that the person who was moaning was *him*.

He opened his eyes.

Piercing blue light seared his retinas, and he groaned, squeezing his eyelids shut. He paused, then opened them again, seeing a dark shape appear above him. His eyes focused, and he realized he was staring at a person's face. A woman, with skin so dark it was almost black. Her eyes were wide, her lips moving. A halo of faint blue light surrounded her head.

I can't understand you, he thought.

He felt hands grip his temples, then fall away. Then he felt a sharp stinging sensation on his left cheek, his head jerking to the right. He gasped.

"...coming!" he heard a woman's voice shout in his ear. He turned his head forward.

"What?" he croaked. He stared at the woman above him, realizing that he was lying on the ground, and that she was laying on her belly beside him, propping herself on her elbows.

Petra!

"Get up!" she yelled. "They're coming!" She raised her hand to slap him again.

"I'm up, I'm up," he blurted out, grunting, then pushing himself up into a sitting position. He rose shakily to his feet, then extended one hand. "Come on," he urged. Petra shook her head.

"I can't," she replied. "My leg," she added with a grimace. Kalibar looked down, spotting her left ankle. It was deformed, rotated at a grotesque angle. Her uniform had torn behind her shattered ankle, the rip extending all the way up to her mid-calf. The skin below had torn as well, yellow fat exposed under the gaping wound. Blue light leaked from the flesh there. Kalibar put a hand to his mouth, then dropped down to his knees before her.

"Petra..." he began, then his voice caught in his throat.

"I filled you with magic," she said between clenched teeth. She took a deep, hissing breath in, then grabbed his hand with her own. "Go," she ordered. "Leave me!"

"I can't..."

"Go!" she shouted, letting go of his hand. "It's my turn to save you."

He heard a *thump* behind him, followed by another.

Kalibar turned around slowly, knowing exactly what he would see. There, standing before them, were two tall men in black, rippling cloaks, their faces shrouded in the shadows cast by their loose hoods.

"Run, damn it!" Petra shouted. But it was too late. He felt a vibration in his skull, then felt a terrible force shoving him downward. He fell to his knees, then onto his back, feeling his head strike the ground.

One of the Chosen stepped forward, staring down at him. Sunlight caught the green, diamond-shaped crystal in its forehead, making it glimmer as the Chosen knelt down before him. Kalibar tried to move, but his limbs were bolted to the ground, locked there by an invisible force. The Chosen stared at him, its eyes barely visible in the shadows of its hood. It reached a hand into its cloak, then pulled it out.

A long, tapered green crystal glittered against the dark skin of its hand.

"No," Kalibar blurted out. The Chosen leaned forward over him, rotating the crystal so its cruel point hovered over the center of his forehead. "No!"

"Kalibar," he heard Petra whimper from behind him. "I'm sorry."

Kalibar saw the tip of the green crystal descend, felt its cool sharpness press against his forehead. He grit his teeth, trying to lift his arms in vain.

"Kill me," he spat, glaring at the Chosen. "I'd rather be dead than be your slave!"

The Chosen's lips curled up into a smirk.

"You'll be both," it murmured.

There was a hissing sound, and all of a sudden the Chosen's head jerked backward, and it tumbled to the ground.

Kalibar stared up at where the Chosen had been, seeing only tree branches waving against a blue sky. He flexed his hands, feeling them move easily, and grunted, rising up into a sitting position. He saw the unmoving form of the Chosen before him, sprawled in a heap on the ground, its face covered by its black hood. A few feet away, the other Chosen was also lying on the ground, also unmoving.

Slowly, Kalibar got to his feet.

"Kalibar?" he heard Petra call out from behind him. He turned to her, saying nothing, then turned back to the nearest fallen Chosen. It still hadn't moved. He walked up to its head, kneeling down before it, and put a hand on its black hood, curling his fingers around the thick edge of it.

He peeled it back from the Chosen's face...and his breath caught in his throat.

"Kalibar, what happened?" Petra asked. He barely heard her, his eyes on the Chosen before him. The thing's eyes were open, staring right through Kalibar, its mouth agape.

And there, in the center of its forehead, where the green, shimmering facets of its shard had been, was an empty, blackened hole.

* * *

Kyle stared at the red, spinning globe created by Ampir's cylindrical device, watching as the countless tiny red dots on its surface winked out. He saw Sabin's avatar blink, saw his mouth fall open, his eyes unfocusing. His ancient face went blank for a long moment, and then suddenly re-animated, his eyes focusing on Ampir's mirrored visor.

"What did you do?" Sabin demanded, his gnarled fingers clenching into fists at his side. "What did you do!"

Ampir said nothing, raising his hand up toward the globe before him. The black and silver ends of the spinning globe retracted suddenly, re-forming the black cylinder in the center. It spun madly for a moment, then slowed, coming to a stop above Ampir. It lowered itself slowly into his hand, and he placed it back into the recesses of his armor.

"What did you do with my Chosen?" Sabin shouted. Ampir smirked.

"I introduced them to the latest version of my spacetime bridge cannon," he replied. Sabin stared at him uncomprehendingly, but

Kyle's eyes widened; he pictured the rifle Ampir showed him on Antara, the one that had locked on to his beating heart.

"Where are they?" Sabin demanded. "Why can't I see them?"

"They've lost their minds," Ampir replied.

Sabin stared at Ampir mutely, his jaw working silently. Then his expression went flat.

"You killed them," he stated, his voice perfectly calm.

"Yep."

"Why?" Sabin asked.

"I don't know," Ampir replied. "Something about 'erasing Man from the face of the planet.'" Sabin's eyes narrowed.

"You know I would never have done that!" he exclaimed angrily. "*You* threatened *me*!" Ampir shook his head.

"I don't trust you anymore, Sabin," he retorted. He raised his visor to Sabin's true body, trapped in its crystalline tomb. "You're not the man you used to be."

"Neither are you," Sabin countered acidly. "The Ampir I knew would never have betrayed me." He gripped his cane with both hands, his jawline rippling. "I invited you here in peace!"

"You'll have peace," Ampir replied, "...when you're dead."

Sabin stared silently at Ampir, his cataract-glazed eyes unblinking, his mouth slightly open. Then he lowered his gaze, bowing his head. When he raised it again, his expression was serene. Almost sad.

"Then you leave me no choice."

The Void crystals in the massive chamber – every single one of them – flashed bright white.

Blue light burst from Kyle's head, and he cried out, feeling the magic in his mind's eye being torn from him. He felt Ariana's hand grip his like a vise, then go slack. He turned to her, seeing cords of blue light shooting out of her forehead in all directions, sucking into the Void crystals beyond. Her eyes widened, her mouth gaping open...and then she slumped over, her body lifeless.

"Ariana!" Kyle cried. He pulled on her arm, drawing her in close, and wrapped his arms around her waist. He turned to Ampir, seeing the man floating there in front of Sabin, his arms at his sides.

"Goodbye, Ampir," Sabin muttered.

The massive cylindrical crystal Sabin's body was suspended in flashed blue.

Kyle felt an intense vibration in his skull, and then an incredible force slammed into him, shoving him backward through the air. He felt Ariana slipping from his grasp, and clung to her desperately. An incredible barrage of flashing lights exploded around Ampir, the air crackling with energy. Kyle flew backward, Ariana in his arms, the wall of razor-sharp Void crystals behind them zooming toward them.

"Ampir!" he cried.

Still backward he flew, the wall speeding ever closer, until he could see the blank stares of the Chosen trapped behind the glittering spikes. He cried out again, thrusting one arm in front of his face and closing his eyes. He felt a horrible, piercing pain in his lower back.

And then it faded.

His eyes snapped open, and he turned, feeling the point of a Void crystal jab into his cheek. He jerked away, then reached down to his lower back with one hand, feeling a narrow spike pressing against his armor there. He almost laughed out loud with relief, until he turned forward again.

There, in the center of the chamber, floating in front of Sabin's encapsulated body, was Ampir. Surrounded in flames and flashing lights, the crackling *boom-boom-boom* of explosion after explosion slamming into his body.

"Ampir!" Kyle shouted. The Void crystals throughout the cavern shifted colors, turning bright white again. The barrage stopped instantly, ending in a brilliant corona of blue light that streaked back to the Void crystals lining the chamber.

Ampir stood there, levitating before Sabin and his ancient avatar, his hands at his sides.

"Pretty colors," the Battle-Runic murmured.

Sabin's avatar smirked, the spotted flesh of his cheek forming deep wrinkles with the movement. He gave Ampir a slight nod.

"Your armor is more sophisticated than I thought," he conceded. "Impressive, to counter that many attacks so quickly."

"If you can weave," Ampir replied, "...it can weave."

"Yes," Sabin agreed. "And with my Void crystals active, draining magic, neither of us can weave."

"A standoff then," Ampir declared. Sabin snorted.

"Hardly," he countered. "I can attack, but if you do, I'll simply pull your patterns out of the air into my Void crystals. And with every attack, I'll be one step closer to completely mapping your armor's defenses." He flashed a grotesque smile. "It's only a matter of time now."

"Then what are you waiting for?" Ampir replied coolly. Sabin's eyebrows rose.

"Very well."

The Void chamber's walls turned a dull white, and Sabin's cylindrical tomb flashed blue again. Kyle felt the air around him crackle, and then an explosion of pure white light seared his eyes, pain lancing through his head. There was an ear-shattering *boom*, and then he felt himself lurch backward against the Void crystals behind him. He felt his grasp on Ariana slip, felt her tear away from him.

No!

The bright light faded, and Kyle blinked the spots from his vision, his eyes darting frantically around the chamber. Then he saw a dark, limp shape cartwheeling through the air ten feet below him, floating away slowly toward the crystal-lined floor far below. He tried to move, then realized he'd been pushed back into the spaces between the Void crystals, wedged between them. He gripped the crystals on either side of him with his gauntleted hands, straining to pull himself forward. He didn't budge; his shoulders were wedged tight.

Kyle lowered his arms, exhaling as much as he could, then sucked his shoulders forward and inward. Then he twisted his torso, pushing back with his legs, his feet braced on the sides of the Void crystals. He felt himself lurch forward, and he grabbed the tapered ends of the crystals on either side of him, seeing them flash blue, then bright white again, strobing through the two colors in rapid-fire succession. He looked downward again, spotting Ariana some thirty feet away now, cartwheeling slowly through the air.

He took a deep breath in, then pulled his legs up behind him, aligning himself with her position. He shoved with his legs, propelling himself toward her. His aim was perfect; he dove down toward her, and stretched his arms out to grab her. There was another flash of light, following by the crackling sound of thunder from above, and a blast of air struck Kyle, shoving him backward right before he reached her. He spun out of control, and thrust his arms out at the last minute, feeling his right hand strike something. He grabbed on to it, discovering to his relief that it was Ariana's wrist. He pulled her in close, wrapping his arms around her back, and clung to her as hard as he could.

There was another flash of light from above, followed by an ear-splitting *boom*, another shockwave blasting into Kyle. He lurched downward, spinning faster now, the chamber a rotating blur around him. He grit his teeth against a wave of nausea, locking his hands together behind Ariana's back, then felt his own back slam into something...hard. Pain lanced across his spine, and he grunted, feeling an enormous pressure on his shoulders. He realized they'd stopping falling, and that he'd been wedged – again – between the Void crystals on the floor of the chamber.

He tried to move, but he couldn't.

He stared upward then, seeing Ampir far above, facing Sabin's avatar. The huge crystal cylinder in the center of the chamber flashed, a monstrous bolt of white-hot energy shooting outward from it, right at Ampir's chest. It struck with terrible force, sending Ampir careening backward into the wall of Void crystals behind him. The crystals shattered as he slammed into them, translucent shards exploding outward from the impact, then falling toward Kyle and Ariana in a glittering shower. Kyle shut his eyes, turning his head to his side. He heard pieces of crystal *clang* off of Ariana's armor, then clatter between the Void crystals he was wedged between. After a few moments, the deluge stopped.

Kyle opened his eyes.

He saw Ampir there, his black armor standing out sharply against the wall of Void crystals he was embedded in.

Why isn't he doing anything?

536

Ampir grunted, trying to pull himself free of the crumpled crystalline wall, but with no success. Sabin's avatar watched idly as Ampir struggled.

"At long last," Sabin declared, raising one crooked finger and pointing directly at Ampir's chest. "The great Ampir has finally been cracked." Kyle followed Sabin's finger to Ampir's chest, and saw a large rent in the surface of the metallic armor, blue light pouring from the misshapen hole in the center of Ampir's chestplate.

Kyle's blood went cold.

"Goodbye, Ampir," Sabin murmured.

The massive cylindrical crystal in the chamber flashed bright white.

Thick cords of blue light burst outward from the hole in Ampir's chestplate, fanning outward to the countless Void crystals lining the chamber. The light brightened, growing more and more intense, until it was almost painful to look at. The Void crystals glowed with an intense white light, voraciously consuming the enormous magical power. Kyle saw Ampir's features contort into a grimace, his hands clenching into tight fists. Small, tight clusters of blue light burst from his forehead, unraveling rapidly and speeding toward the Void crystals around him.

"Don't bother," Sabin stated, his voice almost pitying. "You can't weave here, Ampir." He smiled sadly. "I warned you."

The blue light continued to flow from Ampir to the surrounding Void crystals, a torrential outpouring of unthinkable amounts of power. Ampir struggled to yank his arms free from the crystalline wall they were embedded in again, with no success. Sabin watched Ampir for a moment, then flew through the chamber toward him, until he was only a few feet away. He reached into his tattered shirt, retrieving a long, tapered green crystal. Its facets glittered in the light from the Void crystals.

"It's only a matter of time now," Sabin murmured, staring at the green crystal as he twirled it between his fingers. He looked past the shard, at Ampir. "Soon you will be utterly drained, helpless to resist me." He smiled then, his breath hissing through the rotted stumps of his teeth. He brought the tapered end of the green crystal forward, pressing it against Ampir's forehead. "And then you...and your memories...will be mine."

Kyle felt his blood turn cold.

Ampir shrank back, pulling away from the deadly tip of the shard, but Sabin moved forward, pressing it against his forehead again. Magic continued to course from Ampir's shattered chestplate, shooting outward in all directions like a brilliant blue corona.

Sabin's smile broadened.

"You will be," he murmured, "...my greatest Chosen."

* * *

Marcus sat on his favorite chair at the far end of his small lawn behind his house, only a few feet from the edge of Anatara. He gazed down at the open book in his hands, reading the small, perfect print there. It was slow going, as it was written in English, a language he'd only starting learning five months ago. But he found it utterly fascinating. Written by a philosopher like himself, a man long dead who'd lived in a world on the other end of the universe. Yet despite this vast distance in space and time, the author's wondrous prose and gentle wisdom had managed to touch Marcus's spirit. Each word so clearly proved the universality of human nature, the unique greatness of the human spirit.

Marcus turned the book over, glancing at its cover. "Assays," it read. He was so thankful to Ampir for having given it to him. A gift so precisely fitting for Marcus's temperament and interests, it was yet another example of the legendary Battle-Runic's careful, measured thoughtfulness.

He felt a vibration in his temples then.

Marcus frowned, glancing up from his book. He gazed out across the perfect blue sky above, and the mist-shrouded forests of Doma far below.

The sky rippled.

Marcus felt his heart skip a beat, and he opened his book, marking his page with a fallen leaf. Then he closed the book, bending over to set it down on the ground beside his chair. He gripped the handrails on either side of him tightly, and leaned back, closing his eyes.

It was time.

He felt another vibration in his temples, and gripped the handrails even tighter, taking a deep breath in, then letting it out.

Agony tore through his chest, ripping to his back.

He cried out, lurching forward, and felt something slam into his chest, pressing down with such incredible force that it blasted the air from his lungs. Pain radiated to his left shoulder, shooting down his arm. His hands started to tingle, then went numb. He could no longer feel the handrails he was gripping, could no longer hear, no longer see. Blackness and nothingness surrounded him. The only thing left was the pain.

And then, as quickly as it had come, it stopped.

Marcus sat there, feeling his palms slick with sweat, his breath coming in short, panting gasps. His heart hammered in his chest, and he forced himself to slow his breathing, to calm himself.

Breathe, he told himself. *In and out.*

He waited until his heart began to slow, then opened his eyes, seeing the same blue sky as before. He grunted, then pushed himself up from his chair, rising shakily to his feet. He stepped forward then, toward the end of his lawn, at the very edge of Antara. Looking down, he saw the treetops of the huge forest far below, thick white mist obscuring what lay beyond. He looked straight down, at where the churning gray clouds of the alien atmosphere that Antara hovered over were supposed to be...and saw that they were gone. In their place were a few mountains that stood clustered miles below.

Marcus stepped back from the edge, then returned to his chair, sitting down on it. He leaned over to pick up his book, and opened it to the page he'd marked, tossing the leaf he'd used as a bookmark aside. He found the paragraph he'd stopped at, and continued reading.

* * *

Kalibar stood there, staring down at the two Chosen lying motionless on the forest floor, blackened holes in their skulls where their green shards had been moments before. Then he turned back to Petra, who was still lying on the ground, staring up at him.

"Kalibar, what happened?" she asked. He looked at the Chosen for a moment longer, then turned to her, realizing she couldn't see them from her vantage point. He shook his head.

"They're dead," he answered.

"What?"

"Dead," he repeated. He stepped to the side, allowing her an unfettered view. "Look." Petra did so, her eyes widening.

"How?"

"I don't know," Kalibar replied. Petra shifted her weight, and immediately cried out, freezing in place. Kalibar looked at her deformed ankle, and rushed to her side, kneeling before her.

"Don't touch it!" Petra yelled out. Kalibar studied the wound, then reached out with his fingers to the top of her foot. "Don't!" Petra repeated, taking a sharp breath in.

"I need to see if blood is flowing to it," Kalibar replied. "I'll be gentle," he insisted. Petra said nothing, but she nodded. Kalibar leaned forward, pressing two of his fingers on the top of her foot, trying to feel the pulsing of her lifeblood flowing through the vessel there. It was difficult through the tough fabric of her Reaper suit, but he felt the faintest pulsation there. Then he got up, scanning the ground for some sticks. He found a long, relatively straight one, and picked it up, snapping it in half over his knee. Then he turned to one of the fallen Chosen, staring at its black cloak. He grabbed a corner of it, and wove magic to create a tear in it, throwing the pattern outward. The faint blue light of his magic struck the cloth...and stopped.

He frowned.

Kalibar turned back to Petra, staring at her black Reaper suit, then turned back to the Chosen's cloak. They were absolutely identical in shade.

"Kalibar?" he heard Petra ask.

Kalibar rolled the Chosen over, pulling off its cloak, then removing his own brown cloak, donning the black cloak instead. Then he grabbed the end of his brown cloak, weaving another pattern to make a cut in the thick fabric. This time it worked, and he tore a few long strips of the cloth free, walking back to Petra and kneeling before her ankle.

"Wait, what are you doing?" she asked, stiffening again.

"I need to splint your ankle," Kalibar explained. "It's going to hurt."

"No!" Petra protested. She took a deep breath in, then let it out. "Please don't touch it."

"I have to," Kalibar warned. "I can't move you without stabilizing it."

"I'll stay here then," Petra decided. Kalibar sighed.

"Petra..."

"I know, I know," Petra muttered. She grimaced. "Just give me a second." Kalibar nodded, laying the sticks on either side of Petra's ankle. She closed her eyes, taking deep breaths in and out. After nearly a minute, she opened her eyes, and nodded at him.

"Okay," she stated. "Do it."

Kalibar grabbed her big toe, pulling up on it to raise her foot off of the ground, hearing a *clunk* as her ankle went back in place. She screamed, and he moved quickly, wrapping the fabric around her leg with the two sticks flanking it. He set her leg down gently, then tied off the strip of fabric. When he looked up at her, he found that she was sweating profusely. And even with her dark skin, she looked pale.

"Sorry," he offered.

"Thank you," she replied.

"Come on," he said, putting a hand under her knees, and one behind her back, then lifting her up from the ground. She bit off another scream with the movement. "Let's get you out of here."

"But Ariana," she began.

"I need to make sure you're safe first," Kalibar countered. "Then I'll look for her."

Petra nodded, then rested her head against his shoulder, putting a hand on his chest. She gazed up at him silently. Looking down at those eyes — and feeling her closeness — made his heart beat faster. She smiled.

"One of these days," she stated, "...I'm going to save *you*."

Kalibar smiled back.

"I think," he replied, "...you already have."

He wove magic then, and felt himself floating upward into the air, his black cloak rippling in the wind. Higher they rose, until they cleared the treetops above, the magnificent sky opening up all around them. Kalibar turned to face the Spine of Grimore, staring at the spot where Kyle had been only a short while ago, and felt a surge of grief come over him.

Then something above caught his eye.

He turned his gaze upward, far above the Spine, and stared at the blue sky there. He could've sworn that he'd seen something there. Something moving.

The sky rippled.

Petra lifted her head off of his shoulder, staring up at him, then following his gaze. The sky rippled again, then it *pinched* inward for a split second.

And then it exploded.

Gray mist shot outward in all directions from the once clear sky, high above Mount Grimore's peak. Above the mist, Kalibar saw a massive, hulking shape appear. A sound as loud as a dozen thunderclaps rolled through the air, followed by a blast of wind so powerful that it knocked Kalibar back through the air, making the trees below bow outward violently, the white mist around them blown away instantly. The wind faded as quickly as it had come, and Kalibar recovered, staring up at the monstrosity in the sky once more. His eyes widened, his breath catching in his throat.

It was a massive island, so large that it rivaled the mountain below it, floating miles above Mount Grimore's peak. Its underside was enormous, like a mountain of rock turned upside-down. Halfway down this, the rock gave way to an incredible tapering mass of gunmetal gray, almost as if the rock had been dipped in molten steel. The shadow of the island cast all of Mount Grimore in relative darkness, extending even to Kalibar himself.

He heard Petra gasp, felt her hands grip the front of his cloak.

There was a flash of brilliant blue light at the seam between the rock and the metal portions of the island's underbelly, and suddenly the enormous metallic end broke off.

Kalibar swore, then spun around, weaving magic in his mind's eye. He burst away, accelerating toward Mount Kress in the distance. He glanced over his shoulder.

The metallic base of the island fell slowly through the air, descending toward Mount Grimore miles below, picking up speed as it went.

Kalibar pushed more and more magic into his stream, shoving as much power as he could into it. He felt his blood drain from his head with the enormous G-forces of his acceleration, felt his vision starting to blacken. Still he pressed on, the edge of the island's shadow now only a short distance away. He crossed over it, then glanced backward.

The base of the island fell straight toward one side of Mount Grimore's peak, the tapered metallic monstrosity slamming into the mountainside. Stone and dust burst outward from the incredible force of its impact, shooting outward and upward in an enormous explosion. The shockwave blasted across the landscape, ripping the surrounding trees out of the ground and tossing them into the air.

Kalibar pushed even more magic into his stream, pushing himself beyond his limits, his vision blackening completely. The shockwave rippled across the forest after them with terrifying speed, even as he felt his consciousness starting to slip away. His concentration wavered, his magic stream threatening to collapse on itself. He felt himself slowing down, his vision clearing as he did so, and saw Mount Kress looming a quarter mile away, the steeply-sloped mountainside to his left. He grit his teeth, angling leftward.

If I can just get behind the mountain...

He focused, pushing himself to go faster again, balancing himself on the razor's edge of his consciousness, arcing around the mountainside. He felt a blast of wind strike him from behind, hurtling him forward and blackening the air around him with thick, choking dust. He wove magic deftly, trying to stabilize himself in

543

mid-air, and turned left *hard*, descending toward the rear of the mountain. He aimed between the treetops on the mountainside below, weaving magic rapidly, feeling the blood rush into his head with the violence of his deceleration.

The rocky face of the mountain rushed up to meet him, right as a wall of flying trees and boulders slammed into the other side of Mount Kress, destroying everything in its path.

* * *

Kyle clung to Ariana's unconscious body, wedged between the Void crystals at the bottom of Sabin's massive lair. He stared in horror at Sabin's ancient avatar, at the shimmering facets of the green shard Sabin held against Ampir's bare forehead. The tip pressed into Ampir's flesh, denting his skin. Ampir grimaced, jerking his head to the side suddenly, the shard's vicious point sliding off of his forehead.

"It's pointless to resist," Sabin stated, grabbing Ampir's chin with one hand and forcing his head to face forward once again. He pressed the shard against Ampir's forehead. "You're mine now."

Ampir struggled mightily, his hands curled into fists, and jerked at his arms, still embedded in the crystalline wall. But they didn't budge.

"Go to hell," Ampir growled.

"I've been there," Sabin replied. He pressed the shard against Ampir's forehead, pressed *hard*. But the green crystal's tip did not pierce Ampir's flesh. Ampir's visor flashed, and it vanished suddenly, revealing his blue eyes. They stared right into Sabin's, even as Ampir's lips curled into a smirk.

"Time to go back."

Then the ceiling above them *exploded*.

Void crystals burst free from the ceiling with a tremendous, ear-splitting roar, shattering into millions of glittering pieces that fell downward all around Sabin and Ampir. Sabin lurched backward from Ampir, gravity shields appearing around him. The cords of blue light emanating from Ampir vanished, and his visor reappeared, the hole in his armor repairing itself instantly.

From below, Kyle watched as the massive chamber collapsed inward from above, the entire ceiling crumbling downward in a hail of translucent white crystal fragments.

"No!" Sabin shouted, retreating his avatar to the massive cylindrical crystal that housed his true body. Layers of shimmering blue gravity shields appeared around the entire structure, completely enveloping it. The upper base of the cylinder cracked where it connected to the falling ceiling, large hunks of it sliding off and falling down to the Void-crystal-lined floor below. Kyle saw one of those huge chunks falling right toward him and Ariana, and cried out, throwing an arm in front of his face right before it reached them. But it veered to the side at the last minute, crashing into the floor beside them, shattering the crystals there with an incredible *boom*. The walls around them caved inward and downward, millions of Void crystals falling toward the bottom of the cavern.

And from those shattered crystals, the Chosen began to rise.

Thousands of pale forms lifted up from the gem-strewn floor, many with severed limbs, some reduced to severed heads. They flew into the air, a few of them coming right for Kyle.

"Ampir!" Kyle cried, holding Ariana close. But the Chosen ignored Kyle and Ariana, passing by them and flying toward Sabin's central column. Thousands of them congregated there, surrounding the massive column from bottom to top, blue light emanating from their foreheads. Layer upon layer of gravity shields appeared around the column, chunks of crystal from the ceiling bouncing off of them, leaving the column intact. But huge chunks of the ceiling continued to descend, white crystal shards and huge fragments of rock crashing downward. Some of these slammed into the rising Chosen, knocking them out of the air and crushing them against the floor below. The mass of gravity shields around Sabin's cylinder began to waver as more and more Chosen fell...and then it vanished altogether.

A crack appeared in the middle of the crystal, right at Sabin's pale, entombed waist. More cracks appeared where the cylinder met what remained of the ceiling high above.

Then, as Kyle watched, the massive crystalline column broke free from the ceiling, separating at the crack at Sabin's waist. The flesh there tore as the cylinder broke free...falling right toward Kyle and Ariana.

"Ampir!" Kyle screamed. He kicked his arms and legs frantically, trying to break free from the Void crystals around him. It was useless...he was wedged in too tightly. Again Kyle tried to weave, but his mind was utterly empty. "Ampir!" he screamed again.

And then the massive crystalline column was upon them.

Chapter 36

The air screamed around Kalibar as he pressed himself against the mountainside, dirt, rocks, and ripped-up trees hurtling through the air at deadly speed hundreds of feet away on either side of him. He maintained his magic stream to his gravity shields, knowing full well that they would be useless against such a barrage. He felt Petra clinging to him, her face buried into the side of his neck, and held her tightly.

All around them, the maelstrom roared, surging around Mount Kress's massive flanks.

The barrage eased suddenly, the last of the tree trees hurtling past, a dense fog of swirling brown dust all that remained. Kalibar stayed where he was for nearly a minute, then relaxed his grip on Petra. She opened her eyes, looking around her, then turned to him.

"It's over?" she asked.

"It's over," Kalibar agreed.

"What *was* that?"

"I don't know," Kalibar admitted. He stood up then, carrying Petra in front of him. He wove magic, feeling his boots lifting off of the ground, and flew up into the air, circling around Mount Kress until Mount Grimore was once again visible in the distance.

What remained of it, that was.

For there, miles below the huge floating island in the sky, the once-formidable peak of Mount Grimore was no more, having shattered under the incredible force of the impact from the fallen base of the island. A huge plume of dust surrounded the site of impact, making it impossible to see much of anything through it. The entire base of the mountain was surrounded by that earthen fog. But beyond it, the surrounding forest had caved inward, sinking down to form a deep crater in the forest floor. Easily hundreds of feet deep, the crater extended nearly a mile around, forming a bowl-shaped depression filled with shattered trees and rocky debris.

Kalibar stared, landing on a small clearing on the mountainside, his jaw slack.

"My god," he breathed.

He felt a vibration in the earth then, following a low-pitched rumbling sound that permeated his very bones. He felt Petra tense up, and instinctively he wove magic in his mind, holding the pattern to fly away in his mind's eye. He saw the massive dust cloud covering Mount Grimore swirl, saw a dark shadow deep within rising upward. Suddenly a plume of dust burst upward from that cloud, followed by the silver gleam of metal. It was, Kalibar realized, the fallen base of the floating island, that massive hunk of metal, rising upward through the air. The vibration in the ground stopped, the low-pitched sound ending. Upward the metallic base flew, rising steadily toward the floating island far above. It slowed its ascent as it neared the island, coming to a gentle stop as it reconnected with the bottom of it.

And then the sky around the island rippled, and in an instant, the island vanished.

Kalibar stared at the blue sky that remained, his jaw slack with wonder. Then he felt a vibration in his skull, followed by a sudden gust of wind.

"Kalibar!" he heard a young voice cry from behind.

He turned around, and saw a very familiar young boy standing there on the mountainside before him, an equally familiar young girl at his side.

"Kyle!" Kalibar exclaimed, his heart leaping into his throat. He eased Petra to the ground, setting her down gently, then ran frantically to Kyle, his heart pounding in his chest. Kyle jumped into his arms, and he embraced the boy, holding him tightly, tears welling up in his eyes and streaming down his cheeks. His legs began to wobble underneath him, and he fell to his knees, bringing his hands up to the sides of Kyle's face and staring at him in wonder.

My boy!

To his immense relief, and utter astonishment, there was no crystal in Kyle's forehead. His skin was not pale, or cold. He was *Kyle*, alive and whole!

Then Kalibar turned his head, seeing Ariana – Ariana! – standing there beside Kyle. He gestured for her to come close, and he embraced her as well, holding his two children in his arms. His whole body was trembling.

"My children," he murmured, his voice cracking. Words streamed out of him, and he hardly registered that he was saying them. "Oh thank god," he blurted out. "Thank god."

"Thank him," Ariana replied, pulling away and twisting around. Kalibar opened his eyes, wiping the tears from them, then followed Ariana's gaze. There, standing where Kyle and Ariana had appeared only moments ago, was a man. A tall man clad in black armor, blue light coursing through the countless runes inscribed into its metallic surface. The man's mirror-like visor reflected an incredible blue vista of the sky, and the shattered remains of Mount Grimore.

"Ampir," Kalibar breathed, feeling a chill run through his body. He knelt there, staring at the legendary Battle-Runic, the man who had somehow, someway, come back from the dead. Ampir strode forward wordlessly, stopping before Kalibar and extending one gauntleted hand.

Rise, a voice reverberated in his mind.

Kalibar took Ampir's hand, and the man pulled Kalibar to his feet. Kalibar turned then, seeing Ariana and Kyle kneeling before Petra, still lying on the ground. Petra was sweating, undoubtedly from the pain in her ankle, splinted though it was. Kalibar turned back to Ampir, staring at his impenetrable visor.

"Please," he pleaded. "If you could help her..."

Ampir turned to face Petra, then stepped past Kalibar toward the fallen woman. Petra looked up at Ampir, clearly confused.

"Who is..." she began, then her eyes widened. The runes on Ampir's armor shimmered blue, and suddenly a great flare of blue light burst forth from his body. Kalibar felt a tremendous force slam into his mind's eye, filling him instantly with overwhelming power. He closed his eyes, unable to help himself from savoring the moment, the incredible rapture of it. Within seconds, the feeling ended, the blue light fading, and Kalibar opened his eyes.

Petra stared at Ampir, her eyes wide open, her mouth forming into a perfect "O." Moments passed before she finally blinked, her mouth snapping shut. She reached down to touch her ankle, tentatively at first, then more confidently, running her fingers over the once-mutilated flesh. The wound was gone, her ankle whole again. She gathered herself then, pulling her legs under her and rising to her feet. She stared at Ampir

"Who are you?" she asked. Ampir said nothing, turning away from her, and Petra turned to Kalibar.

"He's Ampir," Kalibar explained. "He was an...associate of Sabin."

"The Outsider?" Petra asked, her eyes widening.

"The same," Kalibar confirmed. He turned to face the remains of Mount Grimore then. The great cloud of dust still obscured the devastation wrought upon it. Then he turned back to Ampir. "I take it you did that."

Ampir nodded.

"Is he dead?" Kalibar asked. Ampir didn't answer, but Kyle nodded.

"He says Xanos is destroyed," Kyle said. Kalibar nodded, turning back to Mount Grimore, a strange feeling coming over him. As if this weren't happening, as if it was just a dream.

It's really over, he thought.

He'd never really allowed himself to believe that it would happen this way. Never imagined, despite what he'd told Kyle and Ariana, that Sabin could ever be destroyed. They'd been teetering on the edge of annihilation for so long now, pummeled by the sheer hopelessness of fighting against such an overwhelming power, that even the *idea* of defeating the self-proclaimed god had seemed impossible.

It's over, he told himself again. He stared at Mount Grimore, expecting to feel some sort of profound relief, a burst of joy. Something. *Anything*. But all he felt was dazed. He'd seen the same looks on the faces of his men back in his military days, after surviving against all odds to win a battle. That blank look, an unwillingness of the mind to admit that the fighting was over...that they didn't need to be afraid anymore.

He felt a cool hand take his then, and turned to see Ariana standing beside him, her eyes on Mount Grimore. She stared for a long time, then looked up at Kalibar, her big brown eyes looking questioningly at him.

"What now?" she asked. And the way she said it, he knew that she was feeling exactly the same as he was. Kalibar smiled, squeezing her hand and pulling her in to kiss the top of her head. Her hair – long again after healing from the Void Chosen's fireball – tickled his bare face.

"Now," he replied, drawing back from her. "We learn how to live."

He felt a hand on his back, and turned to see Petra standing on his other side. She too was staring at Mount Grimore, but she was hardly smiling.

"What about my family?" she asked. "And the tribes?"

"They're fine," Kyle answered. The boy blushed when Petra turned to look at him. "Ampir says so," he added, staring at his feet.

"And the Immortals?" she pressed.

"Gone," Kyle answered.

"Why don't you speak for yourself?" Petra demanded, looking at Ampir. Ampir's lips curled into a smirk, and he gestured at what remained of Mount Grimore with one hand.

I have, his voice boomed in Kalibar's mind. Petra must have heard it too, because she stepped backward, her eyes widening. She swallowed visibly, clearly shaken.

"Where is my family?" she asked.

Safe.

"Can I see them?" she pressed.

Soon, Ampir answered. He lowered his arm, turning to Kalibar. *Go with him,* he added. *I will protect your family.*

Petra turned to Kalibar, then back to Ampir.

"But..." she began. But before she could continue, the air around them shimmered, a burst of blue light shining from the runes on Ampir's armor. Kalibar felt a vibration in his skull, and suddenly the world around him *shifted.*

* * *

The sun shone brilliantly in the bright blue sky, sending its gentle rays to kiss the lush green grass of the seemingly endless manicured lawns of the Secula Magna. Birds chirped merrily from a nearby tree, and in the distance, not a mile away, the Great Tower stood tall against the cloudless sky, the crystal pyramid topping it shimmering like a precious jewel in the sunlight.

And there, standing a dozen feet away from the foot of the tree – Ariana's favorite tree – from which the birds sang, Kyle stood, hand-in-hand with Ariana, hardly able to believe his eyes.

"We're home!" he heard Ariana cry. She turned and flung her arms around him, kissing him full on the lips. Kyle stumbled backward, nearly losing his balance, and felt the back of his head bump into something soft from behind. Ariana disengaged from him, and he glanced backward, seeing Petra standing behind him, Kalibar at her side. A quick calculation made it all too clear what he must have bumped his head into; he felt his cheeks burning, and turned back to Ariana quickly. Luckily, Ariana didn't seem to notice Kyle's mortification. She was grinning from ear-to-ear, gazing across the verdant lawns of the Secula Magna, at the Great Tower beyond.

"We are indeed," Kyle heard Kalibar say. Kyle glanced at Petra, who was wide-eyed, spinning around in a slow circle, taking everything in.

"Where are we?" she asked. "How did we get here?"

"Ampir teleported us," Kyle explained. "We're home. Uh, our home," he added.

"This is Stridon," Kalibar added, gesturing at the campus around them. "A city on the west coast of a continent across the ocean from your home."

"Across the *ocean?*" Petra exclaimed. "We traveled halfway around the *world?*"

"Not quite," Kalibar countered. "But close enough." He smiled at her, putting a hand on her shoulder. "Come on, I'll show you around." He fiddled with his right ear then, and removed the yellow earring there, giving it to Petra. "You're going to need this," he added. He helped her put it in her ear, then stepped forward then, toward the Great Tower in the distance. Kyle and Ariana fell in behind the two, holding hands. Kalibar pointed off at the Tower, saying something to Petra about it. Kyle kept his eyes strictly on the Tower, becoming more practiced at keeping his gaze well clear of the powerful gravitational field of Petra's form. He felt Ariana squeeze his hand, and she leaned in, giving him a kiss on the cheek.

"I can't believe it's over," she whispered in his ear. He turned to her, and found her lovely brown eyes twinkling. He suddenly couldn't remember having seen her so happy. So...content.

"Me neither," he admitted.

"What happened in there?" she asked. "With Sabin, while I was unconscious?" Her eyebrows knit together. "All I can remember is falling...and then waking up to see the whole place crashing down on us."

"That's pretty much it," Kyle admitted.

They reached the Tower then, following one of the many cobblestone paths up to the huge open double-doors leading to the lobby. Crowds of Runic and Weaver students dressed in their white and black uniforms streamed in and out of those doors, on their way to and from their various classes. Kyle couldn't help but notice that those students were staring at them. Or rather, not Kyle or Ariana...and not even Kalibar. They were staring at Petra.

"This is the Great Tower," Kalibar was explaining to Petra as they wove through the crowd and passed through the huge double-

doors. "It's a school for Weavers and Runics, among other things."
Petra nodded wordlessly, clearly impressed by the sheer size of the
Tower...and obviously intimidated by the crowds of people around
it. She grabbed Kalibar's arm, pulling herself close to his side.

"Is this where you teach?" she asked.

"Ah," Kalibar replied, "...not quite."

They entered the lobby, and Petra's eyes immediately widened.
Three stories tall, with tall stone columns rising from the polished
granite floor to the ceiling far above, she couldn't have seen anything
like it back in the Barrens. Her eyes swept across the massive
paintings on the walls, the luxurious couches neatly arranged on the
lobby floor, and the tall statue of a Battle-Weaver standing on its
majestic golden pedestal in the center of the lobby. Then her eyes
rose upward, and she gasped, putting a hand to her mouth.

"Kalibar!" she exclaimed, pointing upward. "Look!" For there,
on the ceiling three stories above, was the *other* half of the lobby.
Men and women milled about on the upside-down floor, sitting on
upside-down couches. Upside-down fountains sprayed their water
downward, the liquid arching back up toward the ceiling under the
power of the reverse-polarity gravitational field. Kyle smiled,
remembering the first time he'd seen what Petra was seeing. It
seemed like forever ago.

Kalibar chuckled, putting an arm around Petra's shoulders.

"Come on," he urged. "I'll show you around."

He led Petra across the lobby, to a long hallway that lead, Kyle
knew, to a riser at its end. Petra gawked at the painted statues on
either wall of the hallway, depicting the fall of the Ancient Empire.
They reached the riser, stepping onto it, and Kalibar turned to Petra.

"This is a riser," he explained. "It goes up quickly," he warned.

The riser did just that, rising upward slowly at first, then picking
up speed at a formidable rate. The forty-two floors of the Great
Tower whizzed by in front of them at incredible speed, and Petra
clung to Kalibar as they accelerated upward. Within moments, the
riser slowed, then stopped at the topmost floor, the large stone disc
leveling perfectly with the granite floor of the hallway beyond. Petra
hurried off of the riser, and Kalibar followed after her, unable to

keep a smile from his face. Kyle stepped off with Ariana, remembering how he'd felt the first time he'd gone up a riser. Far quicker than elevators back home on Earth, it had been quite the experience.

Almost immediately after they stepped off of the riser, two elite guards rushed down the hallway toward them.

"Stop!" one of them cried. Gravity shields appeared around both of the guards, and Kalibar stopped immediately. Petra stepped backward, a gravity shield appearing around her as well. Kalibar put a hand up.

"At ease," he stated calmly. One of the elite guards frowned, staring at Kalibar for a long moment. Then his eyes widened.

"Grand Weaver!" he exclaimed, his shields vanishing instantly. He dropped to one knee instantly, as did the other guard moments later. "I'm sorry," he blurted out. "We didn't recognize you."

"Quite alright," Kalibar replied. "Stand up, please," he added. The guards did so, looking extraordinarily embarrassed. "Is Grand Runic Erasmus around?" he inquired.

"Yes your Excellency," one of the guards answered. "He's in a meeting with Councilman Goran, in the Grand Runic's suite."

"Thank you," Kalibar replied. The guards let them pass, and Kyle followed Kalibar and Petra down the hallway to the door to Erasmus's suite on the left. They stopped before it, and Kalibar knocked on the door. Within moments, it became translucent, and they could see Erasmus standing on the other side. The portly Grand Runic's eyes widened.

"Kalibar!" he exclaimed. The door immediately opened, and Erasmus rushed forward, giving Kalibar a big bear hug. Kalibar laughed, hugging Erasmus back. They held each other for a long moment, and then Erasmus broke away from Kalibar, wiping his obviously moist eyes with the back of his sleeve. Then he cleared his throat, ushering everyone into his luxurious suite. Kyle saw Councilman Goran – looking more exhausted than Kyle had ever seen the man – sitting on one of the many couches in the suite. Goran stood when they entered.

"Grand Weaver!" Goran exclaimed. "You're back early!"

"Councilman Goran," Kalibar greeted.

"What the hell did you do to yourself?" Erasmus stated, a huge grin on his face, staring at Kalibar's bald head and grizzled chin. Tears were flowing down his cheeks, and he wiped them away hurriedly. "You look like a hobo...and you smell like one too."

"It's a long story," Kalibar admitted.

"I've got time," Erasmus said, still grinning from ear-to-ear. Then he noticed Kyle and Ariana standing there. "You too?" he exclaimed, no doubt noticing Ariana's clothes and Kyle's short blond hair. "What the hell is this, a costume party?"

"Uh, well," Kyle began. But Kalibar held up a hand to stop him.

"He knows," Kalibar stated.

"He does?" Kyle asked, turning to Erasmus.

"I do," Erasmus admitted. Then his gaze fell on Petra, and his eyes widened. "Well now!" he declared, stepping forward and reaching for Petra's hand. He grabbed it – much to Petra's obvious discomfort – and brought the back of her hand to his lips. "Who, might I ask, are you?"

"This is Petra," Kalibar introduced. "She's from the Barrens, in Orja."

"Well hello Petra," Erasmus greeted, his blue eyes twinkling mischievously. She pulled her hand away from his, and he chuckled. "So you're not dead," he added, turning to Kalibar. "That's a start. Your mission...?"

"A success," Kalibar answered, grinning from ear-to-ear.

"Hot damn!" Erasmus blurted out. "You're serious?"

"Dead serious."

"You crazy bastard!" Erasmus nearly shouted, grabbing Kalibar and giving him a big bear hug. "You old, crazy, beautiful bastard!" He let go of Kalibar, his eyes once again moist with tears. This time, he didn't brush them away. "Pinch me!" he ordered. "Tell me I'm not dreaming!"

"You're not," Kalibar said, chuckling at his old friend. "It's over."

"Well I'll be damned," Erasmus breathed. "The mother of all suicide missions, and you managed to pull it off!"

"Wait, what mission?" Goran interjected, looking utterly confused. Kalibar and Erasmus turned to the Elder Runic.

"Kalibar may have taken a little...detour on his vacation," the Grand Runic confessed, trying to contain his pleasure at the man's confusion, and failing miserably.

"Detour?"

"To Orja," Erasmus added, breaking into another grin.

"*Orja?*" Goran exclaimed, his eyes widening. "You went to *Orja?*"

"Well, yes," Kalibar confirmed. Goran shook his head.

"Kalibar, the Council...your Battle-Weavers...they still think you're in Bellingham!"

"A necessary deceit," Kalibar explained. "The vacation was a ruse."

"Kalibar, what are you talking about?" Goran demanded. "Your entire security force doesn't know where you are! You could've been killed!"

"Well..." Kalibar replied. "That's actually far less likely now."

"He went to Orja to confront Xanos," Erasmus revealed. Goran stared at Erasmus, then turned back to Kalibar. He looked utterly lost. Erasmus, as usual, looked enormously pleased at having stymied the dour Elder Runic.

"Ampir gave us a weapon," Kalibar explained. "One that he said could destroy Xanos if we could get it close enough to him. Ampir gave us Xanos's location, and we brought the bomb there."

"Wait, Ampir gave you a weapon against Xanos, and you didn't tell the Council?" Goran accused, his tone incredulous.

"Ampir gave *Kyle* the weapon," Kalibar corrected. "I found out about it the same day that these two," he added, gesturing at Kyle and Ariana, "...decided to sneak out and save the Empire on their own."

"That's why Kalibar took his vacation," Erasmus explained. "To go after them."

"So you knew about this?" Goran pressed, glaring at Erasmus. He crossed his arms, his eyes narrowing. "You knew about this and you didn't tell the Council? Or me?" Kalibar put a hand on Goran's shoulder.

"That was *my* decision," he explained. "I had no way of knowing where Xanos's spies were. The more people I told, the more likely Xanos would have found out, and our mission would have failed."

"Wait, it succeeded?" Goran blurted out. Kalibar broke into a grin.

"Yes."

"Xanos is dead?"

"Dead and buried," Kalibar confirmed. Goran's jaw dropped, and he stared at Kalibar, dumbfounded, for a long moment.

"No," he retorted. Kalibar chuckled.

"Oh yes," he countered.

"You're serious?"

"Dead serious," Kalibar confirmed. Goran stared at Kalibar for a moment longer, then turned to Kyle and Ariana.

"He's right," Ariana spoke up.

"Xanos is dead," Kyle piped in. "I saw it with my own eyes."

Goran stared at them for a moment longer, then turned back to Kyle. His jaw worked silently for a moment, and his arms – still crossed – slid down to his sides. Then the surly Elder Runic did something that Kyle had never seen the man do before.

He smiled, so hard that it nearly split his face in two.

"Kalibar, you crazy...!" he shouted, rushing up and grabbing Kalibar by the shoulders. Kalibar laughed, and Goran embraced the Grand Weaver for a moment, pulling away and staring at him with wonder. "You really did it?"

"Not me, I'm afraid," Kalibar admitted. "We were waylaid by Xanos's Chosen. Ampir saved us...and killed Sabin."

"*The* Ampir?" Goran exclaimed.

"That's right."

Goran let go of Kalibar, rushing past everyone and making his way to one of the communication orbs on a nearby table. He touched it, sending a stream of magic to it.

"We have to call the Council!" he declared. "We have to tell everyone!" He let go of the orb, turning back to Kalibar and Erasmus. Then he burst out laughing, his eyes darting from Grand Runic to Grand Weaver. He hopped up and down, then rushed at

Kalibar again, giving the man another bear hug. Then he disengaged, turning to Erasmus, and – after a momentary hesitation – embraced the portly Grand Runic. Much to Erasmus's obvious dismay.

Just then, there was a knock on the front door of Erasmus's suite, and Kyle turned to see a pair of elite guards standing on the other side of it. Erasmus gladly extracted himself from Goran, walking up to the door to let the guards in.

"I want an emergency meeting with the Council as soon as possible," he told them. "In the War room." The guards saluted crisply, and exited as quickly as they had come. Erasmus turned back to face Kalibar...and his eyes again shifted to Petra. And to her...obvious gifts.

"Well then," he stated. "Now, what was your name again?" "Petra," she answered, leaning closer to Kalibar. Erasmus grinned, walking up to her and grabbing her hand again, lifting it and bringing it to his lips as he had before. She shrank away from him, glancing at Kalibar in a rather alarmed way.

"Tell me that this incredible creature isn't your new girlfriend," Erasmus pleaded, looking at Kalibar, who for once was speechless. Erasmus gave another wily grin. "Say the word, my dear," Erasmus continued, "...and I'll have my divorce finalized within the hour!"

Petra jerked her hand back from Erasmus, a look of horror on her face.

"Don't worry about him," Kalibar told her, chuckling despite himself. "He's completely harmless." He raised an eyebrow at Erasmus. "You do realize she could kill you," he added.

"My wife?" Erasmus asked.

"No, she's killing you slowly," Kalibar corrected. "Petra will do it much more quickly."

"Less painfully, though," Erasmus replied.

Goran cleared his throat then.

"Come on," he stated. "We'd better get to the War room."

"I'll meet you there in a moment," Kalibar said, glancing at Petra.

"Me too," Erasmus added. Goran nodded, then walked out of the suite, the door closing automatically behind him. After he'd left, Kyle saw Petra ogling Erasmus's suite. It was extraordinary, luxurious beyond description, with crystalline walls that tapered to form the shimmering pyramid that topped the Tower. She was obviously very impressed.

"So you're from the Barrens?" Erasmus inquired. Petra turned to him.

"The Barren forest," she confirmed.

"A hell of a change of scenery, eh?" Erasmus said with a chuckle.

"Who lives here?" she asked.

"I do," Erasmus answered. "At least for another six years." Petra's eyes widened.

"*You* live here?" she exclaimed. Erasmus raised an eyebrow, running a hand through his long white beard.

"Why," he asked. "Is that so hard to believe?"

"It's just..." she replied. "So rich."

"Well, so am I," Erasmus stated.

"What do you do here?"

"I'm the guy who runs the place," Erasmus replied, gesturing at the crystalline windows giving a magnificent view of the Secula Magna's vast campus...and the skyline of Stridon beyond. "And so is he," he added, pointing at Kalibar. Petra blinked, then turned to Kalibar.

"What?"

"See that city?" Erasmus answered, again gesturing at the window to the city outside. "We run it."

"The whole thing?" Petra pressed, clearly taken aback. Kyle couldn't blame her; Stridon was huge, as big as any city on Earth, and while it of course didn't have quite as impressive skyscrapers as those back home, its architecture was mighty impressive.

"And forty-seven other major cities," Erasmus continued. "Five hundred and twenty-two towns, a few islands here and there, and an army of five hundred thousand infantry, give or take."

Petra's mouth fell open.

"He never told you?" Erasmus asked incredulously. Petra turned to Kalibar, who, it seemed, could only shrug.

"I'm the leader of an Empire," he admitted. When Petra continued to stare at him, open-mouthed, he looked down, clearing his throat noisily. Petra's mouth snapped shut, and she pulled away from Kalibar, regarding him with an expression that Kyle couldn't read, but definitely wasn't the good kind.

"You're an *emperor*?" she exclaimed. Kalibar sighed heavily, not meeting her gaze.

"Yes."

Petra balled her right hand into a fist, and punched Kalibar in the shoulder.

"I almost killed you!" she accused.

"Actually, not..." Kalibar began, but Petra punched him in the shoulder again, and he grunted.

"Lead with that next time!"

"All right," Kalibar muttered. "Next time we meet for the first time, I'll tell you I'm an emperor."

"Oh," Erasmus interjected. "You didn't tell me she was your new girlfriend, Kalibar!" Both Kalibar and Petra turned to him. Erasmus put up his hands and stepped back, no doubt because Petra looked like she wanted to punch *him* now. "Well you fight like it," he added hastily.

Petra paused, then relaxed her fists, turning back to Kalibar.

"*You* two lead an Empire?"

"I know," Erasmus said with a grin, walking up to Kalibar and putting an arm around his shoulder. "Hard to believe, eh?"

"I need to sit down," Petra muttered, turning around and walking up to one of Erasmus's couches and doing just that. She stared off into space.

"Now now," Erasmus said, sitting down beside Petra and patting his impressive belly with one hand. "I hope this doesn't sour things between you two." Petra frowned at him.

"What?"

"Well, that Kalibar's a dirty politician," Erasmus continued. "I've known him for oh, what now? Forty-eight years?"

"Forty-nine," Kalibar corrected.

"That man," Erasmus said, pointing at Kalibar, "...is the greatest, most beautiful damn human being I've ever met." He smirked then. "He looks a hell of a lot better with hair though."

"He's right," Ariana stated suddenly. All eyes turned to her.

"I look better with hair?" Kalibar asked.

"I've seen who he is," Petra interjected, looking at Kalibar. "You told me that I was of fine character," she added. "And that you wanted a chance to prove that you were as well."

"I remember," Kalibar admitted. Petra smiled, rising from the couch and walking up to him. Then she leaned in, giving Kalibar a kiss right on the lips. Kalibar stiffened with surprise, and Petra held the kiss for a moment, before pulling back to gaze into his eyes.

"You *are* the greatest man I've ever met."

Chapter 37

The emergency meeting of the Council went exactly as Kyle expected it to. Which is to say that, after a long period of disbelief and shock, the twelve members of the Council burst into joyous celebration, much as Goran had earlier. It was, Kyle had realized, the first time he'd seen them all getting along. After countless back-slaps and tearful congratulations – and a disturbing number of emptied wine bottles – the celebration died away, and the Council, along with Kalibar and Goran, got to work. On planning a more formal celebration, of course. Kalibar and Erasmus were to announce their victory in Stridon's Central Square, after which a parade unlike anything the Empire had ever seen would be had.

Kyle had left the meeting soon after the celebratory part had ended, both he and Ariana going back to Kalibar's suite. Petra had joined them, at least at first, and they'd spent some time catching up on what had happened to each of them, respectively. Kalibar and Erasmus had returned from the meeting afterward, and Kalibar had insisted that everyone come to his suite to have dinner together, like old times. And that is exactly what they did.

Kyle sat at the dinner table in Kalibar's suite, Ariana to his left and Erasmus to his right. Kalibar sat opposite him, as did Petra at his side. Petra had changed out of her Reaper uniform and into more conventional clothing...a simple dress. Of course, on her, the dress had transformed into something quite extraordinary, by virtue of her natural gifts. Kyle was relieved to see that he was not the only one who was having a hard time resisting the urge to look; Kalibar and Erasmus were clearly struggling with the same compulsion, with little success.

Just then, the door to Kalibar's suite opened, and a very familiar person strode in.

"Darius!" Kyle cried, standing up from his chair. It was indeed Darius, wearing his customary golden armor. The bodyguard nodded at Kyle, walking up to the seat opposite Ariana and sitting down. Erasmus rolled his eyes at the man.

"Late again?" he asked. "Are you *ever* on time?"

"Darius, you're back," Kalibar stated, clearly surprised. Erasmus snorted.

"He's *been* back," he muttered. "Came back a few hours after you left for your 'vacation,'" he added, glancing at Kalibar. He turned back to Darius, a mischievous twinkle in his eyes. "I immediately offered him a lifetime of unpaid vacation."

"Petra, this is Darius," Kalibar introduced, gesturing at the bodyguard. Petra stood to shake Darius's hand, and he stayed right where he was, giving her the slightest of nods. Petra kept her hand extended for a moment, then withdrew it, sitting down and giving Kalibar a confused look. Erasmus chuckled.

"You don't have to like him," the Grand Runic counseled. "No one else does."

Just then, Jenkins arrived. Ever the faithful butler, he appeared with stacks of plates, bowls, and silverware in his hands. Within moments, the table was set, with all of the instruments of eating within easy reach. Jenkins took everyone's orders – which for most of them was the perennial favorite, roasted duck – and then left as quickly as he had come to carry out their requests. He returned minutes later – an assistant butler in tow – with silver platters and a remarkable assortment of wine bottles. After everyone had been served, Jenkins left, his assistant clearly struggling to keep up with the expert butler's formidable speed and efficiency. Everyone at the table dug in to their meals at once, except for Ariana, of course. For

Kyle, the delicious aroma of roasted duck was damn near intoxicating, his mouth watering almost painfully with anticipation. When he eagerly shoveled a juicy slice of it into his mouth, it didn't disappoint.

For a few minutes, the suite was thrust into near-silence, the smacking of lips and sipping of wine the only sounds to be heard. As usual, Darius finished before everyone else, immediately ordering a second course. And, by that time, a third glass of wine. Kyle's eyebrows rose; even Erasmus, whose love for wine was legendary among his peers, had yet to finish his first glass.

"You're celebrating pretty hard," Erasmus observed, eyeing Darius mischievously as the bodyguard gulped down the third glass. "...for a guy who did nothing worth celebrating." Darius smirked at the Grand Runic.

"If it weren't for me, you wouldn't be celebrating," the bodyguard retorted, casually pouring himself a fourth glass. "You'd be dead."

"He does have a point there," Kalibar piped in, grinning at Erasmus, who scowled furiously.

"And he hasn't done anything since," he muttered. He turned to Kalibar, giving his old friend a pleading look. "Can't I at least have him whipped? I won't even ask for the death penalty."

"You can try," Darius quipped.

Kyle grinned at the two men, trying not to laugh out loud. If only Erasmus knew! The old Runic was a huge fan of Ampir's, one of the few who believed that Ampir hadn't been responsible for the destruction of the Ancients. If he ever found out that he'd been mercilessly insulting his greatest hero, he'd never live it down.

"How is your food?" Kalibar asked Petra, in an obvious attempt to change the subject. Petra smiled, jabbing one of the few pieces of duck left on her plate with her fork.

"Incredible," she replied. "I've never tasted anything like it."

"Stick around," Erasmus said with a grin, "...and you'll eat like this every day."

Just then, Jenkins reappeared, carrying more platters, this time filled with various desserts. He made quite a show of displaying each, and everyone chose their favorites, again digging in with gusto. Kyle, loving everything chocolate, chose the chocolate cream pie, one of his favorite desserts back home on Earth. It was, of course, better than any he'd tasted before.

"Mmm," Petra hummed, tasting a piece of her own pie. She'd gotten the same dessert as Kyle. "My god that's good!"

"Isn't it?" Erasmus replied with a chuckle. "Does this mean you'll stick around for a while?" Petra paused, then glanced at Kalibar, who was suddenly concentrating a bit too hard on his own dessert.

"I have responsibilities back home," she answered.

"Damn," Erasmus muttered. "Well, if there's anything we can do to help," he added, "...we *are* all-powerful emperors."

There was silence after that, and Jenkins appeared again, making swift work of clearing the table. The butler refreshed everyone's wine – Kyle had already lost track of how many glasses Darius had emptied – then vanished again, as if by magic. Everyone sat back in their chairs, their hands on their overstuffed bellies and their cheeks rosy with wine. Erasmus drained his glass of every drop of its contents, then heaved a contented sigh.

"Well," he stated, looking around the table. "Now what?"

"Good question," Kalibar admitted. Erasmus chuckled.

"I know, right?" he said. "All I've been thinking about is this damn war for the last what, two months?"

"It seems like longer than that," Ariana stated.

"Well, there's the parade to plan," Erasmus offered. The Council had unanimously voted to fund a huge celebration – complete with a parade – throughout Stridon, and in several other major cities in the Empire. They had less than a week to plan it.

"I'll leave that to the Council," Kalibar replied. "I believe I'm still owed a few more days' vacation," he added, glancing at Petra. "I'd like to show you around, if that's alright."

"It is," Petra agreed.

"Then I'm going to work on that brilliant letter you sent me a few days ago," Erasmus decided, grinning at Kalibar. "You won't believe how pissed I was when I read it, by the way," he added. "A damn Weaver solving Sabin's Void theory!" He shook his head. "I think I hate you."

"Sorry," Kalibar replied, unable to help himself from grinning.

"Oh yeah, you're devastated," Erasmus shot back. Kyle stared at both of them uncomprehendingly.

"What are you talking about?" he asked.

"I'll tell you later," Kalibar promised.

"Yeah, yeah," Erasmus grumbled. He poured himself another glass of wine, bringing it to his lips and taking a generous gulp. Then he put his glass down, and turned to Kyle and Ariana. "So let's hear it," he stated. Kyle stared at him uncomprehendingly.

"What?"

"Your story," Erasmus clarified. "What happened over there?"

Kyle obliged, starting with his and Ariana's escape from the Tower, and their flight to the *Defiance*. He told the tale, and Ariana chimed in from time to time, as did Kalibar, and even Petra. By the time Kyle had finished, Erasmus was well into his umpteenth glass of wine, his pudgy cheeks rosy and his eyes moist. The Grand Runic, ever the sentimental drunk, rose unsteadily from his chair, circling around the table to give Kyle and Ariana each a hug. After teary congratulations were meted out – and after Erasmus's repeated attempts to hug Petra – Kalibar himself rose to escort Erasmus safely to his own suite. Minutes later, Kalibar returned, and bid everyone goodnight. Kyle and Ariana left the table and went to Kyle's room, and they sat in the bedroom together. Neither of them felt like going to bed, Kyle being wide awake, and Ariana of course being incapable of sleep. They sat there, side-by-side, and Kyle snuck his hand into Ariana's, holding it. She smiled at him, looking as beautiful as ever. She said nothing, just staring at him with that strange smile on her face.

"What?" he asked at last.

"Am I making you nervous?"

"A little," he admitted. Her smile broadened, and she squeezed his hand gently.

"Good."

"Why is that good?" he pressed. She leaned in, kissing him on the cheek, then pulled back. She didn't answer, not at first, staring at him for another uncomfortably long period of time. Finally, she turned away, staring off into the distance at nothing in particular.

"I can't believe it's really over," she murmured.

"Me neither," he admitted.

"All I've been dreaming about for the last year is killing the Dead Man, or Xanos," Ariana stated. She turned to look at him. "I don't even know what to think about anymore."

"Think happy thoughts," Kyle offered, giving her a smile. She smiled back, albeit weakly.

"Sounds hard."

"It's not, really," he replied. "I'll help you."

"You always do," Ariana agreed, gently turning his head with one hand and leaning in to kiss him on the lips. As cool as those lips were, it was still magic, sending a chill through his body. When she pulled away, he found himself staring at her stupidly...much to her obvious delight.

"Whoa," he mumbled.

"You still like me?" she asked, a mischievous twinkle in her eyes. Kyle nodded emphatically. "Good," she added. Kyle yawned suddenly, and Ariana patted the bed with one hand. "Time for you to go to bed."

"I can stay up a little longer," he protested. But Ariana would have none of it.

"Come on," she insisted. "You've had a long day."

"That's an understatement," he grumbled. It was hard to imagine that he'd woken up in Petra's parents' house in the Barren forest that morning. No wonder that he was so tired suddenly; he'd scaled a mountain, nearly died on several occasions, and descended miles into the earth to defeat a two-thousand-year-old demigod, all in one day. And to think that a day at the beach back home on Earth used to seem like a jam-packed adventure!

"What are you thinking?" Ariana inquired. "You're staring off into space." Kyle blinked, then shook himself out of his reverie.

"Just that I could use a little less adventure," he admitted ruefully. Ariana smiled.

"Ditto," she agreed. Then it was her turn to stare off into space.

"What?" Kyle asked.

"Oh, I'm just wondering what I'm going to do now," she answered.

"You could go for a walk with Darius," Kyle offered. But Ariana shook her head.

"Nah," she replied. "I think I'll watch you sleep for a while."

"Creepy," Kyle muttered, not at all comfortable with the idea of being stared at while he was snoring...and probably drooling.

"Just for a bit," Ariana reasoned, patting his hand. "Then I'll go and practice weaving."

"All right," Kyle agreed. He hopped off the bed, going to his bathroom to change into his pajamas and take care of all things eliminatory, then returned, crawling into bed. Almost instantly after Ariana had pulled the covers over him and his head sank into his plush pillow, he felt glorious sleep reaching for him, its soft, comforting fingers ready to pull him down into a peaceful slumber. He barely had the energy to muster a final goodnight to Ariana before his eyelids became too heavy to open. He closed them, and within moments, sleep claimed him.

* * *

The next day was, to Kyle's surprise, utterly normal.

Kalibar had gone away with Petra to give her a tour of his mansion in Bellingham, but had insisted that Kyle and Ariana continue their lessons with Master Lee and Master Owens, respectively. That meant that Kyle had been awoken at five in the morning by one of his elite guards, much to his dismay. Led to the Archives, he'd met up with Master Lee, who immediately made him review everything she'd taught him thus far. After demonstrating his abilities, Master Lee sat back in her chair, a smile casting innumerable wrinkles on the thin skin of her face.

"You've been practicing," she observed, nodding in approval. Kyle shrugged.

"Not really," he confessed. "I had to use what you taught me a couple of times, that's all." He explained his adventure on the *Defiance*, describing the simple runics he'd constructed to help save the day.

"That," Master Lee replied, "...is the best kind of practice." Her smile faded, and she leaned forward in her chair, propping her elbows on the tabletop between them. "You'll learn more in one day from necessity than you will in a week from me."

"Maybe," Kyle mumbled.

"Definitely," Lee corrected. "I know what I'm talking about," she added. "I'm old." She chuckled then. "Magic is like anything else," she stated. "You learn it best by using it." She leaned back in her chair again. "I could tell you what to do until I was blue in the face, but until you do it yourself..." She trailed off then, lowering her gaze and sighing.

"What?"

"I guess that's why I stopped teaching," Lee admitted. "Too many students who memorized all their texts but still didn't know their ass from their elbows." She smirked then. "As if everything they needed to know in life could be learned from a book."

Kyle could hardly argue with that. He'd arguably learned more in the last few weeks – about magic and, more importantly, life – than he had in all of the years he'd spent on Earth. And while he probably wouldn't be able to tell anyone what specifically he'd learned, there was no doubt in his mind that he was a much different person than he had been before coming to Doma. And he had one person, above all, to thank for it.

"Well, I'm done," Lee stated suddenly, pushing herself away from the table and standing up suddenly. Kyle blinked.

"Wait, what?" he asked. "What'd I do?"

"Relax," Lee replied, smirking at him. She pushed in her chair with one liver-spotted arm. "You did fine." She walked past him toward the entrance to the Archives, putting a hand on his shoulder as she passed by. "Show me something new tomorrow," she ordered.

570

"Wait, what?" Kyle blurted out, twisting about in his chair to stare at her stooped, retreating form. "What do you mean?"

"Surprise me," she hollered, not bothering to turn around. Within moments, she was gone.

Kyle stared at the entrance to the Archives where Master Lee had been only moments before, then sighed, turning around in his chair. Then he nearly jumped out of it.

There, sitting across from him, in Master Lee's chair, was Darius!

"Gah!" Kyle blurted out, gripping the armrests of his chair. Darius smirked.

"Hey kid," he greeted.

"Geez," Kyle muttered. "You almost gave me a heart attack!"

"Let's go for a walk," Darius stated, completely ignoring Kyle's indignation. Kyle blinked.

"Uh, okay..."

And then the air around them rippled, and the universe tore open.

* * *

Kyle clutched at his chest, the immense pain lancing through his sternum abating as quickly as it had come. His vision cleared, sensation returning to his limbs. He realized that he was sitting in a chair...but not the one he'd been in moments before. He looked around, seeing a very familiar room around him. A large room with a cathedral-style ceiling constructed of bare wooden beams, a few round tables sitting in the center. And he was seated at one of them. Opposite Darius...and another man.

"Marcus!" Kyle cried, grinning at Kalibar's old mentor. Marcus smiled back at him.

"Good to see you Kyle," he replied, pushing a glass filled with ambrosia toward Kyle. Kyle took it, then turned to Darius.

"Hey wait," he stated. "How'd we get here? I thought you could only go to Antara through the Gateway."

"We did," Darius replied. "Then we teleported here."

"I didn't see that," Kyle protested.

"You were still blind," Darius countered. "As usual." Marcus cleared his throat, and Kyle turned to the old man.

"I hear you've had quite an adventure these past few days," he said.

"That's for sure," Kyle agreed. "Thank god it's over," he added.

"Yes," Marcus agreed. "I hear Sabin is no longer a threat."

"We killed him," Kyle confirmed. "Uh, Darius did," he added hastily. Marcus glanced at Darius, then sighed.

"If Sabin is dead," he corrected, "...then he will have brought it upon himself." He took a sip of his own ambrosia, then set his glass down. "How is Kalibar?"

"He's good," Kyle answered. He couldn't help but grin. "Really good; I think he's got a girlfriend."

"Really?" Marcus declared, arching one eyebrow. "About time!" He leaned forward. "Tell me, what's she like?"

"Um, well," Kyle began, then paused. "She's uh, nice," he stated rather lamely.

"And?"

"And really strong," he added. "And um, pretty," he mumbled, feeling his cheeks turning uncomfortably warm.

"She's hot," Darius translated.

"I see," Marcus murmured, leaning back in his chair. "Well, she'd have to be pretty special to win Kalibar over," he added. "I've never seen another man so wary of relationships."

"She's special all right," Darius replied with a smirk.

"Funny how things work out in the end," Marcus murmured, glancing at Darius, then taking another sip of his ambrosia. Darius stood suddenly, turning to Kyle.

"Let's take that walk," he stated. Kyle glanced up at Darius, then turned to Marcus.

"Uh..."

"Go on," Marcus stated, rising from his own chair and stepping around the table until he was standing in front of Kyle. "Good to see you again," he added, extending a hand. Kyle shook it; the older man's grip was firm, but not uncomfortably so. "The next time you visit, I'd like to spend some more time talking with you."

"Sure," Kyle agreed, feeling rather pleased by this. He certainly didn't mind the prospect of spending more time with Marcus; there was something...comforting about the man. As if he could tell Marcus anything, and it would be okay.

"I'll be looking forward to it," Marcus stated. He waved goodbye, and Darius led Kyle out of the front entrance to Marcus's house, walking across the short path in the front yard through the open gate beyond. They continued down the street, then took a turn toward a familiar dirt path between the tall trees to their right. The path narrowed quickly, forcing Kyle to drop behind and follow Darius down it. After a few minutes, the path ended, opening up to reveal a narrow rocky outcropping. Beyond this, there was an endless expanse of blue sky. It was the same cliff – at the very edge of Antara – that they'd visited earlier, when Darius had told Kyle that he was Kyle's grandfather. Darius walked to the edge of the cliff, and Kyle followed. He looked down from the edge, and jerked backward in surprise.

"Whoa!"

There, miles below, Doma's surface lay. But instead of the ocean he'd seen the first time he'd been here – or the forest and mountains he'd seen from Marcus's backyard only a few days ago – there was a vast desert, a huge canyon splitting its surface in two. And it wasn't standing still; the desert was zipping by below them, at a dizzying pace.

"Where are we going?" Kyle asked.

"You'll see," Darius replied.

"Why can't you just tell me for once?" Kyle muttered. He was getting sick and tired of Darius's maddeningly poor communication skills. After all, he'd led Kyle to believe that Sabin had killed him...and had outright lied about the black cylinder. It hadn't been a bomb at all. Even if Darius *did* tell him something, how was he supposed to believe it?

"Why can't you just trust me for once?" Darius countered. Kyle scowled.

"You lied about the bomb," he retorted. "And you tricked me into thinking you were dead!" He rubbed his chest then, remembering the spacetime bridge generator Darius had – supposedly – placed there. "Heck, you probably lied about this spacetime generator too."

"Nope."

"It's really there?" Kyle asked. Darius nodded. Kyle frowned. "Wait, so it really would've taken me back to Earth?"

"Yep."

"But what if I'd used it?" Kyle pressed. He'd nearly used it when that Chosen had pushed its green shard into Kyle's forehead. He'd activated the bomb instead.

"Exactly what I said."

"What do you mean?" Kyle asked, feeling suddenly alarmed. "You would've left me there on Earth forever?"

"Yep."

"You *would* have?" Kyle exclaimed. "But what about everyone else?"

"I would've done the same thing I did," Darius replied. "But you'd never have known it."

"You would've abandoned me?" Kyle pressed, his tone incredulous.

"If you abandoned them," Darius confirmed.

"But I'm your grandson!"

"And you're still here," Darius stated. Kyle chewed on that for a moment, then sighed.

"I don't understand you," he mumbled. He felt Darius's arm around his shoulders, and glanced up at the man. Darius was smiling.

"You don't need to."

They both stared at the passing desert below, the canyon that had once been directly below them now barely visible on the horizon. The flat, rocky ground had given way to huge, rolling sand dunes.

"What now?" Kyle asked.

"I can take you back to Earth," Darius offered. "Or you can stay on Doma."

"Oh," Kyle replied. He thought about it for a moment. "I think I'll stay on Doma for a little bit longer."

Darius nodded, saying nothing more. Kyle stared at his grandfather, then at the scenery flying by below.

"Hey," he stated suddenly.

"Yeah?"

"About my dad," Kyle continued. "He remembers you, you know."

"Maybe."

"He does," Kyle insisted. "He told me he remembered a man in a suit of black armor."

"And?"

"Well," Kyle replied. "...are you ever going to visit him?" Darius said nothing, staring down at the passing scenery miles below. Kyle sighed. "He's still your son, you know."

"I know."

"I think you should talk to him," Kyle opined.

"We'll see."

They both fell silent then, and Kyle felt an all-too-familiar frustration come over him. Why couldn't anything with Darius be *easy*? He sighed, kicking a nearby pebble off of the edge of the cliff. The stone tumbled downward, vanishing into the angry gray clouds of the alien atmosphere directly below Antara. But his frustration soon abated, replaced by the memory of Darius saving him from the Chosen, and bringing them to Sabin to save the Empire once and for all. He couldn't very well be mad at the man, given how Darius had managed to save them all from certain doom.

"Thanks," Kyle mumbled. Darius said nothing, remaining silent until Kyle wondered if the man had even heard him. "Thanks for everything," he added, more loudly this time. Darius smirked, looking down at Kyle, his metallic arm still draped around Kyle's shoulders.

"You're welcome."

"Not just saving us," Kyle continued. Then he paused, considering his words carefully.

"What?"

"Thanks for bringing me here," Kyle said at last. "To Doma, I mean," he added. "And for helping Kalibar and Ariana."

"No problem."

They stared off into the distance then, at the vast desert below, more huge sand dunes flying by. Kyle turned suddenly, wrapping his arms around Darius and giving him a hug. He half-expected Darius to back away, but Darius didn't. To Kyle's surprise, he felt Darius hug him back.

"I'm glad you're my grandpa," Kyle said, his voice a bit muffled by Darius's armored chest. He felt Darius's gauntleted hand pat him gently on the back.

"You're okay too, kid," Darius replied. Kyle scowled.

"Gee, thanks," he muttered. "You're just warming my heart." Darius smirked, giving Kyle a squeeze.

"I'm proud of you kiddo."

Darius turned away from the edge of the cliff then, striding quickly back toward the path they'd taken to get there. Kyle hesitated, then rushed to catch up with the man.

"Where are we going?" he asked.

"You're going back to Doma," Darius answered. Kyle frowned.

"Where are *you* going?" he pressed.

"I don't know," Darius admitted. "But I'm done babysitting you mortals, that's for sure."

"*Babysitting?*"

"From now on, you're on your own, kid," Darius declared. "Good luck."

And with that, he vanished.

Epilogue

Sabin felt his mind rip away from his avatar as an enormous hunk of stone crushed the ancient body, destroying it instantly.

No!

Through his own eyes, he saw the ceiling collapsing before him, his Chosen falling before the incredible weight of the earth crashing down upon them. He heard a cracking sound coming from below, and then felt himself starting to tip leftward and forward from within his crystalline tomb. Horrible pain ripped through his midsection.

No no no!

The massive cylinder that held him continued to lean leftward and forward, until Sabin felt the unmistakable sensation of free-fall twist his guts. He could only watch as he fell, the shattered floor of his once-magnificent cavern rising upward to meet him.

He couldn't close his eyes, couldn't turn away. He could only watch as his world – everything he had created over the last two millennia – was destroyed.

The cylinder around him fell faster and faster, and then it struck the ground with a horrific crash.

And then there was darkness...and pain.

Sabin felt terror grip him, and instinctively reached into his mind's eye, grasping for any hint of magic there. But all of his magic had been siphoned into his network during the battle with Ampir. He had nothing.

Invisible flames licked at his flesh, his eternal curse consuming him. Without the sanctuary of his network...without Xanos...the agony was beyond imagination. Though he'd felt its full force before, it had only been for a few minutes at most...and he'd always known there was a way out.

But now he was trapped. Unable to move, unable to weave, there was no escape.

Sabin screamed silently, willing his arms to move. They betrayed him, as Ampir had betrayed him. As his Chosen had so unknowingly betrayed him two thousand years ago, when he'd woken one day to find himself like this. Lying in bed, unable to move. Only able to breath, and to move his eyes a little. And to feel the incredible pain searing his flesh, worse than he'd ever felt before.

They'd come for him then, his Chosen. His original Chosen...the two men who had volunteered to risk death for a chance at immortality. Alarmed by his absence, they'd come to his bedroom, staring down at him, unable to understand what was happening to him. They'd known about his disease, of course. The strange numbness and paralysis that came and went, but had grown steadily more severe over the decades he'd lived with them. And, of course, the pain.

Amazing how quickly he'd gone from fearing death to begging for it. Or trying to; unable to speak, unable to move, he'd only been able to scream silently at them.

Kill me!

And then the third Chosen had come for him. His wife.

He'd felt a sudden fear then, seeing her standing over him. Beautiful as ever, she'd been turned immortal while still young, undergoing the process after the first two Chosen had been successfully created. But something had gone wrong...terribly wrong.

She'd left then, returning moments later with something clutched in her hand.

A green crystal.

He'd felt terror then. Absolute terror as he'd realized what she was about to do.

No!

He'd recognized the crystal instantly. It was the shard he'd created for himself, to one day join the ranks of the immortals. How long had he waited to use his shard, hoping to first find a cure for his terrible disease? How many decades had passed, his health failing despite his every effort to keep himself alive, far beyond the lifespan of a normal man?

What bitter, bitter irony, that at that moment, at the apex of his disease, trapped in his body and engulfed in pain beyond his wildest imagination, she would grant him everlasting life!

Kill me, he'd screamed soundlessly at his other Chosen. Unable to hear him, they'd leaned over him, the smooth facets of his shard glittering in the morning sunlight. He still remembered the feeling of its cool tip pressing into his forehead, a sharp pain lancing through the front of his skull as it pierced his flesh, sinking all the way to the bone.

Not like this, he'd begged. *Not like this!*

It was only then that he'd thought to end his own life. To weave magic to destroy himself. And weave he had. But his Chosen had stopped him, preventing him from escaping this personal Hell he'd been so suddenly pulled down into.

Furious, he'd attacked them then, tried to kill *them.*

It hadn't worked.

Sabin stared at the swirling blackness before him, pushing past his pain to focus again on his mind's eye. He had only one goal now. Despite centuries of doing everything he could to ensure that his undead life would never end, despite the fact that, only minutes ago, he would have done anything to cling onto his existence, now all he wanted to do was die.

But his mind, again, was empty of magic.

Sheer panic gripped him then, exactly as it had all those years ago. He could almost see his Chosen surrounding him, feel them lifting him up from his bed to carry him through his house, then outside of it. He could almost see the treetops as they'd been then, two thousand years ago. Their branches swaying in the wind, oblivious to the horror being perpetrated below.

How long had they carried him for, to bring him to the largest of the caves he'd spent so much of his life studying? To a deep underground lake over a mile below the surface, one so filled with Void minerals that it was supersaturated? And this, ironically, all according to his instructions.

How he'd begged for death then.

His lofty goal, to become like the Reaper Queens. He'd instructed his Chosen to do exactly as they did. To lower him into the supersaturated lake when he gave the order, to immortalize him and send him to the bottom of that lake so that he might weave a crystalline tomb around himself. So that he might become the great brain that would control a vast army of Chosen, as the Reaper Queens controlled their swarms.

And yet they'd done it *without* his consent, convinced by his twisted wife that it would be his dying wish.

Sabin felt a slight vibration, felt the tiniest thread of magic appear in his mind's eye. He grasped at it desperately, clutching it in his mind and holding it there. He felt it grow slowly within him.

Engulfed by agony, every nerve fiber feeling as if it were being torn from his flesh and roasted alive, his first thought was to end it. Once and for all. He began to weave the thread of magic, twisting it this way and that, forming the necessary pattern in his mind's eye.

Then he hesitated.

His Chosen – the Originals – were still out there, he knew. Never a part of his network, they could not have been killed by Ampir's ingenious weapon. No one knew where they were...including Sabin. But they would know that he had been compromised...would *feel* the sudden absence of Sabin's worldwide communication stream.

They'll come for me, he thought. But not his wife. Without him, she would finally be free.

But the other Originals *would* come for him, as they had sworn to do nearly two thousand years ago. That had always been Sabin's rescue plan, if his network were to somehow fall.

Sabin paused, letting the thread of magic unravel into a straight thread in his mind once more. He held the magic there, feeling it continue to grow. Magic must have leaked out of the crushed rock and crystals all around him. His shard was automatically drawing it inward, exactly as it had been programmed to do.

They'll come for me, he repeated to himself. *And when they do...*

He pictured Ampir then, that smug smirk on his face as he'd betrayed Sabin, destroying everything Sabin had worked so painstakingly to create.

He felt magic continue to pour into him, felt his mind filling with it. Enough magic, perhaps, to allow him to burrow upward through the earth. Not to the surface, where he'd be vulnerable, but at least far enough so that the Originals might find him.

The memory of his Chosen lowering him into the ice-cold water of the pond came to him, the water draping over his bare skin. Sweeping over his eyes and filling his mouth and nose. How he'd panicked then, utterly terrified that he'd drown in that water.

And at the same time, desperately hoping that he would.

Sabin held the growing magic in his mind's eye, his flesh consumed with torment. He hesitated, knowing that he could end his pain once and for all. He could be free of this hell he'd suffered through for so long.

With a single thought, he could finally be at peace.

They'll come for me, he reminded himself.

He hesitated for a moment longer, then gathered his courage, twisting the strand of magic in his mind's eye. He wove quickly, until the strand formed a tight, pulsating ball in the center of his brain. He held the pattern there, feeling one last burst of fear grip him. He ignored it, secure in the knowledge of what he had to do.

So be it, he thought.

He shoved the pattern outward, and streamed as much magic as he could to it.